ISBN 978 1 913313 01 2 Kindle Edition
ISBN 978 1 913313 08 1 ePub Edition
ISBN 978 1 913313 09 8 Paperback Edition

The Heist: Third Edition 2020. Second Edition 2018. First published 2017
The Getaway: Second Edition 2020. First published 2018
Powder: Second Edition 2020. First published 2018
Mama's Gone: Second Edition 2020. First published 2019

For more information please visit LeopoldBorstinski.com

##

The Lagotti Family Series

Books 1-4

By

Leopold Borstinski

The Heist

AUGUST

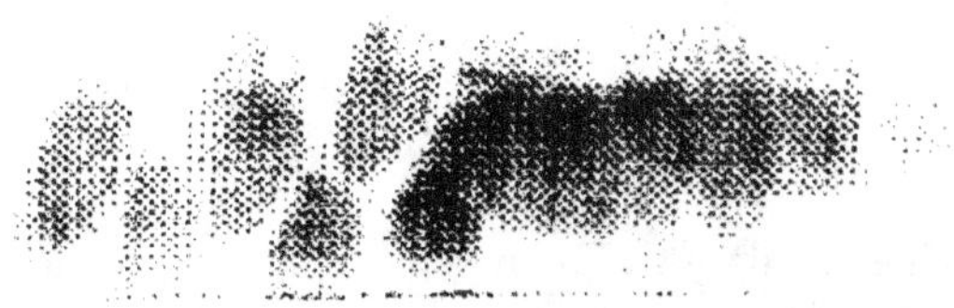

1

FRANK WAS OUT the can two minutes and already he knew he wanted money. A lot of money. So much money he knew he wasn't getting it from the recruitment pages of the local paper. He wanted dirty money. Money you can only get if you mix with the kind of guys who've got ideas. The kind of guys Frank was stuck in a cell with. The kind of guys who've got connections. Real connections with real guys. Frank was hungry for greenbacks.

Like many of us, Frank had dreams, big dreams. Big dreams of a big life. Fast cars, faster girls and a fancy suit or two. The kind of life he'd seen on a million TV shows. Only Frank thought it was real. Thought he really could have one of those TV lives.

There's nothing wrong with dreams. Unless they catch you full in the chest and knock you for seven. Then there can be something wrong with dreams. But Frank's problem wasn't his dreams. It was his wallet and his wallet was empty. So he needed to fill it. To plug his gap.

People say that being in the joint is like going to a criminal university and Frank had passed his final exam with flying colors. He'd spent his two years of incarceration keeping his head down, so he'd get paroled early. And he listened and learned from the men around him. How to pick a good location, how to find someone on the inside you can leverage. All the little details that turn a half-baked plan into a complete apple pie.

So when Frank walked through the gates of the Baltimore penitentiary, he knew exactly what he would do. Knew exactly how to get that pot of money he had spent two long years dreaming about.

Of course, there was something else he'd been dreaming about too. Or rather, trying not to dream about. Because some dreams just leave you weak, not able to concentrate on the matter at hand. And in the joint that kind of concentration can get you killed.

When the last gate clanged shut and Frank was standing on free soil and breathing in free air, there was the other thing of his dreams. Mary Lou's tight-fitting pants and all that was hidden beneath them.

There she stood, with one hand on her hip and the other holding a bottle of tequila in a brown paper bag, nice and legal like. A denim shirt with the ends tied on one side to show off that flat stomach and the tattoo of a rose three inches below her belly button, peeping out from her jeans and a thick brown belt.

Frank smiled and Mary Lou ran towards him, teetering on her high white plastic heels until she reached him and flung her arms round his neck and planted her lips on his. She sure was pleased to see him. How has it been these last few days since my last visit? Do you think my hair looks good as I got it cut special for you, Frank? And this and that and the other. And all Frank wanted to do was to lie down with that bottle of tequila and fuck Mary Lou's brains out.

LIKE SO MANY prisons, the penitentiary was built in the middle of nowhere, surrounded by flat, grassy fields. And as Mary Lou didn't own an automobile, they waited thirty-five minutes for the next bus back to Halethorpe.

Frank stood, back straight, with his left arm draped over Mary Lou's shoulder while his right hand clung to the tequila. Occasionally he'd stroke the back of her neck with his thumb, more to show interest than out of any genuine sense of affection. His mind was split between his dreams, the tequila and her bush. And every few seconds, he would flit from one thought to the next. By the time the bus showed up, Frank figured his dreams could wait until the morning, provided he got a serious dose of tequila and ass tonight.

The bus journey took over an hour, by the time it had made the long stretch into town and zigzagged its way from downtown to midtown to a block away from Mary Lou's apartment. A rented, brownstone affair with peeling paint in the hall and a bare lightbulb in front of her door, 3F.

The first thing Frank did when they got inside was to strip to the waist, throwing his shirt onto the floor.

"We'll get you some fresh clothes tomorrow, honey."

And then he sat down in front of the TV, switched it on and started flipping through the channels until he found something familiar.

He didn't notice his chair was less than one arm's stretch from the double bed and the kitchenette was only slightly further away on the other side. Mary Lou hadn't wasted any bucks on this boutique accommodation. And no one would care about who came and went.

Half a bottle of tequila later and Frank was ready to focus his attention on Mary Lou. He pushed her roughly down on the bed and she undid the zipper on her jeans. He pulled them off, one leg at a time. And stood there, swaying, as he stared at her white frilly panties and the tattooed rose peeking out from the top of them. With one more swig of tequila, he staggered and fell backwards, landing back on the armchair. Snored loudly, drunk-asleep.

Mary Lou sighed, put her hand inside her panties until she came. Twice. "Not tonight, Frank. Tonight's just not your night." Mary Lou fell asleep a short while after, half-content with the flickering thought rattling around her pretty young skull: whether her Frank would ever make her truly happy.

DURING THE NIGHT—and neither of them had a clue quite when—Frank woke up long enough to stand up, undo his pants, walk out of them and lie on the bed next to Mary Lou.

Some crappy time well before nine in the morning a bus wheezed past, waking Frank up with a start. Mary Lou had been living there long enough not be bothered by this municipal alarm clock anymore. He rolled over and eyed Mary Lou's body up and down. First her head, then her neck, belly and legs. He finished with her feet, toes curled in sleepy repose.

He put his hand under her white bra until Mary Lou groaned and half opened her eyes. She smiled slightly and shut them again. Then she arched her back and undid the garment so that Frank wouldn't have to try too hard. He squeezed some more and then covered her breast with his whole palm until Mary Lou groaned again.

She put her hand on his shorts and at that moment, Frank came. He'd been jerking off for the best part of two years and wasn't really ready for anything much more than that. Mary Lou understood and started kissing him on the stomach, moving downwards and pulled his shorts to his knees. It was the least she could do under the circumstances.

An hour or two later, when they were sat in a nearby diner having eggs, toast and coffee for breakfast, Frank told Mary Lou of his dreams and the next job he had cooked up in jail.

He had learned a lot from the last caper he was on. This time, he'd run the gang and not rely on some other guy to look after the little details: like making sure they had a wiring diagram of the joint so's they could cut off all alarms to the cops. And it would need to be a bank because robbing supermarkets and gas stations would only make them chump change and that was no good. Frank wanted a big enough haul so they'd head out west to Vegas or even California, maybe. Somewhere you could live like a king on a small fortune and no one'll ask too many questions about how you came into the money.

A couple of miles down the road was Lansdowne, a town big enough for more than one bank, so they took their pick of whichever one had the richest take. They would spend the next few days checking them out and decide which one to go for. Then the plan would be for Mary Lou to get to know someone on the inside so's they could get hold of plans and have a real good look inside with no one getting suspicious. And then she'd fade away from the scene months before the job itself was done so no one would suspect a thing. It would be like taking candy from a baby.

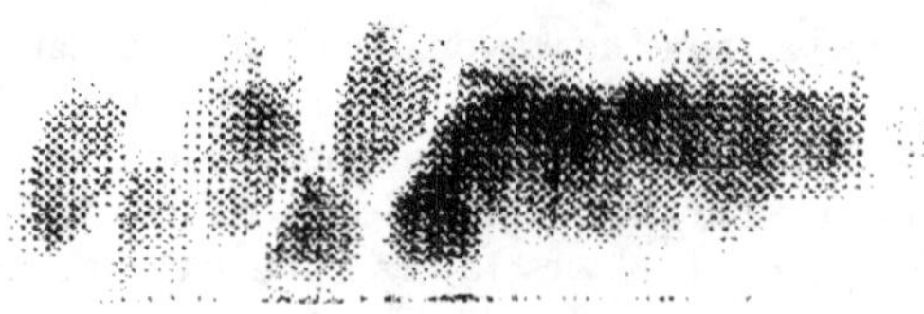

2

MARY LOU WOKE up refreshed, for the first time since she could remember. "Maybe you should lay off the tequila more often, Mary Lou Belle," she told herself. She rolled over and saw the hulk of a guy lying next to her. The hairs of his legs touching hers. She spooned him while he slept, smelling his back and resting her head near his neck. Cocooned in a cuddle that lasted forever. Immersed in a calm state of comfort with a man who cared for her and cared about her. She stroked his side and down his right leg until her arm couldn't reach any further. The corners of his mouth rose in a half smile.

"Hey, babe."

"Hi. You like that?" she whispered in his ear and then grabbed his earlobe between her lips.

"Not as much as if you sit on me."

He rolled over, facing upwards and Mary Lou put one of her legs over his and pushed herself on top of his body.

"Oh Carter, I love it when you're horny in the mornings," she giggled. And they carried on until he'd licked her tattooed rose, following the stem downwards.

Afterwards, they cuddled more and dozed until the sun stopped shining through the Lansdowne apartment window. He had paid a month's rent in advance. Cash, no questions asked. A perfect arrangement for a trysting place.

THE FIRST TIME Mary Lou met Carter she'd gone into the bank to find out about savings accounts because Frank thought that would be an easy in. She planned to wander round the bank, ask for a flyer, check out any security guards and cameras, and then get out quick.

But he caught her eye, sat at his desk with a photo of his wife and his wedding ring on his finger. His hair was greased back to reveal a high crown and widow's peak beneath a shock of black, dyed as the roots were showing.

Mary Lou teetered over to him and asked to sit down. "Sure thing miss," he said, rising and walking round to her side of the desk to pull the chair out for her. As he went back, he adjusted his tie and absentmindedly touched himself. She knew then he was her mark. Nervous and aroused, just by seeing a young woman standing near him. He rubbed his wedding ring before sitting himself down, facing her.

She sat with her back straight just to make sure her breasts were as far forward as she could naturally get them. His eyes followed down her face and stopped at her chest. Mary Lou explained how she'd been putting some money aside—not much you understand, but it all mounts up if you work hard—and now wanted somewhere safer than her mattress to store it. And also a friend had told she could get interest on it if she gave it to a bank to look after. But she did not understand about any of that sort of thing, so needed to know what her options were.

"Let me take down a few details before I can help you, Miss…?" Carter allowed the question hang in the air, drawing Mary Lou into conversation.

"And are you married or single?"

"I'm unmarried, but if I were to meet the right man…" This time she trailed her sentence off and started to play with a complimentary pen attached to a piece of string on a heavy blue stand on Carter's desk. She stroked the end with her thumb, licked her lips slowly at him and smirked.

He beamed back and carried on with his form-filling questions. Having built up a shallow but discernible picture of her personal and financial circumstances, Carter started going through the various potential investment opportunities open to Mary Lou. She stopped listening and started thinking about how she to progress things away from municipal bonds and onto something much more interesting to her.

"I'm sorry, but I find all this talk far too complicated for a simple girl like me. And it's taken all my nerve to come in here today. I don't mind telling you because I trust you. You have an honest face, but do you think we might meet in the coffee shop over on Third Avenue because I'd be a lot more comfortable there? This place creeps me out a bit." And with that, Mary Lou waved her palm around the bank and rested it on Carter's desk, leaning forward so he chest puffed out again as far as it could go and her hand was only an inch away from his.

"Uh, sure. If it'd make you more comfortable. These things can appear to be tricky without someone to guide you through the financial maze. I'd love to do that." And there was something about his intonation that caught her attention. As though it was the first real moment that Carter had left his script behind and was speaking like himself.

They arranged a time a couple of days later and Mary Lou thanked him and stood up. Carter came round and pulled back her chair to help her stand up, like a real gentleman. They shook hands, but she made sure she kept her grip a fraction longer than was right. He had noticed because he squeezed just a little too much in response. Then she giggled, took her hand and sashayed out of the bank. She didn't look but she caught his gaze staring at her hiney as she left the building, her white stiletto heels clipping on the marble floor.

Mary Lou returned from her first memory of Carter and nuzzled him some more. His back was hairy but somehow that worked for her. And he certainly knew how to keep her happy in the sack. And the man sure had prospects.

Frank had prospects too. And big dreams. She loved the idea of spending her days on a sun lounger in some fancy house in Santa Barbara or somewhere. With a couple of kids and a Dalmatian.

Carter started to lick her tattooed rose again and she knew she should lie back and give in to the moment and worry less about Dalmatians and babies. Frank never licked her rose.

3

CARTER HAD TROUBLES of his own, stuck in a loveless, barren marriage and in hock to a local Shylock to the tune of six thousand dollars. With no place to escape and no money to make the debt good. Up shit creek without a paddle. And his problems weren't going to go away anytime soon.

When you double up on your losses to such an extent that your bookie won't take another bet from you, there's definitely a problem. And Carter had got to the point where he was put in touch with Frank Senior who'd taken over the debt. Now, Carter hadn't heard of Frank Senior before but he was in the mire, even though he didn't know quite how deeply in it he was.

He met with Frank Senior at his repair shop and knew to have this week's payment with him. He'd heard tales of people losing their fingers to Shylocks before and that was enough to focus his mind and ensure there was cash, no Benjamins, no consecutive serial numbers.

When Carter walked down the street and found the yard with two broken down limos, he figured he had the right place. Walking to the entrance, trying to avoid the spilled oil, his breathing got shorter until he saw his hand knock on the door, grab the handle and his whole body entered the room.

As he glanced around, he caught sight of two mechanics in dark blue boiler suits and another guy, leaning back on his wooden chair, chewing a matchstick. There were various bits of crumpled paper on the desk in front of him, but that didn't appear to bother him and his gnawing. Carter tried to figure out who was Frank Senior as none of them looked in charge or appeared to be expecting him. But they certainly weren't acting like repairmen either. There was a general air of quiet smugness in the room.

"I'm… I'm looking for Frank Senior?" faltered Carter.

Matchstick guy pointed to a door to his right in the distant corner which Carter hadn't noticed until now. He nodded to acknowledge Matchstick Charlie and proceeded to Frank Senior's door, rapped on it with two short bursts, opened it and walked inside.

FRANK SENIOR WAS at the far side of the room, sat in a leather swivel chair, leaning back with his feet on an antique desk, etched in what looked like gold but was probably off-yellow paint. Frank Senior didn't look up and carried on reading his magazine. Carter saw a lot of full-page photos, some of which Frank Senior needed to turn sideways to view properly.

After a lifetime or about twenty seconds depending on who was counting, Carter gave out a little cough, but Frank Senior ignored him. Carter looked left then right, not too sure what to do. Should he speak or wait for the man to be ready?

The problem was solved for him while he was asking himself the question. Frank Lagotti Senior put his girlie magazine down, opened a drawer and brushed it in, closing the desk with a slam. He leaned back again in his chair, placed his elbows on the armrests so each finger tip touched its counterpart.

"Well," he said quietly after a spell of staring at Carter like he was shit on his shoe. "What do we have here?"

Carter cleared his throat and mumbled his name, eyes facing downwards. They both knew why he was there and neither really wanted to spend any longer in each other's company than was absolutely necessary for the transaction of the day. Carter put his hand into the inside left of his jacket and Frank Senior tensed ever so slightly, but not enough for Carter to notice or understand why a man like Frank Senior would be concerned about a stranger reaching into an inside pocket and whipping out anything.

He held the envelope and placed it on the near side of Frank Senior's desk, who dropped his feet down onto the ground, reached out and grabbed the package. Tore it open and pulled out the greenbacks. Licked a forefinger and quickly counted up all the notes.

"Good," he intoned, "I do not like being short-changed with my payments. Make sure you remember that. If you ever have a problem making a payment: beg, borrow from a friend, steal. Not my problem. Take the money from your mother's purse or from your girlfriend's snatch. I don't give a fuck. Just bring me my cash every week and you'll walk out of here every week. Got it?"

"Yes… sir," stuttered Carter. Frank beckoned with a dismissive hand for Carter to go. Suddenly, he took the cash, rolled it into a cylinder shape and stuffed it into his trouser pocket.

Carter turned around and walked out. This was one scary mother to be dealing with and they were going to be seeing an awful lot of each other unless Carter could think of some way of getting a very large quantity of money together in a very short space of time. Perhaps he should go to Atlantic City and try his hand at poker. But gambling's what got him into this situation.

A WEEK LATER, Carter was back but on this occasion with a slight spring in his step. He'd met Mary Lou only the day before and even though she was only a girl looking for a savings account, he couldn't get her out of his mind. He'd felt a real connection with her and couldn't work out why. They were meeting in a local coffee shop a short walk from the bank tomorrow and maybe he'd figure it out. Meantime, there was Frank Senior's payments to contend with.

If he could explain things to Rita, then maybe her family would help him out. They were well off and they spent almost all their time telling her how much happier she'd be without him. If they handed over some money, he'd suggest a divorce.

But this was not a realistic scenario because, his in-laws would never agree to paying off his gambling debts even if it meant increasing their daughter's happiness because they despised him so much. Also, if he got divorced then his prospects at the bank would be shot to hell. They only promoted married men and if he waited it out a year or two, then Mr. Cranford might retire and then he would end up as the Assistant Bank Manager. And who knows where after.

So that left him making payments to Frank Senior from now until the year after next. If he got the girl to put a large sum into the bank then he might ask for a raise or something, which would at least ease the weekly burden a bit.

But within two weeks Carter was short in a payment and had no clue what to do. He was spending money on Mary Lou that should have been earmarked for Frank Senior. He was besotted with her and spent most of his days at the bank thinking about the next time they would see each other. Thinking about the curves of her breasts and the scent of her rose. She smelled of sex and he wanted more.

Instead, he needed to figure out a strategy to deal with Frank Senior because he had virtually nothing in the envelope this week. Running away might work. No, really. If he fled the state Frank

Senior couldn't possibly get to him. If he changed his name, left his wife, he'd start again with Mary Lou. They'd live off her investment money until he got himself sorted. They could go to Florida. But he'd only just put a down payment on an apartment for the two of them and deep down Carter knew Frank Senior would locate him wherever he went. Even Mexico.

Instead he went to the repair shop with an envelope which had only an insult of cash in it and hoped to survive the inevitable beating or trip to a hospital fast enough to sew back on the end of his finger.

INSIDE FRANK'S OFFICE, Carter stood near the door, waiting for Frank to look up and acknowledge him. Frank always made him wait.

Eventually, Frank said: "Well?" and Carter took out his ever-so-thin envelope out of his jacket pocket. Unlike the previous weeks, he didn't place the package on Frank Senior's desk.

"Mr. Senior," Carter began, "We are both going to be disappointed by what I'm about to say, but I want you to understand I mean you no disrespect and I have surely tried my hardest to get matters… sorted."

Lagotti let the legs of his chair slam down onto the ground to show his displeasure at this unpleasant turn of events. All Carter had done past weeks was to take out the envelope, wait for Lagotti to count the wad and leave. Now the pip speak son-of-a-bitch was making speeches. And that meant only one thing: he was short and was trying to cut a deal.

Usually, this would mean Luigi and Paul next door would have to drag his sorry ass out of the office and beat the living shit out of the pen pusher. But today was Carter's lucky day; his besotted angel, Mary Lou would save him having a new asshole cut out where his kidneys used to be.

Lagotti had already heard of the plans for the job from his step nephew, Frank and how Carter was their mark. Lagotti also understood what kind of man he was: a coward, a weakling gambler who stole from his wife to place bets on baseball games he knew nothing about. But he worked in a bank and that was a establishment with lots of money and now Lagotti had some real leverage with this pin head, which his step nephew need never learn about.

"Young man, before you say another word, stop," said Lagotti quietly, slowly and sternly. "I told you when we first met that the only thing you had to do was bring me my fuckin' money. And I'm guessing you ain't planning on doing that this week."

Frank put a hand up to prevent Carter from responding, which was exactly what Carter had been intending to do.

"I shall give you an opportunity to play double or quits. While you really need to have got me my fucking money," slamming his fist on the table and making Carter flinch where he stood, "I am prepared on this one occasion to give you another chance before I ask my friends to rearrange your body parts and throw you into a dumpster."

Lagotti held back saying anything for a second or two to let that image sink in. Then he continued: "You can take the beating and double your debt or wipe it out and perhaps make some money on top too. Which'll it be?"

"Wipe it out please, sir," whispered Carter, his throat so dry with fear he daren't swallow in case he choked.

Lagotti explained what he had to do. There would come a morning when he would get a visit from Luigi or Paul and the next day, he would go into the bank just like any other day. But before the bank opened for business, Carter would enter the vault and transfer the cash into a case, which he would then hide in the bank. At no point during that time should he do anything unusual, Lagotti made that very clear. Also, Carter had to take out the case when he left that day. He'd receive further instructions in the evening to tell him where to go.

Lagotti informed him if he did as he was told and kept his end of the bargain then his debt would be wiped clean and if there was more than enough from the vault, he would get to keep two thousand for himself. Happy days. If he didn't do as instructed Lagotti guaranteed his body parts would be spread across the greater Baltimore area and his death would be slow, painful and full of unbelievable agony.

Carter was convinced without a moment's thought. This was a big break he couldn't ignore. For the first time in his existence, he would end up with his own scratch and a chance for a new life with Mary Lou. And then the rose popped into his head again and he scurried out of Lagotti's office in case Frank Senior changed his mind.

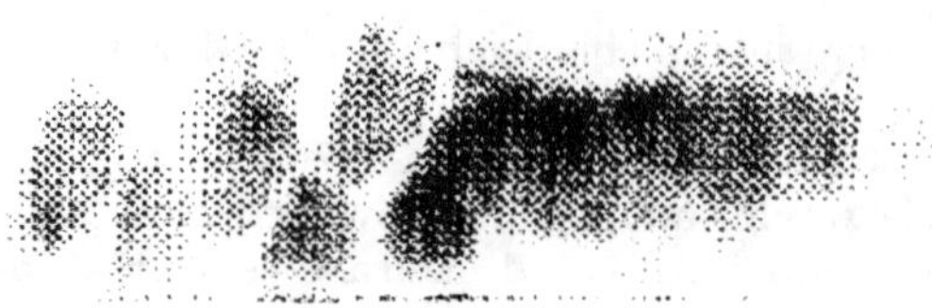

4

THEY HAD ARRANGED to meet in the Lansdowne cemetery and Frank had arrived a few minutes early to find a quiet spot, away from the roads that lined two of the graveyard's triangular sides and off the main path that ran through the middle of the cold, gray slabs.

Frank found a bench, hidden under a tree he figured would do fine. It faced a row of graves with no flowers near them, which showed they were unlikely to be visited this afternoon. Frank Senior arrived in the cemetery bang on time but it took Paul and Luigi a little while to find Frank and his seat. By the time Frank Senior sat next to Frank, the clock in the tower struck a quarter past two.

"Hi, Uncle Frankie," said Lagotti's nephew, with a quiet, contemplative smile on his face. Lagotti nodded in acknowledgement and relaxed on the bench, passing his arm round the back of Frank's shoulders.

"Hey you. Good to see you again," he replied warmly, wanting the boy to be comfortable with everything, even though he wasn't a blood relation, Frankie would give him more than the time of day.

"You too, Uncle Frankie. Mighty fine to see you. I mean, it's fucking great to be out the can, y'know?"

They sat and talked about the good old days for a spell, Frankie letting Frank find out the latest gossip about their mutual family members. They were silent, staring at the graves representing the dead and buried from many years ago.

"Stir was harsh. I mean, I kept myself clean and all, but it's tough always watching your back, never knowing who to trust. The only ones you could be sure of were the screws. You could rely on them to be a bunch of mothers. Apart from that, you never knew…"

"I understand my boy, but you did well. No drugs inside, right?"

"I stayed clean, sir."

"And did your girl come and visit you?"

"Every weekend like clockwork. And she wrote me a letter each week too."

"Good girl. You've a keeper there, mark my words. A keeper there."

"Yessir."

"And all that unpleasantness with Louis, that's all over right?"

"Yes, for sure. Louis got his before I went inside, anyway. So what's done is done, I say."

Louis was the bright spark who'd led his gang into a supermarket safe job without knowing there were two separate phone lines leading out of the building. When they grabbed the bags of cash and left by the back door, the cops were waiting for them. Frank might have only turned thirty, but he wasn't that much of a greenhorn, despite always being called a boy by his step uncle. He figured Louis had fucked up even before they started crouching behind their getaway car and firing at the police. Frank and Louis survived but the rest of them bought it that morning.

After Uncle Frankie posted his bail, Frank visited Louis' apartment and threw him out of the eighth floor window. There was no open casket at that funeral because there wasn't much solid to bury.

"What's done is done for certain. So you made any plans now you're out?"

Lagotti was happy to see Frank but the guy would take up the whole of his afternoon if he let him and there was business to attend to other than his nephew.

"I've one plan, for sure. But I might need your help…"

"Oh? Tell me about it."

And Frank did. He explained about the bank he and Mary Lou had picked only a few yards from the cemetery entrance. And how she had already started to case the place and had connected with a bank worker, Carter something. And how they'd go in first thing after the safe was unlocked, grab the cash, create a road block at the T junction and head out of town.

"Sounds fine, but let's get down to business, what do you want from me?" Lagotti's tone had turned slightly harsher, because this next bit of conversation involved cash and that was always a serious topic of discussion. Frank explained to do this right, he'd need money to get good people he could trust and not a bunch of mooks.

Lagotti said he understood exactly and was pleased Frank had come to him for help. He could find him a driver first, because that was key and that he'd fund the job, but needed appropriate tribute. They'd agree the exact amount later. Frank thanked him and accepted his terms mainly because he had absolutely no choice. He had known whatever Frankie wanted, he got and Frank was in no position to haggle. He had been out the joint three days and only had a hangover and aching balls to show for it. A slice of something sounded a hell of a lot better than a whole load more of nothing. Nothing he could get by himself. And if the take was as huge as he thought it might be, he and Mary Lou could still settle out west somewhere with no problems, anyway.

They shook hands and had a big bear hug to seal the deal and Frank sat down to let Frankie leave first. Twenty minutes later, Frank left the cemetery in the opposite direction, taking the west exit on Saratoga Avenue. Then he hopped on a bus and headed to Mary Lou's apartment.

When Lagotti returned to the auto shop, he made a single follow-up phone call to Pete "The Wheels", the best getaway driver, who wasn't doing time right now.

"How's you? I've got a job for you. Yep, driving away from a bank… Should be simple enough. One thing: it's being run by that kid nephew of mine and I'd like you to keep an eye on my investment… Yeah, Frank as in Frank-and-Louis, rest in peace. Bad business. Let me know if I should be concerned, okay?"

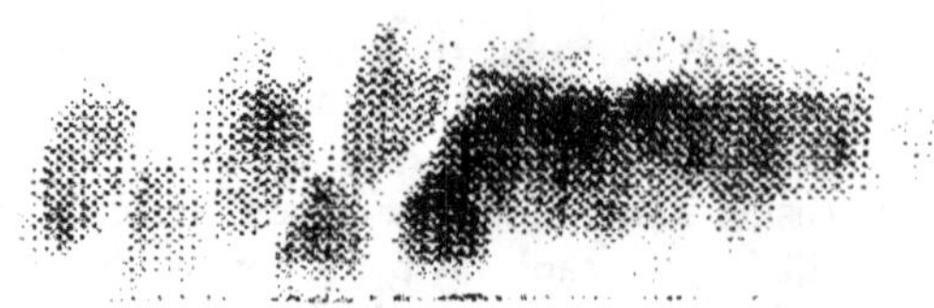

5

PETE SAT IN the Butterfly Arms for a quarter of an hour. He hugged his Heineken bottle slightly more than he would in any other bar. He couldn't entirely put his finger on it but something didn't feel right. If Pete'd been more aware of his surroundings and possessed a stronger level of knowledge of local bars, he'd have noticed there were absolutely no women in the joint. And there was a simple reason: not that this was one of those coincidences and that in the next hour, the gender balance would be realigned. No, the Butterfly Arms was and is a gay bar and was well known by everyone who lived within fifteen miles of the joint, because it was the only gay bar within fifteen miles.

Why Pete didn't know this before he arrived early for the meet is beyond explanation for a man like him. But not only did he not know before he entered the establishment, he really hadn't noticed how close some men were once he settled down and hugged his beer.

And despite this amazing oversight of Pete's, if he figured things out, he would have been mildly annoyed but not upset, because while he might have felt slightly uncomfortable at the thought of being that close to a bunch of queers, Pete was enough of a Republican to believe in freedom of choice even if it creeped him out.

Martin chose the place when they spoke on the phone. Frank told them to hook up before everybody met so they could get to know each other a little better. Two key guys for the job were the driver and the crowd control. The former gets everyone out safely and the latter keeps everyone safe inside so if they both connect the whole thing goes much more smoothly. Safety first–and last.

Martin sounded okay on the phone, so when Martin sat down opposite him in his booth, Pete nearly wigged out totally. Because in front of him was one of the meanest looking niggers Pete ever cast his eyes on. And for choice-loving Republican Pete, this was a problem, a serious problem. He wasn't going to have no coon in his vehicle.

HE KNEW COMPLAINING the guy was as black as the ace of spades would do him no good. Pete might have been a racist, but he was rational. If Frank already picked him to be on the team, he must be okay with him. And if Frank was okay with this black son-of-a-bitch, then Pete couldn't throw his toys out of the stroller just yet. He'd need to speak with Frank Senior and find out what he thought of the dark situation he was in.

Meanwhile, Pete made small talk with Martin and waited. They covered a few war stories from raids gone by, each trying to gently outdo the last tale from the other. After two beers, Pete had more than enough of this black cocksucker and left the Butterfly Arms.

That evening, he called Frank Senior to seek his advice: "Do whatever you think is best. This Martin means nothing to me, but remember he's one of the boy's preferred guys."

So the next time Pete and Martin hooked up, it was Pete's turn to pick the venue and he chose a spit-and-sawdust country and western joint where the toilets were right by the fire exit, which led to the back alley. *The Whiskey Bar*. After making sure Martin consumed all the beer he wanted, Pete waited until Martin needed to hit the head.

He followed the guy through the bar until they had a straight choice between turning left to the john or right through the exit. Pete seized Martin's shoulder, making him lose his balance and quickly thrust him through the door and pushed him out into the alley. Half cut, Martin fell to the floor, confused by what just happened and unable to see his attacker. He landed with a crack, face down, and Pete leaped on him, pushing his knee deep into the small of Martin's back as he grabbed either side of Martin's head and slammed it onto the concrete ground.

Then he whipped out a .38 snub nose from his pants and put a bullet in the base of Martin's skull as he lay face down, gushing blood into the alley gutter. Two slugs to make sure, then he turned the body over and pummeled it in the mouth until there were no teeth left to identify Martin. And then Pete took out a hunting knife and sliced off Martin's fingertips. No nigger would sit in Pete's car.

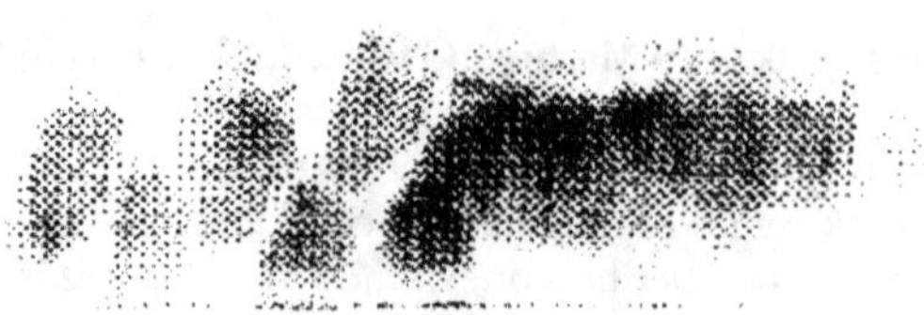

6

THE DOOR CHIME rang out and Andrew got off the sofa and looked through the peephole in the apartment hallway. He smiled as he squinted at Martin's distorted head through the lens. Andrew took the door off the latch, opened it and beamed a smile to Martin, who responded with a similar grin. They hugged in the doorway and then Andrew stood aside to let his friend enter the apartment.

"Hey, you guys have done wonders to this place!" exclaimed Martin after walking around the living room a couple of seconds.

"Thanks. It's amazing what a difference some paint and some soft furnishings can make to the ambience, y'know?" intoned Andrew, who clearly took interior decorating seriously. Martin threw himself onto the sofa where Andrew had been sitting.

"Some coffee or something?"

"That'd be lovely. An Irish would be even better."

Andrew scrabbled round the back of a cupboard near the percolator and pulled out a bottle of scotch. Displaying the logo like an Oscar, he sorted out the paraphernalia associated with making a decent cup of coffee. Eventually Andrew had two mugs of coffees ready, handed one to Martin and sunk into the easy chair next to the brown sofa. Then they got down to business.

"So tell me what happened with you and Pete yesterday."

"The guy seemed okay. I mean he's obsessed with fast cars but in his line of work that'd be a distinct advantage." They both laughed briefly.

"He's strange for sure, but I don't know why just yet."

"How so, sister? Your Spidey Sense is normally reliable."

Martin was silent for a spell, mulling over his thoughts, trying to figure out why Pete gave him a bad vibe.

"There's nothing that he said, but it's the whole way he acted. He was never relaxed, y'know—always seemed on edge, even after we sank a beer or two."

"Where did you go?"

"Well, he let me choose so I suggested the Butterfly Arms."

"You crazy motherfucker. Of course he was on edge. Is the guy straight?"

"Um, I didn't ask. Do you think he could be?"

"What world are you living in nigger? He's straight and you took him to the only gay bar for fifty miles!"

"Shit! I didn't think. It was just the first place I thought of and it's got such a nice, warm friendly vibe… Yeah, the guy's a homophobe."

Martin giggled briefly and then frowned. "Now we have a problem. I took Pete the Wheels to a gay bar to talk about a bank job and now he's pissed at me."

"How'd he leave it with you?"

"Well, he suggested we meet up again tomorrow to make sure we were *simpatico* before seeing Frank next week and I said yes."

"It can't be all that bad between you and him if he's prepared to hook up again. Perhaps he just isn't the sociable type."

"Yeah, maybe."

The conversation drifted for a few minutes until Martin suggested speaking to Frank about getting Andrew on the payroll.

"That'd be mighty Dutch of you."

"No problem, what are friends for? Besides, Frank said he was looking for some good men and you are the goodest I've met." Martin smiled and put his hand on Andrew's and gave it a squeeze. "You're a good man, Charlie Brown."

"Don't start all that up again. We're friends and no more. What's past is past. Anyway, I'm happily married now."

"Yes, how is Brian?" and somehow Martin made the two syllables drip with venom.

"He's fine. Sends his love."

"Sure thing. And right back at him."

"Now, now. Don't start getting all shirty on me after all this time. I'm not saying you two will be best buddies, but the time has long gone when you are both fighting for my affection. I loved you a lot, Martin dear, but you forget how we used to drive each other crazy."

"No I don't. I just choose not to mention it." Martin winked a knowing wink at Andrew, who smirked back and fell silent again. Another Irish coffee and Martin bade his farewell, they hugged and he staggered out the door into the apartment corridor.

Twenty-four hours later, Pete sliced and diced Martin's body parts on a plastic sheet in a safe house before depositing them in various dumpsters around the Baltimore suburbs. He fed the fingertips to some alley cats and put the teeth in a trash can on the far side of town. Pete was particular about who he had in his car.

ANDREW TRIED CALLING Martin several times over the next week. He wanted to find out how the meet with Pete went. If the dude was a homophobe, then Martin would need some help to deal with the guy. When he got zilch by way of reply, he hopped round to Martin's crash pad. He rang the bell , but nobody was home. Three days in a row.

Andrew asked round the neighborhood , but no one had seen him. In fact, Andrew appeared to be the last person to have spoken with Martin. At least before the Pete meet. After that, there was nothing to show for him.

Nothing at all. Now maybe he'd hightailed it out of town, perhaps because of Pete, but you'd think Martin'd put a call through to him before skipping if that was his plan, unless things were so hairy with Pete he had no time at all. And that wasn't good.

Andrew reckoned the best thing to do was to wait another day or two because if Martin had gone to ground, he would eventually find a dime to drop a call to him. And wait is what he did.

When it had been a week, Andrew knew something was seriously up and Brian agreed to act. The question was what. They couldn't go to the cops exactly and it wouldn't look good to go crying to Frank. But the thought of confronting Pete didn't hold much joy either. How do you walk up to a guy and ask if he killed your friend? It's not an easy conversational starter.

Andrew and Brian agreed the first step was to aim their search a little wider, because Martin could still be holed up in some guy's apartment, experiencing the joys of a butt plug and they were worrying over nothing.

They retraced Martin's steps up to where he entered the Whiskey Bar. One of the wizened drunks hanging outside the joint had taken a five spot to confirm Martin had gone inside the joint. While the hobo couldn't be sure, he didn't think he'd seen Martin come out. But by that point in the evening, there was far too much meths in his bloodstream for him to be certain. Or conscious really.

And as they didn't know what Pete looked like, they had no idea if Martin had somehow picked someone up at the bar or if the Wheels had been a no-show or what.

Further enquiry through the use of a ten spot delivered definite info from the barman. Martin had spent at least half an hour sat in a booth with one guy. They'd sank three beers each for sure and the dude had settled the tab; Martin had gone by the time the bill was paid.

"Let's speak with Frank," concluded Andrew and Brian agreed.

ANDREW SAW HIM the following day, Wednesday, and Frank chose the same cemetery he'd seen Lagotti. Andrew explained his concerns to Frank, who sighed a long sigh and continued staring straight ahead, with his hands in his pockets and his legs stretched out in front of himself. On the same bench. By the same graves.

"Martin was a good man," he eventually monotoned, his voice heavy with the weight of the implication of his words. "I'll speak to Pete and get this sorted out, don't worry. Pete's a reliable guy. Not prone to irrational violence. He likes his engines and his autos and not much else. But he is reliable. I'm sure there's a perfectly reasonable explanation. Martin'll probably be fucking his way across Penn. state if I know him," and Andrew agreed that this was the most likely answer. But under his breath, he didn't believe Frank because he didn't know this Pete and he didn't trust him–that was something needing to be earned.

On the plus side, Andrew asked Frank if he would have Brian in the crew. Reliable guy, tough as old boots but calm under pressure and damn reliable. Reliable as hell. Frank said he'd think about it and call him tomorrow with an answer. This time Frank left the cemetery first and Andrew waited fifteen to twenty minutes before making a move out of the graveyard.

Next day, Frank phoned: "Hi. About Brian: it's a go."

"And about the other matter?"

"I'll talk to the guy for sure."

"Good news."

But Frank never asked Pete because he was the best driver not in stir and Martin was just another muscle, no matter how much Frank liked Martin and how little he knew Pete. Uncle Frankie had given him Pete and he wasn't stupid enough to want to put his big dream in jeopardy.

And no one spoke of Martin again.

DECEMBER

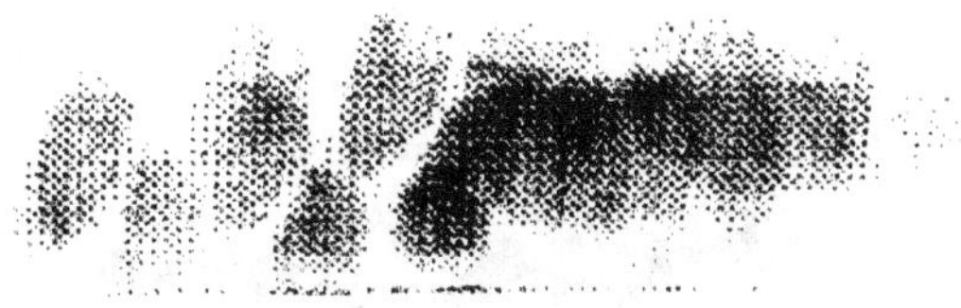

7

WITH SNOW ON the ground, Frank had warned them all to be careful not to break their legs on the ice; Baltimore didn't usually get this cold. It was said in more than just mock paternal concern. The last thing Frank needed was one of his crew not functioning. He wasn't too sure how long it would be before they hit the bank but he did know they needed to be ready real fast. And at that point, there would be no time to think or to replace someone stupid enough to go and break their leg.

But Frank was worrying in vain because not only were all limbs safe that winter, but it would be months before they were ready and extracted sufficient information out of Carter, even though Mary Lou was spending a lot of her time with the scrawny sack of shit.

The much bigger problem they were facing was that any damn fool can stride into a bank, but it takes one special kind of crazy idiot to take the money and walk out with it the same way they came in. Now, the First Bank of Baltimore, Lansdowne branch had a major advantage over its local rivals: it had a back door which led out to an L-shaped alley and a small parking lot, which led straight onto the main drag. That meant in-and-out was more or less sorted, but quite how they were going to get to the vault and extract the simoleon without getting into a whole mess of trouble was far from clear.

Frank met up with the great persuader, Brian. It was his job to handle security during the ruckus and that included old man Joe, the security guard and any civilians who got in the way. At the back of their minds was the knowledge robbing a city bank was one thing, but shooting and killing someone during an act of grand larceny and then crossing the state border was federal. And none of them wanted that shit storm in their lives. Brian might not have been the sharpest tool in the box, but they all recognized he had an exceptional talent for figuring these kinds of things out. It's why Frank was okay with Brian coming onboard all those months ago. Martin was too flakey anyway, as much as Frank liked him.

Brian had been thinking about all this and had decided Frank, Andrew and himself could handle the robbery between them. Any more and it would get too top heavy. With three of them, you could have one keeping control of the civilians, while the others moved into the basement and grabbed the cash. But Brian also knew two kinds of weapons were needed for the job: a loud motherfucker to scare the civilians and that old timer security guard of theirs and some heavy armor for the getaway itself. And something to blow open the vault.

His real concern was the vault because that wasn't down to him and if that bit fell apart they were all screwed. The good news was that they were going to hit the joint just after it opened for business so the safe would be fat with cash and open. They wouldn't even need to rip anyone's fingernails off with a pair of pliers.

But the bottom line was they needed to get hold of some fire power to scare the civilians and in part to take care of any situation that might arise.

PETE HONKED THE horn twice. He'd had enough waiting around for one day and it'd only just gone past breakfast time. He honked again.

"Come on. What the fuck's taking you so long?" he announced to Brian in his head. They had a long, dull drive ahead and Pete just wanted to get it over and done with. There was business to take care of. Gun business.

Pete was generally a happy driver. He enjoyed controlling the vehicle, harnessing the power of the engine. But dealing with gun sellers was a distinct matter altogether. The guys who bought and sold guns for a living were a different breed. They were steely cold, man. Life was cheap when you could blow a man's brains apart with a slight movement of one finger on a trigger. So no matter how well you knew them, you had to give your supplier a respectful wide berth. And that meant close encounters had an edge to them.

So Pete was fine with today's trip except for the destination which was hanging on his mind already. And he didn't need Brian jerking him about before the day had begun. He honked three times in quick succession.

Finally Brian ambled out the building and slunk into the back passenger seat.

"What am I? You're fuckin' chauffeur?" barked Pete, "Get up here!"

"Sorry, man. Wasn't thinking."

"Too fucking right, ya mook."

Brian clambered out and dropped himself in the front passenger seat.

As soon as the door was shut, Pete slammed on the gas and they were off. He switched the radio on and *KWFM 101.2 All Country, All Western* burst out the speakers. Despite his ill humor, Pete was still a professional and made sure his speed never beat the limit. There was no way he was going to get stopped by the cops on this trip.

"Settle in, it will be a while and I ain't gonna stop off for no piss," instructed Pete when they reached the I-95 turnpike.

"Fine by me. Let's get this job done. The sooner we are there, the sooner we are back, 'n' no offense to you, but I don't want to be stuck in this tin can all day myself."

"None taken. I like a man who keeps his eyes on the prize. You and me'll be just fine." And with that Pete sat quiet again, thinking what a coon lovin' cocksucker he had sat next to him. The sooner they got back, the sooner that sack of shit could leave his car. And then there'd only be one or two more times he'd have to be near the cocksucker and the other fag. Not that he had anything against fags, no. But they were both coon lovers and that sat badly at the back of his throat.

Just before the Joppa exit Pete punctured the silence: "I need a piss," and pulled off the I-95 onto the South Mountain Road until they reached a diner he knew a few blocks away.

One thing Pete had not brought with him was any heat of his own. After all, he was just the chauffeur. Up to this point, he hadn't seen the need but Brian had pissed him off. Pete knew he'd hidden a small snub nose in the john at the Steers Rancho diner.

"Stay here, I'll be back in a minute," instructed Pete.

"Sure thing," auto-replied Brian.

PETE WENT TO the right of the main entrance and headed for the washroom door. A check both the cubicles were empty and he went into the left one and shut the door. Lid off the cistern and he felt for the plastic bag he'd taped to the inside several months before. And there it was. He ripped the elephant tape off and grabbed the gun and bullets, secreted for just a day like today.

Then he hightailed it to the car, but no Brian. Again. Coon loving cocksucker. He hooted twice and fumed some more. The crazy thing was Pete would have been very happy to have gone inside himself —if Brian was there—because Pete knew the very horny Lucy who served up hot coffee and more for a traveler passing through. Then Brian would have discovered this was more than a chance stopover at a diner because she would remember him from the last time he was here. He'd doubt that many customers took her from behind on the kitchen table.

As soon as Pete had entered the rest room at the side of the gas station, Brian got out of the vehicle and headed straight for the door of the adjacent diner. He strode to the counter and ordered a coffee to take away.

"Going far, honey?" asked Lucy, the waitress who had a tarnished badge over her left breast. She wore too much blusher and not enough bra but that's how she got most of her tips–and the occasional dose of crabs–from the middle aged locals who came to her counter most days of the week.

"Got a few more miles to go, hon', that's why I need the caffeine," smiled Brian back at her. Lucy poured a hot cup of brown liquid into a paper cup. "Milk?"

"No thanks, Lucy."

Brian placed a dollar bill on the counter. Lucy turned round with the coffee, having wrestled a plastic lid onto the drink.

"Keep the change."

"Why thanks, you can come in my establishment any time you want, darling."

"I sure will remember that," said Brian and he walked out the door and back to the saloon where Pete was already behind the wheel.

"WHERE THE FUCK were you? I told you not to leave the car."

"Chill. I wanted a coffee and here it is, is all."

"Where's mine?"

"As you needed a piss after only twenty minutes, I didn't think you'd need one otherwise we'll be zigzagging our way to Philly all day long from one gas station head to the next. And neither of us need that now, do we?"

Pete was silent and fuming for tens of miles and cranked the radio louder to drown out Brian from his car.

Things weren't much better the following hour but neither of them were in the mood for a long heart to heart, anyway. Eventually, Pete took the volume down on Tammy Tunes low enough so Brian could think without wanting to rip out his eyeballs. Or Pete's.

To keep Pete on-side, as he'd said to Andrew he wanted to do, Brian broke the silence: "My Ma comes from Wilmington," and this odd fact seemed a lot less random considering they were hurtling through Wilmington at the time.

"Want me to stop so's we can pay her a visit?" asked Pete, not sure where this was going and taken aback that Brian had kicked off a conversation after so much silence.

"The crone's long since buried 'n' gone. On the way back, we can dance on her grave if you're so minded."

Pete laughed a wheezy, smoker's laugh. "Hey, I only asked. Family's important."

"Depends what kind of family you got makes 'em important or not."

"S'pose so. S'pose so. Didn't mean nothing by it, kid, okay?"

"Sure thing. I doubt you ever met the bitch anyhow. So no skin off your nose. Don't sweat it." And Brian let out a small, calculated chuckle. Just enough for Pete to know that all was fine between them. "I'm gonna kill that queer baiter before all this is over," he promised himself.

Nothing much happened else on the way there. Pete pulled off the I-95 when they reached Philly Airport.

"I thought we were heading into town?"

"Nope, never was. Always going to be the airport."

"But you didn't say it was the airport, only Philly."

"Yep, you're right there. Never did say," agreed Pete.

Brian wasn't too happy about being misled by Pete, not that he wanted to go to Philly, anyway. More it showed how little Pete trusted him. And on the day, they were all going to need to put all their trust in Pete. He sure wasn't making it easy.

Pete pulled into the long stay parking lot, a vast graveyard of vehicles, all in neat rows as far as they eye could see. You could understand why Pete had picked the place. No one would see them and anyone turning up at random would be heard ages before they drew close enough to notice anything.

They moved three rows left then six right until they stopped near a blue Dodge. Nothing special, just another auto in this field of autos. Game on.

Pete got out and, at precisely the same moment, a guy hopped out of the Dodge, came to the back, shook hands with Pete and popped the trunk. Pete peered in, shook the guy's hand again and banged on the hood of their car: Brian's signal to join them.

"Hi."

"Like what you see?"

"What'm I looking at?" monotoned Brian, in full work mode, eyes and ears open to the slightest sniff of trouble. He'd brought along a snub nose in case of need and, at this point in proceedings, his fingers were coiled around the weapon hidden in his pants' front pocket.

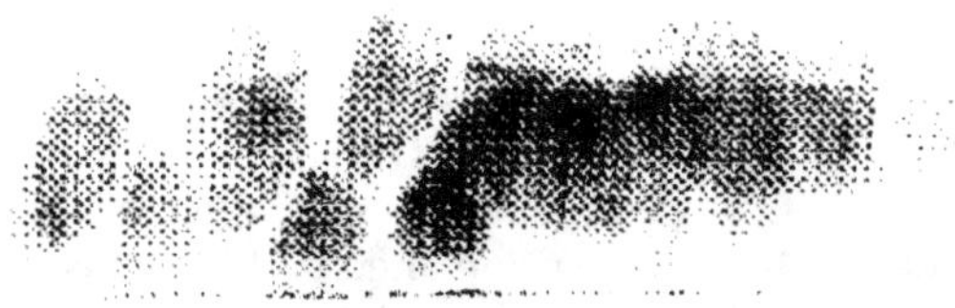

8

"I GOT MAGNUMS, I got Colts. I got Smith 'n' Wessons. I got ammo for all. You tell me what you're lookin' to buy and we can take it from there," intoned the guy, his seller's spiel tripping off his tongue. Chuck had gone through this ritual a thousand times before in a thousand airport parking lots all over the country. Always the same, never a word different. People he came across would not be swayed by any smart chat from him. They were serious men with important business in mind. All they needed was the time to see what he had and make a choice.

In Chuck's experience most people appreciated the simplicity of the Colt but some preferred the unbelievable sense of power that came from the kickback of a Magnum. The noise was also useful if you had to deal with civilians too. Others preferred the S and W. Its rifle made the West if you believe the myth and Jimmy Stewart movies. No, that was the Winchester. Oh fuck, who cares? Different dudes liked different guns. Finito.

Brian pointed at the Magnums. As Chuck had noted, Brian liked them because they were heavy in his hand and they cracked out such a fucking loud bang when you squeezed the trigger you'd have to be Satan himself to want to fuck with whoever held that piece of metal. Brian selected two .44s, and two .38s and enough bullets to fight his own war in Vietnam.

Before they'd set off on their day trip, Frank had made it real clear to both of them that they were not to insult Pete's man. They should not get ripped off, but they might need him again before the job, so leave him happy. So the haggling process involved Brian naming a price, Chuck doubling it and Brian taking a hundred bucks off as some kind of discount. Easy.

Then Brian asked about the M112. Did Chuck have any? He smiled and dragged over a tarpaulin near the back of the trunk to reveal a large black suitcase, locked.

He pulled out a key from his pocket, turned the lock and flipped open the case to show the whole thing packed with C4 explosive forming units about eleven inches long and two inches square: military grade C4 known as M112.

"How much you looking to buy?"

"Just one—and detonators and such."

"That's fine. I have it all here."

Another empty haggle and the C4 was wrapped in a blanket in the rear of Pete's trunk, along with another blanket containing the guns and a small attaché case for the ammo.

They all shook hands and Chuck returned to his car and waited. Pete and Brian hopped back to Pete's stolen auto and they headed for the parking lot exit.

THE MOOD WAS better on the way back, the tension lifted partly just because they got the job done with no hassle and partly because Pete had shown himself to be useful and not merely a country-and-western loving dickwad.

As they drew nearer to Baltimore, Brian asked Pete to exit onto the I-695 to Towson. When they got there, he directed Pete this way, then that, until they'd gone along Allegheny Avenue and stopped at a derelict factory. This time it was Brian's turn to say: "Wait here," and he exited the vehicle. He grabbed the items from the trunk and headed into the warehouse.

The place had been deserted forever because no one round here had the spondoolix to get it back on its feet. Inside the factory was a rabbit warren of storage rooms and the main area was filled with machinery and conveyor belts. This was Brian's preferred hidey-hole mainly because even if you entered the place, it'd take you a lifetime to check out each room and Brian never used the same spot twice. Many years ago, he'd been a security guard here, so it was a home from home for him.

He got back to the car and Pete had already turned it around. Then on the I-95. Pete felt better about life now the stress of the day was over. And the fact he hadn't used his piece on Chuck, who could be quite a volatile motherfucker if he wanted.

Brian was a lot less annoying to him too. So much so Pete suggested grabbing a bite at the diner. He gave up caring whether Brian found out he'd had a particular purpose there and was more concerned about popping the gun back in its hiding place and getting inside Lucy's black crotchless panties. She might have been a waitress, but she was definitely a whore.

The men downed their burgers and fries in short order and Pete approached the counter to pay.

"Was all to your liking?"

"Everything, darling. Everything I can see, for sure. Mighty fine."

"Well, I've got hidden depths, you know, babe." Lucy licked her lips and thrust out her tits at Pete to emphasize her words.

"And how'm I going to get my hands on those depths?"

"I finish at one if you care to pop back. We can party 'till dawn: I'm not on shift until tomorrow afternoon." More licking of lips, more tit thrusting.

Pete stood with his legs apart and his hands in his jeans pockets. Rocking back and forth on his heels, mirroring Lucy's thrusting with his own.

"Party on, Lucy. I'll grab the tequila 'n' you bring your hidden depths."

"I never leave home without them, deary."

All the while, Brian was looking on from their booth, watching the conversation in mime. They were clearly flirting away at each other and Brian thought he might have to call a very expensive taxi to get back to Baltimore.

Then Pete returned and they hightailed it to Brian's brownstone.

"Thanks for hooking me up with Chuck."

"De nada," and almost before Brian shut the door, the car zoomed off into the dark.

ANDREW IMAGINED WHAT he and Brian would do with their share of the loot. There'd be new clothes and a car and a bigger, better apartment and that's all he really ever wanted. A nice place to live with a nice man, who cared and loved him. Not much to ask in the general scheme of things. A lovely man to hold him in his arms and tell him he's safe. That's all.

And Brian was that guy. Okay, he'd go off on the odd unplanned trip to Vegas or AC but, apart from that, he was dependable. Unlike Martin, who had been the love of his life when he first came out. That was one flakey dude. Had opened his mind to so many experiences. Sexual experiences. But had helped him in other ways too.

The trouble was you couldn't live with a person like that. Not all the time. Martin drove him crazy. So that is why Andrew left him and shacked up with Brian: a tender, kind man who loved him greatly and held him in his arms and made him feel safe in this ugly, dangerous world. Hardly without opening his eyes, Andrew got out of bed and went to the bathroom, brushed his teeth, washed his face and hit the head. He lay back down on the bed and fell asleep.

When he awoke at eleven, he sat up with a start and looked around for Brian. He remembered Brian had gone off early with Pete to get hold of the guns and explosives for the job. Nice. He'd chill in the apartment and cook them something for this evening. Brian liked his home-cooked food.

Andrew planned the menu and checked they had all the ingredients in the cupboard. He made a list because it quickly became clear there was almost nothing to eat in the kitchen, unless they had dinner composed of stale bread and some rancid butter.

Paella was the dish *du jour*, so there'd need to be plenty of shellfish, brown rice, spices and some neatly chopped vegetables. A trip to the corner shop was inevitable and long overdue. Andrew would also get some cereal for breakfast, bread and butter to replace the blue versions he threw away a few minutes ago, some milk for his coffee. And some coffee too. The more Andrew thought about food, the longer the shopping list grew until he realized there was no way he could carry it all home with him, even if it was only the other side of the street. He'd have to pay the boy to help, which wasn't a problem. It's just that he and Brian agreed not to allow strangers in the apartment when they were on a job. Basic security and nothing more.

Brian never bought food, so he had no idea of the problems of shopping and keeping to their agreements. Don't let strangers in the apartment. Don't go off with strangers from bars. Don't lie to him at any time about anything. Don't, don't, don't. And Andrew's rules in return? Love me, hold me, make me feel safe. Brian was a prize A fucker really, wasn't he?

Nah, he wanted to be careful and keep them both secure, but those rules were pretty controlling because they sounded as though they referred to both of them but really they only applied to him.

And it wasn't so much suffocating, which it was, as much as untrusting. If Brian couldn't trust him, and had to make up a bunch of stupid rules to hide this, what else was Brian hiding? And why did he feel the need to control Andrew so very much because Andrew didn't want to control Brian to the same extent? At least, he didn't think he did. But Andrew did always want to know where Brian was. Every minute of every day. And it made him uneasy not to be with Brian today.

The last guy Andrew had seen who'd gone to Pete had vanished into thin air, so it was hardly paranoia that made Andrew concerned. Besides which, at the back of his mind was the passing thought Brian might do something stupid with Pete. Kill him or fuck him or both, only not in that order, you'd have to hope.

9

PETE HAD ENOUGH time to grab a bottle of liquor from the Seven Eleven before it closed, dump the stolen car he'd used for the gun run, clean it up and return to his own vehicle. A speedy rush along the I-95 and back to the Steers Rancho. He looked at his watch: five minutes past one and there was Lucy, stood in the doorway. Her curvy hips silhouetted in the moonlight and a brief flash of light near her head as she inhaled deeply on a Marlboro. Man, she sure was a hot babe. He swung by the main entrance of the diner, leaned over the passenger seat and opened the door from the inside.

"Hey, it's party time, doll. Hop inside."

Lucy threw the rest of her cigarette on the floor and stubbed it out under her heel. Exhaled the last breath of smoke and got into the open car. She shut the door, turned to Pete, placing her hand on the side of his face, drawing him in towards her. She kissed him on the lips, parting them slightly with an inquisitive tongue.

"What're you waiting for? You can remember where I live, can't you?"

"Sure thing, babe."

Pete squeezed her thigh and pulled out of the parking lot and headed straight to her trailer around the corner and two blocks south.

When they got into Lucy's pad, Pete popped the tequila onto the kitchen counter but Lucy picked it up immediately and poured a couple of shots for them, using some dusty glasses she found in a cupboard above the sink. She passed a glass to Pete, chinked their glasses together and knocked back the hard liquor in one gulp. Pete did the same and Lucy poured them both another.

Then she sat up on the kitchen counter and Pete stood in front of her, separating her legs with his body so he could be real close. He grabbed the nape of her neck and pulled her mouth towards his. Lucy moaned a satisfied moan, undid his belt and unbuttoned his flies. In response, Pete thrust at her with his shorts round his knees.

Later that night, after most of the tequila had been downed, they fucked twice more: before they crashed out, and once more around ten the following morning when Pete woke up feeling horny. She just about managed to wake up before he had finished, but she didn't mind. She never expected much of the men she hung out with because they were all no-good no-hopers who helped her forget she was a waitress for a couple of hours. And also because that was the only sex she'd ever known. Pete as well.

By midday, he had woken up again properly, made himself handy in the kitchenette frying some eggs and bacon for the two of them. Then he found his shorts and jeans and put them back on.

"See you round, I gotta make tracks."

"Sure thing, babe. You come up and see me any time," she said. Pete slapped her naked ass with a smile on his face, walked out of the trailer and headed home. "Great lay, terrible conversationalist," he thought as he joined the I-95 back to Baltimore, not realizing he'd hardly said a word himself since the moment he entered her trailer in the early hours of the morning.

HIS HATRED OF Pete stayed in Andrew's skull well into the afternoon. While he was chopping the vegetables and preparing the giant prawns, measuring out the rice and generally prepping for the evening meal. Getting everything ready so they could eat within twenty minutes of Brian's return. He was bound to be hungry after spending a day stuck in a tin can with Pete. So the best thing was to feed him before he got any more grumpy than he obviously would be under the circumstances.

The clock ticked past six and there was still no sign of Brian. Past seven and nada. Brian walked into the apartment at around ten to eight, tired, a bit sleepy, to be met with a hug from Andrew.

"Hey, you. How was it with Pete? All go okay? Food'll be ready in a mo'."

"Food? I've already eaten, thanks."

"What d'ya mean? I've cooked you a meal. Paella, your favorite."

"Thanks but me and Pete caught a burger in a diner on the way back from Philly."

"No, you didn't call. I mean, you had sufficient time to stop at some grease joint to eat but you didn't have enough time, apparently, to call me and tell me not to waste my life at the stove."

"Wait a minute."

"No, buddy. Why the hell didn't you call me? You knew I would cook. I mean, you knew that, right?"

"Yeah, but."

"No, buts. You knew I was going to cook, right? So why didn't you at least phone to let me know?"

Silence. Brian's molars were grinding, but he said nothing. Partly because he had a beer or two inside him and partly because Andrew was plain right. He should have called, but it didn't cross his mind when he and Pete walked into Lucy's diner.

Andrew stared at him, glaring into his eyes, flaring his nostrils. Then he turned his back on Brian, went into the kitchen, dished himself up a big bowl of paella, sat down at the kitchen table and ate by himself.

What a fucker, he thought, chewing on a prawn. It's not much to ask. And why would Brian spend time with Pete instead of him? It makes little sense. That homophobic prick. If Andrew got the chance, he'd kill Pete. Not for taking Brian away from him this evening, but because of Martin and the way Brian was so easily manipulated by Pete to eat a burger with him. He couldn't trust Pete. And so Andrew decided to slice the motherfucker's stomach open and let him bleed out. Period.

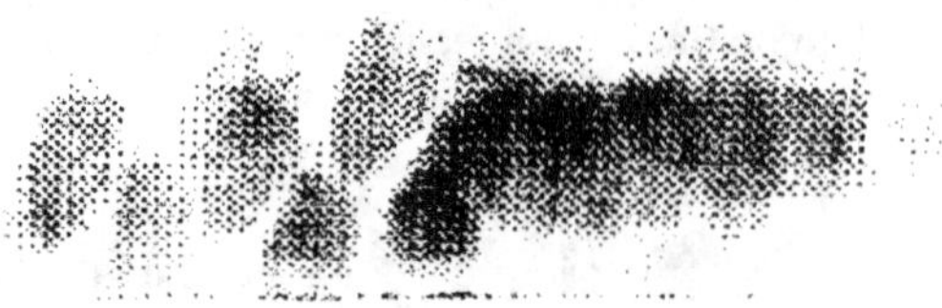

10

A WEEK ON and Frank was pleased with himself. The half tumbledown factory was a perfect location for the group to meet. Mainly because no one would be stupid enough to suddenly walk into the place due to its state of disrepair and it was so obviously empty.

The other reason he liked it was because he had been here several times before and was comfortable squatting among the rubble and broken bits of machinery, which were slowly rusting into oblivion. And this meant the others would be less comfortable and would want to get the fuck out as quickly as possible. So there shouldn't be too many dumbass questions either. He wanted this job to go well, so he led and they followed.

For their first time all together, Frank ran through the whole plan with the group and left it at that. When they hooked up again, they could pick at the plan and find the holes in it. For now, they needed to get their part and see where it fit in the grand scheme of things.

Frank and Mary Lou had arrived nice and early as a welcoming committee for the others. As soon as they get out of the car, Mary Lou complained if she'd known the state of the building she would have worn flats, not heels.

Shortly, Uncle Frankie turned up with Luigi and Paul. The two remained in the station wagon and Frank gave his uncle directions to the area he had cleared to use for the meet up. Lagotti mumbled something under his breath about a room at a cheap hotel. He proved his point when he scuffed his shoes on the way into the building past the rubble and broken machinery. Frank stood outside to make sure everyone got in okay.

Andrew and Brian appeared next. Then finally Pete the Wheels showed up in a loud, mean motor machine.

"Good to see you, Pete, but Jeez, could you have picked a vehicle that was more likely to get you noticed?"

"Sorry, man. Sweet ride. I'll drop it off for a friend after we leave here."

"Shit. Park it round the side, you asshole."

Pete gave Frank one of his trademark looks but Frank was far from impressed. Antics like that land them in jail and Frank had no intention of returning there. Including the two-year stretch he finished three months ago, he'd spent eight and a half years behind bars and that was without the twelve months in juvey. More than enough time. This haul would be the last. He wasn't like Uncle Frankie; he was more muscle than brains but he had his dreams and he'd figured out a way to get that to happen. Unless pricks like Pete drove brand new cars to secret bank robbery meetings. Asshole.

WHEN FRANK CAUGHT up with the group, they were standing around talking to each other in a three-sided room on the side of the building. The fourth wall had fallen down when the termite infestation really took a hold. Not good for a food packaging plant.

Mary Lou was clearly hoping there was a gentleman in the place to offer her his seat but she was wrong. Frank had dragged in the only chair in the factory from a nearby room so his uncle wouldn't need to stand for the proceedings as he was the big bankroll.

The truth was Lagotti really didn't care about the details of the plan. Who did what, when and where was beyond his interest. He only cared about what would happen to his money and if his investment would be safe. So he turned up today to show his faith and support for Frank to the people Frank had picked for his team. Without this, Lagotti would have stayed at home. Besides, Frank Senior knew the key person in the scheme wasn't even in the building: the bank clerk who would actually get the contents of the bank vault for Lagotti.

Frank went through the assault on the joint itself, the drive away by Pete. Great driver that guy. Flakey as hell, but a perfect wheel man. Then talked about the real getaway from the town.

The most important thing Frank omitted to talk through was how the contents of the bank was going to get into Lagotti's hands for laundering. Simple reason: the two of them hadn't discussed it yet. Frank hadn't thought through that piece at all, hadn't mentioned it to his uncle once. Lagotti was waiting to see how long it would take for Frank to cover this off. Without it, he would have nothing but bags full of paper he couldn't spend.

Brian had heard of the money lender and investor ever since he first entered the business, but had never met him. Frank Senior had funded almost every job Brian had been on. He didn't seem that special to be honest, mused Brian. I mean, he's not that much to look at. Quite an ordinary looking guy in his late forties. Two dudes flanked him, who never said a word. Clearly his enforcers. Respect to him for that, thought Brian.

Frank drew out a plan of the area in the dirt on the floor. Then he started talking about how they were going to get in, who would handle crowd control when inside the bank—Brian and Andrew—and then how they would get away. All eyes turned to Pete, but he remained silent.

They all listened intently as Frank described the bank layout, furnished by Mary Lou, and the overall plan to enter just as the bank was opening, hit the vault for cash, notes only if possible, and then get the fuck out of town using a diversion to slow the cops down to a crawl. Simple, effective.

Frank started going through the scheme in more detail, covering each element so everybody understood what was expected of them. While they didn't have much time to figure it out, they needed to see themselves as a team. Only trouble was: they couldn't hang together for very long before the job because they'd be seen together and that was a no-no.

"How're we going to split up when we're in the place?"

"It's cool, Brian. You, me and Andrew will be inside. Andrew and I hit the vault and your job will be to keep the civilians in check. I don't need to remind you that they must keep calm, quiet and still."

"Then don't," retorted Brian. Frank smiled.

"No offense intended. But we both also know if you need to, waste one of them if they step out of line."

They were all silent for a spell because murder in the progress of a bank job raised it from a state case to a federal crime. And that was a whole pile of shit none of them wanted but now they knew how serious this job was. If it fucked up, the Feds would be after them, not a bunch of tinpot cops from the metropolitan district. And now Brian understood how far he could go with them: as far as he needed up to raping a child.

IN THE BASEMENT, Andrew'd crack the safe if anyone had slammed it shut during the furore. They'd have no more than three minutes between entering the joint and leaving, so they'd need to shake their tails to get the money into their bags and out the back into Pete's getaway vehicle.

Andrew calculated if he timed it right, he could take some cash out to the car early, gut Pete and get back in for the second round before the other two knew what'd happened. And he could drive the car: he'd been the driver in previous jobs so that didn't phase him. Besides, in the heat of the moment, neither Frank nor Brian were going to argue over who was behind the wheel.

Mary Lou was an interesting broad to Andrew: Frank had done well for himself there. She still had her looks and, although her clothing was more whore than nun, she might have been classy once. Judging by her body language, she was clearly besotted with Frank. Eyes all over him. And Frank obviously trusted her enough to put her in with the bank manager guy.

That dude was the weak link to this caper. Some employee who would make certain the safe was unlocked. Well, if he didn't do what he was told, bad consequences ensued. Given Frank's reputation for dropping people out of tall buildings, the appropriate motivation was being applied: fear and, presumably, a not inconsiderable dose of lust. That Mary Lou sure cut a slender figure in those jeans. But Andrew questioned her judgment on picking stilettos for today in an old crumbling ruin of a factory or whatever it once was.

"AND WHAT ABOUT security guards, cameras, access, the whole thing?"

"I was coming to that, Brian. We've learned a lot about the interior of the bank's first floor but we are still working on the basement where the safe is."

Frank half glanced at Mary Lou, who stood by his left side, and placed his hand on her ass and squeezed and stroked it with his thumb, all the while talking to Brian and pointing at the map of Lansdowne town center drawn on the dirt of the floor. He felt hot inside standing next to her and touching her. Not warm near his dick like when he felt horny but warm in his stomach from an emotion.

"Who's the mark?"

"Some assistant manager that Mary Lou's got under her thumb and we're gently teasing the information out of him. If there's anything in particular you want to find out, tell Mary Lou."

"I bet that's not the only thing she has under her," muttered Pete and Frank stared daggers at him, while the other men smiled and hid sniggers behind coughs. Frank could feel Mary Lou's butt tense in his hand and her face had gone red with embarrassment.

"Fuck you, Pete. Let's focus on the job at hand and no more smart ass remarks, fella."

Pete's eyes gazed down behind his shades and the group came to order when Frank Senior quietly intoned a second later: "Back to business, gentlemen."

There would be one old guard, called Joe, who lets the staff in through the front door before the bank opens and then usually stands between the door and the Stars and Stripes on the left. He packed a piece, but they'd have no argument from him because he was pure showcase. The man was seventy if he was a day and wanted to spend his time with his grandkids. No way was he going to risk his life for someone else's bag of money.

There were two tellers, the assistant manager and a deputy. They were all trained to cooperate with robbers because the money was insured and the bank didn't want to get sued by the next of kin. So they wouldn't be a problem. No, it was the civilians you had to watch. You never knew when one would put their panties over their stockings and act like a hero. If one of those types was in the room, there'd be blood.

11

FINALLY FRANK STOPPED going on about the vault and the civilians and started to talk about the getaway. Pete's ears pricked up.

"So Pete'll be at the rear entrance, down the alley. Okay."

"Sure thing, boss."

"And we'll use that car with the four us to take the loot out of town."

"Gonna by notes only or coins too?"

"We're not planning on coins so the load shouldn't be too heavy, but there are safe deposit boxes in the basement and if we have time, we will lift them too. There's maybe fifty of them but I'd rather take bearer bonds and cash than grand mom's jewelry."

"Sounds like a plan to me. The more paper, the faster we get out of there."

"I know. I know."

Frank explained Mary Lou would be in a second car, nothing fancy, as she'd be the one to set the C4 off. The idea was to make some loud bangs by the junction outside the bank and cause a bit of chaos and confusion by felling a couple of telegraph poles. If the explosive was placed on the correct side of the pole there was a good chance when it landed, it would fall on the road. This would stop most law enforcement in their tracks and would mean there'd only be one way out from the bank. And Pete would need to take that quickly.

Mary Lou would leave town before Frank, Andrew and Brian entered the bank. Then they'd rendezvous outside Lansdowne and split into three groups. Pete would drop the others off. Andrew and Brian would go in a second fast car and head west. Frank and Mary Lou would first travel south but then make their way east. Frank would hold the take until it was safe to fence or spend the proceeds. Everyone knew they could trust him because they all trusted Frank Senior, who stood quietly showing no emotion on his face.

By this time, Pete had stopped listening again. So three speedsters and a small van, he thought. Might need two of them to have a reinforced floor. Just because Frank doesn't want jewelry doesn't mean he won't grab any gold he finds along the way. Better be cautious and not trash the suspension of the one and only car they had to get out of Dodge. Make that mistake and they'd each by looking at ten years minimum in a high security cell. Fuck that. Reinforce the floors and swap out the engines for something beefier. He'd require a discrete lockup to hide the cars and to work on them in relative peace. So we're talking an oxyacetylene torch and a load of other kit. There were going to be expenses to claim, for sure.

MARY LOU WAS quite worried about the explosives. Frank had explained to her the C4 was safe until it had a lit fuse inside it, but the idea still sounded deeply scary. And without the telegraph poles blocking the roads, there was a near-zero chance of Frank and the money getting away safely. So this meant the success of the whole caper rested on her shoulders. Not only was she taking a huge risk every time she hooked up with Carter and went to the bank with him, but now she was expected to put her life in danger setting explosives in the middle of Lansdowne.

That said, there wasn't anyone else that Frank would trust to do this. He trusted her and she would share in his dreams: they'd be living out west. In California or Las Vegas or wherever. It didn't really matter that much. She'd have Frank and the money and a pretty great life. They'd have a great time together and that was something Mary Lou had not been prepared to contemplate, let alone articulate, at any other point.

All the guys walked away to return to the land of the living, but Frank held back for a moment. Mary Lou stayed by his side, but he patted her on the butt and said: "I'll catch up with you in a moment, hon'," and turned to talk to Frank Senior who hadn't moved either.

Mary Lou made a face and stumbled her way slowly through the rubble back to Frank's battered old jalopy. The bastard hadn't given her the keys though, so she was left leaning against the car until he appeared ten minutes later.

Lagotti watched as Frank spoke with Mary Lou. Seemed a good kid with a fine pair of tits and a great ass. No idea why she'd stuck by Frank all the time he was in the joint, though. I mean, thought Lagotti, with a figure like that she could have had her pick of any man who walked past her, more or less. So why stay with Frank?

Lagotti had heard a story Mary Lou was so besotted with his step nephew she'd got a tattoo on her privates of his nickname for her. But that was just rumor. And it still didn't explain why the fuck she stayed with him when he was in the can. Lagotti's train of thought was interrupted by Frank.

"Now they've all gone, there's something I need to talk to you about."

"Where's your girl? She was here a minute ago."

"What, Mary Lou? I told her to wait for me by the car. I wanted a private word."

"Well, here we are."

Frank looked round and saw they were alone.

"Once we have the cash from the vault and we've driven out of town…"

"Yes?"

"Well. What do we do then?"

"You fuckin' kiddin' me, right?"

"No, not at all. I've been spending these first couple of months thinking through everything up to the point we leave Lansdowne behind us. After that, I'm a blank. All I know is I've got to get all the money together and over to you so you receive your tribute and we obtain some clean cash to spend. Then we keep our heads down until the heat dies away."

"My boy, it'll be fine, there's nothing to worry about. A day or two before the job, I'll give you the location for the drop. We won't meet on the day because you'll be far too hot, but you must make sure I get the money then. Fail to do that and you fail me. Every minute you hold the cash is another you can get stopped by the cops red handed.

"So at the drop, you leave the proceeds for me and I'll have left some spending green for you and your girl. You can play hide the salami for a month or two. Somewhere quiet and keep your heads down. Nothing fancy, nothing flash.

"Then I'll bring word to you when it's all good. You come back to the east coast and get the rest of your winnings. Then you divide up the spoils as you see fit with the rest of your crew.

"And that's all you have to do. You are right to ask about this and I am pleased you've had the foresight to do so. Also, you are right to spend most of your time trying to figure out all the angles that'll play out between now and you leaving Lansdowne. Carry on doing that and leave the rest to me."

Frank smiled, thanked him and shook Lagotti's hand with both of his. Then he walked out to his car. Lagotti followed him until he saw Mary Lou draped over him in an embrace. Frank Senior thought about the missing magazine time torn from him by this afternoon's escapade and hopped into his car and headed back to the auto shop.

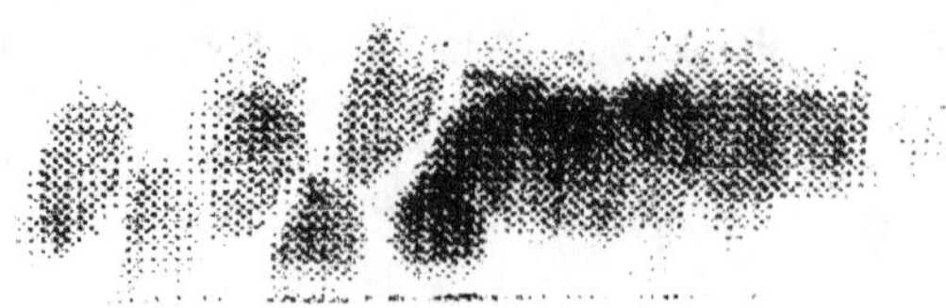

12

BRIAN AND ANDREW motored over to a firing range to get some practice in. Brian liked to go there twice a week if he wasn't on a job to keep his eye in. There's nothing worse than taking aim at a cop who's bearing down on you only to find you've pulled the trigger and the fucker is still standing. So Brian came to the range and kept his guns cleaned weekly too. A carpenter has his saw sharp, a gunman keeps his gun barrels clean. That's what Brian figured and he had a point.

Andrew had a different perspective. He reckoned in his line of work, if you used two instead of one bullet on a guy, it didn't matter because the jerk was dead and you were still standing. Brian and Andrew didn't agree on many things but there was a strong bond between them, anyway.

It'd been great the last year or so working with Andrew and living with him, thought Brian as he pulled the auto into the parking lot of the shooting gallery. At least he could talk about work with him and he truly understood. No questions asked. That's what Brian said as he slipped the shift stick to park and got out the vehicle.

The reality wasn't really matching the lie he'd told himself. Since working together, they had become a tighter unit on the job, for sure. But it was at the expense of their personal lives. Because it's so intense—life and death literally—they both needed some space away from each other during the long months when they were idle.

And the more time Brian spent separate from Andrew, the less he missed him. Until he reached the point when he actually wasn't that bothered about when he was going to see Andrew again. Handy Andy. So called because of what he could do to your dick with just four fingers and a thumb.

And the sex was good, but it wasn't enough for him anymore. Andrew was safe, for sure, not likely to run off to Vegas with the first guy he met in a bar—unlike Martin who only thought with his dick. And safe was always something Brian had sought in a relationship and never had. Until Andrew. The trouble was that safe carried with it the risk of dull and Brian didn't want tedious in his personal life. He wanted love and lust and the feeling of the thrill in the pit of your stomach. And what he had was Andrew, a new sofa and a Magnum .38 in his hand, firing at a classic FBI target.

Andrew looked good with a gun, stood next to Brian in the adjacent alley. Legs apart, hands clasping the butt of the pistol firmly and squeezing off round after round. A keen technical eye in his head. With a big heart but limited imagination. Andrew's idea of a wild night out was not to book a return cab home.

ANDREW'S MIND WASN'T focused on the practice. He was trying to work out if he could still take out Pete and keep Frank and Brian on-side. Now all eyes were on the three of them inside the bank, there'd be very limited room for maneuver. And Andrew would need to show them the getaway was safe by getting behind the wheel and making it so.

He needed to practice for that without Brian beginning to suspect something was up. Wouldn't be easy but he'd better get some high speed driving under his belt otherwise the whole thing would come crashing down around his ankles. And he'd have a bullet through his brains.

Brian was in the zone, standing square to the target, squeezing that trigger and taking out the imaginary cops in his head. Andrew's cock grew hard just looking at that hunk of meat. He was a beautiful guy and really knew his business. No messing. That could make him dangerous, mind. But sexy too. Andrew knew better than to interrupt Brian to get a quickie behind the firing range, but he wanted it. Right here, right now. Andrew stopped concentrating and he fired six or ten inches away from his target.

"What's the matter with you?" asked Brian immediately. He always kept an eye on Andrew on the range because he Andrew was more interested in cracking safes than firing guns at sheets of paper.

"Sorry, nothing. Just thinking, is all."

"Think about taking out the cop who's trained his shotgun at you as you leave the bank…"

"Don't be snappy with me."

"Keep your head in the game, ya putz."

"Hey, don't get like that about it. Jeez. Keep your wig on, you freak."

Brian put away his pistols and stormed out of the building with Andrew following on quickly behind. He got into the car just before Brian pulled off and squealed down the highway.

Why had he let his mind wonder? He knew how seriously Brian took the firing range and he knew Brian was always watching over him at the range too.

BRIAN WONDERED HOW much longer they would last as a couple. He'd do nothing before this job was over. He didn't know Frank well enough to judge whether he'd be whacked for causing a rumpus. And Frank Senior's reputation was as much for violence as it was for his money. So, no. Wait until the job was done and take stock. Not before.

Besides, it wasn't as though Brian didn't like Andrew, he was only a bit bored by him, but he still gave the best hand job on the Eastern Seaboard and that certainly counted for something. Quite a lot really. And the lunk loved him and treated him good—and there were very few men you could say that about. Most wanted some guaranteed sex from a warm and willing body. Shit. Andrew wasn't all that bad. He was safe.

The other important thing about Andrew was that he was Brian's connection to Frank and all that implied. Frank might have been in jail longer than he'd been out these past few years, but he had a cool head on him and some good ideas. Most people would barge into a bank, but Frank had been smart enough to get that toots to fuck the manager for information. And being close to Frank Senior was no bad situation. Brian reckoned if he did well in this, Frank Senior might be a great source of regular income. The man funded almost every job of any scale in the area and you can always trust a fella who's looking to share his winnings with you.

Which thought made Brian's head turn towards Frank and Martin. He'd done nothing about the guy's disappearance as far as Brian could tell. Nada. This begged the question whether Frank got Pete to hit Martin. And if he did, how can you be sure Frank won't want you whacked, thought Brian. The next step was to wonder what would happen after the job. How could Brian be certain Frank wouldn't tidy things up later on and grab a bigger share? There were quite a few people dipping their snouts in the trough.

This was when Brian first hatched the plan to kill Frank and Andrew on the same day but for different reasons. He figured if he took out the two men when they were in the bank he'd end up with more money and fewer problems back home. And no one would be any the wiser because Frank, Andrew and Brian were going to be the only ones actually inside the building. And the rest wouldn't care provided the money got out and they received their cut.

They drove home, parked and went into the apartment without a single word being spoken. Brian sat down at one end of the sofa, leaned his head back and shut his eyes, covering his face with his hands. Hiding in plain sight. Andrew sat next to and facing him, then sighed.

"Sorry," he said and he kinda meant it. He was certainly sorry he'd lost concentration and he was a little unhappy he'd annoyed Brian. Andrew put his palm on Brian's stomach, leaned forward and started nibbling his ear. His hand headed south and Andrew earned his nickname: Handy Andy. He did owe him for the trouble he'd caused this afternoon. Brian kneeled on the floor, facing Andrew and unzipped his jeans.

Later they lay in bed together, curled up and comfortable, each planning a way to place a bullet in someone's skull. Each getting hard again at the thought of someone else's demise.

13

TWO MINUTES LATER, both Franks walked out of the factory together, shook hands and Frank unlocked the car and opened the door for Mary Lou. He gunned it out the weed-infested parking lot and headed towards their Halethorpe apartment.

What Pete said was still running round Frank's head. While the wheel man had been joking around, there was no smoke without fire and Frank wondered what Mary Lou was getting up to with Carter and what that idea really meant. It sent a shiver down his spine and he gripped the steering wheel a little tighter.

"What did you have to say to Frank Senior?" she asked.

"Business, is all." Frank flipped on the radio and rock 'n' roll burst out the speakers. Not because he didn't want to talk, but because he wanted to remove the image from his head of the point where Mary Lou and Carter's bodies met.

"What kind of business, babe?"

"None of your never mind, hon'."

"Aw, shucks. We're in this together. I mean, I'm busting my chops trying to get all I can out of the bank clerk."

"Call him Carter," interrupted Frank.

"I'm busting my chops trying to get all I can out of Carter," she emphasized his name, "so I figure the least you can do is to tell me what's going on with the big man."

"I don't rightly figure that's the case. We are all doing what we need to do to get this job to work." he replied.

Mary Lou was fuming, so she decided not to answer him.

"Right. I had business to do with Uncle Frankie and that's all there is to it. An' you have work to do with Carter. I don't ask you about your business with Carter, so don't you ask me about Uncle Frankie."

"You can ask me anything you want about what I do with Carter and that's fine by me."
Mary Lou mused for a short spell. Initially, she hadn't been too bothered really what the hell he had been doing, but his reticence spurred her on to want to find out. Frank could tell he'd made her mad because her breathing had changed, got faster, more nasally.

FRANK TOLD HIMSELF when he first got Mary Lou to go into the bank and find a mark he wouldn't delve too deep into what she would get up to, because in his heart of hearts, it would end up involving her fucking the guy and, as much as he said it didn't matter, he actually knew it did. And this conversation—of his own making—would be all about precisely what he promised himself not to think about.

"It's just business between you two, right?"

"Just business Frank."

"You sure? You hesitated," Frank heard himself say.

"Jeez, yes Frank. Just business."

Frank still did not know where he was taking this conversation, but it was gaining a very unpleasant edge. One from which there was no going back.

"And in the evenings? What happens…?"

"We talk. So he can trust me and I find out about the bank. So I can walk round the bank with no one blinking at me. So's we can rob the fucking place." Clearly Frank had pissed off Mary Lou and he didn't need to be a professional psychologist to figure that out. He noticed how she was gripping the passenger seat, nails gouging into the leather.

"And what about when I was inside. What did you do then?"

"I came and visited you. Nearly every weekend. Every weekend I was able." What did she mean by that? All she needed to do was turn up and see him. What was so damn important in those odd weeks to stop her from visiting?

"What about when you weren't visiting? Like in your evenings?"

Mary Lou swallowed hard. This moment had been inevitable from the second Frank had walked out of that jail, but she hadn't expected to be sat in a rusty old heap when it happened. The truth was she had been faithful in her mind but not with her body. There had been a string of one night stands but they were never more than fillers until Frank's return. And Ron had floated around for six months but she had finished with him two weeks before Frank got out.

"I'd go to the movies sometimes, meet up with my girlfriends, stuff like that. Other times I stayed in and watched the Ed Sullivan Show."

"The Ed Sullivan Show?" Frank couldn't quite decide if Mary Lou was jibing him or not.

"Yes. He's funny."

"Right. And did you see anybody while I was away?" Frank couldn't believe he'd just asked the one question he didn't want to hear the answer to.

"No, Frank."

"You sure? Sounds like you hesitated again… So you didn't see anyone while I was inside? You didn't sleep with anybody while I was gone?"

There was a silence in the car. Even with the radio station blaring out, Frank was certain he heard Mary Lou grinding her back teeth.

"No, did you?"

FRANK SAW RED. Slammed the brakes and span off the road. Him screw someone when he was in the can? What was she thinking?

"What the fuck did you just say to me?" he yelled near the top of his voice spit flying onto Mary Lou's face, his eyes like slits and pure anger on his breath, not able to believe she'd accused him of having queer sex.

Whatever Mary Lou was going on inside her head, she had stepped over the line. She, too, didn't want to be having this conversation and she, too, had plenty of opportunities to close it down. She was silent for a spell and tears started to well up and trickle out of the corners of her eyes until they became a torrent.

"Nothing, Frank. You're freaking me out with your insinuations. I didn't mean what I said. I wasn't thinking straight," and the crying upped a notch.

Despite his anger, Frank had gone too far—she was only verbally retaliating because he'd got under her skin. And now he made her cry and that was not part of his plan. He moved her left hand away from her face and gently stroked her red cheek with the back of his palm, touching her neck and wiped some of her tears from her eye with his thumb.

"What's done is done. For the two of us. No more questions, eh?"

"No, Frank."

Mary Lou eventually stopped her crying and smiled her cute smile at him. Then she turned to him, kissed him on the mouth and slipped her hand under his shorts and jerked him off.

Despite the histrionics, Frank had got no further knowing what Mary Lou did with Carter and the bottom line was he couldn't face finding out. The mere potential of the truth was more than he was able to actually cope with. But what would happen with Mary Lou and him once they'd done the job? How to be sure he could trust her? What would he do with her if the trust wasn't there anymore? She knew too much about him to let her merely walk away if they split up. After the job, he'd have to put a bullet in her brain.

Frank pulled back onto the highway and drove to Mary Lou's apartment. She cooked them some linguini bolognese, Frank's favorite, and they settled down to watch some television. After the Ed Sullivan Show, they headed to bed.

14

THE CALL FROM Pete came through two days later. Pete was a great driver, really excellent wheel man. But he had issues. He had very specific attitudes which didn't always help him get along with folks. And he had a very short fuse, which meant he could be unpredictable and dangerous. But he was a good wheel man.

Lagotti agreed to meet up with him if only to find out what was going on inside his head. He'd known Pete for about five years and they had first met when Pete came into the auto shop looking for a loan to buy a new set of wheels. Lagotti could tell Pete was no ordinary car freak and hired him for jobs a few months later. Since then, Pete had been on four heists, sliced two throats and shot one guy in the eye. Serious driver with significant problems.

Under these circumstances, Lagotti brought along Paul and Luigi, in case Pete was going through a troubled phase. They met in a launderette downtown, in the kind of neighborhood where no one is stupid enough to listen into anybody else's conversation.

"Thanks for agreeing to see me."

"*Di niente.*"

Pete shoved his hands in his trouser pockets and looked down at his shoes.

"Well," interjected Lagotti after about five seconds of silence.

"I've got something to ask you and I don't know how you will react."

"If you don't ask, you'll never know, will you?"

"No… But…"

"Pete, don't sweat it. Whatever you have to say, I will not be angry and it'll go no further than this damp room." Luigi nodded to Pete, but they both understood if he put a foot wrong with Frank Senior, Luigi would be the one to break his neck and chuck his body in the nearest sewer.

"It's about Brian and the job."

"What about him?" Lagotti was getting impatient with this psychotic gas man.

"Something's not right with him. I don't trust him."

"Really? How so?"

"I can't quite say but I'm not sure we can trust him with the money and he will be mighty close to it for most of the day of the job."

"This is true. Can you tell me why? I respect your instincts but I'd like to understand better."

Pete couldn't think of anything specific apart from the fact Brian was a coon lover, but Frank Senior wouldn't see that as a sufficient reason to have him killed.

"He'll betray us at some point and we shouldn't share our winnings with a man who'll stab us in the back."

"Have you spoken to Frank about your concerns, if you think he will turn on us?"

"No, I came straight to you."

"And how long have you had this… feeling about Brian?"

"Well. It's been a while but our trip to get the guns sealed the deal for me."

"How so?"

"He started whoring around while the merchandise was still in the trunk. That's not what I need in a business partner."

"I understand. So what do you want of me, apart from to hear your concerns?"

"If things go down on the day, I want your backing and your permission to do what needs to be done to take care of matters."

"Of course you do. Is there anything else you want to talk to me about?"

"No, sir."

"Then let's get the fuck out of this shit-hole. It's damper than my wife's pussy." And with that, Lagotti stood up and left, sandwiched between Paul and Luigi, both of whom had remained perfectly still throughout the whole conversation, apart from Luigi's one nod.

Lagotti figured Pete would kill Brian after he came out of the bank with Frank and the other one. But he also knew this would be the least of Pete's problems because there would be no money coming out with them. And that would make him mad and try to do something foolish. So Paul and Luigi would need to be on hand to deal with the inevitable situation.

Back at the auto shop, Lagotti sat back in his chair and flipped his feet onto his desk. A move he'd done a thousand times before. He remained still for a second or two, pondering.

"For a driver, that Pete sure loves to whack people. If he was more stable and less racist, he'd go far. But a man of quality should be able to get along with many folks, not just the ones he can tolerate."

Lagotti grabbed the reading material from his desk drawer and settled back for an afternoon's rest and relaxation.

THE FOLLOWING WEDNESDAY, Carter arrived at Frank Senior's slightly breathless. He'd walked at quite a pace to catch the bus from round the corner of the bank. Cheaper than grabbing a taxi and a damn sight more reliable. But there'd been traffic en route and everyone had taken slightly too long to get on and off and pay and such.

Now he found himself in front of the man instead of just handing over an envelope to one of his goons. Carter was scared shitless. The Shylock hadn't spoken with him for months and now he was stood in front of the guy he owed thousands to. And the last time they'd seen each other, Frank Senior had told him he would rob his own bank.

As usual, Lagotti had his head stuck inside a picture magazine and ignored Carter for quite a while. He always did that to whoever came into his office.

"Make 'em wait," he thought.

So finally, Frank Senior looked up and dropped his feet off his desk and onto the floor.

"Do you have anything for me, then?"

"Of course. Here it is," and Carter took an envelope out of his inside jacket pocket and placed it on Frank Senior's desk.

"You wanted to see me? I usually leave the package for you. I mean, have I done anything wrong?"

"Don't you fret. I just figured it'd be nice for us to have a chat."

"Oh… okay." Carter relaxed slightly because he had an ominous sinking feeling from the second he was told to go in and see Frank Senior until now, forty-three seconds later.

"I wanted to remind you of our agreement. Of how you will help me in your bank. And how Luigi will come to your apartment and tell you to bring the case in. And the next day, you'll put the paper money from the vault into that case and walk out of the place with it at the end of the day."

"Yessir."

"And I mean whatever happens, you leave at the end of the day with that case. Do you understand me?"

"Yessir, for sure. I'll leave with the case."

"At the end of the day."

"Sure."

Swirling vipers twirled around the knots in Carter's stomach. This was real, all too real. Why had he been so stupid to double up all those times? Why had he borrowed so much money from so many people he ran out of options who to borrow from next? Until the only person left was Frank Senior with his insanely high vig and his bank robbing interest. The more Carter thought about it, the more unsettled his belly became.

"Fuck with me and you are a dead man, you hear?"

"I won't."

"Get outta here. You'll be fine."

All Carter could do was to clench his ass cheeks, nod and leave. As soon as he'd left the room, he started to feel better. That was one scary muchachos. And today neither Paul, Luigi nor the matchstick chewing mute could freak him out as much as Frank Senior had just done.

THIS WHOLE IDEA with the case was becoming real in Carter's head. He'd need to find one as inconspicuous as could be, given it needed to hold all the cash in the vault. That'd be a mighty big bag. Unless he could convince Frank Senior he should only steal the racks, which would be worth the most and take up the least space. For interstate business, they also had some thousand dollar bills in stock and they'd occupy nearly no room at all.

By the time this mental meander had finished, Carter was at the door of the First Bank of Baltimore, Lansdowne branch, and entered the building. As always, old man Grimble, the security guard greeted him.

"Hey, Joe."

Joe nodded back at him but maintained his eyes unswervingly on the customers and the main area of the bank.

"Hello, Mr. Reinfeldt."

Carter smiled briefly and walked on, heading for his desk. Grimble was a decent enough guy, but was way past retirement age. He'd been kept on by JH principally because he was cheap and because this was a modest branch of a quiet bank in a peaceful part of town. Their idea of trouble was being two dimes short on the cash reconciliation at the end of the day.

Before he could get to his chair, Carter was accosted by George, the deputy manager who also happened to be JH's son. George Hunkerton got his position at the First Bank of Baltimore's Lansdowne branch by emanating from Joshua Hunkerton's seed. The only job young George could get was working for his father because he was stupid and incapable and everyone knew it. Even George. But to hide the truth from himself, he bossed people around as much as he could because he believed that was the best way to show his authority and to gain respect. He was wrong on both counts, which exemplified how dumb he was.

Seeing Carter head towards his desk when he should already have been sat there after lunch was a perfect opportunity for George to prove his superiority to Carter and the rest of the team.

"You're late back, Mr. Reinfeldt."

"Am I, George? Never mind, I'm only a couple of minutes over."

Like all the staff, Carter called George by his first name precisely because George wanted everyone to use his last name, just as they did out of respect for his father.

George scowled at Carter as he sat down at his desk and fiddled with his index cards and diary.

"Well, keep an eye on the time in future."

"Oh, I will, George." and Carter picked up his phone as if he would make a call. George stood there for a second or two, mumbled something unintelligible under his breath and sidled off back to his own desk.

Across the reception area, Miss. Galtieri and Mrs. Pieck were busy with customers. Mrs. Pieck was counting out five-dollar bills for a local businessman but Miss. Galtieri looked straight at Carter and when he caught her eye, he winked at her and she raised her eyes to the heavens as if to say: "What a pain that George is."

JH stayed in his office in the early part of the afternoon. He was in meetings with the richer customers of the bank or discussing strategy and plans with Bob Cranford. One day Carter would take his assistant manager's job. In most branches it wasn't much to write home about, but with George as useful as treacle, it actually was the second most important role as JH's right-hand man.

Carter was attracted by the power and by the extra few thousand a year. Once he became assistant manager, he'd have sufficient money not just to pay for an apartment for Mary Lou, but have enough to start a new life with her and leave Rita. They could move out of the state and he could get a bank manager's job somewhere else, someplace he could make a mark for himself without being dragged down by Rita and her negativity. About him and about what he did. Mary Lou would be with him and they'd have a lovely house with a lovely garden and a lovely car. With some lovely children too.

BUT, AS EVER, that night Carter traveled home to Rita and not Mary Lou. Their home was a bit out of town on the corner of Hazel and Baltimore Avenue. Not that far from the interstate which made it cheaper to buy, but it still had a white picket fence, flower beds and more rooms than Carter and Rita needed. They had planned on staying there forever with enough space for their family, but there was no family because they had no children. And no prospect of them either unless they adopted, but Rita wanted her own and not to look after someone's reject child, so she said, and Carter agreed with her.

They had found out Rita's tubes were fucked three years ago and since then, things had become tense between them. It had got to where they were two people, sharing a last name, but living entirely separate lives under the same roof.

The only moments of connection were dinner time and the fact they shared the same bed. They'd occasionally make love, but the pleasure was gone. It was almost like it was for old time's sake rather than anything else.

It was no surprise when he came home, Carter found Rita in her sewing room, having put the dinner in the oven a short while before. He ran down into the living room, poured himself a scotch on the rocks, and settled into his leather easy chair, holding the squat glass in his hand, slowly rotating it to cool the drink down with the three ice cubes floating in it. He stayed there until Rita called him into the dining room to eat.

They sat down opposite each other, having only said a couple of words to each other since Carter had entered the house some forty-five minutes ago.

"Thanks."

"You're welcome. Only took me a short while to rustle up."

They both looked down at the casserole and knew that Rita had spoken the truth. Quarter of an hour chopping vegetables and a few seconds to shove it in the oven. Done.

"Tastes good."

The silence of their lives enveloped them as they chewed on diced pieces of beef, carrot, potato and onion. Rita was pretty with light brown hair down to her shoulders and a cute, pointy nose. And pointy breasts. But Carter knew he no longer loved her and believed if he was leaving her he should provide for her too. They had vowed to stay together through thick and thin so he owed her if he was departing her shores.

They had been attractive shores at one point. Now Rita left him cold; no, not so much cold as empty. Besides, she'd be okay. She felt the same towards him. He knew this by the way she looked at him. And she'd find a considerably better guy with the turn of her head. Rita was a fine woman with good looks and a mighty fine way of cooking. He just needed to leave her.

AND THE FIRST real step to do that was to get a case and do Frank Senior's bidding. But the germ of an idea was taking root inside Carter's head. He thought if he was going to take the risk of stealing the cash and get away with it, why not steal the money for himself and leave the state? That way, he wouldn't have to worry about paying Frank Senior back and he'd have more to spend on his new life with Mary Lou.

Now, Carter wasn't absolutely sure about this plan because he knew there was quite a risk. If he tried to pull this off and failed, Frank Senior would most definitely kill him. But if it came good he'd be set for life.

Carter kept on thinking through the germ of this idea over the next few days. He reckoned he needed a few things to happen for his half-formed plan to work. First, he needed to swap the money out of the case so he could give Frank Senior's henchmen what they were expecting to buy himself enough time to get away. The second thing was to make sure his getaway was fast and final because there was no way back. And thirdly, he must line up Mary Lou to leave that evening after he'd passed a case full of bricks over to Frank Senior.

And that was as far as he'd got. The big weakness, he knew, was in switching out the cash for something heavy and not getting caught out. The other approach would be to not do a switch and just take the money and run. Of course, that assumed none of Frank Senior's men would be watching him during the day.

By the end of the weekend, Carter had figured out a third way, which dealt with all the problems of his first two plans. He'd wait until the end of the day, in case he was being watched, and then instead of going to the meet up, he would grab his car, pick up Mary Lou and off they'd go, leaving Frank Senior and Rita far behind them.

While Carter lay awake in bed on Sunday night putting the finishing touches to his thoughts, Rita was beside him, with her back to him. He turned towards her and rested his palm on her hip. She smiled, pleased there was still some connection between them despite all their problems. He moved his hand round to her front and they made a perfunctory attempt at sex.

"That'll keep her happy for a while," he thought as he rolled off and headed towards sleep, knowing a new day would soon be dawning.

Monday lunchtime, Carter sloped off to the Lansdowne store to buy two black cases. They'd be about the same size as each other and large enough to cope with a reasonable amount of notes. He'd grab the hundreds and twenties only because the thousands would be impossible for him to spend without arousing suspicion.

When he got to the store, he explained to Mr. Oakesen he was looking for a couple of Christmas presents for his wife's family. Something that didn't just look good, but would be sturdy too, so they'd actually want to use them.

Oakesen quickly found three contenders and Carter bought two of them, insisting Oakesen put both in big carrier bags. And when he got back to the bank, Carter placed the bags in his locker, having removed them from their carriers. And they remained in the bank until the day of the robbery.

15

CARTER HAD TO work late that evening as far as Rita was concerned. She didn't mind because for the first time in months, he had satisfied her the night before. He'd phoned Mary Lou and met her at their apartment. On his way over, he bought some cut flowers and brought a spring in his step, which she had not noticed before.

She cooked some spaghetti with a bolognese sauce. It tasted like nothing he'd had before, but this said much more about his mental state than it did about Mary Lou's cooking. Not that she wasn't handy in a kitchen, but tonight Carter wore his optimism in a prism through which he saw everything.

He mopped up the remaining sauce on his plate with some bread and licked his fingers where some tomato had smeared itself onto his hand. Something Rita would never allow him to do. Mary Lou wondered what the hell Carter was on to keep him this high. She imagined it might be happiness or hope as she'd rarely experienced an emotion even close to that during her adult life.

"You're in a good mood today, aren't you?" said Mary Lou, after they'd done the washing up and were sat down on the sofa.

"Yeah, it's been quite a few days."

"How so, dear?" While Mary Lou was here to extract information from Carter, she had got attached to him in a way she had not expected. He was just a mark when the game began.

"Well, an opportunity has arisen so we can be together properly. Without Rita in the picture, I mean."

"What opportunity?"

"I might be coming into some money."

"How?"

"Money, yeah," laughed Carter nervously. This was the first time he'd spoken out loud about his idea.

"It's a good news and bad news story."

"Oh?"

"Look, I've been in a bit of bother the last year." With those words, Mary Lou's heart sank. Just another loser with a hard luck tale.

"Owed some money to some people from some gambling debts. But I can get out from under the situation in the next few months. They want me to steal for them and then I'll be square with them." This is too freaky, thought Mary Lou.

"But if I take from them, they can't do anything because they're hardly going to go to the police and complain the money they were robbing has been stolen from them!"

A shiver ran down Mary Lou's spine. In the instant since Carter inhaled for breath, she saw what was happening. Carter was planning on ripping off the bank instead of Frank and the crew. And it sounded as if Frank Senior was putting him up to it. Holy fuck!

"So I'll take the money, leave some for Rita, and then we skip the state and never look back!"

Carter was getting excited now. And Mary Lou's head was spinning, trying to work out what was going on and how the hell to keep on top of it all.

"Dear, I don't know what to say," she responded after two seconds of silence. She leaned into him, kissed him squarely on the lips and pushed her hands under his pants. And squeezed.

SO IT WAS the following weekend, she sat on the sofa with Carter in their apartment, listening to his plans to break into a bank. As she heard what he was planning to do, two thoughts ran through her head. First, she admired him for wanting to get himself out from under his situation. Secondly, she couldn't imagine how he was going to rob their bank and steal from Frank Senior. That took more balls than she knew he had. And besides, he'd hidden from her the fact he had gambling debts so big the only place he could pick up a loan was from the Shylock.

What made her judder was that he was setting Carter up to take the money before the gang got a chance. Sneaky motherfucker.

The implications of that were still seeping into her brain and she knew she had to do something. So she took her mind off the problem the only way she knew how and fooled around a while. She undid his pants and pulled down his shorts until he stumbled off to bed, exhilarated and exhausted, drunk with euphoria, red wine and ecstasy. Mary Lou sure knew how to blow a guy off.

She sat on the floor facing the sofa, head on her hands, leaning on the seat, desperately trying to make sense of it all. Carter called down to her; she hadn't tired him out enough.

"I'll be up in a minute darling!" she shouted. Then did nothing but think. If he stole from both Frank and Frank Senior, they'd be on the run for the remainder of their lives. Neither man would rest until they got their money back and the two of them were dead. If he failed, Carter'd be deceased or penniless or both. The crazy thing was she was feeling a certain affection for the stooge. He appeared to care about her. As her, as an individual and that was something that Frank never seemed to do. Carter might actually be a good provider—for her and their kids. Mary Lou laughed at herself: "Children. Do me a favor," she thought. "What right do I have to consider children?"

But the idea didn't leave her either. Both Carter and Frank were strong men, who could provide for her and make her happy, in their own different ways. How in hell's name was she going to figure this one out?

MARY LOU WALKED upstairs and into the bedroom of their duplex. Carter lay in bed wearing nothing but a smile. She slipped off her miniskirt and panties in one downward dragging motion, undid her blouse and bra before she got in on top of him. Then they both fell asleep, dreaming of what might be. And a pile of stolen money.

Two days later, Mary Lou entered the First Bank of Baltimore for the umpteenth time, nodded at the old security guard and walked to Carter's desk. He looked up and smiled a knowing smile. By now, Joe was used to seeing her visiting, although he didn't approve of what was going on before his eyes. Joe reckoned Carter should not mix his personal life so tightly with a customer—even if she had a body like hers. He also felt that married people shouldn't play the field and Carter was pretty blatantly not just helping Mary Lou with her portfolio. She was here much too often for that and they were far too familiar with one another when she was here. Dirty bastard.

"Why doesn't he care what people think? And why is he treating his lovely wife with so much disrespect?" mumbled Grimble to himself. The truth was he had never even met Rita. To him, she was just a photo in a black frame on Carter's desk. But Grimble was not alone asking those questions.

In particular, JH was singularly unimpressed with the behavior of his senior financial consultant, albeit his only financial advisor. JH would be damned to eternal hell's fire if he gave that bigamist-in-all-but-name a promotion with a harlot paramour on his arm. No sir, that would not happen under his watch.

Mary Lou asked Carter if it was okay to use the staff bathrooms and, as ever, he nodded it was. As she brushed past him, he caught the aroma of her perfume in his breath. She pushed to open the door marked 'Staff Only' and Mrs. Pieck buzzed her in. The door itself was flimsy and the security lock was clearly more for show than protection because Mary Lou reckoned she could kick it down with flats on.

Mary Lou smiled at Mrs. Pieck and mouthed "Thank you" even though she knew the woman did not approve of guests crossing the line into the employee's sanctuary. Again, Mary Lou looked up at the ceiling, ever so briefly, to check the security cameras were still as she remembered them. Their little red lights were still failing to blink. She alone had noticed, because the first time she had come back here she had seen them working, but not since and no one appeared to have done anything about it.

SHE WALKED DOWN the passageway to the restrooms and popped inside, but her real aim was to get down to the basement. So she trotted off away from the cash tellers and headed for the door at the far end of the corridor, near the exit. She noticed this was not a purpose built place because you'd want the vault entrance further from the rear exit, if you had any sense. But Carter had explained to her how it was only a satellite office that acted as a hub for the other sites south of Baltimore. Notes from here would be distributed across ten or more sub-branches, so they were really the most important rep office the First Bank had, even though it looked quite a small affair from the front.

Mary Lou slowly turned the door handle and scurried through and down the stairs just the other side; it was like the basement she'd had when she was a girl.

At the bottom of the steps were a set of bars with two locks and beyond it the open vault. She peered into the safe to see how many shelves it had and, therefore, how much cash there was. Tuesday was the day when it was at its most full, according to Carter. Monday was when head office delivered notes for transportation to the sub-branches and Wednesday was when the distribution occurred. The safe was ripe on Tuesday. Besides, there were around thirty, maybe forty, deposit boxes lined up on the right-hand side. And they'd be crammed with bonds, jewelry and the like. A quick count of the racks alone showed Mary Lou there was more than a million dollars sat a few feet away from her. She drew in a massive breath of excitement and fear. Composing herself, she scuttled up the stairs, closing the door quietly behind her. As she pulled down her dress, which had ridden up a couple of inches when she vaulted up the staircase, she walked to the staff room door, unlocked it using the buzzer on the left door jamb and aimed straight back to Carter.

At this point she knew exactly what she'd do: whichever man had the money is where she would be. And if that meant going off with Carter then that meant Frank would need to die.

THE FOLLOWING THURSDAY, Frank checked up on Mary Lou Belle. Two minutes after she took off for the bank to pay a fleeting visit to Carter and find out whether the surveillance cameras had been fixed, Frank too left the apartment, locked up and exited the block and walked in the bus stop's direction. He watched Mary Lou get on the bus, so he skipped to his battered old Ford, hopped in and headed straight for a parking lot at the public library, near the bank and cemetery. He popped into the graveyard and pretended to show his respects to some long gone corpse and strolled past the bank to see Mary Lou touch Carter's shoulder and head for the back of the bank. Just as she said she would do: checking out the security.

Frank reckoned if his face was visible now and again in the area it would pass for normal if he was seen on the morning of the job walking through Lansdowne. He was absolutely right in that regard, but he didn't consider the fact this same act would make things much easier for those trying to recall his face if the police took eye witness interviews.

Friday, Frank popped back to the cemetery for another sign of respect to the dead man, but on this occasion he followed Carter to see what he was up to. The clerk drove out of the rear lot and headed west. Frank scampered to his vehicle with barely sufficient time to fire up the engine, turn right and get to within two hundred yards of Carter's Dodge before he took a right northbound. Soon enough, Carter pulled into a driveway near Hazel and Baltimore Avenue, got out of the car and walked inside.

Frank kept on driving and parked around the corner. He lingered a quarter of an hour and sallied back to Carter's white-fenced house. There was a big, leafy tree in the front yard. It had clearly been growing there for years and Frank shimmied up its thick trunk to see what he could see. Nothing much as the rooms were cloaked in darkness or had their curtains shut. He waited.

Nothing. So he slid down and made his way to the back of the property. Here the lights were on and the drapes were still open. In what looked like a sitting room on the first floor Carter sat swirling a whiskey around in a glass. A woman, his wife perhaps, was in the kitchen fixing their dinner.

Frank squatted in a bush by the sitting-room window until the woman called out: "Dinner's ready!"

"Coming, Rita," responded the clerk.

Frank stayed there the entire evening, but all that happened was they ate, watched television for a while together and then Rita went upstairs to knit and Carter drank whiskey until the TV went blank and he stumbled to bed, where Rita was already lying asleep.

Frank came home in the small hours and lay next to Mary Lou, out cold. After he'd warmed up under the covers, Frank reached a conclusion. He might not know whether to trust Mary Lou, but he sure as fuck knew he'd kill Carter before this job was over.

MARCH

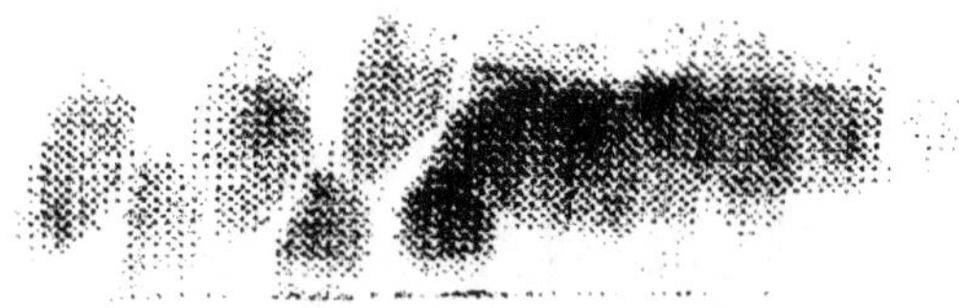

16

OVER THE NEXT three months, Frank kept a watchful eye on Rita and Carter, mainly Rita. He popped over to their house twice a week, during the day when he Carter would be out at work and the woman would be on her own.

At the back of his mind, he probably considered that peeping at Rita counted as some revenge on Carter, but it obviously wasn't, because Frank did nothing to Rita, apart from look at her from the other side of a pane of glass, and Carter was totally unaware it was going on. So no one was particularly suffering at the hands of this retribution.

Most of the time, he'd hide in the tree in their backyard and stare in at Rita as she cooked herself some lunch, watched the color TV or popped into the back small bedroom to do some sewing, which Frank had mistaken for a sitting room. But Frank still returned to the house, despite himself.

One afternoon Frank was perched in the tree when Rita broke the pattern of her behavior: instead of heading to her knitting needles, she sashayed to her bedroom. She sat on the bed and dialed some number on the phone. As soon as she had finished dialing, she rotated her body and lay down on top of the covers. After about six or seven rings, the other party on the call picked up and Rita started chatting away, twisting and curling her hair around a finger. She nestled down, her head pushing deeper into the pillow as the conversation continued. And then the most strange thing happened that almost knocked Frank off his perch.

Rita's free hand stopped playing with her curls and turned to her upper torso; she started rubbing and massaging one of her breasts. Then, two minutes later, the hand moved down her body and slid under her pants. Frank could see the fingers, moving rhythmically beneath the material. He was shocked, even though he wasn't sure precisely what was going on, but he was certain it was something dirty. And he was transfixed.

Ten minutes later, Frank had a much better idea what Rita was up to because, by that point, she had pushed her pants down below her knees. Her legs were bent and her hand was clearly under her panties. She was massaging herself. Frank had heard of such things but hadn't imagined he would see it with his own eyes. He wondered if Mary Lou got up to the same thing when his back was turned.

The one question Frank left to the end, although his eyes remained locked on Rita's hand, was: who was she talking to? That was a fella with a mighty powerful tongue. Besides, Rita was not the faithful little woman he had assumed she was.

"Carter will be in for a hell of a shock when he comes home one day," thought Frank to himself with a wry smile on his face. While all these things were true, they didn't really have much impact on the job or on anything that Frank was actually going to be doing about either Carter or Mary Lou.

ORIGINALLY, FRANK HAD hoped that, somehow, he would discover a way to threaten Carter, but he also needed Carter to be reasonably stable to deliver what they required of him for the job. So although Frank wanted to use what he'd found out about Rita, it would have too great an impact on the little man. Once they had the money, he would happily mess with Carter's head—or put a bullet through it. Just not now.

The important thing was to keep his eye on the prize: the cash in that vault needed to be in his possession and then he could spend it on his big dreams.

In the meantime, Carter must wait and Frank realized there wasn't much point in watching Rita in bed with herself any more.

Frank turned his attention back to Carter for a moment. Now they had learned what the inside of the bank looked like to a high degree of detail: the tellers, the security guard, the vault with safe and deposit boxes, was there any need for Mary Lou to continue to turn up there, risk any kind of discovery and still spend time in his apartment? The job didn't demand it any more and it would make him happier knowing Carter was a part of her past. Then he would have her to himself and could count on her for his future dreams and not be put in the annoying position of having to kill her later on. Because while he couldn't say he loved her, he did feel an affection for her. And, he reckoned, she must feel a certain affection for him, otherwise why did she stick by him while he was in the joint? She was a good-looking girl and fabulous lay. Frank never considered that Mary Lou might actually love him and she felt a strong loyalty to the man in her heart. But the same thought hadn't crossed her mind either.

He pulled himself out of his reverie and noticed he was still in the middle of a tree, so he shinned down, walked at a straight pace back to his car and drove home to the Halethorpe apartment and waited for the warmth of her body and the comfort of her linguini.

THE NEXT OCCASION he met up with his uncle, Frank had just eaten a salami-on-rye from a diner in Lansdowne two blocks away from the cemetery. They hooked up by the same gravestone as the first time they discussed the job.

Things had moved on for both of them and the plan was taking very satisfactory shape.

"How's it going, my boy?" asked the old money lender, investor, business partner and relative.

"Good, Uncle."

"And what exactly does that entail?"

"We've got a great picture of what the inside of the bank looks like, thanks to Mary Lou."

"Great ass, that girl," interrupted Lagotti.

"And the crew is in superb shape too. I've kept them separate in the main. I don't want us to be seen hanging together in case we're spotted on the day, but Andrew and Brian are close so the core of the team is okay. And Pete's a loner anyway so I wouldn't expect him to be a social butterfly."

"He's one crazy fucker, for sure."

"Well, he's certainly the least stable of all of us, but I respect your recommendation. From what I hear, Pete the Wheels is the best driver not in the can by a wide margin."

Frank waited for a second to let that idea hang in the air.

"But some reckon he has, um, homicidal tendencies. There's talk that Martin, who was my initial choice to ride shotgun, was killed by him three months ago. I did nothing out of respect for you."

"Thank you. Pete does have a history, for sure. I know nothing of this Martin situation but it wouldn't be the first time that Pete has spilled blood."

Frank was silent for a second or two, mulling over Lagotti's words and the implication he had a psychopath in his gang.

"I'll keep on eye on him then. The good news is his only task is to drive away from the bank fast and get us out of town."

"Yeah and not kill anyone along the way."

Frank turned to his uncle to see how much he was joking, but Frankie was playing a straight game.

"And then we bring the proceeds over to you."

"Indeed," noted monotone Lagotti, waiting to find out what was going on inside Frank's head.

"So Uncle, what's the deal with laundering the cash?"

"Well, young man, I'm glad you've posed that question. As I said a while ago, I've wanted you to focus on the job at hand, but now is the time for us to talk business."

"So what's the deal, Uncle?"

"What do you think it should be?" asked Lagotti, knowing he didn't want to be the first to name his price.

"Well," smiled Frank, "ten cents on the dollar as there's going to be a lot of our sweat and blood in this job."

Lagotti put up his hand to silence Frank. The initial offer was painfully inadequate and they both knew it. Frank had only started so low because he was negotiating with his uncle, otherwise by now Lagotti would have signaled Luigi to break some of Frank's fingers.

"That's a touch low, my boy. The operation would not be happening if it wasn't for my initial investment for the guns, the explosives and the vehicles. And that ignores the simple fact that without me refreshing the money at the other end of the job, there'll be nothing at all."

"So what do you suggest?" asked Frank, knowing they needed to have this sorted out quickly, because his first offer was close to an insult.

"People usually receive twenty-five cents on the dollar from me, but I can give you thirty as you're family."

"Is that the best you can offer us?" Frank said quietly, facing the ground, eyes searching for the base of the nearest gravestone. Lagotti noticed the change in Frank's tone and recognized his nephew had stepped a bit too far, but also wanted to get a better deal for himself.

"Tell you what," he added, "make it forty cents on the dollar and stop there."

"Thank you. You won't regret this at all."

"I know it, my boy. Is there anything for us to discuss?"

"No, Uncle."

"Then with our tribute agreed, let's get outta this bone yard," he responded. Lagotti unceremoniously stood up, hugged his step nephew and departed the cemetery.

Pleased with the deal he'd got from his uncle, Frank decided things were actually going okay and he could afford some R-and-R with Mary Lou. This would also give him a chance to check her out and try to figure out what she was really up to.

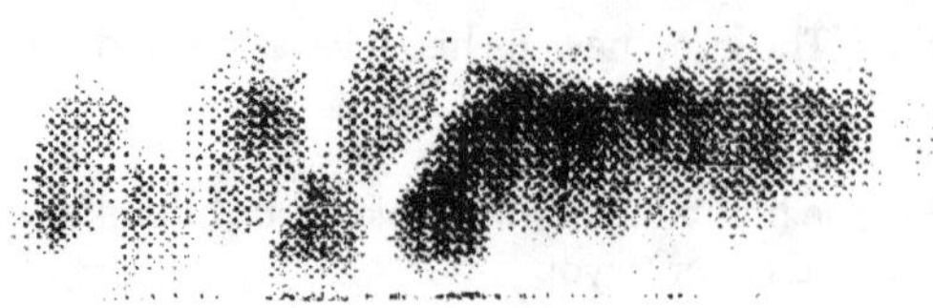

17

CARTER AND MARY Lou waited in line to see a movie, just to break free from the routine of their daily lives, so he said. Besides, the tellers had told him it was funny and that counted as a recommendation. *No Way to Treat a Lady* was a thriller starring Rod Steiger and Lee Remick with George Segal as a cop.

Mary Lou thought Steiger was still rather handsome in an old-man sort of manner. But she certainly wouldn't throw him out of bed if he turned up one night although Segal was far too nebbish for Mary Lou's taste. There was something about his nose she didn't like and, while she couldn't really say what it was, it was a big enough deal to her that she knew he wasn't attractive to her.

Carter had a bookworm charm to himself, but he was a gambler and liked to play the odds. The risk taker in him was what she found tempting. As she mused while the movie droned on, the tricks and turns of the plot left her cold, there was clearly a physical level to the attraction and she was definitely enjoying sex with him more than with Frank. Somewhere inside him was some kind of kindred spirit. He understood her and she got him. Now, he only really knew her as the person she was pretending to be. She made up some stuff to help him believe and trust her, but apart from that, she was being honest with him. Or as true as she could be with a married man out of whom she was extracting information so her fella could steal from his place of work.

Mary Lou shifted her weight onto the other side of her body—these seats sure lacked comfort—and leaned her head on Carter. The film felt as though it had been running for quite a while. She loved his smell and inhaled it off his shoulder and sleeve.

But the movie was boring and she wasn't out with Carter to be bored. That was not part of her plan. Besides, tomorrow she would be flying down to Florida with Frank and Mary Lou was very excited. She had only flown once before when she visited Ron in Vegas and that was scary because she negotiated the airport by herself. This time Frank would carry that burden.

To take her mind off Florida and Steiger, she dropped her arm nearest Carter off the shared armrest and placed it on his leg. She started to stroke his thigh, which made him open his legs slightly to make space for her hand to travel up and down its full length, all the way from his knee to his crotch and back again.

Within a minute, she felt how her manipulations aroused him. She smiled to herself in the dark, pleased with her work so far and the fact she turned him on merely by stroking him until his pants were wet to touch.

AFTERWARDS THEY GRABBED a bite to eat in a chichi restaurant round the corner, called *El Greco*. Carter took a rib-eye and Mary Lou chose the lamb chop. With a choice of potato and vegetables, she picked mint sauce on the side.

Carter had been spending most of his waking moments thinking about cash. The money every week for Frank Senior and the money he was planning to steal from Frank Senior and the bank.

Each chance he thought about these two things, he imagined Mary Lou and himself lying on a beach on the west coast or Mexico, walking along the seashore with his palm on her butt and a bunch of other clichés.

Right now, he was holding her hand in a restaurant in downtown Baltimore, hiding in plain sight from the world and his wife. They sat next to each other but their hands remained under the table, resting on Mary Lou's leg. Even though they were miles away from Lansdowne, the last thing he needed was any trouble from anyone. So he stroked the back of her hand with his and they talked about the show. About how sexy George Segal looked (Mary Lou, gently teasing) and how the film seemed to possess no moral compass (Carter, pompous).

He was so paranoid about being spotted with Mary Lou they didn't meet in Lansdowne to get to the movie; he made Mary Lou catch a bus into Baltimore. To make matters worse, this was the first time Carter braved being seen in the outside world since they hooked up those three or four months ago. This was a big step for him and Mary Lou knew it, but he sure was showing how much he trusted her, loved her and wanted to be with her. Even if he spent most of his time with Rita and hid with Mary Lou in an apartment in Halethorpe—the location for which was suggested by Mary Lou, but he never for a minute asked himself why this single woman hadn't just offered him a key to her own place instead of making him rent out a suite.

Strangely, the conversation in the restaurant was stilted between them. By shifting the context away from that apartment and turning themselves into a normal couple doing ordinary things, the two of them were all out of whack. Their routine constituted an easy meal put together by Mary Lou, some horseplay on the sofa and then the rest of the evening was spent in bed, stroking, sucking and squelching in between chats and licks until one of them fell asleep, which was usually Carter. Mostly, Carter's love making included consideration for her body too.

So, sat in *El Greco*, he found the conversation between them far from relaxed, precisely at the time he was hoping everything would come good for them. Mary Lou sensed it too. His response was to move his hand up her thigh and under her black miniskirt—all the rage in New York.

While they slowly shared their profiteroles, Carter's fingers stroked her upper leg and conversation ground to a halt, while they both thought about the cream in their mouths and the tip of his index finger, curling against Mary Lou's flesh. He paid for the meal in cash, leaving a hefty gratuity. Then they drove back to their apartment.

18

MARY LOU STROLLED through first and flipped on the living room light, while Carter closed the door and hung his coat on a peg. By the time he turned to face the couch, Mary Lou had walked back to stand in front of him. She kissed him squarely on the mouth, hands stroking, rubbing, caressing his back, torso, arms. She put her fingers on his lips to shush him and pushed down her skirt and shimmied it off. When she bent down to finally remove the garment from around her feet, her head was level with Carter's belt. She kneeled down, undid it, pulled down his shorts and sucked him off, there in the hallway. Carter didn't know what to think or do, apart from lean on the wall with his fingertips and allowed the rush of orgasm overtake him.

Mary Lou took his hand and, without a word, led him into the bedroom. She let go of his grip and removed her powder blue blouse. Carter took his cue and started undressing too. He watched as she unclipped her bra to reveal her perfectly round nipples, slinked off her black panties and slid into bed. He realized after his shirt landed on the floor, all he had done was to watch, stare at Mary Lou and breathe in that amazingly beautiful body of hers. He smiled at her as she lay under the covers.

"Hurry, my darling," she purred at him. He didn't need a second reminder. Carter kicked off his pants which were already hanging off only one foot and removed his shorts, which were damp from his hallway encounter with her mouth. Their bodies touched each other and lips, hair, arms and torsos writhed away as they both tried to give as much pleasure to the other that their imaginations would allow.

A half hour later when they were done, Carter was resting his head on Mary Lou's stomach, casually stroking and squeezing one of her breasts as they were talking. His left ear was immediately above the top of her rose and he could inhaled their sex on her groin. He was content in that moment.

They talked about which parts of their bodies they liked to be licked—as any other couple might do. Later the conversation moved on to their kinkiest sex acts. Carter admitted he had once done it in his parents' bed while they were at a dinner party. This was with his childhood sweetheart, Rita, naturally. Mary Lou told him she had once been tied up and fucked repeatedly by a guy named Ron.

Carter was shocked. So much that he stopped rubbing her breast, turned round and faced her.

"Are you serious?"

"Why… yes? It was a long while ago anyway. Does it bother you?"

"Um… I don't think so. It's more I wasn't expecting you to say anything close to that. I mean, I've done nothing like it."

"Well, would you like to try some time?"

"Maybe."

The truth was that while it sounded pretty scary to Carter, the idea also sounded very sexy. He lay back down and Mary Lou sat on top of him until they both came. Later that night, Mary Lou told him she would have to leave town the next day to visit her sick mother who lived in Florida.

"How long are you going to be gone for?"

"Two days is all. I'll be back by Monday; Tuesday at the latest. But she really needs me right now."

"Okay then," his voice trailing off with a mix of disappointment and tiredness. He weakly squeezed her butt cheek—Mary Lou still lay on top of him, her rose and his groin touching—and promptly fell asleep.

When he awoke the following morning, she had already got up and left. He found a note pinned to the fridge door: *I'll call you when I get back. Bring some scarves over and we can tie ourselves up in knots. MLB.*

Carter gulped, but noticed he was getting hard at the thought of it. That lunchtime he popped into the Lansdowne department store and bought six silk shawls, all different colors. Mary Lou and he would have a party when she got back. It was only at this point he really cared about Mary Lou's mother making a quick recovery.

THAT NIGHT, CARTER found himself sat opposite Rita over a bowl of casserole, having downed a glass of scotch before the meal, as he did every evening with her. The liquor deadened his mind to his situation with her.

There was something different about tonight: his head was part-filled with thoughts and images of those silk scarves. And, as he chewed on the cubes of beef and potato, Carter started thinking he had been too harsh with Rita—they hadn't rushed into their marriage. Or he was horny and he knew he wouldn't be inside Mary Lou for many days.

Either way, after they had eaten and the dishes and cutlery had been washed and dried up, Rita was drying her hands on the tea towel they kept by the oven for just this purpose, her back to Carter. He walked up to her and wrapped his arms around her belly, nuzzling her neck with his lips.

"Why Carter," and before she could finish her sentence, he had moved his hands up to her breasts and was squeezing both of them at the same time. She raised her arms, put them over his head and rested them on the back of his collar, helping him get complete access to her chest. She turned her head sideways and they kissed while he started teasing her nipples.

A few minutes later, they were upstairs naked. Carter took out one scarf he'd bought earlier that day and tied it around Rita's left wrist and attached the other end to the bed post. She looked quizzically at him, but smiled and whispered: "Go on."

He did the same with her other three limbs so she was sprawled out like a starfish. At this point he realized he had no idea what to do next. He'd never got involved with anything close to this in his life and it was way beyond his experience or imagination. He thought about lying on top of her but that seemed so tame. So he did the only other thing he could imagine, which was the least bit transgressive. He masturbated all over Rita's body. Not on her face because that would have been too much like the porn films he'd seen when he was at college.

At first, Rita's expression was a picture of surprise, but it transformed into pleasure. When he undid the scarves after finished, she rubbed her breasts, almost as though she was trying to get him inside her body. Meanwhile, Carter kneeled on the bed between her legs, bent down and licked her until Rita came. Like old times—only now he felt more empty than before and wanted to be breathing in Mary Lou's scent more than any moment in his life up to this point, and not Rita's acrid pussy. Instead, all he noticed was his own spunk smeared around Rita's torso and the aroma of sex in the room. And he felt dirty and ashamed, but not so much to stop her sucking him off before they both fell asleep.

By Tuesday, Carter was longing for Mary Lou's return and it wasn't solely because of the scarves, but they helped. No, despite his brief foray with Rita and sex, he was still hooked on Mary Lou and her damn rose.

IN THE MORNING, Mary Lou left the apartment, went straight over to her own place, changed into some comfortable clothes, fucked Frank until he was red sore and they flew down to Florida that afternoon. Mary Lou was happy on the inside for the first time since she met Frank outside Baltimore Penitentiary the previous August.

As soon as the door to the DC-8 opened after they landed, the heat in the air hit them. Even though it was only March, the temperature was still super warm compared to home. Mary Lou undid another button on her blouse to let more of her skin breathe. She watched Frank's eyes look down at her and she was pleased she could even elicit that kind of gaze in the man she'd known for almost ten years now. As a response to what he was clearly thinking in that man's head of his, she glanced up at him and ran her tongue slowly around her lips.

In the cramped aisle on the plane while everyone stood waiting to disembark, Frank's hand got to the back of her jeans and he tried to squeeze her groin from behind, sneaking one finger between her legs so that it curled and pushed up against her. It gave her a frisson of a thrill and a warm sudden burst in down below. She liked him. He was a good man.

Mary Lou bought a bikini with Frank's money in a shore-side boutique and he even found some trunks to wear before they hit the sand. They lay on hired beach loungers all day long and soaked in the rays, massaging each other's backs as they rubbed in sun oil to bring out their tans, which had little chance of coming good given the time they could spend before they returned home.

They held hands with each other as they walked along Ocean Drive, Frank's jaw dropping almost whenever someone sashayed past. For once, Mary Lou thought they were a real couple.

For the second time in twenty-four hours, Mary Lou found herself eating in a restaurant. Now she knew how movie stars felt. Somehow the food was more intense than at home. The tablecloth corners were sharply creased and the bread appeared in a basket in the middle of the table and had its own cloth cover. He sure was treating her well.

AFTER THE WALK back to the hotel in the balm of the evening, they stopped off in the next door bar for a martini. Clearly, Frank was trying very hard because Mary Lou had only ever seen him drink beer, not cocktails. To be fair, apart from the odd shot of liquor—and the glass of brandy with Carter—she was hardly a cocktail queen either. But she got a taste for vodka martinis on that trip. After they emptied their glasses, Frank suggested another but she wasn't so sure. He insisted, saying: "Martinis are like tits: one's too few and three's too many." And she had to agree.

So by the time they got back to their hotel suite, they were both soaked in high grade alcohol and lust.

In their room, as soon as the door was closed behind them, the pair turned to each other and kissed, hugging close and leaning their legs into each other to make their whole bodies merge into one.

And the most amazing thing about that experience was he had done nothing like that with his fingers or tongue before. She knew this as it was happening, but thought about it again when Frank slept with his head on her stomach in the middle of the night. Never made her come like that before. Ever. Period. And the same situation happened the following evening with fewer martinis and a lot more care and time. He was one good man.

Having spent the entire night touching, licking and thrusting themselves until after the sun peeked over the horizon, Mary Lou and Frank exited their hotel room with the strong aroma of their bodily fluids. And left the haven of Miami for the harsh reality of suburban Baltimore.

They were each totally exhausted but completely satisfied. Comfortable with each other's bodies; calm in the presence of the other. In that moment, he decided Mary Lou would survive the job, providing he could ensure he stopped her from spending too much time with the bank clerk.

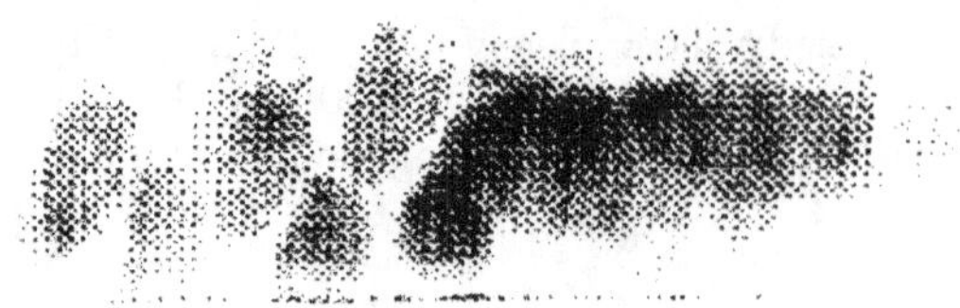

19

THE NEXT DAY Mary Lou phoned Carter and met up with him on the Sunday evening. The good news: Carter was horny and easy to con; his concern for Mary Lou's fictional mother was fleeting, so she didn't need to go into any convoluted explanations or lies. The bad news: he was impossible to distract outside of his tunnel vision sex thoughts.

So this meant, despite all the great times she'd had with Frank the past week, she found herself in bed with Carter with no insight into what was happening at the bank, if anything.

With Miami still firmly lodged in her brain, and Frank's newfound consideration for her body, she was veering towards sticking with Frank and the last thing she really fancied doing was spending the night with Carter, despite his general homeliness and immediate sexual desire.

As ever, she had cooked them a pesto based pasta meal and they sat on the sofa, as they had so many times before. Only now, he truly had bedroom eyes.

"Is your mother better now?"

"What? Er… yes, thank goodness."

"Yeah."

"By the time I arrived, she was on the mend, so all I really had to do was cook her meals, keep the place tidy for her and things like that. No big deal. And because she was sleeping mostly, because she was tired, I lay in the garden for a few hours to soak up the sun."

"You sure are looking good," said Carter, stroking her cheek with the back of one finger. He ran it down the side of her face, down her neck and it followed its natural course along the neckline of her tee shirt to her cleavage. He let his fingertip curl over the material and pulled it towards him, stretching the blouse as he leaned slightly into her enabling him to look at her breasts—or at least as much of them as were visible from outside her bra.

"Sure looking good," he repeated, leaning in further until he could smell her scent and lick her body.

Ten minutes later they lay in bed, with Carter tied up by some silk scarves he had brought for that purpose. He was anticipating extremes of sexual delight and Mary Lou began by stroking his upper thighs.

Maybe it was the resentment of being in that bedroom in the first place, perhaps it was the greater experience on her part and she plain forgot to only slowly ramp up the matter at hand. When she leaned over him and massaged him up and down, it was all he could bear. Unfortunately for Carter and his overactive libido, this caused him a bit too much of a shock and his body shutdown and he blacked out.

THEN IT WAS Mary Lou's turn to be shocked, because she really didn't think she would get that kind of reaction from him. She placed her fingertips on his jugular to make sure all was okay. Once she knew he was merely out of it, she took herself to the living room, leaving him attached to the bed, but he was hardly going anywhere for a while.

Instead, after mopping herself up, she lay on the sofa, one leg propped up on the armrest, musing on the last few days. Her life with Frank, her time with Carter. And the money. After midnight, she untied Carter and fell asleep next to him. He was just the latest in a long line of men who had let her down in the sack. The question remained whether he'd repeat the experience in the bank.

The following day, they both traveled into Lansdowne with the objective of getting to the bank, only Carter walked straight in so he was there before the doors opened at nine, whereas Mary Lou popped over to a coffee shop on Charleston and Forth, several blocks the other side of the cemetery until after ten.

When she pushed at the entrance to the First Bank, as ever she nodded to Grimble, his wrinkled right hand hovering over his revolver as it always did whenever the door opened.

Grimble was a cheap and reliable security guard. A cop who took early retirement because he was shot in the line but still had a decade to go before he could afford to stop working. So sitting and standing near the entrance to a suburban bank was the perfect solution for him. He got the occasional bit of exercise, some money kept flowing into his savings account and he left the house and close the door on Mrs. Grimble, who would otherwise have spent the whole day bitching and moaning about how useless and shitty he was. The First Bank job was the best result ever.

Mary Lou hopped over to Carter's desk and sat opposite him like a customer should. His eyes lit up to see her again even though it had only been an hour since he last touched her lips.

He told her there had been a robbery at a bank branch at Linthicum Heights, north of Baltimore Airport. It happened over the weekend and head office was sending someone over that day to revamp all security cameras and, over the next week, all entry doors would be strengthened and any other vulnerabilities assessed by central services.

Mary Lou's initial thought was that they should hit the bank tomorrow before the real heat came down on this place, but that idea was immediately slapped in the face when Carter mentioned they decided to hold back any big movements of monies until processes improved. First on the list: the security cameras and the security doors. Her eyes veered towards the flimsy excuse of a piece of plywood that currently constituted the staff door. Next would be the vault.

She sighed inside but at least she'd find out early about whatever was done. Because at heart he was a gambler, Carter was always looking for the angles, spotting the flaws in the system and, instead of letting his superiors gain from his insights, he preferred to show off to Mary Lou. One hand job per insight kept him very happy and the gang fully informed. Within a week of the audit which was immediate and swift, she knew what the new layout would be even before it was installed. And Frank had figured out almost all the ways round it before he called the next meeting of his business associates.

20

THEY WERE DUE to all meet up with Frank again on Sunday in the peeling paint and termite-infested walls of the factory, so Pete spent the day before in Lucy's trailer. He had not intended to hook up with her again, so soon at any rate, but he got bored, was horny and wouldn't pay for a hooker: he was short of cash, still waiting for the latest payment from Frank Senior.

Off down the highway to buy coffee and a doughnut and to wait for some sweet dessert. Lucy didn't mind because she liked the company and he helped keep her bed warm. Lucy deserved better than Pete, but he was definitely punching above his weight.

Before he left the trailer the following morning, Pete had a shower and washed the stink of their sex from his body. Lucy was still asleep, one titty poking out from under the sheets. As he was drying himself with a rather small towel he'd found hanging up, he considered doing something about the tit: cover it up or fuck Lucy again. He couldn't decide what he actually wanted, but he looked at his watch and decided he didn't have time to do either. He walked out the mobile home, hopped into the car and headed straight back onto the I-95 towards Baltimore.

As he neared the city, the highway started to resemble a parking lot. For some reason, the traffic got thicker until he was only moving a few feet every five or ten minutes. By the time the vehicles in front had cleared, Pete's blood pressure had risen significantly and you wished you'd had a dollar for each obscenity to come out of his mouth.

ANDREW AND BRIAN drove to the meet together. Andrew rode shotgun. Again. That was fine. It wasn't as if he enjoyed driving that much although he had been practicing behind Brian's back. After Brian ran off to the firing range, Andrew hit a dirt track he'd found. Standing starts, brodying about and massive acceleration after a steady forty.

When Brian had parked, they hopped out of the car and both picked their way around the rubble to get to the rest of the crew, although they still had to stand waiting for Pete for about a quarter of an hour. Andrew was tired and really didn't fancy waiting round, especially not for the likes of some bushwhacker like Pete. But wait is what they did.

"Okay guys," said Frank during the interminable hanging around, "once we're all here I will talk about the new security arrangements at the bank. But Andrew, Brian and myself will need to meet up in a much warmer place to go through things in more detail and to figure out how we will crack the joint wide open."

This concerned Andrew as Frank had led him to regard this as a straight walk-in, walk-out job with no hassle in the middle. Now it was looking as though it was more complicated than that and if the security was the thing that was more sophisticated, the risk was becoming higher too. For the same money.

"Well that's mighty upright of you," he responded, not really knowing what he meant by those words but he felt like somebody should say something vaguely positive, even though he wasn't very positive himself. Brian wasn't going to mention anything for sure as Andrew was by far the more talkative of the two of them. And Brian tended not to say anything in public, in larger groups.

Still, Frank's comment was not good and hung on Andrew's mind even after Pete eventually arrived and Frank could start his briefing.

"Are we not going to wait for Frank Senior?" asked Andrew as Frank inhaled to begin talking.

"No, he's not coming. I mean, he never was coming. I've talked to him separately. He knows what I'm about to say to you and he's okay with that."

Andrew shifted his gaze to Brian, who looked back at him with a brief wink to show he thought the same: that Frank Senior should share their pain and not leave it to his nephew—well, step nephew really—to dish out the shit.

Besides, thought Andrew, they'd been waiting for months with nothing happening and the new security meant they would have to wait even longer. With more risk for the same money. Andrew didn't like risk at the best of times and steel doors were not the best of times. Far from it. About as far from the best of times as you could go without falling into the sea.

Andrew could hear Frank's voice in the background as his mind continued to process the implications of the cameras working now and the steel doors. Frank had mentioned metal cutters at their first meet, but it sounded like they were going to be a necessary piece of kit, which meant it'd have to be dragged into the bank and then dragged out—in daylight to slow them down and to help any passerby civilian see them and remember them. More risk, same money.

PETE WAS THE last to arrive and his embarrassed apologies were way too quiet and slow to make anybody feel better. Bottom line: if your wheel man can't turn up on time when all you're doing is talking about a job, what are the chances he'll be there when you run out of a bank with a bag of cash in your hand? They all thought it but no one said it. Pete knew though and that was enough for all of them. The sheepishness of his apology was the most acknowledgement anyone would hear. But Pete knew.

There were two items on Frank's agenda and he knew neither would make the crew exactly happy. So he offered them a shit sandwich.

"Thanks for making your way over here, guys. I've got some news for you all. First thing is our intel on the bank continues to be excellent," and Frank turned his shoulders towards Mary Lou, who again was stood right by him, wearing flats this time.

"Some of you were probably thinking we'd have hit the joint by now," continued Frank, "and I'd have agreed with you only last week. But if we'd done that, we'd have walked out of the bank whistling Dixie.

"Mary Lou has found out they've upgraded their security two weeks ago, so we must change our approach once we're inside the place."

There was a general murmuring and shuffling of feet to show to Frank that, while everyone would really be all right to get the job over and done with, no one wanted to walk into a steel cage. Mary Lou could sense the men were growing restless, getting itchy to move on with the job and the last thing they needed to hear was about more delays. They hadn't earned since the summer and although Frank Senior had been supplying them each with keeping-safe money, they all knew they'd have to pay that back out of their end of the bounty. So it wasn't really earning.

With that downer firmly under his belt, Frank punched them all in the solar plexus with news about the getaway. On the day, after the job, they would all meet up with Frank, hand the takings over to him and split up for a month or so.

"This'll give me time to get the stolen cash to Frank Senior, who'll launder the cash. His usual rate is twenty-five cents on the dollar, but we're getting a better price as I'm family: forty cents. As you know, the biggest problem with bank jobs is the money's so easy to trace and that's how most people got caught. So, yes, it sounds like we're losing some money but we gain our freedom."

Andrew and Brian looked at each other. Pete ground his molars. Mary Lou could sensed they weren't happy, yet again, but knew they weren't as smart as her Frank to see it was the safest way to deal.

"So it's free money or jail money, then?"

"Yes, babe. And anyway, the bank vault will be full to the brim with cash, because you will find out the best day for us to strike."

"We'll be in clover, Frank."

Mary Lou smiled and turned her head to make sure she caught everyone's eye. Reluctantly, everybody nodded. Deep down they all knew bank money was dangerous to have in your pocket. But no one liked to lose more than half their winnings.

"How much is in the bank?" asked Pete.

"We're talking around a million dollars," replied Mary Lou.

"So even after the cash is cleaned up by Frank Senior, who's been funding us from the start, we will still be left with enough to never need to do another job again. Unless you want to use gold leaf to wipe your ass!" joked Frank.

They all laughed at the thought of that and the tension was eased. Frank carried on describing the getaway and how they'd all hook up again a month later to get their stake and then split up and never see each other again.

Mary Lou looked round the group again and she could tell every damn one of them was imagining how they were going to spend their share of the prize. Frank put his hand on her ass and up her crack from behind, as he had done on the plane. She turned to him and kissed him on the cheek.

"We'll all do fine," she murmured to them all and they nodded in agreement.

"Any questions? Okay then, I'll hook up with Pete, Andrew and Brian separately to talk about the changes to the security. The next time we meet up should be just before the off. See you then."

As Pete sat in his car, he thought of when Frank pat Mary Lou's butt before they all split up and his mind returned to Lucy's ass. So he drove along the highway to get another portion of sweet dessert from his favorite waitress.

21

MONDAY AFTERNOON, HE formed his body into a long straight line for a massive stretch along its entirety. His feet stuck out of the bottom of the blanket and his hands banged against the side of the kitchen unit. That's when he was awake enough to realize he was still in the trailer. He turned his head to see the back of Lucy's and he rolled over to face her; he wanted some fun.

She groaned a little and swatted his palm away, pushing it off her breast and onto her stomach. He sent his fingers upwards and she sighed and grabbed his hand and put it between her legs. If he would rummage around, he might as well do something useful, she thought, as the cloud of unconsciousness was punctured by the sharp stabs of pleasure and pain caused by Pete's fingertips and long nails, respectively.

Later, Pete hauled his tired, half-drunk sorry ass out of the trailer and back onto the I-95. When he got home, there was a message Andrew'd called. He walked to a phone booth across the street from his apartment and returned the call.

PETE MET UP with Andrew and Brian on Tuesday. This time in a venue Brian chose, so only Brian was happy with the decision. For Pete, the White Horse was a touch upmarket for his taste, selling martinis as well as beer and, for Andrew, there was beer as well as cocktails. Brian smiled because to him, the White Horse was just another bar, so it was perfect. Brian bought them a Bud each and they sat down in a booth far back, away from the door.

Pete wasn't too sure why the two men needed to get together with him because they were the muscle, Frank was the brains and he was the Wheels. But he figured it'd be worth it in case they had a side deal on the go. So he let the chitchat last a few minutes but got bored and wanted to cut to the chase.

"So, what's this all about, then?" he slid into the conversation when Andrew inhaled, possibly for the first time since they sat down.

"Well," said Andrew in an almost whisper, drawing Pete's head closer to his just so he could hear the dude, "we're a bit worried, you see?"

"About what? I want the job to be over and we ain't exactly rushing into things but I ain't exactly frettin'."

"No, it's not the waiting."

"What, then?" Pete was getting irritated at this point. If not the job why the pussyfooting around? Spit it out, guys. Man up.

"Well, it's Martin."

"Martin?" Pete acted all surprised and quizzical but he'd been waiting for this day for months now. He thought they had chickened out, but he figured they'd work out Martin vanished in a puff the evening after he and Pete met up. Then again, Pete didn't particularly want this conversation either.

"Yes, Martin."

"What ever happened to him?" asked Pete, raising his eyebrows.

"That's the sixty-four million dollar question, Pete. What did happen to him?" said Andrew, slowly staring straight into Pete's eyes, boring a hole into his brain. Brain leaned forward, his elbows resting on the booth table.

Pete felt his revolver still tucked into his jeans, ready if things turned ugly. But he sat himself back, put both arms on the booth, as open as his body language could be.

"I don't rightly know. We hooked up for a beer, yakked over another one and that was that. Didn't see him again and never got a call from him neither. Plain vanished in a puff."

"Vanished in a puff all right."

"Yep."

"So what do you think happened to him?" said Brian, also staring deep into Pete's soul.

"Fucked if I can say."

"No idea at all?"

"Nope. Sure is a mystery."

"A mystery," repeated Brian.

"But the interesting thing," picked up Andrew, "is that you were the last person to see him alive."

"WAS I? DIDN'T he just skipped town."

"Why d'you think that?"

"Well, I thought that's what you said he'd done and you knew him far better than me. And he mentioned he was thinking of checking out California when I chugged a beer with him."

"Really?"

"Yeah, wanted to check out the Malibu talent or something. Damn good idea if you ask me."

The conversation meandered this way and that for another five, ten minutes and Pete could tell they didn't trust him but they wouldn't possess the cajones to accuse him or do anything real with their mistrust, which was fine by Pete.

Two minutes later, Pete made his excuses and departed, making a mental note not to be left in a room with those two on his own, in case they did something more about their disquiet. He also decided after the job was over he'd organize the end of Andrew. Pete wasn't that bothered about Brian any more: rightly or wrongly, Pete didn't think much of Brian and he certainly cared less about the nigger Martin. Didn't have Andrew's brains neither.

The day after, Pete got in touch with Frank and they met up in Frank's favorite cemetery on the Friday. There was a steel conversation to be had.

As usual, Frank arrived early and Pete arrived ten minutes late.

"Do me a favor: next meet up arrive on time. When we exit that bank, we want to be sure you will be outside."

"Don't sweat it. I'm always there when I'm on the clock." Frank stared at him for a half a second, holding his gaze just long enough for Pete to realize how unimpressed he was with Pete's statement.

"Anyhow… if we cut through to get into the vault, how will that impact our vehicles?"

"Well, as I told you right at the start, oxyacetylene cylinders are damn heavy and we must reinforce the chassis of each vehicle and bump up the suspension or we'll be dragging our sorry asses along the ground. So the issue I've got for you is this: what are the chances we're going to cut into the safe?"

Frank paused for a second, contemplating the enormity of the question.

"We must assume we will need it. If we don't bring it with us, we could end up walking out the joint with only our dicks in our hands."

Pete nodded. He'd reached the same conclusion before he arrived at the cemetery and was pleased he would not need to convince Frank to change his mind.

Frank explained how the best plan would be for there to be a van at the back of the bank so if they needed the kit they could grab it real easy. Either way, they'd use a second vehicle to leave the scene of the crime with. For Frank, this meant he needed to change his plans slightly: the best thing to do with the van would be to torch it before they sped away. It would act as a decoy for any cop who got close and would also mean they wouldn't need to find another driver.

They left via different exits. Pete traveled straight to a scrapyard and bought some steel girders for welding.

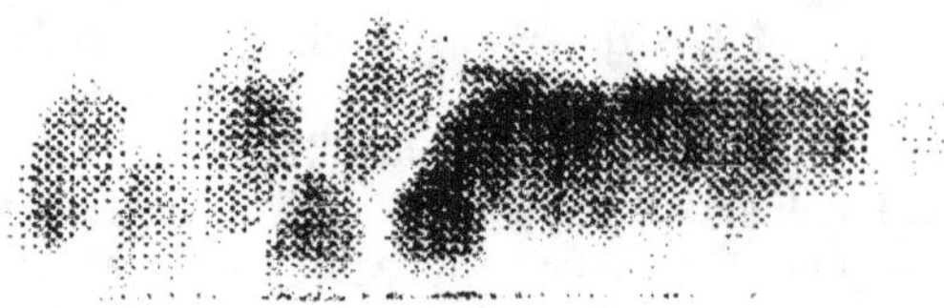

22

WEDNESDAY WAS THE day when Frank, Andrew and Brian hooked up in a Baltimore bar, Finian's Rainbow, where the locals knew each other but tolerated strangers by ignoring them and hoping they'd go away as quickly as possible. This suited the three of them down to the ground as they weren't planning to stick around very long.

Frank kicked off proceedings after he bought a round of beers for them all and made sure he'd left a tip, but not too big as he really didn't want to be the kind of customer who'd be remembered.

"Down to business."

"What's the story?" asked Andrew.

"The simple truth is someone's robbed a different branch of the First Baltimore and they've gone ape shit."

"What the fu'"

"I know. What are the chances, eh?"

Frank took a swig of his beer.

"Trouble is they picked the wrong branch. Bad timing is all. What it means for us is that we're going to have to be more careful and be slightly more prepared than originally planned. We can still take this bank, for sure."

"How?" asked Andrew, who was far from clear that the risks hadn't gone through the roof.

"There's still going to be the old guard at the entrance. Point a gun at him and he should be fine. The staff door leads to the vault. Before it was just a flimsy piece of wood; now it's got steel attached to it and Mary Lou says the lock has been swapped out for a five lever deadbolt. That might sound like a hassle, but they are the same cashiers behind the tills and if we threaten anyone on our side of the door, they'll open it up for us because they are the same bank employees who are told not to put their lives at risk or those of their customers for the sake of the money. They still have insurance to cover them for the loss of the theft and they have a reputation to protect. All that's changed is the material of the door."

Andrew and Brian nodded, because despite himself, Andrew could see the logic in all of Frank's words.

"And once we've got that door opened, we walk down the same corridor we were walking down before. This time, we know we must keep our balaclavas because the cameras will be working.

"So before the day of the job, we all need to go and get some brand new jeans, black tees and a long brown coat and a black balaclava. If we all look the same, it'll be harder for witnesses to distinguish between us.

"When we reach the meeting point, we can change and burn the clothes. But make sure they are new and that you haven't worn them before: that way, no one will say they recognize what you're wearing."

Again, nods all round because, that made perfect sense—even to cautious Andrew.

"FINALLY, THERE'S THE vault," said Frank. "This is the only thing where I can see potential problems because they are likely to have the safe closed instead of open like they've done all these months up to now. It really was a walk-in, walk-out job until last week."

"So why didn't we hit it then?" asked Brian, with a hint of a snarl. Frank responded with a vicious glance and carried on.

"As I see it, there are two approaches. Option one: we bring an acetylene torch to the fucker and cut our way in. Option two: we take the bank manager and threaten to rip off his dick until he opens the safe for us. Option one will take longer but is clean. Option two means we might have to cut off the guy's dick or the tits off a cashier until the dude sees sense, so it could get very messy. That said, in theory there is still bank insurance and none of them are meant to turn into Superman. But civilians respond to stress in strange ways sometimes. How do you think we should play it?"

Brian responded quickly and surely: "Cut off the guy's dick then tell him to open the safe. Saves all the hassle and gets to the point real fast. I can't think what fella's going to get argumentative if you're holding his manhood in your hand."

"Good point," said Frank, curling up his mouth in a near smile, "but maybe we shouldn't replay the Tet offensive."

"Well, we don't want to be hanging about," noted Andrew carefully choosing his words because he didn't want to annoy or upset either Frank or Brian, "so perhaps we threaten the bank manager first as that should be the fastest way to get the safe open. If he refuses, we start cutting. If it takes too long, we take a knife to his dick and see if the pinhead will speed our progress out of there."

Now it was Frank's turn to nod in agreement as this was probably the most sensible approach.

"And how do we all feel about dragging an acetylene torch and all that gear into the bank?"

"Well," said Andrew slowly, thinking as he was speaking, "we could have the gear in the car with Pete and bring it in if we needed it. But if we don't, we won't be wasting time hauling it in or out or drawing undue attention to ourselves."

"Makes sense to me," commented Brian, who almost always liked Andrew's plans because they were simple and generally worked.

"Is that it?"

"Sounds like a plan."

"Sure does. Here's to the job. Get in, get out, get rich."

They clinked their glasses, because Finian's Rainbow only served beer in glasses. It was that kind of upmarket dive. On that note, they left—first Andrew and Brian with Frank waiting ten minutes before his own departure.

DRIVING BACK, ANDREW turned to Brian, puncturing their silence, and said: "Frank still hasn't talked about Martin, has he?"

"Nope," responded Brian, deadpan.

"Well, it's not good enough. Martin hasn't gone off to AC and debaunched himself to oblivion. He's been killed and Pete was the last to see him alive. And I don't intend to forget that fact."

"No, but Frank's not going to bring it up again and Pete looks like he's gonna get away with it."

"Well, let's not be too hasty," added Andrew, "all we know is that Martin was with Pete in a bar. Someone could have jumped him after they parted. But as they left out the back door, I agree it sounds as though Pete did for him."

"So what do you think we should do then?"

"Let's go to Atlantic City. If we don't find Martin, Pete will die."

"Uh-huh," intoned Brian.

The following day, they took off and Brian drove all the way. They stopped only once, to stretch their legs, and were in a casino before the sun had set.

Most of the next couple of days was spent either playing Blackjack, Andrew's favorite card game, and the one-armed bandits, Brian's gamble of choice—or in a men-only drinking club, which they'd been introduced to by a friend on a previous trip to the city. It was called *Birds of a Feather* and they'd drink and dance until breakfast time and go into the VIP suite and party on.

This was a totally darkened room where you could see nothing but feel everything. Brian loved it because he felt truly free in there. Andrew was less comfortable with the randomness of the encounters but he always warmed up by the time he'd had his second blow job. After they'd refreshed themselves, they were able to ask their contacts about where Martin could be, if he was in AC at all.

From bar to bar, club to club, Andrew and Brian showed their photo of Martin to anyone who would give them the time of day. But three days and two nights gumshoe work had delivered them zip. Nada.

Sipping coffee in some dive bar at three in the afternoon, they sat opposite each other, waiting for the energy to continue. A grilled chicken sandwich and fries had been downed by both of them but the entire meal had tasted of stale grease. They were tired and were no nearer to finding Martin than when they'd first driven into the city almost a week before.

"He ain't here, y'know that, right?" said Brian, breaking the silence between them.

"Yeah, I guess."

"You guess? Really man, he ain't here."

Brian put his hand on Andrew's, knowing this meant there was no doubt in their minds that Pete had offed Martin.

"I know. I just don't want him to be gone."

"Yeah, well… he is. And we need to be going now."

"Sure thing. Let's quit this town."

"Shall we go back to the *Birds of a Feather* for one last night?"

"Nah, take me to our hotel and show me a good time instead," smiled Andrew.

"Come on," said Brian and stood up to leave the bar, swigging the remains of his coffee. Andrew mirrored him and they returned to their room and fucked each other until dawn. They had a hearty breakfast in the diner opposite their hotel and headed to Baltimore. And the ever-present knowledge that Pete was a dead man.

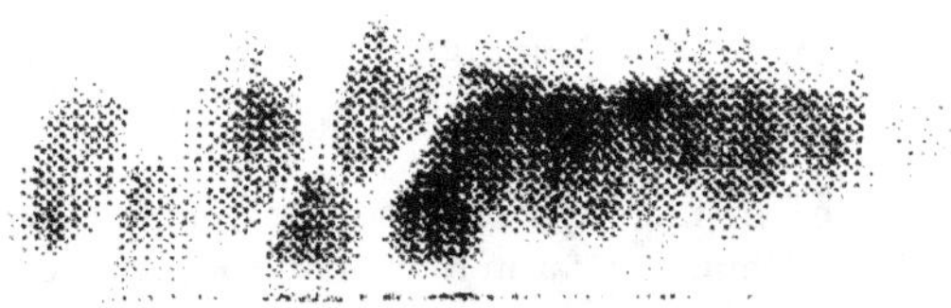

23

LAGOTTI HAD MENTIONED to Frank he should have a chat with Mary Lou as the security was being stepped up in the bank and Frank had no reason she shouldn't brief the big bankroll about the new deal.

So she strolled into the repair shop one Tuesday afternoon, as Paul and Luigi were heading home after a day spent playing penuckle for dimes. Luigi opened the door to Lagotti's office for her and caught up with Paul, who was already revving his engine impatiently.

As she headed to sit down in the only available chair that wasn't occupied, Lagotti signaled her with a beckoning hand and she moved towards him instead. She had no idea why she did that, but the man commanded the room, even without a word being spoken.

He smiled at her as she stood leaning against his desk but he carried on looking through his girlie magazine for another minute, before opening the top drawer, putting the picture book inside and slamming the drawer shut, which made Mary Lou noticeably flinch. Ever so slightly.

He smiled again.

"Don't be alarmed my dear," he said, "only a desk." He laughed for a second, forcing his head back momentarily, and leaned forward and briefly placed one hand on hers, as she was half leaning on the desk using her arms as leverage to stand with her butt against the edge of the fake oak veneer.

She glanced down at his hand as he patted hers and she noticed he was watching her looking at him.

"So tell me about the new security arrangements they are putting in place. My Frank has described the situation to me, but I would like to hear it from the horse's mouth, as it were." He slapped her hand once more and listened intently as she recounted the cameras, doors and reinforced steel to him in great detail.

Finally she stopped talking and Lagotti nodded.

"Can you sketch what the vault room looks like?" he asked, eventually. She scrunched her face up quizzically for a half second, shrugged and said: "Sure."

SHE TURNED ROUND to his desk and Lagotti stood up and scrabbled about the top surface and drawers searching for some paper in the bottom drawer and something to write with—by the table lamp, hidden under some receipts.

As Mary Lou started drawing a rectangle to represent the vault room itself, Lagotti stood behind and to one side of her to not block out the light but also to see. The more she sketched and talked, the more he leaned in.

By the time she had drawn the bars that separated the safe from the main room and the shelving with the deposit boxes, Lagotti was leaning so far in Mary Lou could sense his arm around her neck, lazily hanging there so he could see the whole sketch, she told herself. He volleyed questions about that vault at her for another five, maybe ten, minutes. All the while leaving his arm on her shoulder, eventually leaning in so far she felt his torso against her body. The warmth of his body.

"I assume you didn't just talk with the bank clerk to find all this out? You fucked him, right?"

She decided enough was enough and that he had gone too far. Even if he was Frank Senior. So she bent her right arm to make her elbow stick out and gently point into Lagotti's body.

"Don't be like that, dear," he snarled and quickly whipped his arm off her neck and grabbed her hair, yanking her head back and making her let out a muted scream. They were alone and shouting would not make things any better.

Lagotti pushed her down onto the desk, all the while her hair was tightly bound in his fist. Face down on, his other hand jerking down on her pants until they were past her hips and then she heard him unzip his jeans.

The next thing he was inside her, pumping hard and fast, hurting, hurting, hurting her. When he finished, he pushed her head down against the cold flatness of his desk and intoned: "Get outta my fuckin' sight, you bitch whore."

Mary Lou sobbed as she pulled up her pants and how damp they were at the back where he had dripped spunk on her clothes as he withdrew. Clinging to herself as she left the room, she didn't turn round and didn't close the door behind her. Then she walked out of the repair shop and ran into the evening.

She wouldn't allow Frank to touch her for ten days and it was another week before she'd let herself be naked with either him or Carter.

One thing was certain and she said this to herself every night before she fell asleep for weeks afterwards: "I'm gonna kill that motherfucker." And she knew she meant it.

May

24

THE SUN WAS shining bright and high in the late morning sky. Frank was itching to get the job over and done with so his dreams could become a reality—leave Baltimore behind him and take Mary Lou to Vegas or Los Angeles or anywhere else on the west coast. He wanted to see the Grand Canyon and find some place with a beach and a quiet wood shack to hang out. Most of all he wished to keep his freedom and he knew the best way to achieve that was to hide in plain sight in a different state and be secure with her, to know she was with him and he could count on her. Because once they left Baltimore, there was no turning back. They'd need each other far more than they did now. In Mary Lou and money we trust.

He was sure he could rely on her, but a couple of months ago he was not so confident. When they got home from Miami, she started blowing cold to him and he hadn't figure out why, because they had been so hot together in Florida.

In fact, she was so cool she wouldn't let him touch her for a week. At that point, he thought it was a bad case of the curse but she would not let him inside her for another two weeks after that. No curse, just misery. Frank got to thinking about where she had been and who she'd seen. Had Carter turned her head? Had she met some new guy?

He thought over and over about the events trailing away from Miami. Each conversation with Mary Lou, each touch, each time they'd fucked. Finally, he remembered he hadn't seen her for two days after she popped over to Uncle Frank to talk through the new security arrangements. He figured she'd been hanging out with Carter to extract more info.

Then it struck him: when he saw her next, she had changed. When Mary Lou met Uncle Frank. And if that was the turning point and she would not let herself be touched afterwards that meant that Uncle Frank had upset her. Messed with her. Uncle Frank had fucked his girl. His Uncle Frank. His girl. And if that was the case he was would have to kill that man. Murder his Uncle Frank. Execute the man who'd hurt his girl.

AT THIS POINT in his day, Frank left the apartment and went for a long walk. Halethorpe seemed too small to him and he got on a bus and headed for Lansdowne where there was a comforting cemetery to sit in. And there he sat for an hour or two, replaying the anger in his mind until he calmed down enough to want a cup of Java.

Frank went out of the graveyard, northwards, in the opposite direction to the bank until he bumped into a small diner with no customers and a jug of coffee on the hot plate. He pushed the door open and sat down at the bar, ordered a coffee and slowly stirred the three spoons of sugar and the dash of milk. Over the next nine minutes, he sipped the mug dry, threw two dollars down on the counter and walked out. He glanced around and realized he was only six or seven blocks away from Carter's home so he popped round and check on what Rita was up to. He hadn't been there for at least three months.

When he reached the house Frank looked up and down the street before walking over the picket fence into the backyard and up his tree to peer into the bedroom window. There she was, arms behind her head stretched out on the bed. Like the last time Frank saw her, only on this occasion she was entirely naked and had a man between her legs. And that man was definitely not Carter.

Frank smiled to himself and realized unless he wanted to stick around for his own personal porn movie, there wasn't much to see here. Move along down the bus everyone.

Five minutes later, he crawled down the tree because, despite himself, he couldn't quite walk away. He was transfixed by what his eyes were showing him. When the guy raised his head to catch a breath, Rita sat up and pushed him down so he was lying on his back and she was licking him and then slid up his body until she was astride him. He pumped hard and she rode him like a rodeo buck. Down the tree and off along the street, round the corner and a walk to the bus stop and home to Halethorpe.

THE SANCTUARY OF that small one-room apartment made Frank feel deeply secure. The image of Rita, merging with the imagined fucking of Mary Lou and Uncle Frank, continued to unsettle him to where his anger had abated but he was now feeling a sense of loss. Not so much sadness for himself, but a melancholy for what she must have been through and the fact she didn't believe she was able to talk to him about it.

Given how turbulent their last few months had been, Frank understood why she hadn't said anything, but her silence was even more painful to him precisely because how he'd behaved to her since Christmas. If this was how he treated someone who he wanted to share his west coast dreams with then what was he doing? Why was he not able to let her know how important she was to him?

Frank heard the key turn in the lock, the door opened and there stood his Mary Lou.

"Hiya, hon'"

"Hi babe," he responded immediately. He smiled at her and she frowned, briefly, back at him. An indication of how unusual his smiles were to her. He rose out of the armchair and made the three paces over to her in time to catch her facing the wall as she hung up her keys on a hook. He gently put his arms around her waist and kissed the side of her neck. She giggled slightly and leaned her head sideways to let his lips cover more of her skin with peck-kisses.

"Hey, you. What's all this about?"

Frank stopped briefly, long enough to say: "Just wanted you to know I was pleased to see you. I want you to know I'm always tickled to be with you, is all," and he carried on kissing her neck while she raised her arms and messed his hair at the back of his head with her fingers, which he liked.

Meanwhile, his hands had moved from her waist. His left palm had gone upwards, stroking her belly and up to squeeze a breast. His right hand had gone the other way, over her rose and under her skirt.

"Wait a minute," she said and she turned to face him once she'd extracted herself from his octopus arms. She loosened her blouse and pushed down her skirt so she was standing in only her undies. Then she undid Frank's belt and unzipped his jeans, while Frank pulled off his tee shirt. The pants fell to the floor and he stepped out from the denim around his ankles.

With one swift motion, he swooped a hand under her body and the other under her neck and carried her, Mary Lou giggling all the while, to their bed and deposited her on the sheets as gentle as anything. He pulled off her panties and kissing his way to her groin, licking the rose and everything and anything nearby. The giggles stopped pretty quickly at this point and all Frank heard was the sound of his tongue and the murmurs and moans of his woman.

Vanilla tones in the perfume and the sweet smell of sex. He tasted her for the first time and he didn't want it to stop. Eventually Frank got tired and he kissed the inside of her thighs and licked the rose again and stuck his tongue in her belly button. Then they focused on generating tingles in each other's bodies until the intensity of the moment had subsided.

"I'm pleased to see you too," she whispered and they both smiled and didn't move for a spell.

Unconsciousness enveloped them and within a minute of each other, they both fell asleep, content in their own juices and the pleasure they'd given each other.

25

FRANK WOKE UP early the following morning. Mary Lou was facing down with her cheek on its side, arms above her head and her legs straight, slightly apart. And he faced her with an arm on her ass. His palm slipped down a few inches until his first and second fingers could feel her butt cheeks. She stirred from her sleep and rolled away from him so his hand hung in midair.

"Hey you," she whispered, "don't stop." And he didn't.

After they got up and ate breakfast, they left the apartment and headed off in separate directions: He walked to his car and she grabbed a bus to Lansdowne.

MARY LOU WAS in the middle of a dirty dream: she and Frank were naked, rolling around in a park, over and over. He was inside her and she clamped her knees round his legs and there was an intense energy inside. And then she woke up to find the intense energy was truly inside her, caused by Frank. She laughed to herself and rolled onto her side, the tingles from her groin traveled up her spine and into her head.

"Don't stop," she said. He spooned her with his body while his fingers returned to their earlier work. He smiled, still pleased to be in Mary Lou's orbit; his dreams were on track. She sucked in air and gave into the pulsing waves of pleasure. Once she got used to the spasms running up and down her body, she became aware of Frank poking into her side.

"Sit up with your legs ahead of you," she instructed and, sure enough, he rearranged himself and sat up, leaning on his hands—arms straight—with his legs in front of him, with a quizzical expression on his face. Mary Lou squatted on top of him… intense wave of pleasure.

She rocked up and down ever so gently to give him a chance to recover—his massive inhalation just then meant he felt it too. He placed one of his arms on her back and the other around the nape of her neck and she reciprocated. He was much better in the sack now than he ever was before, she mused, once the tingles subsided enough for ordinary thoughts to resurface. After all these years together, it was only in the last couple of months Mary Lou found she liked the taste of Frank's sperm.

Despite the fucking horrible time with Frank Senior, his step nephew had really grown into a proper man. He'd somehow worked out she needed some space after it happened and he hadn't pushed her or tried to force her into being intimate with him until she was ready. Until the hurting well and truly stopped and the pain of the night subsided in her head.

As she stepped into the shower, she thought how she still had nightmares on a depressingly regular basis, but he had come through for her. Most men would have dropped her as soon as look at her, but Frank had class.

When they both left the apartment together, she kissed him full on the mouth and then said: "Have a nice day at work, hon'"

"And you, babe," he replied quick as a flash, squeezing her ass. Then he turned away and round the corner to get his car.

With a skip in her step, Mary Lou Belle bounced to the Lansdowne bus stop, straightened her skirt and waited for the latest installment at the First Bank of Baltimore.

26

TWENTY MINUTES LATER, Mary Lou sat on the bus as it trundled its way through to Lansdowne and beyond. People hopped on, guys got off, but her mind was more focused on last night and the prospects she might have with Carter after the job was over.

Frank was a class guy but would he still be that classy if Carter was the one holding the haul? Carter might be a gambler, but she'd know how to spend his money without him pissing it on the World Series or whatever. Especially if it was in cash because he wouldn't spend what he wasn't holding in his hand.

The vehicle bounced over a hole in the road and she realized it was turning the corner just before her stop. Lucky pothole. Off the bus and ino the bank. She walked past Carter's desk before she reached the front door and Grimble standing there with his hand hovering over his revolver and a smile on his face. But Mary Lou had seen his disdainful snarl on the periphery of her vision almost every time she visited the place, so she recognized what he really thought of her. Two-faced shit head.

She nodded at him to acknowledge his existence and sashayed her way to Carter's desk and sat down opposite him, just like the day they'd met. He looked up and smiled, leaning back in his chair and talking as a bank official would. Somehow he thought that made their relationship respectable in the eyes of Grimble and JH. But Mary Lou understood what they thought and she kinda agreed. He was a married man clearly playing the field with one of his customers. Her hundred dollar deposit was not worth the amount of attention she was getting from him, but the time she spent naked with him, listening to his problems was more than enough justification in his mind for a few business lunches and a regular coffee date in the late afternoon.

Small talk with Carter and another in a long line of excuses to go to the bathroom. Then she stood up and headed to the staff door. Today Theresa Galtieri was on the till, so she was buzzed into the rear with a smile instead of that old crone Pieck's scowl.

Mary Lou smiled back and placed her hand on her lower belly, over her secret rose, as if to imply her tubes were hurting her. She mouthed "Thank you," as she pushed the door open and closed it behind her.

THE BANK WASN'T taking the new security arrangements very seriously because the maintenance crew had only screwed a steel plate to the back of the same door that was there before. It made the thing heavier to push open, but the lock appeared no more robust. And even if it was, it was still sitting in the self-same door jamb and you could still kick it in with little effort. More to the point, Frank could still kick it in with no struggle at all. True for Andrew and Brian as well.

She scuttled down the hall and saw the exit to the parking lot. Same door, same lock: no change there. Mary Lou peered along the corridor and sneaked down the vault stairs. Here was where the real changes had been made.

The safe was locked shut. Carter had told her it was still left open because they were keeping less cash upstairs nowadays and it was too much hassle to have two of the managers keep coming downstairs to unlock it every time a few more bucks were needed.

Then one of his comments fell into place. He'd said when JH was out at meetings he wouldn't allow George to hold the key so everything ground to a halt. And JH came in late when he went into Baltimore for a managers' meeting first thing. But the flip side of this was they needed to be certain of having JH in the building on the day of the job. She'd book an appointment with him for 9.15 to be sure he'd be there. As their protocols were to slam the safe shut in the event of emergencies Frank and the boys would deal with that problem in their own special way.

Besides which, thought Mary Lou, when they slammed the money shut, the horse would already have bolted into Carter's black case.

Back up the stairs and into the bathroom to flush the cistern, be heard to wash her hands and out again and into the lobby area. She sat down at Carter's desk and smiled at him. He smiled with eyes that yearned for her, but he'd only just got in, more or less. It was only a few minutes past ten and they both knew there was no way JH would approve of him taking an early three hour lunch with Mary Lou just because she'd deposited a Benjamin.

"Would you like us to meet up for lunch?" she asked, sitting forwards on her chair with her knees closed, her arms straight and her hands on the front edge of the seat, forcing her breasts together and up: a natural uplift designed to appeal to Carter's baser nature.

"Yes I would, but I'm not sure if I can," he replied honestly, furtively darting his eyes left and right to see if he was drawing any attention from any of the seniors in the building.

"Oh," answered with mild disappointment.

"But we might grab a coffee immediately after work before I have to go home, if you like?"

"That'd be lovely," she said quietly enough to draw him in.

"Our usual place?"

"For sure. See you there around six?"

"Definitely," and she touched him gently on the arm as she got up and walked out the door, nodding at Grimble on the way out.

FRANK LAGOTTI SPENT most of his days doing what he enjoyed and what he did best. First, was his uncanny ability to find good people to turn money into more money. He also calculated interest rates at an inconceivable speed and accuracy.

The other thing Lagotti was very good at was looking at nude women. Most days he combined both talents, percentages in the morning, naked women in the afternoon. Most of these afternoons were spent using pictures, but occasional he would leave his auto shop in search of real flesh.

One such time, Lagotti was sitting in the Kitkatt Club in downtown Baltimore, stirring a vodka lime. There was an Asian girl wearing a red G-string with her groin inches away from Lagotti's face. He popped a twenty into the front to glimpse her bush. Then she moved on to the next john in the row. He smiled, admiring the curves of her ass and the roundness of her tits.

His step nephew sat beside him and Lagotti signaled to the semi-clad waitress, who stepped forward. He whispered in her ear and a beer appeared on the table beside Frank, who was staring at the Asian girl with the red G-string.

When the music stopped after fifteen minutes, the dancer had earned several hundred for the club owners. Lagotti held a fifty-one per cent stake after a previous owner found himself with an unpleasant debt problem caused by a mix of eightballs and marijuana.

"Well, my boy."

"All going fine, Uncle."

"Good to hear, young man."

"And we've got a full set of plans to deal with the new security arrangements."

"That Mary Lou sure is a talent," mused Lagotti, while Frank's stomach flew around, a cold sense of dread near his heart. But he knew there was nothing to say at this point in the job.

"And now we have the most likely date too."

"Excellent. And when will that be?"

"June 17 until we hear otherwise."

"Until you hear otherwise?"

"Yeah, the dates for the big payroll runs aren't finalized until the week before, but this is when the biggest haul is due in next."

Frank used all his self-control to keep the conversation business-like, because he needed his uncle at least until the money was laundered.

"I understand. I shall prepare for industrial level cleaning to take place mid-July… Anything else for me?"

"No, that's all Uncle."

"Good news. Stay if you want."

"No thanks. See y'all."

Frank chugged the dregs of his beer, stood up and walked out, just as the music started and a blonde with long hair, large breasts and a cigarette got up on stage. Lagotti settled back into his chair and enjoyed the view.

Talking with Frank gave Lagotti a chance to think about Mary Lou for the first time since she walked out of his office and he hitched up his pants. Great piece of ass that girl. He couldn't decide if he had a large dick, or she had a small snatch. Either way, she was a tight fit, but it felt good anyway, even though she whimpered all the way through, which put him off a bit. But not so much to knock him off his stride as he recalled.

If it took his fancy, Lagotti usually had his pick of the pussy at the Kitkatt Club, but sometimes he didn't have time to go down there. And it didn't matter to him where he got it as long as it wasn't from Mrs. Lagotti, who he had ceased to find attractive twenty years ago or more.

The only reason they weren't divorced was because he was Catholic and she was the mother of his children. In any other circumstances, Lagotti would have had her clipped a long time before—without giving it a moment's thought. Mrs. Lagotti was a lucky woman. Of sorts.

The music in the room changed beat and a new girl appeared on stage: brunette in a black thong. Lagotti decided he'd bang her as soon as she got off performing because he liked the shape of her nipples.

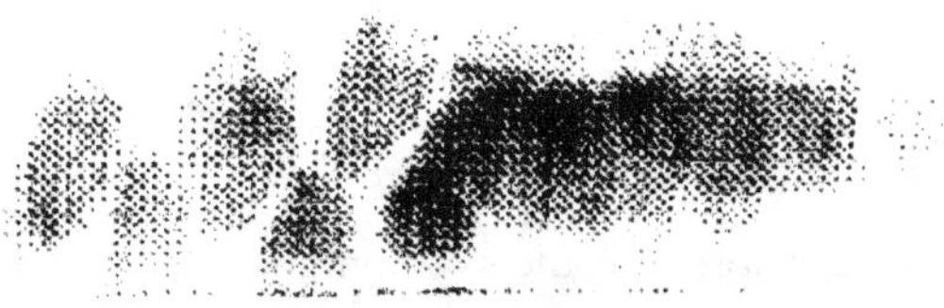

27

JH HELD AN extraordinary staff meeting once the dust had settled on the raising of the security status. When the bank closed at five, they all squeezed into his office, all but JH standing so everyone had room. Carter was one of the last to arrive, so he found himself with his back to the door.

JH coughed slightly to clear his throat—he was never comfortable with public speaking—and droned on about how the bank's biggest concern was that people would get hurt during an attack on the monies and other items they held in safety for their customers. Then he moved on to how there must be changes to their working practices and that, because there needed to be sacrifices, they were all in this together.

Carter thought how some of them would be in it together more than others. And sure enough, he was proved right.

"We will be instigating a new regime for distributions. While the days of the deliveries remain the same for the time being, their schedule will be altered. To reduce the opportunity for attacks, we will concentrate all smaller transfers together to make more significant payroll distributions.

"The other change is the timing of these Pooled Deposit distributions to the satellite offices, such as ours. We are instigating a programme where we receive deliveries at oh seven hundred hours.

"Naturally, this means we will start a schedule for everyone to participate in the distribution receipts. Three of us are needed each time and we shall post the roster on the staff notice board. The precise dates for each distribution will be confirmed only seven days in advance, but they are monthly and the prospective first date is June 16."

And then JH kept talking for another lifetime or five minutes, all the while using the same monotone drone. As soon as he had let them go, Carter and the others moved to the notice board to see if they were going to be hit with the first early rise. George had been given the task of figuring out the schedule so it was hardly a surprise his least favorite people had the honor of waking up early to make the bank a safer place. Carter's name was there for the June drop.

He was far from a morning person and really could do without this intrusion into his personal life, especially as this would put a crimp in his weekends with Mary Lou. Fuckers. This reflected his overall mood when, having been forced to work late to hear the bad news about the Pooled Deposit drops, he arrived back at his house with Rita and her casserole getting cold in the kitchen. He found her sat in the dining room in front of her plate, long since emptied with just a thin film of gravy left on its surface. His plate was there, waiting for him, congealed in a beef and potato sculpture.

HE SAT DOWN opposite her and, before he could say anything, she barked: "You're late."

"Yes, I know."

"You've forced me sit here and eat on my own. You've made me squander my time cooking for you for it to go to waste. Why didn't you phone?"

Carter sighed. He really didn't have the energy to argue with her tonight. He was pissed off having to deal with the Pooled Deposit drop and her moaning at him was doing him no good at all.

"I was busy at work," he hammered out these words, staccato and stood up realizing he hadn't poured himself a much needed scotch yet. He could sense Rita fuming as he scuffed out of the dining room to get to the glass and bottle and returned to his seat.

"I find it hard to believe you couldn't spare two precious minutes to tell me you were going to be late."

"Well, that's exactly the case. We were called into a meeting after hours and then I came home. This wasn't me partying 'till the small hours."

"Chance'd be a fine thing," she snorted. Carter looked at her with steely eyes. He had no patience for this shit, and besides, Rita was normally far more accepting of little things like this.

"What?"

"If you'd told me you were going to be late, I could've spent some more time with a friend of mine in the afternoon."

"What friend?" Carter had always operated on the assumption Rita was at home during the day. He'd never given a single moment of his life wondering what she did when he wasn't in the house. He worked on the basis she was frozen until he reanimated her by getting back into their house. An unrealistic belief if he'd ever bothered to pay attention to it.

"I have friends, bucko. Good friends I like to spend time with."

"Where d'you go to meet your friend?" said with a sneer in his voice.

"We had lunch in the Baltimore Regal Hotel just out of town. If I'd known you would be late, we wouldn't have had to rush."

"Lunch would have been over hours before I knew I was going to be late. Anyway, I wouldn't have been able to get in touch with you if you weren't at home."

"Yes, we had to rush because of you," she said, still a pile of anger at the back of her voice, but a stillness and calmness was present too. She stood up from the table. "We had to rush afterwards." The last word was spoken slowly, clearly, drawing all the life out of it and as she uttered it, she moved one hand over her groin and mimed massaging herself, so he could see the contours of her thighs through her dress and the shape of her body.

"We had to rush because of you… Clear the dishes, boy. I'm going to bed." And while still massaging herself, Rita floated out of the room and up the stairs. Carter heard the bedroom door slam shut.

"Bitch! She's fucking someone else," he thought as he took the plates into the kitchen to soak before he did as he was bid and washed the crockery. "Who the fuck is screwing my wife?"

When he left the house some twenty minutes later, the cutlery was sparkly clean, he'd knocked back half a bottle of hard liquor and his anger had seeped into moroseness.

MARY LOU GOT to Lansdowne that evening in good time given it was her only appointment of the day. Mary Lou sat in the Dolce Caffe for about ten minutes before Carter appeared. He sat down next to her at their booth at the rear and ordered a coffee with milk.

"How was your day?" she enquired.

"Same old," Carter replied, but Mary Lou sensed that wasn't the whole story.

"Yeah…?"

"Well, the new payroll roster is being rolled out and they're changing the drop times at our branch. Now, the money's going to get delivered to us before the bank opens instead of during the day when there are more people around. But that doesn't matter…" A gulp of coffee.

"…as much as I've been co-opted onto the roster. When there's a Pooled Deposit I will be one of the staff who take it in and get it into the safe. Once a month I shall be in at six in the morning, for Christ's sake."

Mary Lou let this information hang in the air. Pooled Deposit simply meant a payroll worth over half a million—this was what they'd been waiting for all these months.

"Goddamn. How much notice are they going to give you?"

"The previous week we will be told if there are any Pooled Deposits the following week, so I'll get only seven days."

"Damn. That's not good for us, is it?"

"No, we'll lose a chunk of one of our weekends if I have to be in that early," he trailed off into his own disappointed thoughts.

"But that still leaves loads of nights when we can be together doesn't it?" she asked hopefully.

"Yeah… yes. And because it's a new roster, looks like the first Pooled Deposit will be on June 16."

They finished their coffees while she stroked his leg to show she felt his sadness, but in reality she just saw dollar signs. Held by Frank or by Carter, finally.

The bus couldn't turn up fast enough for her; the trip home lasted a lifetime. She zoomed off the vehicle and made her way back to the apartment as quickly as her skirt let her.

MARY LOU SHOT through the door with a smile on her face, threw off her coat and skipped to Frank's armchair to fling herself on his lap.

"What's up, babe?" asked Frank having wheezed at the moment she landed on him.

"Have I got some good news, hon'!"

"What news?"

"They've arranged next month's payroll runs."

"Oh?"

Frank set bolt up with a straight back, holding Mary Lou around the middle to stop her falling on the floor.

"The biggest run will be in the second week of June…"

"Do you know when in the second week exactly?"

"Not quite. Usually they use Monday to receive the notes, Tuesday to hold the cash and Wednesday to transport it to the other branches."

"So it'll be Tuesday, then?"

"Most likely, but I won't know for certain until the end of the previous week."

"Okay, game on. Sounds like we have a plan. Sounds like we have a fucking plan."

And they did.

THEY SAT IN each other's arms for a spell, soaking in the meaning of the news Mary Lou had imparted a few seconds ago. She thought about the planning, the talking, the time she had spent with Carter the past nine months. Of the fact this was all going to be a memory soon. She imagined how Frank would react when he got into that vault and found there was no cash in there. How Carter would deal with laundering all that cash. And she asked herself, yet again, whether she would be better off with a class act like Frank or the risky Carter. Who was most likely to actually steal the money? To walk out of that bank with the cash in a bag. The truth was she had no goddamn clue.

As the future seemed so unclear, even amid the almost absolute certainty of the date of the job, Mary Lou decided the best thing to do right now was to live in the here and now, because if nothing else that was very clear and very certain. She kissed Frank repeatedly and so began another night of tasting each other's bodies until they fell asleep.

Beyond the moment and despite the class act her Frank undoubtedly was, she was believing maybe Carter could pull it off. Mainly because no one would suspect him of doing anything as audacious as robbing a bank: not JH, not Grimble and certainly not Frank. And if that was the case she should follow the money and that would be in Carter's pockets.

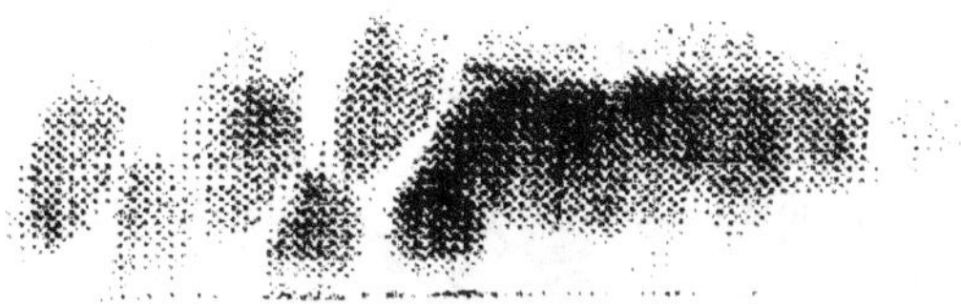

28

LATER IN THE evening Mary Lou headed over to their trysting place to cook linguini and run through everything he'd said to her. He arrived way too late to eat: the pasta had gone cold and she knew that meant he had been back to the house with Rita and they'd had another in a long line of arguments. It was part of Mary Lou's job to hear him and calm him down, so she braced herself for just that task.

When Carter arrived, he was in a foul mood. She could smell on his breath he'd way more than his usual one shot of scotch. That and his generally aggressive air.

"How'd it go at work, dear?" she asked but he snorted and replied: "Shit." But that was all she could get out of him.

Swaying with liquor, he noticed another meal gone cold on a table and rolled his eyes, sighed, turned round and switched on the TV to slump in an armchair, watching blindly at whatever game show was broadcast.

A few minutes later a ham sandwich appeared on the arm of the chair and he grabbed it and stuffed it down without a word. Missing two dinners had made him hungry. Carter put the plate on the floor by his feet and carried on staring at the TV.

"Better?"

"S'pose. Those shit heels at the bank. It just pisses me off, it really does. I've been working there for five years and that pinhead George slaps me with the first Pooled Deposit duty. What's the point of putting the time in, if you get nothing back? I mean…" Mouthful of whiskey. "…is that what I'm worth to them? Just a hired hand to open a door and count some bags of cash, f'Chris' sake?" Another gulp of liquor. "Well, say something for fuck's sake? Am I right, or what?"

"Yes, dear."

"Yeah." Swig of scotch. "And another thing…" Gulp. "…how long do I have to wait for a promotion? I've brought in so much money through investments, they can't have failed to notice, surely." Glug and a dribble of whiskey onto Carter's chin, wiped off with his spare hand.

She hadn't seen him this way before. He'd be grouchy with her if he and Rita had had an argument but this was clearly more than the next scene of the final chapter of their relationship and marriage. There was an unpleasant edge to him tonight and she didn't like it. "Booze changes a man," she thought as he started railing against anything said on the TV program before him. Even the ads.

She had a couple of options at this point. First, she could walk out the door and leave him to stew in his own juices to deal with the consequences once he'd sobered up. She could ply him with more booze until he fell asleep, but that might mean he started getting nasty to her and there was no way she would put up with that—from him. Or she could keep seeing the night out and hope his mood changed because she really wanted to check she'd got the right date in her head for the first Pooled Deposit run.

Mary Lou weighed all the options and figured the smartest move was to extricate herself from the apartment and try again another time. She could be home in about fifteen minutes and that was a much better idea than to stay in the same four walls as this fucker right now.

So while he ranted at the TV, she grabbed her coat and walked out into the Halethorpe night.

CARTER LOOKED ROUND at the sound of the door slamming shut to see the absence of Mary Lou. Later, when the television crackled white noise at him, he fell asleep in the armchair, his whiskey glass out of his hand and onto the floor. The bottle long since emptied.

When he woke up at around six thirty, Carter couldn't feel his toes as the apartment was cold and he'd been in the chair all night. He twisted left and right looking for Mary Lou and ran into the bedroom hoping to find her there, but there were no signs at all. Then he remembered not seeing her before he fell asleep and the door slamming on his rant.

"I am an asshole."

There was no one to disagree with such a clear self-assessment, so Carter nipped into the shower to take the cobwebs of alcohol out of his brain, put his clothes back on and headed to Lansdowne to grab a bite in the Dulce Caffe before starting work.

The irony of Carter's arrival for breakfast before seven was entirely lost on him as he was still sorry for himself. The previous night's haranguing had fled his mind; now he was sad because he'd forced Mary Lou to leave the apartment rather than deal with his mood.

The solitary lucid thought Carter had during his time at the Dulce was that if the Pooled Deposit drop was happening next month, the chances were Frank Senior would want him to grab the cash on one of those days. This gave him a cold judder down his spine and a sinking ache in his stomach, but there was no getting away from it. One way or another, he would pay his debt. And this way, he'd be able to not just be clear of money issues, but he would also rid himself of Rita and all those problems too. And gain Mary Lou if he hadn't fucked everything up with her last night.

At a quarter to nine, Carter left the diner and headed to the First Bank of Baltimore's Lansdowne branch. As usual, he sauntered into the staff kitchen to make himself a cup of coffee, just as he did every morning. Then next door to open his locker with the key he had attached to his house fob. Inside was an emergency cut throat and shaving foam, toothbrush and toothpaste. All on the top shelf along with a spare hair brush. Beneath, resting on the floor, was one of his black cases. Empty, sagging in the middle under its own weight waiting for a time to be used.

He then swung by the kitchen to grab his coffee and headed for his desk. Underneath, leaning on one side, was his other case. Also waiting for the moment to spring into action. Grimble stared at him so he grimaced a smile back just to annoy him.

The cases were ready. All he had to do was fill them with cash and leave the bank before the end of a Pooled Deposit day. June 16 or thereabouts.

TWO NIGHTS LATER, Carter and Mary Lou met up at the apartment. He entered first and he sat on the couch until she arrived. When he heard Mary Lou's key in the door, he stood up and put his hands in his pockets.

Mary Lou entered, looked at him and smiled.

"Hi."

"Hi, dear."

"Um…"

"Yes?"

She hung up her coat and settled on the sofa. The far end, back straight, legs together and palms held on her knees. Carter mirrored her.

"Well?"

"I behaved badly last time we were here. I'd got dreadful news at the bank, had bad news at home and it was all too much for me."

"Right."

Calm voice, head slightly angled to one side, listening.

"So I shouldn't have turned up drunk and all. And shouldn't have laid that shit down on you… Sorry."

"Thanks for the apology."

Carter put his hand out and she held it with a light touch and a gentle squeeze. Her body relaxed a bit and her legs were less clenched together.

"Thank you for coming over this evening and listening to me. Again." He smiled at her because he knew the time she'd spent hearing his problems and talking through their solutions. She looked back, still cautious.

"I just don't want my behavior to change how you feel about me; I was genuinely scared you wouldn't show. Don't know what I'd do without you…"

Mary Lou put her other hand around his so it was sandwiched between hers. Her fingertips touched his knuckles and that was comfort enough for him.

"You mean so much to me. Once Rita is out of my life, we can be together properly."

"And I'd really like that too. It's not easy…"

"I know, I know."

"But I have to be certain we're good. I have to be sure I will be safe with you. I've had relationships before where he's got nasty and I don't want to be in that kind of situation again."

"Oh god! No, I mean. I'd never do anything to hurt you. Christ."

"Or make me think you might harm me. That's important to me too."

"God. I'm so sorry," and Carter crumbled, crying and folding forwards so his head and damp tears were dripping over their hands. Eventually he stopped and she carried on stroking him to reassure the lunk.

He sat up and blew his nose, his red eyes dry but doleful. She was totally relaxed by now, so she smiled at him and stood up.

"There's one thing," she stated with a glint in her expression. Mary Lou turned and faced Carter, still sat on the sofa. She unzipped her skirt and it dropped by her feet. Her rose was in his eye line.

"Lick me until I feel better about you," she said. And he did.

29

PETE WAS IN a strange old mood and he wasn't too sure why. Yes, he had been whoring around for a week or two with nothing to show for it other than a sore head and dick, but he was used to both those sensations and it did not bother him any. No, this was different and he didn't think he'd experienced anything like it before in his life.

After four hours tinkering under the hood of one of the cars, the Wheels gradually began to realize what was up: he wanted the companionship of Lucy again. So Pete finished the work on the engine and motored down to the Joppa exit of the I-95 and scooted down the South Mountain Road in search of Java.

There she was in her tight-fitting waitress overalls and dress, with one hand on her hip and the other pouring coffee into a mug.

Pete walked to the counter and sat down and waited. Sure enough, when Lucy handed the coffee over to the John, she looked up and noticed Pete and walked over to him.

"Well hello, sugar! What can I get ya?"

"A whole heap of lovin' and a mug of your best Java," Pete replied with a smile, or the nearest expression he had on his face.

"You can plonk your spoon in my coffee cup any time you want, my dear," said Lucy. Mostly what she uttered made little sense, but somehow it sounded dirty and that's what the guys liked so she got good tips. She'd stopped listening to herself in the diner about the third day after she arrived. And that was best part of twenty years ago.

"Sure would like to show you that spoonful, darlin'" replied Pete with a twinkle in his eye. "When's closin' time?"

"Late in the night, dear, but my shift ends at five, so you slurp your coffee and I'll be more or less done."

"Mighty fine."

He sipped his cup to the dregs and when he put the mug down and wiped his lips on his sleeve, there was Lucy stood next to him, no overalls but still wearing the dress two sizes too small for her. This was another trick she used to increase her tips: having tits that looked like they were about to fall out every time she bent down kept the middle-aged men's money rolling in.

Pete drove them round the corner to Lucy's trailer and they went inside—like so many times before. Without a blink or turn of her head, as soon as he shut the door, she unzipped her dress and threw it in a wardrobe.

There Lucy stood, wearing a red bra, striped blue panties and flesh-colored panty hose, which she rolled down and shove into a drawer.

"Pete, have you suddenly got shy on me or do you want to watch?"

Pete's cheeks reddened ever so slightly, because watching very much appealed to him at this point in the afternoon.

"I ain't shy, 'n' I sure as shit like what I see."

Lucy smirked and started slow dancing in front of him, using both hands to accentuate her bosom and swayed to the beat of some imaginary music in her head. She leaned back, pushing and pulling at her tits and then she undid her bra, still swaying from side to side. The underwear dropped towards the floor but she scooped it up with a foot and kicked it up to catch it. Then she threw it straight at Pete's face—during this time, he'd sat down on the sofa bed, all the while grinning and licking his lips, clapping along to the rhythm in Lucy's mind.

She put her hands on her belly and eased them downwards so her fingers were under the top of her blue striped panties and Pete stopped needing to imagine what was beneath. Lucy pushed down a half inch more on the material each time, staring at Pete as she danced, watching him react to her teasing him.

Finally she shoved her panties all the way down and paused in front of him, bare ass naked like the day she was born, only with great curvy hips and the scent of sex.

"STOP YOUR LOOKIN'" now and earn your keep," she whispered to him. Pete rose, dropped his trousers and grabbed her with both hands. Five minutes later, it was all over and they shared a cigarette both lying on the couch, although two of their legs were firmly on the floor.

"In a couple of weeks, I'm gonna crash here like I did before, okay?"

"Sure thing, dear. You can plant yourself in my trailer any time you want."

He stuck around for a day or so. The following morning she worked the day shift and was back by just gone five in the afternoon. He spent his time sleeping and watching daytime TV on the black and white portable she had bought the previous year. There was only a mix of chat shows and quizzes, neither of which he found interesting, but he was fascinated by the television itself, because he had only seen one in department store windows or in the joint.

He was lying on the sofa bed with his feet up when she returned and she smiled, hitched up her tight-fitting dress. The hem rode a good six inches above her knees so the men could imagine seeing her crotch—more tips, thank you—and sat astride him.

In less time than it took her to pour her famous cup of coffee, Pete had come and lay back, satisfied with himself and his world, but he knew he had to return to his yard and finish off fixing those cars. He slapped her on the thigh, kissed her and said: "See you soon, babe."

"I'm countin' the days, dear" she responded, lying down to watch the TV still blaring out in the background, relaxed, legs apart. After he left the trailer, and she heard his car growl back onto the main road, she hitched up her skirt again and this time made sure she climaxed too.

Pete spent the next three days and nights in his Glen Burnie yard, partly because he'd stolen a day from himself to get some R 'n' R with Lucy and partly because he just wanted it all to be over. There could be no job until he had done this work and he was getting impatient with all the waiting. Hanging around was his worst time.

Some might worry about all the things that could go wrong and figure out how to mitigate against those risks. He just got bored and that's generally when he did stupid things. Like the time he stabbed Willie Bob in the eye with a screwdriver for looking at his woman funny. He didn't really have anything much against Willie Bob, but he was fatigued and an anger welled up in him that would never have seen the light of day if he'd had something proper to do, such as driving a getaway vehicle instead.

So he worked damn hard on those cars: tweaking engines, replacing shocks, increasing the size of gas tanks. Anything to give the guys an edge on the day, should they need it.

The yard had a small one-room building, which housed a zed bed, a sink and a chair and a fridge. He kept the latter well stocked with beer and a carton of smokes were placed on top to cover all of life's eventualities. And there was a transistor radio tuned into the best Country and Western station he could find.

FRANK APPEARED ON the fourth day of Pete's hermit-like retreat into grease and auto parts. The good thing about the yard was that it was in the middle of fucking nowhere, so no one would stumble onto his projects without an invitation. The bad thing was it was in the middle of fucking nowhere, which meant even if you had an invite, it was a bitch to find and Frank normally ended up stumbling upon it by accident, having zigzagged his way around a thousand units in an industrial wasteland known as Glen Burnie, caught between the I-97 and the 176, by the south-east corner of Baltimore airport. If you didn't appreciate the stench of the oil and gas, you could always inhale the diesel fumes from the planes flying feet above your head. At least, it gave Pete an excuse to play music as loud as he did on the radio.

Frank tooted his horn twice as he and the jalopy arrived in the yard. Pete stopped and cleaned his hands on a rag tucked into the top of his jeans. By this time, Frank had parked and was heading towards him, palm outstretched for a firm shake. Pete looked at his own greasy fingers and laughed.

"No need to stand on formalities round here," he jeered, "you can buy me a beer sometime if you want to say hello."

Frank put his hand away and asked how things were going, no smile. Pete didn't quite know how he did it, but there was always a way of interpreting what he said to Frank as though it had a sharp corner. It was rarely something he did intentionally and he could see it annoyed Frank much of the time. Frank said nothing about it, apart from give him the odd filthy look, so Pete didn't pay no never mind. But he knew he pissed Frank off.

First, the workaday van Frank would use to take Andrew and Brian to the bank. The floor had reinforced steel to take the weight of anything they caught in the haul and the gear they'd be taking with them to cut through the vault door, and the safe itself if needs be. There'd also be enough gasoline canisters to blow the thing off its chassis if the cutting tool wasn't needed as part of the exit plan.

Second was a sport sedan which Pete intended to use to take them from the bank to the split up point. Because its top speed was only 100mph, he had tweaked it to give more bang for their buck. Just in case. Again, it would be torched to disconnect them from the tools of their crime.

Next were three getaway cars: a white, blue and red high-performance number for Pete himself; these were family saloons, nothing fancy, or out of the ordinary. All the same brand because Pete noticed Frank liked them and Pete knew they just had to be reliable. All the group needed was a full tank of gas and no one to break the speed limit or drive with a broken tail light. Pete made certain there were a spare set of bulbs in each vehicle. The man might not turn up to their meetings on time, but he sure as hell took care of his end of business.

Finally, there was a high-performance convertible Mary Lou would use to drive through Lansdowne in the morning, plant the C4 and head off to the split up point.

"That's one beast of an automobile for a girl, isn't it?"

"Yes and no, my friend." Frank stared at him, waiting for a fuller response which would contain some information or explanation.

"Thing is she will have half a dozen blocks of C4 in the rear and if she has to hightail it outta there for any reason, we don't need the whole fucking thing blowing up now, do we?

"Also, if she gets stopped, she'll have half a dozen blocks of C4 in the back, so we don't want her to be stopped neither. Ways I sees it is she needs to have a lotta power under them hood to see her stay clear outta trouble.

"If that ain't enough for ya, if all the other cars go to shit on the day—they shouldn't, mind, but stranger things've happened on jobs before now—then we've got one hot rod to snake our way outta Dodge."

Frank grinned and winked at Pete. "Only asking." Pete smiled back, pleased Frank was trusting his judgment and checking his auto knowledge.

"Just make sure she wears flats. Her feet'll slip right off them pedals if she's in them fancy heels of hers." Frank nodded and they moved on to the next, then the next.

Once they'd checked out all the vehicles, Frank stopped and asked: "And where do you hide them at night?"

"In plain sight, here in the yard, but they's covered by tarpaulin so they want be receiving no unwarranted attention."

"Good man. We're close now, Pete. Just need to wait for the next big haul and then it'll be show time."

Frank punched Pete affectionately on the shoulder, greasy hands were still greasy hands, and drove back to Halethorpe to wait for the time to finally kick off the job.

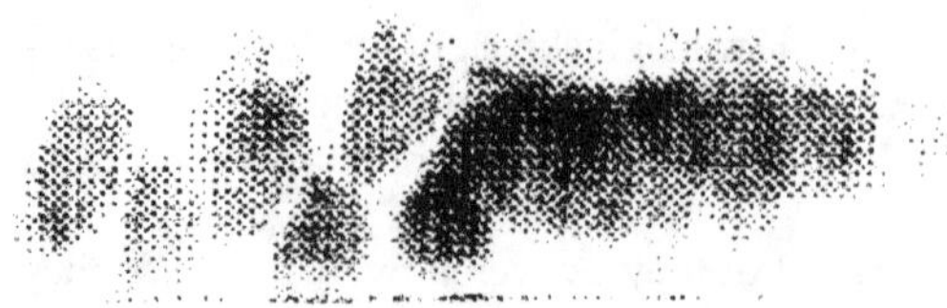

30

PETE FINISHED UP his work on the convertible's engine, which he'd started before Frank's arrival. Slammed the hood down and covered each auto with a tarpaulin. The only thing left to do was fill each with gas and drive them in rotation each day until the job. That would keep him busy enough to not get bored, because then he did stupid things. And he didn't want to fuck up on this job, not with Frank Senior watching so closely.

Pete went inside to clean his hands, locked up the yard and headed home to wash and eat a burger.

After his shower—but before the burger—he slumped down on his easy chair, the towel still wrapped around his waist.

With all the hustle and bustle of sorting out the autos, Pete hadn't had much time to think about Andrew and Brian and their little conversation. They were getting dangerous and like a mangey old hound, they didn't appear to want to let go of that bone.

That was okay. The important thing was the job at hand and having sufficient people to take care of it. If he moved on Andrew now that might set back the job by weeks or months and Pete sure had had enough waiting around already. He didn't need to stretch things out any longer than they had to be.

So he chose to do nothing at this point but after was a different matter. If he did nothing, there would definitely come a day when there'd be a knock on the door and that coon-lover Andrew would be on the other side of it with a sawn-off shotgun and a snarl on that face of his. Bad idea.

There were only three obvious opportunities for Pete to take matters into his own hands: during the job itself, at the scatter point or after he'd got his split of the haul and freely track down Andrew and do whatever he wanted to the motherfucker.

The trouble with tracking him down was that it gave Andrew exactly the same opportunity to find him and those odds didn't sound so good to Pete. If he used the scatter point, he'd also have to negotiate with at least Frank and Brian, if not Mary Lou too. The girl was not a problem for him; one slap would send that bitch flying. The issue would be Brian more than Frank. Clearly, Brian's allegiance was to Andrew: the guy had brought him into this job and they worked together. Sounded as though they'd been working closely for quite a while. Brian would be a problem. Frank would be pissed if he whacked Andrew but it wouldn't be a big deal to him because he'd already have done his part.

There was the option of hitting Andrew before the end of the job. Maybe if he clipped him either when he was on his own taking money out into Pete's car or just as they were leaving. Brian would still be a problem and Frank might not be happy. If things turned nasty with Frank, he might clip him and take the proceeds to Frank Senior himself. That way, he'd keep all the winnings and there'd only be Mary Lou to deal with. Or to clip. Whatever.

And so the plan began to form more solidly in Pete's head to kill Andrew and Brian, either at the job after the money was in the automobile or when they all hooked up before the month's hiatus. Best case? The guy takes a bullet in the line of duty and Pete doesn't have to lift a finger. If he drove carefully and near enough to a cop car that could happen quite naturally.

All this thinking made him tired, so he jerked himself off, wiped himself down, put some clothes on and headed out to his local diner for that burger he'd promised himself.

THE FOLLOWING WEEK Luigi visited Pete's rundown apartment and knocked on his door.

"The boss wants to see you," said Luigi factually.

"Um… Now?"

"Nah. Tomorrow will do."

"Okay. When 'n' where?"

"Not that fucking launderette again. He was most displeased with that location. Why not use the derelict factory, Frank's favorite, y'know?"

"Yeah. When?"

"Let's say noon."

"Suits me, I'll bring my own chair," said Pete with a smile on the corner of his mouth.

"No need," replied Luigi, "you won't be standing for long." Pete looked at him, shook his head and closed his front door.

"What a mook," he thought.

So he throttled down the I-95 to get to that shitty factory to have a talk with Frank Senior. Standing in the remains of that building, Pete didn't see how this was any more preferable than a Glen Burnie launderette, but apparently it was. At least there were seats in the laundromat.

Them Lagottis sure picked crumby places for business meetings. Derelict factories, cemeteries. Jeez. But he knew better than do anything other than keep those sorts of thoughts in his head.

"Glad you made it, my boy."

"Hey, anything for you Frank Senior."

"How's tricks?"

"All good, thanks."

"Excellent news. And our Frankie?"

Pete hesitated. Not because he had something particularly negative to say about his step nephew, but because it was concerning to hear Frank Senior might be concerned.

"All's okay. The job's going fine."

"Good. Anything else?"

"Well, we'd all like the business to be over with by now but we also recognize it's better to plan and wait for the perfect moment rather than rush in all guns blazin'."

Lagotti nodded. Frank was right to wait. A bigger haul due to land in their laps next month was proof. And clearly the Wheels had yet to hear the good news on that front. Lagotti would let Frank be the bearer of those glad tidings.

"And is there anything about the organization you feel I should know about?"

"Um, no?" Pete was getting more confused because he couldn't work out quite what Frank Senior was after. What or who was he trying to nail?

"No. Nothing more then?"

"Not that I can think of. I mean, is there anything in particular you want to know from me? I'm not being funny, I just don't know what you're getting at."

Lagotti peered at Pete for a long moment. The Wheels was a bit of a joker but he wouldn't fuck with him or be intentionally disrespectful. Pete might have the habit of clipping the odd guy unnecessarily, but he wasn't a disrespectful psycho, otherwise Lagotti himself would have sent the dude to hell many jobs ago.

"HOW COMFORTABLE ARE you with the information you are getting about the bank?"

"You mean from Mary Lou and the mark?"

"Exactly, my boy!"

"Oh… She's got a lot of useful intel for us from the mark, for sure. I dunno if she could have got it faster as I've never even seen the mark. Don't know how easy it would be to make him talk. But," sly dirty smile erupted across his expression, turning his mouth into a nasty grimace, "I'd slash my old mother's face with a bolo knife to taste at those tits and ass."

Pete's words trailed off as they both started mentally undressing Mary Lou until she was standing before them in just her undies.

"I understand what you are saying," and Lagotti raised his eyebrows to show Pete her breasts and tuches were also on his mind.

"And is there anything you are concerned about with this job?"

"Just getting the money out of the safe. I mean, we've planned and planned, but knowing it might be all locked inside a vault means we won't have much time for fucking about. Apart from that, nothing."

Lagotti thought to himself the fellas wouldn't have to worry about the safe, simply because he knew Carter would have removed it all before they opened the door and stepped into the bank.

"You don't have to worry about a thing," he said with a straight face, "it'll all work out fine, my boy."

Lagotti patted him on the shoulder and walked away back to Paul in the car who drove off as soon as his boss shut the door.

PETE MADE SURE Lagotti was the first to leave and he waited at least ten minutes before traveling in the opposite direction. As he was relatively close to Joppa and the I-95 beckoned, he paid an extra visit to luscious Lucy, his dessert delivering doll.

He parked in the lot and headed straight for a booth to grab some food and take a pinch of that ass. He perused the menu slowly because reading was not his strongest skill and some of the more tricksy items didn't come with pictures.

"What ya havin', lover man?" asked a pair of tits in a uniform that was definitely not his Lucy.

"Coffee. Burger. Fries. Where's Lucy?"

The waitress chuckled. Pete caught sight of her name badge thrusting at his face. Glenda whistled.

"Gee, honey. It's our Lucy's day off. Still be wantin' the burger and fries?"

"Sure thing, Glenda. I've got a hunger on me."

"I'm sure you have, babe," and the rest of Glenda's sentence trailed off into silence as she winked at him, turned and walked over to the kitchen to deliver his request to the short order chef sweating buckets by the hot plate and frying oil.

Pete left a five buck tip for Glenda, wiped the grease from his lips and teeth and got back into his auto. Then he drove round the corner to Lucy's trailer and saw there was a light on inside. Quietly, he closed the door of the car and tiptoed to the trailer to hear if Lucy had any visitors—he was turning up unannounced and there was nothing between them enough for her not to fuck other guys. But there was just the sound of the television set and the heehaw sounds of a game show host and audience.

Pete pushed open the door of the trailer and stepped in with his back heel still holding it ajar. He smiled and pulled his tee shirt off over his head.

"Hi, I'm here for some of your lovin'."

"What you doin' at the door, papa? Close it 'n' come inside your mama, now."

Lucy pushed down on her jeans and panties until they were below her knees, let them separate and Pete whipped off his pants and shorts and lay on top of her, pumping hard, while she carried on watching the TV, occasionally slapping his ass and making an appropriate moan or two. It was good to keep her men happy, she found. That way, she got punched a lot less later on.

BACK AT THE Kitkatt Club, Lagotti went to his usual table and ordered a vodka lime. There were two beauties on stage, working the room hard. One was naked except for a headscarf and a belt round her waist where the johns hung notes. She was bending over and slapping her ass. She had brown hair on top but her bush was black. The other blonde was still in her underpants and was collecting a pretty penny just by walking around with her thumbs in her panties, letting the members get a glimpse of her pubes. "America is a wonderful country," thought their boss, as he took a twenty from his roll and sauntered towards the blonde to profer her tip. She recognized him and made sure she was at the edge of the platform by the time Lagotti had wended his way around all the tables. Unlike the other men, Lagotti was allowed to touch the merchandise, so he pulled at her thong, holding the greenbacks that were already there and pushing his Jackson down the front so he gave himself an excuse to have her hairs brush past his hand. He smiled up at her as he patted her knickers back into position and she carried on with her performance.

When he sat down, he beckoned for the waitress who scurried over and he asked: "What's the blonde's name?"

"August."

"Find somewhere for August and me when she's finished, my dear." He pushed twenty dollars into her bra and patted her ass as she left.

Ten minutes later, Lagotti and August were alone in a private members room. He had a fresh vodka lime and she was wearing a faux silk dressing gown. There was a table, two chairs and a sofa. He sat on the love seat and placed his drink on the glass table top.

"Sit down, my dear," he said patting the space next to his and she immediately obliged.

"My what fine pale skin you have," he added, brushing the back of his finger up and down her leg nearest to him. Then he led his fingers up her limb and up her torso until he was stroking her breast.

He stood up at this point and undid his pants so they fell to the floor.

"Take off your things. Let's get this done," he instructed and August removed her dressing gown and let it fall off her as she rose up and pushed her panties down until they plopped on the ground. Then she kneeled down and slobbered on Lagotti for a while. He grabbed her by the hair and threw her onto the sofa, climbed on top of her and fucked her until he was finished. He replaced his pants and dropped a C note on the table and picked up his vodka lime.

"There you go. Put your things back on, whore," he snarled and walked out of the private members room leaving August to stop crying and to place the dressing gown over her body.

31

ANDREW HAD KNOWN he was gay from the age of fourteen, although later he would admit to himself he actually was gay from the day he was born. By the time he was sixteen, he'd had his first fumbling sexual experiences with a boy from his school.

But he only came out when he left home at eighteen and discovered his best aptitude was stealing from gas stations, local marts, anywhere with a cash till. And he spent his first night in jail the same year.

Now for many guys away in gaol for the first time, this can be traumatic, but Andrew's experience was different. Under cover of darkness, he found there were plenty of men, straight and gay, who would share a bed with him and that meant jail was more a sexual university to him than a valid deterrent for inappropriate thieving behavior.

Andrew met Martin in prison when he served two years for attempting to rob a gas station. While Andrew was great at stealing, as a young man he was not good at thinking through the consequences of his actions. It was then he recognized the need to plan a robbery rather than just grab a gun and run to a counter and shout: "Give me all your money or I'll shoot you in the face!"

When he got out on probation, Martin introduced him to working with a bunch of guys and they operated as the muscle on several medium scale jobs. They moved in together but, because of the times in which they were living, they always rented two bed apartments.

Later on, Brian appeared on the scene. By the time Andrew headed towards his late twenties, he had changed his outlook. Gone were the days of rushing in waving a gun. Now he was more concerned with being alive for the next job and not just surviving the one he was currently on.

So Martin, the risk taker, was replaced with dependable Brian and the rest, as they say, was history. Only now, dependable had turned into dull and Andrew knew this was because he had allowed them to slide towards mediocrity as much as Brian's fault for not evolving as fast as he would have liked.

That said, Andrew wasn't sure he could face being alone again. He'd been with a partner all his adult life and he was not really in the mood for a solitary existence. Quite the reverse, he really wanted to find a guy to settle down with. Brian simply wasn't that man.

Despite the problems with Brian, there was another issue looming over Andrew: the homophobe, Pete. Even if the man wasn't prejudiced, he still killed Andrew's ex-lover and that was reason enough.

But the fact the guy was a southern bigot made the need for revenge all the more poignant. In an ideal world, Andrew would take Pete back to his auto yard, tie him up and inflict as many of his tools on his body as he could get away with, before the fucker bled out.

BUT ANDREW UNDERSTOOD, more than most, what constituted the perfect crime. It needed means, motivation and opportunity. He had plenty of motivation; motivation he was not short of. The difficulty was the opportunity. His earlier thoughts had been to hit Pete on the way out of the bank, but the more Andrew thought about this, the less convinced he became. The problem was Frank. While clipping Pete wasn't the worst thing in the world to do, killing him in the middle of the job, when his role was to drive them all away from the scene, might not be the smartest approach to keep on Frank's good side. And everyone knew what he'd done to his previous sidekick—and that was someone he liked, respected and admired. Andrew knew he was just a guy holding a gun and in ordinary circumstances that would have been fine. Because that was what he would be paid to do.

But shooting Pete in the head while the dude sat in the getaway vehicle is not a great way to leave a robbery and Andrew could see tremendous downside to this plan of his.

So maybe it would be better for him to hit Pete just before they split up. That would remove the risk of Frank thinking Pete still had value to the group when his work would be done. And it would also mean Andrew and Brian would be more likely to reach the separation point alive. An important consideration in any bank job. He'd need to make it clear to Frank in a matter of seconds he wasn't about to rip off the guys for the money, just deal with Pete for whacking Martin.

Perhaps Andrew should revert to his original plan but ensure Frank knew beforehand that he could be a wheelman too—to de-risk the whole dead-Pete situation in Frank's eyes.

The reality was no matter what Andrew thought, no matter how he tried to rationalize the situation to himself, the basic rule of bank jobs was for members of the crew not to shoot each other until they've at least got away from the crime scene safely. Any attempt to derail that essential, undeniable piece of the plan would be met with short shrift from the leader of the gang. But Andrew's desire for revenge clouded his judgment; a terrible character flaw.

ANDREW SNAPPED OUT of his reverie and saw he was still on the couch next to Brian, who was reading a magazine, flipping from one picture to another until something caught his fancy.

"Martin's dead," said Andrew under his breath.

"I know," said Brian, softly, continuing to flip, "but they'll get equal rights some day, probably before we do." A profound statement for a man who claimed not to follow politics and be more concerned with keeping a good shooting eye than national rights and laws.

Andrew turned his head to look at Brian, the most confused expression on his face he had ever mustered.

"What the fuck… What the fuck are you on about?"

"Huh?"

"What are you on about?"

"Me? You brought it up. What are you chatting about?"

Andrew sighed. "I'm talking about Martin."

"Me, too. Martin Luther King."

Silent beat.

Andrew slapped his forehand with the fleshy bit of his hand to make a loud clapping noise.

"No, darling. I meant our Martin. King might only be dead a month, but our Martin's been gone a lot longer."

Brian smiled.

"Oops, sorry."

"De nada."

Andrew threw an arm round Brian's chest and kissed him on the cheek.

"Silly boy," he murmured and draped a leg onto Brian's lap, who put his arm around Andrew and they stayed that way for a spell. Both basking in the comfort they received from each other amid the ongoing sadness of Martin's loss.

Andrew thought about the first time he met Martin, in a cell in Baltimore Penitentiary the month of his arrival there. Andrew had the bottom bunk and Martin was above him. He heard Andrew's whimpering and popped down beside him. He held him and hugged him and eventually he kissed him and that was the start of their beautiful friendship.

The summer of '62, they spent in San Francisco. Free love might not have been declared yet, but they sure had an amazing time, fucking their way from club to club, night after night. Andrew came of age that season.

When they moved back east, Martin chose to carry on partying through life and there was nothing wrong with that. But Andrew didn't. He figured out he wanted more than just sex with strangers in the same room as his partner. He yearned for the love of a good man and Martin could have been that man, but he got into some bad drugs and poor dependency and Andrew had to have the strength to let him go. Trust the one you're with; Martin was stealing from them to feed his habit.

Andrew's tough love worked and Martin used the opportunity away from him to clean up his act, kicking the heroin and working hard again. But by this time, Brian was on the scene and inside Andrew's heart, so there was no going back.

BRIAN CONTINUED LEAFING through a gun magazine, many articles about the latest firearms and close-up photos of them too. He admired the intricacy of their design and the beauty of their construction. Despite Andrew flopped on top of him, he placed the glossy on his lap and flip the pages with a free hand.

Brian was not as dense as he appeared, but he wasn't one for book learning. Instead, he found out about the world through doing. He'd known his sexuality differed from most of the kids in his class when he gallantly tried to have sex with Anne Schuster, not the most attractive girl in eleventh grade, but she was certainly the most available. And while mechanically, there were no problems, Brian knew he didn't want to repeat the experience either.

So began Brian's real education. Like Andrew, his time spent in jail proved an invaluable source of sexual learning and yearning. And he also honed his skills in two other key areas: the use of firearms and handling the public. Brian found he had a knack for scaring Joe Citizen into doing what he asked of them, without too much violence. This gave him a competitive advantage over other men in his field because cash tills and safes were opened faster and jobs ended sooner and more effectively too.

Brian turned over a couple more pages of his journal. Andrew had rested his body on Brian's and, while it wasn't uncomfortable, the situation was limiting Brian's ability to read his own magazine.

He thought about Andrew and his inability to cope with change. The man just couldn't deal with the idea things don't stay set in concrete. Andrew could extricate himself from Martin and take up with him, but it appeared that was the last time in his life Andrew would do anything close to make a change. Since he forced Martin out of his home, Andrew had tried to create the perfect living environment and once each element of perfection was discovered, nothing about it was allowed to be altered. From the color of the drapes to the pattern on the cushions.

Brian needed a little more out of his life than a weakened relationship in an atrophied apartment. He craved excitement, danger and the comfort of a good man at home once the adrenalin stopped pumping. On the other hand, he'd never really had any trouble out of Andrew either. Safe really meant safe, so while there were few surprises, there were very few tantrums pulled in return. Sometimes in life you get what you ask for and then realize you've asked for the wrong thing.

BIZARRE, TO BRIAN'S point of view, was the near obsession Andrew had gained with Martin's death. Obviously, Brian would never rush to defend Martin, given how he and Martin ended, his ongoing drug habit and the fact Martin permanently resented Brian's presence in Andrew's life. All quite normal for an ex-boyfriend, really.

Andrew was a sucker for injustice and thought of himself as a much less promiscuous Errol Flynn in some Robin Hood movie. But he'd been brooding on Pete's guilt for the best part of six months now doing nothing concrete about it. As far as Brian was concerned, he was pretty much certain Pete had whacked Martin, but the guy was a dope fiend and a shit heel and probably had it coming to him, although he wouldn't admit those thoughts to Andrew. Criticizing your partner's ex is normal but being overjoyed to see their murderer walk free overstepped the bounds of forgiveness.

Brian was conflicted. He was in two minds whether to clip Pete when on the job to make Andrew happy or to whack him because the man was dull and not going away. He'd take any shit from him and instead of walking or throwing Brian out, Andrew'd suck it in and think of the good times they had—mainly because he'd used up all his real emotional energy dealing with Martin, caring for Martin and mourning for him. And that pissed off Brian even though he was quite an easy-going guy—for a hired killer and thug.

The biggest problem hitting Pete during the job was the simple fact he was the wheelman. So no one would appreciate Pete's brains dripping onto the sidewalk before they had left the vicinity of the bank. And even then, the only real opportunity would be just after they'd pulled the winnings and before they split for a month. But Brian knew at that point, everyone would be completely stoked, adrenal pushing through every vein. And that meant any slight deviation from plan would cause a major disruption to everyone's day and there'd be lots of guys with loads of guns and itchy trigger fingers. Never a good time to despatch one of your own to God's Kingdom without at least some warning, if not an actual trial by a jury of his peers.

But did Brian really want to get rid of Andrew that much? Couldn't they just split up and move on? Probably. And with the money from the job, Brian could live a very lovely life, with or without Andrew. And Andrew at least offered some domestic perks. But their time together was exceptionally dull.

And so the thoughts echoed around Brian's mind, over and over, until he was knocked out of this loop when Andrew placed his palm under Brian's chin and forced him to turn his head and kissed him on the mouth.

Meanwhile Andrew's other hand rubbed Brian's chest and stomach, eventually arriving at the bottom of the tee shirt. It went under the tee and up Brian's torso, stroking and kneading his flesh as it went up and then down again until it reached the hem of the tee and carried its journey on down to Brian's thigh, which caressed it from the knee up. In return, Brian started stroking Andrew's back and sides. A few moments more and they were writhing and squirming around each other's bodies until they were both sated. Then they fell asleep.

Andrew woke up in the small hours of the morning, thinking it was later than it was. He misread twenty to four for twenty past eight and the shock kept him awake with a rush of adrenalin.

The question that entered his head when he saw Brian lying next to him, all naked and cute, was not whether the money they were getting from the job would change them, but by how much and would Brian cope with the cash, because he wasn't the brightest spark in the firmament. The thought echoed round his skull several times and then Andrew drifted back to sleep.

Monday, June 16

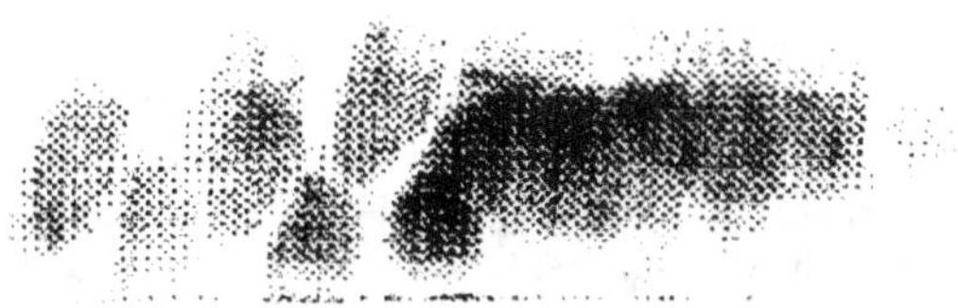

32

MARY LOU AWOKE just after Carter—he'd opened his eyes and registered the light of the day, but had done nothing more with his day than that when she stirred and rolled over to face him.

Carter touched her upturned cheek gently with the back of his first and second fingers and she smiled at him, still to open her own eyes.

"Morning," she whispered and took his stroking hand and kissed it, then let it return to Carter's control.

"Hey," he replied and twisted his wrist so his palm could touch her face. She smirked and he carried on caressing her. Next he drifted down to her neck and she settled into the experience. Then he moved down to her breasts where they remained for a while—so much so Mary Lou rolled onto her back to give him better access to her torso and to make herself more comfortable. After a few minutes, his fingers wandered down to her rose and then further down still until… He caught sight of the alarm clock and shouted: "Shit!"

"What is it?" exclaimed Mary Lou taken aback by the sudden violence of his words and worried Carter'd found something in her pubes.

"Fuck!" was his only response as he leaped out of bed, taking most of the covers with him, leaving Mary Lou naked and confused.

"I'm fucking late!" was all the answer he needed to give.

He threw his clothes on, splashed water on his face and rubbed a finger against his teeth instead of a proper brushing. Then he ran out the door. At the back of her mind, she thought it was sweet how Carter was concerned about such things. It mattered to him, because they were normal, the usual phenomena most Americans had to worry about every day of the week. And part of her yearned to be that Norma Joe.

Carter ran into the bedroom having reached the front door but not quite beyond it. Into the bathroom and the sloshing sound showed Carter'd realized he hadn't shaved in all the rush. Mary Lou laughed as he ran back, kissed her on the forehead and sprinted to the door, this time slamming it shut behind him. Then silence.

CARTER GOT TO the bank at one minute to six, receiving the latest in a long line of disapproving looks from Grimble on the door. Ex-cop and strutting cock.

Taking his coat off and throwing it under his desk, Carter sat down, opened a file and started moving papers about to look like he was engrossed in his work. He stood up and walked to the rear exit to wait for the Pooled Deposit drop, the first for the Lansdowne branch of the First Bank of Baltimore. This was a proud day for JH who, despite not being on his son's roster, had got up especially early to make sure he was there to receive the consignment.

Just after six, an armored truck reversed to the rear and a guard, with a pistol on his hip and a peaked cap on his head, knocked on the door using a pre-arranged signal. JH indicated to Theresa to open up which she dutifully did.

An appropriate form signed by JH and the guard and his companion brought the racks of notes into the back, down the stairs and into the vault. JH remained there counting the $10,000 bricks as they passed him and once all were in the basement, he counted them again. All present, correct and accounted for, so he autographed another piece of paper, keeping a copy for himself and passed the carbon to Theresa to dispose of appropriately. All the while, Carter stood there not sure quite what his role was apart from to remain standing and, presumably, catch JH if he fell or somehow injured himself.

After twenty minutes of this futility, Carter settled into his day and was considerably calmer than when he entered the building. He started to get his head together.

On his list of things to do for the morning was a coffee, because with the rush first thing, he had not consumed a drop to drink apart from the sweet touch of Mary Lou's body—and that would not sustain him until lunch time, no matter how beautiful that woman was.

Second was his regular Monday morning audit of the cases. He'd brought this into his routine about a month after he got them. One day he stretched his legs under the desk and accidentally kicked the bag and was surprised it was there. Somehow he'd forgotten its very existence; it had literally become part of the furniture. So now, every week, without fail, Carter would open each case and check he knew where the keys were and remind himself of their capacity.

Finally, he should carry on with some work. There were a pile of quotations he needed to write: those investments don't get made without him, you know. So the most important task of the day kicked off as Carter stood up and ambled over to the staff door and waited for Theresa or Mrs. Pieck to open up the steel door for him.

As soon as their sole customer had left the counter, Theresa smiled and buzzed him in. She sure had a cute smile, he thought. But he also knew there was never a moment in his life when he would have done anything about that grin. There was Rita, but even without his wedding vows, Carter would never have made a move on someone in the bank, no matter how cute the lips attached to the curvaceous body. It was something he just wouldn't do, at least not since his affair with Monica, which caused the move to the Bank of Baltimore in the first place.

He set the coffee machine in the staff room to brew and popped to his locker, opened the door and looked inside. He made sure he was alone and took the case out and checked its innards. All was well. It was larger than the one under his desk and he figured that, when the moment came, he should be able to get most, if not all, of the big notes from the vault into the pair of cases. He had decided there was no point worrying about the small ones because they would take up a lot of space, but wouldn't score him any points with Frank Senior.

Locking up, he grabbed his mug of coffee and returned to his desk. Just as he sat down, his phone rang.

"FIRST BANK OF Baltimore, Lansdowne Branch. Carter Reinfeldt here. How can I help you?"

"Hey darling."

There was only one female voice in his life who might start a conversation like that. He knew the days of it being Rita had long since paled into impossibility.

"Hey, you." His words emanated warmth, happiness and a calm air of satisfied pleasure.

"You left in a flash this morning. I thought we were having fun."

Carter's mind zoomed back to the two of them naked, with his hand on her rose. The inkling of an erection formed in his trousers.

"Yeah, sorry about that. If we'd woken earlier, we could have had more entertainment, but a man's gotta do what a man's gotta do."

"Sure thing… I know." He discerned disappointment in Mary Lou's voice.

"There's always tonight…" and Mary Lou let her words hang in the air for him to catch, because Monday wasn't one of their usual days.

"Hell yes. We must keep arrangements loose though, because I don't know what time I will be finished here."

"Oh?"

"Yeah, it's the first of the new payroll deliveries, remember?"

"Shoot, yes."

"But we can still hook up, right?"

"Sure thing, darling. You call me when you're leaving so's I know to get ready for you, okay?" The erection got ever so slightly harder.

"You bet your bottom dollar I will," he reported, perhaps a bit too eagerly.

"See you tonight, then."

Carter heard a kissing sound in his ear and just as the phone clicked, he whispered: "Love you," but there was nobody heard his words at the other end of the line because Mary Lou had replaced the receiver and taken a deep breath. They'd been waiting for months. This was the big one. Another inhalation and she dialed Frank back home.

"Game on tomorrow," and she hung up. There was nothing else to say and Frank needed to hear nothing more.

MARY LOU SAT on the sofa in the living room, with her left foot tucked under her right knee. There was a strange silence, which she'd never experienced before. Like the whole world had ground to a halt and reduced in size to her, the couch and the surrounding space.

After a year, it had come to this. Tomorrow morning, Frank would walk into that bank with a gun and Carter would leave just before with a case full of money. Before nine fifteen the First Bank of Baltimore, Lansdowne branch, would be robbed. And another thing that was certain was she would be by the side of the man who had the cash in his hand.

Quite what ended up happening tomorrow was beyond her knowledge, but Mary Lou knew it would be scary and by the time the roller coaster came to a halt, she would live in a totally different place.

The question she had to face was this: should she just follow the money or should she chose between the men instead? The former was easier, but it was so passive Mary Lou had to wonder if she possessed any backbone at all.

But deciding between Frank and Carter was far from easy. For sure, Frank had his big dreams and if Carter and Frank Senior didn't get in the way tomorrow, his dreams would become the reality, but Mary Lou wasn't sure that was sufficient for her in some strange way.

Of course, the money was enough for her and nearly anyone on the planet, but was Frank the right man to be with? Carter was as much a risk taker as Frank, but he had a different manner about him. Carter knew less of the underbelly of life and that was the core of his magic—and helped Mary Lou feel superior to him. But there was also a gentleness to his bearing Frank lacked. Sure he had become a more caring lover over the last while, but that was learned and Carter's was a natural charm.

The other practical question was how Carter would handle himself when Frank Senior came a-knockin' to retrieve his cash—and how would they spend the money if it was dirty. Mary Lou didn't have many good answers to that thorny chestnut, but she was sufficiently street-wise to realize crossing her fingers and hoping for the best was no solution. The world—or at least her world—would be better off if the old gizzard was a goner.

Then again, if there was any trouble from Frank Senior, her Frank would deal immediately. During the time she'd known him, he might have spent more days in jail than out, but he had been a wonderful provider—even when he was in the penitentiary.

Carter talked a good talk, but he had stolen enough cash from his wife to land himself in a whole world of trouble with Frank Senior. Basically, he'd borrowed money off every other Shylock in town so the only person left to get cash from was Frank Senior. And you don't put yourself in that situation without incredibly bad gambling judgment and a bunch of dumb on the side.

But careful, considerate and clear of jail time were all positive aspects of Carter's calling card. The man might have leeched off his wife—she sounded like a bitch—but he was filled with good intentions and dreams of his own he wanted to share with her. That was cute.

Mary Lou felt her pinky finger getting tickled, which snapped her out of her daydream. She was still sat on the sofa and her pinky was definitely getting a slight tickling sensation on one side. She looked down at her hand, which was lying on her lap. The cause was simple: somehow she had let her palm rest upside down and it was next to her pubes, rising and falling with her breathing, tickled by her hairs.

She blushed with the realization she was naked on the sofa. There was no real reason for embarrassment: she'd spent so much time naked in this apartment, but her nudity shocked her, perhaps because her thoughts were so personal, so intimate. Mary Lou strolled straight into the bedroom, there and then, and put on clothes to hide her body from herself and then went into the kitchen to make some breakfast.

FOR THE NEXT couple of hours, Mary Lou went round the apartment gathering anything that was hers and putting it in a travel case—however Tuesday ended, she would not be coming back to this apartment and all her things needed to vanish before the day was over.

After making a quick call, Mary Lou was done. She walked through the joint one more time and took the travel bag and brought it round to Frank's place. She unpacked the case and stuck around for the afternoon, only returning to Carter's place when she thought he might call her to tell her when he'd be home. It was a good idea to at least check all was still right before spending the night away from him so she could be fresh for the morning.

At the back of Mary Lou's mind was the fact she would be setting off some explosives the next day —and she hated dealing with things like that. C4 made her nervous because she didn't understand quite how it worked and that was scary.

So there she sat in an empty apartment waiting for a call from Carter, with only a TV, one of his suits and his toothbrush for company. Carter never actually kept his possessions in the place. It was like he never really believed he lived there. For sure, he paid the rent and dealt with the landlord and so on, but his footprint was so light in the place, if you sauntered around, you'd be forgiven if you thought he just wasn't there. Maybe, that's how he coped with his flitting between Rita and herself. Maybe it reflected how he actually felt about their relationship. Mary Lou couldn't tell, but all his other actions made her believe he was serious about her.

33

FRANK RECEIVED THE call from Mary Lou at nine thirty. He heard three little words and she hung up: "Game on tomorrow."

His whole world reduced to five small syllables; dreams for the future encapsulated in that singular thought.

Frank sat down after the call. There was a tense, fluttering sensation in the pit of his stomach. The back of his throat was intensely dry and he cleared his throat. Again and again, until the clearing became a cough. which morphed into a retching sound and he rushed to the bathroom, in time to throw up in the sink.

He spat out the gunk in his mouth and sloshed a mouthful of water round to remove the acid taste still lingering. Then he left the tap running and washed away the remnants from the sink and, finally, grabbed a toothbrush to clean his teeth. Frank looked up at the mirror on the bathroom wall and saw his red stained eyes staring back and was glad it was over. This always happened to him before a job and the good thing was it had occurred early in the day, so he could get on with the rest of his life and dreams.

Having shaken his body around with the retching and vomiting, he sat on the toilet and pondered the world a while. He thought about what he needed to do between now and the end of the evening and he imagined how the first few hours of tomorrow would pan out—until he segued from imagination to fantasy.

He knew even his plan, which was well thought through, would go awry. Something always got in the way of your intentions on jobs like these. The successful people were the ones who made the right decisions at the time when things went wrong. The failures ended up back in jail or with a bullet through the chest and neither option sounded a great idea to him.

He played the movie of Tuesday morning through his mind again, anticipating anything where reality might force him to shift away from his imagined scenarios. There was nothing obvious, but if there had been then the hours of talking the matter through with Mary Lou, Pete and Uncle Frankie would have been completely wasted.

Frank replayed his list of chores for today. There were only three things he absolutely needed to do. First, he needed to kick off the chain so everyone knew the job was finally on. Then he must hook up with Frankie some time before evening and, finally, he had to be on the receiving end of the chain before nightfall—otherwise all bets were off and he'd have to nix the game before anyone made any foolish moves in the morning. But he knew better than to get ahead of himself. So he finished on the toilet, washed his hands and face to help give him a super clear head, put on some clothes and left the apartment. First stop, Andrew's place.

FRANK FIRED UP the jalopy and headed over to the apartment on the other side of Halethorpe. He parked a couple of blocks away and walked over to the brownstone, just as a precaution. Up the stairs to the second floor, turned right at the hallway and third on the left. Frank knocked and waited.

An eternity passed, the door opened up and Andrew stood there. And quite surprised to see him, judging by his expression. Frank was hoping to be invited in, more out of curiosity than anything else. He'd never been inside Andrew's pad and he was interested to find out what it looked like. But no. Andrew stood, barring Frank's further progress, so he spoke out in the corridor.

"I'll make this quick, Andrew," said Frank, trying to crane his eyes around the wooden entrance to get a glimpse of at least the decor.

"Okay. What's up?" snapped Andrew back at him. A bit sharp for Andrew, thought Frank. What was the matter with him? Or he wasn't expecting Frank to appear at ten in the morning.

"The job's tomorrow. Game on." Frank let the words hang in the air because he knew how immense the impact those words would have on the rest of the gang. They were all going to galvanize behind that single phrase.

"Game on, Frank," replied Andrew with a smile, although his eyes showed more fear than the pleasure showing on his lips. Before Frank could say another word, Andrew shut the door on his face. He shrugged and decided not to take it personally, but it was damn strange behavior. People react weird at the best of times.

Andrew smiled as he closed the door on Frank, his heart racing with the adrenaline Frank's words generated. Game on tomorrow. A simple code for a classic game. They each passed on the words to another fella and until the message reached all of them. The last person fed what they were told back to Frank. That way he could be certain they hadn't been playing the Telephone Game.

Andrew sat on the sofa and let the news soak in, dripping into his brain. First, the sheer immediacy of it all: tomorrow morning they would wake up and two hours later, they would be in the bank with guns in their hands and cash in their pockets. Second, the thudding realization this meant he was shooting Pete as well.

Third, and this was taking the longest time to feel real to Andrew: from some point in the morning, they'd be lying low for weeks with only a phone number, and a pre-arranged hour, provided by Frank, to hold them together. He and Brian wouldn't be seeing their condo for a while. They'd better not leave anything open in the fridge or it will walk out by itself by the time they got back.

Finally, there was the thought they wouldn't be seeing this apartment again, because they hit easy street or they were either dead or in jail. The last two options didn't appeal, but Andrew tried to process their implications.

After two minutes, a wave of melancholia descending upon him and he decided the best option was a long walk. The smart thing was to roam around Lansdowne and give himself one last chance to get the street map in his head before the game began.

HALF AN HOUR later, Andrew stood in the middle of the graveyard getting his bearings and headed off northwards, moving away from the bank to swing round later and catch a few other streets along the way.

He exited the cemetery and turned west until he hit Saratoga Avenue. Then he sauntered south and reached fifth. Next right and he walked parallel to the south side of the graveyard along Hollins Ferry Road.

When he'd got about three hundred feet, Andrew realized what he really wanted was a cup of coffee. As luck would have it, he stood outside a place called the Dulce Caffe, so he popped right in and sat down at a table by the window.

A waiter let him sit there perusing the menu for a minute or two then swooped in and asked what him wanted. The answer of a coffee was met with a curt smile and a shuffling of the card back into the slot in the menu holder, which each table had included on its surface, as well as napkins, cutlery and a bowl of sugar cubes.

Andrew leaned his elbows on the counter, holding his head in his hands. He looked out the window and watched the world go by, not that there were too many people walking past. The time for workers to be out had ended and the hardened shoppers were not yet in town or in another part of Lansdowne where there were shops. This stretch of the road was fairly bare: a connector between the residential roads further south east and the city center further north west after the cemetery.

The same thoughts he tried to shake off in the apartment flooded back now he was in the cafe as if Andrew could only exorcize them through physical movement. His Java arrived and he added a drop of milk, then he plopped two sugar cubes into the cup with a splash and stirred them round with a coffee spoon. The sugar dissolved and he returned to his musing.

Thoughts of jail were the biggest thing haunting him. Not that the building itself held much sway, more the people. Between the guards and the hardcore inmates, they could stir up a lot of shit for a man like Andrew. He was smarter than the average—he found that the last time he was in gaol—and his lifestyle was upsetting to some of the jail straight community. And they reacted with violence rather than an inquisitive nature.

So jail was far from an ideal location. And he'd be split up from Brian, almost inevitably, which would be another layer of pain on top. Or relief, depending on his mood on the day.

But Frank was a reliable guy who'd got the planning down to a tee. The more likely issue was dealing with killing Pete while keeping everyone else on-side. Brian would get the joke immediately, but Frank or Frank Senior? Mary Lou would fall in line behind Frank.

The waiter dropped the bill onto Andrew's table and he threw out a buck and left.

34

BY THE TIME Andrew got home, Brian had woken from his tequila coma from the night before and was sat up in bed. Just.

Andrew inhaled the musty smell in the bedroom which had accumulated all of Brian's liquor breath and opened the window nearest Brian's head. A blast of cold air hit the man's body and he was most definitely awake.

"Game on tomorrow," said Andrew loudly. Then he turned round and walked out the apartment, making sure the front door was firmly, and far from noiselessly, shut.

Andrew carried on wondering around the roads, his hands in his pockets and his head down low, meandering along the sidewalk with no particular purpose in mind. He crisscrossed streets, sometimes going left or heading right, but never paying much attention to where he was heading. He turned a corner and walking towards him was Pat.

Now Pat was an old flame, long since extinguished, from Andrew's past. His hair was shorter than when Andrew had seen it last, but this was Pat with no dispute. And the sight of Pat slapped him out of his reverie and snapped him back to planet Earth. The big question at the front of Andrew's mind was why Pat suddenly appeared out of nowhere, only a day before the job.

"You gotta be kiddin' me!" Pat exclaimed when he looked up from the sidewalk and saw Andrew for the first time in seven years.

"Holy moly!" responded Andrew, in mild shock from seeing this guy after so long and still wondering why the coincidence on this of all days, not realizing what happens when you randomly walk around a town you've lived in all your life.

They shook hands and rolled that gesture into a brief hug. Then they stepped back and grinned.

"What brings you here?"

Andrew smiled again and shrugged.

"I was just wandering around, to be honest, clearing my head."

"And you were walking round the neighborhood?"

"Yep. Just strolling from here to there."

"Nice. What are you up to when you're not having a walk?"

"This and that, y'know," replied Andrew, trailing his voice into nothingness. Pat picked up on the evasiveness and let it lie. He knew Andrew worked on the wrong side of the tracks so he didn't push the matter. Part of Andrew's attraction to him was his criminal tendencies. So they small-talked for a minute, another hug and off they walked, carrying on in their respective original directions.

But from that point on, Andrew was awake and aware, focused on where he was and where he was going. He grabbed a cab and went across town so he could take a bus home, just in case Pat—or anyone else—was following him. It was time for him to get his brain in the game.

BEFORE ANDREW RETURNED to the apartment, he made a minor detour to the train station and went to the left luggage area and zoomed straight to locker number B21, one of the smaller lockers at head height. He took out a key from a compartment in his wallet, turned it in its lock and opened the B21 door just enough to enable himself to put his hand into the dark abyss and retrieve a metallic gadget and a cardboard box the size of his fist. Pistol and ammo.

All that practice in the firing range with Brian was shaping into tomorrow. But this rod was not for the job itself. No, this was a special gun. If the opportunity to cap Pete only arose after they'd ditched their firearms, Andrew wanted the necessary tools. If Pete handed his revolvers over that would be the best time to hit him. When he was naked.

Also Andrew had kept up his driving practice, because if the Wheels had to go before they'd left the scene, he needed to show Frank all was well with the world—apart from a dead Pete, that is.

Now today was not the day for spinning round a track, but it was a an opportunity to make sure there were no loose ends in their lives, so when they vanished for a few weeks, no one would notice their absence. They weren't the kinds of people to buy a newspaper regularly. And they only occasionally visited to the same diner twice in a row for breakfast—Brian was always too cautious to let them do anything as normal as that.

Andrew knew the most important thing, therefore, was to throw out all the food and empty the trash. The very last issue they'd want in two weeks time would be for the Super to unlock the place with his master key to find an unoccupied apartment harboring the aroma of death and decay. Nobody must notice they were gone and absolutely no one should notice when they were gone.

A COLD BLAST of air caught Brian in the neck and he awoke with a start. Andrew was right in his face.

"Game on tomorrow," he said with an unbelievable volume, slammed the door and left.

Brian's head was filled with a wooly, fuzzy sensation, which made his hands shake and caused him to crave a long drag on a cigarette. Tequila hangovers were a killer for him.

While Brian's body generally followed the rule that clear liquor didn't cause headaches, no one bothered to explain that simple fact to the alcohol coursing through his veins. He faced the ceiling with both hands by his side and, for a man his size, he was too afraid to open his eyes, in case the room carried on spinning the way it did last night before he crashed out.

When Brian fell into the apartment, he literally moved around the place from memory as his eyes weren't working in the normal fashion. It was only luck and habit that meant he landed on the correct side of the bed, instead of squashing Andrew with his not inconsiderable frame.

Brian knew he needed to get a serious hangover recipe inside himself before too long because he really couldn't spend the day with the tremors. Not today. Not with the news Andrew had just left in his ear. Game on tomorrow.

He bumbled into the kitchen and cracked two eggs into a tall glass. Next he poured in some buttermilk and a splash of tabasco. He whisked the mixture with a fork until the raw egg had turned the milk an eerie pale yellow. Then he swigged the concoction down in one, clinging to the sink as he did, partly to stay upright and partly to manage the foul taste of his own devising. Finally, he made himself an extremely strong coffee to jolt his body back into life. And then another.

By the time he showered, shaved and got dressed, Brian felt more like a human being and thought beyond the quivering moments he was experiencing. If he'd known tomorrow was game on, he wouldn't have drunk that much hard liquor. But you only know what you know although he would have preferred if Frank had given them all more notice.

Brian left the apartment and slunk down to a phone booth two blocks west. He dialed Pete's number and waited. No reply after ten, twenty, thirty rings. Pete had his head stuck in an engine block or he wasn't in his yard.

"Fuck," thought Brian, knowing this meant he either had to spend the day chasing phone calls to Pete or he'd have to drive over to the lot and just sit and wait for him to appear. Both involved effort on his part and neither sounded like fun.

Brian decided to try again in an hour and, if there was still no joy, he'd pop over and deal accordingly. Pete had until noon to show his sorry ass. In the meantime, Brian decided the best thing he could do was to get some proper lunch, so he walked across the street to the Lansdowne Steakhouse. What the restaurant lacked in terms of inventiveness of its name, it sure made up for in its product: the steaks were to die for.

BRIAN TOOK A table away from the window and ordered a sixteen ounce rib-eye and fries. He had a hunger on him brought on by the recovery from the tequila slammer evening and the thought he'd need to be in best shape for tomorrow. So today had better have some protein in it.

He also had the good sense to start drinking a lot of water so he could wash away the sucking dryness of the tequila and get his brain back in gear.

In his booth, Brian sipped the umpteenth glass of water, sucked the remains of his steak caught between his teeth, and swallowed it all down. Slowly. These were the last moments of silence and isolation he would experience for weeks at the very least.

He and Andrew would hole up someplace in Manhattan, somewhere busy where they could get lost in the crowd and no one asks questions of strangers. And there would be no quiet there. Even when they were alone together, there'd still be Andrew warbling in his ear about something scaring him. And the repetitiveness of their relationship would wear Brian down more than it had over the past year.

Ultimately, Brian knew Andrew was going to have to go. Go away from his life, that is, but Brian hadn't had the energy to deal until now and with the job happening tomorrow, he knew Andrew would have to wait at least until they'd got their fair share. Worst case, Brian would end up with a double quota if Andrew really began to piss him off, but he was dull rather than dangerous, so there was no reason at this point to think it'd be anything other than an amicable split. Screaming, shouting, tears.

Brian ordered a piece of key lime pie to balance out the steak. The food arrived almost immediately and Brian got the feeling the waiter was trying to hustle him out the restaurant. There was no reason because the place was half empty. There was also no reason because the waiter was merely being prompt and had picked up on some tetchy vibes coming from Brian. The tensions in his mind were revealing themselves to those whose job it was to pick up on such things.

The bill appeared as soon as Brian asked for it. He carried on finishing his dessert, threw down some greenbacks and left the eatery. Back to the phone booth and he dialed Pete's number again.

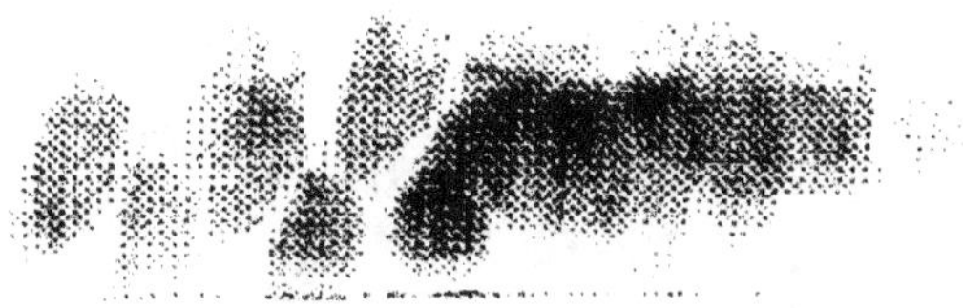

35

PETE HAD SPENT the night until six a.m. playing five stud poker with a bottle of vodka by his side and Lady Luck waving him goodbye through an open window. By the time he collapsed onto his bed, he was six hundred dollars down and couldn't taste the insides of his mouth. This counted as a good night's gambling for Pete.

So when the phone rang around eleven, there was no way on this planet he would be roused from his slumber to answer the dang thing. An hour later and his body was sufficiently recovered to acknowledge the constant ringing noise by his head. Pete fished for the receiver keeping his eyes shut as the brightness of the room was not something he was prepared to deal with at this point in his life.

"Yep?" he muttered when he finally got the handset near his ear.

"Who's that?"

"You called me butt features."

Brian thought he recognized the accent and that response meant it was definitely Pete.

"Game on… tomorrow."

Bolt upright. Eyes open. Swallow hard.

"Bye," he said to Brian's voice and, without thinking, he put the phone down.

"Fuck," as he realized he needed to speak with Brian more. Luckily, Brian had given him the phone booth number which he'd use for this important message and Pete had taped it next to the phone. Just in case. So he rang straight back and hoped Brian hadn't walked away too fast. After a couple of rings, Brian answered.

"Is that you?"

"Yes," said Brian. It was Pete on the line.

"Need some help. Can you come over this afternoon?"

"Sure thing. When?"

"Around three?"

"Got it. See you then."

That done, Pete poured water over his face and head from the little sink in his room and put on a pot of coffee. He opened the fridge and found cans of beer and some moldy ham, which he threw in a bin bag.

With nothing to eat, Pete took the bin bag and walked round the place looking for crap to throw away. He'd be gone a few weeks and the festering stench of his rotten past shouldn't be used to drag anyone's attention towards his yard. He tied up the bag, throwing it on the sidewalk, ready for whenever the refuse truck came to collect. Finally Pete's brain kicked into gear and he placed one short call to Frank Senior.

THE CALL FROM Pete came into Lagotti's office around twelve twenty and, luckily, Luigi took it. He wasn't usually keen on answering as he found the telephone a difficult device. He preferred to figure out what was going on by looking at your expression.

"Hallo."

"I've a message for Frank Senior."

"Okay."

"Will you pass him over to me or are you going to take the message?"

"Yes," said Luigi already feeling uncomfortable, wishing Paul had been in at the time when the phone's little bell began to ring-a-ding.

"Which one, numb nuts?"

The voice at the other end was getting annoyed and a touch abusive. If he had been in the place, Luigi would've slugged him one. But to be fair, if Luigi had been in the same room as the guy, he'd have seen how pissed Luigi was and might well have altered his tone all round.

"Um… I'll take the message."

"Okay. Listen carefully. The message is…"

"Yes, I'm listening," Luigi interrupted.

"Listen good and say nothing for a second, numb nuts."

"Uh huh." Heavy sigh from Pete, who was on the edge of losing his patience.

"The message is: game on tomorrow. Got it?"

"Yep."

"Good," said Pete as calmly as he was able. "Say it back to me so's I know you heard it right."

"What?" Luigi was getting confused again. Phones shouldn't be this complicated.

"Say the message back to me, shit head."

"Game on tomorrow got it."

"No, no, no! Just the three words: game on tomorrow. Nothing more, nothing less. Say them back to me, for Christ's sake!"

"Game on tomorrow."

"Abso-fucking-lutely. Make sure Frank Senior gets that message in the next half an hour. Tell him the Wheels left the message."

"The wheels?"

"Yeah, the Wheels. He'll know who it is."

"Let me get this straight. You want me to tell Mr. Lagotti that some wheels left a message that the game is on tomorrow?"

"Close enough, shit-for-brains. Just make sure you fucking tell him." And with that, Pete hung up.

Now Luigi might not be the brightest wrench in the toolbox but when he had an errand, he had an errand, and nothing would force him to deviate from his chosen aim. He was flustered by Pete's aggression and found the message unusual, but he would get it to Frank Senior before he forgot it come hell or high water.

The good news was Lagotti was only in the next room, reading his girlie magazine, so Luigi knocked on the door.

"Enter," called out Lagotti.

Luigi walked in and waited for Lagotti to put down his picture papers, which always took a while.

"A guy called the wheels called and left you a message."

"Why thank you, Luigi. And what was that message that the Wheels has left me?" Lagotti knew Luigi was the slowest in the race but as a reliable son-of-a-bitch as you could find in the Northern hemisphere. So he knew patience was the key to extracting information out of this Rottweiler.

Luigi thought for a moment, not wanting to let his boss down and knowing he had heard the phrase not once, but twice at least, just a few seconds ago.

"He said the game was on for tomorrow."

Lagotti smiled.

"Did he say: Game on tomorrow?"

"Yeah, those was the self-same words he used!"

"Good news then. Well done, Luigi."

"Thank yous."

"Now I've got a job for you and it must be completed today. Without fail, you understand?"

"Sure thing, Mr. L."

"I want you to pay a visit to that bank teller, Carter Reinfeldt before he gets home from the Bank of Baltimore tonight. You inform him you'll be back again tomorrow evening to collect the case he should have for me."

"Okay."

"Tell him Tuesday night is when you will get the item from him. Got it?"

"Do you want me to do this alone or can I bring Paul?"

"Whichever you prefer, Luigi. The man won't give you any bother, but if you'd like some company on the ride over, that's fine by me."

Lagotti knew Luigi didn't need chaperoning, but he needed someone who to remember a couple of basic facts for over ten minutes without having to read it in a notebook. And Paul was far brighter than Luigi, but not nearly as fearless—mainly because he was far brighter and understood what risk was. But they both had their uses and handled themselves well if it came to that.

Luigi left Lagotti, still with his feet up on the desk, and went to find out where Paul had gotten to.

LAGOTTI PUT HIS magazine onto his lap and smiled to himself. This was as close to a win-win situation he had ever conjured up. Heads he won, tails he won. The only way to lose would be if the coin landed on its side and even if that somehow happened, he would not lose: he'd still have the bank adviser by the balls and his step nephew would still want to rob another bank for him. Thinking further, Lagotti realized there was only one scenario that might play out where he actually lost—if Reinfeldt was killed in the robbery and couldn't pay him back. The chances were slim because Frank may be a vengeful man, but he was a professional and wouldn't let the chance to kill the guy, who'd been fucking his girl for best part of a year, get in the way of grabbing some bags of notes.

Talking of which, Lagotti decided now matters were finalized with the job, he should sort out the cash transfer agent. The basic idea behind money laundering is to swap out any cash that can be identified with other currency that is clean. A smooth running capitalist system operated in this murky world: every person along the chain between dirty and clean money needed to create a profit for themselves, so there was an essential mismatch between the amount of dirty money provided and the value of clean money handed back at the so-called retail end.

Specifically, in our example, the total profit across the entire supply chain was sixty per cent as Frank would only pick up forty cents on the dollar which was a shockingly good rate. This was achieved mainly because Lagotti didn't believe he would need to accommodate it as he thought Carter was giving him all the cash and Lagotti would wait a few months before shifting it and he'd receive a wholesale price, anyway.

The first step for Lagotti was to line up Jimmy the German, a Baltimore based gentleman of European heritage, who was able to take in amounts of half a million plus and perform magic on the cash within a period of about two or three days. This came at a price which was fifty cents on the dollar so it was well within Lagotti's profit margin.

After the transaction was complete, Lagotti would need to get the clean money over to Frank and the boys so they could finally split the spoils and part their merry ways.

Were it to happen, this would be the most dangerous part of the escapade because there would be clean money—a lot of it—and many people with access to firearms. And one of the basic courtesies, when you are returning less than half the money a gang has given you, is to turn up in person with their loot. Otherwise you look like you're robbing them blind yourself, which you are—hence why you don't want it to appear to be the case.

Lagotti would need to be standing next to the clean dough when it was handed over to the gang and that made him nervous. It was why he paid Paul and Luigi to stand around looking mean near him because they were the kind of guys more likely to spill blood than ask questions.

And depending who showed up at that point, at the back of Lagotti's mind, was the thought that maybe Paul and Luigi could deal with the remnants of the group if everything at the bank had turned messy. This entire scenario was predicated on the teller not walking out with the money as some bad shit has to go down when you rob a bank with an empty vault.

Lagotti put the call through to Jimmy the German to prepare him for some financial Spring cleaning. Then he left the repair shop to meet his step nephew in their favorite derelict factory.

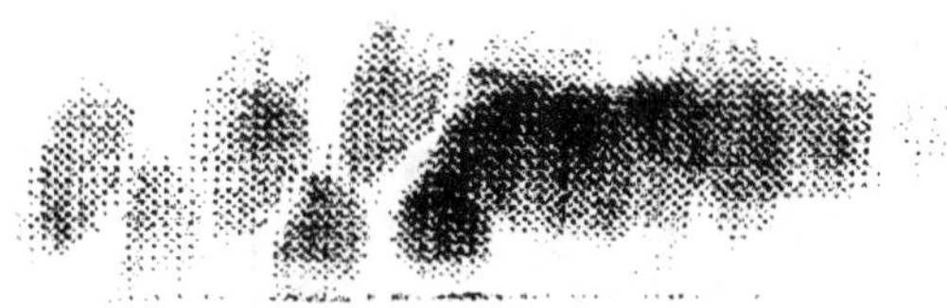

36

TO KILL TIME as much as anything else, Frank drove into Baltimore to find somewhere to eat and tried a little Italian on the corner of West Lexington and Park, which was half full—a good sign given this was a Monday lunchtime. As ever, even here, he took a table at the back—although there was no reason for him not to be in Baltimore having lunch.

Frank ordered some linguini e salsa Napoletana and the waiter delivered a basket of bread and olives while he was waiting. The pasta was fine, but the sauce was no great shakes; Mary Lou's was better. He knew that for a fact, but he could spend a bit of time somewhere different and relaxed, given the tension and mayhem soon to engulf him as he woke up tomorrow. This made Frank feel happier about himself despite the sauce not being worth the gas to travel here.

He had a good crew even though he still had his doubts about Frankie's choice of Pete. They were tough enough to get through the next twenty-four hours, but they had sufficient brains between them to improvise when his plan inevitably hit the skids.

Frank's final thought at the table was for Mary Lou. She had been through so much over the past year with him, Carter and Frank Senior. And still she was there, double checking the vault was full to brimming with that bank's money.

He paid the check and headed out. Before he did, Frank turned round and asked the waiter to direct him to the pay phone.

"THANKS FOR TAKING my call."

"No problem. You have an assignment for me?"

"Yes, yes I do."

"Good. Who is it?"

"Frank Lagotti Senior. Is that an issue?"

"Not for me. When?"

"In a week's time?"

"It's short notice. Any flexibility on the timing?"

"For sure. Just no sooner than a week. Can be a week, two weeks, a month. Whatever works for you. I just want him dead."

"Okay. Leave half the money in the location we discussed a day before the hit and deliver the second half to the same place the day after the assignment is completed."

"Understood."

"Bye."

"Goodbye."

AFTER YET ANOTHER trip down the I-95, Frank arrived at the factory. His uncle's car was nowhere to be seen, so Frank parked round the back and made his way to the usual ramshackle room, filled with rubble and a solitary chair.

Frank sat down on three breeze blocks he built into a seat, so he could let Frank Senior see the seat had been left for him, to show full respect to his uncle.

While he rested there, waiting, Frank thought how conflicted he felt about his uncle. There was tremendous gratitude for all the old man's help in setting up the job and sorting out the laundering of the cash afterwards. Then there was what Frankie had done to Mary Lou. Cocksucker.

A wind blew through the building and sent a shudder down Frank's spine. And the shiver kept going after the breeze died down.

At this point, Uncle Frankie arrived in the room, Frank stood up and walked over to greet him. A brief hug and Lagotti sat down in his chair and Frank resumed his position on his makeshift seat.

Once they'd settled down, Frankie cleared his throat and spoke with tremendous seriousness.

"I have one thing to say to you, my boy: Game on tomorrow."

Frank discovered a flash of happiness surge through him when he heard those words. His plan was coming good.

"The circle is complete, Uncle Frankie. We're all ready to go," he heard himself say, but he was still thinking about how the line of communication between them all had turned into a loop. It was such a beautiful thing to behold.

"Is there anything for us to do before tomorrow?" Lagotti asked after a minute. Frank said there wasn't and outlined what was left for the others to do before the morning.

Frankie asked Frank if there was anything he could do on the Tuesday. Again, Frank could think of nothing in particular and thanked Frankie for all his help. It was important his uncle only thought positively of his nephew—without him, they would face serious problems holding onto a large amount of dirty money.

"We're all in this together. When one of us succeeds, we all succeed," noted Lagotti, but while the words sounded reasonably warm, Frank had no real idea what he was talking about. For a moment, there was an awkward silence between the two of them, something that hadn't really happened since Frank entered the slammer after his previous job and his uncle had tried to rig the jury and failed, so he said. But that was all water under the bridge. Frankie looked after him when he was in the penitentiary and made sure Mary Lou had a roof over her head and money in her pocket.

"We won't be seeing each other for a while—not until the heat's died down, so good luck and take care of yourself and your guys."

Frank let the warmth of those words soak inside him; Frankie knew how to say the right thing at the right time.

"I don't need luck; I need steel," replied Frank, not too certain quite what he meant, but it sure sounded good. The two men hugged and Lagotti squeezed Frank's cheek as he had down when Frank was a boy. Frank smiled, patted Lagotti at the top of his arm near his shoulder and walked away.

Lagotti sat back in the chair and waited until he heard Frank's junk heap depart the lot. He stood up and shivered—he hated this fucking place and was glad to be seeing the back of it, more or less.

When they found the vault empty, he would suggest they meet up here. He'd point out the source of their information was the girl and get Luigi—or maybe even Frank himself—to cap her there and then. The rest would flow naturally from that.

The old man strolled to his car and drove back to the auto repairs where he parked it in its usual spot. Now to pay a visit to the Kitkatt Club.

LIKE FRANK BEFORE him, the first time Brian visited Pete's yard, he spent twenty futile minutes driving round trying to locate the damn place. Unlike Frank, Brian's spatial awareness meant he always found it easily after that. But they both discovered Pete might be great behind the wheel but was useless when riding shotgun. Couldn't give you directions to find your dick during a hand job.

Pete gazed around his yard at all the vehicles in his domain before Brian's arrival. Everything appeared fine. All the engines turned over okay, nothing sounded out of the ordinary and there was a full tank of gas in each car and truck. Locked and loaded.

Pete sat back on his bed with a cup of warm Java in his hand. He sipped the brown drink until Brian showed up about a half hour later.

First, they set about getting the saloons at the split up point outside Lansdowne. There was an a decrepit barn, long since used, Frank had scouted out and it looked fine. There was plenty of space away from the road for everyone to park and ride without being seen. And no one would poke their noses in a dirty old place like that between now and the morning.

Each car was driven by Pete, and Brian followed him, so they could go back and forth to set things up. And Pete chose a different route each time in case someone was following them—not that anyone had any reason to.

Next they took Mary Lou's convertible to an underground parking lot in Halethorpe for her to collect in the morning. The C4 and timers primed for action resided in the trunk. All she had to do was flip the switch on the timer and attach them on the telegraph poles near the bank.

They drove the van into the same lot, but at opposite ends so Frank could start his route and pick up Andrew and Brian with no hassle. Finally, they headed back to the yard. Each trip together, they'd hardly said anything to each other. Not because of any tension between them like the last time when they bought the guns. There was silence simply because there was nothing they needed or wanted to say to each other.

Pete got out of Brian's car and Brian repeated the two magic words:

"Game on."

He drove off, leaving Pete on his own in the yard.

BY FOUR O'CLOCK Brian was off to the firing range, secure in the knowledge the rides had been sorted and the handguns appeared mighty fine. He only used up fifty rounds, but it gave an excuse to clean the barrels again, so he had sufficient confidence in the proper working order of his revolvers.

He planted his feet squarely and imagined taking down the guard or a do-good civilian. Brian never enjoyed shooting civilians even if it was only a graze-shot or a through-and-through. He figured Johnny Come Latelys should keep their noses out of his business and not get themselves shot. He didn't like clipping them. It wasn't his fault if they got in his way. If he'd ever sat in front of a psychologist, he would have been asked why he felt no responsibility for his actions under those circumstances. But Brian would never be with a shrink, not while there was breath in his body.

Instead, he was squaring off against an FBI target, pretending the silhouette was someone getting in his way. And the stupid thing was there would be no trouble tomorrow because Frank had been planning this for goddamn months. The guy had been eating, drinking and pissing the job since last summer. Andrew'd told him he'd planned it while he was still in the joint. This was one seriously planned takedown.

Brian knew if Frank hadn't got it under control, his broad would sure as hell know what was going on. She'd been fucking the teller since the summer too. She was the one who'd saved their bacon a couple of months ago when the bank stepped up security. Brian trusted Mary Lou and Frank completely, unlike Pete, who was a prize motherfucker 'n' no mistakin'.

The bullets kept on squeezing out of that barrel and virtually every single one formed a cluster around the primary target of the silhouette, the heart. Only two missed because Brian couldn't resist aiming for a couple of head shots, but he knew the best way to take someone down was to aim at the torso. It was the largest part of the body so you were almost bound to hit something. Figured.

With the practice over, all they had to do was be patient and wait for dawn's early light to cast a shadow on their land.

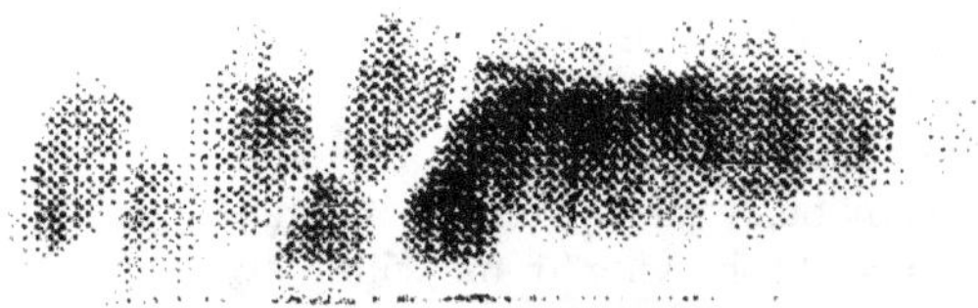

37

FRANKIE SLUMPED DOWN at his usual table, which has been cleared especially once he had arrived. Two girls were on stage and everything was good in the house of Lagotti.

A waitress in red hot pants and matching bra sidled up to him and took his order of a vodka lime. All during the transaction, Lagotti kept his eyes squarely on her nipples, which were more than clearly visible under her underwear. Still staring at the breasts waving in front of him, Lagotti asked: "Where's August?"

"Oh, we have no August here, I don't think."

"Don't shit with me. You new? Haven't seen your… face?" An upward curl of the left side of Lagotti's lips.

"Yes, started this week… Maybe August just hasn't been in recently."

"Doesn't matter. What's your name, missy?"

"April."

"Call me Frank. Ask the other girls about me if you fancy."

"I will Frank. Shall I get your vodka lime now?"

"That would be wonderful. On the rocks, mind."

"Sure thing."

April swished away leaving Lagotti with the opportunity to survey her underage firm buttocks as she departed for the bar. Jailbait ass. She'd be up on stage by the end of the week and on her back before the end of the weekend. That's the business we are in, he said to himself, strumming his fingers on the armrest to the beat of the music engulfing him.

The girls changed around and two more appeared wearing nothing more than their underwear, a pretty smile and a pout. One was ebony with pointy tits and the other was pale white with round ones. Lagotti focused his attention on the round titties. He didn't believe in miscegenation or anything close and with Kennedy gone, the niggers would stay in their place, he thought.

Lagotti stood up and placed a Jackson in Blondie's G-string. It was dark blue and contrasted with her skin gloriously. She kept on dancing and nodded a thank you to him. He smiled back at her and remained by the stage until she came round again. Then he dropped two Jacksons inside the thong and made sure his hand brushed her front when he put the notes in her underwear.

This time he received a wink from her and, at that moment, he got the prize of being up close when she threw her bra to the side of the stage. That placed her nipples only inches from his face, almost near enough to bite.

Lagotti sat back down in his seat and sipped at his drink, keeping an eye on the dancer all the while. He signaled to April, who came over and said: "How can I help, Frank?"

"What's the name of the blonde on stage?"

"She's… um… May, I think."

"You gotta get better at the names, April."

"Sure thing sir." April had obviously had a word backstage about Frank.

"Don't sweat it. Arrange a private showing for me with May when she's off the stage."

"Okay, Frank."

He left fifty on the table for April and took the remains of his drink with him. After he fucked May, Lagotti stuck around just to watch the show. Despite him having funded countless jobs, Lagotti was still excited about this one and knew he wouldn't be going to sleep soon.

NOT FOR THE first time that day, Andrew headed back to the apartment. He walked from Lansdowne Station to the front door on autopilot. Key in the lock and stepped inside.

Brian was sat on the sofa with a cigarette in one hand and a glass of clear liquid in the other.

"Smoking?" he enquired.

"Game on, game on."

"Drink?"

"No thanks, already have one." Andrew smiled out of the corner of his mouth.

"Funny. What are you drinking?"

Brian's turn to smile. "Water, don't worry. Game on, remember."

Andrew returned a genuine grin this time.

"Game on. At last."

He walked straight to the bedroom and hid the gun and ammo in his bedside table drawer. Then Andrew slumped down on the sofa next to Brian, glad to take the weight off his feet. With his arm around Brian's neck, Andrew pecked him on the cheek and whispered in his ear: "How's your head?"

"Just fine, thanks. Two strong mugs of Java and the room stopped spinning. Eventually."

Andrew stroked Brian's upper leg and planted his lips on Brian's cheek again.

"No worries. Our world is changing from tomorrow. Changing for the better."

"Sure thing, muchacho."

"Come to the kitchen with me."

"Oh, really?" in a suggestive manner.

"Yes, we've got some vegetables to chop. Tonight is casserole night."

"Oh, really?" no longer seductive, more wondering where the meat on his plate was coming from.

Brian was glad he'd had a steak for lunch. A casserole was a very sensible way to use up as much of the fridge contents as possible, but it was a boring meal for a last supper before the game tomorrow.

They had fun in the kitchen though, rudely holding carrots and licking the oddly shaped ones like dicks. Once they sat down to eat, the laughing ceased. Both Brian and Andrew turned their thoughts to the following day and all they wanted and expected of it.

BRIAN FACED ANDREW at the table they'd squeezed into the kitchen. He smiled and chewed on his food, mulling over the state of things. The man was a stayer, for sure, and the great thing was Andrew would totally have Brian's back tomorrow and knowing that made the day a lot safer than it could be. Safety on a job was real important; the difference between jail or freedom. Or worse.

But yet again, even though this was not the time for these thoughts, Brian couldn't help imagine what the next month would look like if he didn't have Andrew by his side but only that money there instead.

Brian could party until he dropped in some Castro dive bar. Or not. The choice would be his. Andrew was less inquisitive than Brian who wanted to see the world—or at least the west coast—before he died. If he had the money the idea of checking out Europe or Asia also appealed. He didn't know which places to travel to but he was prepared to get a passport and find out. Not Andrew. Going to a new diner for breakfast was as adventurous as he got.

Brian smiled again at him as his thoughts turned to the best of their times. When they'd first hooked up, he was much needed stability in his life. The sex had been satisfying and the companionship comforting. Brian had felt at ease with him and they were a respite from the storms swirling all around them.

They chatted some more over the remnants of the casserole and then Andrew washed their dishes and Brian dried. A perfect domestic scene; Brian died a little on the inside.

Afterwards, they sat back on the sofa for a spell but Brian got bored and edgy. Bored with that domestic bliss and uptight about tomorrow. If one of those events had occurred on their own, his natural reaction was to aim for a bar and get too drunk to care. The fact these two things were happening simultaneously meant he had to go to bed instead. A tequila hangover on the day of a job was just downright unprofessional.

Brian kissed Andrew goodnight and hit the hay; Andrew followed shortly after. Brian closed his eyes and made his breathing slow to convince Andrew think he was already asleep. Andrew's snoring kept Brian awake for fifteen minutes, but his world lapsed into blackness too. Game on.

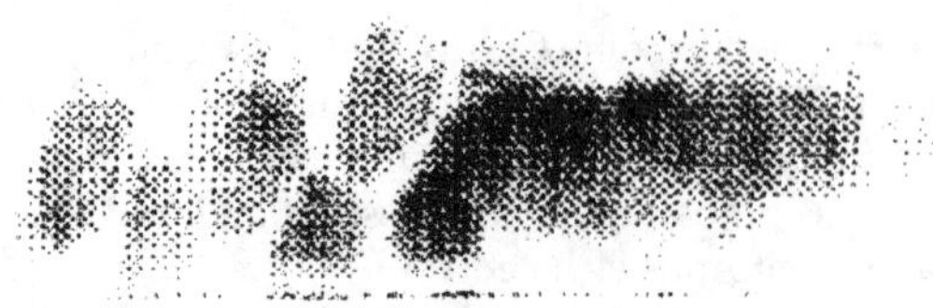

38

ONCE THE BANK'S shutters were nearly down and everyone was leaving after the extra work for the Pooled Deposit—bank reconciliations are incredibly long-winded and dull to perform—Carter thought about seeing Mary Lou again and butterflies flew around his stomach. He turned right out and said goodbye to Theresa and Bob, who walked in the opposite direction to him. For one moment, he considered the possibility they were having an affair, but remembered they were both in relationships. Or so they claimed.

He strolled down the street with his hands in his pockets and halted at the bus stop. There were a few people already waiting and he leaned his back against the wall, imagining soon being in Mary Lou's arms and then nuzzling between her thighs.

After two minutes Carter began to get a sense he was not alone, which was not that strange given he was standing on a sidewalk in midtown Lansdowne. His eyes had firmly and squarely zoned out staring at the paving stone under his feet so he raised his gaze to find out why the sensation of being alone had altered.

Luigi stood next to him on his left and Paul was by his right-hand side. Frank Senior's two goons. Carter swallowed hard and a queasy feeling entered his stomach and ran straight down to his bowels.

They said nothing and remained there. Luigi whistled and Paul just stayed perfectly still, not looking at Carter, not even acknowledging he existed. Two long minutes later and his bus appeared. The people in front of him in the line got on board and he moved one step forwards to do the same, but Paul held out his hand to block his body. Carter looked at him, ashen faced. Paul stared back at him and shook his head slowly.

The bus pulled away, leaving a plume of diesel smoke and an empty space. Once the fumes had cleared, Luigi turned to him: "We have a message for you from our boss." Carter just stood there, palms sweating and his stomach knotting up.

"Do you remember the task he requested you to carry out?" asked Paul, making him turn his head to face Paul's direction. Carter nodded, not trusting his throat to deliver any sound at this point in his life.

"Good. Tomorrow is the day when you shall perform that task. Do you understand?"

Again, Carter nodded.

"Speak to me."

Swallow. "Yes, I understand."

"Excellent. Just remember to carry out the job as soon as you get in, nice and early. And before the doors open at nine."

"Okay."

"And don't leave until the end of the day, no matter what happens. Got it?"

"I've got it."

"Not until the end of the day. Understand?"

"I understand."

"Good. Now go and catch your bus and we'll see each other again tomorrow night."

"Okay."

Before he could finish that simple word, Luigi and Paul walked away and around the corner. Although he thought of following them to make sure they were gone, Carter realized that would mean he would get nearer to them again and was the last thing in the world he wanted to do right now.

His hands shook and his palms were dry as hell. He considered going to Mary Lou's apartment but thought better of it. Frank Senior had made it very clear to him that, once he got word from his boys, Carter should do nothing but either be at home or be in the bank and there was no way he could be with her tonight.

Instead, he walked to a pay phone and called the apartment. Mary Lou answered almost immediately.

"That was quick, baby," he commented as she took the call.

"I was right by the phone, is all."

"Okay. Look. I hate to say this but I can't pop round this evening…"

"Oh." Mary Lou let out a disgruntled child's two-syllable groan.

"Something happened after we finished the Pooled Deposit reconciliation. Listen, can you meet me tomorrow morning when the bank opens for business at nine?"

"Sure thing, darling."

"But I need you to see me at the back where the parking lot is round the side and to pick me up in your car."

"In my car?"

"Yes, you told me you've got one, right?"

"Why yes, I treated myself to a convertible earlier this year."

"Well then, in that."

"Sure thing, but why? Where will we be going?"

"No more questions. It's a surprise for tomorrow. I'll tell you everything then. But promise you'll be there just before nine."

"I do."

"Love you," and this time Carter made certain Mary Lou heard him before he put the phone down on her. Saying those words was a risk and making her the getaway driver was risky too. But he figured that when she looked at the cases, she'd get the picture.

Anyway, he didn't really have chance to ponder the possibilities too closely, because the next bus trundled along the road. He reached the stop in time to hop on.

Carter hopped off the bus and scurried back home to find Rita in the kitchen and an empty whiskey glass with his name on it in the living room. A double shot of Scotch steadied his nerves and he just let himself sink into his easy chair until he became a normal human being again.

The impending tomorrow didn't go away, but his head stopped buzzing with fear and he could focus on the matter at hand, even if it was only for brief spurts before his anxiety took hold and he turned his mind to other things.

RITA CALLED HIM in for dinner and Carter was pleased that at least it wasn't another casserole. This time there was spaghetti with meatballs, which was a welcome, but chewy, change. He understood the reason why there were so many casseroles—they involved nearly zero effort on Rita's part—just chop up whatever was in the fridge, chuck it into a pot and leave it on the heat for a while.

This got Carter thinking about Rita's lover and what they did together: merely displacement activity for his own troubles tomorrow. He and Rita sat opposite each other, as ever, slurping spaghetti and cutting up meatballs until their bowls were empty.

"That was nice, thank you," he commented once he'd mopped up the last of the sauce with a piece of bread.

"You're welcome. I thought we both deserved a bit of a change," she replied without the usual hostile timbre in her voice. In fact, she undid a button or two of her blouse so he could view the shape of her breasts. She hadn't done nothing like that—at least not for many years.

"Well thank you, I really appreciated that," he said, not sure if he was referring to the food or the sight of her flesh, which was merging in his mind with Mary Lou's body.

Rita stood up and yanked out her blouse from her pants and walked over to his side of the table. She took his hand and said: "Let's fuck," and pulled at him to get him to stand up, which he was happy to do, and they both padded to their bedroom, disrobed and climbed into bed.

Throughout the time he was with her, all he could envisage was Mary Lou, because if he hadn't known before, tonight was the night he became certain he didn't feel very much for Rita any more. Watching her breasts jiggle up and down as he lay on top of her thrusting, he thought of Rita not as his wife, but as just a woman to fuck. He was cold inside while they were naked together although clearly he wasn't honest enough to behave as though he did.

Later, after they'd gone back downstairs to do the washing up, they snuggled on the sofa watching TV. he sipped another Scotch, but he made sure it was his last one. Tuesday would be a hell of a day and the woman sat next to him would be no part of it—nor any part of his future.

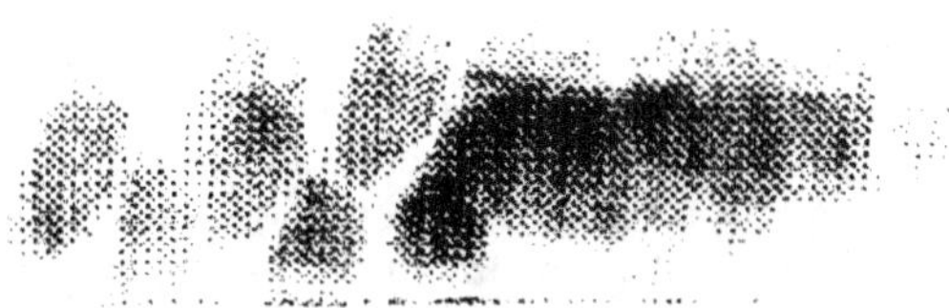

39

PETE GRABBED A duffel bag—filled with clothes, two packs of smokes and some emergency money—
and threw it into the back seat of his car. He whipped out the yard and aimed for the Joppa exit on the
I-95. The diner was packed with late afternoon truckers, looking for a bite to eat before the last long
haul of the day. Pete strode to the outhouse bathroom to get his piece where he found it still hidden.

One bullet he fed into the clip had Andrew's name on it. That cunt would keep hounding him over
the dead nigger and he might as easily settle all business tomorrow. If bullets were flying—and it was a
bank robbery after all—one might as well go through Andrew's heart or brain. As long as the fucker
was deceased afterwards, Pete wouldn't pay no never mind.

Pete popped into the diner for a Java and a sniff of Lucy. The coffee was poured for him and, like
before, Lucy was not there but in her trailer. She'd been in earlier and they'd been so quiet in the
morning, she was sent home and boy they wished she'd stayed now.

Pete took three sips of the horse swill that passed for coffee and exited the place forthwith. Around
the corner was Lucy's mobile home and that was a much more interesting prospect than slugging down
shit coffee, listening to some old bitch moaning about her life. Like he cared.

At the trailer park, Pete grabbed his duffel bag from the back seat and sauntered up. Knocked
twice, rat-a-tat, on the door and strolled in and dropped the bag near the door.

LUCY WAS LYING on the sofa with a pink dressing gown on. There were ties holding it together, but
they had loosened over the past couple of hours since she had lain down to watch TV. Pete could see
one titty peeking out and half a bush too. She could sense he was looking but did nothing to cover
herself up with the night attire.

He took that as an invitation and removed his pants. Lucy smiled and said: "Hey babe, nice of you
to drop in. I've missed you 'n' I know exactly where I need you right now."

He needed no more encouragement than that, but to make matters clear, She opened up the
dressing gown completely as Pete scurried towards her and took his shorts down. Thirty seconds,
maybe a minute, of thrusting later and he was done, dripping spunk on the sofa and floor. Always the
gentleman, he rubbed her nipples a couple of times to show how much he'd appreciated the fuck.

Lucy switched off the TV at this point and rustled them up some eggs and beans. Pete ate it like it was his first meal that day, which it was, and he was ready for seconds. In this instance, that meant another round of eggs and beans but once he'd cleared his plate, he was ready for seconds again.

This time Lucy was less interested, probably because of the lousy time Pete had just shown her. But after five minutes catting about, she figured she'd either have to let him do something or he'd force her to and that was not a a healthy option. So she took the easy way out and kept what was left of her dignity by kneeling on the kitchen floor and waiting until he was done. Once it was over, she turned round and patted his cheek.

"Good to have you back, Pete."

"I reckon so," he smiled, standing up and scooting over to the sofa wearing nothing but his socks.

"I WILL HAVE to be off in a short while, but I'll return tomorrow and will be here for a few weeks, like I said before."

"*Mi casa es tu casa.*"

"Mighty kind of you to say," and Pete patted the space next to him on the sofa to invite her to lie on her own furniture. The guy sure was making himself comfortable early on.

She followed Pete's instruction and draped herself over him, still both naked, but she grabbed her dressing gown off the floor and sprawled it over them like a blanket.

"Will be good to have a man about the place," she whispered, putting her palm on his dick again and giving it a playful squeeze.

"Enough of that young lady," replied Pete and he took her hand away from his groin and dropped it on his stomach. "I need to keep some of my Samson strength for work tomorrow. But after that we can play all day long if ya like."

"Ooh, sounds fun!"

"It'll be a fucking blast, baby."

He flipped the TV on with the remote control and they ogled the moving pictures before them until he glanced at his watch and saw the time.

"Why don't you finish what you wanted to start a while back," he said and brought his hand round the back of Lucy's neck and pushed and encouraged her head down his body. When she finally got the message and pulled off the their blanket, he let her get on with her work.

Afterwards, he put his clothes on and kissed her on the lips for the first time that afternoon.

"See ya tomorrow."

"Bye, lover man."

AS PETE WALKED out of the trailer, Lucy wrapped the dressing gown over herself to keep warm and wondered how long he was actually planning on staying. Great to have a man to fuck at home, but all this while and he still couldn't string a sentence together to call his own, let alone hold a conversation.

Pete kept just under the speed limit all the way to Glen Burnie. When he arrived in the yard, he parked his car right into the far corner and pulled a large piece of tarpaulin over it, so any eyes looking into the lot would have zero chance of seeing his usual wheels hanging around without him.

He studied his vehicle one last time, hit the head and then hit the sack. With an early start tomorrow—much earlier than he was used to—he knew he had to get some rest. But he also knew there would be very little chance for a sleep over the next couple of days and he would be running on adrenaline and not much else. He double checked he had some smokes for the next two days, and afterwards he drank four glasses of water. Ten minutes later he needed a piss but at least he knew his body was rehydrating and would put him in a good place in the morning. There was nothing worse on the day of a job than having chapped lips and losing focus because your throat was dry.

Pete set an alarm clock and lay down on his bed with his arms behind his head, acting as an extra pillow. He thought about the logistics for tomorrow and how he and Brian had planted enough gas in the Econoline to burn the whole of Atlanta down, with sufficient to spare at the barn to torch that place to kingdom come.

A run-through of which car was where and who was driving in what direction and all that felt fine too. Tthe C4 and Mary Lou riding that convertible through rush hour traffic and dropping off those little bundles of joy from the shopping bag provided. He'd put the timers together himself so he knew they'd go off on cue.

All that remained was the takedown itself—the one thing he had no control over. But he had sufficient faith in Frank to execute that piece of the job well. He had a history with safes and the man was a stand-up guy if the stories about his last robbery partner were anything to believe. Even if it wasn't true that he had pushed him off a twentieth floor building, there was no smoke without fire. He clearly had the balls for people to believe he'd done it. And that was good enough for Pete. Then he fell asleep, snoring loudly.

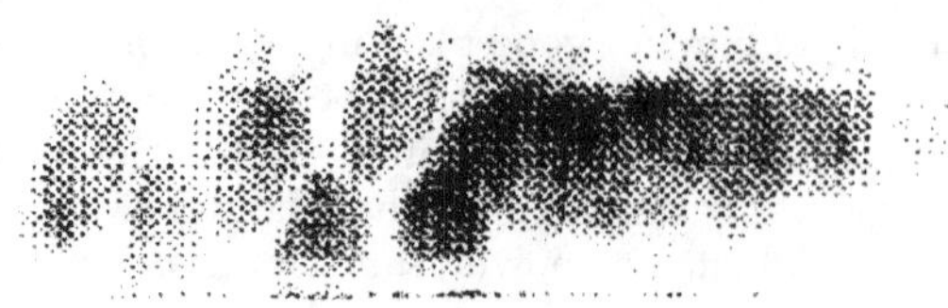

40

MARY LOU PUT the phone down on Carter. Jesus Christ! He wanted her to be part of his bank robbery and rob Frank Senior and, more to the point, to steal the money from Frank.

Head spin. No chance to think. Heading into a panic. Stay calm, goddamn you. Mary Lou sat still for a second. Tension in her spine as she her free hand embedded its finger nails into the seat of the sofa. She let go of the cushion and remembered to breathe.

Decision time.

Carter's last two words span round her like a shiny ball running around a roulette wheel until it finally came to rest inside her head.

Decision time.

Frank was someone you could trust and was strong and handsome and had dreams, but if she didn't turn up tomorrow morning and let Carter into her car, he was a dead man and she would have killed him.

But if she did that she'd have Frank and Frank Senior—and the rest of the boys—chasing her down until they found her and no matter how close she was to Frank, Mary Lou knew between Frank Senior and Pete alone, she would have the most painful, disgusting last few hours any woman could imagine on this earth.

She glanced at the clock hanging on the living room wall and realized she needed to leave this joint. She walked through one final time to check she had left nothing of hers lying around in the back of the wardrobe or at the bottom of the drawers. A pair of panties discovered, she stepped out of their trysting place and locked the door behind her.

WHEN SHE RETURNED to her apartment, Mary Lou prepared some food. Everything needed to be normal and calm, because Frank would be tense enough the night before a job and she was stressed for the two of them. But after all these months with Carter, and countless times with so many men before, she knew how to hide what she was really thinking from him.

She started cooking, guessing Frank would be back before long and she caught sight of him from the kitchen window and put their steaks on. A moment later, he appeared at the door. She smiled at him and came over to kiss him on the mouth, one hand round the back of his neck, the other on his side. She was wearing a blue tee shirt and a short red skirt that revealed a lot of her thighs. And an apron because she was still cooking.

The onions, garlic and ketchup sauce had been on the go for a while and was nicely sizzling, waiting to be a mattress for the beef. And now they were only minutes away from eating.

Frank took out crockery and cutlery and laid the table in their small apartment. He squeezed her butt as he grabbed two glasses from the cupboard and poured a glass of red wine each, knowing this was the most they'd be drinking tonight.

Seven minutes later, both steaks were on plates, the potatoes had been drained and the carrots strained too. They sat opposite each other, holding hands and he made a toast:

"To you, babe. None of this would have been possible without you." He raised his glass and she clinked hers against his. She pushed her hair behind one ear and smiled.

"Thanks, hon', but it was the both of us. Not only me."

Now it was Frank's turn to smile. He leaned forward and kissed her hand, let go and picked up his cutlery.

"Fit for a King. Thank you."

"De nada."

TO BEGIN WITH, they ate in silence, allowing the taste of each streaky mouthful to linger on their tongues, savoring the textures and the mix of flavors. They started talking about what happened in their days and how each had got ready for tomorrow. Mary Lou provided a circumspect summary omitting much of her later interactions with Carter.

When it came to the point in his day when he met up with Uncle Frankie, Mary Lou stopped in her tracks, her hands frozen in front of her. Frank quickly moved on to his return and hiding the jalopy in the parking lot. She relaxed again and carried on eating. His uncle would have to pay for what he had done and that time was coming soon.

He and Mary Lou kept on chatting, talking about anything and everything apart from Tuesday, the next day. They both knew it was there, looming large on the horizon and neither wanted to talk about it. They were merely enjoying each other's company.

After they'd done the washing up—he'd rinsed while she dried—they moved onto the couch and their chat continued. Mary Lou made sure they were as relaxed as they could be given the takedown was the next day and how she was suffering inside. He didn't appear to notice, mainly because he was wrapped up in his own thoughts about the job, repeating every conceivable nuance of events that could occur in the morning.

By around ten, they were getting tired and, at the back of his mind, Frank knew they had an early start and a long time ahead of them. He wanted to get to it as soon as possible. Tuesday was when his dreams would unfold into reality.

Mary Lou moved close to him, leaning her head on his shoulder and he casually placed his hand on her upper leg, where the hem of her flimsy skirt met the flesh of her thigh. Although he thought about it, he didn't stroke her or move his fingers up to her panties. He let it rest there, doing nothing but providing reassurance about tomorrow and companionship during this evening.

He knew no matter how comfortable they were right now in this moment, Tuesday was coming hurtling into view, so he stood up, took Mary Lou's hand and walked her into the bedroom.

THE CONVERSATION CARRIED on when they were naked in bed. Frank removed all his clothes before they got under the covers and Mary Lou mirrored him. He got in first, so he had the pleasure of watching her pull her tee shirt over her head and witness her breasts rise and fall, cosseted by her bra.

She shimmied out of her skirt and he stared at her red panties, which matched the bra. She looked down on the ground and saw Frank's shorts and she smiled at him, with a slightly dirty grin. She shrugged and undid the fastening of her bra and pushed her panties down so she stood before him totally exposed. He gawked at her nipples and at her tattoo. And below the rose at her perfect triangle of a bush.

She got into bed and they were silent with Mary Lou's hand resting on Frank's groin and his palm occasionally stroking her rose. They absentmindedly played with each other. If nothing else, this took her mind off everything playing out in her brain.

After a few minutes her tingles kicked off. Sheu let out a slight, almost audible moan and Frank carried on as she opened her legs ever so slightly. Neither said a word as they kept on their gentle teasing; both their breathing much heavier by now. Thoughts of tomorrow gone from their minds as they lived inside this isolated moment of trust and pleasure. It felt so good. The tingles were intense like her rose was screaming Hallelujah. She grabbed Frank's hand to stop its movement. Just for a second. Pure. Intense. Pleasure. For. What felt. Like an hour. And then it was over.

They lay still, facing each other for who knows how long, stroking and massaging the other until both could breathe normally again.

"Good night, babe."

"Good night, Frank."

"Game on."

He licked his fingers, twisted the right way, rolled over to face the outside of the bed and was quickly asleep. Mary Lou was nearly unconscious and the last thoughts she decided before she went under was that, despite that being the deepest orgasm she had ever experienced, she'd be better off with Carter by the end of tomorrow. And then she too was sleeping.

TUESDAY, JUNE 17

41

FRANK LAGOTTI SENIOR woke up, not too sure where he was. Then he stared down at the red satin sheets and realized he hadn't moved from the Kitkatt Club: there were three VIP rooms and, clearly, he was in one of them. He looked left and saw a girl's head and recognized May and, beyond her, April. As he couldn't get to sleep, he'd chosen partying to knock himself out instead.

The two whores were still unconscious, so he slapped May on the backside—just because she was the nearest—and Lagotti saw her eyes open wide real quick.

"Hey. Find some water in this goddamn place and then bring your ass back over here."

May nodded and stretched her arms to help wake herself up, then she slid over Lagotti to get out of the oversized bed, found a towel to wrap around herself and left the room in bare feet.

When she returned, Lagotti was sitting up, but April was crashed out. He'd pulled the covers up over himself to keep warm to reveal April still had her underwear on. Perhaps he hadn't fucked her. Or maybe he had but hadn't bothered to get her to undress first. Whatever.

Lagotti took the water from May, who let the towel drop around her feet and clambered back into bed. He sipped the start of the glass to moisten the inside his mouth and then he glugged the remaining two-thirds straight down to quench his vodka thirst.

Only then did Lagotti pay any real attention to May's body, whose firm round breasts had first caught his eye the previous night. He thought of fucking her again and half thought of getting her to suck him off again. But he didn't really want her to touch him anymore at all. He just liked ordering her about.

"Wake that bitch up," he instructed May, "and lick her out until I get back."

May shrugged and started to rouse April by pushing the fabric of her panty's crotch out of the way so she could get down to business. Meanwhile, he stumbled round the VIP suite, put on his clothes and left the girls to it.

As soon as Frank Senior removed himself from the room, May stopped what she was doing and grabbed four of the five C-notes Lagotti had thrown down onto the bedside table—April's contribution was to dance near the bed while she had fucked him with every orifice she possessed. She'd earned her money that Monday night. April took the remaining C-note, found her hot pants where she'd dropped them on the floor and followed May out.

Lagotti pushed open the front doors of the Kitkatt Club, blinked and covered his eyes in what felt like the sharp brightness of the morning. In reality dawn was only a half hour old and the sun had hardly penetrated the daytime sky.

A cab pulled up right where he stood, he got in and headed home to freshen up for the day ahead.

AS HE OPENED the front door to his modest four-bedroom house on Tudsbury Road in Windsor Mill, due west of Baltimore itself, Lagotti heard his wife, Francesca pottering about in the kitchen. The clock had yet to strike eight, but she was already cooking the tomato sauce for tonight's meal.

Fran was the mother of Lagotti's three children, a fabulous cook and home maker. As his young bride, she'd been the pick of the crop, but now her good looks had receded inside her, leaving the husk of a smile and layers of fat to hide herself in. Frankie loved her but he had no carnal desire for her anymore.

They had found a comfortable way to share the same domestic space and that was all he really wanted out of her. He had his magazines and the Kitkatt Club to pander to any sexual gratification required and that worked out well for him because he got what he required and didn't have to waste his time taking cute girls out for meals or pretending to listen to them as they told him about their lives. Fuck and done. Easy.

Lagotti strolled into the kitchen to get some breakfast and Fran was busy watching the sauce simmer away, adding a little of garlic here and some more onion there. She turned round with a start and smiled at her Frankie.

"Hi, love."

"Heh."

"Shall I put some coffee on for you?"

"That would be nice. Thank you, my darling."

Fran stopped what she was doing and took a jar of freshly ground beans out of a cupboard for the percolator. She filled the base of the machine with water from the tap. Finally, she measured out the Java into the top half, screwed the two pieces back together again and put the unit on the hob and started heating up the coffee. Five minutes later and Lagotti had a fresh cup of piping hot Java in front of him where he'd sat at the kitchen table when Fran had commenced her coffee mission.

"Breakfast, dear?" Frankie nodded and in a short while, bacon, eggs and toast appeared, which he dutifully consumed with gusto and verve.

"Thank you, my dear," he said once his plate was cleared, "and what are we going to have tonight?"

"Oh nothing special. Just pork sausage, meatballs with spaghetti, that kind of thing." And she was right. It was not exceptional, but place those ingredients near her Bolognese sauce and you'd cream your pants.

He smiled, stood up and walked upstairs. Into their bedroom—the children had moved out to get married several years ago—and took a shower, then a shave and changed into a fresh set of clothes.

AT THIS POINT, the door bell rang out, which meant Lagotti knew it was eight fifteen and Paul was right on time. Sure enough, a quick glance at his watch proved this.

Lagotti put on his shoes and traveled downstairs, opened the front door and declared: "I'll be out in a minute." Frankie did this not for his benefit or for Paul's—the man could wait all day as far as Lagotti was concerned because he was paying for Paul's time. He did it for Fran, who used to fret about poor Paul waiting outside all on his own. So Frankie would acknowledge Paul's existence to stop himself getting nagged by Fran, which never looked good in front of his men.

Frankie kissed her on the cheek, told her he would be back later, but he didn't know when, and left the house to be driven by Paul to the auto repair shop, where he'd hold court on the day of the robbery.

As ever, the first thing was to place some calls and catch up on business. Then he could dispatch Paul and Luigi to make their morning collections while Lagotti considered strategy. This mainly comprised staring at hardcore pornography until the boys came back with the bags of cash.

Today was a special day and he wanted his men near him in case of need, so they would wait until later in the morning. He told Paul to fill the car with gas, in the unlikely event there was a journey to be made and Lagotti sank bank in his chair and waited.

Luigi brought him in a cup of strong coffee about fifteen minutes later and left the boss on his own. He knew better than to hang around unless he was explicitly told to do so. He understood he creeped most people out and had accepted this as part of his normal way of life quite some time ago.

Apart from the sound of Lagotti's breathing and the music hurtling out of a radio, all was silent in the auto shop. One thing that never happened was a car coming in for any kind of repair. The same vehicles had been on that forecourt from the first week Lagotti become its proud owner when Harvey Titchford handed over the deeds after he found himself unable to meet the debt repayments of an incredibly foolhardy bet on the World Series.

The clock next to the radio in Frank Senior's anteroom ticked and tocked and slowly, but surely, the big hand lurched from the number eight towards the nine.

Lagotti was unaware of this massive journey as he was ensconced in his office, staring at women's body parts, occasionally sipping from his cup and generally enjoying his working day. Most of Lagotti's effort involved finding new debtors and calculating an appropriate vig. Nowadays, with his reputation and existing clientele, the customers came to him. The days of him having to hang out at late night poker games had long since faded.

Instead, he used his connections to lure insects into his web and, worse case, with businesses rather than inveterate gamblers, he could find himself with an interest in something unusual like the Kitkatt Club or this auto shop. But mostly, Lagotti wanted to generate money by lending cash and not by getting an income over time based on how well someone else was doing. He didn't enjoy relying on other people to create his wealth.

Paul knocked on the door and Lagotti called him in. The obligatory wait over, Paul said: "There's something on the news I think you'll want to hear. It's about the Bank of Baltimore." Lagotti leaped to his feet and went straight to the reception area of the auto shop. There, on top of the fridge, was the radio which had been piping out music from the moment he had arrived this morning, as it did most every day. A DJ was talking about the bank and Lagotti stood next to it, intensely listening…

42

FRANK OPENED HIS eyes and looked at Mary Lou's body—or rather the small part of her he saw. One eye was buried in his pillow so all he perceived was the few inches in front of his functioning eye. Mary Lou was lying on her side, her head facing him with a nipple a tongue-stretch away from his mouth.

Frank stretched his neck and clipped the tip of the breast with his mouth. Then he moved his body over an inch or two and licked the areola. One of Mary Lou's eyes opened.

"Don't stop," she whispered. There was a flush of guilt, knotting in her stomach because she knew she would betray him in only a couple of hours. But she wanted him to have happy memories of their time together. Besides which, she was really, truly enjoying this moment.

Frank carried on, whirling around until he was flicking his tongue on the nipple itself and covered it with his lips and licked and sucked it until she breathed more deeply.

To encourage him to keep going, she wrapped a hand round the back of his head and dug her nails gently into his hair. The increase in tongue motion validated the decision. This started waves running up and down Mary Lou's spine, so she scooped him up in her arms and a spare leg, rolling him on top of her. And they carried on like this until the buzzer sounded.

"Damn. Goddamn!"

"Shoot."

Frank pulled himself up and reached out to shut off the alarm.

"Any other time, babe… Sorry."

"I know," she replied and they both swung out of bed to face the new day.

Frank ran into the shower first and she wandered through the bedroom, looking for personal items that needed to be thrown out or put into a carry bag she had from the time they'd been on that ill-fated job with Louis. With a quickly-formed pile on the bed, she heard he was still showering. So she hopped into the bathroom and pulled back the curtain and joined him.

FIRST SHE SCOOPED some soapy froth from his chest over his torso and on his arms and, stepping forwards, round to his spine so the front of their bodies touched. Frank wrapped his arms around her, rubbing her back with the soap so she was slippery and, leaning into her neck, he kissed her and reached down so his hand caressed her buttocks and his fingers moved in between them. She shifted her legs apart, ever so slightly, so his hand could continue its journey.

Over the last few months—and only then—he had realized Mary Lou was an integral part of his life. That they truly were a couple: in a two-way relationship and not just a body to fuck when he wasn't in jail.

After breakfast, he took one final look in his tool bag. Metal cutters, hammer, pincers. All sorts of things to get into vaults, safes and to persuade people to help him open them up. He kept his gun in his jacket.

They kissed just before they left the apartment.

"I'll catch you in a few hours."

"You take care of yourself," she replied, "Remember that I love you."

She wanted to be the first to leave. She didn't want a real goodbye even though she knew this was the last time they would see each other. She missed him already and he was still standing in front of her.

"And I love you too," said Frank honestly. He tapped her on the ass and she flew downstairs to street level while he locked up and threw out a refuse sack.

She turned and walked down the stairs, not waiting for him to lock up. As she scurried down the steps, she wondered why she had uttered those last three words and, more importantly, whether she meant them. Twenty seconds later he walked briskly over to the underground parking lot and unlocked the van. He got in and turned the engine over. Nothing. On the second attempt, he pumped the gas pedal at the same time as twisting the key and the motor sparked into life.

43

WHIPPING THE VEHICLE out of the lot, Frank saw the remnants of smoke that had exited Mary Lou's exhaust seconds before, although she was nowhere to be seen.

He gunned the van down the street, kangarooing until he found fourth gear. While he didn't feel that nervous under the circumstances, clearly there was some tension in his body and he reminded himself to stay totally focused in the moment at hand and not to let his mind wander to what was happening later in the day.

Left, right, onwards, pushing his way through the commuter traffic with a steadfast concern to reach Andrew and Brian in good time. Frank was pleased he only had one pick-up to do. The fact they shared an apartment was helpful. There was a rumor about town they were queers but he didn't give a shit. Andrew was a reliable guy and Brian had showed himself to be the same over the last year.

Frank reached their street and pulled in to park almost exactly outside their apartment door. Lucky. He honked the van's horn twice and waited. Looking at his watch, he saw he was about ten minutes earlier than planned, but that was no bad thing. So much better to be early than late. True at a wedding, true on a bank job.

The two eventually showed up, sauntering out of the building and ambling to the van. This annoyed Frank, because he was hoping and expecting for some greater energy, today of all days.

They opened the door and got inside. First Andrew, then Brian. And as soon as he saw Brian was in, he hit the gas and off, leaving Brian to slam the door shut and for the pair of them to figure out how to sit down on the mattress in the back. In the front cabin, in the passenger footwell, was the gasoline they would be using shortly to destroy the vehicle once they'd left its usefulness all behind.

Zooming along the road, Frank focused on the route to Lansdowne and on keeping under the speed limit and avoiding the other vehicles. He'd practiced the journey in other cars Pete had supplied him over the last few weeks, even getting up at the crack of dawn to get used to the commuter traffic, which often became quite sticky on the entrance to the I-695 from Washington Boulevard. But there were no problems today. No hold ups whatsoever.

Frank took the van all the way to the lot behind the bank. This was an L-shaped lot with the bank standing on the first leg with spaces nearby. The other was a right turn past the bank and fed the backs of a couple of other buildings on the street. He lurched the automobile to a halt and reversed into a space two cars away from the bank, pointing outwards for a fast getaway—if needed. They'd arrived at the bank. Early. The planned ten minute wait in the bank parking lot appeared more like thirty. All three sat, not making a sound.

Frank looked at his watch and said: "I have eight thirty-five so I suggest we take a walk or we'll go stir crazy stuck in here."

THOUGHTS OF NEVER seeing Frank again stayed in Mary Lou's head as she walked away from him round the corner from the apartment and into the lot. Pete had done a good job of parking the convertible almost exactly where he said it would be. She popped the trunk and checked the C4 parcels in the shopping bag he had promised would be there.

She got in, turned the engine over with one twist of the car key and exited the lot. Mary Lou looked in her rear-view mirror but no Frank or his van. So she headed off to Lansdowne, making sure she was always at least five miles per hour below the limit—even if it was an open road and nobody behind her —as Pete had instructed.

After about ten minutes at the wheel, Mary Loushe reached the Baltimore Public Library and its parking lot, which was two buildings up from the First Bank of Baltimore, Lansdowne branch.

Out the car and she whipped the bag out of the trunk. She looked inside again and saw there was a block of plastic attached to a timepiece by a set of wires. The minute hand of each countdown clock was already set. Straps hung from both sides of the plastic and all she had to do was flip the little switch on the side of the clock face. It would go bang eleven minutes later. Simple.

Mary Lou trundled across the street to a telegraph pole, which was adjacent to the traffic lights opposite the bank. She bent down to pretend to tie her shoelaces and attached the straps to the base of the telegraph pole.

She moved onto the next pole on the other side of the road, right by the bank. Again, damn those shoelaces, tie them up again. Another pole with an explosive at its base. So that meant Hollins Ferry Road was fixed to be wonderfully blocked except in the southbound direction. Finally, she walked over to Third Avenue and repeated the same operation each side of the road.

All this setting of bombs was based on the false idea there would be a bank robbery by Frank and the guys whereas she knew Carter was taking the money from right under their noses. She reckoned the least she'd do was to give them the best chance possible to flee the scene even if they had nothing to take with apart from their anger and disappointment.

MARY LOU WALKED back and drove the hot rod to the bank just a few feet away. When she got into the parking lot, she saw it was split into two parts, one of which was by the bank exit and the other half was round the corner.

She knew Pete and Frank would stop right by the entrance and that was the last place she should be—being seen would be the worst of all possible worlds for her. So Mary Lou drove round the corner and reversed into a space where she couldn't see the bank door. If the door wasn't visible, she was invisible to anyone hanging out near the door. Carter would know to check out the whole of the lot because he'd mentioned to her, repeatedly, the complaints from Theresa and Bob about how hard it was to find a parking space by the bank exit.

And then she waited for Carter… She waited and nothing materialized and no one appeared. Mary Lou looked at the clock. Where was he? He should have been in the car and they should be well away from the bank before the damn thing opened.

She tried to think through what had happened and what options she had to play with. Okay. First, Carter hadn't exited by the back door, because he'd gone it alone and left by the Hollins Ferry Road front entrance and, because she was tucked into the rear of the lot, she hadn't seen him leave. If that was true she had to escape as soon as possible.

Secondly, Carter might have backed out of the deal and stayed put, in which case she must get the fuck out of here and hightail it over to the barn to stand a chance of remaining with Frank. Carter may have been the better man for her, but only if he could be relied on. If he was a flakey fucker, he was useless to her.

Frank was about to walk into the bank with only those two scenarios she thought of that might have played out the other side of the bank wall. Either way, it was time for her to get out of Dodge, because something was seriously wrong in the state of Maryland. She scorched out the lot without looking at the bank door and swung right. Mary Lou turned left onto the I-695 and, right at the first exit, onto the I-895 southbound. Off to the barn or she keep going. It was nine eleven and she had no idea what she would do.

FORTY MINUTES EARLIER Pete woke up with death on his mind—the thought of the upcoming day's job at the forefront of his thoughts. And then he looked at his clock.

"Motherfucker!" he exclaimed to the world at large and no one in particular. He had set his alarm but the time to which he had selected was eleven o'clock. It was now eight and the shit was about to hit the fan.

Flying out of his cot bed, Pete threw his clothes on, grabbed his cigs, lighter, keys, wallet, coins and pistol and pelted to the car and gunned the engine awake. He took it only a few feet, outside the gate, leaped out and back to lock up. He would not return for quite a while. Hell of a way to leave. Cutting out on himself. The only positive thing about Pete's departure was he didn't have to waste any time thinking about the day ahead—or brushing his teeth or putting on any deodorant. Pete pulled out a cigarette from the pack and flipped his lighter open, thumbed the flint wheel and lit it.

Eight ten and he was on the road. The professional within Pete knew no matter how late you are for a bank robbery, the getaway driver should not be stopped by the cops for speeding, having a busted taillight or any other misdemeanor. So, despite his desire to catch up on himself, he kept the vehicle a steady five miles per hour below the limit all the journey long.

Now he was on the road, he had a chance to think for the first time in the day. The game was on and everything was resting on his shoulders. When the guys left the rear entrance to the bank, he was the one who would torch a vehicle and driving them to safety—at high speed. And Frank Senior had entrusted him to keep an eye on Frank himself.

Pete had tried not to think too much about why Frank Senior wanted to watch his nephew. He always thought the best way to manage some situations was not to think too hard about stuff and let things happen. This ethos was especially true with dangerous men like Frank Senior, but, Pete had been intrigued whether he was being put in the middle of some long running family feud. He'd not been in that position since he was a kid. Hadn't seen his ma since he was eight and hadn't even got a letter from his brothers or sisters in over a decade. He didn't know if any of them were alive or dead.

Pete reached the I-97 turnpike and headed North, always keeping the speed under control. In his mind's eye, he ran through all he had set up the previous day and the precise list of things he needed to do before he drove away from the bank.

From the exact position and location of each vehicle to the C4 packages he'd left for Mary Lou, Pete had driven the getaway route countless times before—in the afternoon at first when he was learning the various routes out of town. Then in the evenings because he really needed to drive on instinct as the streets always looked so different at night. And finally, he spent three weeks following the same route in the morning, so he got a real good feeling for the traffic black spots. He had put all that information inside his head back in April and had given himself top-up lessons every other week since. He was comfortable no matter what happened on the roads, he would be able to leave town safely and out to the barn.

The guy had done his homework for his own getaway after that. He'd figured out the best routes to circle round to reach Joppa without heading straight there. Meanwhile, he exited at Arundel Hills Park and turned left onto the I-695, aiming north west.

A RUMBLING IN his stomach told Pete skipping breakfast was not a good idea. He snagged the glove compartment handle and the little door popped open. Two Twinkies lay where he'd thrown the previous week. He guzzled both down and, within minutes, he was receiving the benefits of the artificial sugar high he had induced in himself. He promised himself he'd grab some bread along the way if there was time and opportunity, because he knew he wouldn't get through to the end of the afternoon without something more filling inside himself.

The final piece of Pete's jigsaw was the problem of Andrew. That shit heel was going down today. Either at the bank or at the barn, but he would not be waking up tomorrow morning—of that Pete was certain. He felt for the gun in his jacket pocket to reassure himself. And he smiled as more country music blurted out of his radio speakers and the car ate up the I-695. Andrew would be dead and likely Brian would hit the dirt too.

There was something to be said for not shaving. He'd been planning on leaving some fur on his face to make it harder to be recognized, especially after he'd shave it off tomorrow. But this morning he'd not even thought about it. No time. Frank was right. Pete sure had promptness issues.

Turning onto the 295 just after Overlook Park and he knew it wouldn't be long now. He felt the fuzz on his face and noticed there was a small triangle under his lower lip where he was bare. A little bare triangle surrounded by fuzz. Then he thought of Lucy's triangle of fuzz surrounded by bare skin.

He shook his head to whip the idea of Lucy out of his mind. Now was not the time. Two minutes more, he hung left onto the I-895 and almost immediately took the Hollins Ferry Road exit. Half a mile later and he passed the Mount Zion Cemetery and reached the left and stopped in the lot, reversing next to the van which was parked but empty.

There was no time for bread or for anything apart from keeping his head clear until the job was over. He lit another cigarette and waited. Pete looked at his watch and saw that it was eight forty-six. Quarter of an hour and the fun would start. He should be inside Lucy's trailer by eleven, twelve at the latest. What a trailer that woman had. Always available, ever welcoming. And the great thing was he never had to ask twice. She was always willing to have him come round.

Lucy represented a port in an otherwise troubled sea. She fried eggs, cooked bacon and let him fuck her pretty much any way he wanted. As he only had three ways of fucking, this meant he was very happy and she was well within her sexual comfort zone, given the weirdos she'd slept with over the years. If he had known, he'd have run away in disgust.

Instead, he had a safe place to stash his firearm and to pitch his tent when he needed to lie low. The added advantage: there was nothing to connect him to her apart from the fact one day he'd strolled into the diner when he was desperate for a piss after a long journey and he knew he wasn't able to wait the extra half hour to get to Glen Burnie.

The coffee was terrible there, but he'd sparked well with Lucy and he went back to her trailer and found her more than welcoming. Now, he hadn't been in for about six months or a year until he and Brian had rocked in on their way to making the connection with Chuck. But it was like he'd walked out only the day before.

Pete didn't pay no never mind to what she'd been up to in the meantime. He was only concerned to make sure the trailer would be safe for himself when the time was right. And this was one of those times. Beyond that, he didn't really care at all—but it was nice to know she'd be there to keep his bed warm while he was lying low. And his dick hard.

Afterwards, he'd make sure he'd get her something to keep her sweet. And quiet. Pete knew he could take her to AC for a weekend and that would be enough. Besides, that only meant he had to pay for a hotel room so they'd fuck in a different place.

44

FRANK LED THE three men out the bank parking lot and walked a hundred feet down Hollins Ferry and into Third Avenue, carrying on five hundred feet until they came across a side entrance of a graveyard. This meant they could sit outside, but without being seen particularly from the road. The tombstones offered an oasis of calm in the heart of Lansdowne.

Frank led them to the cemetery and to his bench, on which Brian sat down almost immediately. Still there was a silence between them all the while.

He stood there alone in his thoughts: Frank had allowed himself this time to daydream about the future. He ran through what he would do from the moment they entered the First Bank of Baltimore, Lansdowne branch, through to leaving the parking lot with the money in a sack. In particular, he thought about the likely responses from the bank staff and how they'd respond if any civilians strolled in, unexpected and uninvited.

With the comfort of knowing he and the guys were as ready as they could be—Frank's attention turned to his future with Mary Lou. Naturally, the first image that loomed into his consciousness was her rose. The taste of her returned to his mouth from the night before. He'd enjoyed the shower this morning too—having her limbs wrapped round him, her pubes against his dick as water cascaded all around them.

And then he thought of California. Of Mary Lou and him lying on a beach, sipping cocktails while the poor saps beavered about, working. The truth was he was merely replaying their Miami vacation, but that did not matter to him. His big dream was so close to him now he could almost touch it. And that sensation felt good.

Frank looked up at the sky and down at his watch. "It's time," he said, casually, to help keep everyone at their ease, while being very aware how tense the other two were feeling.

He took them out through the south entrance of Mount Zion and pounded the streets the few hundred feet until they turned left onto Hollins Ferry. Frank checked his watch again and slowed his pace down a touch. Ideally, he wanted them to arrive exactly on time so they wouldn't have to hang around near the bank before the job. Would be too easy for someone to remember them when the cops came calling.

When they reached the alleyway that led to the parking lot, Frank turned his head leftwards to check Pete was in place. Everything looked good.

RIGHT ON CUE, Pete spotted Frank—then Andrew and Brian—walking past the entrance to the alleyway. They would be in the bank soon and all the hullabaloo would begin. In the final few seconds of calm before the shit hit the fan, Pete's mind turned to Andrew. He had decided he shouldn't cap the nigger lover during the job itself. Not professional. Not at all.

Instead, Pete figured the best time would be at the barn. That way, the money would be safe so Frank and, more importantly, Frank Senior would not be bothered quite how many people got to split up the cash. If he separated him from Brian, that would make things even easier, but if he had to shoot out the tires and kill both of them, so be it. The whole thing would be pure self defense. Pete knew either he took out Andrew or Andrew would take him out—and Pete's plan was to be top dog.

Pete glanced around the parking lot, surveying each of the vehicles to make sure everything was square. From his position all in the L-shaped lot was cool. But he was aware he couldn't see the other side of the lot: the half that went from the bank in the L's corner towards the dead end. Pete reckoned there shouldn't be any trouble from there mainly because if it did, the perps would block themselves in, which would not be a wise move if guns were drawn.

So he kept his eyes trained on the back door of the bank which he caught in the right-hand rear-view mirror of his auto, and the exit onto the street. This moment was not the time for a dumper truck to break down there—or any other shit for that matter.

Frank and the crew must be inside by now. They were only five seconds away from the door when he spied them. He looked at his watch and saw it was nine oh-one and he knew the game had begun.

Pete stiffened in his seat and grabbed his balaclava and placed it on his lap. Sitting in that head gear would draw attention to himself but as soon as the guys came out, he'd need to be anonymous as hell. He also placed the revolver on his lap. Again, close but not visible. In case of trouble.

He looked around the lot again. Nothing. Checked his gun and the balaclava. Switched the engine back on. Ready. Any moment now there'll be a robbery in progress...

THE THREE CROSSED the alleyway entrance until the bank's brickwork was to Frank's left. The first window then the second. Followed by Brian and Andrew two feet behind, Frank put his right hand in his coat pocket to hold on to his revolver, inhaled deep into his lungs, shoved the balaclava over his head and pushed the bank door open and stepped inside. After all the waiting, all the planning, his moment was here. His hopes, his dreams: they were all coming to the boil just... about... now.

45

"THIS IS A stickup! Don't any of you motherfuckers move 'n' no one'll get hurt!"

Frank pointed his gun straight at old Joe Grimble, who immediately put up his hands, allowing Brian to take Grimble's firearm out of its holster. Brian and Andrew walked further into the bank and ensured there was a piece aimed at every member of staff they could see.

"Everyone, out here and lie face down on the ground. No talking. No messing about!" Frank had learned the best way to get a fast response from civilians was to keep the instructions short, sweet and to the point. Andrew and Brian stood over the clerks and Frank counted heads. There was one missing. He looked around and found the manager's office. Walked straight over and kicked open the door. JH was hiding under his desk, hoping what was taking place outside his room simply wasn't happening. No luck.

Frank dragged his sorry ass into the main reception and dumped him on the ground. At that point, Grimble decided to be a hero and raised himself up near Brian's foot. Brian saw what he was up to, bent down and slammed the butt of his gun into Grimble's face, causing him to fall back unconscious and for a little ripple of blood to trickle past old Joe's nose and onto the floor. The rest of the staff took in a massive breath, almost like it had been choreographed.

"No messing about is what I stated and it's what we mean," intoned Frank in case they hadn't already figured that cold fact out. He looked at Brian and said: "Look after the shop while we're downstairs."

"You got it," replied Brian with a real sense of menace behind his words. This was what he'd been waiting for. This was the game he was playing.

Andrew followed Frank to the staff door which he opened with a simple shove of his shoulder. Mary Lou had been absolutely right: they'd added some steel to the surface of the door, but it was purely for show. The lock and hinges were as feeble as they were when she first visited the joint.

They hurried down the corridor and down the stairs to the safe. As expected, all the doors were open—into the vault and into the safe. The only problem was the damn thing was empty. No money, nothing. It made no sense.

"What the fuck?"

ANDREW AND FRANK stood for a second, looking quizzically at each other.

"Don't get it," said Frank and they sprinted back to the others without even a turn of the head at the safe deposit boxes on the other side of the room.

Frank headed straight to JH and put a gun barrel in his mouth.

"Where's the fucking money!"

JH looked at him like he was crazy.

"The cash, you fucker, where is it?"

Again, JH's eyes scurried from one side of his head to the other but JH had no idea where the cash had gone any more than Frank did.

Frank inhaled a deep breath and took the barrel out of JH's mouth. Frank sighed, placed JH's right hand flat on the ground and slammed the butt onto JH's first and second fingers. Broken.

JH screamed in agony and Frank slapped him to get his attention.

"The money. Bring me the money!"

"It's in the safe!" screamed the bank manager.

"No, it's fucking not, numb nuts."

JH looked at Frank like he had no idea the meaning of Frank's words.

"In the safe," he whispered, half asking, knowing his response was plain false.

Frank opened his bag and pulled out a kitchen knife and walked over to Theresa, ripped her blouse with it and stared at JH.

"Look at me!" he screamed, "Tell me where the money is or I'll cut her."

"I thought it was in the safe."

Frank swung the blade down and sliced Theresa's left tit open. Blood gushed out and, in a few seconds, she was sitting in a pool of her own red. Then she fainted with shock.

JH shrugged at him and shook his head; he had no idea where the damn money was. Frank knew JH didn't know: there was no way he would have allowed the girl to be injured just to save the money because all staff know how insurance works.

Frank strode back to the manager and hauled him up so he was sitting L-shaped.

"Okay everyone, listen to me carefully."

All eyes stared at Frank and he carried on.

"At least one of you must know where the money has gone. I don't give a shit who has got it or who knows. But if someone doesn't tell me before I count to five then this man will get his throat cut.

"Do you understand?"

They all nodded.

"One... two... three..."

FRANK CHECKED OUT everyone's faces, desperately seeking a guilty expression. One of them would say or the bank manager would die in two counts.

"Four..."

One of the other men. His face twitched, his cheeks reddened ever so slightly.

Frank dropped JH like a stone and headed over to Carter. Grabbed his hand.

"Tell me where's the money or I'll chop your cocksucking fingers off!"

"I... I dunno."

His mouth said one thing but his eyes kept darting back to his desk. Frank dragged him by the wrist over to the table and kicked it upside down to reveal the two cases as the contents flew onto the floor. Pens, forms, a paper weight and Carter's triangular name plate.

Frank let go of Carter and threw him down, picked both bags up in one hand and started to walk away until, out of the corner of his eye, he noticed what was written on the name plate: Carter Reinfeldt. He gritted his teeth and, still holding his gun in the other hand, shot him in the groin, who keeled over screaming as another pool of blood spread across the bank floor.

"Let's get out of here. Where's the other one?"

Brian shrugged, as he had no idea himself. Andrew had been stood near him only a few seconds ago, but Brian had focused on the staff while Frank was torturing his way to the money.

"Have you killed the phones?"

"Sure thing. When we first came in."

"Good news. Listen up everyone. This is nearly over for you. We will leave and all you have to do is wait two minutes before you do anything. If you follow us out any earlier, we will shoot you as soon as we see you. No questions asked."

Frank and Brian walked towards the staff door, still aiming their guns at the personnel lying on the floor. They made their way over, avoiding the bloody pools they'd created spewing from bodies.

"Start counting down from 120 seconds."

The two men raced down the corridor and out the rear exit, Frank first.

Out in the parking lot, Frank saw Andrew stood next to Pete's vehicle. There were red speckles on the windows of the auto and Frank couldn't see Pete. As Frank got nearer to Andrew, he could see a body slumped in the driver's seat and blood splatter across the whole of the insides of the Chevy. Click, whir. Andrew's shot Pete dead. Fucker.

FRANK RAISED HIS gun to Andrew and squeezed the trigger. He dropped straight to the ground and Frank stood over him and put another bullet through his heart.

Brian pointed his own revolver at Frank; the man had just shot down his lover in front of his eyes. Frank swung round and aimed his own piece back at Brian.

"Lower your hardware or I will shoot you dead. Andrew died because he nixed one of our own."

Brian thought for a long second and then lowered his gun. Frank put his away too and then opened the rear passenger door. They picked up Andrew's body and dragged it in. Then Frank opened the Econoline and grabbed two cans of gasoline, handing one to Brian. The pair of them doused the car until both canisters were empty.

Frank fired up the van and Brian hopped into the front passenger seat. Then Frank got out, with the engine running, and threw a match into Pete's saloon, which lit up like a Halloween lantern gone mad.

Only at this point did Frank realize he hadn't heard any of the C4 packages go off. None. And he didn't think it was just because they'd been inside the bank. Why hadn't Mary Lou set the explosives? In the far distance, Frank heard a siren. A goddamn police siren.

He jumped back into the van which squealed forwards and Frank shot out the lot and turned right, the two cases by his feet and Brian by his side. He didn't know what had happened to Mary Lou and couldn't figure out what Carter had been doing with the money. But something had sure as hell fucked up and someone had surely fucked him over.

All Frank had left were his dreams and hopes, stashed in two black cases by his feet, built on a litany of betrayal he didn't think he could ever forgive. Thoughts of himself pushing Louis through that fucking window flashed through his head.

The only thing he could focus on was getting to that barn and seeing Uncle Frankie. He'd sort everything out. And Frank gunned the gas pedal to get to his destiny just a little faster.

THE END

The Getaway

1956

46

MARY LOU BELLE'S father died when she was only eight so her mother, Alice brought her up, along with her two brothers and two younger twin sisters. The eldest sibling was six and the youngest were born three years later. Times were tough in Texas for everyone and Alice's lack of a man to support her made life even harder for her family.

Tied to tending her young offspring, Alice rarely left their side and her only escape was the baptist church around the corner from her home. In particular, she leaned heavily on the kind words and understanding ear of Pastor Neil.

In 1956, Mary Lou turned fourteen and he started to look after the kids for Alice on Sunday afternoons so she could take some time to devote to herself and not just to the family. She spent these invaluable hours in the bar with her girlfriends sipping Long Island iced teas where she listened to them complain about the men in their world.

Pastor Neil brought along board games for the children to play. First, he showed the youngsters the rules, then he would sit and let them have their fun with snakes and ladders or checkers. Because of the age difference between herself and her brothers and sisters, Mary Lou sat back too. Apart from her one male teacher, Pastor Neil was the only constant man of any significance in her life and she didn't want to squander that time with children's games. This father figure was all she had and they enjoyed each other's company. She liked the fact he didn't spend Sunday afternoon talking about god like all the other priests felt the need to do.

Just before Mary Lou's next birthday, he asked her if she'd ever seen God's Trunk and she confessed she had not. While the youngsters were playing their board games, they wandered into her bedroom and he showed her his Trunk and got her to touch it. Within three weeks, she was so used to God's Trunk, Mary Lou would stroke it until its sap would rise and rush out of it. She made him very happy.

On her fifteenth birthday, he bought her a large bar of chocolate, which he told her she did not have to share with anyone—just like their secret times together. He asked her if she'd started her woman's bleeding and she confirmed she had.

The following week he encouraged her to take off her panties for him and over the next month instead of touching the Trunk and releasing its sap, Pastor Neil got Mary Lou to let him put his Trunk inside her Rosebush.

The next school year came and went. He kept up his visits and Alice leaned more heavily on him. He would pop over of an evening during the week and they would talk. Sometimes she would cry and he would give her a hug for solace but always he would listen and be respectful of her, something her long-dead husband failed ever to do.

Mary Lou's school career bumped along near the bottom but she finally made some real friends and could engage in honest conversation with people her own age. Being seventeen, many of the girls were putting out for their guys, describing their sexual explorations in lurid detail during Monday recess. This was the point when Mary Lou discovered her Sunday afternoons with this man were not normal by any stretch of the imagination.

She knew her mother wouldn't believe her. She eavesdropped on Alice's conversation with him one evening and they talked about getting married. They planned to move the family to the Pastor's house next to the church.

Mary Lou packed a bag she found at the back of the cupboard by the front door and stole a knife from the kitchen and hid it under her bed until Sunday arrived with a thud in her life.

As always, the kids played their games while her mother got drunk in a bar. Pastor Neil took her into her room and sat on the edge of the bed. She kneeled down between his legs while he pushed his shorts down from under his cassock.

Then without a word, she grabbed the knife she'd placed so carefully at exactly the right position and stabbed and sliced at his groin. Blood poured everywhere and he rolled off the bed, writhing in agony. She reckoned she had carved his dick clean off.

She took the bag out of her wardrobe and stuffed her last few possessions into it. Then she turned back to Pastor Neil, picked up the knife she'd left on the bedside table and plunged it into his throat. As much as she wanted to watch that man suffer, Mary Lou Belle didn't stay to witness him bleed out. She walked out the room, out the house and out of that town—never to return.

TUESDAY JUNE 17, 1968

47

FRANK LAGOTTI DROVE his white van south at high speed down Hollins Ferry Road in the suburbs of Baltimore, ignoring any red lights trying to impede his progress. Next to him sat Brian and jammed under their feet where two black bags stuffed with banknotes, which a short while ago had been resting in the vault of the First Bank of Baltimore, Lansdowne Branch.

Even though he'd extracted the cash from a bank, Frank was not a happy man. He had left two of his gang dead on the ground, but what really made him angry was his girlfriend had not kept her word to him that morning.

Police sirens wailed behind them; they had exited the bank minutes earlier and the cops were already chomping at their heels. The noise remained in the distance and Frank couldn't tell if they were gaining on him. Foot flat on the gas pedal, arms rigid-straight attached to the steering wheel, he stared ahead and continued to fume.

Brian sat in total silence, an occasional glance towards Frank the only discernible movement in his entire body. Surviving the raid was one thing, but they weren't clear just yet. He was lucky to be alive although there was no guarantee that state would continue. As a reflex action, he checked his guns were in their correct place in his coat, having refilled the chambers in case of need.

"Check mine."

Frank passed his revolvers to Brian who repeated the process and returned them to his boss.

"I think they're fading."

"Maybe, Frank."

The men sank back to silence as the wagon sped along the road heading for a barn which was the gang's rendezvous. Frank was right, the sirens were disappearing: must have taken a wrong turning because even though Pete the Wheels spent a lot of time souping up their vehicles, the van was no competition for a police car in a high-speed chase.

That was why Frank planned to set charges along the telegraph poles near the bank—to make it real hard for the police to follow them. But they hadn't blown and the cops were behind them now. Brian tried not to dwell on the events that had gone down in the bank. He knew he needed to keep his wits about him and remembering the blood pour out of Andrew's chest was not the way to go.

"Hop into the back and tell me if you can see anything."

Brian loped over the shift stick and landed on the mattress he'd found so uncomfortable on their route into Lansdowne. He shuffled to the small window at the rear of the van. He peeped out and stared.

A lot of dust from the van's tires and an empty scene: road, verge, fields. Amazing how quickly the suburban sprawl gives way to the countryside. The land was flat and the road was straight so the tarmac looked like it fell away at the curvature of the Earth. Just at that point. Brian thought he spotted a glowing light, flashing red, but he couldn't be sure. He stared again, but the sunlight was at precisely the wrong angle for him to be certain.

"Well?"

"Give me another minute. Might be something, might be nothing."

Frank knew Brian well enough to allow him the time to decide—he was a professional. He rode shotgun for many jobs before this one. If the man demanded a moment, he needed it.

Tick tock.

"And?"

"There's a red light on the horizon. Not catching us up but not going away."

"Hang on, I'll give ourselves an edge."

Frank waited two seconds and then flung the wheel hard right, forcing the vehicle to career off the road, onto the dirt and into a field. He gunned the vehicle as it made its way over the bumpiest field in Maryland. The steel reinforcement attached to the chassis kept the van in one piece. It headed straight for a clump of trees and bushes. He skidded it to a halt, facing the road a thousand feet away.

Five minutes later a single cherry top sped past staying on the road. Both men had guns drawn and had stepped out the van ready to let rip if anything left the safety of the highway. They stayed a minute to make sure the blue and white didn't return and hopped back into the van.

"Gonna stay here all day?"

"Nope. But if we're not being chased, we don't have to drive like we are."

Brian thought about that for three seconds then nodded understanding and, by extension, his consent. Not that Frank was asking for it.

Nothing appeared. Not from the left or the right. There was the occasional chirp of a bird and the rustling of leaves in the breeze but apart from that: zip.

Another ten minutes of silent waiting. Frank put the van into gear and drove at a sensible pace back to the highway. Then he rejoined the road and traveled at five below the legal limit. He was right: if you travel at high speed, every cop will want to stop you. If you drive legit then they'll arrest you for a bust tail light. And Pete already checked them the day before.

Fifteen minutes later, the destination loomed in the distance. There were no automobiles out front but he expected that. Pete and Brian parked the vehicles away from the line of sight from the highway.

Frank turned off the road and idled the vehicle round the side of the barn. There were three cars, filled with gas and ready to go. All were family saloons; nothing to raise an eyebrow of a hero citizen: a white Galaxie, a blue Falcon and a red Ford Torino. Brian noticed they remained in the exact location where he and Pete set them up the previous night.

There was one exception: a black Cadillac parked at the end, blocking all three vehicles from exiting the makeshift parking lot. Stood next to the saloon were two men Frank and Brian recognized.

Paul and Luigi were there to collect the take for Frank's Shylock and money-laundering uncle, Frank Senior. Frankie to close family and friends. Nothing was out the ordinary so they stepped out the van to greet Frankie's heavies.

WHEN MARY LOU sped out the back of the bank lot, she contained a maelstrom of emotions. Her Barracuda took her away from the man she thought she loved and back into the arms of a man who'd have worked out she'd betrayed him.

South onto Hollins Ferry Road and her thoughts were with Carter. He'd spent months telling her he would clear his gambling debt to Uncle Frankie by stealing from the bank on the day the gang was due to appear. Then he hatched a plan to steal from Frankie too. Instead of fleeing for her life, he was meant to be sat beside her with a bag full of cash.

When he was a no-show, Mary Lou figured the smartest thing was to head to the barn and see if Frank got to the money. This would have been perfect were it not for one small detail. As she drove away from the First Bank of Baltimore, she noticed the silence. She might have placed the explosives on the poles near the bank but with all the stress of the morning, she'd forgotten to set the timers. Frank would be pissed.

If that wasn't awful enough, Mary Lou had no notion why Carter hadn't appeared. Frank might have singled him out and done who knows what. She couldn't let herself pursue that idea for too long as it made her want to cry. If Carter was a sap, so be it, but he deserved nothing bad to happen to him.

She remembered the words of advice she'd received repeatedly. Drive under the limit. Don't jump any lights. Don't give the cops any excuse to pull you over. You're just a single girl in a powerful sports car out for a tour of the countryside.

Far off in her rearview mirror: a flashing red light. Mary Lou's heart sunk and her stomach tightened. Her bowels churned. A blue and white gained on her every time she checked its position.

"Steady, steady. Keep your nerve."

Within a minute, she caught sight of the face of the driver clear as day, his car tucked in behind hers. She took her foot off the gas just for a second to give him the opportunity to pass her more easily, which he did. Hers was the only vehicle in the vicinity so he gunned his Chevrolet and sped off in front. Five minutes later, it had gone beyond the horizon. Almost instantly, so it felt, the barn appeared and Mary Lou slowed down and passed the building by six hundred feet or more.

She let the Barracuda glide to a halt hidden among some undergrowth next to two trees. If anyone was already at the meeting point, she hoped they wouldn't have heard her arrival. She popped open the glove compartment and took out a small snub nose Pete had left for her in case of any trouble. He was a great getaway driver. Despite that, Mary Lou reminded herself the guy had been a creep every time he'd been anywhere near her and she should cut his throat before they were through.

She opened her door as quietly as she could and kept it ajar. She scampered out of the undergrowth and ducked from one tree or bush to the next until she made her way back to the barn.

The building itself fell into disrepair a decade before and the far wall had collapsed several years before then. The wooden structure contained a window on each of its short sides and a door and two windows on the remaining front wall. These were just shutters now: the glass shattered and fallen away long ago.

Mary Lou pushed the side shutter and revealed the derelict and empty building inside. There was a fence running down the middle to tie up farm animals and she made out pens on the far side. She barely lifted the shutter a few inches, so her view onto the back was limited. The automobiles were out there somewhere but she couldn't see them. Mary Lou closed the shutter to make sure it didn't slam shut and sneaked along the wall toward the rear. At the corner, she espied the three cars but saw a fourth black one parked in front of them all. Strange, that wasn't part of the plan.

She inched her head out further and recognized two men leaning against the far side of the car: Luigi and Paul, Frankie's goons. She shivered because they creeped her out. Old school mafiosi in the making. Uncle Frankie was connected for sure.

The white van appeared which was strange as Pete drove a Chevy Impale, not that lump of a thing. Mary Lou craned further and witnessed two men get out, not the four who went to the bank. The others could be in the back but she'd thought they'd all want to head the fuck out of Dodge, as Frank used to say.

First she recognized Brian. He'd been in the passenger seat. Due to the morning's sunlight, the other guy was in the direct path of the sun so all Mary Lou could see was his silhouette. Five seconds later, she saw Frank's face and a tear rolled down her cheeks. He was safe.

The men stood and talked a while. She couldn't hear a single word because they were too far away. Then they pulled out guns and fired at each other.

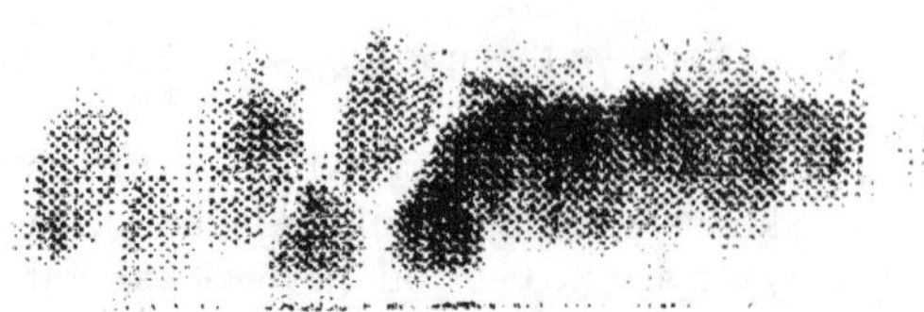

48

"LET'S BE CAREFUL out there, Brian. Frank Senior won't be happy with the way things have turned out so far."

"Okay, Frank."

The men slipped out the van leaving their doors wide open. Frank eyed Paul then Luigi and they both stayed leaning against their limousine. Relaxed.

Frank took two steps toward them, stopped and Brian mirrored him.

"Hey boys."

"Hi, Frank."

Paul had never spoken so much to Frank the whole year since he was out of the jail. Luigi remained his usual silent self.

"Radio said you robbed a bank this morning."

"Yep. Shows there are some things you can believe on the radio."

"Big haul?"

"Big enough, I reckon. Not like we've had any time to count it."

"Got it with you though?"

"Yes. It's safe with us."

"What about the others? Four of you walked into the bank. That was the plan. There's only you two and your goomah's missing."

"Plans change. Andrew and Pete didn't make it. No idea about Mary Lou."

"Any loose ends?"

"Nope. Both bodies in the getaway car and we torched the fucking lot."

"That explains the van."

"It brought us here… So you haven't seen Mary Lou? She's not been here?"

"Uh-uh. No sign of the skirt."

"And did you bring some seed money? Frank Senior promised us cash while he laundered the take."

"He did."

"So you got it?"

Frank became tetchy. Why was Paul so casual when Frank hoped they'd be on their way within minutes of arriving?

"Sure. You in a rush?"

"Paul, we've robbed a bank and the police are swarming all over the place. Can we get a move on?"

"Thought you might want to wait a while for your blanket warmer."

"She knows the score. Be here or don't and take the consequences."

Frank looked around as though mention of her would make Mary Lou appear in a puff of smoke. "Let me grab your working capital."

Paul lifted his body off the Caddy and opened the front passenger door, while Luigi stood upright. Brian turned to go into the van but Frank glared at him until he stopped. Brian edged nearer the door without noticing himself do it.

As Paul spun round, Frank spotted a black barrel and whipped out his revolver and aimed it at Paul. A flash and a roar as Luigi's gun let rip and Frank hit the dirt. He rolled over and hid behind the driver's side door.

Bullets flew and amid the whizzes and bangs, red spurt out of Luigi's left shoulder but he didn't go down. Instead, the ox stood there and blasted towards both himself and Brian. Frank aimed at Luigi's heart and squeezed out a shot. It landed square and true and Luigi crumpled in an instant. One down, one remaining.

"How you doing Brian?"

No answer.

"Brian?"

Nothing.

Frank hunkered down as slugs continued to fly in his direction. He checked his revolver: two left in the chamber. Patted his pockets and found he had no spares. Rolling under the van, he got close to Brian's body which was lying face up. One pool of blood around his stomach, another round his forehead. Two good shots.

Frank dragged the corpse behind the passenger door and checked each of Brian's coat pockets. There was a box, but it only had three shells in it. He stuffed them into the chamber but he knew it wouldn't be enough. He squeezed off one shot at Paul and missed. Paul responded with a dozen slugs which flew over Frank's head and around his feet. No time to think.

Paul scampered round the other side of the Cadillac and Frank couldn't figure out where he was. Another burst of fire aimed where Frank was squatting so Paul still had him in his sights. Frank rolled back under the van and stayed there. Five seconds. Ten seconds. Silence.

This was not the OK Corral and he had too few pills for any kind of gunfight. Either Frank needed to be nearer to Paul or he should wait for Paul to come to him.

The space between the cars gave little room for any sneaky maneuvers and there was an open field further out. Get into the barn and scoot round the wasteland which had grown up since the place became derelict? Not a great idea.

Stay put and wait? A hail of bullets landed around the driver door as Paul assumed Frank had gone back to his original side. Perhaps Paul didn't have as good a line of sight as Frank thought. Didn't mean the new plan should change though.

All he could think about was his breathing which sounded like a hurricane to his ears. He focused on looking at both sides of the van to wait for Paul's calves but the sound of his hair swooshing the dirt was far too noisy. An earthquake in his head.

His bright idea quickly turned the space below the vehicle into a death cell. He realized that now. There were no more stray bullets. No more bursts from Paul at all. Frank strained to hear Paul's footsteps, but the wind picked up and the rustling of the trees took over from any other noise.

Two feet appeared just out of reach from Frank's head, facing towards him. He aimed his revolver at one calf and squeezed the trigger. Click. The damn gun jammed. He tried a second time. Click. Nothing. Damn. Paul bent down and Frank saw an eye looking right at him with the guy's semi-automatic pointing straight to his forehead.

A SINGLE SHOT rang out and Paul slumped to the ground, parts of his brain flying to the left and landing on the van door.

"You okay?"

Mary Lou's voice echoed under the wagon with genuine concern but with an edge of fear.

"You alone?"

"Yep."

"Okay, I'm coming out on the other side."

When Frank got up, she held her gun in combat position and continued to point it at Paul.

"Relax, Mary Lou."

She ignored him and Frank stormed round and stood next to her. Then he placed his hands on hers, gently. Her fingers clasped the snub nose more tightly until he kissed her on the neck and the tension in her arms eased off. He took the gun off her and they walked away from the van until he'd made sure Mary Lou stayed with her back to the carnage she'd created. Then he pocketed the piece.

"Thanks."

"You're welcome."

They kissed and hugged even though Frank still hadn't figured out what happened at the bank and whether she had betrayed him.

"You hurt?"

"No. You?"

"All good."

Frank surveyed the scene.

"Where's your car?"

"Down the road a ways. You got any of the money?"

Frank ground his molars.

"Yes. We took the entire haul. Eventually."

"Huh?"

"Tell you later. Now is not the time. We gotta get out of here."

A siren wailed in the distance. Faint but wailing nonetheless.

Frank sprinted to the open van and leaned over to grab the two bags under the front seats and yanked them out.

"Which car?"

Mary Lou shrugged as they all looked the same to her.

"Blue one."

Frank traipsed over to the Falcon and opened the driver's door then halted.

"What about your Barracuda? It'll be faster than this thing."

"Yes but it stands out. That's why Pete chose these family cars for us."

They'd go further in the Barracuda but it turned too many heads.

"Okay, you're right. Bring it over here and we'll deal from there."

Mary Lou ran off leaving Frank to scavenge through the Caddy. A semi-automatic, several boxes of shells, but not much else. He lifted Luigi and Paul's wallets. They had a hundred bucks on them, which was now in his coat pocket. Before getting out of their vehicle, he shunted the shift stick into neutral and pushed it but got nowhere. Instead he dragged the two bodies into the back of the wagon. Then he kneeled down by Brian.

He put his fingers on Brian's neck. No pulse. Frank took the cash from Brian's wallet and threw his body into the van too. He looked around for the gas cans left in advance by the gang. Mary Lou appeared inside the sports car and Frank gestured for her to park in the field behind the barn.

"We've a couple more guns and a pile of shells. And about two hundred bucks spending money."

"I've only got a few dollars on me."

"Same as me before I swiped the wallets."

Mary Lou noticed the feet sticking out the back of the van.

"What do we do first?"

"Help me push the Caddy towards your Barracuda."

Once they had the two cars close to each other, they scurried round the barn looking for the gas cans. Meanwhile the sirens felt like they were getting louder. Every minute, one of them would hold their head up, ears pricked, trying to gauge the distance. Always failing.

Mary Lou walked into the barn and cried out.

"Found them!"

Frank hunkered over and counted six black cans.

"Come on. Dowse the Caddy and Barracuda and I'll make a start on the others."

She walked away to follow his instructions until he gave out a shout.

"Stop! What are we thinking?"

Mary Lou swung round and scrunched her face up.

"We gotta be better than this, Mary Lou. This is gasoline we're about to splash around. Why don't we move the Falcon away from it all so when we fire up its engine, we don't make ourselves a bonfire?"

She slapped her forehead with her palm, nodded and drove the Falcon round the corner. Now it was visible from the road if you were traveling slowly enough to notice it, hidden under a tree. Mary Lou returned and slopped gas all over the remaining cars until all the cans were empty and thrown inside the vehicles.

Frank pulled out a match, struck it and threw it on the Caddy which lit up in twenty seconds. Orange flames licked across the bodywork and flowed along the interior leather. The yellow tongues grew in size until the wind blew in just the right direction causing a spike to transfer to the Barracuda until it, too, was a ball of reddish melting.

He passed the matches to Mary Lou and picked up both black bags.

"Light 'em up, babe. I'll be in the Falcon."

Mary Lou took the matches and watched him disappear round the corner. For a second she wondered if he would drive off without her. What had happened to Carter, Andrew and Pete?

She shook herself out of her reverie and threw one match into each of the cars and two into the van. Only once she was certain the flames had taken hold did she walk away. Mary Lou looked back to see the clothing of the bodies catch light.

"It's a goddamn crematorium in there."

She ran to the side of the barn to watch Frank revving the engine of the Falcon. Mary Lou jumped into the passenger seat and closed the door.

"Let's get the fuck out of Dodge."

Frank slammed his foot onto the pedal and the car skidded around, the back end swerving right then left until the Falcon reached tarmac and its tyres found some grip.

"Easy, Frank."

He laughed, gunned the saloon along the highway for about two minutes and slowed down to below the speed limit.

"We're out for a drive to enjoy the countryside."

"You said it, Frank."

"If the police stops us, it'll be for a blown sidelight. The guns are in the trunk. So's the take. There's nothing of interest in the glove compartment. If a cop pops the hood, we're dead. Do whatever you need to prevent that from happening. Understood?"

"I got it, Frank."

"Good."

Frank switched on the radio and swiveled the dials until he found his favorite station.

"WFTX 96.4 FM, where you're never more than 60 seconds away from quality Rock 'n' Roll."

Both hands on the wheel, he tapped along to the songs while Mary Lou sat there sinking into the passenger seat. His silence bore down on her because she thought he'd want her to explain about the explosives, if nothing else. And she knew the robbery itself was still too raw for her to ask what went wrong.

Meanwhile, Frank was desperate to not think. He walked into the bank at 09:01 with a balaclava on his head exactly one hour ago. The security guard was dead, two of theirs were gone. No three: Brian. And Uncle Frankie sent Paul and Luigi to kill them.

That was before he could figure out what to do with the woman sat next to him. The lack of explosions meant she sabotaged the whole job to take the money for herself and Carter. But she hadn't been out there in the parking lot to go with the chump when Frank left the bank. So what was exactly happening? And those sirens were only getting louder behind them.

He Lagotti had no clue and, as far as he was concerned, the best thing right now was to drive and hum along to a bunch of songs. It had not been a good morning. In the rearview mirror, a plume of smoke rose from the barn. The flames must have reached the building itself. Halloween had come early this year.

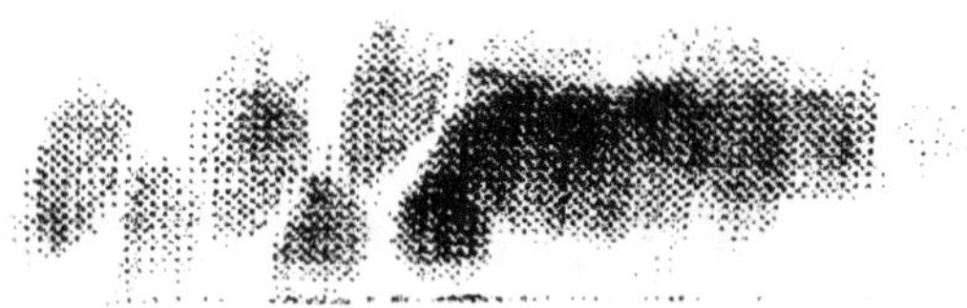

49

FRANK TAPPED AWAY at his steering wheel and focused on keeping just below the speed limit. He avoided the freeway in case there were any cordons but there were too many alternate routes for the cops to prevent a felon from fleeing the scene.

The plan had always been to head off in the wrong direction from their intended destination and Frank saw no reason to deviate from this sensible decision—even though that siren was getting louder.

He kept checking in the mirror for some sign of a red flashing light but there was nothing. A few cars and the occasional truck behind him.

"Any idea where the siren's coming from?"

"No. But if you listen carefully, only sounds like one."

"You reckon?"

"Yes, Frank."

Mary Lou opened her window to get a better fix. A blast of cold air entered the cabin due to the speed of the car. Her hair flapped around and whipped her face. Frank's short back and sides unaffected by the airflow.

"One for sure—unless they're so far away…"

Frank was certain the cop was getting closer, but there wasn't even the dust trail from a high pursuit vehicle behind them. Nada.

Mary Lou shook her head and shrugged.

"Wind your window back up. If we can't hear the siren, then I might as well listen to my music."

"Okay."

He carried on tapping and Mary Lou put both feet on her seat, turning her body into a ball. And the car stormed along despite traveling at exactly five miles an hour below the limit.

"How far east should we go?"

"Long enough so that if any local recognizes us, they report to the cops we were heading for Philly."

"How long you reckon that is?"

"Another hour tops. Then we can head north and round until we are on a straight line for California."

"California? Wow."

Frank sucked in air. He didn't want to have this conversation now.

"Not planning on heading to the west coast then?"

She stared at him.

"I had total faith in your ability to take out the bank. We spent enough time preparing for the robbery to be sure we'd carry it through right."

"But?"

"There were complications for both so us, I'd say. Me before you hit the entrance and for you once you'd told everyone to stick 'em up."

"Complications. Nice description. Yes, there were problems inside. No one knew where the money was. Not even the bank manager."

"Crazier things have happened."

"Did Carter tell you he would run off with the take?"

Mary Lou's eyes widened as Frank had nailed the situation perfectly. Carter was their mark inside and she'd been playing him for months. Squeezing him for information, spending time with him, sleeping with him. Falling in love with him.

"He spoke about it but I didn't reckon on him going through with it. Talked big but acted small."

"Is that why you didn't mention his plan to rob the take from under our noses? Not even a word. Not once."

"He didn't name a date. Said it to impress me. Nothing more than that."

"Then any idea why he chose the exact day we came in to lift the money?"

"Well, it was the largest amount of notes in their vault for months. That's why…"

Frank's eyes showed he wasn't buying a word she was saying. To be fair, she was skating close to the truth but withholding certain key facts. Like she was planning to run away from him. Or Uncle Frankie's involvement in the whole deal. That could wait until later. Much later.

"Not now, Frank. It's too complicated and I doubt you're happy with what I've said, judging by your expression."

He nodded in agreement.

"But at some point you need to tell me what happened in that bank. There's next of kin to call."

"Pete had no one: he was a cantankerous little shit who had no friends and no family. And don't spare a tear for Andrew. He's the guy who blasted a hole in Pete's head."

Mary Lou sat and stared at Frank with a stomach cramp reflecting the pain of his words.

"Now is not the time."

"For sure. We can talk later. Let's get further away from the scene of the crime. There's a lot to figure out."

"You said it."

The siren got nearer but still only a handful of cars and two trucks. And a plume of smoke receding in the distance. The noise was loud and Frank listened hard. Mary Lou was right: there was only one noise blaring out. Nothing in the rearview mirror. He looked at the road, at the mirror and noticed beads of sweat dribbling down the side of his face.

"Put your legs down. If this goes belly-up, you don't want to be crushed by the dash."

Mary Lou sat properly again although Frank's comment didn't help her anxiety levels, which were through the roof.

There was a bend up ahead which shifted the highway about eighty degrees right. A clump of trees stood at the inside line of the road's curve. As if from nowhere, a blue-and-white hurtled toward them and then past heading back into Baltimore. Its red light flashed and the siren wailed. Frank recognized the driver from the car which overtook the van earlier. He relaxed.

"Looks like we're not the ones being chased."

She leaned over and planted a kiss on his shoulder—she couldn't reach his mouth.

THE MILES STRETCHED out behind them until Mary Lou thought she'd been to this place before. When Frank pulled into a faded parking lot next to a tumbledown building, then Mary Lou knew for sure. He'd taken them to the disused factory where they'd held their meetings as a crew.

"What we doing here?"

"You'll see."

Frank drove round the back of the rundown warehouse. Originally it stood four stories tall but now half the building was a pile of rubble and the surviving bricks comprised a series of small rooms missing walls, ceilings and, in two cases, floors.

They had used the only space with functioning walls, complete floor and ceiling, which was located in the middle of the space. The location was obscure and even if someone followed them to the site, finding the room was a trial in itself.

They both walked round the fallen bricks and Mary Lou trailed Frank into the room they'd been in so many times before. A sole chair lay on its side, which Uncle Frankie used while everyone else stood around. Four feet away from it was the flat ground Frank had drawn a map of the bank.

He went past the seat and headed towards the far wall. She couldn't tell quite where he was going, but he certainly had a destination in mind. He halted in a corner and counted fifteen footsteps heel-to-toe. Then stopped and faced the whitewash.

Mary Lou watched him squat and pull out a brick to reveal a gap containing a box. He dragged it out of the cavity and flipped open the lid. Inside: papers. He passed two items up to her.

"Here's a passport with a fake name and a matching driving license."

"How long have you had these?"

"Long enough."

Frank smiled up at her and winked.

"Got them sorted a month after I departed the Baltimore State Penitentiary. Never knew when they might be useful."

"You said it. What else is in there?"

Frank slammed the box shut and crammed it into the cavity.

"Never you mind."

He stood up and shoved his passport and photo ID into his pocket.

"Does that mean we're going to leave the country? I thought we were off west."

"Never hurts to have a plan B. And these will give us options if we need then."

Mary Lou flipped over her ID to find her new name: Claudia Starr. Sounded like a porn actress.

"Who's Claudia?"

"You."

"No, silly. I mean who d'you know called Claudia?"

"Nobody. It's just a name."

Mary Lou nodded, but she found it hard to believe.

"And I'm Karl Todd."

"Hi Karl.

"Hi Claudia."

They both laughed a little and then headed to the Falcon.

"Can we get a bite to eat? I'm starved."

Frank sat there for a second.

"I am too. I know a place a few miles down the road. Brian mentioned it to me. We can go there then head west."

"Cool."

Out the parking lot and back onto tarmac. Stubbornly remaining under the limit, he drove off, still avoiding the expressway. Thirty minutes later they understood why the interstates were built. Straight lines with faster traffic. If they weren't concerned about police cordons they would already have been tucking into bacon and hash browns.

Instead, they made their way safely along the back roads. Whenever a blue and white crossed their paths, Mary Lou froze in her seat. Frank appeared more relaxed, but he always stopped tapping on the steering wheel until the cop car faded into the rearview mirror. While there was stress in the automobile, there was nothing but rolling hills and the great outdoors beyond the Falcon.

Mary Lou noticed they traveled under the I-95 as they passed the exit and entrance ramp signs. A minute later they went by a gas station on the right and twenty seconds further on, a diner appeared on the left: *The Joppa-de-Doopah.*

They parked and she stared at the ramshackle venue. It looked like it hadn't seen a lick of paint since 1945. The slime of oil seeped into every corner of the lot and the brickwork. There was a large and one small building. The smaller one clearly was an outhouse and the larger was filled with light, tables and women wearing waitress uniforms. You didn't need to be a genius to figure out what went on inside the Joppa-de-Doopah. Even though the smaller outcrop from the diner appeared basic in the extreme, Mary Lou knew she needed to use the facilities before she ate.

"You go ahead. I'll catch up with you in a minute."

"Huh? Oh, sure."

She was taking a risk: Frank could drive off and leave her stranded but she'd already tested him with the same quandary at the barn and he had waited for her. So the chances were he'd do the same again.

50

WHEN SHE PUSHED open the door marked with an enormous 'W', Mary Lou held her breath. There were two mirrors above cracked sinks and on the other wall were a pair of cubicles. Only one had a lock.

Given the amount of grime on the faucets, she decided against washing her hands and went into the diner to find Frank in a booth by a window. She sat opposite him and realized they could see the entrance to the lot as well as the Falcon. No surprises there.

"What d'you kids like to wrap your lips around?"

The waitress's voice carried over the two feet tall menus which she'd earlier deposited on the table when he first arrived.

Without looking at her, Mary Lou asked for coffee and a glass of water. Frank ordered the same. She lowered the laminated menu in time to see a middle-aged woman waddled off to behind the counter to prepare their drinks. She was no spring chicken. Mary Lou eyed her up and down. The woman's blouse was too tight for her; each button was about to burst. Perhaps because of this, one too many buttons were undone. Or she did it to get more tips. Most of the clientele were men, who'd left the expressway for a bite to eat and an ass to ogle.

"Thanks."

"Call me Lucy."

"Thanks, Lucy."

"You're welcome, fella."

She turned to Mary Lou.

"He's a big hulk of a man, isn't he? You better hang on to him. Take my word. You lose sight of him for one minute and I'll be all over his bones. No offense dear."

"None taken."

They ordered too much food and Lucy left them alone for a while. What she lacked in subtlety, she made up for in efficiency. Soon they tucked into their feast: bacon, eggs, hash browns, toast, home fries.

There was no conversation, just chewing and slurping of coffee. Frank and Mary Lou both deep in their own thoughts, playing over the last two hours and projecting into the future without knowing what would happen one moment to the next.

"What went down in the bank, then?"

He put his silverware down and folded his arms.

"It was a fucking mess. That's what happened. The money had gone from the vault. No kidding."

"Jeez."

"I had to break a few heads before I believed the bank staff when they said they didn't have a clue."

He replayed the images in his head of him torturing the manager, slicing a cashier and cutting her tit.

"We were walking out with nothing when something didn't look right in the state of Maryland. One pinhead couldn't keep his eyes straight. Kept on looking below his desk and I figured he'd stashed the cash. In the two black bags in the trunk. That was your Carter."

Mary Lou continued to stare at him but said nothing.

"Maybe you know what the fuck he was up to. You can tell me in a minute. Brian was standing next to me but Andrew was nowhere. We exited the bank and found him outside, by Pete's driver's door holding a gun. He'd shot Pete in the head. The interior of the vehicle was a fucking mess. You never want to see what that car looked like."

Frank sank the rest of his coffee and Lucy came over for a refill and walked away. He watched her return to the counter and turned his gaze back on Mary Lou.

"So I shot him dead. Couldn't have a killer in the crew. One minute it's Pete, the next it could've been any of us. Then we met up a few minutes later."

He sipped the now hot coffee and drank a mouthful of water.

"The cops chased us out of Lansdowne. Any idea why?"

Mary Lou nodded.

"Because you failed to the explosives. Why?"

"It might be hard to believe but it was an honest mistake. I placed them all, but I got flustered and just plain forgot to flip the switch to set them off. I told you all I wanted nothing to do with the bombs but y'all insisted."

"You forgot?"

"Yep."

Frank remained silent for five minutes, staring at Mary Lou and sipping his coffee. Eventually, she broke the tension.

"Carter had the money, but he was in the bank?"

"Yes. Hidden under his desk, like I said."

"Any idea what he was doing with it?"

"He was gonna rob our bank. Actually, he had robbed the place, if you think about it. But he had missed a key element of any robbery: he forgot to get away."

Mary Lou let out a nervous laugh and he carried on staring. She had known Carter would steal the money for a while before the job but, for whatever reason, instead of leaving before Frank arrived, he had gained a yellow streak down his back and hadn't stolen anything from anyone. Shifting the cash from one part of a bank to another meant nothing. And she had been planning on spending the rest of her life with this sap.

"It's the little things that count."

"Any idea what your Carter was gonna do this morning?"

"First, he's not my Carter. Just plain Carter. Second, no. If I had known he would run off with the money then I'd have met him and we could have bushwhacked him with no one going into that damn bank."

"And you hadn't schemed with him to steal the take away from us?"

"Frank? Listen to yourself. Please."

He continued to stare and then it was Mary Lou's turn to sip at a coffee mug. To her, it was only a partial lie. Once Carter failed to come out the bank then she was telling the truth. Until then, her plan was to follow the money. She was attracted to both men and, although she'd selected Carter, Mary Lou knew Frank was a decent man. Didn't mean he would believe her.

"Listen. If I wanted you gone, I'd have let Paul and Luigi do you in at the rendezvous. But I saved your life."

She allowed those four words to sink in because his staring was annoying her. He had good reason to be angry over Carter but he should show some gratitude too, she reckoned.

THE PROBLEM THEY both faced was simple: neither trusted the other enough. In the last few hours, Mary Lou and Frank had supported the other but the bliss they felt yesterday before the heist had dissipated into thin air. She had withheld vital information before the job and understood he was wary of her.

When those detonators failed to blow, Frank was well within his rights to hunt her down and throw her out the window. That's what he'd done to his last partner when a robbery went sour. Mary Lou plain didn't know if he was just biding his time, waiting for the right moment.

"Where do we progress from here?"

"I don't know. We could split up the money and go our separate ways."

"Is that what you want Frank?"

"Me? No, but I understand if that's what you wanted. I wouldn't choose that to happen but I'd get it."

"I don't wish us to split either."

"Then where shall we go from here?"

He smiled because he understood the double meaning to his words. He had only intended the geographical question.

"West like we said a year ago?"

"That's been the plan all right. Cali-forn-I-a. I've always wanted to see the Pacific Ocean."

"With our new passports, we could always head to Mexico. Swift shuffle over the border and then we vanish."

"Sure could. I love the sound of the weather they have down Tijuana way but neither of us speak Spanish."

Mary Lou thought about how much she'd hate to move south. She had spent her entire life trying to escape from those murky depths of the country.

"There's also Canada, Frank."

"It hovers over us and enough people have gone over the border to dodge the draft, we know we could slip through the customs barrier no problem. But man it's cold up there and I don't fancy that. If we will relocate the least the place should offer us is a warm environment."

"So does California sound the best option then?"

"Does to me."

"Me too."

Mary Lou reached out her hand and Frank squeezed it, briefly. They were far from reconciled but there was still enough connection between them to carry on together. At least for a while.

"But there's a problem with the cash, isn't there?"

"We're stuck with dirty money and we have no idea how much we have."

"Do you think Paul and Luigi got greedy or were they following Uncle Frankie's orders?"

"Good question and right now I don't know. He's always been kind to me even though there's no blood tie."

Mary Lou bit her tongue. There was more to Frankie than a benign step uncle.

"Should we go over to Frankie and sort things out?"

"Any other day, I'd say yes. But if he called a hit on us then we shouldn't be going into the lion's den. Besides, we need to get out of Baltimore and out of Maryland as soon as."

"Where can we launder the money instead if we're not touching Uncle Frankie?"

"We must make a detour."

"Huh?"

"Vegas. I know a guy who knows a guy out there. And worse case, we can hit the wheels."

"Are you serious?"

"I've got some connections out there. It'll be fine."

"And after Vegas, on to California?"

"For now, but we can decide for sure later. Depending on how much heat is after us, we might have to head over the border—north or south—before coming back or leaving forever."

"But we don't have to worry about that right now."

"Not at all, Mary Lou. Without laundered money, we might as well make a break for Canada now because at the moment all we have in those black bags are bunches of paper. They are useless to us. If we pass any of those notes over, the cops'll be all over us within thirty minutes. Make no mistake: we can't do anything with those notes until we've got them washed and dried."

"I understand, Frank."

Lucy strolled over and refilled the mugs which killed the conversation at the table.

"No need to stop just 'cause I came around. I heard just about everything over the years in this diner. There's nothing that'd embarrass me."

"We were just trying to decide where to go on vacation. Which do you prefer: Mexico or Canada?"

"I've never been to either. Never left the States. I reckon the heat of Mexico'd lead to some sexy nights for a woman and a man like you two."

"What are we like?"

"Young. In love. You know."

"Do we look like we're in love?"

"Sure do, hon'. Are you married?"

Mary Lou glanced at Frank.

"No, we're not."

"Oh kids. If you love each other, then do it right. I've been hitched twice but I'm single at the present."

"No guy to keep your bed warm?"

Lucy chuckled.

"No, hon' but I have a man aiming to heat my mattress tonight."

Now it was Mary Lou's turn to chuckle; Frank didn't respond.

"Can we have the check?"

"Sure thing, babe."

Lucy pulled out a pad from her apron and wrote out the total on the bottom of the chit. She placed it face down in front of Frank and went away.

"Why did you encourage her so much?"

"Just being nice."

"But you've basically told her where we're thinking of going."

"Sorry, I didn't think."

"You said it. Think before you talk next time, okay? We can't afford any slip ups."

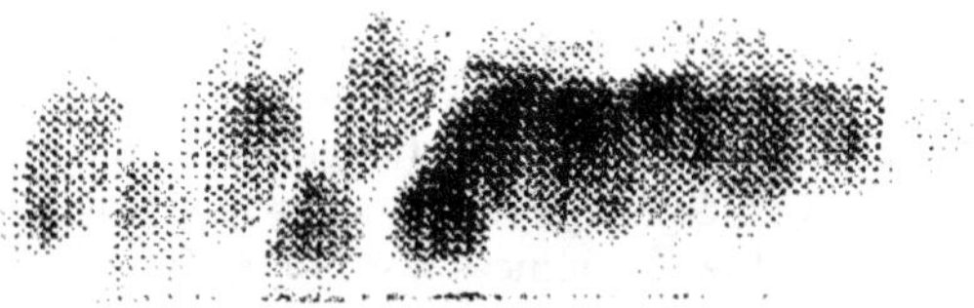

51

FRANK LAGOTTI SENIOR switched the radio off just before ten. No news for ages and the music annoyed him. He returned to his office, sat down behind his desk and took his mind off the bank robbery by focusing on his favorite pastime.

He pulled open the top right drawer of his bureau, picked out a girlie magazine and opened it. Leaned back in his chair and stared at the pictures. This was his morning routine and the heist had disrupted it.

Frankie told himself the robbery was a win-win for him. On one side of the coin was step-nephew Frank. He'd funded the boy and his crew, knowing the place would be fat with cash and was ripe for picking.

The other side was a deal Frankie'd made with one of the bank employees who'd run up a hefty gambling debt whose marker Frankie had purchased. He gave the schmuck a choice: spend the rest of his life paying back his bill or take the money out of the safe.

Frankie set Carter up to grab the greens the morning of the heist. He told himself the only way he could lose was if the coin landed on its edge. And what're the chances of that? Whatever the probability, he sent out Paul and Luigi to extract the take from Frank and head back to his auto repair shop.

The fact the radio announced the robbery meant Carter owed him forty thousand dollars and a huge explanation. Frankie would deal with the mook later; there was more than enough time. He had told Frank he'd need two weeks to launder the take, which wasn't exactly true. An arrangement had already been reached with a connection and within twenty-four hours the cash would be returned. Frankie intended to use the rest of the time to invest the cash and make a little on the side.

What concerned him was the time Paul and Luigi had been gone. Their primary orders were to bring the money back at whatever cost. If Frank bought it that was an acceptable loss, he'd said to Paul. With the guy toast, he could keep the whole take for himself as none of the rest of his crew would come after him. Apart from Pete the Wheels who was a homicidal maniac. If his two did for Frank, Pete was a dead man walking. He'd cap the crazy fucker; great driver but a sociopath for sure.

If Paul had misinterpreted his words, who knows how Frank might react. He could be volatile at times. Either way, Luigi would do whatever Paul told him to do because he was a fine bodyguard but not one of Nature's natural thinkers. A simple soldier though.

Frankie's concentration was distracted by a particular image of a naked body stretched out before him on the page. He turned the publication sideways to not strain his neck. A true connoisseur of free creative expression, Frankie liked the shape of her tits.

Of an evening, Frankie would pursue his artistic interests at the *Kitkatt Club*, a venue he acquired as a result of a different failed attempt to pay off a gambling debt by some other degenerate. This strip joint did good business thanks to its location near the expressway. It also served as a great place for Frankie's R&R—he never paid as he was the owner.

His mind drifted even further as he thought about the girls he had banged there. Some wild nights. Mrs. Lagotti made him breakfast but asked no questions where he'd been. They had been happily married for decades and the source of their happiness was Frankie's porn collection and titty bar. He and his wife hadn't been intimate with each other for over fifteen years and that was how they both liked it.

Frank Senior preferred younger flesh; much younger. And the Kitkatt Club was a feast of fresh naïve pussy ripe for plucking. Those girls made a lot of money and earned every dime. It was the American way.

A foot slipped off his bureau and this knocked Frankie out of his reverie. Despite himself, Frank Senior jolted upright and his mag fell on the floor. He threw it back into the desk drawer and stormed into his anteroom. There was only one person there: Anthony, who was sitting forward in his chair playing cards, chewing a matchstick.

"Any word, Anthony?"

"Nothing."

"Why's the radio off? How do you know what is happening?"

"You switched it off, so I reckoned you didn't want me flipping it on the minute your back was turned."

Anthony was right. That boy was brighter than Paul and could handle himself better than Luigi, who was an aggressive fighter who'd give no quarter ever.

"Okay. Put it on, we might learn something about the heist and if they got away with it."

Very disappointing about Carter. Next week Anthony will pay him a visit. Until then Frankie wanted to get his hands on that money. He looked at the clock and he gave up on waiting.

"Anthony. You have reliable guys you can call on now?"

"Guess so… yes."

"Bring them over to the rendezvous. You and them. As soon as you can paint a picture, find a payphone and tell me."

"Right boss."

Anthony made two calls and promised Frankie he'd phone with information about the money. Paul and Luigi could wait until later.

"Sure thing."

Anthony put his playing cards back in their cardboard packaging and placed them neatly in a drawer. Then he stood up and left the auto repair in search of the take.

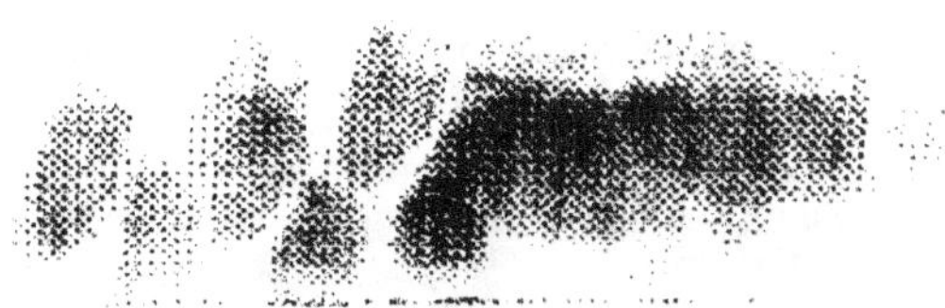

52

AFTER ANTHONY LEFT the premises, Frankie returned to his office and spent some time examining the visual poetry of his girlie magazine. He made a mental note to pop over to the Kitkatt Club on his way home tonight. He needed the relief on offer from one of the girls.

Frankie settled into his chair and the day passed uneventfully. The place was quiet: no vehicle had been in for repair since the day he took over the auto shop. Visitors came and went but none had any car business. An hour later and a knock at his door.

"Enter!"

Anthony walked in and stood waiting. Frankie always forced everyone to wait at least a minute when they entered the room. It was his way of reminding you of the power he held over you. Tedious.

"So?"

"We found the barn but we couldn't get too close."

"Why not?"

"The place was ablaze. Flames forty feet in the air. Too many fire trucks and blue-and-whites for us to get near the joint."

"Okay. You've told me what you don't know. Got anything more useful for me?"

"We talked with the rescue servicemen and there were several cars set alight. They reckoned that was the cause."

"Did they say how many vehicles had been torched?"

"Three saloons and a van, they said."

"Any bodies?"

"Yes. They found some incinerated remains in the vehicle but they aren't too sure exactly. The inside was like a crematorium."

"Jeez."

"Three or four corpses for certain, but they need to sift through the bones to count up accurately."

"Do you think Paul and Luigi got themselves cremated?"

"They ain't nowhere to be seen and there are bodies turning to ash in that van. I reckon two will be Luigi and Paul."

"Rest in peace. Let's get some flowers sent over to their widows."

"Right, boss."

"If our two bought it that means the money is still out there and that step nephew and his skirt are on the lam."

"We asked about, but no one had heard or seen anybody else. A cop remembered seeing the van and a couple of cars on the road before the barn burned. And they mentioned passing a blue Falcon."

"That's them. Frank gave way too much detail for me and listed all the vehicles Pete had acquired for them to use."

"What now?"

"Wait outside. I need to make a few calls. Are the people you've brought in reliable?"

"I trust them."

"With your life?"

"Well, I'd trust them with my money overnight. There's no one I'd trust my life to."

"Trusting them with money speaks volumes and is good enough for me. I'll call you when I'm ready."

Anthony shut the door behind him and Frankie sat at his desk seething. Looked like that step nephew of his skipped town, possibly with his girlfriend in tow—depending how many bodies were in that van. The other possibility was that she had survived and the rest of them were goners. Either way, he and his men would find the survivor and extract the take from them—whoever they were. And a bonus if they wind up dead.

Carter let him down and Frankie would have smiled had he known the man was fighting for his life in hospital suffering from gunshot wounds to the groin—administered by Frank after he took the cash off him and before he left the bank.

Instead, the Shylock was planning his own revenge for the gambler which involved a workshop vice and a lot of pain. This train of thought only increased his anger because he was dealing with the loss of his money and two doses of betrayal on top.

Frankie's sister remarried after her husband met an unexpected end when a mechanical digger crushed his stationary car with him in the driver's seat. Her second fella played poker with Frankie before they were hitched and, to his regret, he felt he had introduced them to each other.

The problem with Giuseppe was five-card stud. He had a series of tells you could read a mile off and many did. This meant him a loser and like gamblers before and after when he lost he often would double up hoping to turn things around. When the deadbeat had borrowed to the max from everyone else, the only person left to get cash from was his brother-in-law.

So Frank Senior spent ten years keeping this guy afloat to ensure his sister lived in the lap of luxury she deserved. That annoyed the moneylender daily, but what hurt him more was Giuseppe's son from his previous marriage.

The schnook was short of brains and long on mistakes. Frequently Frankie had organized work for him—a variety of crews hitting different venues—but he got caught more times than was good for a professional.

And the boy had the family name. How? Maria had reverted to the Lagotti moniker after the car crush and then refused to change it when she remarried. Frankie regretted the age in which he lived and the bra-burning feminists who inhabited it.

Then his step nephew decided he preferred his mother's name to his own and used that instead. Frankie ground his molars as the memory of these events raised his blood pressure even more. He hoped Frank's body was on the funeral pyre and that Mary Lou had survived. He could have some more fun with her if Anthony caught her alive.

The money became his focus again. That and an amazing ass which appeared in his field of vision as he flipped through more of the pages of his magazine.

What annoyed Frankie most was he had no handle on the amount of the take. The radio DJ had been vague at the start and then his update implied there was a big haul. Frankie knew the heist was large because they'd planned it that way. In his mind, he imagined a pile of notes and counted them out. His fear was that the news was exaggerating the size to beef up the story.

While the accuracy of the radio was not Frankie's primary concern, the fact there was talk of a six figure sum was very important to him. And if he could listen to the broadcast, so could his boss back in New York—and that built up expectations he couldn't meet. When the Five Boroughs wasn't happy then bloody retribution often ensued.

THE BEST THING was for Frankie to place a call. He didn't need to look up the number as it was tattooed to the inside of his eyelids.

"Is Charlie available? It's Frank Lagotti… Sure."

Charles Pentangelo was a made man for the Bonanno Family, who controlled much of the significant criminal activity in the Five Boroughs.

Frankie was left holding the receiver for several minutes. The six minute wait stretched to eternity.

"Charlie! How's that wife of yours and your wonderful children?"

"All fine, thanks Frankie. And how is Mrs. Lagotti?"

"She's cooking me up a storm."

"Great news. What can I do for you?"

"Wanted to give you an update on a matter I mentioned to you a couple of weeks ago."

"Oh yes, how is that proceeding?"

"Good and bad, hence the call."

An audible sigh.

"Talk Frankie."

"Is it okay for us to speak on this line?"

"Sure thing."

"They got the money out. That's the good news."

"And the bad?"

"I sent my men out to collect the take but something went wrong. My people are dead and the holders of our cash appear to have flown the coop."

"How big is the yield?"

"That's not well defined right now. We were waiting for a large haul but the only count I have comes from the radio so it's not reliable."

"What do you intend to do about it?"

"I will send a different crew to chase after the cash. So far what's left of the gang have been careful. They've burned evidence and kept under the police radar."

"Are they smart?"

"I wouldn't have said so. My step nephew is not the sharpest tool in the box."

"But he's been clever enough to steal the money from a bank, wipe out your people in a puff of smoke and still evade capture."

"Yes."

"So perhaps you should have the decency to give him the respect he deserves."

"Yep, it's the trouble with family—from the wrong side. It's a bad business but I shouldn't let it cloud my judgment. My apologies."

"Accepted, Frankie. How reliable is this second crew you are planning to send after them?"

"They are fine. I trust them—with my money if not my life."

Charlie laughed and Frankie was pleased to steal Anthony's words and turn them into a joke to lighten the mood.

"But what about with my money? That is the question, isn't it?"

"Of course."

"Just messing with you. We all have a vested interest in your success. Any help required, say."

"Thanks, Charlie. I wanted you to know what was happening. We are still only a handful of hours since they took the bank, so it's early days."

"Sounds like you are trying to tell me our money may be in the wind."

"It is possible. Hence my call."

"I appreciate you calling me. You were correct to do so: always pass on bad news quickly."

"That's what I expect of my people and I wanted to offer you the same curtesy."

"How certain are you that this second team will succeed where your first crew failed?"

"Pretty sure. Paul and Luigi were fine upstanding guys but you could never accuse Luigi of having too many brains. God rest his soul."

"Luigi? Shame, I knew his family well, but no one shall mourn his passing—not even his wife."

"That's for sure."

"Sounds to me you've underestimated your step nephew and overestimated your own people. Don't make that mistake again, Frankie. These errors can compound each other and become dangerous."

"I understand. But you need to know I won't be able to offer tribute tomorrow as I originally indicated."

"I figured that out myself, but again it is good to hear you voice these concerns instead of pretending they aren't out there."

"Thank you. I do these things because I respect you."

And because you'd whack me if I didn't.

"Once you have a reliable figure, tell me. And once you have the money, call me too."

"Of course."

"I ask a second time, is there anything I can do to help?"

"Not right now. They've left a trail of destruction in their wake but they're still on the road."

"The radio said there were deaths at the bank even before they torched that barn. Was it a rendezvous point?"

"Yes, it was. The good news is that Frank shared the plan with me in great detail as I was funding the venture. Once he's circled away from the Baltimore area, he will head for California. It's what's driven him to keep going all these months."

"I'll have a word with our west coast contacts and get them to prepare a welcoming committee."

"You need not do that just yet. They might not have left the state."

"You and I know they'll wave Maryland goodbye. The question in my mind is whether they will actually strike out for California or pick anywhere apart from there."

"I may have underestimated him as you say, but I saw his eyes light up every time he mentioned that state. If they leave Maryland then they'll head for the west coast."

"So be it. California will be the destination."

"Trouble is it's a long way from here to there."

"Frankie, send your people off on the trail at your end and I will handle any of the other details."

"Okay, Charlie. Thanks again."

"It's what I'm here for."

Click.

FRANKIE CALLED ANTHONY into his office.

"Pack your toothbrush, you're gonna be on the road for the next few days. Come back with the cash."

"Frank and the girl?"

"Get me my money. If they hand it over to you, then that's fine."

"And if they don't?"

"Find me my money, anyway. Two more dead bodies won't make much difference given the trail of blood they've already caused."

"Okay, boss."

"And if you find them alive and you want to keep them in that state then do so. I'm happy to have a conversation with them. But if you have to shoot them between the eyes, do it. There is no need for any of us to be precious around them."

"Sure thing."

"But remember, do not come back without the take and make certain your crew doesn't dip their fingers in the cash. Every dime is mine alone."

Anthony nodded and closed the door behind himself. This gave Frankie an opportunity to return to his porn journal and soak in the exquisite beauty of the naked girls on the pages.

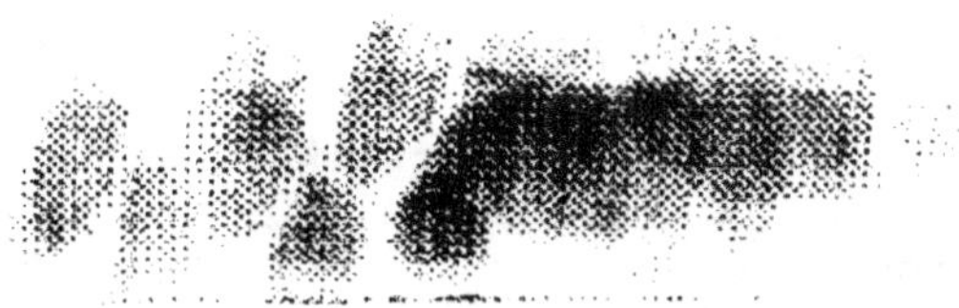

53

MARY LOU AND Frank walked out the diner and back toward the car.

"You drive for a while, okay?"

"Sure thing, Frank."

She adjusted the seat and the rearview mirror, fought the shift stick into first and pulled out of the space.

"What route are we taking? I have no idea how to get to Vegas from here."

Frank laughed.

"Neither do I. Hang on a minute."

He shut his eyes for five seconds and then opened them. Frank described how they'd go cross-country to Frederick off to the west and join the I-70 for a straight run to Pittsburgh. Beyond that was another day. She nodded.

"Let's hit the road."

She punched the gas pedal and they squealed out the lot.

"Take it easy, babe."

Mary Lou eased off the pedal and took the vehicle down to a sensible pace.

"Five miles an hour under all the way, right?"

"Got it, Frank."

Her voice contained no annoyance. Calm personified. He settled into his seat, folded his arms and focused on the road ahead. No mistakes, Mary Lou. No need to get pulled over by some lazy cop with a quota to fill. Before they'd stepped back into the Falcon, he'd walked round to check all the lights, a task he'd perform every stop they made from here to California. If they got that far.

"This sounds totally crazy, but I missed you today, babe."

"When?"

"From the moment we said goodbye and split up this morning. I didn't want you to go."

Mary Lou reached over and squeezed his knee then took it away for a gear change.

Ever since he got out of the penitentiary this time last year, their relationship had gone from distant to extremely close. Frank discovered how to be a loving human being. It had been quite a journey, but he was getting there.

"We've had a bumpy ride, but after our Miami trip things were good between us..."

"But?"

"But after this morning I don't know. I told myself that what happened with you and Carter stayed with you and Carter, and I haven't asked questions any more."

There was a silence in the cabin as they both recalled the argument they'd had on this same topic—only in a different car.

"What about Carter and the money? You didn't explain."

"It was complicated."

"Just tell me. I want to know."

Mary Lou sighed a deep heavy outpouring of breath.

"Carter has a gambling problem: he loses way more times than he wins. And Uncle Frank holds a forty thousand dollar marker on him, so he gave him a simple choice: take the money or spend the rest of his life paying off the debt. Refuse either option and finito."

"So…"

Frank was taking his time putting the pieces of the jigsaw together for himself. Mary Lou helped him out.

"Frankie ordered Carter to remove the cash from the bank on the morning of our hit. Either Carter followed his instructions and got Frankie the take or we did. Whichever way, Frankie wins."

"Uncle Frank?"

"Yes your uncle, Frank."

The words sank into Frank's skull. The man had always been so good to his ma and the family. To turn on him like this while pretending to only have his best interests to heart.

"And the barn was a double-cross?"

"I reckon. If Carter had succeeded, I'm sure he'd be buried in a field by now. He didn't even own a gun."

"And you held this back from me because…?"

"I couldn't see how you'd believe me. I doubt if you do now."

"The double-cross I believe. Paul and Luigi fired first. They were operating under orders. Paul wouldn't have been dumb enough to steal from Uncle Frankie and Luigi was plain too stupid."

"I just didn't know how to tell you, hon'. And the explosives?"

"A terrible mistake. I forgot. The stress of tying the damn things to those telegraph poles did me in. It took longer than I thought and I was so obsessed with getting them all done that flipping the switch flew out my head."

"And you expect me to accept that?"

"It's the truth. You believe what you need to."

"A cop car followed us out of town because that C4 didn't blow."

"What happened?"

"Was way behind for miles, then it kicked up an extra gear and passed us."

"Huh?"

"Yes. They must have been expecting something more like your Barracuda for a getaway vehicle and not a white van."

"Pete was a smart cookie."

"And a pain in the ass the rest of his waking hours."

He stretched out and rested his left hand on Mary Lou's thigh below her black miniskirt, occasionally stroking her skin as they talked.

"ARE WE BEING honest, Frank?"

"I've been. Yes."

"I'm scared, here in this car. With you."

Mary Lou felt Frank's fingers stiffen, which made her even more nervous.

"Because you see me as someone who's failed you, I can't be certain you have any faith in me at all. On top of that, the last job when you lost confidence in somebody they took a trip out a window. And you've already whacked Andrew today."

"He'd clipped Pete before we'd got away."

"Frank, I'm not saying you were wrong to take him out, but you have to admit you're a dangerous man to be around."

His fingers relaxed, but the stroking stopped. Mary Lou kept both hands on the wheel.

"And that makes me nervous. Especially when I look at what happened at the barn."

"What went down there?"

"After it was all over and you hopped in the car, I had no idea if you were going to drive off and leave me."

"Of course I wasn't, babe."

"But that's not how it felt. You were angry with me and you've said yourself you can't figure out if there was anything between Carter and me. So how am I supposed to know?"

The stroking started up again.

"It crossed my mind. It's true."

"If I was going to double-cross you, wouldn't I have struck a deal with Uncle Frankie or got Carter out the bank and run off with him or… beats me. There are a thousand ways you can punch someone in the face but only one way to kiss them."

"And do you love me?"

"I did this morning. Now I'm building up a wall so I don't get hurt by you. But I did earlier today."

This lie tripped off her tongue with remarkable ease. A week ago Frank was the one—or at least he was after Florida. Then the idea took hold in her that Carter was a better catch. That he had a stronger chance of getting the money and she should go with him instead.

Carter found the cajones to remove the cash from the vault but didn't leave the bank for whatever reason. That was the moment she stopped trusting him and loving him. If a guy can't do a simple thing, like keep his word, then he was not a man at all. Besides, Carter was always going to lift the money for Uncle Frankie but it was only the day before she discovered the game Frankie was playing with all of them. And she was right. Frank would never have believed her. The proof only existed at that point in Carter's words.

"Remember. Carter was just someone to get the crew into that vault and out without obstruction. What I did, I did. But for us."

"I know."

"Do you?"

"Not sure, to be honest. I want to believe you but there's so much up in the air right now. And what you're saying about Uncle Frankie."

"None of this easy."

"Nope."

Mary Lou kept them at a steady pace and passed through Cockeysville, a small nowhere town with a crossroads, shops and people who notice a stranger's car flying past even if it's not stopping. Both hands gripped the wheel and only relaxed when they were back on empty roads with fields or dirt either side of the road.

"You never answered my question."

"No? Which one?"

"Were you definitely going to wait for me at the barn?"

The hand stroked her again.

"When I left you with the matches… I was angry and I wasn't sure if you were with me or the take."

Mary Lou sighed. He was right and he was wrong. When she exited the parking lot at the bank she was following the money but by the time she arrived at the barn she was following Frank. That's hard to explain though—even to yourself sometimes.

"And when I appeared at the car?"

"You were there and I waited for you."

"Sure. But why?"

"Like I said before. I cared about you; I care about you but did I trust you at that precise moment today? Don't know, but I wanted to."

"I shot Paul so you would live. If I was so intent on getting hold of the money, and nothing more, then I'd have let him take you out and then clipped him. You were a sitting duck, Frank. Without me, you would be a corpse."

Mary Lou's words scratched deep inside Frank. This was the first time he'd had to consider today's events. She was kinda right but did that mean he could forgive her for what she did with Carter?

He ought to because he inserted her in the situation with the financial adviser. However now he'd seen the guy, so up close and personal, didn't remove the image of the two of them naked together from his mind's eye. It hurt each time it flashed across his brain. Yet part of that self-same thought—with Mary Lou's body in it—turned him on. The lust he felt for her was real and consistent. It was fucking her again that kept him going in prison. At night. Those lonely nights. After his first stint inside he understood why some men became fags in jail.

His hand moved up her thigh and under the skirt almost reaching her panties. She grabbed it and dragged it back nearer her knee.

"You won't be getting anywhere near that until we can trust each other."

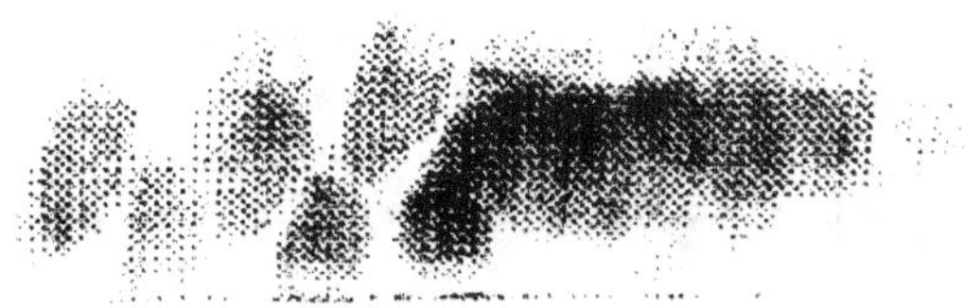

54

SILENCE FELL OVER them as they experienced the isolation of their own thoughts. Without admitting it to themselves or the other person, they both had been in the wrong and both had right on their side.

Mary Lou carried on driving, catching the occasional sign for Westminster forcing them to make a wide arc, leaving Lansdowne and the city of Baltimore behind and heading towards Frederick and the expressway beyond.

As they left Westminster, Frank tapped her thigh.

"Pull over, now!"

She slammed on the brake and drove off the road.

"What is it?"

"Saw me something of use."

Frank popped the trunk and grabbed what looked like a stick and ran back two hundred feet. Through her side mirror, Mary Lou watched as he took a screwdriver to the rear plates of a rusted carcass of a car standing with flat tires in a ditch. He replaced the Falcon's plates with his newfound spoils and dropped the old ones into the trunk.

"Pennsylvania plates. Spotted them as we flew past and soon we'll need them. Besides, if anyone has somehow figured out who we are along the way, this'll throw the cops off the scent."

"Paranoid but beautiful."

"That's me."

Mary Lou carried on down the highway, five miles an hour below the speed limit.

"Should we have waited until we crossed the state line for the new plates?"

"No, we're close enough to not raise suspicion from passersby. This way we look like we're returning home."

"There's a thin line between appearing to go home and looking like we are on the run."

"Sure but I can't see how the cops'd even know they were chasing a man and a woman, let alone knowing what we look like or what kind of car we're driving."

"Wasn't expecting this to be the getaway, Frank. I imagined the cars crammed with the crew laughing and celebrating."

"You and me both. We don't even know how big the take is. We have two bags stuffed with notes but that doesn't mean I have any idea how much we're talking about. How about you? You were in those vaults often enough."

"They brought in half a million yesterday to distribute to other branches so it's a lot. I shouldn't say this so soon but…"

"Our share of the haul has gone up in the last few hours. I know. Only thing is that without Frankie's connections and family discount, it will cost us more to clean the cash."

"We need to take care of that trunk. Should we bring the money inside, Frank?"

"It'll be safer where it is. The most likely problem we'll encounter is a traffic cop and those bags must be out of sight."

"Sure. Makes me nervous though."

"Yeah. It's quite a sum. Shame we can't spend a single cent of it yet."

"Really?"

"Not. One. Dime."

Frank squeezed her knee in time to his words to reinforce their importance as the Falcon continued on its journey from Westminster to Frederick. Dusk approached and as the light faded, more houses came next to the highway and eventually the outskirts of a town formed round them. She flipped the headlights on and three minutes later a neon sign appeared up ahead.

"Pull into the motel, babe."

She stopped the car near the reception and he walked inside. As she hung around the bank and Frank had worn a balaclava, he reckoned his face was less likely to be recognized than hers, even though he spent so much of his time walking the streets of Lansdowne these last nine months.

Five minutes later he emerged with a key and Mary Lou moved the car to park it outside their room. They dropped their two bags of cash on the bed and drew the curtains so they could open them and count the money in private.

They split up the notes into their respective denominations and then they each counted every pile. This was a simple way to spot errors and ensure they would agree on the final amount. Five hundred and fifty thousand dollars. Even losing most of it to whoever laundered the money, they could still live out their days like royalty.

Once they discovered the total, they put the notes into the cases, careful to keep the money split evenly.

"I'm hungry."

"Me too."

Taking the bags with them, they walked round the corner and along half a block where a fast-food chain had dumped a building. Thirty minutes later they were in the room filled with burger, fries and a shake. Mary Lou brought back her drink as she couldn't finish it at the burger bar.

"The trouble with you and me, Frank, is that we've known each other for a long time."

"Met in '62."

"We've both been through a lot of shit over the years."

"And?"

"And we've always been there for each other. Even in the bad times. Now the trust between us is breaking down. You think I'm in love with Carter and I think you're ready to dump me for the money. Right?"

"More or less."

"Today has been one hell of a day but we're never moving back to Lansdowne and you are never returning to your family. What has past is long gone. We only have what we've brought into this room: you, me and the take. If you're not satisfied with that then we should separate now because it will not get any easier if we stay together and the other wants to leave."

"Do you want to split, Mary Lou?"

"No. That's what I've been saying to you this afternoon. I choose to be with you. I chose you over Carter because you are the better man, Frank Lagotti. In the car I got to thinking how much we need each other. Not just to escape the cops today but how you fill me up. How you are a part of me."

"I don't want us to split up either."

"Then we shouldn't."

"But I gotta tell you I find it hard to think about what the two of you got up to."

"Then don't think about it Frank because I can't spend the rest of my life apologizing to you for extracting information from Carter Reinfeldt. It's what you wanted me to do and you never said there were any restrictions on how I should go about doing it."

Frank nodded. They both sat on the end of the bed as there was nowhere else for the two of them to perch. He returned his hand to her leg, just as though they were still sitting in the car.

"And I won't keep asking you if you'll drive off and leave me. If we're with each other, it has to be because we want to be."

"Mary Lou, you're right. If we trust each other then we depend on each other. And if we don't we've got nothing."

She nodded in return and kissed him on the lips.

"Let's go to bed."

He undressed first and snuck under the covers still in his shorts. She came out of the bathroom and removed her blouse then her skirt as he stared at her rose tattoo which peeped out from her pubes and headed up until it nearly reached her belly button. She slipped off her bra and panties and lay beside him.

Frank threw his shorts onto the floor, rolled over to face her and wrapped himself around her body until his groin moved just below the rose. Mary Lou didn't push him away.

CHARLIE PENTANGELO PUT the phone down on Frank Lagotti Senior. He had already listened to the radio to know the robbery had taken place and had been waiting for the call so he could press the button on the money laundering. The last thing he wanted to hear was the take was on the lam.

Ordinarily, Charlie would have shrugged this off but the news broadcast had mentioned a heist value much higher than any sum Frankie had offered him. This meant either Frankie was withholding money from him or that the bank was involved in an insurance scam by overinflating its claim.

If Frankie was hiding money that was the same as stealing from the Bonanno Family. The punishment for that crime was anything from having your hand cut off through to death, depending on the sum involved. If the bank was lying to the insurers then this created its own set of problems. While Frank had selected the First Bank of Baltimore for logistical reasons to make a heist most successful, he had picked a financial institution where the Bonannos had made a series of investments.

Banks inflate figures only to hide losses and this sum was big. The implication was clear: if the bank was claiming more than had been stolen in Lansdowne that was because the amount was gone elsewhere and needed to be recouped. Chances were that was Bonanno money which had been silently lost.

Charlie made a mental note to instigate some enquiries about their First Bank of Baltimore investments. The chief executive would receive a phone call and that should straighten matters out.

The other outstanding issue was that Charlie's cash was in the wind and if Frankie was stealing from him, then he couldn't be trusted to recover all the take and deliver it for laundering. That meant only one thing: Charlie must recapture the money himself.

Pentangelo picked up the receiver and made a local call.

"Hi there."

"I told you not to phone me."

"This is an emergency: I need your assistance in a small matter."

"How small?"

"Some objects of mine have gone missing and I'd like you to help me find them."

"The usual recovery fee?"

"Of course. And given the importance of the materials to me, there'll be a healthy bonus if you succeed."

"And the location of the items is known?"

"Not precisely but we know the individuals holding them right now. My people will fill you in with the details. You'd better pack a suitcase; it'll take a few days to track them down."

55

TED GOODWIN HOPPED out of his vehicle and walked into the Lansdowne branch of the First Bank of Baltimore. The call had come through at five past nine and by the time he arrived, there was a police line in situ and he had to fight his way to the front: the numbers of passersby who'd stopped to stare was remarkable for an ordinary Tuesday morning.

He flashed his detective's badge and the officer let him duck under the tape and go into the bank. The first thing he noted was the sheer quantity of blood—it looked like the robbers had smeared red over the floor and the walls. A uniform stood near the door as a defense in case someone crossed the line.

"How many dead?"

"Two out back we reckon but the bodies turned to ash when they set the van alight."

"Injured?"

"Three in hospital and the rest in shock."

"What happened to the three?"

"The security guard was pistol-whipped and was unconscious when they took him out. Another man shot in the groin and one cashier… Well, they slashed her breast, sir."

"Where are the rest of the staff?"

"Right now we have them all in the manager's office, but it's pretty cramped. Doubt if we can keep them there much longer."

"Until we've got enough vehicles to take them back to the station, let's hold them where they are. It won't be long and they're out of the way."

The officer nodded and Goodwin moved tentatively around the bank trying to figure out what happened and when. Once they interviewed the staff, they should have a reasonable picture. Goodwin spotted Sam Parrish squatting next to a pool of blood, so he scooted over.

"Hey Sam. Here before me. What you see and what you got?"

"Yeah, I was round the corner buying a coffee."

"Did you get here before they left?"

"Nah. The cashier only pressed the alarm after the perps had exited via the back door."

"And then they killed two out the rear?"

"Yep. It's all strange. From what one cashier was saying: the money hadn't been in the vault but an employee, Carter Reinfeldt, had taken it."

"Say again."

"Sounds crazy, but it definitely happened."

"Any news on the identities of the bodies in the parking lot?"

"You're kidding, right? Have you been out there yet? They torched a sports car and stuffed what we think are a pair of corpses inside before they lit it."

"How are we so sure there's two if the car's been in flames?"

"There were twin bursts of gunfire. One happened when at least two of the gang were in this room and the other burst occurred after they departed."

"Are all bank staff accounted for?"

"Yes, so the bodies are likely to be crew members, not civilians."

This case would take a while to crack. Dead 'uns, money stolen from bank staff who'd pilfered it from the bank.

"And the vault?"

"Clean as a nun's conscience."

Sam pointed to a security door next to the counters. Goodwin followed the finger and entered the staff-only area. Cashier desks to one side and a corridor in front. As he walked along the narrow space, Goodwin noticed a kitchen and a locker room.

At the far end, by the exit was a staircase leading downwards. At the bottom of the stairs: a wall filled with deposit boxes and on the opposite side behind bars was the safe itself. It was open and there was no sign of the large denomination notes. None of the security boxes appeared disturbed.

The gang come down here to take the money. At least one guy upstairs to maintain order over the staff. Possibly more. Someone's hit the safe before you so you'll be spitting venom by the time you get back up top. Then you torture people to find out where the cash is.

Goodwin couldn't understand it: two hits on the same bank on the same day. That was a new one. So unlikely it couldn't be true, could it?

What next? You scream for the money and the staff look blankly at you. Reinfeldt knows but doesn't say and lets a woman get slashed for her troubles. Gangs rely on bank staff to hand over the loot in a breath because it's covered by the insurance. Policy would demand they hand it over but still Reinfeldt refuses. How did he give the game away?

Strange fact number two: if they were professionals and they had the money, why shoot Reinfeldt? Why the unnecessary violence? They'd be able to interview him in the next day or so—assuming he survived. The chances were he was part of the gang and had tried to double cross them.

Detective Goodwin sauntered upstairs and popped his head into the locker room and kitchen, but neither appeared to be the source of anything interesting. The boys would have a look-round before they left.

Ted made his way out the back into the parking lot. He gagged with the stench and covered his mouth and nose with his handkerchief. The last fire wagon was heading off to leave a husk of a car— black, charred—and a large puddle of water hiding any forensics that might have been on the ground.

He peered into the remains of the automobile and made out two bodies—one dumped across the front seats and the other at the back. Doors were open, but the fire had done its worst. Shards of melted glass lay on the floor. They came prepared to burn evidence: no matter what happened for two people to get killed, they were expecting to destroy a vehicle here. And why were the pair dead? An unsuspecting civilian bumped into the waiting getaway driver, perhaps. That doesn't explain the second body though. Strange fact number three.

Goodwin walked out the parking lot onto the street and made his way left, then same again two hundred feet later, to arrive at the front of the bank. Into his car and back to the station to interview the staff before their memory for details faded.

TED SAT AT his desk and stared at his typewriter. Most bank jobs were simple affairs: some men enter a building, take the money and leave. End of story. But this was peculiar around the edges and plain weird in the middle. His phone rang and he carried on focusing on his typing. The ringing continued until he snapped out of his thoughts and picked up the receiver.

"Detective Goodwin."

"The staff from the robbery have arrived. They're in the interview rooms."

"Thanks. I'll be right down."

Goodwin headed over to meet Sam organizing drinks and food for the witnesses.

"How are they shaping up?"

"Fine under the circumstances. All seem eager to help but it's hard to tell if they know anything."

"What we got?"

"Bank manager, assistant manager, deputy manager, cashier. Other cashier, the security guard and financial advisor in hospital."

"I'll take the bank manager and the assistant. You take the deputy and the cashier. First one to finish gets the donuts."

He winked and walked off to bring Joshua Hunkerton into an interview room. Food and a coffee arrived a few minutes later and Goodwin waited for the guy to settle down. He sat with a straight back and a dignified air the whole time.

"How're you doing?"

"I'm fine. Shaken, you understand and obviously concerned about poor Miss. Galtieri and Mr. Grimble."

"The cashier and the guard?"

"Yes."

"You didn't mention Carter Reinfeldt."

"Well, it looks as though he was involved with those people, so forgive me if I'm less worried about that fellow."

"We'll come back to that later. Let's go over the events of the morning a piece at a time, starting with your arrival at the bank. What time was that?"

They burrowed through the minutiae from Hunkerton's breakfast rituals through to the moment just after nine when three men wearing balaclavas entered the building and announced the start of a stick-up.

Hunkerton was in his office. The gang came in and forced him at gunpoint to join the others in the middle of the floor in the customer area. One of the crew made them lie face down and the other two left to go to the vault. A few minutes later, they returned empty handed. The leader was furious and threatened him to say where the money was.

"I didn't understand. I had opened the safe as usual at eight in good time for some smaller denominations to be taken upstairs by the cashiers. I was dumbfounded. I'm sure that made the felon more angry, but I plain had no answer. That is when he walked over to Miss. Galtieri and…"

The bank manager sank into silence as he recalled Frank taking a knife and slashing open her breast to force Hunkerton to spill his guts. But he had nothing to say. And the blood…

"Then what happened?"

"They looked like they would give up. Him and the fellow who had been with us earlier."

"What about the third guy?"

Hunkerton squinted to improve his memory.

"I don't recall him being in the room at that point."

"Go on."

"The leader strode over to Mr. Reinfeldt and demanded the money from him. It was as though he knew him but Carter didn't do a thing. So the man upturned Mr. Reinfeldt's desk to reveal two bags. He took them and made to leave but then he stopped, turned round and shot poor Carter in the…"

Another introspective silence as the image of the red pool forming around Carter's groin returned inside his head. And the screaming. Carter had lapsed into unconsciousness before the robbers had gone out of the staff corridor.

"Did you hear any shots?"

"Only after they left. Two, I believe. Then a roar and Mrs. Pieck was brave enough to move and press the alarm."

Goodwin checked a few more details and then was done with him. Meantime, Sam had interviewed the deputy manager, George Hunkerton.

"Related by any chance?"

"Yes Ted. My Hunkerton is the son of yours. And I figured out why such a small branch needed an assistant and a deputy. My Hunkerton couldn't find the end of his nose."

"Good that nepotism is alive and well in the banking industry."

"For sure. And we're not even in Alabama. But the goofball had one useful thing to offer. While they were being minded, my Hunkerton heard a single shot go off."

"He's certain of this?"

"Told me he'd already pissed himself when the gang came into the bank and he was trying to hold it together by listening to anything happening outside the room. And he definitely caught a gunshot while two of them were in the building."

"So one left early and clipped the fourth?"

"That's what I'm thinking."

"But why?"

"Beats the hell out of me."

"What did your little Jimmy have to say about Reinfeldt?"

"Not much. The guy had a roving dick and problems at home but George knew nothing about the money."

"Trouble?"

"Reinfeldt transferred over to the Lansdowne branch after he slept with a young floozie at his previous office. Now he was carrying on with a customer. Been seeing her for months, apparently."

"Where is she?"

"Not clear as yet but I'll work on it."

"And was anything else happening at home?"

"Dunno. He and his wife have no children but they weren't happy. Not getting along. That's all I got so far."

"Let's keep going and catch up later. The girlfriend might tell us if Reinfeldt was mixed up with the gang. One of the uniforms can put together a description from all the staff. If we're lucky, we'll even get an address."

56

FORTY-FIVE MINUTES later a blue-and-white called in a blaze on the outskirts of town. The uniform had been chasing a suspicious vehicle when the smoke hurtled into the air. He'd swung back to find a barn on fire and steel shells billowing flames.

Goodwin left Sam to finish the interviewing and hightailed it northeast of Lansdowne via the scenic route to Philadelphia. A pair of melted cars in an hour were too much of a coincidence in a day filled with them. This marked the trail of the gang out of town.

When he arrived there three uniforms in front of the barn and two fire trucks. Smoke was still visible, but no flames were in view from the highway. What once had been an outbuilding lay in seared carbon on the floor, one corner of a wall refusing to collapse. Behind this mess was rough ground containing a melted vehicle with another blob of former cars standing on the edge of the field.

Goodwin strode around the devastation at the front and reached the vehicles, where uniforms and a medic were hard at work.

"Hey, doc."

"Hi Ted. Quite a morning."

"Telling me. What you got?"

"Three bodies all piled into a van and torched. The fire service arrived in time for them to douse the crime scene in gallons of water. But at least the corpses are partially intact. By which I mean there are clearly three Caucasian males thrown in the back of that vehicle: all shot. The boys have already searched for shells in the vicinity."

"Thanks, doc."

"More for you once these fricasseed felons are back to the lab."

The detective winced at the pathologist's gallows humor. Goodwin was facing a major robbery with violence and five dead souls. Word from above was that the take had been over a million. Unimaginable. What was a small-town bank doing with that much cash in its vault?

Who knew? Someone had piled those bodies into the van and had sufficient gas to burn the fucking lot up in smoke—just like at the bank. They had been prepared and there must be at least one of them still alive. Chances were they were in a vehicle this minute high-speeding out of Baltimore and, most likely, out the state too.

Without a description, all he had was person or persons of unknown gender and racial profile. So he had nothing to hang his hat on. Just a trail of carnage running parallel with the I-295. Trouble was they were only ten minutes away from the 895 which meant the person or persons unknown drove from the vicinity east or west and he'd have no way of knowing in which direction to try. This would need to be a mighty wide net to cast.

Instead of focusing on the great unknowns, Goodwin examined what was visible to him, in front of his nose. Eye witnesses reported seeing a white Ford Econoline leaving the bank area after the robbery and he was standing next to the shell of a van right now. There was a saloon, a once-feisty sports car and a beast of a Cadillac. He recognized the logo lying on the floor.

Presumably the saloon and Barracuda were used by crew members now deceased but the Caddy? It didn't fit. Perhaps the inhabitants came to meet the crew. If bullets flew that meant there was some disagreement and discussions went south from that point. So he either had the gang in the back of the van and the owners of the limo ran off with the money or vice versa.

A glimmer of good news for this crime scene was the collection of slugs found by the uniforms. There were five different calibers bagged up and ready for inspection. Five guns and only five people in total: anyone holding a knife to this gunfight would be first into the back of the van. With three dead, there were only one or two at large.

His best bet was a search for a single vehicle with two inside. What kind? Dunno but probably a saloon. What do the people look like? Arms, legs, torsos, a head each and a million dollars in the trunk.

Goodwin scuffed the scorched earth with his foot and came back to his car. He sat inside and knew this was not enough information to keep his boss happy.

When he returned to the station, his prediction proved accurate.

"Goodwin. Looks like you got jack for me."

Lieutenant Fred Hester stared at Ted over his glasses while seated at his desk. Goodwin remained at attention.

"Tomorrow's headlines will say the Baltimore Police Department knows zip about a million dollar heist. No description. Nothing. We don't even know how many are alive in the perps' gang."

"They are professionals, sir. Covered their tracks well. In our favor is Reinfeldt in hospital, who stole the money before the crew hit the joint. Doctors say he's survived surgery and when he regains consciousness, we can interview the hell out of him."

"Is that the only lead?"

"There's also his girlfriend who visited him most days these past nine months. Even though uniforms stayed at the bank all day, she hasn't appeared. Sounds like she's hit the road. If she doesn't show tomorrow then she has gone for certain."

"And what about today? I can't believe your best idea is to hang around and wait a while."

"The chances are they've flown the coop. I think we should call on the resources of the FBI, sir."

NO POLICE FORCE likes to seek federal assistance. It's almost written into the Constitution, but Lieutenant Hester had little choice. They had a violent armed robbery and an enormous haul to chase down with no tangible leads to work with. The press was baying at the Mayor's feet and soon they'd be clamoring for his blood. It was the natural way of things. Hester gave the order for Goodwin to place the call.

"Outside line, please."

He dialed the number and waited until a girl on reception answered. He explained his mission and she put him on hold.

"Phil McNamara. How can I help?"

"Detective Ted Goodwin of the Baltimore Police Department. We need your assistance."

"I thought we might get a call from you. No offense, but our Intel informed us you've quite a case on your hands."

"Well, yes."

"Look, I know asking for our support wasn't easy and I don't want to tread on anyone's toes, okay?"

"For sure."

"I'm in the area so why don't we meet in an hour's time. Does that work for you?"

"Sure, Phil."

"Gather what you got and we'll take it from there, Ted. See you at your station house in an hour."

Sixty one minutes later, Phil McNamara arrived at Goodwin's desk. The piano had stopped playing the minute he entered the building and you could hear a pin drop within two hundred feet of where McNamara stood.

Goodwin hustled him into an interview room and fetched him a coffee. And brought a cup each for himself and for Sam.

"Thanks for coming."

"Don't mention it. Just to be clear: I'm not here to take over your case. I'm here to offer you resources you can't access so we can catch the bad guys."

"Okay."

He knew not to trust Hoover men: their reputation traveled before them but this guy appeared reasonable—at first glance at any rate.

"What do you need from us right now?"

"We're sitting on a lot of burned corpses and no identities to attach to them so anything to help with that…"

"You got it."

"And we have a poor description of a girl who is a person of interest with no address for her."

"Give me what you have and we'll see if we can figure something out for you."

"Right. Also, it doesn't take a genius to work out they ain't staying in Maryland."

"One step at a time, Ted. Once we have a better idea of who we are looking for then yes, I'll get sufficient men on the ground to search for them interstate. We don't have enough to wipe our asses right now. No offense intended. Just saying what needs to be said."

"None taken. My boss isn't the least bit happy to see you—as you no doubt know. But Sam and I are fine with anyone who can help us catch these guys. They slashed a woman in the tit for Christ's sake."

"How's she doing?"

"Twenty stitches and she'll be on the road to recovery in a few days. Her biggest issue at the time was the amount of blood she lost. Next week, the docs tell her she's scarred for life."

McNamara nodded and allowed everyone's thoughts about Theresa Galtieri's tit to hang in the air for ten seconds. Then he sighed and carried on.

"They'll get theirs. Robbery with violence at a state bank, murder in the first degree, arson. Sounds like the gas chamber to me."

"Phil, now who's getting ahead of himself?"

Goodwin smiled at McNamara, who returned the favor.

"You're right. Just want to get to the end of the journey."

Sam had been silent until then, allowing his older colleague to take the lead.

"Do you need to pitch tent here or are you in the local FBI store?"

"Here would be good. I used to live in Baltimore but moved away five years ago."

"Where are you staying?"

"In a nearby hotel. Don't worry. I'll be okay. This is how I spend my life—on the road living out of a suitcase."

"The least we can do is take you out tonight for a bite to eat and a drink."

"Sounds like a mighty fine plan. Is there somewhere with a phone to call the cavalry?"

WEDNESDAY JUNE 18

57

MARY LOU WOKE first and enjoyed the time to stare at Frank and feel the warmth of his body next to hers. He appeared to be back on her side. She only hoped his words would translate into action and he wasn't about to double cross her. There was a lot of cash in those bags and people make bad decisions because of money.

She dozed twice and finally remained awake. Frank had rolled over to face her and had draped an arm on her hip. It slithered down to land between her legs. His eyes were shut, but he was conscious. Mary Lou took his fingers and placed them on her groin.

One of Frank's eyelids opened and stared at her, soaking in her head and upper torso—all he could see without moving his neck.

"Sorry babe, but we should get going."

"I know."

He removed his hand and kissed her rose, got up and threw on their only set of clothes.

"We can't wear these things all the way to Vegas."

"Better buy some more."

They checked their cash and realized they had enough for gas and some diner meals but not much else. A thrift store would be handy and if they couldn't find one, they'd have to be creative.

Back to the diner for breakfast with their bags and into the car for Frank's turn to drive. Before he hit the expressway, which ran round the edge of town, they drove until they found just the right place.

They could tell by the quality of the eaterie in what part of Frederick they'd landed: there was a lot of grease and not much else but the coffee wasn't bad. A store with clothes for next to nothing was an inevitable consequence of the local demographic. Frank and Mary Lou hopped into the place and grabbed jeans, a tee-shirt each and underwear. They each threw one top into the shopping basket too for some variety. He also found a jacket to hide his handgun and back to the motel so they could change before the journey.

"We've spent too long here. We'll need to make a move before people notice we're hanging around."

"Sure. A sweep of the room before we go. Let's not leave any incriminating evidence behind—like a black bag or two."

Out the door, into the car. he hit the gas pedal hard until they joined the on-ramp for Pittsburgh.

ROCK 'N' ROLL continued to spit out the speakers and Frank drove and tapped on the steering wheel in time to the warped blues of the music. Over the years Mary Lou had got used to Frank's taste though it was far from her favorite. She was a Country and Western girl.

On the hour the news cut into the musical extravaganza to reveal the FBI had been called in.

"We've dead people strewn all over Lansdowne. That was inevitable even if you ignore the size of the take."

The broadcast carried on to say the haul was over one million dollars.

"Brilliant. The bank's doing an insurance fraud! Why else would they lie about how much we stole from them?"

"Don't know but it will not be good."

"Yep. Let's make some distance between us and Maryland. Then we'll deal."

"Sure Frank."

He drove for ten miles, both sitting in silence while the world flew by five below the speed limit.

"We need to get off the freeway."

"Why's that?"

"If the FBI are on our trail, they'll man the largest roads so we should avoid them while the Hoover men put up road blocks."

"Good point."

Two miles later and he left the expressway. He didn't want to turn up at a gas station to buy a map because that would make them too visible. Instead Frank used his vague memory of the countryside and a careful eye on the signs to help them wend their way to their destination.

Vehicle after vehicle in Frank's rearview mirror looked like a G-man to him. The cropped hair and inky black color of the car conspired in his mind to equate to an unmarked FBI team. He would take extra side roads to lose them and they'd stop following him but another unmarked car appearing further down the route would only feed the fire in his head.

"Do you think they've found us so soon?"

"No idea. I'm just being cautious."

"The only way to catch us is if someone saw you and I leave the barn, but there wasn't anyone for miles around."

"Apart from that cop car that screamed by."

"Yeah, but it didn't stop us—twice. If they were doing something, they'd have pulled us over then."

"I s'pose."

"And they don't have either of our descriptions and you swapped the plates. Frank, they've got shit."

"We still need to be careful."

"I know. All's I'm saying is that losing FBI cars that aren't there is slowing us down. Take it easy, hon'."

Despite her words, he kept off the expressway and rattled along the narrower roads in and out of towns with no names. The Falcon trundled out the other side and they headed towards the next place further down their route.

One hour later and the vehicle edged into yet another conurbation—only this time it was the outskirts of Frederick, announced by the usual signage: 'Welcome to Frederick'. Frank drove past a used car lot and a diner stood immediately after on the right-hand side.

"Let's pull in here. If you're correct about the Feds, we can get back on the expressway and be in Pittsburgh before midnight."

ANOTHER MEAL COMPRISING a burger and fries. Frank ordered a coffee and she took a vanilla shake.

"Is this all we're eating?"

"You still hungry, babe?"

"No, I mean there's more to life than flipped burgers."

"Mary Lou, once we get to our destination we can eat steaks for the rest of our lives. Right now, we need to keep under everyone's radars, so that means coming to a lot of crappy diners and having the shit food. That way we fade into the background, never to be noticed or remarked upon."

"Sure, Frank."

"But places like this do sell good homemade desserts."

Mary Lou's eyes lit up and she ordered a piece of key lime pie as soon as she caught the waitress's eye. The dessert gave Mary Lou a frisson of nostalgia for her childhood. There wasn't much for her to remember that was positive but the treat of her mom baking key lime pie for Sunday afternoons before her father died enabled a small ripple of happiness to echo on her face.

"We'll take turns at the wheel, okay?"

"Of course, Frank. As long as we are creating some distance between here and us, everything'll be fine."

"There's more to it than leaving Maryland. We must sort out something with our packages."

Both pairs of eyes pointed below the table to reinforce the circumspect language Frank chose whenever civilians surrounded him and he needed to talk business. Once his look returned above the ceramic surface, he glanced around the room to check everyone—if they'd reacted to his words and if anyone appeared too intent on their conversation. He eased back into the seat of their booth until he slumped onto his coccyx. Mary Lou realized the rest of the world was eating, sitting and chatting as the afternoon degraded into the night.

Like every diner in America, there were truckers on their own taking a pit stop before the next leg of their cross-country haul. Frank noticed they always sat at the counter—almost as if they wouldn't allow themselves the comfort of a booth or a normal table. There was an occasional couple, chowing down before they heading home to destroy their brains on beer and game shows hosted by men who used to be comedians.

One exception to this scenario sat next to Frank and Mary Lou: a mother and her child. The child was three, maybe four but no older.

"Sit on the seat like a good boy."

A pair of feet appeared on the shared backrest between Mary Lou and the kid. She twisted as she noticed small movements in her peripheral vision. The legs disappeared and were replaced by his head. The boy was staring straight at her.

"Eat your burger like a good boy."

The skull bobbed down and resurfaced as soon as Mary Lou turned away to resume her conversation with Frank. She looked back at him and he vanished for a second time but she was not in the mood. She scowled at him until he cried and leaped off the seat to perch next to his ma on the other side of the table, far from Mary Lou.

The woman hugged the boy and stroked his forehead. With his mother's attention secured, the tears stopped flowing.

"You shouldn't bother the lady. Remember: nice things happen to boys who behave nicely."

Mary Lou eavesdropped on this maternal advice and pondered for a second. Was that true? What did it say about her time with Frank?

"You all right?"

"Yes thanks. Just thinking is all."

"Don't make a habit out of it."

He winked and squeezed her hand. She smiled back, knowing he was not demeaning her. The trust between them was building.

"We will need to hit the road. Are you okay to take a turn behind the wheel?"

"Yeah. I prefer it to being a passenger."

"Me too. Watching America fly by is no fun, is it?"

"Nah. Do you think we'll make it?"

Frank looked into Mary Lou's eyes, boring a hole straight through.

"It won't be easy but we have an advantage: we've no idea quite what our route will be. So no one else can predict it either."

Mary Lou nodded.

"You reckon they're after us?"

"You can bet on it."

"Everyone?"

"Everyone who's breathing. Yes."

Mary Lou imagined the Feds and Uncle Frankie sending out their hordes to capture them.

"But we'll be okay?"

"We're ahead of them now. All we have to do is keep going and once we clean up our act, we will be home and dry."

Frank emphasized the word 'clean' to ensure she understood what he meant. Mary Lou felt better hearing his reassurance but she could not tell if he was only boosting both of them up before the first of a long series of car hops.

"Home and dry."

She mulled the phrase over her tongue to hear how it sounded out loud. She didn't remember a time in her existence when she'd felt home and dry. So the idea this state was around the corner from her seemed alien.

"Will we have a home one day?"

"Sooner than you think. Once this is behind us, we can settle down and start a whole new life for ourselves."

She took Frank's hand in hers and stroked her thumb over the back of his fingers. They leaned forward over the table and kissed.

"You love birds good or you want the check?"

The waitress waded into their moment and dissolved it to nothingness.

"Check'll do."

58

ANTHONY FACED TWO major problems with following Frankie's orders. First, he had no guys to bring with because Luigi and Paul had been incinerated earlier in the day. Second, he had no idea which way Frank and Mary Lou were heading.

The initial problem was resolved with a quick call or two. Mickey agreed to help as there was money attached to the deal and he had nothing else on the cards the next day or so. Bobby was harder to track down because he was in greater demand. While he was a paid goon like Mickey, rumor had it that he was a mob hitman, so he was tough, tenacious and took no quarter. Precisely the dude you want on your side when you're chasing across the country to kill people and get your hands on their pile of cash.

Anthony waited three hours for Bobby to finish a job he was on. If he was on your team, you needed patience and not to ask too many questions on his whereabouts. If he wanted an alibi, you gave him one. By late afternoon he was free and Anthony gained his attention. A large amount of money as a finder's fee proved sufficient to motivate Bobby onto Anthony's crew.

His two new recruits met Anthony on the outskirts of town at the Kitkatt Club because nobody asked questions in a strip joint. The lights were low and Anthony could get a discount by having a boss who owned the flophouse. There had to be some advantages to living in a crap heap like Baltimore.

Anthony positioned himself at the back of the auditorium so there were no tables behind them: no one to notice them arrive or leave. He ordered a bottle of scotch from the big-tittied girl who wandered by holding a tray and only wearing a pair of purple panties.

Once she'd delivered the hooch, he told her to scram but pushed a Jackson into the front of her only item of clothing so she didn't feel too bad or remember too much of what he looked like. Then he waited for his guests to make their way to the club.

Within fifteen minutes they sat, drank and made plans.

"Do we have any idea where the bums are heading Anthony?"

"Mickey, Frank said he was doing the job to go to California. Told Frankie several times."

"You reckon he's clever enough for a double bluff?"

"No Bobby. Besides when he mentioned it he thought Frankie was on his side and had no reason to lie."

"So you think they ran straight out west?"

"That's not Frank's way. His plan was to head east a while and then double back westwards."

"Should we try to follow his tracks?"

"Worth spending a morning on it. If we get a sniff then fine. If not then we just turn tail and think like a fugitive who's aiming to end up on the other side of the country without getting caught along the way."

"I can do one better than that."

"How Bobby?"

"I know a guy who might know a guy."

"And?"

Mickey sounded impatient, but he was smart enough not to let his annoyance at Bobby show through too much.

"And this dude has a connection in the FBI. They'll have been pounding the pavement today asking the same questions as we just did only they've got a shiny badge and a lot of men on the ground to do the searching. I'll put a call through and see if he can give us a nod."

Although Frankie told him he was only really interested in retrieving his money, Anthony knew the best result would be to walk into the auto repairs with the bags of cash, the two of them tied up and still alive. But if only one of those things happened, he had better have the take.

"So we hit the road to Philly in the morning."

The other two nodded and all three settled in to watch the show. As their conversation ended, two girls—one black, one white—were slowly removing bikini tops on stage while a third sprayed oil over her torso and walked near enough to the edge of the stage so that patrons could seize the opportunity to stuff greenbacks into her hot pants.

An hour later, Anthony spotted Frankie walking across the room and a table set for him near the front of the auditorium. Anthony nudged Mickey with his elbow.

"My boss has just sat down. Time for us to split. He'll want to think we're spending every waking minute searching for his nephew."

Mickey nodded and Bobby shrugged. The hit man didn't really see the point of watching girls not quite take all their clothes off for tips. If he bought a whore, he just paid for a slut and didn't bother pretending otherwise. A man after Frankie's heart.

Under different circumstances, Mickey would have spent a hundred or two on the girls only to see them wrap themselves in circles on stage. He never paid for ass but he was a sucker for a floor show. Anthony occupied so much of his time waiting for Frankie at the Kitkatt, he forgot there was tit on display. He thought of the place as a glorious liquor bar and nothing more—unless he felt like an afternoon fuck.

With the bottle empty, he threw down sufficient notes to cover the cost of another round of scotch and called it a night. He knew they had some long days ahead of them.

"See you outside this joint at seven. We've got a lot of driving to do."

Mickey and Bobby nodded while staring at a bouncing nipple on stage. Anthony shrugged and headed home for a good night's rest.

ANGELO BIANCHI PUT the phone down after Charlie Pentangelo hung up and remained sat down for three minutes. This gave him enough time to conjure up a plan. He considered what he would pack in his overnight case and who he would call to join him on the hunt for a bag of money and two heads on a plate.

He stood up, walked into his bedroom and squatted by his open wardrobe to pull out a soft leather holdall he used on these occasions. Angelo threw in shorts, socks, a spare pair of pants, two shirts and some toiletries. Then he grabbed a box from under the bed to remove a pump-action shotgun and a revolver, along with enough ammo to last a week on a firing range. With the rifle in the holdall, Angelo placed the pistol in a holster he wore under his jacket. He always exited the apartment wearing a black three piece suit and a brown fedora. Today was no exception.

Mulberry Street was a shabby place to live but he called it home. Along the street, left two blocks and right one brought him to a small restaurant where men in suits sat at tables and talked in hush tones. He melted into this tableau and waited.

Soon a sallow complexion of a man appeared opposite and ordered a double espresso. Angelo nodded at him and leaned in, elbows on the white tablecloth. The new arrival mirrored his position.

"Thanks for coming at short notice, Rico."

This nickname hung around his neck since his childhood. Before he'd been a mobster, he had loved gangster movies and Rico was his favorite character. Now he lived the dream.

"Happy to help a friend, Angelo. What seems to be the problem?"

"We have two fugitives carrying money that is not theirs. Our job is to retrieve the cash."

"And the escapees?"

"My associates don't care about them. Alive or dead. It doesn't matter: it's the money. Their bodies breathing or otherwise is of secondary importance."

"But there's benefit to them being conscious?"

"I am sure if we hauled their asses back with us, some appreciation would be shown."

Rico sat in his chair for a minute, pondered and sipped his coffee. After two mouthfuls, he added a small amount of sugar.

"Where's the cash now?"

"Location unknown. The ultimate destination is California according to the Shylock whose problem has been dumped on our laps."

"Where did the money start its journey?"

"Baltimore. The good news is that the FBI is on their tail and my associates have connections there who can give us the inside track."

"Although I have no desire to pry, Angelo, by any chance did the green reside within a bank until recently?"

"That is my understanding."

"Holy Mary. That's a lot of cash to chase down."

"We should assume we are not the only ones with an interest in the recovery of the money. I expect the Shylock has sent after it and if he succeeds, then my associates will be happy but you and I won't receive a dime for our time."

"So we need to be the first to the greens."

Rico nodded again, mulling over the conversation.

"Where to then?"

"If you were running for your life to the Pacific, how would you get there without drawing attention?"

"Car or bus."

"Yep. And if you wanted to clean the dirty money along the way?"

Rico thought for ten seconds.

"Vegas."

"Why?"

"Casinos and enough Shylocks to cut a deal fast."

"I agree. I think they'll be sufficiently desperate to head straight for the biggest concentration of mobsters outside the Big Apple and the Windy City."

"When shall we leave?"

"We fly tonight and hole up until they catch up with us."

"And if we're wrong about Vegas?"

"I'll check in with our associates so we keep abreast of the Feds. Those G-men know how to track a fella down to the ends of the world."

Rico smiled. He enjoyed working with Angelo. The man had a good head on him: looked for the angles but was a stand-up guy when times were tough and bullets were flying. They finished their drinks and headed for LaGuardia.

Thursday June 19

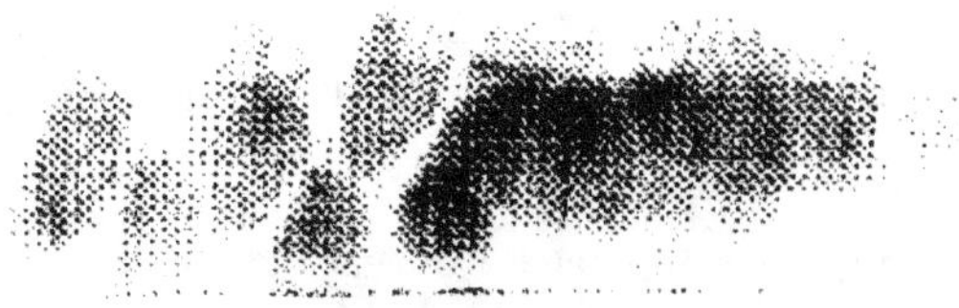

59

MARY LOU SNORED in the passenger seat: her head flopped backward to open her windpipe and maximize the airflow to her brain. Frank gripped the wheel and tapped fingers along to the rock 'n' roll beat. The Falcon went straight through a pothole and bounced violently causing her skull to bob around.

She awoke with a start and glanced into the darkness.

"Where are we?"

"Outskirts of Pittsburgh."

"Did I fall asleep?"

"Judging by the snoring…"

"I don't snore."

"Okay. Judging by the heavy breathing, I'd say you were snoozing."

"Do you think they're still after us?"

"Better believe it."

Mary Lou rubbed the sleep out of the corner of her eyes and glanced at her watch: midnight.

"Are you tired?"

"On the way."

"Wake me next time and I'll take over."

"I wanted you to get some rest. You deserved it. But we'll pull over as soon as we see a motel."

Ten minutes driving landed them outside the reception of the Pittsburg Plaaza, which was nothing more than a string of prefab cabins and a hut with a desk where you wrote any false name you chose and signed next to it. Customer privacy was a priority at the Plaaza.

Frank asked for a quiet cabin away from the main road implying they were a young couple up to you-never-your-mind and didn't want to embarrass any of the other guests. The clerk sneered a lecherous glance at Mary Lou in the car and Frank gave him the space to conjure up pornographic images in his head.

With the key in his hand, he took the Falcon to the far end of the parking lot. Bags in tow, they shut the door on the world and sat on the edge of the bed.

Frank stood up and switched the TV on, loud enough to mask any conversation.

"We've made it to Pittsburgh but what should we do now?"

"I reckon we need to assume that everyone has seen the Falcon, change of plates or not. So we should ditch it first thing tomorrow. Then our next stop should be Cincinnati. If anyone has followed us they'll be searching for a couple. So the obvious move is to split up. We can both slip by any Fed because we will not be what they are looking for."

"I dunno, Frank."

"We'll be fine. One drives and the other goes by train. It'll mean a day apart but make it so much safer by nightfall tomorrow."

"We're a team though?"

"Yes we are, but strong enough to be separated from each other. For a single day only. That's all."

"I don't like it. Remember, when I get stressed I forget to do things. The explosives: I didn't set them. What happens if I screw up when you're not there?"

"Mary Lou: I've complete faith in you. You'll do well. I know it. We take one bag each from the heist just in case anything goes wrong."

"Wrong?"

"If I get caught, then you still hold half the money and can carry on."

"Caught?"

"I'm covering all bases. Nothing more. We shall meet up at Cincinnati and everything will be fine. You'll see."

"Now you're scaring me, Frank."

He put his arms around her and she let his body engulf her. Mary Lou felt safer than she ever had before in her life surrounded by the smell of that man and the comfort of his breathing near her ear.

She hugged him back and they sat holding each other until the stress of their conversation left her shoulders and they both relaxed.

"One day, right?"

"That's all. We'll be miles away from the Feds by then and changed our MO along the way. They'll never catch us then."

"And do you think Uncle Frankie will give up too?"

Frank didn't answer. His silence spoke volumes but Mary Lou waited, hoping the response would be what she wanted to hear and not reality.

"One day at a time, babe. Uncle Frankie'll be harder than a bunch of G-men, but we'll get away from him too. Somehow."

They remained hugging another five minutes, she closed her eyes and soaked in each moment of tranquility in the cabin, although she noticed roach traps all along the walls.

"Ever been to Cincinnati?"

"No."

"Me neither."

He kissed her on the forehead and they allowed themselves a laugh.

"Rob a bank and see the sights of America."

"Yeah, I didn't count on this happening."

"No one did, babe. It's how the cards landed. You only play the hand you're dealt."

"Ain't that the truth."

She pecked him on the cheek twice. Tenderly.

"Once we meet up in Cincinnati, where to then?"

"I was thinking Oklahoma City. It'll be a long drive but then at least it won't be too far to Vegas and we can relax in the anonymity of the bright lights and one-armed bandits."

She distracted him by kissing his cheeks then poking her fingers under his shirt to caress his chest. Frank placed a hand on a breast and squeezed until she felt a tingle running up her spine from her groin to the back of her neck.

Mary Lou undid his buttons while he pulled at her bra until they were both under the blankets and naked. An hour later with him fast asleep, she slipped out from under the covers long enough to switch the television off and remembered the nights soon after his last stretch in the State Penitentiary.

FRANK WOKE FIRST and couldn't remember switching the TV off the night before. He smiled as he recalled what they'd got up to before he'd fallen asleep. He felt calm and a sliver of happiness soaked into him as he looked at Mary Lou—until a roar of lust exited past his throat which she mistook for a belch.

"Good morning to you too."

He laughed and licked her back as it was the nearest part of her body to his mouth at the time. His fingers landed between her thighs.

"Not now dear, there's traveling to do."

Mary Lou took his hand and placed it on his dick. Then she flung the covers off the bed and scampered into the bathroom. Frank let his palm rest where it was and used the moment to consider what they had to do before leaving town.

He got dressed, put the bags back in the Falcon then waited for Mary Lou to be ready. He liked to watch her get undressed and he loved to gaze at her as she took off her clothes, slowly revealing her soft skin and curves to him. There was something deeply satisfying about being the only one privileged to experience those moments.

In the car and out for breakfast and a place to swap vehicles. A mile down the road they found a diner to eat. It was a popular venue and cars crammed until it nearly burst. The Falcon got lost in the sprawl as soon as Frank drove in.

Coffee and pancakes later, Mary Lou stared out the window from their booth and watched the world go by.

"There's a bunch of trees at the end of this lot."

"Yeah?"

"Lots of shrubs too."

"Okay."

"You could hide a car in that undergrowth."

Frank pricked up his ears as he worked out why Mary Lou cared so much about the details of the parking facilities. The pancakes had landed at the pit of his stomach and he was feeling sleepy while he digested them.

"Where should we get our next ride do you reckon?"

"Out there, maybe?"

"Yes but if we boost something here, chances are someone will connect us to the vehicle."

"There's another restaurant half a block down the road. I can make out its neon sign from here."

"Much better idea. You ready to head out?"

Mary Lou swigged back the last mouthful of coffee and Frank paid up. They sauntered over to the nearby lot and took their pick of the saloons. Nothing too fancy, new or old. Just a sensible ride that'd turn no heads.

A black hooded family saloon squatted three spaces from the end. Mary Lou stood in front of it pretending to check her make-up in her handbag mirror while Frank opened the driver's window, popped open the door and slid inside to kick-start the engine. It roared into life within two seconds and she jumped in as he drove off.

"That was fast."

"Sometimes I'm lucky. There's a full tank of gas too so I can make it all the way without stopping."

Back to the other lot where they transferred their possessions into the new vehicle and pushed the Falcon into the copse. They kept going until it got stuck in a rut or ditch. Then they grabbed some branches and threw them on top for camouflage.

Frank remained behind the wheel as they headed for the station. She was quiet, aware they would split up soon and still not happy about the situation—even though it was the safest thing to do.

Twenty minutes later they were in the middle of Cincinnati and the main building was in front of them. Frank and Mary Lou divided their spending money, so she'd enough for the train fare and a bite to eat on board and he could still buy food and more gas.

"Would you like me to come in with you until you're on the platform?"

"Yes I would, but no you shouldn't. If the cops wired a description, it'll be of me, not you, Frank."

"All the more reason for me to ride shotgun until you are safe in a carriage."

Before she could argue the point any further, he pulled in and got out the car. Mary Lou knew she wanted him by her side and stopped any further attempts at protesting. They each carried a money bag and she stuffed her clothes on the top of the notes so she'd have less to carry. There were only two passengers in the line and soon she held a one-way ticket in her hand and the knowledge she was facing a twelve-hour journey ahead of her.

The next train for Oklahoma City was due to depart in fifteen minutes so the couple had enough time to saunter to the platform and for Frank to hug and kiss her before he helped her find the right passenger car and settle into her seat. He put her bag in the rack above her head and passed her a fashion magazine he'd found on a bench.

"I'll be waiting for you in the station when you get off. We'll be lying in bed together tonight."

He kissed her again and walked out the carriage without looking back because he was certain he had seen a tear roll out her eye and that broke his heart.

60

FRANK KNEW HE would take less time than Mary Lou because he could go a direct route and she'd have to follow the train tracks as they zigzagged across the country. So he took it easy, never going over five miles an hour under the speed limit and letting folks pass him as they saw fit.

Even though he chose not to use the expressway, he still found straight roads and desolate countryside. The highway was as flat as this morning's pancakes. This gave him the advantage of seeing any impending traffic coming from the rear or head on. And nothing appeared on either horizon.

Frank cranked the music up and opened a window because this would be one long dull journey. The black bag with the cash was back in the trunk and his clothes were strewn on the backseat. He had dumped them there when he returned to the car after leaving Mary Lou. He figured if any prying eyes were to take an interest then levels would subside at the sight of his shorts and a tee.

His plan was to travel parallel to the expressway as that represented the shortest distance between cities but he needed to avoid the freeway itself. There was nothing to see but painted lines on the highway so Frank got to thinking about Mary Lou and her rose.

A man's mind was bound to wander on a journey such as this. The more he thought about the tattoo nestling below her belly button, the more he wanted to savor it there and then. For a second, the car rumbled and Frank found himself in the dirt and dust of the side of the highway heading towards the gulley edging the field. He swerved the steering wheel hard right and the rear of the vehicle swung sideways. The rear passenger tire lost footing and dangled in mid air over the ditch as he tried to cling to earth. Another twist of the wheel and the back end lurched in the opposite direction until all four tires were eating tarmac and he settled the automobile squarely in the middle of the only lane pointing to St Louis.

With the car stable, he pulled over to the side of the road and stopped. A minute later the cold sweats ceased to pour out of his armpits and back and he breathed again. His stomach churned, so he leaped out just in time to spew into the ditch which had tried to kill him less than sixty seconds before.

Frank slumped into the dirt to regain control of his body, which seemed to be trying to escape from him. Mary Lou was right: they should never have split up. He was safer with her by his side. Too late though—and the thought of her rose entered his mind's eye yet again, almost taunting him with the lust of his poor decision.

He found spittle returning to his mouth and he sloshed it around to take the taste of vomit away from his teeth. Frank'd have killed for a glass of water then. His heart rate subsided to a normal level and he considered standing up but waited another minute before doing anything so ambitious.

Four minutes later Frank sat behind the wheel and released the clutch. The vehicle kangarooed forwards and, ten feet further, he regained control and the saloon purred onwards while he accompanied the rock 'n' roll with loud singing. He hit two or three of the right notes but no one was judging, which was just as well given the noise he generated.

The car carried on following the lines of the road all the way to St Louis. Frank drove round the outskirts rather than open himself to the possibility of the city cops somehow having his identity to match with his face but he needn't have worried. No police around here were watching out for him.

His stomach rumbled and he realized he'd been sat in the damn car for three hours without a piss or a bite to eat. The boredom of escape took over and he allowed himself to be consumed with the idea of a cheese burger with fries, onion rings and a coffee.

All the places he passed in the burbs were way too empty, making him far too memorable a patron, or jam packed and he wasn't prepared to wait too long for his food. Thirty minutes more and he was the other side of the urban sprawl heading towards Cincinnati.

A sign appeared announcing the nothing town and Frank parked in the House Springs Deli, which claimed short-order cooking was their speciality. The lot was half filled with cars but there were sufficient spare tables he could get served fast enough for his stomach.

As ever, he brought his bag with him and placed it under his feet beneath the booth. Norma Richardson approached Frank and asked him what he'd like to drink.

"Coffee, please."

As she walked away to grab the pot, he noticed the bottom two buttons on her dress were undone. He watched the flesh of her legs rise above her knees until it vanished in the murky shadows of her clothing.

With those thighs locked in his mind, Frank inspected Norma's face and the rest of her body. Long brown hair with a slight wave. Bright blue eyes with a pointy nose. Average height. Breasts that created a pronounced cleavage because she had big tits or because her blouse was too small. Either way, he liked what he saw. The image of her decolletage and Mary Lou's rose merged as he ordered the food he'd been salivating over for the last hour.

NORMA LAUGHED AT another of Frank's jokes. He knew he wasn't that amusing but the falseness of her reaction didn't stop him continuing to like her. The tension in her blouse caused a gap between the top buttons to emerge and revealed a bright yellow bra beneath the light blue material of her uniform.

He mopped up the juices from his burger with a slice of bread Norma had brought over.

"Is there anything else I can get you?"

"Something sweet would be neat."

She chuckled once more and touched his shoulder.

"I got a mighty fine piece of pie to offer you."

"I'm sure your pie is mighty fine, Norma."

He winked and could not believe he'd said what he did. Norma giggled again and slapped him in jest.

"Now Frank, talk like that is liable to get you in trouble."

He glanced at her left hand and saw no wedding ring.

"You got a fella then?"

"Why Frank, no I ain't. Whatever are you thinking of?"

He knew she knew and this was part of the game they were playing.

"Just wondering when you're off your shift."

Norma leaned down so he could get a good look at the space between her tits and whispered.

"About five minutes time if you play your cards right."

He threw down a bunch of notes to pay for his meal and waited for Norma to return with his change. He was still on a budget.

"Meet you out back."

She then walked up to her boss and he heard her spin some story about women's trouble. The guy shrugged and she hung up her apron and trundled through the kitchen. He took his cue and scuttled round to the rear of the building in time to see her walk out and light a cigarette until he stood next to her.

"You near here?"

"Frank, you are so forward."

A giggle and she led him down three blocks and left onto another until they arrived at a shabby condo. Nothing a lick of paint and replacing all the pipe work wouldn't fix.

Up to the second floor and into Norma's one-bedroom apartment. She dumped her clutch bag on the kitchen table and Frank placed his black holdall next to it.

"You always carry something that large with you?"

"Don't get fresh, Norma Richardson. A man has to look after the tools of his trade."

With that, he cupped her cheek in his hand and they kissed. Within five minutes a trail of clothing formed from the kitchen where a yellow bra lay on top of a woman's blouse and a man's shirt covered them both. At the door a skirt nestled in the folds of a pair of jeans and at the foot of the bed: panties, shorts and socks. Two pairs of feet stuck out from the end of the covers—Norma's pointing upwards, Frank's down. Both were deep-breathing and she had wrapped her legs around his hips, preventing him from getting inside her. This momentary pause caused Frank to think and realize what he was doing. His lust had overpowered him and he was about to make a mistake.

"Where've you gone?"

Norma let the disappointment ooze out her voice. They were having fun and this breeze-through man had all the right moves for her. Then he curled up and vanished.

"What gives?"

She repeated her question wanting to know why Frank had just turned off to her. He remained silent.

"Was it something I did?"

"What? No? No. Sorry. Look, I should never have put us in this situation."

"Is there another woman?"

"That obvious?"

"'Fraid so, mister."

"While you are mighty attractive, I should leave before things go any further. And they almost did."

Frank rolled off Norma and sat on the edge of the bed. She wrapped herself around him so tightly he could feel her hairs against his buttocks.

"It was fun while it lasted. Shame it didn't last a minute or two longer."

She nibbled his ear and he inhaled her vanilla perfume. Later, she made him a coffee while wearing her yellow underwear and they sat together at the kitchen table while he put on his socks.

"Frank, if you're ever passing through…"

"…I know. Keep on going."

She giggled and kissed him on the forehead before he popped on his shoes and left the apartment. A short hustle back to his car and he hit the road—but always five miles an hour below the limit. Even with this layover, he would arrive in Cincinnati six hours before Mary Lou.

61

GLENDA'S SHIFT AT the Joppa diner ended at five. She sat in the staff room smoking a cigarette and sipping at a coffee to give herself the energy to leave the place and head home. A small portable TV was on and the news anchor showed an artist's impression of three men from the Lansdowne robbery. While not a great likeness, Glenda thought she recognized Pete and placed a call through to the cops.

Four hours later and a knock erupted from the front door of Glenda's apartment. She shared it with her girlfriend, Annie Price but she was out working shift in a local shoe factory. Glenda put on a housecoat and sauntered to the entrance. Two men stood on the doormat, backs straight. One in black jacket and pants, the other in uniform. The suit spoke first.

"Inspector Philip McNamara from the FBI and this is my colleague, Detective Edward Goodwin of the Baltimore Police Department."

"Come on in. We've got enough for a party if you don't tell my super."

The two men eyed each other and entered the premises. Glenda pointed at some seating and the gentlemen made themselves comfortable.

"Coffee?"

"We're good thanks."

The suit crossed his legs and the uniform took out a notepad.

"When you called, you told my colleague you recognized one of the deceased from the Lansdowne bank robbery."

"Yes."

"How did you know him?"

"I hadn't so much been acquainted with him, officer. I'd seen him before."

"Call me, Phil."

"Okay, Phil."

Glenda eased back in her chair and worried less whether the two front pieces of her house coat met in the middle.

"Where had you seen him?"

"In the diner. The Joppa-de-Doopah Diner—where I work."

The uniform scratched away with his pencil and pad, saying nothing but staring right at her.

"Was he a regular?"

"No, I wouldn't say that but he had been two times over the past few months."

"If he only turned up once or twice, how can you be sure it was him?"

"He was a guy you'd never forget. A sharp tongue and never left a tip. I always remember the ones who don't show any gratitude."

"Harsh words?"

"He just thought he was better than everyone else and didn't pretend to hide it. A thin long streak of piss if you'll pardon my language. Can I rustle up a coffee for you fellas?"

"No thanks. We're fine."

"You sure are, Phil."

Ted laughed and covered his mouth to generate a cough while Phil's cheeks turned a shade of red.

"When did you see him?"

"Last week I think. He came in looking for Lucy."

"Another customer?"

"No, we work together. When I told him she wasn't around, he finished up and left. Didn't even order any food."

"Any idea what business he had with this Lucy?"

"He was Lucy's latest ride."

Phil rarely experienced such directness from waitresses.

"Did she often have gentleman callers?"

"Don't get me wrong—she's no whore. Like me, she enjoys the company of men during the dark lonely nights, right?"

He noticed Glenda's knees had separated a few inches. What did they put in the water round here to make these middle-aged women so horny?

"And had this guy been around much?"

"Only a couple of times. From what Lucy told me, he was quite a cold fish to her too. Hardly spoke a word before or after any… intimacy they might have had. But he had smokes and was a warm body; none of us are getting any younger."

She stretched her arms out across a neighboring chair and Ted saw her look down to check she had revealed the curve of one of her tits.

Goodwin took down a description of Pete and then they left Glenda's apartment.

"What you think?"

"Horny old vixen."

"About what she said."

"Sounds like Pete the Wheels liked to dip his dick in the local service industry."

"Good move."

"Not if Lucy looks anything like Glenda."

"Smart move to set yourself up to hide away in this backwater from nowhere."

"Ah yes."

"Sometimes Ted, the trick is to look at their faces and not their tits."

"Yes Phil, but not always."

LUCY GAVE UP waiting for Pete a day before. She wasn't sure when she figured he wasn't coming back. Perhaps when she heard about the bank robbery on the news or that night when he failed to show up. Men were unreliable at the best of times and after the previous night's tequilas, today was not the best of times.

She woke up in her trailer not clear what day it was or quite where she was. Only after ten minutes was she able to open her eyes and let reality seep into her consciousness. Before the morning took hold, she reached out and grabbed a cigarette and a lighter, combining the two deftly.

In a moment of paranoia mixed with amnesia, Lucy flitted her head sideways to make sure she hadn't brought anybody home with her. The bed was empty. She inhaled, leaving the filter to hang from the corner of her mouth. Lucy's next challenge was to remember when her shift started at the Joppa-de-Doopah Diner. The good news was that her trailer was nearby: a six-minute walk. Her blurred memory held onto the idea she had the late shift which ran from five until they shut the place up for the night at midnight.

The fling with Pete had been fun but now all she had left was an itching sensation in her groin and a fat travel bag. Lucy switched on the radio and the news gave an update on the robbery. The description of one of the dead sounded a lot like him. She sighed. He wasn't a talker but they'd had a fabulous ride together.

After she got dressed, she fixed a coffee and cracked an egg into it. Sometimes that made the pounding fists in her head go away. As she tried to swig back the awful concoction, her eyes caught sight of Pete's holdall. She'd thrown it on a chair because the lummox had dropped it on the floor and her trailer didn't enjoy spacious accommodation.

She dragged the bag onto her bed and unzipped it. Nestling on the top of Pete's clothes was a carton of cigarettes and beneath the smokes was a roll of notes. She took both and counted the greenbacks. Five shy of two hundred dollars. Quite a find. She added up a second time to make sure. Under the clothes: a metal object. She didn't need to pull it out to be certain it was a revolver. Pete had left a gun in her trailer. Nice move.

She removed the carton and roll of notes and zipped up the bag. When she felt better, she'd take the contents and scatter them in the trash around the area. Until then, she placed the smokes on the small table near the kitchenette and stuffed the money into a drawer.

The only question left for Lucy was what to do with the cash. She could splash it on a new hairdo and a pretty dress—or take a trip with a girlfriend to Atlantic City or travel even further afield. To help her decisions making, she fried an egg and grilled some toast while in her dressing gown.

Once she'd sat down at the kitchenette table, Lucy's mind whirred as she thought through all the possibilities Pete's cash could buy her. It wasn't enough to quit her job at the diner and take her chances on the open road, but she sure was sick and tired of serving donuts and coffee to the middle-aged men who frequented the place. She might make good tips by thrusting her chest out through that tight blouse and bending down, but there had to be more to life than pouring brown liquid into mugs.

At this point in her reverie, a knock erupted on Lucy's trailer door. She opened it and greeted two men: one in uniform and the other in a suit, both holding badges.

"Can I come in, Miss.?"

62

MARY LOU WATCHED Frank step off the carriage and she felt alone. Really alone. The bag was in the rack and she didn't feel she should go anywhere in case someone stole it. Their future hung above her head.

The passenger car was composed of row upon row of pairs of seats all facing forwards and Mary Lou sat three rows from the back. Just far enough away from the exit to not catch a draft when the train pulled into stations but not so distant that she couldn't run off.

The head-high baggage compartment was nothing more than a shelf with no attempt made to prevent bags from falling. Mary Lou kept her eyes on the black bag. Not because it was in imminent peril but because it might be in danger during the journey.

The last few days had shaken her. She wasn't that kind of person until then. She'd spent years with Frank in the can staying out of trouble. With the bank job going south, her self-possession was ebbing out of her.

Perhaps this was just her way of coping with the sudden change in their lives. They both waited for the day of the robbery for such a long time—months—and she hadn't given a second's consideration what life would be like after the takedown.

And now she lived that moment for real—and it was nothing how she was expecting. They'd talked about spending three or four weeks together while Uncle Frankie handled the money end of the business and they laid low. In theory, once the dust settled, they would hook up with Frankie, get the laundered cash and split up from the crew forever.

Instead, she was stuck on a train running from the Feds and Uncle Frankie without even Frank to offer reassurance. As she looked around, half the seats contained heads but she had no sense of how many passenger cars there were or where potential danger may lie. She needed to go scouting and prepared to get up from her seat. Her one quandary: to keep the bag with her and stand out as unusual or leave it and risk it getting stolen. A middle-aged woman sat on the other side of the aisle.

"Sorry to bother you, but I need to… freshen up. Would you mind keeping an eye on my luggage up there?"

She pointed at the rack and the harridan nodded.

"Of course, love, don't worry about a thing."

Mary Lou thanked her and stood up. It was a risk but lugging the bag down the aisles would have made her more visible if she was heading toward trouble.

Four sets of doors further on, she reached the dining car where people were ordering a late breakfast. She carried on and six cars down she hit the end of the line. Just a baggage wagon in front and nobody would be getting past that.

On the way back, Mary Lou paid more attention to the individuals as she passed them. Three guys caught her eye. Two wore hats and one sported a crewcut. All reeked of cop. She noted where they sat but did nothing more than that for the moment. They might have just been cops going to Cincinnati or beyond. Being on the train did not mean they were on the lookout for her.

Back at her seat, she thanked the woman again for watching her bag.

"You have a long journey ahead of you?"

"Ten hours. And you?"

"Much longer: all the way out west."

"How exciting. Are you visiting friends?"

"Oh no. My husband died last year so I'm seeing my inlaws. We never got on and this'll be the final time I have to put up with them."

Mary Lou considered this news. The social awkwardness of hearing about the disquiet in her family gave no wiggle room for further conversation. They both lapsed back into their own little worlds.

THE CREWCUT LINGERED in her head until Mary Lou could no longer sit still in her seat. She forced herself to investigate what he was up to. Another excuse to mind her bag and off she went to find him. He had stood up and was talking with the guard: a peaked cap, starched shirt. She carried on walking past to eavesdrop.

"Do you think they'll catch 'em?"

"Not if I've got anything to say about it."

"And what'll you do?"

"I aim to arrest me some bank robbers."

"Is that right?"

"Sure is and why not? I've as good a chance as anyone else. The FBI have said them two are heading west. And so's this train. Who's to know if they ain't even on this train?"

With this statement Mary Lou shuddered. She kept on walking down the aisle and waited for a rest room to become available. When she'd closed the door on the world, she splashed water over her face and leaned on the walls. Why had she and Frank agreed to split up? She was a few feet away from a transit cop who mistook himself for Eliot Ness.

After an indecent time, she left the confines of her sanctuary and walked past the officer to return to her seat.

"Do you have a description?"

"Sure do. They issued one this morning. Man and a woman carrying some heavy duty bags. Let's face it if they are on this train, it won't be that difficult to spot them. They are walking around with a million dollars between them."

The guard whistled at the sound of the size of the haul.

"Tell me," he leaned in. "If you found them, wouldn't you be tempted to take the money for yourself?"

"I am a fine upstanding member of the police force. I'd grab the cash for myself."

They both laughed but only one of them knew if he was joking.

"Have you got any leads?"

"Two Caucasians, one male, other female."

"That narrows it down."

"Yeah, but how many couples do you see walking round with a million bucks in their back pockets?"

"Now that is a great point."

"Say that again, bud."

The guard chuckled.

"And how do you know they haven't split up? I mean, you called them a couple but they might just be two gang members, if you get me?"

"Hadn't considered that. You're right. I should look out for one or both of them."

"I've made your life a lot more complicated."

"Sure have, but I forgive you. If I make the reward, I'll remember you."

"Don't remember me; share the bounty."

"Yeah, like that's going to happen. I'm off for a recce."

Mary Lou scooted back to her seat while the cop headed toward the baggage car to start his search. She stared at the bag above her head and wondered what the hell she should do. There were too many notes to hide them—this was not an option.

Perhaps the holdall needed to go. Mary Lou thought hard and fast. Just because one overzealous cop was on the lookout for a woman—or a man—on her own carrying a stash of cash did not mean he would look at her and know she was worth searching.

And if she didn't hide the notes or the bag, should she hide herself? Make a beeline for the washroom and stay there for the rest of the journey? Mary Lou gave this more serious consideration.

But that middle-aged hag across the aisle had spoken with her and might provide a description of her. She was sat there now and Mary Lou got the feeling she was staring at her this minute. There was one car Mary Lou hadn't explored, which she and Frank had skipped when they boarded the train.

She turned round to get a sense of what was there: a buffet car. Somehow she missed the fact there was food behind her and ahead. She looked up at her bag and tried to imagine seeing it for the first time. Did it say money or undies to her? Even though her chest was tightening and adrenaline was coursing through her veins. The holdall was too dreary to raise any suspicions unless she created a reason for the cop to think ill of her.

She did not want to sit here and wait for him to arrest her. Mary Lou stood up—yet again—and walked behind to the buffet car. There were tables and seats along one side and a bar area where people ordered food and drink. At the far end were a series of windows for passengers to stare out at the passing scenery as it shot past at sixty miles an hour.

Mary Lou headed for a seat near the viewing area so she'd have plenty of warning when the cop burst through the doors. Then she grabbed a menu and held it in front of her to hide behind when the time was right. This was the best plan available to her. It wasn't the greatest idea but a piece of laminated card would protect her from the might of the local law enforcement.

Ten minutes later, the door opened and the cop walked in, checking everyone's expressions who made direct eye contact with him. Mary Lou gulped and gripped her menu tighter.

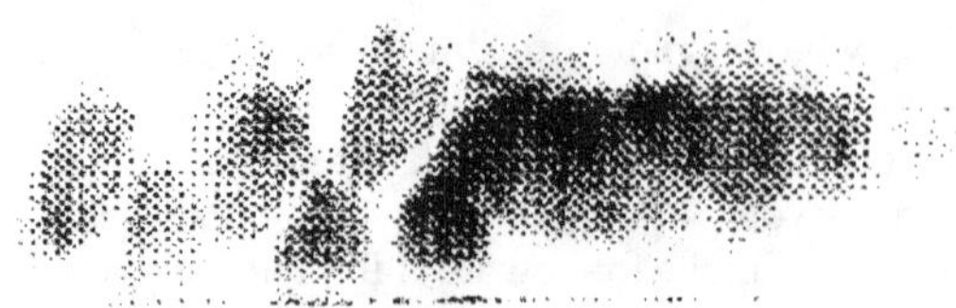

63

MARY LOU RAISED the menu in front of her face as she'd planned to do. This prevented him from taking too close a look but also meant she couldn't see quite where he was in the car.

"Can I get you something?"

She ignored the voice as she was concentrating too much imagining how long he'd take to walk the fifteen steps to reach her.

"Miss?"

"Huh?"

"You want to order anything?"

The buffet barman had a point as the place was filling up and she was taking up valuable counter space. He had left her alone for enough time. An answer was required.

"Java and a slice of cake if you have any."

"We got cake. What you want?"

"Coffee cake?"

"You sure like your coffee?"

Mary Lou had lowered her menu so she could speak with the barman just as the cop sauntered past.

"Huh? Yessir. What girl doesn't love a nice piece of coffee cake?"

"What indeed, honey."

The conversation petered out, much to Mary Lou's relief, and the officer carried on until he reached the end of the car and made his way back. He passed her a second time but on this occasion, he stopped right behind her and she wished she'd kept a gun in her clutch bag.

He leaned past her so she could smell the acrid stench of his aftershave. His hand brushed her shoulder and he took a menu from the counter.

"Excuse me, ma'am."

Her throat was too dry to respond and she half-nodded instead. The menu disappeared beyond her peripheral vision and the cop considered his food and drink options. Blasts of stale breath launched onto the back of her neck and she sensed he was stood there.

"Coffee to go, bud."

"Sure thing, Simon."

Mary Lou noted the cop was a regular on the route else the waiter wouldn't have known his name. Ordinary flatfoot on his usual train journey shooting his mouth off to the guard about his chances of a big break. She relaxed knowing he wasn't here as part of some special detail. He was just a uniform with no imagination trying to put food on his family's table. Deadbeat gumshoe with hopes and dreams and no opportunity to reach them—like every other schnook in the country.

The guy dropped a coffee and cake in front of her. Soon after, another Java landed within an inch of her mug aimed at Simon. He leaned in again and ensured his arm touched hers as he picked up his drink. She did her best not to react. He was a cop and the last thing she needed was to draw attention to herself. That said, she didn't need some dirt ball rubbing himself against her: peaked cap and uniform or not.

Mary Lou unclenched her jaw to chow down on the cake and sip her brown drink without turning her head. She had no desire to catch his gaze or engage him in any conversation. Mooks like him needed only the slightest invitation and she was in no position to deal with him in her usual manner: her hot coffee lingering on his crotch as she walked away.

Instead she threw down some coins on the counter and dismounted from her bar stool. Simon gave her enough room to get past him without moving a single muscle of his body. She considered elbowing him in the balls but the train came to her rescue as the driver took a bend too fast. All the standing passengers in the buffet car lurched to one side including Mary Lou, who reached out with her fist into Simon's stomach. His gut took the entire weight of her blow as she ensured he received the full brunt of the impact.

"I'm so very sorry, officer. I completely lost my balance."

"Don't mention it. The driver needs to stop speeding."

This wheeze of a response created a warmth of happiness inside her and Mary Lou ricocheted back to her seat as the train steadied itself along the tracks.

As she reached the door, she looked behind and saw Simon the cop heading her way. She kept on walking past her possessions and on to where she had found the washroom before. If he was following her, she needed to find out. Besides, she was trapped on this train whatever happened. She felt for the knife she'd stolen in the buffet car and hidden up her sleeve. The blade was far from sharp but it could still do some damage if aimed right.

Inside the washroom, she closed the lid of the toilet and sat down, ear pinned to the door listening out for Simon. Sounded like there was a constant shuffling outside but she wasn't so panicked she couldn't tell the difference between the noise of the train, the sound of her blood pumping in her ears and cop footsteps two feet away.

Someone tried the door and she bit her lip: the desire to yell out was beyond painful but she said nothing, holding her breath trying to hear what was happening inches from her head. The footsteps got quieter and whoever it was—Simon or some other passenger—moved on to find a different place to freshen up.

Back in her allotted seat, she saw a hulk of a man sat next to the middle-aged woman. Mary Lou surveyed him. They were not a couple for sure as the hag was doing her level best to ignore the Neanderthal. After eyeing him up and down the length of his body, Mary Lou felt a severe pang of fear run down her spine and land in her stomach. The slick black hair cut neatly above the ear lobe, crisp suit and what looked like Army-issue shoes. He had a newspaper opened but his eyes were looking above and beyond the paper along the car. He was a Fed.

WHERE HAD THE G-man come from? This stress would be the death of her. Then in a moment of clarity, Mary Lou remembered the train had stopped at least twice since she'd done her first walk up and down the cars so there had been plenty of opportunity for this dude to hop onboard. Didn't make it any better he was here but removed the mystery of his appearance.

She eyed her bag yet again, hoping somehow that she could convince herself it didn't look as though it contained half the proceeds of the robbery at the Lansdowne branch of the First Bank of Baltimore. The black leather appeared sturdy—like it had been purchased from a quality shop. Carter would have been dumb enough to spend good money on bags to rob a bank he'd throw out at the earliest opportunity.

Only there it was hanging above her skull with a Fed camouflaged by the Cincinnati Chronicle only feet away. If the cop was searching for Frank and her, then the Fed must be prowling round sniffing them out.

He turned his head toward her and she pretended to stare out the window, all the while straining her peripheral vision to figure out whether he was still looking at her. After twenty seconds, which felt like a lifetime, Mary Lou turned to look at him.

She smiled at him hoping to disarm his gaze. To prove he was a Hoover boy, he didn't respond at all, preferring to grind his eyes at her, boring a hole into her. He was one mean mother.

Simon the cop arrived and tapped the Fed on the shoulder. He grinned and stood up to shake Simon's hands.

"How goes it in Federal law enforcement?"

"No complaints, Simon. How's life in the sheriff's office?"

"Don't be like that. I'm a city cop not some local yokel."

"Whatever helps you sleep at night."

The G-man play-punched Simon in the upper arm so she knew they were buddies kidding around.

"You in transit or on the hunt for a master criminal mastermind?"

"Out hunting—and keep your voice down: this is serious."

Mary Lou strained her ears yet again as the men leaned into each other to carry on a private conversation in the middle of the train. She heard 'Baltimore' mentioned and 'couple' which was enough for her to know the Feds were on their case.

A bead of sweat dropped off her ear and landed on her neck; she hoped this wasn't visible to anyone but herself. A transit cop was one thing, but the G-men operated in a different league. With all the whispering she couldn't tell if they had her likeness plastered over local news. They might even have Frank in custody already.

Another drop of perspiration on her neck and a sinking feeling in her stomach. The rational part of her brain processed the information which was panicking her. If they knew what she looked like, they'd have grabbed her by now: they were unlikely to have spotted her and were waiting for her to lead them to Frank. That's not how cops operate.

Mary Lou took a deep breath and considered her options. The longer she stayed in the seat the greater the chance one of these lunks would notice that bag and try to do something about it. She checked her watch and saw she had another hour before she reached Cincinnati. Time to hide in the washroom again.

She shuffled past the two cops and hustled down the aisle hoping her movement wouldn't catch their attention. They'd have to check everyone: the amount of talk could not exceed their efforts to find the felons. The question was how she could avoid them. Despite her strongest desires, Mary Lou knew the washroom was not the long-term solution she craved.

Instead, she considered the problem from every angle until she arrived at a conclusion. The train guard was a pushover and not worth consideration. Simon was a local cop: greedy but fundamentally lazy otherwise he'd have got a promotion and moved on in his life. The only dangerous guy among them was the Fed and he was the one she'd need to charm. But how?

Mary Lou left the washroom and carried on until she reached the baggage car—and walked through. There were a series of cages either side of the usual central aisle. Each cage door was on a latch with bags packed in behind them. There were no locks: the entire system kept the luggage from floating around during the journey and to speed up disembarking.

Flipping the lock mechanism enabled the doors to swing open and for suitcases to fall out of their secure lodgings. Mary Lou bent down and unstrapped a couple of cases to make sure a proper mess was made. She dragged a case along the floor until it was right by the carriage door and visible from outside the car.

Back to the washroom to catch her breath and a wait until the guard spotted the chaos she created. Ten minutes later and she caught the stomping of feet and only then did Mary Lou return to her seat. Simon stormed past her making for the baggage and she knew her plan had worked. She banked on the suspicious flatfoot believing someone had caused the mess as they rushed through. He was close but no cigar.

The Fed was slowly walking along the car and stood between Mary Lou and her seat. He was leaning over people, asking them questions and moving onto the next row of seats. She swallowed hard and headed back past him.

"Excuse me, ma'am."

Mary Lou stared at him to give the impression she wasn't in the habit of talking to strange men on trains just because they looked like cops. The train juddered to a halt and she peered out the window.

"Sorry, but this is my stop."

He lifted his hat and stood aside. Mary Lou rushed past and tried to reach the holdall on the shelf but Frank'd pushed it to the back to prevent it falling and now it was too far away to get any purchase. She only had a minute or two before the train would set off again.

An arm stretched up and took the bag, resting it on a seat. She turned her head to thank the stranger and saw it was the Fed.

"Safe onward journey, ma'am."

"Thanks."

Mary Lou picked up the holdall and got off. She remained there desperately wishing to find Frank and, at the same time, not wanting him to be within a thousand miles of this place until the train—and the Fed—had carried on their way.

FRANK STOOD THE other side of the gate for platform two and saw the train pull in. He waited but there was no sign of Mary Lou. Where was she?

Just before the train pulled away, she appeared with a single black bag and headed toward the gate. The station guard had already explained that Frank was not allowed on the platform without a ticket so he remained where he was until she got past by herself. Then he rushed towards her and picked her up and squeezed. He put her down and they hugged and kissed.

She smelled vanilla around his neck but thought nothing of it because she was so relieved to see him again. She didn't want to let go because she had missed him so but eventually their bodies parted.

Frank and Mary Lou held hands as they sauntered out the station while he led her to the car.

"How was the train?"

"Surrounded by cops."

"Kidding me."

"Not at all. There was a city cop and a G-man."

"Jeez. What happened?"

"The Feds know there's two of us and that we're a couple."

"How?"

"No idea. Man and a woman they said."

"Any descriptions?"

"None that I heard."

"But we don't know."

"No clue. We need to get the hell out of Dodge."

Mary Lou put her bag in the trunk and sat in the passenger seat while he got behind the wheel.

"Take me away from this place, Frank."

He squeezed her knee and reversed out the space before joining the road and heading out on the long haul to Oklahoma City. Once they were trundling along in a straight lane, his hand returned to resting on her thigh.

She enjoyed experiencing the warmth of his fingers on her flesh and relaxed for the first time since they'd parted in Cincinnati. The thought remained at the back of her mind of G-men catching them and dragging him off but, for now, this wasn't her primary concern. Instead, she focused her angst on the long car journey ahead and how she needed to get some sleep before she'd have to take over the wheel from him. Three hours on, three off. Repeat for the fifteen hour trek.

SATURDAY JUNE 21

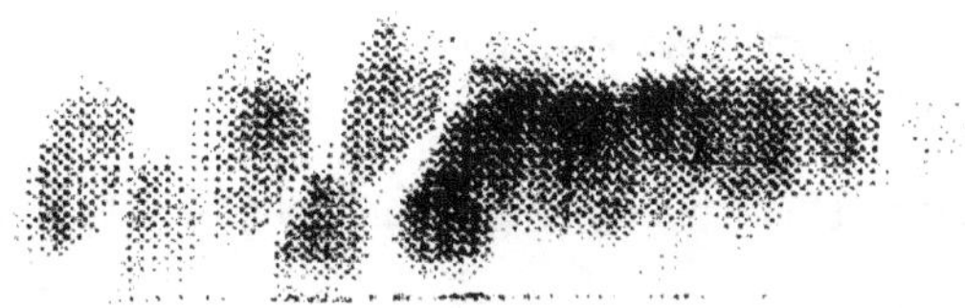

64

IN THE EARLY hours of the morning, Mary Lou woke up with a jolt. Frank had taken the car off the highway and had parked in yet another motel. They all looked the same: he found the ones which were slightly run down with a dark corner in which they could hide. The run-down establishments cared little about their customers provided they paid for their rooms up front.

The other advantages of these low-rent dives was that they were surrounded by equally low-rent bars where characters prop up the counters and deals are available to be done. For this reason, They headed off to grab a bowl of peanuts and a beer.

Food was still being served so Frank grabbed a steak sandwich and Mary Lou took a lamb cutlet. When he made enquiries to the barman where to go if he wanted to buy some weed, the guy carried on wiping the glass in his hand and nodded in Hank's direction at the far end of the bar.

"Hi."

"Hiya."

"I've been told you're the man to see if I'm interested in getting hold of some goods."

"You reckon?"

"That's what I've been told."

"You a cop?"

"Nope. Just a guy with his gal hoping to make a trade."

"Well, I'm going to ask if you are a cop first."

Hank laughed.

"No. What you looking to buy?"

"Are you in the buying and selling business?"

"I can get hold of stuff, for sure."

Frank looked into Hank's eyes. The dude was seventy at least but didn't look like a hippy. If marijuana was his game, he wasn't getting high on his own supply.

"I might have something for you to buy but I need some discretion. Are you up for that or isn't it your bag?"

"I can be cool. What you got?"

"Couple of hundred bucks."

Hank chuckled again.

"You're selling money? Man, you've been at the reefers early buddy."

"I'm serious."

Hank stared at Frank long and hard, sipping at his drink. Eyes checked out every aspect of Frank's appearance.

"The only guy who will be moving cash is sitting on notes they can't take to a financial institution. That money is the cash that's come from a bank—without authorization."

"And?"

"That's outta my league. Love to help a rogue in trouble but I don't get involved in business like that. Not good for my health."

"Thanks for your honesty."

"De nada. If you're feeling the heat, I can offer you a place to hang. Commerce is one thing but helping a rogue is another."

Now it was Frank's turn to stare at Hank. How far could he trust a barfly he'd only just met and whose claim to fame in the local dive bar is that he was the neighborhood drug dealer?

"Got space for me and my lady?"

Frank pointed at Mary Lou with his thumb. She'd stayed by their beers so Hank didn't feel crowded out.

"I have me a plot of land in the woods west of here. I live in one shack and a little way on there's another hut. You and your missus can hole up there for a day or two if you'd like. Nothing fancy but it's dry and no one'll come sniffing around. And if they do, I'll shoot the fucker before they get near you."

Frank raised an eyebrow.

"Don't appreciate trespassers. See?"

"I prefer people who mind their own business too."

The two men shook hands. Frank returned to Mary Lou and explained what he'd agreed.

"Do you trust him?"

"A little. He's smart enough to know we're trouble and sufficiently clever not to ask questions in case he gets answers he doesn't want to hear."

"Will we be safe?"

"Safe enough. Besides, if we don't travel at the speed the Feds expect that'll make it harder for them to pick up our trail. Vanishing for a day or two could be just what we need."

"Or just the opportunity for him to squeal to the Feds."

Frank kissed her on the lips.

"I got a good feeling about him and besides, if he double crosses us I'll put a bullet between his eyes."

HANK HOPPED INTO his car and Mary Lou drove behind him—to give Frank free rein in case matters took a turn for the worse. Instead, they rode for ten minutes until the lane burrowed its way through twists and turns in a wood. Hank slowed and then halted.

"Wait for it."

He ran across the road and opened a gate, hidden by ivy creepers. Lit by the car headlamps, he gave a thumbs-up and used both arms to point at the now-open space. Mary Lou followed him down the dirt track and they both stopped. This time, Frank got out and closed the gate.

Onwards half a mile until they arrived at a clearing inside the wood with two log cabins. Hank drive rightwards and signaled in the opposite direction so Mary Lou drove to the left cabin and parked outside. They were five hundred feet away from Hank and there was nothing but short grass between: nowhere to hide. On the other side of the hut were dense trees as the forest continued to choke the world around it. Frank and Mary Lou took in their bags and Hank appeared a moment later.

"You guys should be fine here. Come end go as you please—just keep the gate shut so's we don't encourage any visitors."

"Thanks Hank."

"Folk like us need to look after each other."

"Like us?"

"Yes missy. People who work outside the conventions of the law."

Mary Lou smiled. Hank was all right.

"One thing I want you to respect though."

"Name it."

"Two hundred feet that-away is a field of vegetation I don't want touched. Reckon you can keep your hands to yourselves?"

"We reckon we can. Is that the weed?"

"Yep. It's my livelihood."

"We respect folks who work hard for what they earn. We won't go messing with the crops."

"Much obliged. Oh, and one other thing, if you want to have any heat in here, you must chop wood out there."

Hank closed the door and was gone.

The cabin comprised a sitting room, a bedroom, a kitchen and a bathroom. All the essentials for life and nothing much more. Mary Lou checked the cupboards and found a tin of condensed milk and some coffee grounds. The living room and bedroom shared a wall with an open fire.

"It is cold in here."

"Yep. I'll get some logs."

Fifteen minutes later, Frank returned with both arms steeped in chopped tree. He threw a match onto the kindling and the flames roared after a moment. They both sat right next to the fire to keep each other company and to gain from the heat of the licking flames. Frank wrapped his arm around her and they relaxed in silence, regaining lost energy from the stress of the day.

"Fancy some Java?"

"For sure, babe."

They went in the kitchen and opened all cupboards until Mary Lou found a small saucepan in one and Frank discovered more matches in another. The faucet produced water and the hob had gas. Within ten minutes two mugs of black coffee sat on the table.

"There'll be bits at the bottom but it should be fine until then."

"Hot and wet. That's all I ask, babe."

"Don't talk dirty. I'm really not in the mood."

Both smiled and they pecked each other on the lips. Then back by the fire, mugs in hand.

"How was your journey?"

"A long road, diner, more driving. The usual. And the train?"

"A lot of stress for one day. A local cop and a Fed sniffing around for bank robbers."

"Trouble?"

"Nearly. I was lucky Cincinnati arrived when it did. I spent way too much time hiding in the john."

"Do you think they made you?"

"Nah. Way too many people on that train with far too much going on for them to notice me in the crowd. But they were planning on doing a more detailed search just as I got off."

"And you reckoned they don't have a description?"

"No, not yet. They've figured out we are a couple. That was the Fed; the locals know nothing—only what the G-men tell them."

"How did they figure out about us?"

"No idea, hon'."

"I mean, who's left alive to snitch?"

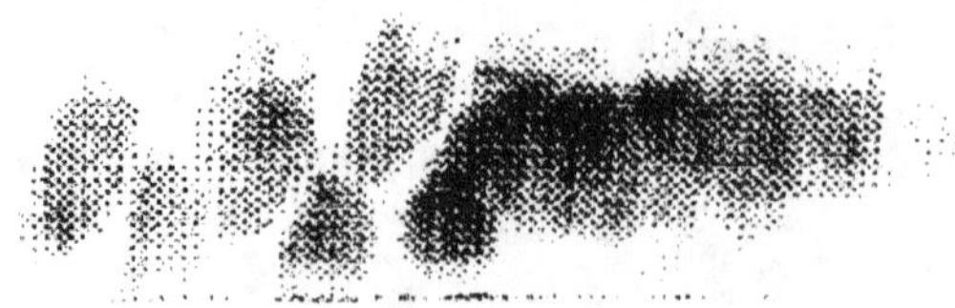

65

MARY LOU HAD not wanted to open up these wounds so soon after a sticking plaster had been placed upon them but she had no choice if they were to survive.

"Uncle Frankie. He's alive and we know he's double-crossed you once already this week."

"Makes no sense. Not to me, anyway."

Silence while she stared at him.

"Frankie had more than one heist planned for the same money."

"Huh?"

Frank considered for a minute.

"Carter?"

"Yes."

"That's why he had the bags under his desk."

"Yes."

"How long had you known?"

She felt the tension in his shoulder that was leaning into her body.

"A day. Maybe two. I didn't tell you because I was confused. I wasn't sure what to do. And I was afraid: scared you'd take your anger out on me."

"I see. And was the plan for you and Carter to transport the haul to Frankie and sell the gang down the river?"

"No. This is why my head was all over the place. Carter intended to steal the money from Frankie and leave both of you high and dry. And I did not know what to do. Anyone I told would assume I was lying. I couldn't tell Frankie…"

He put his arm around her and squeezed her shoulders. He understood there was no way she could go near Frankie, given what his uncle had done to her.

"…and I didn't believe I could go to you."

The complex unspoken triangle between Frank, Mary Lou and Uncle Frankie conspired to destroy them all.

"I get it. How did Carter think he could succeed?"

"Well he didn't think you guys would storm into the place first thing. He reckoned he had all day to take the money and run."

"And what about you?"

"Carter's plan was for me to meet him at the back of the bank and drive him out of Dodge."

"And your strategy?"

"Take the money, shoot him and get the hell out of Dodge."

"Nice."

"Heads, Carter escapes with the money and we win. Tails, you leave with the money and we win. I never expected the coin to land on its edge."

"You and me both."

"I'm telling you the truth Frank. I don't want any lies between us but I'm afraid how you'll react now I've told you."

"What's done is done, babe. All we have is each other. We all do things we might regret later on. Stand up people are the ones brave enough to admit the truth out loud."

Mary Lou turned to Frank and they hugged. She nuzzled her head deep against his neck and noticed that vanilla aroma again.

"As we are being honest with each other, I should tell you I missed out a detail about the robbery."

"What was that?"

"I shot Carter in the balls before we left."

Mary Lou pulled away from Frank, recoiling in shock. Tense.

"Wh… why?"

"Because I was jealous of him and because he looked like he was stealing my money. Besides, he was a coward. He let me hurt the bank manager rather than handing the cash over. That was dishonest of him and I didn't appreciate that."

The image of the cashier's slashed breast flashed across Frank's mind but he laid it to rest as soon as it appeared. Another detail he had omitted to mention to Mary Lou.

"So Frankie has informed on us to the FBI?"

"No babe. There's only one thing Frankie'll have done when he worked out we did for Luigi and Paul."

"And that is?"

"He would make phone New York. Give them the bad news early. If the bank was claiming a million dollar loss and it was only half that then you can bet your last nickel that he had over promised and under delivered. So a call was the least that man would need to do."

"Then what?"

"Two things. First Frankie will have sent out other goons after us. And New York will send out some of their guys too."

"Jeez Louise."

"Yep. The New York connection will have influence with the Feds. They always have someone planted in the Bureau. So I'm guessing Uncle Frank told them who was in the gang and they figured out the rest from there."

"So you are saying Frankie's guys and the mob are after us—and the Feds."

"I reckon. To be honest, the Feds are the least of our worries. Frankie won't just need a return of the take: he'll want revenge."

"And the mob?"

"Just the money. For them this will be business and nothing personal—but they are more ruthless than anything Frankie might ever be. And relentless."

"So what are we doing by this fire, Frank? We should run as fast and far go."

"Yes and no. You see, they can calculate how the distance a train, a car and a plane will take us each day and they are able to figure out which cities we are likely to appear in because of that. But if we don't run, then that throws out their calculations. They'll arrive at our destinations too early and we won't show. I'm hoping they will give up and try somewhere else instead."

"And if they stick around and wait to catch us?"

"Wherever we go that will be a problem. Once we obtain some clean money in our wallets, then we can get new identities or leave the country. The ID we are using now? It's fine for now, but Frankie'll figure out who I used to forge them eventually. And the Feds will know soon after."

"What about the mob?"

"Cut them a deal or find out why the take was so low."

"Do you think JH embezzled some of the money?"

"Who?"

"The manager."

"No way. That sniveling lump? Wouldn't steal a dime that wasn't his."

"The rest were too straight too."

"Well if it wasn't someone inside the bank, must be an outside job."

"I always thought it stupid to make that office the one to carry so much cash overnight when the security was hardly there."

"Set up?"

"Yeah. Do you think the branch was dirty? Mob run or owned or something?"

"No idea, babe. Uncle Frank was too low on the totem pole to be anything close to that and the most I saw when I was clambering up it was his ass bearing down on me."

"Might explain a thing or two though."

"For sure. Right now we are in the middle of a wood where only one person knows we are alive. Hank might sell weed instead of earning an honest buck, but I trust that hemp weaver more than I do my family."

"Know what you mean, hon'. He seems a stand-up guy."

"He'll be a local yokel who wants to stick it to the man."

"You know a man who wants to stick it to someone close?"

"Now who's talking dirty?"

Mary Lou cupped her hand around Frank's cheek and they kissed. With the flames still roaring away, they skipped into the bedroom and hurried under the blankets. Clothing flew out from under the covers: pants, blouse, shorts and panties. Before the fire turned into glowing embers, they fell asleep wallowing in their own juices.

FRANK SLEPT FITFULLY despite the pleasure of sharing a bed with Mary Lou. His mind flitted in a thousand directions—from Uncle Frankie to the Feds to the mob and back to the woman sleeping beside him. Every time he thought about one idea another thing pushed to the front of his consciousness. Lying naked and sticky next to Mary Lou, all he could smell was that waitress's vanilla body.

As he drifted off to sleep, Frank thought about the three men who'd died in the last few days: Pete the Wheels, Andrew and Brian. They had all known the risks, for sure, but that didn't mean he was freed from the responsibility for their bullet-riddled corpses.

Pete was a vicious piece of work. Would spit on your shoe soon as look at you. A classic Southern States redneck with grits coursing through his veins, He was a great driver but showed himself to have anger management issues and was intolerant of people who didn't share his white skin color. A streak of sadistic violence ran through him too so you needed to be careful what you said and what you did near him.

His no-nonsense approach to life was in stark contrast with Frank. He might get hot-headed but his nuanced perspective meant he had been able to keep Mary Lou and manage a gang of bank robbers. She grounded him well; spending time in the joint calmed him down and helped him to focus on what was important. First getting out the can and now California—almost a year since he'd vowed to himself that was where he was heading.

Pete's scrawny face hovered in Frank's mind's eye. He was a scary dude when you were in the same room as him but his clinical approach to every heist was the one benefit of having him around. Apart from the fact he could drive a car.

What would Pete do if he were Frank? Simple: run like a crazy mother until he reached Vegas. Then he'd play fast and loose until he had enough scratch to create options for himself. The man would kill to stay free—the same way he had murdered Martin almost a year ago.

Frank lapsed into unconsciousness with the image of Pete the Wheels driving from Vegas to the Canadian border. And just as he got to the customs house, he vanished from his sports car in a puff of gun smoke leaving the vehicle awash with blood pouring out the windows like a burst faucet.

SUNDAY JUNE 22

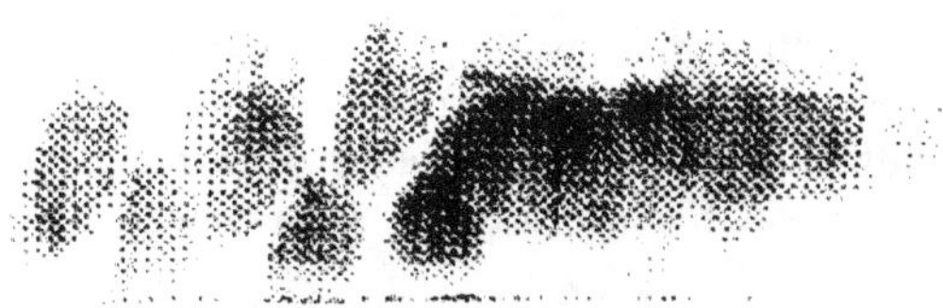

66

FRANK WOKE UP before six in a sea of sweat. Although he had slept, he was not refreshed. He rolled over to see Mary Lou's ass, round and perfectly smooth. One of his fingers stroked her to appreciate her beauty and she stirred, flicking his finger away like it was a fly.

He moved his head to lick her and she swatted him in the face. Dang insect. She turned over onto her back and he was close enough to the rose to reach the stem. Mary Lou giggled a sleepy joy.

"Go on then. While you're down there, you might as well do some good."

THEY DOZED FOR an hour and later, Frank awoke feeling more refreshed than before. He rubbed his eyes and found himself alone. Then Mary Lou appeared with a mug of coffee for each of them. She nuzzled next to him and they petted in between slurps of brown liquid.

At nine, she glanced at her watch, rolled off her man and jumped out of bed, leaving Frank without any blankets.

"We've a long drive ahead if we're ever to make Vegas."

"Eighteen hours I reckon."

"Another overnight motel, then?"

"Yep."

By the time they got to Vegas, the mob would be there waiting for them and, as Frank had pointed out, there was no need to rush into their arms. An extra night's sleep would set them up for when they did eventually arrive in town, but the cabin was a little snippet of luxurious safety they hadn't known in a long while—and were unlikely to see again for even longer.

They shuffled round the rooms searching for clothes and anything else which might tie them to this place if the cops ever came calling. Bags packed, money accounted for, they put everything back in their car.

Frank stomped off to the other cabin to speak with Hank but no dice.

"Not there."

"Shall we leave a note?"

"No, nothing but our memories."

Mary Lou pecked him on the cheek.

"Let's meet our destiny."

She scuttled off and got behind the wheel, waiting for Frank to catch up. Once they returned to the tarmac, she hit the gas but never went more than five miles below the speed limit until it was Frank's turn to take over. Mary Lou shifted the passenger seat rearward as far as it would go to give plenty of stretch. His hand landed on her leg and the comfort of his fingers helped her to drift off to sleep.

TUESDAY JUNE 24

67

MARY LOU DROVE the car into Las Vegas, crossing the city line just before one in the morning. They came in off the Salt Lake Highway and followed the train tracks until she halted outside the Union Pacific Railroad Station.

"You want north or south?"

Frank eyed both options in the neon-lit night.

"It's the same either way. Mint or Queens Hotel: you decide."

She chose North Main Street and stopped the car in the Mint Hotel parking lot.

"Looks like we've arrived."

Frank fished out their fake ID and left Mary Lou while he walked inside to book a room. They'd have a soft mattress and hot running water soon. When he returned with a key, they carried their bags themselves and, for the second time, Frank refused the offer of help from the bellboy. He had the smarts to give the guy a tip, anyway. The last thing they needed in the first hour in Vegas was for some teenager with an attitude to spill his guts to a fella with connections.

Their room faced onto Fremont and looked almost directly at the Queens Hotel and the Golden Nugget. This was a gambling town for sure. The entire city reeked of greenbacks and hard luck. Even though there were famous names packing the theaters with cabaret chic, if you stayed in Las Vegas long, you needed money to burn and a barrel of self belief.

"We can't keep these bags with us the whole time and they can't stay in this room either."

"Trip to the lost luggage at the station?"

"I reckon."

"In the morning, honey."

"We have to assume the mob will be here soon and all they want is the money—and that's all we got."

"Jeez."

"It's getting real, babe. I can taste it too."

"Let me with you."

"No. Stay hear and run us a bath: I'll only be two minutes. It's a swanky hotel: let's take advantage of it."

Mary Lou watched as Frank pulled out a handful of notes and zipped the bag back up. He placed the extra green in his pants pocket and walked out the door with both bags. Down in reception, people were coming and going—unlike any other hotel he had seen. The casinos never sleep.

Over the road, he found the lockers for in-transit folks and opened one at the far end of a row near the floor-to-ceiling window. Nobody could get close to them without being spotted—and they couldn't leave without getting cornered.

Frank stuffed a bag in a locker and found an adjacent one for the second holdall. He popped quarters into both and held the two keys in his fist all the way back to the Mint. Through the busy reception and up the elevator to the fourth floor. Turned left then right and used his hotel key to enter room 409.

He heard Mary Lou singing to herself and the splashing of water. Frank appeared round the bathroom door and saw a bath filled with soapy bubbles and Mary Lou's head bobbing above the surface. He imagined he made out the curves of her body but all he saw was the white froth.

"Come in and get warm."

Frank threw his clothes off and stepped in to join her. She rubbed the grime off his torso as he sat between her thighs and then they lay in the suds stroking and massaging each other. She had thrown a towel near enough for her to dry her hands and light a cigarette which they shared.

Then they wallowed in the tepid liquid as the silence of the night engulfed them—interspersed by the giggling drunk sounds of patrons heading out to the tables or back to their rooms to console themselves over their losses. But Frank and Mary Lou were content in that bathtub sensing each other's hairs without words.

Twice they emptied the water and topped up with more hot. Mary Lou saw her wrinkled fingers and wondered if that was what she'd be like when she was in her eighties. Then she laughed inside, knowing she and Frank were not the sort of people to grow old at all.

They dried each other off with the abundant quantity of towels provided by the Mint and slipped into bed.

"These are crazy days, babe."

"Sure, hon'. We've just got to be ready for whatever comes our way."

"You said it. They're after us and chances are they are already here waiting."

"If we're getting the take laundered, this is the best place to be."

"Yep. Which is why they're here. They know that too because the mob cleans all the money in this town."

"But then we will be free to head for the border."

"Sure will. Get away from this hell hole."

"Together."

Frank looked at her, smiled and touched her cheek.

"Yes, together. We'll make it out of here."

"Or die trying."

He nodded, not wanting to express that thought out loud. Mary Lou didn't mind: the truth never scared her—lies and secrets kept her awake at night and the two of them had their fill of both these past few days and weeks.

"We're in this together. Don't you forget that mister."

"I know. That's what keeps me going: being with you and wanting to spend the rest of my life with you on some beach."

"Steady Frank. Next thing you'll be down on one knee and proposing."

"Would there be anything wrong in us getting hitched?"

Mary Lou thought for a minute and realized this man may not be perfect, but he was the only guy she'd ever met who looked after her without a slap or a punch.

"Nothing at all but I'm too tired to think about it tonight."

Frank fell asleep first and snored straight away while she stayed awake thinking about marriage and the mob. Half an hour later, she was snoring loudly too.

THEY WALKED DOWN South Main until they turned right onto Charleston. This end of the strip contained several bars and financing firms. They catered for a particular segment of visitor: the ones with little money and even lower chance of getting any.

The couple were heading to a loan shark recommended to them by the concierge at the Mint. This was the best option in the absence of any of Frank's own contacts because he'd admitted to Mary Lou he couldn't be sure he could trust them. Inside the building, Frank eyed the pawnbrokers and checked out the loot lining the shelves behind the counter. The usual mix of jewelry, musical instruments and firearms were packed onto every inch of the walls.

"Wonder if you can help?"

"What you got?"

The proprietor sat on a stool, elbows leaning on the glass surface.

"I have some merchandise and I've been told you're the fella to see."

"Oh? A recommendation. Who's been so kind?"

"The concierge at the Mint Hotel."

"Good guy."

"He brought us to you, so yes."

"So what you got?"

"It's tricky."

"Come into the back for a more private conversation."

He nodded and they followed Richard through a door behind his stool. The room contained a desk and three chairs.

"Talk to me about your delicate situation."

Frank looked round and could see nothing to give him a clue whether he could trust this man.

"I have some money."

"Then you don't need me then."

"Well, this cash can't be spent—not retail."

"How dirty and how hot is it?"

"Very hot and exceedingly dirty."

Mary Lou stared at Richard's expression desperate to divine if he was a stand-up guy.

"I see. And the obvious question: how much you got?"

"Right now I'm looking to offload a few hundred dollars."

"But there's more?"

"Don't you worry about that. Let's deal with what's on the table."

"Okay. Nothing personal but how hot is the cash?"

"Hot."

"Hot as in traceable or fresh from a robbery?"

"You need to price up your services. I get it. And yes, this is larceny hot."

"Your East Coast accents make me think you're from somewhere like Baltimore."

"Do they?"

"I reckon. And if you've come from out there then I cannot help you. Nothing personal you understand."

"Why does that put us out of your reach?"

"Word from above. That's why."

"You connected?"

Richard sat back in his chair and strummed his fingers on the armrest.

"If you're in my business, you can't work alone. You always need others in a similar line."

"And?"

"And if I take on a risk, I must offset it somewhere."

"I thought all the junk out front was collateral for secured loans."

Richard laughed.

"The trash is collateral but you know I make more money out of the conversations here. For those kinds of deal I call for backup—and some of that support is Italian."

"Thanks for your honesty."

"No problem. Just telling you how it is."

"And will we get the same response from everyone else we approach?"

"Pretty much. Anyone who can afford frontage here is tied to our Italian cousins. There may be an independent operator in Vegas but you won't find them anywhere near the strip."

"And they'll be small potatoes?"

"Yep. They could work your few hundred but nothing else. You'll need an outfit without East Coast connections for that much action."

Frank and Mary Lou looked at each other.

"And once we leave, are you going to mention this conversation to your associates?"

"Not planning on it. This is a deal that didn't happen."

"Is there no order to report our whereabouts then?"

"But I operate based on trust. How could conduct any transactions if every time someone entered my shop they wound up dead? That'd be bad for business."

"No bounty on our heads then?"

"You're not Bonnie and Clyde."

Mary Lou laughed out loud and the two men turned to her.

"Sorry."

"No harm done."

"I won't lie to you. Tomorrow, I'll make a call and let a person know you came visiting. But I'm in no hurry because the percentage isn't big enough for me to want to rush and rat you out."

"Honor among thieves."

"I'm no thief. I offer cash for clear repayment terms."

"Don't kid yourself. Takes one to know one."

They all shook hands and Richard led them back into the shop. As they headed for the door, Frank stopped to check out some gold jewelry.

"This for sale?"

He pointed at a tray in the display.

"Yes but not with your money. I won't be able to use it."

Frank nodded and walked away.

"What are you interested in?"

He showed him the item and Mary Lou smiled.

"You got any real green on you? The sort you can spend without the cops coming down like flies on shit?"

Frank put his hands in his pants pocket and drew out half the notes from his wallet. Richard took a dollar bill and Frank pocketed the goods.

"Must be your lucky day."

"Much appreciate your generosity."

"I hope you get where you're going before our Italian friends catch up with you."

Out the pawnbrokers and right down Charleston until they went on Las Vegas Boulevard. Two blocks away ran a line of casinos. As they approached, the number of people on the sidewalk increased until they slowed to a crawl by the time they reached the Sahara, the Thunderbird and the Riviera at the end.

"Where's your locker key?"

Mary Lou had one and Frank the other—if they caught either of them, the other still had a quarter of a million to play with.

"In my panties. I figured if I'm stopped nobody's gonna frisk me down there."

"You are a sexy smart cookie. Do you think Richard kept his word?"

"Would you, babe?"

"No, I'd take the money."

"You and me both."

"Better keep an eye out."

"Like never before."

They held hands and judged the expression of every single face that passed them on the street.

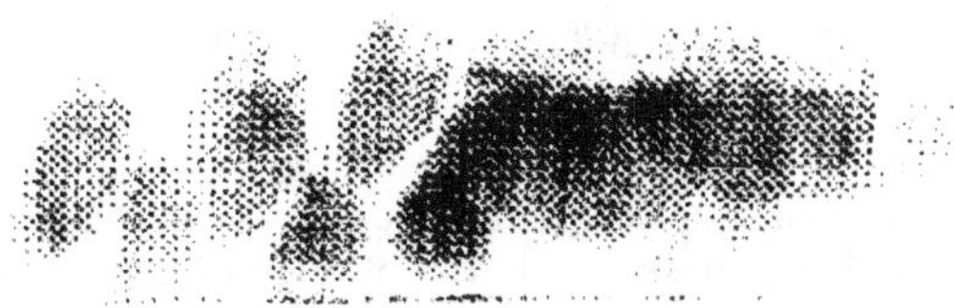

68

"WE NEED TO find an independent operator, wouldn't you say?"

"Yes, hon'."

Frank led them left onto Desert Inn Road and right to Paradise Valley. With a golf course on one side and the Convention Center on the other, they both looked out for anything like a pawnbroker without mob connections. Neither had any clue how to recognize one, but they searched anyway.

In the hinterland beyond the back of the Sands lay a row of shops which bled into the desert ahead. There was a market, a gunsmith and a pawnbroker.

"What you reckon?"

"Only way to find out is to go inside."

"Yes, babe."

"But what if it's not safe? Then what?"

"Okay. I'll pop in and browse to check it out."

Mary Lou stood there and lit a cigarette to pass the time until Frank returned two minutes later.

"Well?"

"Can't say. There are no Italian accents if that's what you mean. But I have no idea."

"Better give it a wide berth."

"Yep."

As they carried on walking down the street, Mary Lou kept deciding every man she sauntered past was a gangster. No matter what they looked like, she couldn't shake the memory of that train journey from her head. Greased-back hair and a three piece dark suit: this was the uniform of old-school New York organized crime.

Frank was no better. He saw the same men and asked the same question: is this guy connected? He had no way of telling the answer by looking. Then he considered the possibility the mob weren't heading towards them, but were behind them instead.

He forced Mary Lou to duck into a shop window to give an opportunity to check who was walking a block away. Just a bunch of people minding their own business.

"They know what we look like, don't they babe?"

"Yeah. Is it time for a change of appearance?"

"Fresh hair color for both of us and a cut for you. New clothes and see what happens."

"A hair cut for you too?"

Frank stared at her and ran his fingers through his locks.

"I could shave it all off but there's only one way to brush this mop."

He had a point. His average hair length was about half an inch.

"Turning you bald will make you stand out more than ever. Are you going blond?"

"Dunno. What color do you want to go to?"

"Jet black with a bob. It's all the rage."

Frank nodded like he knew what she was talking about and they carried on until they reached a pharmacy to buy hair dye and a pair of scissors. They continued on their journey to find an elusive Shylock without mob connections.

An hour later, they had traveled to the far edge of town but found nobody to fit the description. Instead they circled around several times to evade potential mobsters although none appeared to be real. The one thing they could be certain was that if the outfit tracked them down, they'd know about it.

Back at the Mint, Mary Lou cut her hair while Frank watched inches of blond fall onto the floor. His Mary Lou was altering before his eyes and, no matter how disappointed he was feeling, she would hurt more. Women hold a different attitude to their looks than men, he noted.

Before she'd finished, he strode into the bathroom and ruined some hotel towels with his hair dye: from brown to a yellow blond in less than an hour. Mary Lou joined him and blacked out what was left of her mane. With the bottles of chemicals spent, she turned to the mirror and stared at herself. She appeared so different, but the bob suited her, even though it looked so jarring right now.

Frank glanced at his reflection as a final check he hadn't missed anywhere but he didn't care either way. What was important to him was surviving their time in Vegas and laundering the take.

"What are we going to do? We're still stuck with the dirty money."

"I've got an idea about that we can try tonight."

"Oh?"

"But first I should check if you did a good job on your hair."

"What do you mean?"

Mary Lou headed straight back to the mirror in the bathroom and could see nothing wrong. Frank followed her in and stood behind her. She watched his arms wrap around her torso and his hands land on her breasts.

"I need to check whether the carpet matches the drapes."

He pushed his fingers under her skirt and panties until a shiver ran up her spine from her crotch to her neck. She pulled out his hand and led him to the bedroom, giggling.

THEY WOKE IN the middle of the afternoon, Mary Lou first by the noise of her stomach rumbling. For a second she wondered what her head was doing at the foot of the bed. She remembered and smiled. Stretched her arms and legs, almost kicking Frank in the face. The covers were on the floor and she grabbed a corner and threw it over them.

He opened an eye and hugged her ankles, then he licked her calves and carried on working his way up her body, stopping near her rose, until his head took over her entire field of vision. She felt the warmth of his crotch on hers and relaxed into the tenderness of the moment.

"Wait one minute."

Frank leaped off her and Mary Lou frowned—she'd been enjoying what he was up to and could see no reason to stop. The day was a washout, but they sure had fun in the evening, a brief respite from the horrors of their situation.

He bounded back and kneeled in between her legs, forcing her knees apart. He placed one hand on a thigh, stroking it occasionally but his other formed a fist, tightly clutching something.

"We've been together a long time, right?"

"Sure, Frank."

Mary Lou couldn't help letting her mind wander as he spoke because of the tingles he was generating with his palm and her thigh.

"Through thick and thin."

"Oh yes."

He realized his fingers were getting too much attention, so he removed them from her, damp as they were.

"No, listen."

"Ow, all right."

She chuckled and placed both her hands on his dick.

"No, stop it, Mary Lou. I've got something serious I want to say."

She relented and lay there, listening. The last time Frank was this focused he had told her about the bank robbery and his plans for California.

"You've been there for me—even when I was inside. And I hope you think I've been there for you too."

"You have, hon'."

Mary Lou remembered how supportive he had been when his uncle had laid hands on her. She gritted her teeth and relaxed them again as Frank's words soothed her.

"And I may not have always done the right thing, but I always tried."

"I know Frank. We work well together—and you fit so brilliantly inside me."

Another giggle.

"There is that. But more to the point, there's one phrase I have never told you: I love you. And I do."

She'd spoken it to him but Frank found a way to not respond in kind. To be fair, when Mary Lou said it she didn't always mean it. But sometimes it's the right thing to say—like when a guy has fucked you so much you can barely breathe. Memories of Miami floated into her head and she smiled inside.

"And I love you, hon'."

"We've never been as close as we are now. Here in a cheap Las Vegas hotel room, I feel we're inseparable, you and me."

She beckoned for him to kiss her and then he sat back up.

"So, if we are indivisible, we should do something about it."

"Like what?"

He unclenched his fist to reveal a gold ring and Mary Lou's eyes widened.

"Mary Lou Belle: will you marry me?"

"Francis Lagotti. Yes I will."

She uttered those words without thinking. He was the only guy ever to consider such a thing. Every other guy wanted to fuck her and walk away. No one else cared about her. Not even Carter. She realized he was just a lonely man swimming in seas he didn't understand.

But married. How crazy was that? If anyone would make her happy, it was the fella sat with his dick dangling in front of her face right here and now.

Frank tried to put the band on her finger but it was too large. Instead, he bent down to kiss her and Mary Lou wrapped her legs around his body. She didn't let go until all the tingles ceased running up and down her spine many minutes later.

FRANK GLANCED AT his watch and placed three fingers on her cheek. She smiled but kept her eyelids shut. He stroked her skin and then stopped.

"Aw. I was enjoying that."

"As much as I'd like my hand to go wandering again, if we haul ass now, there's enough time to get a license before the place shuts."

Mary Lou's eyes opened and she grabbed his fingers and put them in her mouth for a second.

"What're we doing here? Let's go!"

She leaped out of bed and threw on some clothes—the ones left lying on the floor were easiest to find. Frank did the same. They ran down the strip to reach the Marriage License Bureau before five. They had twenty minutes.

One fast walk along Fremont from their hotel and a brisk right three blocks south took them to the Bureau. Two couples were ahead of them and they waited on line.

With moments to go, Frank and Mary Lou sat opposite a Clark County official who read them their legal obligations and duties while they provided various bits of information as requested. While they were heading over, they agreed to use their real names so the marriage wouldn't be some sham affair. By the time the County had filed the paperwork and made it available for public view, they'd be long gone out the state. They completed and signed the forms using the guy's fountain pen. The ink flowed smoothly onto the administrative pieces of paper.

"Congratulations. Now you have a year to get yourselves married anywhere in the state. You can find a chapel or there is always the Office of Civil Marriages."

His eyes narrowed, with disapproval showing across his face. They thanked him for his help and left clutching their license.

"You want a church, babe?"

"Hell no. God turned his back on me when I was fifteen and I've no need to go looking for his approval for anything that I do, sonofabitch."

"Fine by me. God's done nothing for me. And if he has, I'm damned if I noticed."

They kissed and sauntered over to the Mint, all the time keeping an eye out for the mob, the Feds and Frankie's boys.

WEDNESDAY JUNE 25

69

THE OFFICE OF Civil Marriages was around the corner from the License Bureau and contained all the charm of a municipal building. High ceilings offered a cathedral quality to the venue but you couldn't mistake the smell of musty paperwork and old files. If someone threw a match in the wrong direction, the whole place would go up in flames.

Mary Lou stood at the entrance and looked up at the vaulted ceiling.

"Hold my hand: I feel tiny."

Frank did as he was bid and they sauntered inside. He couldn't help but notice the security guard at the door and scoped out the reception area for police and other armed government officials but a squeeze from Mary Lou reminded him why they were there.

One brief enquiry with a woman at a counter sent them in the right direction down a corridor. At the far end were a series of benches and several couples sat waiting. Each time a couple returned, everyone shuffled forwards until Frank and Mary Lou were next in line, in front of a never-ending slithering snake.

The betrothed talked to each other about where they'd come from, honeymoons and how they met. They tried not to engage with them because every person they spoke to was another rat. Suddenly Mary Lou turned to the girl sat next to her.

"Will you be our witness? We've been in such a hurry, we forgot to ask one of our friends to come along."

"Sure thing, if you'll return the favor."

"Happy to."

Frank scowled, but Mary Lou leaned in to him and whispered: "You need a witness, hon' otherwise it's not official."

She was so wrapped in her own thoughts, this was the first time she looked around to see what everyone was doing. With disappointment, she noticed she was the only one not wearing a wedding dress.

"Frank. My outfit: all the girls are in their Sunday best. And what have I got?"

Frank saw her eyes redden.

"It's not your clothes that count, but what's in your heart that matters, babe."

He was right and she smiled and wiped the dampness off her left cheek. The door opened and a happy couple appeared. Now it was their turn. Rows of chairs lined the room; a desk stood at the far end, a chair and an official sat upon the latter.

"Come in."

The man behind the table beckoned them nearer and Mary Lou, Frank and their witness scurried toward the distant figure.

"This won't take long—and don't worry. Everything will be fine."

Frank held Mary Lou's hand and the girl stood to one side. Chuck got up and walked round to stand with the two of them.

A marriage ceremony is the verbalization of a contract between willing parties and once you've stripped out all the guff about God and worship, you're left with a simple proposition: do you take— and so on. Once Chuck covered all the legal bases, he pronounced them man and wife.

"You may kiss the bride."

The girl smiled and gave them a brief ripple of applause. Everyone with a writing hand signed paperwork and Chuck ushered them out the room. They turned round immediately to witness Trudy's nuptials. Stood outside the Office of Civil Marriages, Trudy and her new husband William asked them if they'd like to go to a bar to celebrate but they declined.

"We're heading out of town this afternoon. Off on our honeymoon straight away."

"Ooh, where?"

"Hawaii."

"Sounds wonderful. We'll stay in Vegas and then head to San Francisco tomorrow."

Frank shook hands and Mary Lou kissed Trudy. Then they walked in whatever direction was the opposite to their newfound friends.

"Let's hole up at the Mint, babe. The longer we are on the street, the worse it is for us."

As they headed up Las Vegas Boulevard, Mary Lou saw a suit a hundred feet behind them.

"Kiss me."

She twisted round on the sidewalk so she could face what she thought she'd noticed in her peripheral vision and Frank complied because he detected the note of authority in her voice. He remained with his back to the potential threat.

"What you seen?"

"Possible Fed. They all dress the same and he looks as though he is in the same uniform as the G-man on the train."

"Spotted him?"

"Yes, he's stopped to check out a shoe store window. Must like the heels."

"Let's walk half a block and see what happens."

Arm in arm, they strolled along the sidewalk allowing everyone to storm past them. If the guy was a civilian, he'd have to catch up with them soon because of their ridiculous slow pace. One minute later they stopped to kiss again, like the lovebirds they were.

"And now where is he?"

"Still hundred feet behind. Maybe a hundred fifty."

Frank eyed their vicinity and took Mary Lou toward a women's boutique.

"He won't want to follow us in here or stand outside."

She knew he was right: the place was a lingerie store and no Hoover man wanted to hang around lady's panties for long.

They grabbed some items off the hangers and she asked the location of the cubicles. A sales assistant pointed to the back of the retail outlet.

"You don't mind if my husband joins me. We've just got married."

Mary Lou giggled coquettishly and the helper agreed.

"Well, as there's no one else trying anything on."

The changing rooms comprised a series of cubicles with a curtain and a door leading out. Frank tried the handle and it opened without effort. He took a glance outside and came back inside.

"It's an alleyway."

"Can I take the bra and panties set? They're divine."

"You're not a thief, babe. We're hardened criminals on the lam. Come on."

Mary Lou dropped the underwear and followed Frank out the door. Ten minutes later they were at the Mint with no sign of any G-man in their wake.

PHIL MCNAMARA AND Ted Goodwin stepped onto the Union Pacific platform with one carry bag each and headed out the Las Vegas station. Fed sources were certain the couple was in the city but Phil had no idea who were these sources. If he had known the mob was the source of their information, he might not have been so keen to head west.

They stood on the sidewalk and hailed a taxi to their hotel, the Hacienda was near the interstate and opposite the Tropicana, way down Las Vegas Boulevard at the far end of the strip.

After they checked in, McNamara called his local office.

"There've been several potential sightings of our couple but nothing confirmed."

"How many men are on the ground searching?"

McNamara looked down at the floor.

"Just the two but I'm assured they're very good."

"They'd need to be to cover an entire city. What gives, Phil?"

"Upstairs wants to catch the Lansdowne gang and recover the money but you have no idea the rivalry between all the offices. The FBI is a series of mini kingdoms. Hoover plays one against the other. The whole thing is a mess."

Goodwin listened in disbelief.

"I always thought you guys would be different. It's just like in Baltimore only with bigger cases. We are in trouble."

"Yeah. The good news is that the information we've gathered has been mighty accurate. First those waitresses gave an excellent steer on the couple and our New York sources have sent us here."

"How did New York here about this?"

"We have several undercover operations in progress and they pick up all sorts of gen."

Goodwin nodded to show he understood but Phil hadn't answered his question. If well-placed persons in the Five Boroughs knew about the Lansdowne gang, there was far more to this caper than a bank robbery.

Sounded more like something mob-run and that made Ted nervous. He was a small town cop out of his home state chasing down a million dollars in cash. What world was he living in?

"Let's get out there and catch us some bad guys."

"Yep, Phil."

They strolled up and down the strip hoping to see a man and woman matching the description Glenda and Lucy had provided but no joy. Hardly surprising—they didn't even know if the pair were still in town. Needle in a haystack.

"Shall we split up and cover twice the area?"

"Sure. Can't hurt. Let's meet at the hotel in two hours."

"Sounds like a plan."

Goodwin prowled round the strip until he reached the Union Pacific Railroad where he took a right onto Fremont past the Mint Hotel. Then back on Las Vegas Boulevard followed by the left fork of Paradise Valley Road. The places on this drag were less fancy and would be where criminals might head.

As he sauntered, hands in pockets, he noticed a couple kissing in the middle of the sidewalk. This was not what people did: strange. He halted at a store window to keep an eye on them and realized he was facing shelves of women's shoes. Too late. Looking for his wife, maybe?

The pair continued and Goodwin carried on following from three hundred feet away. They stopped again, so he ducked into another store window. Had they made him? Again, off they trawled twenty feet and then it was their turn to duck into a lady's emporium. He continued walking towards them hoping to get a better look.

By the time he'd caught up, they were inside somewhere. Then his cheeks reddened as he saw the underwear—panties and bras in all shapes, colors and sizes—hanging in the window. There was no way he could stay outside here to wait for them to come out. Goodwin moved on, not even certain if the pair was anything less than a lovey-dovey type. An hour later he met up with McNamara.

"Any luck?"

"Perhaps. There was one couple I saw but I can't be sure. She had a black bob and he was blond."

"That's not the description though."

"No, but their features looked like the artist's impression. And anyone can dye their hair."

"If you thought it was them, why didn't you carry on following them?"

"Because I wasn't sure and because… well… they popped into a lady's apparel boutique."

McNamara laughed. "You were afraid of a pair of panties?" He carried on chuckling so much so that Goodwin got annoyed.

"Keep your wig on. It's not that funny. And besides, a single man walking into a place like that would have let them know they were being followed."

"You crack me up. You fell for the oldest trick in the book: embarrass a cop with lace and fluttering eyelashes."

McNamara broke out into laughter again and Goodwin sat and seethed. Once he'd calmed down, McNamara called the Vegas FBI office and let his people know the description might be wrong about hair color. Later they dined in their hotel. Steak and coffee, then they agreed to hit the casinos hoping to spot their fugitives in the hustle and bustle of life on the nighttime strip.

FRANK AND MARY Lou stood in the lobby, holding hands. The adjusted wedding band still felt strange on her finger, not so much digging into her flesh as just there. Married. It was good if uncomfortable.

"Best if we lie low for a while. The streets aren't safe for us, babe."

"You said it. Where shall we go?"

"I owe you a honeymoon."

"We owe each other a honeymoon, Frank. Where were you thinking?"

"I know a little place not too far from here."

Mary Lou's expression scrunched up quizzically. He dragged her toward the elevators and hit a button. Perhaps they were off to the top floor. Two seconds after they'd started their ascent, the elevator stopped and the doors opened. Frank took them out. No rooftop bar, then. They padded along the carpeted corridor until they arrived at their room. He looked at her and smiled.

Inside he helped her take off all her clothes and then she reciprocated. They stood naked opposite each other soaking in the sight of the other. Then he stroked her fingers—ever so gently—and their fingertips touched. He ran a finger over her palm, up her arm and around the front of her neck. Then it followed a downward trajectory and cascaded over her left breast, over her heart, and toward her belly button. Then it reached the top most petal of her rose and downwards, heading to the base of the tattoo's stem.

Tingles ran up and down her spine but she stood there, soaking in the rapture of the moment. Motionless.

Frank stepped closer and kissed her on the lips, his other hand caressing the back of her neck. She raised one leg and wrapped it around his calf—and then as high past his knee as she could manage. He held her so she didn't lose her balance. They carried on kissing and the tingles increased.

Within a few minutes they were lying on the bed, Mary Lou licking Frank's chest and stomach. She looked up, along his torso to his head. His eyes were closed and she sensed the strength of the muscles in his body. This was the man she was married to. With his brown-dyed hair and half a million bucks. Mrs. Mary Lou Belle Lagotti. She carried on kissing him until his moaning began. Then she giggled and stopped.

Frank opened his eyes, questioning, as she made her way back up his torso to kiss him on the lips. As she did so, the intensity of Frank's kissing meant he'd figured out her plan too. Ten minutes later, Mary Lou slithered off and lay next to him. He stared at the ceiling and moved an arm so Mary Lou's head could use it as a pillow. She stroked his chest with a hand.

"Happy honeymoon."

"Straight back at you, babe."

"That was lovely."

"Straight back at you, babe."

"Is that all you can say?"

"Pretty much, yes. You've a mighty powerful rose down there."

A flashback to the tingles which screamed through her brain in intense pulses only a few moments before.

"I love honeymoons!"

"Me too, babe."

Given the physical exertion, they dozed until the late afternoon merged with the early evening and her stomach rumbled loud enough to wake Frank and stir herself.

"Should we call room service?"

"It is our honeymoon after all."

Half an hour after they ordered food came a knock on the door. Mary Lou scuttled into the bathroom, still naked, and Frank put on a robe and held a gun behind his back.

The bellboy walked in with a tray and Frank hid the weapon before pulling a note out of his wallet, passing it to the boy in a handshake—the time-honored method of delivering a tip.

Once they'd eaten, Mary Lou flopped onto the bed to rest and digest. Frank cleaned his firearm and then he checked the revolver he'd given to her. Never can be too careful.

"What we gonna do now, hon'?"

"We need to get ourselves some clean money, babe."

"Any ideas?"

"Yep. We should play the wheels."

"Huh?"

"By the time we come back tonight, we'll have two hundred bucks in good notes. But you must put some clothes on before we can start."

Mary Lou used one finger to beckon him toward her.

"In that case, you'd better finish your marital duties before we do anything else, Mr. Lagotti."

She opened her legs and Frank lay in between them. Forty-five minutes later, they left the room hunting for a roulette wheel. In any other town, that would have been a tall order, but this was Las Vegas, the gambling capital of the world.

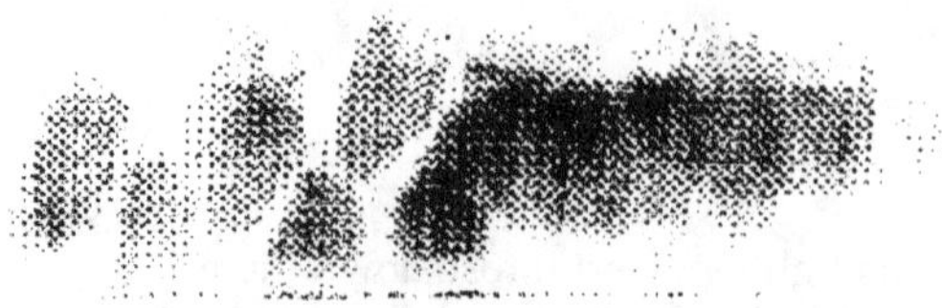

70

CHARLIE PENTANGELO SENT word to his Las Vegas colleagues that he needed some help. The promise of a finder's fee also focused minds. The Jewish community arrived early in the city when Bugsy Siegel saw the potential for an oasis in the sand and, in liaison with some Italian New York friends, several casinos sprung up as vehicles for the East Coast gangs to make a thundering amount of money.

Charlie's interest in Frank and Mary Lou reached Paulie who oversaw the mob operations throughout the Flamingo casino and hotel. What Charlie asked, you wanted to deliver—especially when greenbacks were involved.

Paulie greeted Angelo and Rico from the Five Boroughs and they hit the streets to find the man and woman who'd stolen Charlie's cash. There's nobody worse than a thief who steals. Paulie felt nothing but contempt for Frank and Mary Lou.

The three men walked all day and found nada. Lots of couples but none fitting the description provided by their source in the FBI. They also had the inside track from the Baltimore Shylock.

Rico reckoned the smart thing to do was not to walk round town trying to find two people in tens of thousands. The way he saw it, neither Paulie nor Angelo cared whether they found the man and the woman—what they wanted was the money. So instead of asking about the couple, Rico thought he should ask himself where he had hide a million dollars in cash if he was new to the city.

His answer was telling: bury it somewhere or shove it in a safe. Vegas was surrounded by a desert, so if he buried the take, there was no way anyone would ever find it. If he'd stored it with a hotel, he had a chance. A trip around town revealed only one new couple who had asked reception to put aside sufficiently large bags to fit that much cash. Trouble was they were thirty years too old to be Lagotti and his moll.

This left Rico with a final idea: there were only two other places with locked boxes he could think of: the lockers at either the railroad terminal or the airport. The other guys were obsessed with stalking the wide streets of Las Vegas to catch the couple but Rico was convinced.

He popped over to the airstrip to scout the joint but the lockers were too small. That left the station. So he hunkered down and waited for his prey to come to him.

After five hours sitting in the corner of the depot, nothing had happened, no one had appeared and Rico was in desperate need to visit the head. The only thing that stopped him was the fear that if he left his post for even a minute, that would be the time they grabbed the cash and exited the city. And Paulie did not want to be the guy to give them a free pass out of town.

Meantime the three others had given up on the streets and looked inside the casinos. What else do people do when they come to Vegas? Without the gambling there is literally nothing to occupy a person in a city stuck in the middle of the desert.

It's too damn hot to stay outside for more than thirty minutes and the only places open are hotels and casinos. So stood to reason the two thieves were playing poker, blackjack or trying their hand at the roulettes or slots.

Their problem was that they were outnumbered. Three of them and countless gaming dens to search but they had something no law enforcement officer could call on: the influence of the mob.

Each casino was awash with guys behind the scenes watching. Watching for card cheats on the tables and checking the staff weren't taking a sneaky dip in the house winnings. There was an army of eyes staring at the inside of the casinos and once they received descriptions of the Lansdowne robbers, all those eyeballs were in the pay of Paulie's men. It would only be a matter of time before someone spotted the two and they'd be done for.

Having passed the description to every casino they could find, the three guys headed to the bar at the Sands and waited for the word.

"Like taking candy from a baby."

"Or a million from a pair of douches."

Meantime, Charlie Pentangelo sat in his loft apartment in New York and wondered why everyone was spending so long recovering his money. Two small-time crooks shouldn't be that hard to find—not in a city where there were so many hoods hanging around.

THE NEON LIGHTS of Vegas were shining when Frank and Mary Lou appeared in the Mint reception after their honeymoon.

"Where do you feel lucky?"

"Caesar's Palace."

"Let's do it."

They walked down the strip passing the Riviera, the Stardust and the Desert Inn until Caesar's loomed on the right-hand side. Into the lobby, past reception and off into the casino.

They left the neon lights behind and passed the fruit machines to reach the cards. First thing, Frank stopped near a blackjack table and watched, draping his arm around Mary Lou's shoulders.

"We need chips."

Off to the side, between the card tables and the roulette wheels stood a glass-fronted cashier counter. He pulled out two hundred dollars in dirty notes and handed them to the cashier who swapped them for a series of colored chips: ten blue and twenty red.

He split the chips fifty-fifty between them and they headed to a table with three others already playing.

"Just bet the opposite color to me, okay?"

"Sure thing. This will work, right?"

"Should do. You go first and I'll be over in a minute."

Mary Lou approached a table and sat down, watching the bets land and the wheel turn. She kept the chips tightly in her hand although the others left theirs lying in front on them. After a lifetime of waiting, Frank appeared on the other side of the table.

He placed a red chip—five dollars—on red so she did the same on black. They were almost certain of one of them winning—there were two green zero and double-zero options too. The small white ball stopped bouncing around the wheel and settled on black. She couldn't remember the number—it didn't matter. She had won and Frank had lost so she received a ten-dollar blue chip. Ten bucks bet and ten dollars returned but with some different chips. They carried on like this for a while, churning through their chips. For the first minute, Mary Lou was up and then for the next two, Frank won.

She was down to her last two chips: one red, one blue. He winked at her and placed two chips over four numbers each. She didn't know what to do because she couldn't cover his bet. His two chips were on both black and red numbers: he was gambling for real now. He'd thrown their scheme out the window. The past three balls had come up red-black-black so Mary Lou went for broke with a fifteen dollar ride on red.

The ball hurtled along the edge of the wheel and settled down into a slot. Red. She'd up their ante by fifteen dollars. Then she looked up at Frank who was grinning from ear to ear. The croupier pushed four green chips over toward him—that was one hundred dollars off that single spin, along with the two hundred they'd already moved around the table.

Frank winked and stood up, followed by Mary Lou a moment later. They headed off to a poker game and perched with several spectators watching a round with over a thousand in the pot. A man with a beard won and they all applauded.

"Let's wait awhile and do that again."

"You confused me at the end."

"Yeah? I had a good vibe about the number two and fourteen. No idea why, but it worked."

"The important thing isn't the winning though, is it?"

"No, but it sure feels great, babe."

There was no answer to that because Frank was right. There was nothing in this world like knowing you've beaten someone. And beating the house on a roulette wheel is a mighty difficult task. They both knew the only way to succeed was to play for a short while—and stop if you ever look as though you're sitting on a losing streak. Not following those simple rules makes you a terminal loser.

He placed all the green chips into his pocket.

"That's what we walked in with so it's safe. This time let's play to win."

"Just don't bet against each other."

"We can have some fun if you like. Don't place any even bets."

"No black-red or odd-evens?"

"Nope. If we lose what's in our hands it won't matter, so we can earn ourselves a little scratch."

Two minutes later they sat at a different wheel and placed a small bet. Frank covered four numbers each time and Mary Lou saw what he chose and picked other sets of a similar value. She reckoned that would maximize their chances of winning something.

The first time, the croupier took all their red chips but the second and third attempts, chips headed first to him and then to her. For the next set of three, first she won then they both lost with he chalking up a win at the end.

She looked down at her chips: one hundred dollars minimum without counting and he appeared to hold about the same. She stared at him as he considered placing more chips onto the green baize. He glanced up and saw her expression and nodded.

They both stood up, took their chips and strolled away from the table.

"I've got around one hundred fifty dollars. You?"

"Hundred forty plus the two hundred in my pocket."

"Let's cash out."

"Shame we can't do this with the whole half a million."

"They'll notice if we did and besides, shifting two hundred an hour would mean we'd be stuck in Vegas until a man landed on the moon."

Frank and Mary Lou headed towards a different cashier counter and handed over their chips. The cashier counted them twice and fished out a bunch of notes.

"Small denominations please."

The woman nodded and swapped out twenties for tens instead. She checked the money and passed them over to Frank, who thanked her and walked away.

He looked around the casino and leaned into Mary Lou's ear.

"Looks like we've got trouble."

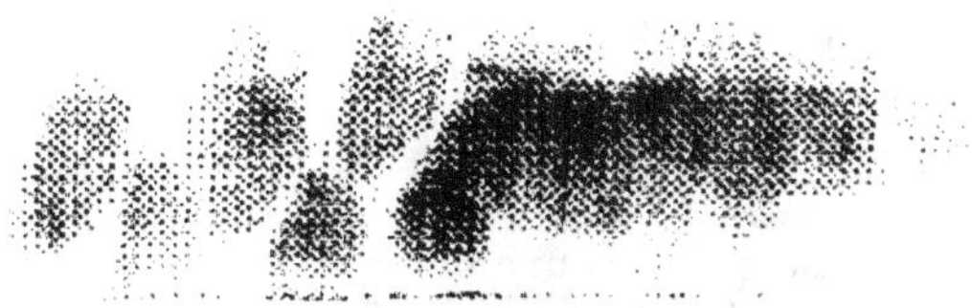

71

FRANK LOOKED LEFT then right, grabbed Mary Lou's hand and they headed straight ahead down the only aisle without a heavy stood in their way. Past the first table, he picked up the pace ever so slightly but not so much to make the casino staff figure they were about to bolt.

Two thickset guys in uniform walked along their own aisles in the same direction as Frank and Mary Lou.

"What we gonna do?"

"Gimme a minute, babe."

She fell silent and kept looking all around her to spot a clear line of escape but nothing was visible. Frank was doing the same and reached the same conclusion. They carried on one step at a time, brushing past blackjack players as they walked. On each occasion, a head turned and someone else expressed their displeasure at being interrupted.

The two continued stomping down the aisle annoying patrons. The heavies were no nearer—but no further away—than when they'd collected the clean money from the counter. At the end of the blackjack tables were a set of roulette wheels. A lightbulb pinged on above Frank's head.

The little white ball had just been thrown into a wheel on the left, so he leaned into another table, picked up a handful of chips and threw them up in the air. The players screamed—one of them tried to punch him but Frank sidestepped and dodged that bullet.

More usefully, everyone leaped to the floor to grab as many pieces of plastic as they could. Bedlam. A pile of people appeared from behind them. The casino guys had nowhere to go. As much as they wanted to carry on pursuing the pair, their more immediate problem was to stop the fight breaking out right in front of their faces. Punches rained down on a young man and a middle aged woman. Every gambler grabbed at the free money lying on the carpet.

Frank led Mary Lou past the rest of the roulette wheels until he caught sight of an exit. They hightailed toward the sign and out into the night. She looked back over her shoulder: no one appeared for at least two seconds.

"Keep running."

They did so until they vanished in the crowds marching along the strip and that was when they stopped, dusted themselves down and walked at the same pace as everyone else on the sidewalk. Sometimes the best way to hide is to melt into the crowd.

"Did they make us somehow?"

"Could have been the money we deposited, babe."

"Or the mob tipped them off?"

"We were in one of their casinos but that's true of almost every place in the city."

"But they were after us, weren't they?"

"Definitely. They were trying to corner us, for sure."

"But was it the mob or the Feds?"

"No fucking clue, babe."

Mary Lou nodded and fell silent to figure out quite who it was they'd escaped from.

"How much longer can we stay in Vegas, you reckon?"

"If we survive until tomorrow morning, we'll be doing well."

"Think we'll make it?"

"Yeah. The crowds work in our favor and at most they've seen our hair color. Don't mean they know who we are."

"Could it have been the funny money?"

"The First Bank of Baltimore would have issued a list of the notes we stole and they'd have wired the serial numbers to anyone who wanted them."

Mary Lou hoped he was right otherwise they were as good as dead.

"We shouldn't go back to the hotel."

"Is there anything we need from there? Where d'you put your locker key?"

"It's still by my rose, Frank. Where's yours?"

"Heel of my shoe?"

"Doesn't that hurt?"

"Once you've been in the joint, you learn to take the pain of hiding objects in places you hope nobody dares to search."

Those words soaked into Mary Lou and she stopped thinking about it because it created unpleasant ripples in the night. And things were bad enough without images of keys hidden in Frank's crevices popping into her head.

"We need to get off the streets. If they're a few hundred feet behind us, we're sitting ducks out in the open."

"Yep. Where to?"

"Another casino?"

"I wonder if there's a movie house anywhere in this town."

"For the locals maybe. Why?"

"Who'd be stupid enough to catch a film if you're on the lam?"

"Dillinger and no one else."

For reasons that escaped her understanding, Frank's argument made sense. In a warped way that defied logic, but in the absence of any other idea, this became the best plan they had.

At the far end of the strip, they turned left and walked up to the Rialto box office and bought two tickets for whatever had started most recently. They were in luck as *The Thomas Crown Affair* was about to begin. What better movie for them to watch than a tale of robberies, deceit and love.

They sat near the emergency exit in case of trouble but none came calling. They were right: no one expected them to be in a cinema. All eyes were searching for a couple in a casino or in a restaurant.

By the time the end credits rolled, Frank and Mary Lou were tired and needed somewhere to sleep that wasn't the Mint. They took the car out of town and turned off into the desert. When they couldn't see the highway any more, he hit the brake.

"It'll get cold later but no one'll find us here."

Until the sun rose, they both slept fitfully but at least they got some rest. Only problem was they'd have to go back for the take before they could kiss goodbye to Sin City.

OVER THE LAST few days, Anthony had spent all his time with Bobby and Mickey. As entertaining as the guys were, Anthony would have been happy never to live another moment in their company ever again.

Anthony realized Bobby was okay: the fella whacked people for a living, so he wouldn't be the most fun guy to hang around. At least he kept his trap shut most of the time; the same could not be said of Mickey. He'd run off his mouth at a moment's notice and keep going until no one was listening. Then carry on for another minute at a bare minimum in case someone regained consciousness and needed an update on his views on life.

When this happened, Anthony would glance at Bobby who looked like he was planning to ax murder Mickey. With anybody else, this might have been a metaphor but Bobby's expression showed he was giving the idea serious consideration.

As soon as Frank Senior received word from the Feds that Mary Lou and Frank were off to Vegas, Anthony and his merry men took the first plane over and holed up in the Sahara, next to the Thunderbird and on the edge of casino land. Two days in a row they'd toured the station and the airport to find zip. Then they walked around the casinos hoping to spot the pair but nada.

Now they were bored and tetchy. The only thing keeping Anthony together was catching them and dragging their sorry asses over to Frank Senior. If he was lucky, he'd get to torture them before he killed them. If not, the finder's fee would keep him in clover for a while—long enough to buy two girls from the KitKatt Club for an entire night of debauched fun before he came home and bought a necklace for his girlfriend. He might take her to Atlantic City for a weekend too and he could win back the cash he spent on the dancers. Everyone'd be a winner.

First, he had to get the pair of them—and the money. Bobby and Mickey needed to be separated for several hours as there was a limit for any human being to be in the same space as Mickey. Anthony made a mental note never to call on the guy again. A big mistake not to be repeated under any circumstances.

"Mickey, you walk the strip and see if you can find our pair there. Bobby, do you want to check out some casinos? Me, I'll take a stroll toward the airport and then off to the railroad station. Let's meet back at our hotel in three hours."

"Why me?"

"Because I say so and I'm paying your wages. Don't turn everything into a major case."

"I'll cover the Sahara, Thunderbird, Riviera and right on through to the Tropicana. Mickey, which end of the strip will you work first?"

"Dunno."

"Decide."

"Huh? Okay, the Hacienda."

"Fine. As you'll be at one end, I'll start at the Sahara on the other side. That way we'll have more eyes on more places. Right Anthony?"

"You said it, Bobby. For the same reason I'll hit the station and hop over to the North Las Vegas Air Terminal. After that, McCarran Airport."

"Jeez. You guys will be warm and comfortable indoors while I'm pounding the streets."

"Let it go, Mickey. Now is not the time for belly aching."

Bobby and Anthony stared down Mickey until even he understood to shut his mouth and headed out onto the street.

"Thank you for doing that."

"No problem, Bobby. Wish I'd come up with it sooner. I didn't think Mickey would behave this way. Every other occasion I've used him, he might not be the sharpest tool in the box, but he's always been effective."

"I understand. We've all had dealings with his kind before."

"But you get parole after a year."

They both laughed and Bobby tipped his hat before heading out the door himself, followed by Anthony who headed for the station.

When he arrived, there was nothing to see. He stayed for an hour and two trains came and left. Four passengers in total made their way along the concourse. The only unusual activity was a solitary guy hanging around the platform gates.

He wore a normal suit—three piece with a tie—but he was noticeable by being there at all. Anthony was loitering in the station at a dumb time of the night, but no one else spends an hour there for kicks.

If you're meeting someone you don't turn up that early when fifty feet away is a hotel bar and casino. Made no sense.

Also, for a man stood by the gates, he showed no interest in any train on any platform. Instead, he spent his entire time facing the left luggage area. As much as he was leaning casually on a wall, Anthony gained the distinct impression those eagle eyes of his were trained on one location and no other.

He considered the suit some more along with the obsession over the lockers. Something clicked inside Anthony's head. Frank Senior was right: they were not the only ones seeking the First Bank of Baltimore robbers. The New York mob must have dispatched their people too and he was staring at one of them as he stood and waited.

This sent Anthony into a flurry. Until this point he had assumed all they had to do was be in the right city at the right time and he'd make Frank Senior a happy man. But seeing the dude in the suit: Anthony knew they'd have to up their game and fight hard to be the ones to catch Frank and Mary Lou. Mickey was a eunuch in a harem so Anthony needed to invest in Bobby if they were to go back home with their heads held high.

THURSDAY JUNE 26

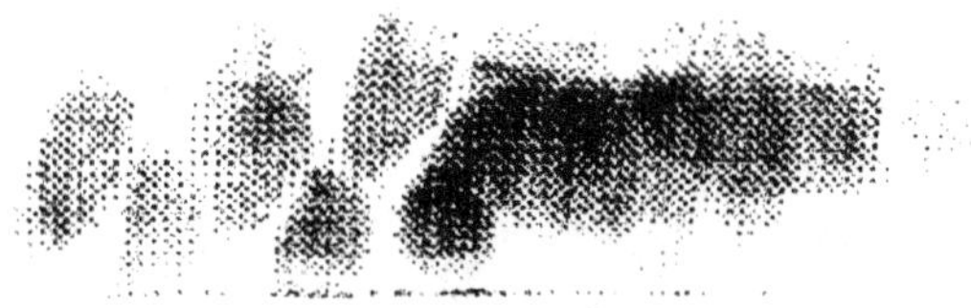

72

MARY LOU'S TEETH chattered her awake in perfect synchrony with Frank's. The sun shone into the driver's side of the car casting a Frank-shaped silhouette on her. He switched on the engine and waited before pushing warm air into the cabin. Ten minutes later, Mary Lou felt the tips of her fingers again, having placed them between her legs next to her crotch all that time.

"Can we get a coffee somewhere?"

"Sure thing, babe. It was Alaska in here last night."

"You're telling me."

Frank drove back onto the highway and they headed further away from Vegas until they hit a diner and gas station, all isolated in the middle of the desert. Four trucks were parked outside and nothing else for miles.

Coffees, scrambled eggs, toast for two. They sat in silence for the start of their meal, thawing out. Frank gobbled down his breakfast faster than Mary Lou could blink. She took longer, not wanting to choke on each mouthful.

The heat from the warm food sunk down her gullet and landed with a splat in her stomach. Then she washed the mixture down with the mug of coffee. The waitress topped up their drinks twice before they declared themselves full.

"Needed that."

"Me too. Warmer now?"

"And some. I'll have to shift the button on my skirt."

Frank grinned and thought about Mary Lou's belly and the rose beneath it. He smiled some more.

"We can rest here a while before we make our next move."

"And what should that be?"

"Well, we need to collect our bags so first we're going back to Vegas."

"They're on to us, aren't they?"

"Yep. For those casino guys to pick up on the money so fast means the mob knows where we are."

"And if they have it figured, then the Feds will know."

"Along with Uncle Frankie."

"Last night you thought the casino had matched the serial numbers on our notes."

"I did but I've been thinking about it. If it was just that, I can't see how they'd have spotted us so quickly by the tables. They had more information than that."

"Jeez. And you want us to go back into the city?"

"We have no option if we're to get our money. I don't want to but we have no choice. Else all we've got is a few hundred dollars in our pockets. And we didn't come all this way to live off chump change until the end of time."

"I don't like it."

"Who does?"

He reached out his hand and placed it on Mary Lou's. They stared at each other for a moment, not needing to express the thoughts their eyes conveyed instead.

"And if we get in, out and survive. Where next?"

"What do you mean?"

"We've always said we're heading to California, but that means Frankie knows too…"

"…and if he knows it then so do the Feds and the mob."

"Right."

"So they'll be waiting for us again."

"California's a mighty big state."

"Yes, but there's only a handful of places to launder half a million. And they know them faster than we can find 'em."

"Where should we go instead?"

Frank's intonation implied a decision had been made but Mary Lou wasn't sure she agreed with it herself: she was only voicing a concern.

"North or south—take your pick."

"Canada or Mexico. You know any Spanish?"

"Enough to order a burrito."

"More than me then."

"That makes Canada our number one destination of choice."

"Perhaps. What would we do there? You got any connections?"

"None that'd give us a line on a wholesale money laundering operation."

"Say that louder, not all the waitresses heard you."

Mary Lou blushed and her eyes darted every which way as her entire body tensed.

"Relax, I was teasing."

She slapped his hand, playfully without spite.

"Don't. That wasn't nice."

"Sorry but this is quite an intense conversation, wouldn't you say?"

If Mary Lou had worn glasses, she'd have looked at Frank over the rims—with disdain. They sat in silence again, ruminating on the possibilities before them.

"Canada might be a good place to hide."

"But not a great location for us to launder the take."

"No. Sounds like we're off to the West Coast, anyway."

"Do you have any connections in Seattle instead?"

"None. You?"

"Nope."

"Done. We'll stick to the original plan and head to California. Once we've cleaned the cash, we decide at that point whether we're Canada bound."

"We are though, right?"

"With what we have now, yes. But we worry about it later. Our only real hope is the mob doesn't know our car so we can move around the city without too getting spotted."

Mary Lou sipped her coffee and thought for a spell.

"How much ammo you sitting on?"

"Enough to get out of trouble but not enough for an all-out gun battle in the streets of Las Vegas. What you planning?"

"Nothing. Just wondered if we were heading into a death trap."

"The Feds will want to capture us alive. It's their job. If we don't produce any heat, they'll keep their end of the bargain."

"Sure, Frank."

"The mob is only interested in the cash. They will only take a pop if we stand between them and the notes."

"Makes sense. What about good old Uncle Frankie?"

"He'll want the money first and foremost."

Mary Lou smiled.

"And then he'll want us dead."

He squeezed her hand and she squeezed back.

"We'll deal with that cocksucker before all this is over."

"Sure will, babe. But right now we gotta focus on getting into Vegas and grabbing our earnings."

They paid up, returned to the car and gunned the vehicle toward the entertainment capital of the world.

FRANK DROVE IN utter silence. Neither he nor Mary Lou wanted to say a word, both wrapped in their thoughts: these might be the last few minutes of their lives.

Along the Salt Lake Highway and into Vegas, the car passed by the Silver Nugget and reached the fork that split North Main from Las Vegas Boulevard. He turned left onto the Boulevard and then right on Fremont. The railroad station loomed straight at them and Mary Lou peered into the distance hoping to catch sight of the mob, the Feds and who knows what.

"Drop into the parking lot, hon'."

He pulled into a space pointing at the exit in case they needed a fast getaway.

"Ready?"

"Let's do it."

They both left the car at the same time and closed their doors in tandem. They took the long route to the building, around the edge of the lot, so they stayed in the shadows as much as possible.

A steady trickle of people came and went: it was still early enough for rush hour. When they reached the main entrance, men and women jostled them as they stood staring into the large open space that made up the station foyer. To the left, ticket counters and to the right, lockers. Straight ahead were the gates leading to the platforms.

They headed off to wait in line for a ticket. He stared at the lockers and she kept her eye on the passengers as they scurried around the concourse.

"See anything?"

"Dunno. Maybe."

"Where?"

"By the entrance to platform one."

She followed the platform signs counting down: three, two, one. Ten feet from the gate stood a guy who spent his entire time staring at the lockers. He remained stationary, leaning against the wall with his full concentration on the left luggage area.

"Three-piece suit in Summer?"

"A mob guy…"

"…or a Fed."

"Not with those shoes."

Frank was right. No Hoover man would wear brown brogues: not regulation footwear. Either he was an honest Joe citizen, or he was in the mob. Mary Lou wasn't certain, but she doubted he was one of Frankie's boys. Over the years, she'd seen almost all of them.

"Let's not waste any money on a train ticket."

They left the line and sauntered, arm in arm, off to a newsstand fifteen feet further away from the main entrance. Frank bought a paper and Mary Lou grabbed some gum. The couple stood next to each other, pretending to read the front page together while staring at Paulie, the guy in the three-piece. He never moved.

"What we gonna do?"

"Have to assume he's not kosher."

"If someone looks like a rat and smells like a rat…"

"…chances are he is a rat."

"And he is gnawing on a scrap of cheese right now."

Mary Lou giggled and dug an elbow into Frank's side.

"That's a mouse, silly. Rats eat anything. They don't care."

"If he's got a description of us, we're toast."

"Where are the bags?"

"Second column at the far end by the window."

"So there's no way to sneak around the lockers, grab them and leave without him spotting us?"

"No chance. He is perched there for a reason."

The two carried on looking, desperate to find some leverage.

"We could always plain shoot him."

"Not from this range, babe. Besides, do you not think people might notice? We need time to reach the lockers and get the hell out of Dodge."

"Okay, shooting him isn't the way but as far as I can tell, we've got to convince him to leave his post. Killing him is one method."

"What do you have in mind?"

"I suck him off in the bathroom and we kill him there."

"Sure, but mobsters tend not to let themselves get lured off the job even by a siren such as beautiful you."

"Charmer."

"You're right. If he was an average Joe it'd work, but this suit is a professional."

"So we must figure out how to whack him if we can't fuck him off his perch."

"Yep, hon'."

"And shooting him is out of the question."

"I've no silencer. A single shot will ring out in this building and bring a ton of shit raining down on us."

"We don't need that, for sure. You got a knife?"

"Um, no. You seen me with a knife these past few days?"

"No but I thought it might be worth asking."

"Let's focus on what we can do rather than making up kit we don't have."

He turned the page to continue the charade of news reading. Meanwhile, they both looked, pondered and peered again.

"Stay here for a minute."

Mary Lou walked off to the other side of the main entrance, leaving Frank to wonder what was going on. When she returned, he noticed the sparkle in her eyes and the upturned corners of her mouth.

"I've got it."

"Spill."

"There's a door in the wall he's leaning on. It leads somehow from platform one to the lockers. Must be a service room in between."

"Go on."

"One of us goes onto the platform, through the service room and sneaks up behind him while the other walks across to the lockers. He'll be staring ahead at the bags and the other can break the fucker's neck."

Frank nodded.

"Like it. Who'll snap the guy's spine and who will risk being shot by the dude as we open a locker?"

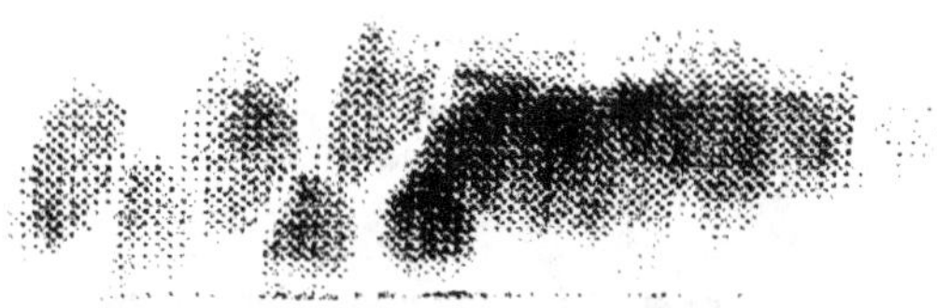

73

FRANK BOUGHT A ticket to New York from the kiosk as that was the next train to leave platform one. Mary Lou stood some way off so they wouldn't appear to be a couple. He showed his rectangular piece of card to the station guard, who let him proceed.

That was her cue to head towards the lockers—not too fast but with enough speed so Joe would recognize her and stay glued to his spot. As she walked across the railroad foyer, a man approached her. She gripped the strap of her handbag: he didn't alter his trajectory.

"Excuse me, miss."

She looked at him and carried on walking.

"Sorry, miss. Can I have one second, please?"

He wore a blue suit with a white shirt and no tie and no hat. She remained silent and tried to ignore him.

"Just a moment of your time."

The john wasn't going away soon. If she didn't stop, there'd be a commotion and she couldn't afford that to happen right now. Not at this precise minute.

"What?"

"Did you drop these?"

She glanced down at his hand, which proffered a pair of white silk gloves.

"No. Sorry. Not mine."

Mary Lou started walking again having disposed of the guy nice and easy.

"Well, can I help you with wherever you're going?"

"No thanks. I'm good."

"I'm sure you are but can I help you?"

"Now why do you want to do that?"

"You are an incredibly attractive girl. I can't think of a better way to spend a single second more in your company."

"Get out of here, bud, before I call the cops. I'm a married woman and don't need your sort soiling my day."

"Only saying…"

The guy wandered off to find another person to schmooze. She turned her head to the left to discover whether Frank had got through the service corridor yet but no sign of him. She was almost at the lockers and she must already be within Joe's field of vision by now.

Mary Lou walked down the first line of metal boxes, pretending to check on their numbers. Her key was still hidden and she had no intention of taking it out until they were ready. Having arrived at the end, she worked her way back via the second row passing their own lockers. Then she did the same with the third and final aisle. Then she sauntered nearer the platforms and spotted Joe continuing to lean against the wall. Bad news: he should be dead by now.

FRANK SHOWED HIS ticket to the guard who clipped it and let him through. On the left-hand side was the New York train and on the right was a wall. A hundred feet along Frank made out a door marked for staff only.

He marched for about seventy feet then stopped and leaned against the brickwork and pretended to read the contents of his paper. Once he was sure the guard was busy with another passenger, he moved down the platform and tried the handle. Locked, Goddamn it.

Two deep breaths and he tried the door knob again. This time he twisted it in the other direction and the wood pinged open. A quick dart inside and he entered a darkened room. He'd been so fast at closing the door, he had no light to find the switch. He felt along the wall either side of the entrance until he arrived at a large enough square under his fingertips. In the middle was a flipper which he pulled upwards.

A solitary bulb sprang into life in the center of the ceiling and an array of filing cabinets and a desk appeared before him. On the far side of the room was another door. This is the one he assumed would lead him to Joe. He padded over and tried its handle. This time it was actually locked shut.

A trip to the table revealed nothing but the acid taste of disappointment and none of the cabinets contained anything but papers, files and more sheets. He bent down to examine the lock and breathed a sigh of relief. He pulled a hair pin from his wallet—kept for just such occasions—and twiddled it around the opening while he listened to the sounds inside. He heard a clunk and he knew he'd picked the mechanism.

Aware of the noise he'd generated on the other side, Frank opened it a crack to check what was happening and scanned the reception foyer and Joe leaning against the wall not twenty feet away. The only reason the guy hadn't noticed the door open was because of the hubbub in the station and that his attention was taken up by some activity at the lockers.

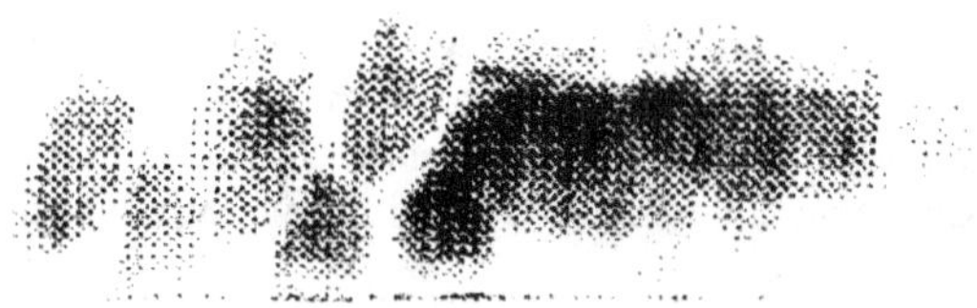

74

RICO WAS BORED rigid. He had been waiting for a lifetime and had achieved nothing apart from a stiff back and aching legs. But that didn't stop him: he was certain he was in the right place if only the thieves would show up and prove him correct. Each time someone walked close to the lockers, Rico watched their every move but there had only been two people so far who'd even gone near that part of the station.

Now a woman had surfaced who kinda looked like the description in his pocket—only she had black hair, not blond. That could have come out of a bottle. The behavior which piqued Rico's interest was that she walked up and down each line of lockers but did nothing more than that. Strange. People know which locker they need to return to. When she got to the end of the last row, the dame hurried back to his side of and stared straight at him. He was sure of that.

Rico stood upright, no longer leaning against the wall. He put his hand in his pants pocket to remind himself he was packing heat. Then he took a step forward—and halted. The dame was acting weird, although that didn't mean she had a million in bank notes in her panties. Yes she looked cute and had caught his attention, but did that make her one of the robbers? He hung there and waited to see what she did next.

Without warning, a hand covered his mouth and an arm engulfed his throat. He choked, but no sound came out because of the vice-like grip of the palm over his lips. Tried to scream but nothing. Four seconds later, Rico ceased to feel anything as Frank twisted his head and snapped his neck. He slumped to the ground and Frank dragged him back into the staff room. All they had to do now was get the money and leave the station.

AS SOON AS Frank returned to the foyer, Mary Lou slipped to the end of the lockers and fumbled inside her skirt and panties to grab the key.

"You okay?"

"Sure thing, babe."

He took the warm metal proffered to him and headed straight to a locker and pulled out one of the black bags. Then he bent down to tie his shoe and flashed the other key in the palm of his hand. Twenty seconds later, he was carrying a bag too and they both walked, fingers entwined, out the main entrance and into the parking lot.

At that point, they heard an enormous bellow ring out around the foyer. Joe had been found and the word 'murder' was carrying in the air. A whistle blew and they had only a few seconds before the cops cordoned off the station and swarmed round the place.

He picked up the pace until they reached the car and threw both bags into the back.

"You drive."

"Are you sure, hon'?"

"Not a discussion. Let's do it."

Mary Lou left the parking space and headed out the lot. A Vegas cop was already standing at the entrance looking in on every vehicle. When Mary Lou's turn came to pass him, Officer Sanchez stopped them in their tracks.

"Steady, babe."

She wound down her window and opened her mouth to speak.

"Hello, ma'am."

"Hi, officer. Anything the matter?"

"There's been an incident inside the station and we're just checking everyone at the moment."

"Oh, how unpleasant."

"Yes, ma'am. Who's in the car with you?"

"My husband."

"Morning, sir."

"Morning, officer."

"Not driving, sir?"

"A long journey to get here and I'm tired. Thought I'd let the little lady take the strain."

"Where you traveled from?"

"Seattle. Been stuck in a tin can for a lifetime."

"I bet. There's no direct route from Seattle to Vegas, is there?"

"Nope. Had to change in Chicago."

"Okay, move along now then."

Sanchez waved them forwards and stopped the car behind them instead.

"Nice and steady, babe."

"Five miles under the speed limit, hon'."

"Let's take a trip to the Convention Center."

Mary Lou did as instructed and rode down the strip, turned left and left again. The convention parking lot was huge.

"Time for a fresh ride."

They drove round a while, like they were in a store choosing a dress. Every so often, she would slow down for Frank to take a better look at a vehicle but either it was too new or too old, too clean or too dirty.

"How about that pickup?"

"Bit big for our needs isn't it?"

"Maybe but it'd be the kind of car to get stolen in this lot wouldn't you say?"

"Good point, but it doesn't feel right somehow."

"We must steal something soon or we'll run out of gas, Frank."

"I know, but I don't want to mess this up."

More slow-mo driving until Mary Lou reckoned they'd covered every aisle in the lot—and still no decision made. She was getting impatient. Each minute they remained in Vegas was another opportunity for the Feds, the mob, Frankie's boys or the local cops to catch them. She ground her molars.

"Let me find one, hon' 'cause we gotta get outta here."

Frank nodded and squeezed her knee. He was paralyzed by indecision but didn't want to admit it to himself or Mary Lou.

She drove round some more until she stopped next to a green saloon.

"Here we are."

"Why?"

"The passenger window is ajar so they're asking for us to steal it. And should be easier to get inside."

"Done."

Less than a minute later, Frank sat in the driver's seat fiddling with wires below the dashboard. Ten seconds more, the engine roared into life.

"You follow me out of town and we'll ditch the old ride in the desert. Pass me one bag: just in case."

Steady as a rock, the two cars spluttered away from Vegas and Mary Lou kept three vehicles behind the green car. She always had a clear line of sight on Frank but, at a glance, they didn't look like they were a convoy.

Four miles out the city, he pulled off the highway and headed inland for six or seven hundred feet. Then he stopped by a dune.

"We can't burn this one—even if we had the gasoline."

"It's a hell of a dramatic signature though."

Instead they searched through every inch of the car making sure there was not one personal item left inside to connect them to that lump of metal. Trunk, rear seat, glove compartment. They both went over the whole thing so nothing could be missed. Frank got behind the wheel and Mary Lou sat beside him. The engine had been running all the time. He was about to move off when she put a hand on his.

"Are we sure we should go to LA?"

"It's still the easiest place to launder the take. I know one or two people there. Anywhere else will be the same as Vegas."

"Won't they be waiting for us again though?"

"The City of Angels is sprawling and spread out. Nothing like compact old Sin City. You could spend a hundred years in LA and never come across someone who lived on the other side of the metropolis to you."

The edges of Mary Lou's eyes were reddening up and a tear was welling in one corner.

"We'll be okay. When we hit town, I'll make some calls, do the business and then we're out of there living the high life where Uncle Frankie and the lot of them can't touch us."

Mary Lou smiled nervously. He kissed her full on the lips.

"Trust me. It'll work out just fine."

He hit the gas pedal and the tires turned but no motion occurred. Frank sighed.

"Damn sand."

He put the shift stick into second gear and tried again. This time they lurched forward until he regained control and the wheels found solid highway.

"Next stop: Tinseltown."

Frank tuned in a rock 'n' roll station and they headed south west. Mary Lou stared out the window and thought about the ending to The Thomas Crown Affair.

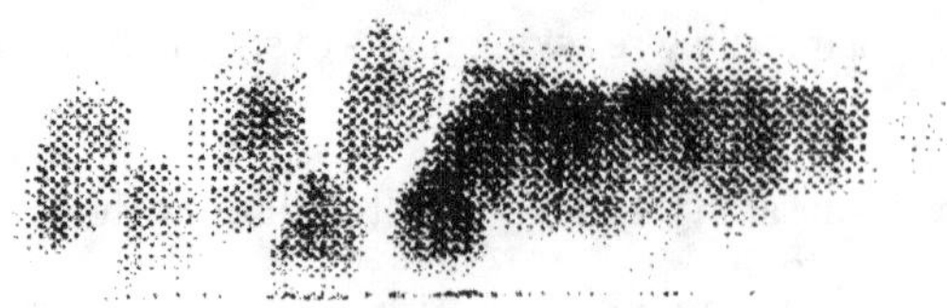

75

WHAT FELT A short time later, they crossed the state line and watched as the highway forced itself through woods and forests: like the trees would take over the road and were chasing them down the tarmac.

"Before we reach LA, we need to get a game plan. We were lucky in Vegas. And we might kid ourselves but it'll be worse on the coast. I know it's a big bad city but we must operate carefully if we're to survive laundering half a million dollars under the radar, babe."

"Well, the least we should do before we arrive is to find some clothes to put on our backs. We've been wearing this lot since before I can remember."

"Sure thing, babe."

"And a toothbrush."

They passed a handful of cabins at five miles below the speed limit. A store broke the monotony of their journey and he pulled into one of the four spaces provided at the side of the road.

They could have been forgiven for thinking it was another log cabin but its neon sign attached to the front flashed that it was a general store. When Frank and Mary Lou walked in, they saw almost any item they could think of available for sale. In one aisle were two piles of red plaid shirts and jeans. They rifled through until they found the correct sizes and picked toiletries, along with some other essentials.

"We're gonna look like quite a pair."

"Yeah, not what I had in mind."

"Let's see if we can find something a little less…"

"…Hicksville?"

"Yep."

A scout round the store revealed a variety of garden tools, digging implements and many cans of food, but no other clothes. Frank took a shovel.

"We'll get more things to wear somewhere else but at least we've got something different for now."

"Sure, hon'. But we'll dress like we're cousins."

"That's normal round here."

They chuckled and proceeded to the front to pay using some of their clean casino cash. Once they'd returned to the car, they changed into their new belongings and Mary Lou took over the driving.

"What do you think we should do?"

"We need to get the Feds, the mob and Frankie off our backs."

"Any ideas?"

"The G-men are looking for the money but what they love is to arrest people. So we should give them some bodies to find."

"Bodies?"

"Yes. We must get ourselves a pair of corpses."

"You're kidding me."

"Nope. Two burnt bodies all crisped and singed. That'd be ideal."

"Frank. Are you saying…"

"We don't have to go murdering anyone, only if we have to."

Frank's expression was more serious than she could remember. He was right though: if the Feds thought they were dead they'd have to give up the chase.

"To the morgue?"

"I reckon—unless we want to become the honeymoon killers."

"Not if we can help it."

"I agree."

Mary Lou set off and headed to the nearest town once she'd spotted a road sign: where there were people, there were deaths. And when folk died, they went to the funeral home.

Fifteen miles down the highway, she stopped the car two hundred feet from the Kingston Range mortuary. The building stood on the edge of a forested area next to a surgery. The doctor must have been out on call because no lights were on—nor in the morgue. In small-town America, the doc was the mortician too so there was little chance of a flurry of concerned citizens arriving to open up for the day's business.

They hopped round the back in their matching jeans and shirts. he jimmied the door free using the newly acquired shovel and they hurried inside.

"Should have bought a flashlight."

"Yes, babe."

Frank improvised by switching the light on and they scurried to a side room to hunt out some bodies. There was a row of small chrome doors on a shelf, as they'd expected. Each door, four feet square, housed a gurney big enough to fit a corpse. One by one, they opened the doors to find what they needed. The first two were empty and the third held a woman, the fourth and fifth contained an old man and a younger guy.

"Frank?"

"Yes, babe?"

"If we take two of these corpses and burn them, even the Feds will work out what we've done and will carry on chasing us."

Frank leaned back on a wall and thought for a spell.

"What if we steal more bodies than we need?"

"Make it look like there's a body snatcher loose?"

"Why not?"

"Won't that bring a ton of G-men down in the area?"

Frank considered the idea some more.

"How about taking the bodies from here and razing it to the ground?"

"We burn this joint down to hide that we're burning two bodies somewhere else. Hon', this won't work."

More silent thinking from Frank as he mulled over various scenarios.

"We need to get outta here, don't we?"

They shut the gurneys, closed the doors and switched off the light. There was no way to hide the smashed door jamb, so he broke open a glass cabinet and took some meds out to make the break-in appear to be kids stealing drugs.

Back in the car and down the road some more.

"We gotta kill ourselves a man and a woman."

"Not a couple though."

"No. Too hard to do and too obvious for the cops."

THEY WERE SILENT as they came to terms with the reality of what they were contemplating. Mary Lou understood why they had to murder two people but she wasn't happy about the situation. Frank saw matters differently: the deaths of strangers would give him his freedom and secure his life with her.

After twenty minutes they reached a town called Baker. There were at least three streets with stores and behind the residential area lay a small airfield. Planes arrived occasionally but there were enough coming and going to create a flow of people through what would otherwise be a tiny gathering of country folk.

Frank and Mary Lou waited in the airstrip lot because someone flying out of town would not be missed for a while. The wait lasted only ten minutes as a car pulled in at the edge of the parking area away from the terminal. They followed it and parked nearby.

A man in his early thirties got out of the vehicle and took out a case from the trunk. The guy was around Frank's height and build.

Mary Lou stood back as he walked a few paces behind him and looked both ways. He saw no one, raised the shovel and slammed it into the guy's head. He stumbled forwards and collapsed. She caught up and helped drag the traveler to his automobile and dump him in their trunk. He returned to grab his bag so it could join its erstwhile owner.

"And now we have a replacement car equipped with keys and free baggage filled with clothes for me, I hope."

They drove round the lot twice in case a woman turned up to make their job easier, but no luck. Instead, Mary Lou motored out with the body in the back and let the vehicle purr around the Baker residences. An hour later she was still driving up and down but no single females were on the streets that day.

"Let's make some house calls. This is getting ridiculous."

"Sure, babe."

She pulled in and parked next to a huddle of suburban bungalows. Mary Lou got out and headed towards one property while Frank walked round the back and vanished from her sight.

The first residence she tried gave no reply, but the second produced more success. A man appeared and she asked directions to the airstrip. She thanked him and hunkered two houses down before trying again. This time a woman opened the door.

"Hi, before you start, I'm not interested."

"Oh, I'm not selling anything. I'm new in town—just moved in across the street—and I was hoping I might borrow a cup of sugar. It'd be most neighborly of you."

"Sorry, we get so many sales reps round here. It's a defense mechanism."

"I understand. I'll end up doing the same in a few months time, I'm sure."

Those were the last words the woman heard because Frank's hands clamped around her throat and he dragged her backwards and snapped her neck in a single twist. Mary Lou ran inside and closed the door. She scampered into the bedroom and took some clothes out of wardrobes until she had a reasonable sized pile on the bed. She rifled through the woman's toiletries too, grabbing a perfume and a hairbrush. When she returned to the hallway, he had thrown a wallet on the floor and was stuffing notes into his pocket.

"This can look like she cut and run away. We'll leave the cops to figure the reason."

There was no evidence of anybody else living in the bungalow—something Frank had checked before he'd scratched the life out of Emily. That was the name on her ID.

He and Mary Lou rolled the woman into a blanket, careful to tuck in both ends. They carried her over to the car and dropped her into the trunk too. With the guy's body already there, he pushed down hard to get them both to fit. But all was good.

Next Frank sat behind the wheel and returned to the airport lot so she could follow him in the new car back toward the general store.

Half a mile short of that destination, they stopped and Mary Lou turned the vehicle round to face in the opposite direction. She parked on the verge, ten feet away from the highway. There were few cars on the road that afternoon which gave them the opportunity to wrestle the bodies into the front seats.

Frank siphoned gas from the tank and spread it inside the vehicle. He placed some bank notes in a valise he'd stolen from Emily. Not much: three hundred dollars.

Mary Lou lit a match and threw it through the window. Orange sparks licked the upholstery and traveled across the rear interior. With the windows open, the small lights grew into yellow flickering wisps and leaped onto the driver's seat until the whole inside filled with heat, darting flames and acrid smoke.

They hopped into the guy's car and motored towards Baker—still in silence.

"That should get the Feds off our tail."

"And if it doesn't?"

"We'll figure out something else—but it should. They'll have two bodies and some bank notes. Even they should be able to work out that equation."

Mary Lou nodded, knowing Frank was right and that once you've murdered one person, you might as well make it three because you can only fry in the mercy seat once in your life.

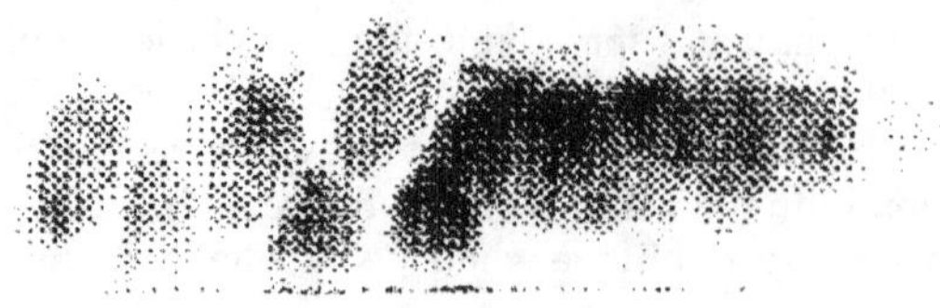

76

DRIVING DOWN THE road, Frank kept a hand on Mary Lou's thigh and left the other hanging on the wheel, five miles below the limit. They remained without talking for an age until she punctured the silence.

"That's not the end of our problems."

"No, babe."

"There's the mob to deal with and then Frankie."

She spat out the last word like a ball of mucus had landed on her tongue.

"Once we've laundered the cash, we should be able to negotiate with New York. If we give them their tithe, we might survive if we stay in this country."

"So if they don't catch up with us that'll leave Uncle Frankie."

"Yeah."

"He'll want the money."

"There'll be guys on the road after us by now. Who knows who it was watching those Vegas lockers."

"Do you think we did for one of Frankie's men?"

"Or the mob's. Neither is good."

"No, murder isn't good."

"Not quite what I meant. If it was Frankie's goon or an East Coast goon. We've killed one of theirs. Spilled blood gets paid with spilled blood—not an apology and a payoff."

Mary Lou pondered for a minute, eyes darting left and right as though she should now be hyper-aware of any sudden movement in case it is a goon seeking revenge with a gun.

"What are we going to do? We can't live like this for the rest of our days."

"We must make peace with everyone. It's the only way."

"Even if we leave the country?"

"They can cross the border as easily as you and I."

"What'll we do about Frankie?"

"Reason with him and convince him to give up the chase."

"We have gunned down his men, hon'."

"And he was expecting to get his hands on a large amount of money we have in our trunk."

Mary Lou giggled.

"There is that."

"He's not laughing though."

"Do I look like I care?"

"Probably not, but he does and we must focus on that."

"We're in the middle of nowhere but when we find a phone, we should talk and try to get him to agree to call off the hounds."

"Do you think he will?"

"We've got a better chance if we ask than if we carry on running."

"That's not what I asked."

"I know. Truth is I have no idea at all. But if we do nothing, he'll keep on coming until he takes all the money off us."

FRANK LAGOTTI SENIOR liked the Kitkatt Club—not because it made him an amazing amount of cash each week, which it did, but because it gave him wonderful access to pussy. These two items were the most important things in his life—passions he could not quell.

While he counted his marriage to Fran Lagotti in decades and not years, they remained together for a simple, irrefutable reason: they were Catholic and a divorce was impossible. And anyway, she was a good cook and ensured his clothes were cleaned and pressed.

When you are a Shylock, you don't always get paid back. On these occasions you can break bones or take advantage. Frankie became the majority owner of the Kitkatt Club because its founder was a terrible gambler and handing over the stock was the only way for him not to be thrown off the top of a tall building. Fair trade.

The reason the club made so much money was that it had two revenue streams. First was the bar where men came to drink overpriced hooch away from their wives and girlfriends. Second, there were the girls: the place was a strip joint and an occasional cathouse depending on the clientele.

Frankie sat near the back so he could keep an eye on his investment and enjoy the show. With all the troubles with his step nephew, Frank and the skirt Mary Lou, he needed to relax a little. The last few days had been stressful. He never wanted to deliver bad news to New York and his conversations with Pentangelo had been tense at best.

To relieve this tension, he had taken the girl known as June into one of the private rooms and fucked her from behind. After, he threw her out because she'd been stealing notes from patrons' wallets. That was not good for business. Now he sat and watched April and May on stage. April wore red panties and May sported green. They had both already got out their tits and he enjoyed the scene. June's titties had been too small for his taste but he wouldn't have to see them again.

There were only a handful of customers in the room but it was early yet, only seven. These guys were on their way home and would leave in the next thirty minutes or they were from out of town and were here until dawn.

August came over and replaced his cocktail.

"Thank you, but no. Get me a coffee."

Too many drinks this early in the night would not help Frankie's head the following morning. And clarity was king. As the girl walked away with his drink returned to her tray, he stared at her powder blue hot pants and the way her ass cheeks moved in a wonderful rhythm and bounce.

Two minutes later, she came back with his coffee which appeared with milk, sugar and three biscuits on a small plate.

"Thanks for the meal."

"You're welcome."

"When does your shift finish?"

"I've another six hours, Frankie."

"Anyone else working the tables right now?"

"Only me. It's quiet, but March starts at eight."

"See me once she's arrived and we can have a private conversation."

"You got it, Frankie."

He took another opportunity to stare at her body but this time watched her back and her hair. Then returned to her best feature: that ass.

After ten minutes, he was bored by the floorshow. There was nothing wrong with April and May's performance but with little energy in the room, everything was dull. And he didn't like the shape of their tits either.

He wandered into the office to look at the books. If semi-naked girls weren't working for him, counting cash would. The Kitkatt Club represented a mountain of money because nobody paid for the girls' services with a credit card. When Frankie took over the joint, one of his first acts was to improve security: dancers, bartenders, everyone were taking from the till and nobody had a clue. That stopped within a week. A barman lost a finger and a girl was thrown out after her face was slashed. No one dipped their beaks in his register anymore.

The Kitkatt was a regular depositor of large quantities of cash and Frankie also withdrew huge amounts too. This was a simple and easy way to launder bills for the mob. Dirty money goes into a bank and clean comes out. It was a useful method for laundering drug receipts but not great for the proceeds of robberies because those notes had known serial numbers.

Frankie checked that cash was flowing and went back to his table at the rear and sipped some water. September and November were on stage now but had done nothing more than a few dance steps. The warm-up would soon be over.

August padded over with a coffee and some liquor on her tray.

"Which would you prefer, Frankie?"

"I'll pass, dear, and stick to my water."

"Okay. March has arrived."

"Let's go."

He stood up and headed to the side of the auditorium leaving the girl to carry his tumbler. She followed him into a private room and watched him slump into the red leather couch with his legs apart —wide enough for her to fit in between his knees.

She shut the door and placed his drink on a small table, kneeled down and unzipped his pants. August was only too aware how rough he would be but she had no choice. Besides, if she handled him right, there'd be a Benjamin for her though she wouldn't be able to take a piss for three or four days without it hurting.

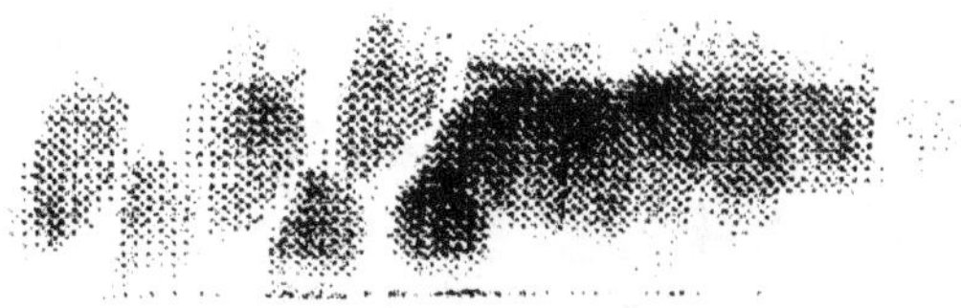

77

FRANKIE LEFT A Jackson on the small table after he'd finished with August, who lay on the couch tired and in pain. He collected his water on his way out and reminded her to get back serving tables in a minute.

He was bored. The sex had been all right but not as enjoyable as he had hoped. Frankie returned to his table and watched the girls on stage for five minutes but got restless. He nodded at his driver who stepped out of the auditorium. Soon after, he stood up and left: the car pulled up outside the entrance as he walked into the night air. Perfect timing. Although it caused him no pleasure to think this, new Luigi was so much smarter than old Luigi.

"Take me to the auto shop."

Frankie never liked talking in the vehicle, instead preferring to melt into the silence in the back seat and watch life unfurl around him. This was his only opportunity to see the normal world—he spent all the rest of his time huddled with crooks, poor gamblers or failed businessmen.

In his office, Frankie grabbed a magazine from his desk drawer, swung his feet up and sat back to enjoy the contents of his latest journal. For fifteen solid minutes, he considered each of the pictures before him with great intensity although none particularly aroused him that evening. Then the phone rang next door.

Luigi popped his head round and waited, knowing Frankie never responded immediately to anyone appearing to get his attention.

"Yes?"

"Call for you."

"Who is it?"

"Says he's Frank."

"Put it through for fuck's sake."

"Hi, Uncle Frankie."

"Hello Frank."

"How are you?"

"All the better for hearing from you. It's late here and you're lucky to catch me still in the office."

"I'd forgotten the time difference."

So the boy had been in the same location for a day or two.

"Four hours?"

"Just the three."

Useful to know.

"And why are you calling me now? It's been a while."

"A lot has happened since we saw each other last."

"Sure has. And how's what's-her-name?"

"Mary Lou is fine."

"Pleased to hear it, dear boy."

"I wanted to speak with you."

"Otherwise you'd have sent a telegram."

"Seriously, Uncle Frank. We need to talk."

"I am being serious, dear boy. You have something which does not belong to you. You are a thief."

"Under the circumstances, I don't think there's any point in name calling—else I've got a few choice ones to throw at you. What you made Luigi and Paul do was not right for an uncle."

"Step uncle."

"It wasn't right, Uncle Frank."

"And what do you propose we do about all this?"

"I was hoping we could come to some form of arrangement."

"What were you thinking?"

"Well, we have merchandise you want."

"You do."

"And we must get away from all this."

"So?"

"If we give you back most of the merchandise, we've had to incur various expenses along the way, can we agree to go our separate ways?"

"What constitutes 'most'?"

"All but a hundred grand. The rest is yours. If you believe the radio, we took more than we were expecting."

"That's full of shit: we gave them the insured amount. The take was around half a million. Right?"

"How well informed for a man who hasn't seen a single red cent of the cash since it left the vault ten days ago."

"Let's say I have friends whose business interests include using a small-town bank for laundering." Frank whistled.

"Nice. Funny because Mary Lou and I picked that branch as the easiest to steal from in the whole of Baltimore."

"Your whimsical nostalgia is noted but irrelevant. I want it all because it is mine and you have my belongings. This is not a negotiation."

"Uncle Frank, you seem to forget that if I put the phone down now, you will see none of your money again."

"The Feds and our friends in New York might have something to say about that."

"They might. Or they might not. Truth is they've been after us for quite some time but have not got close to catching us. And that means you're no closer to getting your money back. We are your best chance of that."

Frankie knew his step nephew was right. Despite Pentangelo's men and the FBI following them, the nearest they got was in Vegas and that had gone horribly wrong.

"I can be satisfied with ninety per cent of the merchandise."

"Eighty. That'll leave us with enough to keep going for the rest of our lives. We'll never need bother you again—or the guys from New York either."

"Accepted. Eighty per cent of something is better than a hundred per cent of nothing. Where shall we meet?"

"Los Angeles. Sunday. I'll call again to arrange the drop."

"I hope you understand this is purely business."

"Sure is, Uncle Frankie. On Sunday, you'll have the cash I'm promising you, and the mob will not need to find us. That's the deal."

"I promise on the souls of my grandchildren, if I get the money I shall call off my men."

"Speak Sunday. Bye."

"Goodbye dear boy."

The phone purred in Frankie's ear until he replaced the receiver. He laughed. Frank wasn't very bright or not a good listener. Lagotti Senior had only promised to step down his crew; nothing about the mob.

Frankie threw his magazine back into the drawer and called for a mug of coffee. When it arrived, he told Luigi he could go home. Then Frankie dialed New York.

CHARLIE PENTANGELO HAD managed the affairs of his Family for many years. While he was not the man in charge, he held a significant role in the organization. Frank Senior had promised him delivery of half a million dollars from the First Bank of Baltimore—and it hadn't arrived.

This state of affairs fell far short of ideal. More vexing was Lagotti's constant barrage of calls. There had been two in less than a week and each time, there was only bad news. Failure was not something Charlie wanted to be associated with—if matters carried on as they did, he might take action against Lagotti. For now, the man had three or four more days before Charlie would need to make a phone call. As if to reflect how often he was being harangued by the man, Frankie Lagotti chose this moment to put another call through.

"I have news."

"Talk."

"Frank Lagotti has approached me to return the money he has stolen from us."

"And?"

"I've arranged for a collection in Los Angeles in a few days' time."

"You know he killed one of my men. In Vegas."

"No, I did not."

"Well, you should bear this in mind when dealing with your nephew."

"He's my step nephew but we cannot allow him to live."

"You cannot. Robbing from us and murdering our members is unacceptable and you must send a clear message to everyone about the consequences of such decisions."

"I shall."

"Do you think you will recover all the money?"

"I intend to get every red cent they haven't spent."

"That is all I ask. And you will make up the shortfall. It was your project and I've lost a man along the way so that's the least you can do."

"Understood."

"I hope you do, Frank. We are not pleased with the situation you have placed us in and we expect you to resolve this matter."

"I will, Charlie."

A whir and a click in Frank Senior's ear and the phone went dead. Pentangelo rarely behaved that way. When he'd been angry in the past, Charlie explained the reason for his anger and what Frank needed to do to sort out the problem. But he never slammed the phone down on him before. He must be real pissed about losing one of his goons.

His step nephew was more resourceful than Frank Senior had thought him capable of. But now he knew where the fool was heading and would play that hand out to the full as he had a crooked deck.

He wanted his money back—no one likes a thief, but he also felt cheated. Frank Senior had set himself up with the perfect playbook: either the step nephew grabbed the cash or Carter the bank employee hustled out with the take. A win-win for Frank but it didn't pan out that way. And Frank resented that Mary Lou had screwed everything up for him. She had Carter in the clutch of her hand and her talons were into the boy Frank too. They would both need to pay—and not with greenbacks.

The Shylock put a call through to Anthony and told him to get his sorry ass over to City of Angels. He pulled out a magazine and checked out the pictures again in case he'd missed any details earlier on.

FRIDAY JUNE 27

78

THEY WOKE AND hit the road early, not wanting to stay in one place any longer than they had to. Mary Lou took the first turn behind the wheel and they hoped they'd get to LA and strike a deal with Frankie.

"Do you think we'll make it?"

"Yes, babe, but not with all the money."

"He's got to let us keep some of it. That was the arrangement before he double-crossed us. That's at least the deal on the table now."

"And if Frankie disagrees?"

"We must help him change his mind."

Mary Lou turned briefly at Frank to judge his mood beyond his deadpan intonation but she had to turn back as she carried on staring at the road ahead.

"Any idea how we'll do that?"

"Not right now but we've got time: first we hit the city and contact a guy I know. Afterwards, we deal with Frankie."

"He'd kill us if he had the chance."

"Sure would. Our job is to make certain we don't give him the opportunity."

Mary Lou fixed her attention on the four hundred feet in front of the car and stayed in lane, five miles below the speed limit. She had faith in Frank but his uncle would do anything in his power to keep the money and end their lives. She swallowed hard to rekindle the saliva in her throat.

Frank's hand maintained its position on her thigh and his touch put her at ease—the stress in her stomach abating. They'd been through all sorts over the years and had come through fine. But this time Mary Lou was less certain about the future than she had ever been in her entire life.

The car hurtled onwards until the needle on the fuel dial pointed to the empty position. Ten miles later, a gas station beckoned them onto its forecourt. They both got out to stretch their legs and Frank instructed the attendant to fill her up.

Mary Lou walked away and to the side of the small convenience store with its cash register, newspapers and snacks for the hungry motorist. Behind the cash till was a miniature black-and-white TV with a local news channel. She wandered inside in search of chocolate and grabbed some chips for Frank. As she looked outside, the attendant finished dribbling the last drops of gas into the fuel tank. He pointed at her to tell the guy to take payment from her.

Carl walked behind his counter and waited for Mary Lou to complete her purchases. As she idled along the aisles, nothing tempted her. Down one aisle away from Carl and back up the other. As she sauntered toward him, she caught sight of the TV above his head. There were two photos on display: a mugshot of Frank and the other was hers. The only good news was the sound was off, but she stopped short of the register and let her jaw drop.

She twisted around and grabbed some gum to hide her unusual behavior. Mary Lou dropped the items for purchase and put on her sunglasses to cover her face. Money swapped for goods, she smiled a thank you and left the store.

She got into the passenger seat and slammed the door shut.

"Drive, Frank."

"What?"

"No questions. Drive!"

He did as he was told and sped out the gas station.

"Keep it steady, Frank. Five miles remember."

"Sure thing, babe. What happened?"

"We're on TV."

"Huh?"

"Our faces are all over the local news."

"What the…"

"Exactly."

Frank kept at a constant pace and the car lurched along the highway.

ANGELO SPENT AN entire day trying to find Rico, only to discover the guy had his neck snapped at the railroad station by person or persons unknown—according to the local news. Angelo realized as soon as he saw the broadcast: Frank Lagotti.

With that information and another call from the East Coast, Angelo's instructions were clear: it was time to head west and grab Frank and his wife when they reached LA. Dead or alive—but bring back the money. A short conversation with Paulie and they agreed to go together—with Charlie's blessing—but the dude took half a day to get the Flamingo's count room sorted with a trustworthy overseer.

They had one of Paulie's men to drive while he and Rico sat in the back of the black sedan and stared out the window. In their line of work, small talk was unnecessary and led to people knowing more than they should about the other guy. So there was no false tension in the vehicle. Three guys on an afternoon spree to the west coast to chase down two bank robbers.

As the journey would take five hours, they agreed to stop off along the way to grab a bite to eat. The sedan pulled into a hick town with one main drag with nothing of note apart from a cinema and a row of storefronts. Paulie and Rico walked the half-block to a diner and sat in a window booth.

"You reckon they stopped here too?"

"Might well have done. Who's to say, Angelo?"

The tumbleweed of their conversation span out the door, leaving the men with nothing to talk about. With so many hours spent together since they left New York, Paulie and Rico felt little need to supplement their food with idle gossip. Two professionals sat at a table with burgers and fries for company. Rico punctured the silence once their plates contained only crumbs.

"Where are we going to go when we get to LA?"

"What you reckon?"

"They like stations."

"But are they likely to repeat the same game?"

"Maybe not."

Rico stared at his mug of coffee, hoping for inspiration from the brown liquid and white crockery.

"Airport lockers?"

"Possibly. They've got to put the take somewhere."

"Yep. But they also need to launder the money."

"Lagotti has contacted the Shylock to arrange a meet. We should save our legs and turn up to the rendezvous to grab the cash."

"And if the moneylender's people get in the way?"

"Our orders are to retrieve the money. No instructions about anything else."

The corner of Paulie's mouth curled up and Rico understood the situation. His shoulders sagged and he relaxed into the conversation.

"When do we hear about the meet?"

"It's scheduled for Sunday some time. We need to be patient and to get there prompt."

"Hire a car and lie by a pool?"

"Like the plan."

"It has a simplicity even I can remember."

"Works for me."

"Throw the net into the sea and wait to catch a fish."

Rico nodded and they lulled back into silence. Then he looked up.

"Not a fish: a shark."

"Two sharks."

"We'll need a big net."

They both smiled and continued to stare into their mugs. Neither had anything to say to the other by now.

"Let's get going. The sooner we're in LA, the sooner we're soaking in the rays."

"You said it."

Paulie threw a few notes down onto the table and the two besuited men left the diner and headed back to their vehicle.

"Need some smokes first."

Rico nodded and leaned against the car while Paulie sauntered down Main Street to get to the nearest convenience store. Before heading to the counter, he walked up and down the aisles in search of something he couldn't quite put a name to. He noticed the clothing at the back of the store and wondered whether the Lagottis had been here earlier. He tried to memorize the patterns for future use but doubted he had done a fantastic job.

At the counter, he took a carton so if they holed up somewhere, he'd be fine for cigarettes until this escapade was over. Nothing worse than being stuck without nicotine. Back at the car, Rico nodded at him and before he opened the door, he posed a simple question:

"Will the West Coast syndicates leave us alone?"

Paulie left the key in the lock and stared at his colleague and blinked once.

"No. No, we won't. We'll need to be circumspect—they won't appreciate our trampling over their turf."

"Is there anything your connections can do to ease our passage?"

"Let's say there's some bad blood between the families."

Rico stared back at Paulie and took in this new information.

"So we're going into alien territory for the sake of some money two robbers stole?"

"That sounds about right."

"With no backup?"

"None."

"Are you not bothered?"

"Concerned: yes. Worried: no."

"And the difference is…?"

"All we have to do is get to the meet with the Shylock and shoot every dumb fucker who's breathing. After, we walk over, collect the money and leave town before any of Nicolo Licata's men find out we're there. By the time they're checking for fingerprints, we'll be back in Vegas shacked up at the Flamingo with pussy coming out of our wazoo."

Rico's expression glazed over as he imagined what he would do to the women covering his naked flesh with their tongues and other body parts. He smiled.

"I thought you'd see it my way. That's why I'm not worried. We have to keep our wits about us and be handy with our firearms."

"A pistol each and a few rounds?"

"Nah."

Paulie pointed to the rear of the car and popped the trunk. At the back of the space, behind their overnight bags, was a wooden box with a metal latch. He hauled it nearer for him and Rico to see its contents. When Paulie opened it, Rico let out a whistle.

"Semi-automatics: respect."

"Received with thanks. I like to go on a job when I am fully prepared and not a second before."

"That improves the odds in our favor. You kept that stash under your hat."

"A carpenter doesn't brag about his saw."

"Those are serious fucking saws, man."

Paulie closed the box and pushed it to its earlier resting place.

"Shall we go?"

"You bet. We have a date with destiny."

"Close enough."

PAULIE DROVE THEM the rest of the way to LA and they managed about twenty words across the hours in proximity to each other. Rico allowed himself to get lost in the radio station Paulie put on and time passed by.

Once they reached the outskirts of the city with no discernible center, Paulie decided where to head. The West Coast mob was a threat only in as far as it held nominal control of Los Angeles and the surrounding areas. There were only a few dozen men left in LA ever since Old Man Nick took over the family the year before. Even though Nick was under-exploiting his territory—much to the annoyance of Charlie Pentangelo—didn't mean he was without power in his home town. They'd need to fly below the radar for their time by the sea.

They headed to Huntington Beach south of Santa Ana. It was about as far away from the center of Californian life while still being in LA. Once arrived, they checked into a nondescript hotel overlooking the sandy front and waited.

Rico suggested trawling through local fences but Paulie pointed out this would only increase their profile with the West Coast syndicate and do nothing to help them track down the Lagottis. Much to Rico's annoyance, Paulie was right. So making up for their inability to do anything constructive, the pair headed to the rooftop of their hotel, sank some martinis and sat in the sun until Frank and Mary Lou Lagotti appeared in LA.

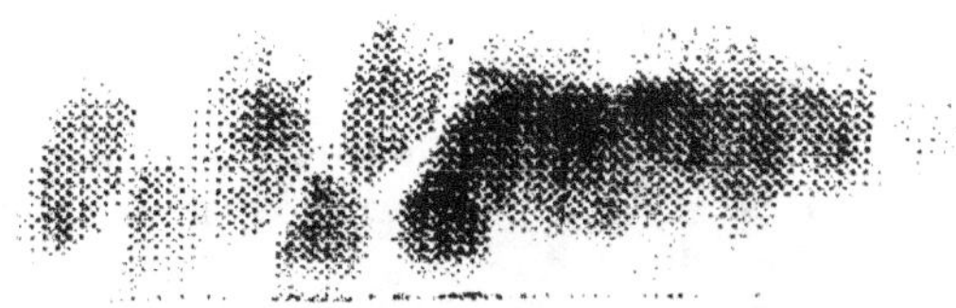

79

WITH THEIR FACES all over the local news, there was no chance to stop anywhere within the forests of the East Mojave National Scenic Area. A silence descended in the automobile with Frank's hand still resting on Mary Lou's thigh—the only comfort in the cabin apart from the slow warm breeze emitting from the air conditioning.

"Let's ditch the car, Frank."

"But we need to be careful where we're seen."

"Sure thing, but I'm scared."

"We'll get through this."

"They know what we look like and where we are."

"We'll dye our hair again and change our clothes. And they got a handle on where we were—not where we are heading."

"Frankie knows it's LA and so the mob will too."

"But we have the advantage. We set the meet and pick the location. We control the situation. They'll have no choice: we will get through this."

"I want to believe. I don't want to die and I don't want to go to prison either."

"You and me both."

Husband and wife smiled together.

"How well do you know LA?"

"Never been there in my life."

"You're kidding me."

"No. Why?"

"You said you met some people there so I…"

"I have connections but that doesn't mean I've visited the place."

"Oh. But your connections…"

"…are real. This guy was with me in the joint. We got on well—we looked after each other. Mark was from LA and returned there after his release."

"Do you trust him?"

"With my life."

"That's good enough for me."

Mary Lou watched as the car sped past the line of trees at the side of the highway. Nothing but foliage as far as she could see. A small window of light up ahead like a tunnel etched out of the trunks as they looked over them. Always five below the limit.

Fifteen miles later and he barked an order.

"Buckle up!"

Mary Lou didn't need to be told twice: not with that tone of voice. Frank removed his hand from her upper thigh and placed it on the wheel. He maintained their speed at a constant rate and she saw the blur of a state trooper vehicle as it scooted past. Chances were it was out to fill up on a daily quota of speeding tickets but they weren't sure.

Frank kept most of his attention on the rearview mirror for the next minute. Mary Lou tried to use the side mirror to check on progress—she didn't turn around as only the guilty look back.

Another sixty seconds and Frank's hand returned to stroke her thigh. She felt like breathing once more and, despite the lightness of his touch, a small tingle spread from her crotch up her spine. Ten miles more and the trees thinned out until the openness of the country was visible from the highway. Twenty further and they entered Barstow.

On the outskirts was a picture house. Five hundred feet later, they passed a convenience store, restaurant, clothes outlet, a place to pick up a rifle—the usual contents of a hick town with nothing to offer but the dream of departure.

Frank pulled in around the corner from this main drag.

"Time for a change, babe."

"I'll go. You stay here."

He looked at her and thought for a second.

"Sure. Safer than both of us on the street."

"Clothes. Hair color. Something to eat."

"And a coffee if you can find one."

"Will do, hon'. If I'm not back in thirty, get the fuck out of Dodge."

"I'll wait for you for an eternity. Take as long as you need."

Mary Lou kissed him on the lips like she would never see him again. She got out and walked over to the main parade. There was almost no one about. She checked her watch: lunch time. Why was the place so empty? She felt her stomach tighten as her nerves kicked in and the adrenaline flowed around her bloodstream.

First she hit the convenience store, careful to put on her sunglasses to hide her face. She grabbed all she could find and paid, not saying a word to anyone. The storekeeper wanted to chat—not enough customers today—but Mary Lou was having none of it.

In the clothes outlet, their lumberjack look would make them stick out in LA so she sought some city things at the back. Two miniskirts for herself, a pair of slacks and some pants for Frank. Black and white tee shirts for both of them, a pretty blouse and a plain shirt in Frank's colors. And a jacket each to hide any hardware they'd need to carry.

Shoot. She'd forgotten hair dye and had to go back to the convenience store and the talkative owner. She took advantage of her return to buy more pairs of sunglasses and two hats—a beret for herself and Fedora for Frank. He wouldn't be happy about it but it'd help to make his face harder to see.

A glance at her watch again: thirty-five minutes since she left the car. Why had everything taken so long? She scurried back to where he had parked but he wasn't there. She spun round but nothing. He had promised her an eternity and given her less than an hour. Her breathing kicked into overdrive and she leaned against the wall of a building.

In the periphery of her vision, despite the blurring in her eyes, she noticed a vehicle had pulled up in front of her. She ignored it for a second and tried to regain her composure. Then she looked up.

"Frank!"

"Used the time to get us a fresh ride."

She threw her purchases onto the backseat and jumped in.

"I thought you'd gone."

She squeezed his thigh briefly as he drove off.

"Mary Lou, I said I'd wait for you for an eternity—and I meant it."

She smeared away the tear falling down her left cheek.

"Let's go a few miles so we can bury what we're wearing."

Their new dark brown saloon traveled at five below the speed limit out of Barstow and headed toward Victorville on the way to LA.

ANTHONY PUT THE phone down and thought about Frank Senior's instructions: head to LA, meet up with the Lagotti couple, secure the money and torture the pair of them. If they die, bury them in the sand. If they survive, bring them to Baltimore.

"The Lagottis' time in Vegas is over, my friends. They are off to Los Angeles."

Bobby nodded and Mickey stared at Anthony awaiting further information. Anthony looked straight back at Mickey, not understanding what the man was waiting for.

"And?"

"So we will follow them to Los Angeles."

Each word was spat out so Mickey could understand the line of argument with no further repetition.

"Mickey. Let's pack up."

Bobby savored the moment because Anthony's eyes were misting over into rage—and there was no need for any of them to get hot and bothered. Mickey would come into his own very soon. What he lacked in brains, he gained in muscle. The guy handled himself in a tight corner: with a gun, a knife or with his fists. On those occasions he was handy to have hanging around.

Ten minutes later and the three men walked out the lobby with a bag each. Into their car with Anthony behind the wheel and the other two in the back.

"To the City of Angels."

Bobby issued the command after Anthony had pulled away and was on the highway. Anthony scowled at him in the rearview mirror but the corner of his mouth revealed he got the joke. The complacent smile on Mickey's face showed he very much had missed the point.

"Do we wait for instructions from Frank Senior when we arrive?"

"Yep. As far as I know, Frank and Mary Lou are due to arrive in town soon and will arrange a meetup with Frank Senior for Sunday. We go there, we grab the cash and we are done."

"And we can torture them if we want?"

"Once we have the money safe and secure, Mickey. Yes. Only once we have the money."

"Got it, boss."

Bobby's expression showed Anthony he too was finding Mickey difficult—they had been cooped up with the fella for far too long. In the past, Anthony gave the guy a call and, two minutes later, Mickey had sufficient information to whack some dude.

These past few days had tested everyone's patience. Anthony tried his best not to snap at Mickey but, as every day passed, this was getting harder. The guy meant well, but he had only a few brain cells to call his own. Anthony heard a story that Mickey used to be a boxer but had to quit because he got punch drunk. He found the tale difficult to believe: the man was slow on the uptake but possessed a clarity of thought and precision in the art of maiming and killing. He was no Jake la Motta.

The car sped out of Vegas and hit the highway to Barstow, Victorville and beyond. Mickey stared out the window at the wonders of the forestry that surrounded them for much of the first leg of their journey. Bobby tapped his hand on his knee in time to the music Anthony played on the radio.

Like everyone on the Vegas to LA run, Anthony pulled the car over at Barstow and they ate a burger and stretched their legs. The town existed only as a place for drivers to stop and get a breath of fresh air. Inhalations paid for every brick in town.

One diner, three men and two burgers and a steak then back to the road and an uneventful journey to LA. Once they arrived, Anthony took them to a hotel in Long Beach. It was a location he'd heard of before as he had no clue where the meetup with the Lagottis would take place. So Long Beach sounded as good a locale to wait as any other.

Compton Plaza was a small family-run establishment whose income relied on the kindness of strangers passing through town on their way to somewhere else. Anthony reckoned this meant the three men would be left well enough alone and, if anyone came sniffing by, the proprietor knew better than to provide any real information. Discretion in fleapits is quite common.

Anthony and Bobby nested in the hotel room and Mickey talked about planning a tourist trip the following day. Anthony explained how they should stick together and wait for Frank Senior's call but Mickey was having none of it.

"If they ain't showin' until Sunday that means we got tomorrow off."

His logic was sharp and, because he could handle himself so well, he didn't consider the possibility he should lie low until he was needed. From Mickey's perspective, he was in LA for the first—and only—time in his life and he should make the most of the opportunity.

Pizza boxes mounted in the room and the wait for Frank and Mary Lou continued. Anthony would return to Baltimore with a heap of cash and two warm bodies, only slightly mutilated.

SATURDAY JUNE 28

80

FRANK DROVE TOWARD Burbank as it sounded as good a place to aim as any other in Los Angeles. They circled round several times passing three motels and one hotel. He pulled over on the other side of the road to the Clement Fitzrovia Hotel. Then they watched the entrance for twenty minutes.

"Quiet spot."

"Yes, babe."

"Big enough for us to get lost among the other guests."

"That's what I'm thinking too."

Mary Lou continued to gaze at the frontage with its stucco designs alluding to a 1920s heritage. The entrance comprised faded bronze swing doors set in an oak frame. A patio area separated the hotel from the main drag and lent the place an air of refined dignity. Closer inspection of the lobby revealed crumbling wallpaper, botched paint jobs and an overwhelming need for basic maintenance.

If they had been holidaymakers, Frank and Mary Lou would have turned around and found somewhere with more pleasant surroundings. But this was the venue they needed: some place where few people showed up and the staff cared little for the patrons who bothered to show.

"How long will you be staying?"

"At least two nights, but maybe a week."

"Well, if you could be here that long, let's put you in a junior suite."

"No need for special treatment."

"Not at all. We like to give the rooms an airing."

He liked the implication their room would be isolated from the rest of the clientele. The front desk clerk summoned a bellboy to help them with their bags but, despite his best efforts, Mary Lou refused to allow him to take the black holdall out of her hand. To placate the teenager, Frank handed him the bag with their clothes: like every other bellhop before and since, he needed to make his tip.

They followed Tom into the lift and up to the seventh floor, below the penthouse level. Through the hallway and into an area with a couch, an armchair and a TV on a stand by one wall. Opposite the entrance to the room was a wall of glass with a balcony the other side. To the right, and close to where they were standing, was another door to the bedroom and an en suite shower. Along the corridor between the living space and their bedroom was a separate bathroom for guests.

The boy showed them all the rooms and opened the curtains wide to reveal the balcony in all its glory. Then he ceased his talking and stood, almost to attention.

"Is there anything you need?"

"No thanks."

"Then I'll be going."

Despite his words, Tom didn't move a muscle until Frank pulled a greenback or two out of his pocket and placed them in the boy's palm. He looked down and beamed.

"Thanks, mister."

Frank smiled back, knowing he had made a friend he could rely on. Love a town where a stranger can buy loyalty with five one-dollar bills. Financial transaction ended, the boy shuffled out and closed the door behind himself.

The couple placed their black bags on the coffee table by the couch. Frank went into the bedroom and Mary Lou checked out the furniture in the living room. There was a sideboard with sliding doors. If she removed the shelf, both holdalls would fit in fine. As she bent down to her task, Frank came back.

"Let's hide the bags under the bed."

"Isn't that a bit obvious?"

"No more than stashing the take in the first piece of furniture you see when you walk into the room."

She tilted her head, thought for a moment and nodded.

"No better, no worse."

"Let's split the difference."

Mary Lou took one bag and shoved it into the sideboard, sliding the door shut while Frank hid the other in the bedroom. Then they both sat down on the couch to take stock.

"Do you have the number of your LA guy?"

"Mark? Yes. I'll call him soon. We also need to decide how to handle Frankie."

"You told Frankie we'd meet up tomorrow."

"Yes, I know, but I've been thinking…"

"Do you not think we should get him off our back?"

"Of course, but if we clean the money, we could go to ground and reappear somewhere different. And not deal with Frankie or anything."

"I reckon you're right, besides we won't need to worry about him for very much longer."

"Huh?"

"Nothing, just mumbling. If we focus on the money, Frankie will take care of himself."

"That leaves us only having to handle the FBI and the East Coast."

Silence descended as they both thought about the seriousness of what Frank had said. Mary Lou nuzzled into him and they hugged while they sifted through ideas about what to do until the dying embers of Sunday. One step at a time: there was no point planning too far ahead.

Frank placed a call to Mark but the voice at the other end said he was out and wasn't expected back for a few hours. Mary Lou suggested they order delivery pizza—a luxury for the pair of them as they'd been on the road forever.

They told the concierge to get Tom bring the food up to them and handed him another fat tip.

"Tom. You going to be around for the rest of the weekend?"

"Sure am."

"Good. If you hear of anyone asking about us, let us know, right?"

"Sure will, mister. You expecting trouble?"

"Nope but we've eloped see and we don't my wife's family come storming in here giving her hell. They don't like me, okay?"

"Oh, I understand. I'll listen out good."

"Thanks, Tom."

She had opened the box by the time Frank sat back down on the couch and, within ten minutes, they had devoured the large pizza. Mary Lou took the carton and walked round the living room until she spotted the trash bin. She bent the card in two and squished it in. Then she turned to return to her seat.

Frank watched her all the while.

"What're we going to do now?"

In response, Mary Lou slipped out of her skirt, pulled down her panties and unbuttoned her shirt, letting her bra fall to the ground to join the rest of her clothes. He stared just below her tattooed rose. She smiled and looked at his face while she soaked in the desire of his gaze.

"I can probably think of something, hon'."

Mary Lou walked into the bedroom, followed by Frank, who had already removed his jeans before her bra had hit the floor.

PHIL MCNAMARA AND Ted Goodwin took a plane from Las Vegas—one advantage of being on a government salary. Phil had received a report that the Lagotti pair were heading for LA and he saw no reason to prolong their stay in the casino capital of the world. The place seethed with organized crime and this G-man did not like the smell.

They landed at Los Angeles International Airport and grabbed a taxi to the local FBI headquarters on Wilshire Boulevard. McNamara showed his badge and the receptionist let them through—Goodwin signed in as his guest. The Fed hightailed it to the bureau chief: politics are the same wherever you go in the world.

"Just checking in, boss. We're hunting the First Bank of Baltimore robbers and have word they've hit town."

"Thanks for the heads up. Make yourselves comfortable if you can find a desk."

"Much appreciated. If our source is correct, we'll be out of your hair by Wednesday latest."

"Take all the time you need—and if there's a warm body spare, feel free to ask for some help."

"Will do—and thanks again."

"Quick heads up: two burned bodies were found with some cash fluttering around them out in the wilds north east of the city. Serial numbers match the Baltimore heist but the corpses have yet to be identified."

"Mob hit on the Lagottis?"

"Possibly."

They left the suit's office and walked round the floors until they reached the basement where two empty desks stood opposite each other.

"Time to pitch tent."

Ted nodded and flopped down on his chair. McNamara settled in and filled the desk drawers with files he'd been lugging from his case.

"What now? And you never told me the identity of your source."

"That's because it's not on the up and up."

"Oh?"

"You see my agency is hopelessly conflicted as far as I can tell. We spend our time trying to capture the biggest, most-organized criminals the country has ever produced."

"Okay—and your problem is…?"

"But sometimes you need the help of a thief to catch a thief."

"So you have an informant out east who's feeding you their whereabouts?"

"Close enough."

"Not exactly right either though?"

"No. The relationship is closer than that."

Ted's quizzical expression stared back at Phil, who felt no need to expand on anything he'd said.

"Does it go into the mob?"

Ted whispered the question for fear he might hear the answer. McNamara looked left and right but there was no one within earshot. He nodded and Goodwin whistled in a mix of disbelief and the utmost respect.

"While I'll be…"

"So the best information has come from the East Coast, if you get my meaning."

"And what do they expect us to do if we recover the money?"

"Ted, if you have to ask, I'm sure as hell not going to dignify it with an answer."

"You're kidding me?"

"No. If we get the money off Frank Lagotti, we will make damn certain the cash gets lost in the evidence room."

"And the Lagottis?"

"Rumors of their deaths may have been greatly exaggerated. We'll have them in custody and they'll be safe with us. It's not like Lagotti is Lee Harvey Oswald."

Ted stared at him in abject horror.

"You tellin' me…"

McNamara laughed.

"Joke. I was joking with you."

Goodwin tried to guffaw but couldn't bring himself to do so.

"Focus, Ted. Just because we know they are in the same city as us doesn't mean we have any idea where they are. Follow me."

He stood up and Goodwin tailed him as McNamara strode to the stairwell and headed up. He knew his way around the building because he reached the computer room without asking anyone for directions.

"Why do you think they traveled across the country to get to LA?"

"My early investigations told me it was the place Frank Lagotti always wanted to go."

"Sure but why still head here after the bodies piled up?"

Ted shrugged.

"There must be someone or something here to draw them all this way."

McNamara turned to a technician and explained they were looking for any connection with Lagotti who might reside in the city. He was fed some background by Goodwin and the computer scientist sat down at his console and typed away.

"Let's get a coffee. This could take some time."

Ted nodded and they left the building and walked along three blocks until they reached a restaurant. McNamara ordered two coffees and a slice of cake each. And then they waited. An hour later they returned to the computer room where Harry the technician greeted them.

"Some good news, gents."

"Oh?"

"I've got some matches for you. One is a man who shared a cell with Lagotti in Baltimore. Mark Tucker, now in Glendale."

He passed a piece of paper to McNamara with the address and other personal details.

"And the other match is much warmer. Local news has been running mugshots of both your felons the last two days in Nevada and California and they were spotted this morning in Burbank."

Ted nodded and McNamara shook Harry's hand, followed by Goodwin.

"Time to wear out some shoe leather."

81

FRANK LOOKED IN between Mary Lou's legs to see the time on the bedside table clock. Almost two. He kissed her on the nearest cheek and pecked at her rose with his tongue until he remembered he shouldn't get distracted so easily.

Mary Lou watched as he left the bed and headed for the living room to grab a notebook from his bag and place a local call.

"Is Mark there?… I'll hold."

He turned to check out the rustling sound as she sat beside him on the couch. Both were naked.

"Mark? Yes, it's Frank L. How's it going?"

The first minute was catchup chatter with nothing worth Mary Lou listening to but she leaned into Frank's side in case hearing Mark's words later became important. He let his free hand slide down onto her thigh and played near her groin, which she found distracting but tingles mounted up and down her spine.

"Listen, bud. I've a favor to ask you."

"What's that, my man?"

"Are you still in the same game as when we last met?"

"Well, I'm a lot more free nowadays, but the play is the same."

They chuckled and then got down to business.

"Do you have any goods you want to pass my way then?"

"Sure do. Only these goods need a fantastic clean first."

Mark let out a whistle of approval.

"Glad to hear you've been moving up in the world, Frank. All the time you spent going on and on about your failed coup must have paid off for you. Respect."

"Thanks. We are in a much better position than last we spoke."

"We? You riding with someone else?"

"Sure am. She's my business partner."

"She? How open-minded of you. Good job you're in California—it's mighty used to hep cats like you."

"Can we meet up and talk some more? Phones attract the wrong people, you know."

"Understand, Frank. Best place for our kind of conversation are some flat, wide spaces. You play golf?"

"Huh? No. Have you joined a club or something?"

Another chuckle.

"No way, José. But there's a course right next to the airport and I like to meet associates there. Could you get near the tee off for the fourth hole tomorrow morning? Say ten?"

"Sure thing."

"I'll be easy to spot: I'm the dude in the golf cart who looks exactly as you remember him—only now I shave once a week."

Another chuckle and Mark hung up. Frank put the receiver back onto its perch and returned the phone to its side table.

"You hear all of that, babe?"

"Yes. Sounds like we got the rest of the day to ourselves, hon'."

"We should stay in the suite."

"Are you sure? I wanna be a tourist."

"It's not safe for us out there."

"What if we go in disguise? This could be our one chance to enjoy California. You've spent too much time dreaming of getting here to spend it stuck in a hotel room in fear of your life. Come on, Frank. Let's do it."

He sat back thinking through Mary Lou's argument. She was right: there's no point living like a coward: face the unknown. Of course, he wasn't stupid. He waited a few minutes before starting his trip so that she could finish her slobbering around his groin. The man liked the mystery of California and all it represented to him, but he loved having Mary Lou go down on him even more.

More hair dye, a shower for both and they were ready to take on the world wearing dark sunglasses and hats, turned-up collars and long coats. In case of trouble, they carried a piece each. When they hit the lobby, Tom the bellboy was standing to attention waiting for his next mission.

"Any news for me?"

"Nothing yet."

"Keep your ears open and your mouth shut."

"Will do, mister."

Tom pocketed the dollar without raising an eyebrow. They hopped into a taxi and headed to Grauman's Chinese Theatre on Hollywood Boulevard.

THE CAB DROPPED them off next to the Chinese Theater and they joined the throng staring at the ground, looking at the footprints and signatures of the famous from yesteryear. When Mary Lou looked down, Frank kept watch glancing left then right. After she'd had her fill, he would look at the concrete floor and she would be the guard.

With no conversation between the two, both maintained their hands on their guns throughout the entire experience. Panhandlers filled the area: Marilyn Monroe lookalikes, Bogart buffs and Cary Grant impersonators. If you had a camera around your neck, you were fair game to pay them to stand near you and have a photo taken.

One Marilyn made the mistake of approaching Frank but he used a direct approach to sending her off without fuss:

"Beat it, cutie. This john isn't for sale."

"Suit yourself. This girl's only trying to earn herself a living."

"Then do something honest like turning a trick, you blond whore."

"Take it easy, Frank."

"Sorry, babe. She got on my nerves. Hard to trust people nowadays."

"I know, but a hooker's still only a hooker. Her hot pants don't make her a member of the mob."

He slung a glance at the teenager as she slunk off looking for someone else to punch her card. Mary Lou was right though. He needed to stay calm to survive until the end of the weekend.

As he double-checked the sidewalk for the millionth time, he noticed a heavy-set dude who stood out from the crowd. Not only was he the only guy in a black three-piece suit within ten miles of the place, but he was heading in their direction at a fast pace. No way was the man a tourist—unless he'd just left a meeting and was a stranger in town.

The hat was the final item that set Frank on edge. Despite all the wannabe lookalikes who'd surrounded them the previous ten minutes, this fella looked as though he was trying to be Humphrey Bogart. Only too hard for his own good. Something was wrong in the state of California.

Frank tapped Mary Lou on the shoulder and she stood up as he pointed in Three-Piece's general direction.

"What you reckon?"

"Give me a minute and I'll tell you."

They stepped back from the crowd and inched to a nearby wall. She opened her bag as though searching for some long-lost family heirloom. He positioned himself opposite her looking in all directions but squarely staring at Three-Piece, who kept pounding toward them.

"Well?"

"Not good."

"Yep."

Three-Piece was twenty feet away and they could make out the contours of his face. Frank pulled out his gun and held it lowered. Fifteen.

Mary Lou tried to sink into the wall having pretended to find the mystery object from her clutch bag. She saw the revolver, saw Three-Piece and looked at the gun again. Ten feet.

"Frank…"

Five…

"Quiet!" snapped Frank.

Three-Piece had brown eyes entirely focused on the ground, like he was hurrying to get to his destination with no interest in his surroundings. Given he was marching past one of the most famous sidewalks on the planet, this was unusual behavior. Neither Frank nor Mary Lou liked it.

The suit continued walking as Frank swiveled to continue to face him in case he was about to turn around and act. When he got twenty feet away, he stopped right outside the Chinese Theater entrance. She stepped forward to mask Frank's gun from the passersby.

The guy bent down and appeared to tie his shoelace but she couldn't quite tell what he was doing for real. He stood up and twisted to face the theater. Frank's arm remained poised to extend, aim and fire.

She strode to the kerb and put her hand out to hail a taxi. Whatever happened in the next five seconds, she didn't want to stick around much after. A yellow cab pulled up and she grabbed open the door as Frank stood his ground, waiting.

Three-Piece continued to stare at the theater and turned his head down at the sidewalk. Then he shifted his weight and Mary Lou felt he was staring right through Frank, whose arm stiffened and she braced herself for the crack of the gun barrel. He dug his heels into the paving stones as he too noticed the change in Three-Piece's stance. Mary Lou gripped the door handle.

She blinked and, in that instant, Three-Piece shrugged his shoulders and walked away from the pair, continuing on his way along Hollywood Boulevard. Mickey never knew how close he got to receiving a bullet in his skull, but Frank did and Mary Lou had a good idea too.

Frank slid his gun back into his pocket and hopped into the taxi, followed by Mary Lou.

"Let's hightail it to Riverside Drive and the Warner Brothers studios in Burbank."

The driver nodded and hustled them over as quickly as his cab would take them.

"Why there?"

"We might spot us some movie stars, babe."

She smiled and pecked Frank on the cheek. That was what she wanted: to soak in the glitz of Tinseltown. They stood outside the studio gates along with all the other nobodies waiting to catch a silhouette they recognized in the rear of a stretch limo. But none appeared.

After an hour, they'd both had enough. The surrounding conversations dragged them down—ordinary people leading normal lives.

"Can we go back to the hotel?"

"I'm right with you, babe."

"We could grab a bite to eat on the way."

"Pizza for lunch. Shall we find Chinese for this evening?"

Mary Lou nodded and Frank walked fifteen feet away from the huddled masses to hail a taxi to separate them from the edge of the magic factory.

Sunday June 29

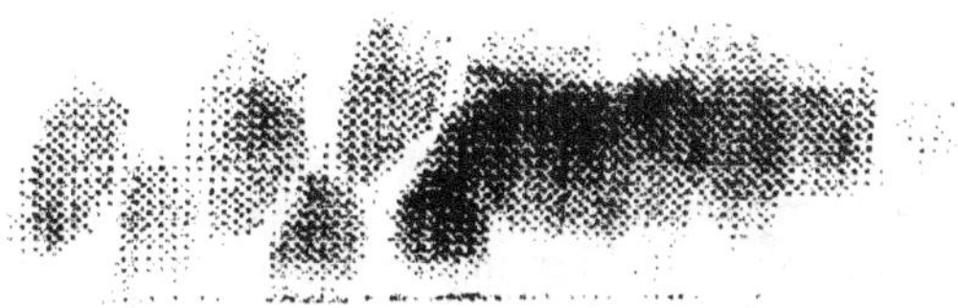

82

THEY TOOK TWO cabs to get to the Wilshire Golf Club: the first was to a random destination made up by the concierge. Then they walked three blocks and caught a different car to where they stood now. The course itself perched on the edge of Los Angeles International Airport. Planes flew over their heads but the site was vast and the noise of the engines didn't drown out conversation.

Frank and Mary Lou crouched behind some bushes next to the tee until Mark sauntered up to them. Frank smiled in recognition and they hugged, patting each other on the back they way men do.

"Damn good to see you again, Frankie L!"

"Mighty fine to catch sight of your face, Mark T!"

"And this must be your accomplice."

"Mary Lou, meet Mark Tucker. We were cell buddies in the day."

"Not that long ago, Frankie L."

"Plain old Frank nowadays, Mark."

"Gotcha."

Mary Lou shook Mark's hand for a greeting.

"Any buddy of Frank's is a friend of mine."

"I'm sure we'll get along just fine, Mark T."

He eyed up the pair, watching how they stood and the relaxed way Frank leaned in towards her body. His eyebrows rose and he whistled.

"Frank, you've got more than an accomplice with you, I'd say."

"You may well be right there, Mark, but we are here for business. We can catch up on old times later in the day."

"You betcha."

Mark walked away from the tee, making sure they stayed behind the bushes and wandered into a clump of eight to ten trees. Smack in the middle was a clearing with some stumps left flat, like they were Nature's own seats.

"Make yourselves comfortable. No one can see us from the fairways and unless we scream at each other, they won't hear anything either."

The three sat on a stump each but only Mark appeared the least bit relaxed on the makeshift wooden stools.

"Let's get down to business, Frank. First off. Are you a cop?"

"No. Are you?"

"No, I am not."

Although law enforcement officers were not the brightest sparks in the firmament, the judiciary had put in place a requirement that undercover cops didn't lie when entrapping felons. This meant the opening to criminal discussions begun with a standard mantra.

"So what do you want to send my way?"

"We've got a large amount of cash needs cleaning yesterday."

"How much money and how fast?"

"About five hundred and fifty thousand. And as soon as you can turn it around."

"First Bank of Baltimore was your hit? Don't answer that. What I don't know can't hurt me."

"It is a sizeable sum."

Frank looked over at Mary Lou who responded in kind. Then they both returned to stare at Mark.

"I thought that haul was twice as big."

"Can't believe everything you hear on the news."

Mark smiled and pondered.

"You got the FBI on your tail? They don't take kindly to people who rob banks."

"I didn't say we robbed a bank but Hoover has taken an interest in our journey across country."

"Is he the only one who's after you?"

"There are other parties involved."

"Baltimore cops?"

"Yep."

"That all?"

"Nope."

"Anyone I should worry about?"

"There are some guys with East Coast connections, Mark. Only fair to let you know. And some Baltimore locals who are less of an issue—for you at any rate."

"Risky business, your line of work."

"And yours. You get stuck with the notes."

"Only for a few hours. With a haul like yours, it's out of my hands before the end of the day. I'm old-fashioned enough to not let incriminating evidence languish at the bottom of a drawer."

"Good policy, my friend. So can you help us?"

"Frank, the question isn't if we'll do some business, but how much it'll cost you."

"If the cash is only with you for a few hours then your risk is minimal, wouldn't you say?"

"You're kidding me, man. It's all mine. You walk away with the clean bills and I'm left holding the baby and the bath water. Your notes can get traced back to me. The only thing stopping the cops knocking on your door is what I tell them. And that's a price worth paying."

"Mark, you know me well enough to be certain of this: if anyone crosses me, I'll kill them. Simple."

"You'd better watch out for him, love. Frank's business partners have a nasty habit of getting buried."

"Don't you worry about me. I know his past. From way before his arrival at the Baltimore Penitentiary."

Mark looked at her with cold eyes, deciding how much to believe this woman. Truth was Mary Lou and Frank got together soon after she arrived in Baltimore, some six years before he did time for the store heist.

She stared back at Mark, letting him make his judgements but not wishing to give him a moment to think she was some pushover. The fact they'd only just met meant Mark did not understand about her and Frank. He might not have mentioned a word about the man since he got out of the can, but Mary Lou could tell there was some special bond between the men.

THE BALTIMORE STATE Penitentiary had never been the most luxurious of penal institutions but it followed a series of protocols designed to keep the prison population as placated and secure as it could be. Two guys per cage was the rule and when Frank's cell mate finally got parole in '66, a new arrival was inevitable within a few days.

Mark waltzed into his life by throwing himself into the top bunk, declaring his possession. As Frank was lying on the lower bed, he didn't care as he wasn't planning on budging from his perch.

The first two weeks passed without incident, both men engulfed by the tedium of their position. Mark kept his mind alive by doing what came natural: buying and selling anything he could lay his hands on and sometimes that included property owned by the prison staff.

Nooks and crannies stuffed with contraband filled their cage. Frank didn't care as he got the occasional perk and nobody would believe he was the perp. Mark's import-export business was thriving, but it relied on him getting goods of interest to the inmates. He operated a barter system which meant other convicts were invited to offer items they'd found to swap for objects in his cell.

The big problem was that it encouraged criminals, many of whom were habitual thieves, to rob from each other. The more desperate prisoners would take the biggest risks, leading to Mark rubbing shoulders with the more dangerous elements of the prison population.

In the third week, Donald "The Hatchet" O'Reilly came into the cell. His nickname said it all: never cross him unless you wanted to be wearing an ax embedded in your skull. Frank was on his own, polishing his shoes.

"Where's Tucker?"

"Dunno, O'Reilly."

"Not good enough. Where is he?"

"I don't know. He's been out the cell most of the morning."

"Tell him he needs to find me."

"Sure thing, O'Reilly."

The lumbering giant, bedecked in tattoos of every conceivable pattern and image over every visible inch of his skin, lurched toward Frank, grabbed him by the throat and yanked him upwards.

"Listen closely, Lagotti. You don't appear to be taking this matter seriously enough. When Tucker gets back from fucking whoever he's fucking, send him over before he nestles down between your great hairy, white ass cheeks. Get me?"

Frank nodded as best he could, blinking acknowledgement to the bearded behemoth who ran the block. O'Reilly's hand relaxed around Frank's larynx but maintained a basic grip.

"The slug has my property and I want it back."

"Okay. Understood. What is it?"

"Are you his agent?"

Frank thought for a minute and realized O'Reilly was right. The last thing he wanted was to get involved but here he was with a hand around his throat and a question out his mouth.

"Smokes. Ten cartons."

"I'll let him know. That's a lot of smokes."

"Better believe it. If I don't receive restitution by four this afternoon, he's a dead man walking."

O'Reilly growled and exited the cell, leaving him alone knowing Mark was due to die. Just before five, Mark entered the cage, torn overalls, bruises around his cheeks, mouth and forehead. One eye was closed up; Frank couldn't work out how the man could see.

"Jeez, Louise."

"Shoulda seen the other guy."

He attempted a smile but the pain of moving the muscles in his face was too much for him.

"O'Reilly found you then."

A nod.

"He set you a four deadline."

Another nod. Mark sat down on Frank's bed.

"I tried to find you but you vanished. Thought you might have had the good fortune to have escaped."

Further attempts to chuckle by Mark but winced with the pain.

"It's not over yet."

"Still wants his smokes. You got them?"

Mark shook his head.

"Sold them on?"

A nod again.

"Anything worth ten cartons to trade?"

Another shake.

"Huh? You always have stuff coming and going."

Amid the spit and drops of blood:

"O'Reilly owns all my stash now. I owe him twenty cartons on top of it all. I got zip."

Frank stood and thought. Mark made this problem for himself but he guessed the guy didn't realize he was trading in O'Reilly's cigarettes.

"How long to pay the debt?"

"Two days."

"Jeez."

Mark looked up at him with plaintive eyes. The men shared a cell, but that was about all.

"I might be able to help."

He gave a quizzical expression in between the cuts and bleeding. Frank kneeled next to the head and pulled a small plastic bag out of a cubby hole. Without letting him see the entire contents, he took out a roll of notes and replaced the pouch.

"First, I must find a new hidey place. Second, you can pay O'Reilly off with the green here. It's at least the price of twenty cartons, but you have to understand that was my bribe money. Without it, I can't keep the guards away—and I haven't been too friendly with some of them in the past, see. So if I hand over this cash, you must look after me instead. Got it?"

If Mark had been able, he would have smiled, but a ghoulish set of teeth showed across his expression.

That night, Frank went to bed first and Mark slipped in under the covers beside him. He did nothing to push him out and Mark looked after Frank's interests from that moment until he got parole three months before Frank himself stepped out into the bright Baltimore sunshine.

83

MARK AND FRANK stared at each other, the memories of the penitentiary flickering across their expressions.

"You guys will be off out the state while I'm stuck with a bunch of questions from the Feds or a bullet from the mob. So be serious, my man."

"Mark, let's not get ahead of ourselves. Yes, I want us to do business but we need to remember what is what and what has passed."

"The past is gone and all we have is our future."

"Past but not forgotten."

"Sure, Frank. But gone."

He fell silent as he didn't think it wise to push the guy too far because he so needed him, but he thought Mark and he had some connection the boy wanted to ignore. Maybe it was just negotiation.

"What of the future then?"

"You've got racks and you want me to swap them for greenbacks. Untraceable and with no consecutive serial numbers unless I miss my guess."

Frank nodded, knowing his old friend had the upper hand—but that had been the case before he'd picked up the phone and contacted the only person from California in his address book.

"What can you give us?"

Now Mark was silent as he mulled over his opening offer.

"Your uncle: what deal did he throw at you?"

"Forty cents on the dollar."

Mark smiled.

"That was the offer. In reality he planned on taking it all and leaving you with nothing, so anything I put forward will be better than the only offer you currently have on the table."

Frank ground his molars because Mark was squeezing him. There was no need to behave like this. Why play a power trip on him?

Mary Lou watched the proceedings and wondered why Frank was trying to do business with this guy. Better for the two of them to torture him until he spilled where he stashes his clean cash. Must be somewhere and not that far from here either. But that's not how Frank wanted to play it—and she respected him too much to take action now.

"Me and Mary Lou can slice your throat open right here and take all the money you've got stored around the city. But you and I have a history and I'm hoping you remember that as we carry on our conversation."

"Stay chilled, Frank. Just jerking your chain. Nothing more. How about twenty cents on the dollar?"

"That won't give us much. We'll have to leave the country—at least until everything dies down and that could take years, not weeks or months."

"I hear you, but you understand I have overheads and I'm trying to do the best I can for you under the circumstances. If you flee the heat, chances are it'll descend on me and we must factor that into the price."

"You and I appreciate there's plenty of fat in the eighty cents you're talking about keeping. All I'm asking is for you to share a little—like I shared my stash with you when we were inside."

Mark gazed down at the earth, eyes unfocused. Mary Lou couldn't tell if he was having an attack or had fallen under some hypnotic spell. After fifteen seconds, he blinked and looked up.

"Twenty five cents. And that takes account of everything that happened in Baltimore."

"Appreciate that, Mark. Is that the best you can do for us?"

"Better believe it. How much are you sitting on again?"

"Five hundred and fifty thousand."

Mark's eyes widened until he got them under control and let out a quiet whistle.

"Total respect man. And to you, lady."

Mary Lou nodded. She was seeing a different side to Frank than he'd shown these last few days. Almost like she'd forgotten how he spent a year planning the heist and leading the gang all that time.

"Tell you what. Round the total up to one hundred and forty thousand and we'll call it quits."

"Frank, as it's you, I'll show a splash of generosity. You and your missus have yourselves a deal."

He had managed to squeeze an extra two and a half grand out of Mark. All three stood up and shook hands to seal their fates.

"Unless you've got the racks stuffed in your pockets, you'll need to collect the goods."

"Yeah, we decided not to bring it with us. Nothing personal, but it's a dangerous game we're playing."

"No explanation necessary. You didn't know if you could trust me. No worries. I'd have done the same."

Frank seized Mark by the cheeks and planted a kiss square on his lips.

"I knew you were the right man to come to."

A long hug as they relived their shared past. Mary Lou stood by, wanting to join in but knowing there was a private experience connecting the two felons. Once they'd separated, she gave Mark a peck on the cheek.

"Thanks for everything. For helping us now and being there for my Frank through his prison time. He's always refused to talk about it, but I can see you too had something special."

She squeezed Frank's hand and he placed an arm around her shoulders. Everyone was square.

"How long will it take you to get the money together?"

"It's ready now."

"Seriously?"

"Yep. I've been doing well since you last saw me."

"Good for you."

"The stash is in some lockers, nice and secure. I need to go back to my pad to pick up the keys."

"Shall we meet in sixty minutes? Will that give you enough time?"

"Sure thing. We're off to Burbank Airport."

"That still going?"

"Yeah, for cargo now, which is why I like it. No screaming kids but plenty of traffic."

"An hour then."

"You get outta here first. I'll go five minutes later once you're safely away."

Frank and Mary Lou crunched to the edge of the tree line and waited until two men had sent their golf balls flying down the fairway. Then they boosted a car in the parking lot and headed straight back to the Clements.

84

FRANK PARKED FOUR blocks away from the Clements and they walked back to the hotel. Through the lobby and up to their room. He pulled out their fake ID from their nightstand drawer while Mary Lou grabbed the two black bags from their hiding places and dropped them onto the coffee table. She went into the bedroom to find out what was taking him so long.

She found him sat on the bed, head in his hands, fake driving license and passports lying next to him. Mary Lou kneeled in front of him, her body between his knees.

"What's the matter, hon'?"

She wiped a tear off his cheek. He'd never behaved like this before and a fear was gripping the middle of her stomach.

"Nothing, babe. After all this time, I can't believe this is coming together. That's all."

Mary Lou's shoulders relaxed and she kissed him, holding the sides of his face in her hands.

"We'll be okay. The only thing to think about is getting the money today. Nothing else matters."

"I know. We'll figure everything out later on. It's Mark we need to focus on now."

"You bet. In a year or two we can come back to California."

"To be honest, babe, for me it's never been about California. It wasn't where we went that counted: it was about leaving. Baltimore was killing me and it would have killed the pair of us if it had the chance."

"That's thousands of miles away."

"Good, isn't it?"

Frank kissed Mary Lou again and let one palm slide down her spine and reach her ass. She put a hand on his groin and separated their lips. In a whisper: "We can fuck ourselves to oblivion later. Now is the time for money."

He squeezed her cheek and sneaked a finger in between her thighs making a single tingle race up her back and reach the nape of her neck. She kissed his hand and placed it on his lap.

"Let's go, hon'."

"You bet."

As ever, they took one bag each, holding hands while they waited for the elevator. In the lobby, Tom stood near the concierge. He walked toward them as soon as he noticed their arrival.

"Mister, I got news for you."

"What's happening?"

"There's been men asking after you and I thought you should know."

"How many?"

"Two pairs. All in suits."

"Four in total?"

"Yessir. I heard them ask the receptionist about you. The first turned up an hour past. You almost bumped into the second set. They were here ten minutes ago."

"They in the lobby now?"

Tom searched round but shook his head.

"You done good."

Frank planted another five spot on the bellboy.

"We're off out again but keep your eyes peeled and your ears open. We'll be back later and you can give us an update. Okay?"

Mary Lou and Frank scurried out the lobby. Before they left the confines of the building, he checked up and down the road but nothing appeared suspicious. At a brisk pace, they hurried along the four blocks to their boosted ride.

Bags on the back seat, he sat behind the wheel. They both pulled out their guns and each counted six slugs in the chamber. Mary Lou looked up and down the sidewalks trying to find the two sets of men. One pair must be Uncle Frankie's goons and the other from the East Coast, she reckoned. The knot of fear in her stomach returned but for a different reason than before. She was more confident because she'd handled dangerous fellas all her life but she couldn't handle things if he could not cope.

"See anything?"

"No."

"Me neither, babe."

"We better get to Mark then."

Frank played with the wiring under the steering block until the engine fired up. He looked over to her and winked. She smiled back: there was something magical in starting a car without the use of a key. And the magic rubbed off on the conjuror who performed the feat.

AS THEY ARRIVED at Hollywood-Burbank Airport, Mary Lou studied the L-shaped building that straddled two sides of the rectangular parking area. The short side was at the far end by the arrivals, whereas the long edge ran the full length of the lot and was designated for departures.

Frank parked the car near the arrivals. They had driven for five minutes before they found any space at all, but the place only coped with two hundred vehicles, so they shouldn't have been that surprised. The advantage of driving round in circles was that it gave them a chance to spot anyone who'd previously visited the Clements Fitzrovia but there were no obvious candidates.

"Keep one hand on your gun, okay?"

"Got it, hon'."

They walked through the parked vehicles until they reached the far end of the departures. With most planes picking and dropping cargo, there were only two gates for passengers left open nowadays. In the previous five years, several major airlines had moved to LAX and Burbank was heading for a decline. A perfect rendezvous location and a great place to hide money in plain sight. Mark was a clever cookie.

Once inside, Mary Lou's and Frank's eyes followed the long corridor that made up the main building. There was a fair buzz of people despite the lack of passenger flights. Mark had failed to mention the number of private jets that still called Burbank home. A series of concession stands broke up their line of sight.

"It's going to be hard to walk down this building without getting spotted."

Mary Lou nodded as she was thinking the selfsame thing. Then she froze, legs unable to move from their position.

"Three hundred feet ahead. By the coffee concession. Two guys. You see them?"

"Got 'em."

"Recognize them?"

"No."

"Might have seen one of them before. On the strip in Vegas. When we hid in the lingerie store."

They both watched Ted Goodwin talking with Phil McNamara, each holding a mug with steam pouring out. Conversation and sips for five, ten minutes while Mary Lou and Frank remained where they were.

"They're not moving any time soon. Has he recognized us?"

"If he's any kind of cop, he should make both of us."

"Let's go."

Mary Lou followed Frank out the building. They stood by the entrance in case of trouble but nothing came. So they padded down the sidewalk until they reached the next door. The wall of the terminal was pure glass, which meant they could see they'd passed by Goodwin and McNamara. If Goodwin made either of them, then he saw where they were standing too.

When they walked inside, they were still amid the gates and concessions, only this time the nearest ones were sealed up, unused. The airport authorities had established a clear separation between the departure area past Goodwin and McNamara and the arrivals section, which Mary Lou and Frank had yet to reach.

They strode away from Goodwin, following the overhead signs for lost luggage. As they walked, both sets of eyes were flitting from one group of people to another. Mary Lou figured that if the FBI were here, then the mob or Frankie's men couldn't be far behind. What she couldn't understand is how they knew to be at this airport at all. An hour ago, she and Frank had zero clue they would end up here before lunchtime, so how could the Feds know? Either they're covering all airports and train stations or Mark dropped a dime on them after he left the golf course. Frank nudged her side as he stared straight ahead.

"Looks like we have more company. Anthony and the guy from the Chinese Theater."

Mary Lou scanned the end of the cavernous room which Frank was facing until she spotted Three-Piece. She gulped.

"What now, hon'?"

"Time to find Mark and get outta Dodge."

"Okay."

They skipped back outside and carried on further along the sidewalk. Anthony and Three-Piece were so busy checking out everyone in the building, they didn't bother to keep an eye on anyone on the other side of the glass wall. Frankie only ever hired the cheapest; never the brightest.

Mary Lou and Frank reached a door with an enormous Arrivals sign above the entrance. Inside there was an arrow for lost luggage.

They walked past the two carousels for baggage collection and sauntered, as casually as possible, round the corner to reach three rows of lockers. In the middle of the second row stood Mark whistling to himself as he leaned against the metal containers. When they approached him, he half-saluted and took his hands out his pockets.

"The place is crawling with fellas. Let's make this quick."

MARK NODDED AND wasted no time as he hurried to the far end of the row and pulled out a bunch of keys from his jacket. Mary Lou and Frank sidled up next to him, both facing away from his activities to keep an eagle eye on anyone who might be intent on getting their money. She heard various clunks, slams and twists of metal. Brown holdalls appeared at Mark's feet.

"Do those bags hold the loot?"

Frank nodded and passed his over to Mark who threw it into a locker and slammed it shut. She did the same.

"I trust you not to have to count it."

"If when you open it there's just cut-up bits of newspaper, find me and shoot me where I stand."

"I will, my friend. And your missus too."

"I wouldn't have it any other way," Mary Lou added.

Mark smiled and picked up the two holdalls he'd retrieved.

"One has a hundred grand, the other forty. Count it if you need to."

"We don't. If it's shreds of newspaper, you know where to find us."

"Standing over my cold, dark grave."

"You said it, muchachos."

Then from the far end of the row of lockers:

"Put the bags down, place your hands over your heads and no one will get hurt."

Goodwin and McNamara trained guns on the three of them and Mary Lou's stomach clenched in knotty fear.

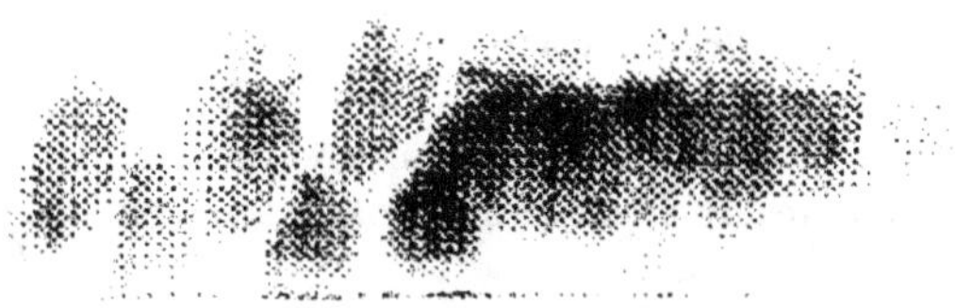

85

MARY LOU AND Frank looked at each other and stared at McNamara. He was the older of the two and had been the one to issue the warning. They clung to the holdalls, gripping tighter than before.

"I said to put the bags down."

"Hands on your heads!"

McNamara's voice contained authority and he was attempting to sound reasonable. Goodwin barked an order at them. Mary Lou watched as McNamara winced at Goodwin's instruction.

The two men edged along the row of the hundred-foot lockers until they were only seventy feet away; McNamara's gun remained pointing at Frank all that time. Goodwin's barrel flitted from Mary Lou to Mark and back again. Behind the three was the glass wall of the terminal building so they had to get out of this metal alley. Whichever other aisle they chose—even if they split up—the cops could pick them off from the other end. The only place to go was nowhere.

A single shot rang out and the they dropped to the ground. Mary Lou and Frank pulled their guns out and Mark fumbled in his pants trying to yank out his piece. She looked around to see red gushing from Goodwin's chest. McNamara had his back to them and was firing off into the distance. Anthony and Three-Piece had made their move—but too early.

Frank, Mark and Mary Lou scurried towards McNamara and crouched down, pressed against the same side of the lockers. The Fed got to one knee and carried on shooting. This gave them time to reach him without catching stray shrapnel.

"This bunch your men?" commanded McNamara.

"Nope."

A bullet whizzed past, missing McNamara's ear by a hair's breadth and Mark spun round and fell to the ground. Blood poured out his neck. Mary Lou screamed and Frank grabbed Mark's gun. He gritted his teeth and fired back at Anthony and Mickey. The only way to escape those two was to kill them.

The cover offered by Frank gave McNamara the opportunity he needed and he ran to the end of the aisle and burst past the corner to get a better line on the snipers.

Frank kicked his holdall forwards. He and Mary Lou perched at the edge of the lockers and watched as McNamara put a bullet straight through Mickey's heart. Clean shot. Then he reloaded his pistol as they gave him cover. Anthony was staying his ground: he knew he was so close to the money, he could almost taste it.

Alarms were spitting out high volume bells by now and the citizenry were running left and right behind Anthony, desperately trying to avoid the gunfire but too scared to think straight and run in the opposite direction and outside.

With fresh slugs in his handgun, McNamara took aim at Anthony, who raised up on his haunches to get a better chance of a hit. Slugs rained out of his piece and McNamara ducked. Then he kneeled back up and sent two bullets into Anthony: one in the gut and the other in his chest. Anthony's body hurled itself in the air and came to rest five feet further on. He screamed in agony, grabbing his torso. McNamara stood up to deal with the felon.

Mary Lou put her hand to her forehead to wipe off the sweat. When she took it away, her fingers were red. Strange, she felt no pain. Then she looked down and gazed at the bullet hole in Frank's upper body and realized his blood had ricocheted onto her, plastering her face with his vital fluid.

WITH A SCREAM of agony, Mary Lou let go her holdall and kneeled down to hold Frank in her arms. Tears lashing down her cheeks, she kissed him on the forehead, kissed him on the mouth and sat with his body hauled on her lap.

Tears, air bubbles of mucus and spit fell down onto his lifeless torso, mixing with the blood puddling out his corpse. Mary Lou sobbed and wailed, crying for the only man in her life who had ever shown her even a hint of kindness. She was alone in this godforsaken world and her honey was dead in her arms.

The alarms carried on ringing and she continued to cry, not caring what happened next. One of Frank's feet twitched slightly in his death throes. The knot in Mary Lou's stomach ceased to ache as the overarching pain of her situation engulfed her completely. Her world reduced itself to her throbbing head and the man she'd loved in her arms. And the pool of blood coalescing around her.

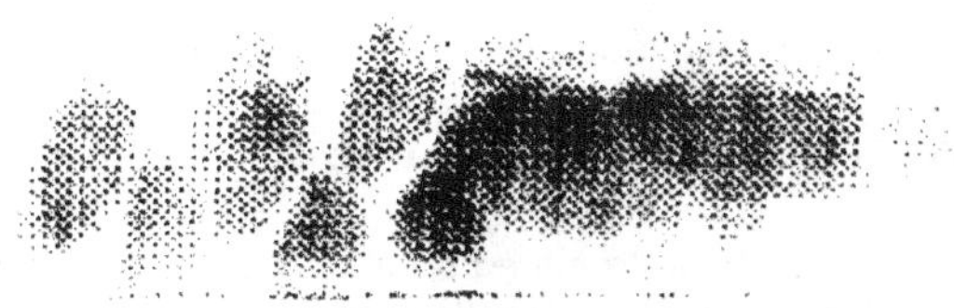

86

FRANK SENIOR WAS spending the last vestiges of the night pleasuring himself in the Kitkatt Club with a girl called May. He had plied her with vodka and fucked her in every available orifice. She hurt across the entirety of her body but knew better than to stop him. The receiving end of Frankie's ire was not a good place to be.

So she sat astride the moneylender, letting his half-erect penis flop near her bush. He was tired enough to be dozing and she was almost unconscious too.

Arnold Roach had received his instructions from Mary Lou by phone around lunchtime on Monday, June 16. The plan was simple and clear. Fifty per cent of the money arrived as requested prior to his task and she would send the rest on its completion.

Roach walked into the Kitkatt and ordered a drink at the bar. He kept his sunglasses on and the lapels of his coat pointed upwards, hiding part of his face. He leaned on the counter and watched the show on stage. Nothing special, just the relentless sight of semi-naked teenagers revealing their bodies in the hope of a Jackson in their G-strings.

He finished his watered down drink and left a dollar tip for the barman. Sauntered around the back edge of the seating area and arrived outside the private rooms. Arnold nipped into the first one but it was empty. Then into the second and closed the door behind himself.

Walked up to the bed where May had flopped on top of Frankie. Roach grabbed a pillow lying on the floor and pushed the sleeping girl off the moneylender. Cushion over his head before the guy could wake and react—and squeezed the trigger. Feathers flew into the air in a ball. Frankie's face was welded to the back of his skull.

May woke as she landed on the ground only to see white fluff. Before she could call out, Arnold stuffed the pillow over her mouth and pulled the trigger again. He didn't wait to check if she was alive because she hadn't seen his face either way. He walked out the room, out the Kitkatt and got into his car to drive off, knowing the second payment from Mary Lou was only days away.

HER PAIN WAS undiminished, but Mary Lou couldn't stay with Frank for an eternity. She pushed him gently off her lap and looked down at her bloody clothes, arms and legs. She wouldn't get far looking like that. This thought forced her to think about the world beyond herself and she saw the blood, the lockers, the terminal building and McNamara walking toward her, gun in hand.

If he got back to her, then there'd be handcuffs on her in less than ten seconds. She picked up one gun lying on the floor and took aim. A crack rang out and McNamara fell to the ground. She smiled as she hit her mark: the right leg. Mary Lou might ache with the loss of Frank but she was thinking clearly enough not to kill a cop.

She stuffed the gun into her waistband, grabbed both holdalls and exited out the nearest door. Mary Lou zigzagged in between the parked cars until she spotted a set of keys in the ignition of a green sedan. She jumped into the driver's seat and threw the bags next to her.

Out the lot and down the road. Tears still dribbling down her cheeks, she exhaled deeply and dragged the vehicle away from the air terminal, five miles an hour below the speed limit. The money sat in the footwell and Mary Lou's dreams lay shattered by the lockers back at Burbank Airport.

THE END

Powder

LOS ANGELES, SUNDAY JUNE 29, 1968

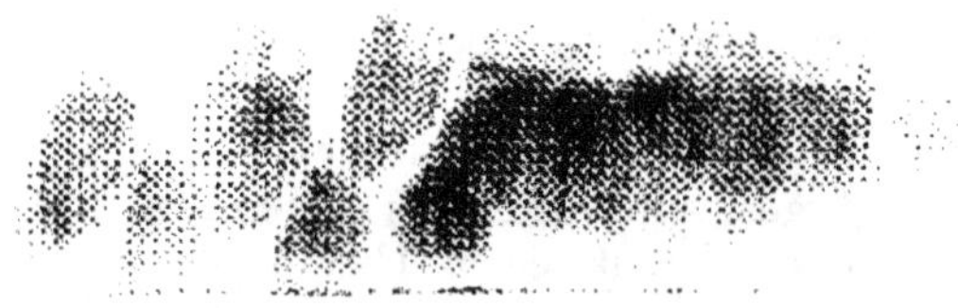

87

MARY LOU LAGOTTI drove at five miles an hour below the speed limit away from Burbank Airport. The first time since 1962 she felt alone, certain there was nobody on this planet who she could rely on for anything.

Always checking in the rearview mirror for signs of trouble, she headed to the Clements Fitzrovia Hotel. Occasionally, she'd glance down at her bloody skirt and glimpse the red ovals on her arms—the small globules of her husband's blood which had splattered over her while he was shot twice as he kneeled beside her.

Tears still dribbled down her cheeks as the shock and torment of those few moments juddered across her mind. No matter how much she concentrated on the road ahead, Mary Lou couldn't shake off the image of Frank bleeding out in her arms. Of her shooting the Fed before he arrested her. Of her zigzag escape from the parking lot that brought her to within three blocks of her current location.

She drove the green saloon to the back of the hotel and grabbed the two holdalls she'd stashed in the front passenger footwell. Mary Lou looked around, saw nobody and bent down to open the lighter bag and move its contents to its heavier twin. Then she zipped it shut and dragged it out the vehicle. She fingered every cent of the one hundred and forty thousand dollars contained inside. Laundered money from the robbery at the Lansdowne branch of the First Bank of Baltimore. And she was the sole survivor of the entire gang now that her Frank was no more.

Into a side door, Mary Lou hoped to find a service elevator but somehow she headed straight for the main reception area. She spotted the bellboy, Tom who strode over to her.

"Jeez, miss. What happened?"

"No time to explain, but I need your help."

"I'm not surprised. Housekeeping will be hard pushed to take those stains out."

Mary Lou looked down at herself and realized how blood-drenched she appeared. Never mind.

"Has anyone else been asking about us since we left this morning?"

"No, none."

"Good. I'll come down in ten minutes and I want you to call a cab and have him wait at the side of the hotel. Got that?"

"Sure, miss."

Mary Lou laid a clean Jackson on Tom who nodded, smiled and went off to find that taxi. Meantime, she hauled straight up the stairs to the second floor and then ran all the way to their room. She fumbled with the door key but after a lifetime the lock pinged open.

In front of the bathroom mirror, Mary Lou stripped out of her bloody clothes and stared at herself. Her legs and arms were splattered with too much blood. She used the shower attachment to wash away the red from her limbs but she still felt dirty inside. Unclean.

That unfathomable sense of disgust clung to her skin as she put on fresh underwear, a shirt, a pair of jeans and sunglasses. A walk around the suite enabled her to gather every ounce of possessions they'd scattered round the place since their arrival in LA. She stuffed all her clothes on top of the cash and shoved all Frank's things into the empty holdall. Mary Lou checked her revolver and filled the chambers with slugs.

One final trip around and by the time she returned to the bed, she knew it was clear. Another image flashed in her head as she recalled Anthony flying through the air with the force of the bullet slamming through his body. His death meant nothing to her—he was one of the thugs Uncle Frankie hired to hunt them down, kill them and return the money. The Shylock had played fast and loose and was left with bupkis. Not even his life.

Mary Lou reckoned the hit she'd arranged on Uncle Frankie must have been executed by now. All that stood between her and some kind of future was the New York mob and the Feds. Her best hope was to leave the country soonest and wait for the heat to die down.

One last check of herself in the mirror, Mary Lou grabbed the holdall and left the room. Down the stairs and into the lobby where Tom hustled over to her.

"The cab is waiting like you asked."

"Thanks."

"Is there anything more I can do for you?"

"No, you've been great."

She placed another Jackson in his palm.

"If anyone else comes wandering past asking questions…"

"…I know nothing."

"You said it. You keep your mouth shut. Even if it's the cops."

"Especially if it's the pigs."

She gave him a peck on the cheek to seal the deal. There's no way that sixteen-year-old boy would spill his guts even to a G-man.

Without turning her head backwards, Mary Lou strode out the Clements and into the back of the cab. It was less than thirty minutes since Frank drew his last breath. She sank into the rear as the taxi dredged its way to the depot.

She bought a ticket for the first vehicle leaving town. After only a quarter hour, she stepped onto a bus, shoved her bag in the overhead shelf and slumped into the aisle seat so no one could grab it without her taking direct action against them.

Ten hours later, she reached San Francisco where she laid overnight in a fleapit near the station. Her time in the city was uneventful but unpleasant. She picked her way past the hookers plying their trade as she entered the hotel.

The following morning, Mary Lou returned to the depot and purchased another ticket—with Vancouver as her destination. There was a two hour wait, so she trooped over to a diner to fill up on food. Her appetite was still shot to hell from the previous day's violence but she ate, anyway.

Thirty hours later and Claudia Starr stepped out into the Canadian sun. She showed her fake ID to cross the border so once the Feds identified her, they'd not be able to trace her departure from the land of the free.

As the mob used intel from the Hoover boys, Mary Lou figured the trail of carnage around the city of Angels would stop at the Clements Fitzrovia. Even if someone worked out she had made it to San Francisco, they wouldn't be able to follow her any further.

As she walked on the foreign concrete sidewalk, Mary Lou removed her sunglasses and tried to breathe and act like a normal person. Only trouble was: she couldn't remember how to do it.

88

CHARLIE PENTANGELO ACCEPTED his mob money had floated into the wind. He was calm about not seeing the money ever again, but he continued to fume at the people who'd taken the proceeds of the heist from him.

As he never held the cash, he was no worse off than before the robbery was mentioned. The Shylock, Frank Lagotti Senior, felt differently. He had the money almost in his hand before his step nephew snatched it out of his grasp. The real issue for Charlie was that people shouldn't steal from him. Rob from a bank? Knock yourself out. Take from Pentangelo? Not if you want to see your next birthday.

Earlier in the day, word reached him about a gunfight in LA and how the Feds had done for his boys while they were trying to get the money back. Details were scant, but he knew the proceeds were gone and two of his own needed a funeral.

Now he sat on his own in his favorite chair contemplating his next move. Frank Senior had been wise to let his step nephew take the First Bank of Baltimore and its half a million even though the man himself was a parasite on the carcass of the world.

The phone rang.

"Hello?"

The voice on the other end of the line spoke flat, no intonation. Just the facts with no comment.

"The money has left Burbank Airport. Our two are deceased, the Shylock's men are offed."

"And?"

"Our FBI sources confirmed Frank Lagotti and one unknown guy are dead. The woman took the proceeds and ran. She is still at large."

"Any good news for me?"

"Nothing to put a smile on your face."

"Keep me informed."

Charlie heard the click of the receiver as the call ended. That girl, Mary Lou, held his cash and would need to pay for her mistakes. The phone rang again—a different voice on the line.

"Bad news, Charles."

"What now?"

"There's been a death."

"Who?"

"Frank Lagotti Senior."

"The Shylock? How?"

"Bullet through his face."

A professional hit.

"Any idea on the perpetrator?"

"Not yet but we're working on it."

"Where did the deed take place?"

"In his cathouse. No struggle. The hitman walked in, plugged Lagotti, did for the girl sat on his dick and strode out. Too much of a coincidence for Lagotti's murder to occur the same day as the fracas in LA. Make some enquiries. I want to know more details."

Pentangelo waited ten minutes and dialed a special number—it was never written but always memorized by those who used it. When serious men needed professional help to complete their murderous tasks, they contacted Murder Inc: the nickname for a unique group of killers who originally came out of Brooklyn. These fellas were the most dangerous the mob families knew. If anyone would take out a hit on someone outside their territory, these were the people to call.

Charlie booked a requisition on the head of Mary Lou and it was immediately sanctioned even with a specific request. He wanted the best man for this job: Arnold Roach. A killer's killer. An elite fiend with a knife or a gun. A relentless murdering machine. Once you hired him, he never gave up. Whoever he held a contract on always wound up demised.

As the sole survivor of the heist, Mary Lou must take responsibility for all that has happened: to the money, to the men and now to Frankie. Roach would track her down and slash her throat. Or cut her open from one side to the other. Whatever Charlie wanted.

Safe knowing Roach was on the case within a matter of hours, Pentangelo put on an aria on his record player and settled back down in his chair. Mary Lou was as good as dead.

Monday July 7, 1968

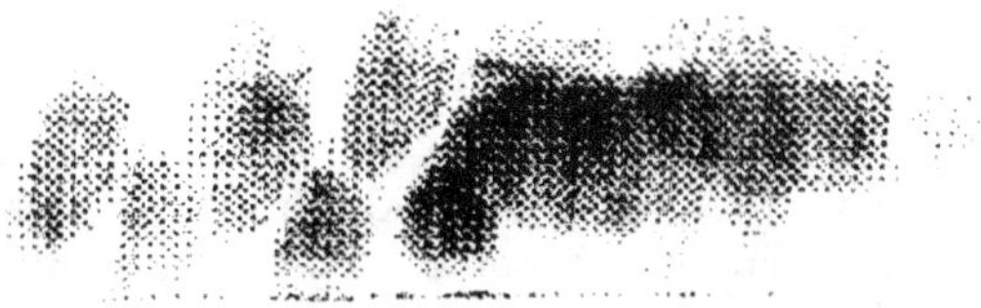

89

THERE HAD BEEN a Murder Incorporated since the day the Big Bankroll formed the Five Families back in the Thirties. Out of Brooklyn—and only Jewish—mobsters turned to these guys when violence between clans was required.

When not wreaking revenge on those they were paid to kill, the members spent their time playing penuckle and performing freelance assassinations instead. Arnold Roach was the best of the baddest and you could always rely on him to get the job done quickly, effectively and without leaving a trace of his passing through town.

As a result, he had little time to engage in extracurricular subversion but, and for the right price, he'd lend a hand to a stranger. A month ago Roach received a call from a woman seeking revenge on a moneylender. He never wanted to know the justification for his services being rendered. It was of no concern to him what the beef was about. He would happily kill anyone who moved, provided there was green in it for him.

The Shylock was based in Baltimore and the down payment arrived as requested. When the time was right, he drove down to the city, found the middle-aged man in his flophouse and shot him in the face.

Standard terms applied and Arnold waited a week for the second half of his money. He had learned to leave several days before getting the final payment as word needed to spread sufficiently far for his employer to hear the good news about the demise of their nemesis.

But the money didn't appear. One day late was of no concern to him as he was off on Murder Inc business and did not return home until a further two days. The absence of an envelope primed with cash caused consternation, but nothing more. Once a full week had lapsed, Roach was like a bear with a honeypot jammed on his nose with an angry bee inside.

Arnold sat in his armchair with one eye on the fire escape and the other on the door. The leather surface leaned him comfort, but he gritted his teeth every time he thought about Mary Lou and Frank Lagotti Senior.

The walls closed in so he grabbed his wallet, keys, checked his jacket holster and headed onto the street. Round the corner was a little cafe where everyone minded their own business and nobody listened too carefully to the conversation of adjacent customers.

Arnold strode to his usual location—at the back, half in shadow and an extra five inches from any other table in the joint. The owner ambled over and placed an espresso by Roach's elbow, who nodded and let the world pass him by.

He had been a fool: why take a job away from home and from a virtual stranger. Roach knew the answer before the thought had tripped out his head. Because the money was good and she was a woman aggrieved.

Something about her voice when they first spoke made him agree to the proposition she lay before him. Killing the moneylender didn't cause him a moment's lost sleep—before or after the event. There was an angry edge to her tone which screamed out how much she wanted the guy to suffer before he died.

Roach wasn't in that business. He was a murderer, not a torturer, and made that clear to her before they struck their deal. If Mary Lou was dissatisfied with the job he performed, she should tell him and they could discuss the matter but her absolute silence? That showed she'd flown in the wind.

And there was no way he could allow someone to fleece him. If word got out you could stiff Arnold Roach, his professional reputation would be over. Kaput.

He swigged down his coffee and headed back to his apartment. Arnold would have to find the woman and extract his money from her. If the cash was not forthcoming, he'd put a bullet between her eyes. Sometimes life can be as simple as that.

SATURDAY OCTOBER 20, 1962

90

MARY LOU BELLE left home when she was fifteen and never looked back. Her mother, her sisters and her cold dead father ceased to feature in her existence from the moment she walked out the family bungalow and into the world. She headed straight for New York but never got there, instead alighting upon Atlantic City and, when the chips were down, over to Baltimore.

As a girl with no book learning, Mary Lou mixed with the wrong sorta guys because they were the only kind who'd give her the time of day. She paid no tax, and she surrounded herself with interesting characters from the dark side of town—a place she'd lived for six years.

One Saturday, her closest girlfriend suggested they go to a neighborhood party and Mary Lou agreed. What better excuse to drink too much and enjoy the laughs and indiscretions of youth?

She shared a fleapit apartment with Vicky Fischer. They'd met within a few days of her arrival in the city and split the rent for living quarters two weeks later when she grew tired of sleeping on strangers' floors and became disillusioned with sleeping in strangers' beds.

The party was one block from home—a neighborhood affair—and Vicky assured her there would be some fresh meat as well as the local boys. Mary Lou'd had her fill of the juvenile young men, who frequented the dive bars near the apartment. They never showed the level of seriousness nestling deep inside her own heart.

When she and Vicky arrived at around eleven, they discovered a full living room heaving with people and a kitchen rammed with liquor. The perfect combination. They remained a close partnership for the first thirty minutes to ensure no octopus hands got fresh while the night was still young.

After midnight, different rules applied and they split up. Vicky hunted for Jamie, a sweet kid with his own Harley. Mary Lou spent an hour chatting and dancing with a string of guys but none of them held her attention for longer than the record took to play.

One fella caught her eye. He sat on the edge of an armchair, laughing with another guy. The way he rested on the end of the furniture grabbed Mary Lou's attention. Self-assured but not arrogant. Grounded. She headed past the two of them, wending her path among the herd of twentysomethings congregating inside this single apartment.

The men were laughing about who knew what and she stopped as she sauntered by, clinked a glass with the brown-haired one and joined in the conversation.

"The thing is, you know…"

Calling it a conversation was generous: these were drunk musings and no more, but Mary Lou enjoyed hearing him talk and she enjoyed looking at his body, hidden under a skin-tight white tee shirt and a pair of jeans. Nothing special: like he was trying to appear as though he hadn't tried at all. His friend wandered off to get more drink.

"I'm Mary Lou."

"Frank."

A clink of glasses again.

"You from round here? I don't think I've seen you in the neighborhood."

"Lived here for years but I have been… away for a while."

She recognized that code. Jail, but the guy was an attractive felon. She liked the sparkle in his eyes and the muscles of his upper arms. And the small twitch in the corner of his mouth as he tried to smile but didn't know how. She understood that facial tic only too well.

"I moved here two weeks ago, so that explains it."

"Sure does."

Mary Lou was leaning on his shoulder: her heels were hurting and, besides, she wanted an excuse to touch him.

"You wanna dance?"

She nodded so he grabbed her hand and they walked a few feet to where the rest of the room was gyrating to the beat of the music. Mary Lou and Frank hopped from one foot to the other for over half an hour. Occasionally, she'd lean into him and say something in his ear and he would respond. Twice he did the same.

They smiled, laughed and danced. Like everyone the world over, each checked out the other to decide if they were attractive for more than a boogie with or without booze.

Some wise guy changed record to a slow number and half the people moved to the edge: either not drunk enough or not interested in getting that close to their current dance partner. But they stayed on. She took a step towards him and Frank placed an arm behind her back. She laid her head on his shoulder and she felt his chin on her hair.

Frank's thumb stroked her neck—slow, slow—until little tingles erupted from the point where he touched her. She nuzzled closer and he put his other hand on the lower portion of her spine.

Three-and-a-half minutes later the music stopped but Mary Lou and Frank remained stationary. She turned her head to look into his eyes and their mouths touched. All around them bodies jumped, hopped and wriggled to the fast tempo but they continued as they were: kissing and stroking, enveloped in the moment between them. She looked to find the world had moved on and she parted their lips and smiled at him.

"You wanna go somewhere quieter so we can talk?"

"Sure thing, babe."

Mary Lou stole some red wine from a nearby table, led Frank out the party and over to her apartment. She opened the bottle and poured two glasses but they never got to consume them. Instead, by the time Vicky came home three hours later, a spent condom lay on the floor and snoring emanated from the room.

SATURDAY OCTOBER 27, 1962

91

NEXT DAY, FRANK left early but not before he scribbled down an address for Mary Lou to find him if she wanted. Under any other circumstances, she'd have scrunched the piece of paper into a ball before going to the stove to make herself a morning coffee. But she had to admit this man was different.

Although she couldn't pin down what it was about him, he made her feel something: an emotion. Not that she'd hit the sack with him on the first night. Mary Lou had done that countless times before. What else was the point of going to a party? The difference with Frank: there was more to the experience than the thudding scream of an orgasm in her head spread across her entire body.

Despite only being with the guy for a few hours, she felt a strong affection for him. Crazy. And he fit so well inside her too.

On Monday she found the address he'd given and popped over. When she buzzed the apartment, a different male voice told her to wait. Then Frank appeared about thirty seconds later.

"Hi."

"Hiya, babe. You free for a coffee?"

She nodded and they headed to a place round the corner and chatted for an hour. The man explained how he wasn't getting on with his step-dad otherwise he'd have invited Mary Lou in.

"I understand. Families are strange beasts. Never trust a step-parent."

Frank eyed her and nodded. Conversation twisted and turned until his time was up.

"I gotta go or I will get shit at home."

"Sure. Why don't you move out?"

"It's complicated. If you're free on Saturday, we could have a bite to eat and I'll tell you all about it."

She thought for less than half a second.

"Yes. I'd like that a lot."

TO SAY MARY Lou thought about nothing else until the weekend would be an obvious lie. The woman had a job to hold down and weekdays were filled with the dullness of life. But to say she pushed the date to the back of her mind would not be true either.

By the time Saturday arrived, Mary Lou knew exactly what she would wear: dress, panties with matching bra and heels. She'd considered hair styles and nail polish. The whole enchilada.

Frank chose a local pasta joint for their rendezvous and they settled into a corner table, sitting on adjacent sides of the square surface. He ordered a bottle of red and she suggested a glass of water on the side. First order of business was to scan the menus for something worth eating.

"I'd recommend everything. There are no bad dishes here."

"Come here often with your lady friends?"

"Don't be like that. The food's good is all."

She squeezed his nearest hand while it held the menu.

"Only teasing, Frank."

He emitted another of his trademark side-of-mouth tics and she knew all was fine. Food ordered and drink delivered, they began the serious business of conversation.

"So where are you from?"

"Away from here. There's nothing to tell."

"Really? What about family?"

"I'm an orphan."

"Wow."

"Joking. My family's dead—or at least dead to me. Papa died when I was in diapers and he really is deceased. I have no idea about my mama and anyone else. Left home when I was fifteen and never looked back."

"What made you leave so young?"

"God and his minions."

She laughed, aware this trail of conversation could only lead into a dark, cold place she didn't want to enter.

"Jeez."

"Fuck him too."

Frank let go her hand and pulled a quizzical face.

"I didn't mean to touch a raw nerve. Sorry."

"Don't be. Not your fault, but some stuff will never be right."

"Say that again."

"And what's the deal with your step-dad?"

"The usual story, I guess. Mom remarried after my dad died. Mysterious circumstances they said, but he was with the mob so you join the dots."

"Fuck."

"Yep. And mom found herself a loser and I don't mind reminding them of that every opportunity I find. Means I'm not popular at home."

"So where do you spend most of your time because it ain't going to be in the bosom of your family? Do you seek out other bosoms instead?"

She tittered and squeezed his hand again. The comment was a joke although she was intrigued to know how much he slept around. Vicky said he was a small-time crook fresh out of jail but she didn't mind. To her, Frank had some oomph. More than most of the schmucks she bedded with since she arrived in Baltimore.

"Nothing wrong with seeking solace in a bosom, Mary Lou."

Another twitch at the side of his mouth.

"And what you get up to when you don't have your head nestled in a bosom?"

He laughed.

"There haven't been too many bosoms in my life. Some, but not many."

"We'll come back to that."

"Sure. I'm between jobs right now but I am cooking up an interesting project with a friend of mine."

"Oh?"

"Yeah. Me and Louis think we can make ourselves some easy money at a drug store or two."

"Is that how you see yourself making a living. In drug stores?"

"God no. I've got plans. Build some seed capital and invest it wisely in a convenience store. Then who knows?"

"I'm sitting beside the next Rockefeller?"

"Next Dillinger, babe. There's a difference. I won't rob from poor people. That's not right."
"I love a man with principles."
Mary Lou leaned over and pecked him on the cheek just as their antipasti arrived.

AT THE END of the meal, Mary Lou offered to pay but Frank had none of it. She thanked him and they sauntered out the restaurant and walked down the block, hand in hand.

"Fancy going to a pool hall to hang with the fellas, babe?"
"I'd rather hole up in a bar and have another glass. Or we could pop to my place…"
He smiled a full-lip toothy grin.
"I hoped you'd say something like that."
With a quickened pace, they headed to her apartment where Vicky sat in the living room reading a magazine. One minute's conversation and Mary Lou and Frank closed her bedroom door behind them.

They threw off their clothes and, once in bed, investigated each other's bodies. The previous week had been a drunken express train of a fuck. This time, they were more sober and more interested in discovering the other as a person.

After much kissing and licking, Frank found Mary Lou's tattooed rose, an inch below her belly button. She liked the way he didn't ask her about it like everybody else did. He accepted its existence and moved on up her body until she felt his groin near her thighs.

Then it was over before anything had begun. Frank squeezed her breast, rolled over and went to sleep. As he snored, she finished herself off and lapsed into unconsciousness too.

November 1968 to November 1969

92

CLAUDIA STARR MADE a new life for herself in Canada. When she stepped off the coach, she swapped two hundred dollars for Canadian and vowed not to do it again. Her accent was a big enough giveaway she was a foreigner without turning up at a currency exchange screaming out to the world she was an American.

She considered traveling to the far side of the country in case the Feds or the East Coast mob followed her, but she realized this was paranoia. Mary Lou changed coach en route from LA to Vancouver so there was no way anyone could guess where she ended up.

A year and a half later and not a solitary fat soul turned up in Canada seeking to chase her down. Her escape was complete. She spent the first two weeks in a hotel and found a job working in a dress store. With a paycheck in her back pocket, Claudia rented a one bed apartment on 13th Avenue and Victoria Drive—in between Clark and John Hendry Parks on the east side of the city.

She kept to herself in the evenings, not wanting to make any mark in this foreign community. Within two months she came down with a bad case of morning sickness and she visited a local doctor to find out what her belly and sore nipples already told her: pregnant.

With Medicare not implemented in Vancouver, Claudia worked her ass off to get the money to fund her antenatal care and the delivery itself. In the third trimester, her bump was kicking away in all directions. Three weeks before her due date, she gave birth to Alice and Frank Junior.

WITH THE NEEDS of her two children paramount in her mind, memories of Frank and the loss she felt over his death faded fast. There was no time to pander to her own emotional state.

By the summer, Claudia had organized a schedule at the store which gave her sufficient money to get by and had kept in contact with some women in the maternity suite from the hospital. They were all married and sympathetic to her plight and the old lady who lived on the same floor in her apartment block agreed to look after the twins when she worked.

She was on as even a keel as any single mother with two babies could be, living in a strange city in a foreign land. But she kept her head down and plowed on through these worst of times.

One ray of happiness Claudia gave herself every week was a trip to a park. The area was ripe with gang related violence which ensured inquisitive folks stayed the hell away. This was the perfect cover for Claudia as her discovery was always around the corner.

Given her background—and the fact she walked with a double buggy—she didn't bat an eyelid when a few young guys up to no good appeared to hang out near the swings. They knew better than to hassle a dame with babies. And if they tried anything, she'd have plugged them full of lead.

Over time, the boys acknowledged her presence and she would listen in on their conversations—not that they were interesting, just different from the domestic chaos that engulfed her daily.

They talked about who did what to whom and the hourly travails of teenagers, nitpicked to within an inch of its life. She smiled inside as their chat reminded her of the snatches of conversation she'd heard when she used to go to school. Before she left home and met Frank and everything seemed to be so simple.

Even though it was too early to say, Alice looked like Mary Lou and Frank Jr was the spitting image of his father. At least, that's what Claudia thought as she watched the two asleep in their cots. Her daughter was four minutes older than her son and Claudia knew this would be a bone of contention between them some day.

In the meantime, she worked hard in the store, grabbing any shift going, and when she got home, she'd slave away to make her children happy. Although she hadn't considered herself someone with a strong maternal instinct, truth was she would do anything to protect her two darlings.

The apartment itself was too small for three people but it was the best she could afford. Violence erupted on the streets most nights but none of it affected her. She watched from a window as one young man beat on another or a car was broken into. Cheap robberies by little hoodlums. Nothing to get worked up about.

Anita on the other side of the corridor complained how the neighborhood had gone down hill. She pretended to empathize to keep in Anita's good books, but none of it bothered her. This wasn't her place; this hadn't been her home for thirty years.

As the twins put on weight and grew, Anita felt more comfortable looking after them. So much so that by winter, Claudia went out once a week. She found a bar one block south with leather seated booths and a slightly older crowd who were amiable enough to welcome her into their fold. Her story was known around the neighborhood and Faye was a friendly face in the tavern.

"How you get through the day beats me."

"Oh, you do what you have to, right?"

"Sure but—I'm not being rude—I don't think I could cope with two kids under one by myself without a man to help."

"And David helps with your brood, does he?"

Faye thought for a minute, sipped her beer and laughed.

"Hell no. He's about as useful as a prophylactic with a hole in it, which come to think of it is how we got our third to turn up in the first place!"

They chuckled at the futility of the male of the species and Claudia carried on as the poor girl with the dead husband and twins.

93

CLAUDIA HANDED THE kids over to Anita and traveled to work. It might have been in November but the same set of events recurred daily. The drudge of keeping a low profile bore down on her. The weight of knowing she was a stone's throw from living the high life dragged her feet along the floor.

Alice and Frank Jr were beautiful, wonderful, fabulous sparkling lights in her world. But they couldn't talk and didn't know or care about her troubles. She loved them with all her might but they weren't enough to fill the void in her existence. The gap left by Frank and the absence of spending opportunity offered by the money she kept at the back of her wardrobe, hidden behind a coat and two long dresses.

If she moved somewhere else in this country, she would face the same set of problems. Her accent would make her a stranger and an avalanche of questions would follow. Then she'd find a crappy job so no one would see how much she really had. Here, in the east side of Vancouver, was as good as anywhere.

Claudia kissed Alice and Frank Jr goodbye, thanked Anita for the millionth time in her life and walked down the stairs, off to the Courtney Boutique where Mrs. Courtney held sway over the middle-aged women in the area.

The woman had been kind enough to offer her a job, so there was gratitude at the heart of the relationship but Courtney paid her bottom dollar as there was no better option available. And they both knew it.

One side benefit was the gossip Claudia overheard as she helped dress the ladies or hang back the clothes once they were done. The great thing about women of a certain age—irrespective of demographic, race, creed or color—was their insatiable desire to dig up shit on those near to them. If anything happened in Clark Park, that boutique knew about it almost before it had occurred.

"Did you see that out-of-towner in McAdams last night?"

"Who?"

"A new guy's moved in on 12th and Commercial."

"Do tell."

"I don't know much, which is why I was asking you."

"Oh."

Disappointment in that voice as the customer who'd picked up three jumpers and dumped them back down in a messy pile, carried on perusing the merchandise.

"He's handsome, I'd say. If you like a man in his forties."

"They have seen the world."

A titter.

"Not just the world if you get me."
Another giggle as lewd thoughts permeated across both minds.
"If I wasn't married, I'd be in the market for a dishy guy who knows his way around."
"Wouldn't we all, darling?"
"Where's he from?"
"Dunno but he sounds as though he's from over the border."
"You've spoken with him?"
"Oh no, but I heard him pay for his groceries in the convenience store."
"Well I never. An American in Rain City."
"Don't be like that."
"I'm kidding with you. Tell me more."
"For a guy just arrived, he was well dressed: three-piece suit. And it looked expensive."
"Anyone know what he's here for?"
"Nobody I've spoken to yet."
Claudia's ears pricked up when she heard about a stranger in town and they almost ripped off the side of her head when she heard about the suit. Only Rockefeller and the mob wore a vest…

She told herself to remain calm because the evidence of a gossip was not the best place to start a panic attack. Her stomach muscles tightened and she took herself off to the bathroom for five minutes to recover.

Two nights later, she sat opposite Faye, each with a beer in the hands.
"Have you heard about the new come-over who's moved in down the block?"
"Someone in the boutique mentioned it. You?"
"Bumped into him by the oranges."
"Say what?"
"At the grocers. He's a man who does his own shopping."
"What a modern world we live in."
A chuckle.
"What's he like then?"
"He looks dapper. Wears smart clothes with oil in his hair. Nice hands: clean fingernails."
"Huh?"
"You notice these things when you're both trying to grab the same clementine."
"And he's definitely a come-over?"
"Has an accent, so he was definitely born in the US. Hey, you might know him."
Claudia stared into her beer and counted to five. The next words were uttered with as much calm as she could muster.
"What makes you say that?"
"No reason. It's a small world though, isn't it?"
"Yep."
"If I see him again fondling fruit, you want me to hook you guys up?"
"What? Hell, no."
"What's wrong?"
"Nothing. Sorry. Just not been a good day. Kids were crying and wouldn't settle."
"Must be tough what you're going through."
Claudia nodded.
"You have no idea how difficult it is being me."
Faye smiled not understanding how deep a truth had been uttered.
"What else you picked up about him?"
"I wasn't sure you'd be interested."
"It's not that I don't want to know about fresh blood on the block. I said I didn't need you making an introduction."
"Polite. Lovely fingers. You can tell he's a white collar fella."
"Did he mention what he did for a living?"
"Well enough to afford a sharp suit."
"Seriously."

"Salesman. Sold typewriters."

"You've got to shift a lot of them to make any money."

"Maybe, but he looked like he was doing all right for himself. Did I mention he wore a beautiful hat?"

"No. That makes all the difference."

They chuckled and Claudia moved over to the bar to get another round of drinks in. This also gave her a chance to ponder the information she had on the guy. The more she thought, the greater her anxiety grew.

If he looked like a mobster and he sounded like a mobster then the chances were: he was a mobster. The time had come for Mary Lou to get the fuck out of Dodge.

MARY LOU CARRIED on talking with Faye as long as the beers lasted despite her overwhelming desire to flee. Nothing screams out guilty more than a woman running away for no obvious reason.

Around eleven, Faye called it a night as she received a glance from David that said it was time to go home. They hugged goodbye as they left the bar and Mary Lou walked off without looking behind. As soon as she'd turned the corner, she picked up the pace and scurried in the opposite direction to the apartment. She checked out every vehicle she passed until she found one to her liking.

Opened handbag. Removed a hat pin. Door lock unpicked. Forty seconds later, the engine roared into life and she drove it home. A race up the stairs and she stopped to catch her breath. She snuck past Anita's door so she could get into the apartment and deal without the twins. A suitcase stuffed with clothes. Bags filled with everything else and downstairs to shove it all into the trunk.

Back upstairs. Mary Lou leaned against the wall next to Anita's. Breathe, babe. The woman knows zip and all you are doing is getting your kids like you've done every week for months. She reminded herself there was nothing special about today.

Rat-a-tat-tat.

"Hi there. Hope I'm not too late."

"Of course not dear."

Anita walked away from the door, letting Mary Lou follow her in. The twins were asleep on a mat rolled out for them.

"Have they been any trouble?"

"Not at all. Slept all night."

"Good. Thanks. For everything."

"Huh?"

"Nothing. Same time next week?"

"You betcha."

Mary Lou scooped up the sleeping babes, one in each arm, so their heads flopped onto her shoulders. As she left Anita's, Alice curled an hand around Mary Lou's neck and Frank Jr gurgled contentedly near her ear. She walked toward her apartment and fumbled a little to poke the key in the lock—to give Anita enough time to close her door behind her.

As fast as she could without waking her bundles of joy, Mary Lou slipped downstairs and flopped them into the back seat. She shoved a blanket over them so they didn't get too cold, got into the driver's seat and headed out of town.

Throughout her life with Frank as they fled across country, a simple mantra echoed in her skull: never go over five miles below the speed limit. She hoped family car wouldn't be missed until the morning to give her enough time to leave the vicinity before the local cops were asked to investigate.

Mary Lou's first thought was to hit another town in Canada but if the guy was following her, then he'd know her false name by now and she'd be an easy catch. The mob had tentacles in every city of influence and they'd used Canada ever since the Prohibition.

She figured the trick would be to go to the one place where the trail had grown coldest: the United States. The Feds must have given up on finding her otherwise they'd have done so by now. Hoover and his merry band have bigger felons to fry than a woman who robbed a bank and vanished into the mist.

There was the minor matter of her shooting a Federal office in the leg, but again, if it was that big a deal to them then they'd have tracked her down and they had not.

Over the border in the small hours of the morning without a customs guard even twitching.

"Purpose of your visit?"

"Popping over to hook up with family in Seattle."

"Unusual time to be traveling?"

"Well, they're asleep and it's much nicer to do it then."

She nodded into the back seat as Alice and Frank Jr carried on snoozing despite the rush of cold air from the open window.

"Stay safe on the roads, ma'am."

Men in uniform were the easiest ones to play, she thought. All you had to do was meet their bigoted expectations and you were home and dry.

Four miles down the road, she pulled over and took out the cuticle scissors from her clutch bag. Mary Lou cut up her Claudia Starr ID and ripped up the passport until it was in small enough pieces to chop into shards.

As she carried on down the highway, she grabbed handfuls of the identification confetti and released it out the window. Over the next ten miles, Claudia was sprinkled along the road until there was nothing left of her apart from Mary Lou's memories.

Being back in the US created its own set of questions: the pressing need to escape gave her no time to decide where to head. The east coast was out: living in the backdoor of the people most interested in seeing her dead was a bad plan. And she was damned if she'd return to the south—Mary Lou had spent all her adult life getting away from that hell hole.

That left only two options: the Midwest or the west coast. She needed a city; there was no space in her head for fields of wheat, which took her westwards. Mary Lou considered the craziest idea: who would think she'd go back to the place where she shot the Fed? No one. And LA was such a sprawling metropolis, she could hide in plain sight forever.

The coach ride to the Rainy City had taken over thirty hours and that was without the need to look after the twins. She followed the I-5 down to Ferndale where she ditched the car and stole another, changing the kids diapers in a diner.

Then a stretch to Seattle and a layover in a dive hotel. The journey echoed in her mind, mirroring the days she spent with Frank the last two weeks they were together. Some roads were familiar because she'd seen them the previous year on her way from Burbank Airport and the bloodshed she left behind.

Madness, inspiration: call it what you will, but Mary Lou plotted a return to California with her children in the back seat and dawn's early light streaming into the side of the car.

February 1971

94

NO ONE FOLLOWED Mary Lou into LA. When she looked back on her last few days in the Rainy City, she never could decide if she should have run. It felt right and she and the kids were living through the consequences of her decision.

The City of Angels was warmer and drier than Vancouver and the twins, who were toddlers by now, enjoyed the outdoor life offered by the glorious weather. Another advantage of being back in the States was the cash in her black holdall could be spent—carefully and with consideration. But she didn't need to live on skid row any more.

Mary Lou found a two-bedroom apartment to rent as soon as she could physically place a down payment and six months later, she looked around for somewhere to buy. A year and a half since the heist, she believed it was all over. That she could ease into a life with the children and become part of a community. Have some sense of belonging.

What was the point of having money if she couldn't enjoy a few creature comforts and buy her way into a bunch of acquaintances she'd eventually call friends? As much as she enjoyed LA life, Mary Lou wanted a quieter existence for her family so she moved a hundred miles west into Palm Springs and further away from the San Fernando epicenter.

A new development had popped up on Oakcrest Drive, a square loop of a road. Each house suffered from an enormous backyard, and sculptured lawns beyond, so there was ample play opportunity for the twins even if Mary Lou got a tennis court built for fun. There were four bedrooms in the south facing home she purchased and an attic fit for a live-in maid.

Downstairs boasted a huge open plan living space, a dining room and kitchen. At the rear was a conservatory leading onto a patio and swimming pool. Beyond was a summerhouse and the rest of the backyard.

As she walked around the area before deciding to buy, Mary Lou noticed how many young families festooned the drive. She and her brood would fit in well here. And she was right.

Within days of getting hold of the keys, she used a local agency to hire a maid. Cindy Magdaleno had barely reached her twenties but possessed impeccable references and seemed to love Alice and Frank Jr.

She sported a tight bun in her head which hid a mane of long black hair. Brown eyes and thin lips. A straight back reflected years of healthy living, which was far from the norm at this point in America's history and not usual in the couch potato paradise of Palm Springs. Cindy was taller than Mary Lou and skinny: like she hadn't been fed enough as a child. She could almost get away with being described as white, but there was a Hispanic tinge to her skin color.

Mary Lou wasn't prejudiced. She didn't care where the woman came from as long as she cared for her children and kept the place tidy. Cleaning would be a bonus.

While Cindy spent her time entertaining Alice and Frank Jr, Mary Lou seized the chance to leave her home and meet the neighbors. She walked from one house to the next holding an empty mug. With a knock on the door, she'd wait until it opened:

"Hi. Sorry to bother you but I've just moved in nearby and I was wondering if I could borrow a cup of sugar?"

The technique worked when she and Frank murdered that girl when they were on the lam. What was her name? And it came up dixie now too.

She first met Janet Frazzini who lived in the house to her left. The woman was a stylish brunette and her son was handled to within an inch of his life by a German nanny. A photo of her spouse, Milton took pride of place above the fireplace. No ego there.

On the other side was Sylvia and Raymond Amante. Again the woman was immaculate and the husband was absent. Mary Lou wasn't surprised. Despite the sexual revolution and the rise of feminism, men worked and their women stayed indoors to tend to the kids. Opposite number twenty— Mary Lou's paradise on Earth—were Vivian and Roy Canepa. Another picture postcard perfect home and missing spouse.

After that day, she thought Sylvia was her favorite, not just because she was the first but because she was the friendliest. Like Sylvia knew how ridiculous her life with Raymond was. While they were sipping cocktails and glancing at manicured lawns, there were sixteen-year-olds losing half their faces and a limb or two in Vietnam.

The following evening, Sylvia invited her over for a barbecue—the twins too. All the families gathered round, adults and children of various ages. They welcomed Mary Lou as if she was a returning friend they hadn't seen for several years rather than the stranger who landed in their street a few minutes ago.

Wine was poured and the men stood around the grill offering advice to Raymond how best to cook his burgers and hot dogs. Meanwhile, the women huddled on sun loungers discussing home improvement ideas and the state of their nails. This was hardly the conversation Mary Lou was used to, but it was calm and worry-free: an experience she relished due to its absence in her life for so long.

Memories of fleeing Burbank Airport faded for an evening and the bloody pool of Frank's chest melted into the back of her mind. Instead, she smiled watching Alice enthrall a crowd of women and Frank Jr climb up onto the diving board before being scooped up and cuddled to within an inch of his life by Janet.

CINDY AGREED TO move into the attic but explained how she still had rent due until the end of the month. Mary Lou considered paying off the rental for Cindy but stopped herself. The flush of joy from having money to burn needed to be tempered: you only have green by not spending it. All those months of counting out the dollars to eke out the cash to the next weekly pay check seemed to have flown out of her mind.

Instead, she made Cindy commit to arrive in time for breakfast and only leave once the kids were in bed and waited for her to move in. Part of the deal was to have Sundays off—or any other day of the week if Mary Lou fancied.

Only when Cindy left after the first night of work did Mary Lou internalize what her life would be like sharing the home with someone else. It's one thing to share a bed with somebody: there's more than physical space as part of that union. But this was a housekeeper, a maid. There would be no privacy once Cindy appeared on the doorstep.

This meant Mary Lou had work to do. There was a holdall at the back of her closet containing just under one hundred and ten thousand dollars—enough money to last the rest of her natural life.

The financial cost of Frank's death lay in a wardrobe and needed to be secured from prying eyes and sticky fingers. Perhaps she should put it somewhere safe, like a deposit box in a bank. Mary Lou smiled at the irony of that consideration. Not a good idea.

Walking round the first floor of the house, she past the cascading staircase which was far too ornate for a woman of her simple tastes. Into the kitchen: keeping paper money near an oven or a sink? Fire and water were not greenbacks' best friends.

She stood in the living room, staring. In the corner, behind the door that led from the hallway was a loose floorboard. The builders hadn't nailed it completely down. Mary Lou could see the gap from the window. Perhaps this would work. The cash would always be near her but nobody would know it was there. Almost perfect.

On closer inspection, half the plank that made up the floorboard was under the sideboard. To get that baby up would need a saw and then the subtle nook would be a home improvement disaster. She sighed, stood up and walked to the floor-to-ceiling window that led out to the conservatory. Keeping an ear out in case one twin called out, Mary Lou sauntered into the glass enclosure and stared out.

Dusk was falling into the night and she wallowed in the orange, purples and reds of the sky caused by the dwindling sun. The summerhouse looked inviting. It'd be a great place to spend long afternoons with the twins. She could turn it into a playroom. A sanctuary for the kids no matter what went on in the main house—not that she had any plans. She reckoned they'd want their own space as they got older although she couldn't imagine Alice or Frank Jr as teenagers—them going to school was beyond comprehension.

The summerhouse: that was the answer. First, she crept upstairs to check on the children and, satisfied that all was well, she nipped downstairs and scurried outside with a torch. There was a key dangling in the lock and she wandered inside.

The space was enormous—fifty feet by twenty—and empty apart from stacked chairs in a corner. Mary Lou stood at the entrance, shining the light into every cranny hoping for inspiration. Then something caught her eye: two sides were glass to let the sun swarm in. One of the other walls remained solidly brick and the fourth had wooden cladding on it. No biggie. Except there was a door handle.

She strode over and entered. It was an empty store cupboard with no lock. If she removed the handle from the front and added a single hole for a lock, then the walk-in store room would be a perfect hiding place for the money and anything she might acquire that needed discretion. Her firearms were a good example of this. A quiet life was all she wanted right now, but she'd been on the run for so long, she hadn't convinced herself that world was over for her.

The next day she found a local hardware store on South Cerritos Drive: left out of Oakcrest and left again after a five-minute walk. The man behind the counter was more than helpful.

"You want some help putting this into the door, little lady?"

"No thanks. I'll be fine."

"I am happy to come by and finish the job for you, honey."

"Really. You're very kind but I know what I'm doing."

"Oh?"

"My husband died two years ago and I've had to fend for myself ever since."

"Mighty sorry to hear that darling."

Had she revealed too much about herself? There's a world of difference between saying your spouse was shot and killed robbing the Lansdowne branch of the First Bank of Baltimore and admitting he was dead at all. The twins were a testament to the fact she'd had Frank's sperm inside her. He had existed and now he was gone. That was inescapable. So better to glide past the truth as often as possible instead of creating some cockamamie story she would be stuck repeating for the rest of her life.

Armed with a toolkit, Mary Lou set to work removing the handles, adding a lock and making the front appear seamlessly smooth. She reminded herself to buy drawers and cupboards for the room— and some furniture. Later she intended to add steel reinforcement to the hidey-hole so the door couldn't be kicked in but for now she needed to prevent Cindy from opening the bag—and not much else.

95

THE EMPTINESS IN the pit of her stomach still lingered every day since she held Frank in her arms and watched him bleed out before her. Now there were two things that put a sparkle back in her expression: Frank Jr and Alice.

As each glowing parent in the past has known, they were the light of her life. Despite the pudgy face only a toddler can get away with, Frank Jr's eyes reminded Mary Lou of his father and Alice had his lips without a shadow of doubt.

Time spent with the two of them was magical—in part because she had been forced to work in Canada. Even though Faye reassured her, the kids were all right, she knew they would grow up to be better people if they were with their mom. Her own childhood showed that truth.

Mary Lou converted one bedroom into a playroom—at least until the summerhouse got sorted—and while Cindy dusted and cleaned the place, Mary Lou would sit on the ground playing with Alice or tickling Frank Jr. Small cuddly islands of hope in a sea of loss.

Other times she and Cindy would fight coats and hats onto the twins and Mary Lou'd push them in their two-seater buggy around the area. The sole entrance to Oakcrest Drive had a three-minute walk to flat park land with a view of the white-peaked mountains beyond. For Mary Lou, this was the best of both worlds: she was urban through and through but she enjoyed beauty when she could find it.

She lit a cigarette after she laid out a picnic blanket and released the twins out of their harness. The two sat still for a second and then Frank Jr reared onto his haunches and skedaddled off on an adventure of his own. Alice watched as he raced twenty feet off and kept the same expression on her face as he collapsed and rolled on the ground.

She took longer to get up but made her way over and sat next to him, picking out blades of grass and daisies from the park lawn. Mary Lou remained on the blanket enjoying the view. The giggles of her children causing a mimicking effect on the corners of her mouth. This moment of pleasure sparked a memory of the night she and Frank had met. A judder slithered down her spine as her thoughts turned to darker times.

Mary Lou did not allow herself to wallow. Instead, she leaped up and ran over to the twins and gave them each an enormous hug. Then she pulled at Alice's striped top and blew a massive raspberry on her tummy. The girl created the most amazing chuckle she had ever known. No one could be sad with that noise in their ears.

"Me! Me!"

Frank Jr wanted in on the action and Mary Lou saw no reason to disappoint. His guffaw was fabulous but Alice's was the best.

"Think it. Don't say it."

Mary Lou had no favorites: she loved both the same, but she knew Frank Jr had the advantage of being born a boy. Even though she was older by four minutes, Alice would have to fight to be seen above the herds of young men vying for top dog. She wanted her daughter to be strong enough to beat them.

She returned to the blanket and threw a ball over to the pair. Both children ran toward her and they kicked it around until everyone needed to lie down and rest. Peanut jelly sandwiches appeared out of the voluminous contents of the buggy and, stoked on a sugar high, the twins played chase for ten minutes, returning to her to refuel.

An hour later and Frank Jr got tetchy, so Mary Lou knew it was nap time. Before they arrived home, he was asleep and Alice wasn't far behind him.

"That was fun."

"You've certainly tired them out."

"All three of us will sleep well tonight."

Cindy helped take them upstairs and the two women laid their charges out for the rest of the nap. Mary Lou returned downstairs and Cindy took her post in their room—in case of need. Mary Lou never wanted them to be alone, not for a minute, ever in their lives.

A WEEK AFTER Valentine's Day, Mary Lou attended yet another house party hosted by Sylvia and Raymond, the epicenter of the neighborhood social scene. This time there were more than just the immediate neighbors: people packed the first floor was packed. Some from Oakcrest Drive but most from around town—Sylvia's Country Club buddies, Raymond's business contacts. Mary Lou felt that if you had met Raymond or Sylvia at any point in your life, then you got an invitation to this do.

"Lovely to see you."

"Thanks. Been quite a while since I've been surrounded by so many people."

"Can be daunting, can't it? Don't worry though. They're all nice. And I need to introduce you to loads of them. Grab yourself a drink and we'll catch up later."

The hostess with the mostest swanned off to another part of the house to engage in chitchat with some other social butterfly. Meantime, Mary Lou headed for the bar at the side of the living room and took her beer outside as the air was still warm and hadn't succumbed yet to the evening chill.

The layout of their house and backyard was the same as number twenty; only the decor was different. A scan of the patio showed several huddles of couples and she couldn't face any more conversation about the travails of husbands and wives. It only drew her attention on how much she missed Frank near her.

Instead, there was one guy leaning against a post sipping his drink and watching the world go by.

"Penny for your thoughts?"

"I'll pass, thanks. Nothing personal but you don't want to know what's going on inside my head."

"Oh? Not too malicious I hope. You haven't had time to judge me."

He smiled and clinked his glass against the neck of her bottle.

"Bobby. Pleased to meet you."

"Mary Lou."

"You're the single mother who moved in a week or two ago."

"Yep, guilty as charged. I have other hidden shallows a sentence can't cover too. Don't know about you but I love being reduced to a series of stereotypes."

Bobby laughed and took another sip of what looked like scotch and cola on the rocks.

"You know everything there is about me but you are a Palm Springs man of mystery. Spill your guts, mister."

"Nothing to tell. I have some business interests in LA but I live here. Enjoy seeing the mountains when I wake up in the morning."

"I can understand that."

She glanced at the hand holding the whiskey and saw no wedding band.

"You got family round here?"

"No, I'm not married. Not any more…"

The last words were spoken with a sadness weighing down his heart. Mary Lou echoed how that felt.

"Divorced or dead?"

"Divorced."

"Mine's dead."

"So I heard."

"How long since the ink dried?"

"Couple of years."

"Any kids?"

"Not any more."

Bobby's response caused a chill in the air. Most times when a child dies, the parents split within five years. This was his story, she guessed.

"Fuck. Happy days, huh?"

"Like a fucking Halloween party."

"I'll drink to that."

Another clink and a sip to let the words fade and the images play out in their heads.

"You know many folks here?"

"Fair few. I've lived round here most of my life."

"And you don't need this come-over poking her nose into your affairs."

"I didn't say that."

"But implied."

"Not intentionally. You're right that I dreaded you opening your mouth as you walked toward me. No kidding, but now we're talking I'm warming to you."

"Gee, thanks. Is that what you tell all the girls?"

"What girls?"

"You telling me you go to parties in your home town and always get into bed later alone?"

"You've got me confused with another man."

Bobby smiled. Was it her directness or the fact she was prepared to speak with him and not tread egg shells? Either way he suffered but not in silence. This could go in two directions. Bobby could be a depressing individual who should stay at home until he gets over himself. Or he might be the only person in town who knows the meaning of loss.

"You look just like the one standing in front of me. And I like what I see."

"Straight back at ya."

"And how do people round here to enjoy themselves when they're not hanging around near a swimming pool on someone else's patio?"

"The usual."

For a man who'd revealed his heart to her two minute ago, Bobby was making this conversation heavy going.

"Like…?"

"Golf is good."

"Never tried it. Are there any decent places to eat?"

"You're kidding me, right?"

"Why?"

"The number of people with… business interests… round here. You can find a a decent restaurant or two. You really are fresh to the streets."

"Never pretended otherwise, Bobby."

"I'll show you the sights if you like."

"That'd be good. Real nice."

"Give me your number and I'll call you."

She pulled out a pen from her bag and they went inside to find something to write on. By the time he placed the strip of paper into his pocket, Sylvia had swooped on Mary Lou and taken her to the far side of the room.

"I see you've met Bobby Trevisan."

"Yes, a kindred dark soul."

"Are you that sad?"

"Now and again, Sylvia. I keep a brave expression on my face but there are wounds still sore."

Sylvia hugged her and took her by the hand upstairs into a bedroom.

"Listen, honey. Don't take this the wrong way, but be careful with Bobby."

"Why?"

"He's prickly and you'll only end up in more pain."

"I can look after myself. Don't worry about me."

"But I do. Bobby mistreats women. He pushes them away so he won't get hurt again. And you deserve better than him."

"What if he's the best that there is?"

March 1971

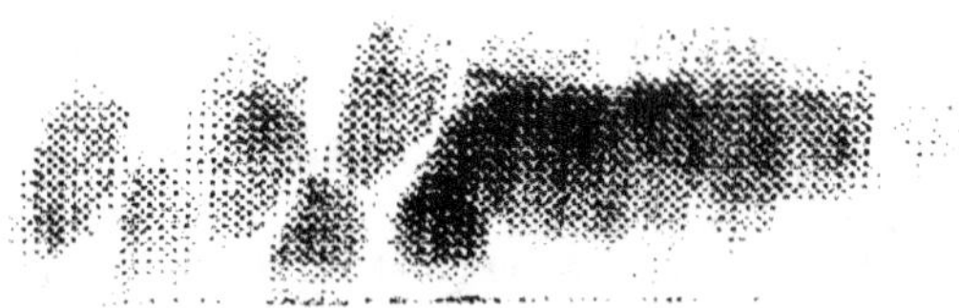

96

MARY LOU SAT in a booth at the Palm Springs Country Club. This was a lovely plush affair where members of the golf club mingled with those who liked to watch and lunch. The seating was red leather and screamed out money although she had never spent a penny since she first visited a week before. The remarkable prejudice in this part of California was that the man always paid. As far as she was concerned, this made the men fools for parting so swiftly with their cash. And she owed them nothing.

Janet and Vivian arrived a moment later, and they settled in for the afternoon with a selection of cosmos and martinis. Mary Lou never finished hers but let the other women get fractious as the hours progressed. They also had the habit of letting their guard down and saying what they meant instead of maintaining the facade built up over the years.

Along with everyone else in America, they were unhappy. They didn't like the houses they lived in, the places they went to and they were dissatisfied with their husbands.

"I know he spends all the week slaving and working to support our family, but when he turns up at the weekends, he's dead beat. No good to me and no good to the kids. And definitely no good in bed."

The two others giggled at Vivian's comments and Janet nodded in appreciation.

"Same here. He goes, returns, sleeps. That's not a life; that's not a way for a man to behave."

"So what do they do to tire themselves out? Running a business doesn't wipe you out. It's not like they are lugging bricks, is it?"

A cold silence descended on the group after Mary Lou spoke: she'd stumbled onto something without realizing.

"Listen, darling. Our men are fine workers. Great providers. You know what they say? What goes on in LA stays in LA."

"And what sort of stuff goes on in LA?"

The words were barely audible from Mary Lou's lips. Vivian eyed Janet, who responded in kind.

"Tell her."

"Okay then, I will. We all come from Italian families with a long tradition running from Sicily, you get me?"

Blank face. Eyes opened wide then relaxed back to normal.

"I see."

She tried to hide the fear within her, knotting her stomach and causing her hands to grip the edge of the table, creasing the white tablecloth. She knew the mob had its tentacles in California but had been unaware that it had an enclave in Palm Springs.

"Don't worry, dear. It is not how you think. Roy and Milton don't go around whacking people who don't pay their bills or nothing."

"It's like a union for business owners. They look after their own and give better rates to their members."

Mary Lou processed these statements, knowing what bullshit she was hearing. Uncle Frankie had ties to the New York mob and look what he had done: raped her, sent men the other side of the country to take the heist money and kill Frank and herself. You couldn't get much further from preferential terms if you tried.

"And that's all?"

"Oh yes. Roy isn't tired from gang shootings. He's tired from banging his mistress. Why do you think the guys stay in the city all week long?"

Good question. These women sipping cocktails at this table produced children, looked pretty and paid someone to keep the house clean. That way, their men could lead a sweet life in the City of Angels and come home to feel great about themselves at the weekend.

"You don't mind?"

"You're kidding me, right? Listen. While he's spending his nights fucking some whore and not making demands on me, I have no problem provided she's clean. And while the cat's away…"

A knowing glance to Janet.

"You mean?"

"Baby. You better believe it."

There were so many double lives being played out, Mary Lou didn't know what to think. She and Frank might have had their difficulties, but they were sexually honest with each other. At least when he was out the Penitentiary.

"Jeez, you girls."

"Are you shocked?"

"Surprised to be honest. Everyone looks so normal. I don't mean that in a bad way. You all appear settled and happy."

"We are, just not the how you thought."

"And your fellas have connections?"

This was Mary Lou's problem. She didn't care who fucked whom in Palm Springs or Los Angeles. If these guys were hooked up with the New York mob, she was as good as dead.

"They know members of the club, yes."

"That's not what I mean."

"I understand, but we don't know each other well enough for me to respond to your question. You a cop?"

"No, I'm not. Are you?"

"Nope."

"So answer my question then."

"Let's just say they have allegiances."

"To the east or west coast?"

"West. Why?"

"No reason. Just interested in the details."

A waiter arrived to deliver another round of drinks. Mary Lou ordered a coffee: she needed to think straight. While she enjoyed her time with the twins in the house, she lacked something in the outside world.

Unfortunately she knew what it was: for years she'd spent every day working toward some goal whether it was to rob the bank, launder the money or flee for her life and survive. There had been an aim to shoot for and right now she had nothing. Apart from the kids who she adored with all her heart and all her soul. But that wasn't enough. she couldn't define what would be sufficient but she ruminated on the problem.

"Don't worry. The men do their thing and we do ours. Fancy some olives?"

DEEP IN THE center of the West Coast mob territory, Mary Lou sat in the passenger seat of Bobby's sports car as they drove round town. The twins were home with Cindy.

The airport lay to the north but Bobby refused to make it one of their stopovers, despite Mary Lou's fake protestations.

"Don't you love the smell of gasoline spewing out of an aircraft's back side?"

"Mary Lou, you need therapy."

Instead, he concentrated the journey around the more scenic elements of Palm Springs, like the Tahquitz Wash which was a feeder river from the lake to the east toward the west and beyond to LA. The water crossed through parkland and unkempt grass, but the way the town was growing, there would be months not years before the land turned into condominiums or retail space. This was an up-and-coming area where the inhabitants suffered from plenty of money.

Bobby took them around the main drag. It reminded her how she imagined Fifth Avenue was in direct contrast to anything she saw near Clark Park.

"You wanna do some shopping?"

"Not right now. I am getting hungry though. Why not take me to one of the many places you promised me that have good food and an impressive atmosphere."

"Not quite my words, but there is a nice little place around here we could try."

He turned left at the next junction and parked outside a restaurant. A valet in uniform smiled at him as he threw the keys over and the guy swapped them for a ticket. The car vanished round the corner and they stepped inside.

The maitre d' greeted Bobby with a warm handshake and ten seconds later they sat by the window, watching the world chug by as water was served to their table.

"May I recommend the prawns?"

Bobby nodded in acquiescence as the waiter jotted down the order.

"Steak and fries for me, please."

The waiter looked to Bobby.

"You heard the lady."

Then to Mary Lou:

"You want something to drink?"

"A cola would be nice."

Bobby laughed.

"A girl of simple pleasures. I was thinking of something stiffer."

"I'm sure you were, but I'll stick with the soda thanks."

"Make mine a scotch on the rocks."

"As you wish, sir."

Bobby blushed for twenty seconds as Mary Lou's comment entered his head and popped out the other side.

"Teasing. That's all."

She winked and took a sip from her iced water.

"So I don't even know where you live."

"Oakcrest, same as you."

"Where?"

"Number three near the entrance."

"Do you find the noise from East Mesquite Drive too much?"

"Nah. There's a solid line of trees between the house and the road. Besides, the traffic's not that bad most of the time. Not even in what we laughingly call the rush hour."

"And how do you spend your days when you're in town?"

"Sleep, eat, drink. Play the odd round of golf. Nothing special."

"They're playing golf on the Moon now."

He smiled.

"True, but it's hard to figure out your handicap when there aren't any pins to drop the ball into."

Mary Lou imagined him floating around a golf course with baggy trousers and a tightly fitting V-neck jumper.

"And where are the business interests you mentioned at the party?"

"In LA. Like everybody else's."

"Does that mean you're fucking some bimbo during the week and come back here for eighteen holes at the weekend?"

"Woah! Hold on there. I came out for a quiet drive and pleasant company. Not to get a grilling."

"Sorry. The more I discover about this place, the more direct I seem to get. I'm only like this because I am interested in you. Otherwise I wouldn't give you the time of day."

"Thanks for the backhanded compliment."

"You're welcome. Most men round here lead a double life—at least according to their wives and they should know."

"Not me. I have a solitary quiet existence. I have my work and I have some friends here. That is all there is to me."

"Hmm. I don't think that's all you are. Not for a minute, but I'll leave you be for now."

"Why thank you kind lady."

He squeezed her hand across the table but Mary Lou withdrew it onto her lap. The gesture might have been innocent, but she wasn't ready to touch another man—even if he was only a friend. And she didn't know if Bobby was that to her yet.

The food arrived with appropriate ceremony and they hunkered down to dine. The steak was superb, the best she'd ever eaten and Bobby's choice of broccoli as a side dish was well-judged.

After a polite amount of time, the menus reappeared for dessert.

"I couldn't eat another thing, but go ahead if you want to."

"Very kind, but I'm only looking out of politeness."

"A coffee perhaps, then. So in what business are you involved? Everyone is so mysterious about how they earn their money."

"A bit of this and a bit of that."

"Come on, Bobby. I won't be embarrassed whatever you do. Sell blow-up dolls? Nurses uniforms?"

"Jeez, nothing like that. What do you take me for?"

"You are so cagey, you might have been a sex toy sales rep."

"Yeah, right. My work is far more mundane than that."

"And?"

"I used to make accommodations for people, but I'm semi-retired."

"You're in construction."

"Huh? No! Make accommodations: I'd help folk out, y'know?"

Mary Lou thought for a minute and joined the dots between Janet, Sylvia and Vivian's husbands and the West Coast mob—through to Bobby.

"Fuck."

"Stay calm. I'm in semi-retirement. They keep me on the payroll so they know I am safe and because I've been a dutiful soldier."

"Mother. Fucker… You never said how your son died."

"I did not."

"You gonna tell me now."

"Had nothing to do with work."

"And your divorce?"

"That was business, yes."

97

THERE WERE NO need for coats and hats in March. Truth was there wasn't much point the previous month either, but Mary Lou wanted to know she was looking after the twins to the best of her ability.

The trip to the park went without event and she checked out a play area Cindy mentioned the preceding weekend. It would give the afternoon a focus and she might bump into other parents too. A shared experience can be a great foundation for a friendship.

Back onto the sidewalk and east to South Campadre Road as directed by Cindy. And there it was. Swings, slides and a sandpit for the adventurous pre-schooler.

There were a huddle of adults, either sitting on nearby benches or holding the hands of the younger users. Every person apart from Mary Lou conformed to a single racial demographic: Hispanic female, eighteen to twenty-five.

She didn't mind about who they were, just they might be speaking Spanish. She and Frank had always planned on hitting Canada rather than Mexico because neither of them spoke the language.

She let the twins loose on a ladder which reached four steps up into a playhouse. Frank Jr sprinted up without consideration for himself or anyone else in the vicinity. Alice stood at the bottom and weighed up her options. She only tried the lowest rung once her brother was ensconced at the top and had declared the territory owned by the Lagottis. Once she caught up at the top, he allowed her to rule the roost and they pretended their lives away in a game that only existed in Alice's head.

Mary Lou stood apart from the Latino maids and watched her children enjoying the equipment. Three minutes later and she noticed there was somebody next to her. She glanced over and there was a man in a brown jacket, white shirt and jeans. Mary Lou hadn't given herself enough time to make a complete clothes judgment.

"Cute, aren't they?"

"Sure are. Which is yours?"

"Over there."

He half pointed in the vaguest of directions toward the other end of the play area but she was more concerned with checking Alice wasn't getting stuck on the ladder as she journeyed down to the ground.

"And yours?"

"Right in front: there."

Her first finger aimed direct at Alice's back ten feet ahead. The guy felt like he stood closer than when she'd originally noticed him.

"Do you come here often?"

"First time. You?"

"Constantly. Great location and wonderful facilities, wouldn't you say?"

"For sure."

Again, when she glanced at him next, he was within two feet of her. Something wasn't right in the state of California.

"Where are your brood again?"

He leaned into her so their shoulders touched.

"Just there."

Mary Lou followed his arm and his finger, by extension, but there were no children in the line of sight.

"See them now?"

He put his hand on her shoulder so she could follow his direction more closely. No one else appeared to have noticed what was happening. She could smell his breath on her cheek and she was not happy about it.

The inevitable consequence of his actions came to a head as his groin nestled against her side, just above her hip. On instinct, she elbowed him in the stomach and used her weight to spin around and push him to the floor, all the while grabbing a hand as he fell so she could twist the attached arm.

He rolled over causing his elbow to flip round his back and Mary Lou pulled upward until she thought the upper shoulder might pop out of its socket. A kick between the legs finished him off. She leaned in and whispered through clenched teeth.

"I see you again: I'll kill you, you motherfucker."

By now, four of the Hispanics had gathered around her but Mary Lou ignored their inquisitive stares.

"It's all right ladies. He just had a bit of a fall but everything is okay. Isn't it, buddy?"

"Yeah. All fine."

The guy still had one hand on his groin reflecting the aggressiveness of the kick. She marched over to the twins and, without making a scene or scaring them, took them softly by the hands and walked away from the play area. The dude limped off refusing to speak to any of the enquiring housekeepers and maids surrounding him.

Mary Lou considered calling the police but thought better of it. The fella wouldn't go bothering her for sure and the chances were he would not be seen in this part of Palm Springs again. Not unless he had a death wish.

She took the most direct route she could to get home but only picked up the pace when the twins were safe in the buggy. Back in the house, she reviewed what happened and realized how quick her reactions had been and that she could still handle herself.

If she'd had a knife in her hand, she knew would have sliced his throat open from ear to ear. A gun would have created a large red hole in his chest. All the years which brought her to this point in her life conspired to make her ready for anything. She was an unashamed fighting machine and that could never be taken away from her. Never.

NOT FOR THE first time, Mary Lou sat in an upmarket booth at the Palm Springs Country Club surrounded by her girlfriends. Today's topic of conversation was whether there was any point in having a golf course next to this eaterie.

"It keeps the men away for a few hours."

"Longer if they don't haven't learned how to swing a club."

"Less if they know how to get their thing into the hole."

"Stop it!"

Janet was unaware of the double entendre that came out of her mouth. And the others were feeling frisky. Mary Lou hoped they'd catch up with their boyfriends soon because they were getting hysterical and it was doing her head in.

"Have any of you ever been tempted to have a go?"

Laughter all round.

"Darling. A lady who lunches should not be a lady who swings."

"Not like that, anyway!"

Janet continued to appear bemused while Vivian and Sylvia tittered over the cleverness of their wordplay.

"I'd be up for having a go. Anyone with me?"

"Would cut into my cosmo time."

"Same here."

"Me too."

Mary Lou looked forlorn. None of these women were prepared to do anything. They sat on their well-toned asses and did nothing but prepare for the next cocktail hour. She couldn't stand it even though she liked them as individuals. Each of them at the table had been so welcoming when she arrived in town and had continued to be friendly since then.

"If not a round, how about knocking a ball around a putting green?"

Blank expressions across the board. This group was not for budging off the red leather. Mary Lou didn't think her expectations were too unreasonable. Women had been admitted as members here in their own right for at least three years. No blacks as yet, but girls were acceptable.

A flicker of memory of Martin turned into a red soaked scene of Frank's blood drying on her arms and legs on the way to the Clements.

Back in the moment, Mary Lou shrugged and allowed the chatter to meander around whether the men should spend longer on the course. This being a weekday, there were few males out playing anyway, but there was a guy four tables down who was punching the hour with his voice. Sylvia called a waiter over.

"Is there any way someone could have a word with the fella over there. He likes the sound of his vocal chords far more than anyone else in this place."

"I understand, ma'am, but he is the son of the club's owner so I can't make you any promises. Would you rather move to a table further away?"

"I'm damned if I'll shift because that man's being an oaf."

The waiter shrugged and walked off, knowing his job would be on the line if he told the twenty-year-old boy to shut his trap. Sylvia remained unhappy with the situation.

She bowled over to him and words were said—too soft for Mary Lou to hear. The boy replied, Sylvia slapped him and stormed back, sat down and finished her cosmo in one gulp. A calm descended on their table but the guy kept his volume down, not least because a trickle of blood rippled from his cheek toward his neck. Sylvia ensured her nails hit his skin instead of the palm of her hand. Clever girl.

MARY LOU WAS true to her word and spent the next week getting private golf lessons. She was not a natural—and it involved the purchase of a new outfit comprising some shockingly unflattering trousers and unpleasant-looking shoes. But she kept at it, practicing daily until she believed she could face a hostile golfing world. Then she got Bobby to agree to a round with her.

"Don't be too critical and we'll see how we get on."

"Golf is the only game I know where you play against yourself and nobody else."

She had no idea what he meant by that but she'd heard others say the same.

Two holes in and Mary Lou watched Bobby tee off. His swing was smooth and effortless. He stood over the ball, moved the club back and forth and the little white sphere flew in an arc heading straight for the flag. A joy to behold.

Her effort continued to involve staring at the ball and waiting for the anxiety to subside long enough to ignore the eyes she imagined bearing down on her, a rush of metal and the ball popped forward cutting the fairway and rolling to a stop within a hundred feet walk.

"Slow your game down and you'll have a better chance to control what you are doing."

She nodded and agreed she was rushing.

"Take your time and focus on the moves you will make. Ignore me, the wind, the world. Keep your head over the ball and everything will flow from that."

His voice was calm. Soothing. There was no annoyance at how she was dragging down his game to a crawl. No sense he'd rather be playing with somebody else — anybody in fact. Bobby was a classy guy.

When the eighteen holes were over—several hours later—they changed out their golf clothes and Mary Lou took a shower. Once suitably refreshed, they met up in the Country Club.

"Hope that wasn't too painful for you."

"Not at all. We all started with our first game. It's normal—and you showed promise."

"Yeah?"

"For sure. You have a good, natural swing. Once you stopped overthinking what the coach told you, the ball flew onto the fairway and your hand-to-eye coordination makes you a solid putter."

She smiled. Compliments were scarce and she wasn't intending to fish.

"You're a good golf buddy. You are patient—and to be honest, you are the only person I know who wanted to play with me. None of the ladies in our little group were prepared to leave this room."

Bobby laughed.

"Cocktail versus a long walk chasing a ball? Most would choose a mojito."

Mary Lou's turn to chuckle.

"It has its own attraction."

She briefly touched his lower arm, near his wrist. Something she had not planned. Involuntary. And, as she was aware, definitely flirtatious.

98

ANOTHER DAY, ANOTHER party. Mary Lou found the constant get-togethers quite tiring. She had no problem being sociable, being in the company of other people. As days and weeks rolled on, she realized she felt less of a loss when she had her nose to the concrete in Canada.

With time on her hands every day, there were greater opportunities to recall Frank and the life she had with him. It had been far from plain sailing—his time behind bars; her time sleeping with other men—but they had been good together for so many years.

And the parties got her down. This lifestyle was not hers. She might have bought the swanky house and have money to burn, but that didn't make her like the neighbors. Mary Lou worked hard for everything she had and would defend her children to the death. Literally.

Part of her needed to keep busy and her recent sporting exploits had been a displacement activity. In the absence of anything meaningful to do, she found an excuse to learn a skill and spend time with Bobby.

But golf was not a sustainable option. While the weather was great for a year-round outdoors pastime, Mary Lou understood herself well enough to know that hitting a small ball was not sufficient to keep her mind from atrophying. And as much as she loved Alice and Frank Jr, she could not spend all her time looking after them. Cindy was better placed to do that day in, day out than her.

That didn't mean she'd ignore her kids. Far from it. She vowed never to disregard them, the way her mother had disregarded her. There would never be a Pastor Neil in her children's lives.

All these thoughts bundled into her brain, Mary Lou stood in Janet's living room with a beer in her hand and Roy, Milton and Raymond talking on the sofa four feet away.

"Will he recover long enough to keep running things?"

"Hard to tell. The Feds are breathing down our necks. That's for sure."

Roy looked up and noticed she was within earshot. A hush descended as they hoped she'd walk back out to her girlfriends sat next to the pool but she remained resolute in her stance. The men changed tack to discuss football while she stood her ground.

"The Baninno Family have always held interests this side of the country."

She let these words hang over them so the men were sure she was listening, but also could understand she wasn't some stupid wallflower.

"They have. Doesn't mean any of us must like it."

"No. When I was out east, you always heard stories of the family seeking to extend its reach in California."

"That so? Where d'you say you lived?"

"I never mentioned it before, but I'm telling you now."

"You have connections with the Baninno Family?"

"Me? Oh no. My husband's family did, but I lost contact with them when he died. It was loose at best."

"But you were connected?"

"At arm's length. What do you guys say? Yeah, we had business concerns that aligned with the Baninnos—for a short while."

"And once he passed away?"

"Those interests receded rather fast."

"But you weren't ever in the Family?"

"Nope. Mixed in circles that mixed with them. Only that."

"When did you say you left the east coast?"

"Never did. And at this point in my life, I'm not going to tell you now. It's nothing personal, okay? Just we're in the middle of a house party and this information is precious to me. Capice?"

Perhaps she had revealed too much, but she wanted some action and these guys were the most direct route for her to get to it. As a precaution, Mary Lou took a gun out the summerhouse and kept it with her for the next three days but nothing happened.

No one followed her, nobody asked any more questions. The dust settled on the conversation as though it never occurred. At least, that was the appearance to the outside world.

The irony was she knew next to nothing about the Baninnos. Her most recent info was no less than two years old and had been gained via Frank and his Shylock uncle. The trail was thin as could be. Frank Senior funded local Baltimore operations sometimes, according to Frank, but he always kicked back ten per cent to New York. The Baninnos ran Baltimore, so she assumed they were the beneficiaries of the tithe.

That meant Baninno's men sprawled across country through Las Vegas to LA when she and Frank were on the lam straight after the heist. So Baninno hoods had been in Burbank Airport when Frank was mortally wounded.

A fragment of image: driving with blood drying all over her thighs to avoid capture and get away from everyone and everything.

Back to reality and barbecues, cocktails and more gatherings without the men picking up on her comments from the few days before. Mary Lou couldn't tell if she imagined this, but she got the feeling the women were treating her differently. Slightly standoffish. She was aware she might be distancing herself from Sylvia and the gang but there was a sense conversations died as she walked into the room or sat down at their booth in the Country Club.

Bottom line: she needed to do more than sip cocktails and die a little inside every day.

MARY LOU USED her car the next time she hooked up with Bobby because his two-seater had insufficient space for the twins. She reckoned if he was going to be a part of her life then he needed to be in theirs too.

The four headed for a picnic near the base of San Jacinto, the mountain that loomed over Palm Springs like a concerned parent over a toddler. Left onto Mesquite until she turned south on Palm Canyon Drive west of the city. As soon as East Avenida Granada appeared on the left, Mary Lou grabbed the first available right turn.

No more than a dirt track leading nowhere, the turning ending five hundred feet away from the main drag at a flat piece of ground, covered in grass. The base of the mountain rose up almost as soon as the vegetation petered out. Mary Lou had done her homework. Bobby whistled as she stopped the car.

"Beautiful. Lived here all my life and never once came here. This is a wonderful country, isn't it?"

"Has its moments, Bobby."

She patted his knee before hopping out and freeing the twins from the back seat. He opened the trunk and pulled out two rugs and a food basket prepared by Cindy.

The kids ran around in empty circles playing chase while the adults smoothed out the wrinkles in the blankets and checked out the contents of the picnic. Before she sat down, Mary Lou scooted over to the trunk and revealed four cushions.

"I wasn't sure how lumpy this place would be."

She tossed one over to Bobby who placed it near his rump, took another for herself and threw the others down for the twins.

"Want a drink or something?"

"Scotch?"

"Nope. I didn't pack hard liquor. Got coffee, though?"

"Sounds good to me."

"Milk?"

"Nah."

Mary Lou smiled, poured him a cup and one for herself.

"I hear you've been annoying the locals."

"Have I? How'd I manage that?"

"By expressing opinions on men's matters."

"Say again?"

"You spoke to Roy and Milton about the Baninno family."

"Oh, yes. I got bored listening to their hushed tones so I reminded them there's more to women than looking pretty."

"And some sure look cute."

He gazed into her eyes until Mary Lou looked away.

"They said you spoke with some authority."

"I know a thing or two."

"I have every faith you do. Doubt if you care, but you freaked them a little."

"Not much."

"Caring or freaking?"

"Both I guess. Does it bother you I had a life before arriving in Palm Springs?"

"Makes you even more attractive as far as I'm concerned."

"But you had to bring this up as soon as we arrived here?"

"More I wanted to mention it and move on without taking up the whole day. What's past has passed. It's part of who you are, so it is interesting but not to any extent that my finding out about it might stop you from wanting to be with me."

A tentative smile from Mary Lou.

"And if your earlier interests have any interconnection with my current ones: yes, I'd like to find out."

"All my old business affairs have well and truly run their course. Believe me, I have no desire to rekindle my east coast contacts."

Bobby nodded. Just then Frank Jr threw himself on top of him causing the man to exhale a loud wheeze while Alice came up to Mary Lou and gave her a hug around the neck. She scooped her daughter up and swung her to land on her lap, carrying on the cuddle until it had spent its force.

The boys carried on playing rough-and-tumble for a minute more. When Bobby was lying on his back with Frank Jr cudgeling his sides, Mary Lou called a halt. He might have been in control of the situation the entire time, but the boy needed to learn he didn't always have to win every fight. Mercy is an important trait.

To save him from her son, Mary Lou revealed peanut jelly sandwiches and chocolate muffins. Cindy could bake too. Ten minutes of near silence as the contents of the basket were devoured. Their ball was released from captivity and the twins shot off to kick the sphere around, enabling the adults to continue their conversation.

"You said you didn't want to hook up again with your east coast contacts. How do they feel about you?"

"Let's just say there was a parting of the ways."

Bobby chuckled.

"Thought so."

"Huh?"

"I've been thinking—about you, the age of your kids, the death of your husband. And the fact you can afford to live on Oakcrest Drive."

Mary Lou bristled.

"And?"

"And I guess you were in the news two or three years ago."

"Oh, you reckon?"

"Yep. Doesn't bother me. If you are who I think you are then I owe you a huge dollop of respect."

"And who am I?"

"If you haven't mentioned your past, would be rude of me to do so. But I believe there might be a hint of Baltimore about your southern accent."

Mary Lou stared cold at Bobby. Her secret was out. Her fingers felt damp with sweat.

"Who else have you told?"

"Nobody. It's not my story to tell, as I said."

"And why are you letting me in on your thoughts now?"

"So you can trust me and that you'll let me be your confidante. I am growing to like you, Mary Lou and I want you to believe I'm safe—given what went down in Burbank Airport."

"How d'you find out what you think you know?"

"Thought about dates, checked a few public records. Nothing fancy."

"So anyone can work it out."

Her mind raced.

"Well, only if they know you enough to bother. You're hidden away in the heartland of the West Coast mob. East and west haven't played nicely in the sandpit since Bugsy Siegel first cut the turf in Las Vegas. There's no love lost between those two gentlemen's clubs."

"And the others?"

"They can probably guess, but again, nobody out here cares to do anything and no one'll be placing a call to the Baninnos. There's no money in it for them. You are as safe today as you were yesterday."

"Is that enough, though?"

99

MARY LOU WANTED to believe she could trust Bobby, but in reality she knew so little about him other than he had some connections with the West Coast mob. Yes, he appeared considerate—and hadn't tried to hit on her since they first met. Perhaps that was the reason there was any relationship between them: they both respected each other's boundaries enough not to ask too many questions or try to speed matters up through sex.

She wasn't even sure she wanted his dick anywhere near her. The absence of a man since Frank hadn't weighed down on her as much as the pre-twins Mary Lou might have expected. Her loins needed attention now and again but she no longer experienced that pressing yearning inside for a fuck. Either the kids put paid to that or Frank's death. Both had blurred into each other, she couldn't quite remember any more.

If she took the children and ran away again, the good news was she still had enough green to start from scratch and leave the house. Few people had the luxury of being able to walk away from a thirty thousand dollar piece of real estate. Mary Lou knew how fortunate her life had become despite her tenuous circumstances.

She took an overnight trip into LA. The twins would enjoy the razzmatazz of Hollywood even if they didn't know who the stars were just yet. Mary Lou brought Cindy along to ease the burden of the childcare and to have someone to talk to during the adventure.

The two-hour journey passed quickly thanks to the simple plan of feeding the twins before shoving them into the car so they crashed out by the time Mary Lou hit the freeway. They missed the commuter crowd heading into Los Angeles, so they sailed into their hotel and up into their adjacent rooms: one for Cindy and the kids, the other for Mary Lou.

The plan was simple: check out the Chinese Theater, pop past a studio or two hoping to see someone famous, sleep then travel home the next day. The overnight piece was there so the kids wouldn't be trapped in a car for four hours solid. Without the sleepover, there would be guaranteed tears before bedtime.

Feed-and-go meant they stood outside their first studio before one as the crowds abated with pangs of hunger. Fifteen minutes later and there was nothing to see—just like the previous time Mary Lou stopped by the same entrance, only with Frank by her side. Their last days together.

"It'll be more interesting at the Chinese Theater."

"Sure thing."

Into a taxi and off to the excitement of seeing hand prints set in concrete. When they arrived, Mary Lou had a huge flashback: a genuine deja vue as clear as day. The moment she held onto a cab door as Frank was about to rip the head off a mobster who walked past them outside the Theater. Once that had passed and her breathing was back to normal, Mary Lou took the kids and marched them along the road.

Occasionally, they'd stop so Cindy and Mary Lou could discuss some star or another, but generally the twins enjoyed the noise and pizzazz but were oblivious to anything more that that. Impersonators pan-handled their way through the crowd hoping to convince someone to take a photo with them in shot.

Unlike the last time when Frank had sent a Marilyn Monroe off with her tail between her legs, Mary Lou allowed a Laurel and Hardy double act to relieve her of two dollars. The twins giggled and chuckled at the silly antics and she felt the money was well spent.

Ice creams for everyone and then back to the hotel. The kids were ready to drop so Cindy put them to sleep and popped into Mary Lou's, leaving the adjoining door ajar.

"Thanks for letting me come along today."

"Don't mention it. You being here means we're all having a much better time."

"Thank you anyway."

"De nada."

"Your family is a pleasure to spend time with."

"No need to blow smoke."

"I'm not. The last place—you wouldn't believe. The kids ran riot around the parents who did nothing to stop them."

"Nightmare. I wasn't brought up that way and the twins will not be either."

"Of course. Firm boundaries with love in the middle. That's best."

Mary Lou cracked open two beers and handed one over to Cindy.

"I shouldn't when I'm on duty."

"I won't tell your employer if you don't."

Cindy smiled and half-raised the bottle before taking a small swig. The agency would disapprove but she was sitting in a classy hotel having a drink with the client. When in Rome…

"Where's your family?"

"Back in Chihuahua City."

"Do you get to see them?"

"Not the past four years, since I arrived in the Land of Opportunity."

"Tough break."

"I send some of my earnings home—to help out—and I receive a letter at least once a month."

"I'm glad you're still in touch. Families can be difficult beasts."

"Not being rude, but I noticed your family never comes round."

"Because they're all deceased."

"I am so very sorry. I didn't mean…"

"Not a problem. Been dead for years. I was orphaned when I was fifteen."

"Oh man. So young."

"Grew up fast."

"Can imagine."

"Tonight, if you want to go out to a club instead of hanging with me, I'll totally understand. Think of it as an extra night off, if you like."

"Well, if you don't mind."

"Not at all. Just remember not to bring anyone back to the room…"

"I'm a a decent Catholic girl!"

"…and we leave at ten so you must be in the land of the living in good time to help the twins in the morning before we get breakfast."

NOTHING HAPPENED AND no one appeared on Mary Lou's doorstep demanding money or shooting her between the eyes. Bobby had been true to his word: what he knew stayed inside him. She didn't want to trap herself in the house, but she wasn't confident enough to hang out in the local bar.

Palm Springs Country Club was a good compromise with a healthy mix of west coast connections surrounding her. The first time out there since the picnic, Mary Lou sat facing the tables even though her usual position was to have her back to the room.

The weekend's arrival meant Roy and Milton returned from the course as she sipped her second coffee of the day. As they walked to the bar on the far side, she waved at them and they acknowledged her as they bought their drinks.

Despite the unwritten rule that the men and women didn't mingle, the two waltzed over and settled down in the booth with her.

"Hiya."

"Hey, you."

"Drinking alone?"

"A morning Java. The girls are still in the nail bar."

Roy smiled and Milton raised his eyebrows.

"Who won?"

"Draw. We both played appallingly. You deserved the win more than we did."

"Is there a prize?"

"Buy you another?"

Mary Lou laughed and shook her head.

"Keep the coffee all the same, but you could do me a favor."

"How so?"

"At the party last week, we talked about business interests. You remember?"

The men nodded and stiffened their backs.

"Well, would you be able to make an introduction for me?"

"To whom?"

"I'd like to carry out an investment or two and I reckon you know the kinds of people I should speak with."

"What sort are they?"

"Come on, Roy. None of us were born yesterday. There's no need to be coy with me. We've all been hanging round together for long enough for me to work out what's what."

"Nothing personal, love, but my connections won't want me to pass on someone like you for business. Men work with men where I come from."

"Although I have no desire to go into details, I have a track record, which has left me with a chunk of cash which I'd want to turn into a bigger pile of green. If you won't hook me up, is there anything you guys do that needs some extra funding?"

"Really, Mary Lou. The answer is no."

She hid the disappointment behind her eyes as she had no desire to show these mooks what she thought of them. Mary Lou stared at Roy and ground her molars instead. Was it so difficult to get a piece of the action in this town?

Milton turned his head sideways and continued to look at her. Even though Roy had looked at him to join in his smirk, Milton had not.

"Is funding all you're interested in?"

"Not necessarily, to be honest. I'm used to being hands-on in my affairs and it'd be good to jump back in the saddle, if you see what I mean."

"I do. You understand you have no track record here, which is why we're skeptical."

"I get that. The only problem I have is that if I tell you what I've done, I must kill you."

Roy laughed but the other two remained stoney faced.

"Let's say I'm sitting on a significant investment potential and it exists through honest hard work. People have died for me to own this money. Ten. Twelve. I've lost count."

Roy removed the inane smirk from his expression, but Mary Lou continued looking at Milton. She had no desire to work with anyone who couldn't imagine her being a serious business partner.

She carried on sipping her coffee until the impact of her remarks had soaked into their heads and the men swallowed. Milton took a large swig of his drink and placed it back on its coaster.

"So you want to make some more money?"

"Yep. That's what I said."

"I can help. If you'd like me to."

"Sure would. Is that all right with you, Roy? I wouldn't want you to be out of sorts."

Roy mumbled something, stood up with his drink and slunk off. Milton and Mary Lou watched as he sat on a high chair at the bar with his back facing them.

"Don't mind Roy. He's just prejudiced."

"Pig."

"Yes, but I always like the sound of cash registers filling up with greenbacks. I have an opportunity which might interest you. Make tenfold profit minimum."

"Sounds serious. Why d'you want me to get involved? If it's that good, why not handle it yourself?"

"Cash flow. Right now I have no liquid assets otherwise you wouldn't see me for dust."

"And you'll drop me once I make some money for you?"

"I'm loyal. If we work together well, then I'll want us to do so again. Success breeds success."

"And if we both build a stash of cash, then we can invest in ever bigger projects."

"That's how I see it. Yes."

"Here's to a bright future."

They clinked coffee mugs and drank down to the dregs. A smile and she called for the check. Despite Milton's protestations, she made the waiter take her money. Mary Lou Lagotti had arrived in town.

GOOD FRIDAY APRIL 9, 1971

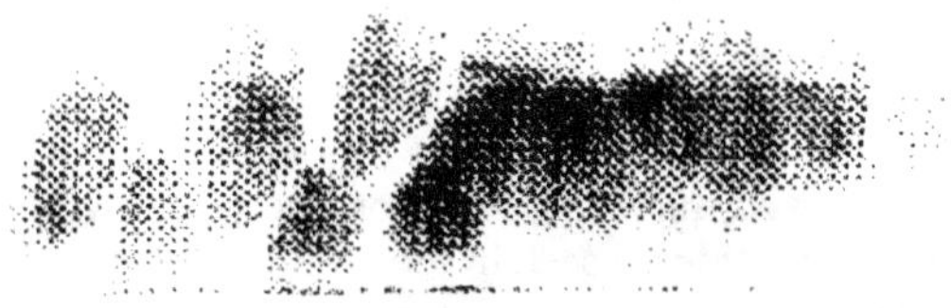

100

MILTON DROVE AND Mary Lou sat beside him. Destination: a warehouse on the far side of town where business could be conducted in relative privacy. All had been quiet since their last conversation until a week ago when Milton knocked on the front door and checked she'd be free today. She wasn't planning on going to Mass: why would she? Mary Lou stabbed god in the balls years ago and slashed his throat for good measure.

"You been to this place before?"

"Couple of times. We usually meet in LA."

"And you trust this guy?"

"He's a capo. Of course I trust him. What's not to trust?"

"Just running through everything in my head. Pay no never mind."

Plush homes flew past them until the buildings got smaller and packed closer together. Then they petered out to reveal some office blocks and light industrial usage. Just before they left Palm Springs altogether, heading north beyond the airport, stood a series of warehouses. Each had four foot high digits on the front, black on a white rectangle.

Too many cars to count were parked outside number five and Milton's vehicle joined them.

"You ready?"

"Yep. You?"

"Sure, but I'm not the one on trial today."

The hundred feet to the main entrance took a lifetime to walk. Mary Lou sensed her breathing getting tighter. Memories of Frank's disused factory and the countless meetings before the heist flashed into her mind's eye.

Through the door and into a large space. An enormous atrium four storeys tall with a row of smaller rooms and offices to the right. A tall and a short guy leaned against a wall chewing toothpicks. A stereotype in all but name.

Milton nodded like he knew them and headed to one of the closed doors. Mary Lou followed. On the other side were another pair of men at a table and three others wearing long coats strung along the walls of the fifteen by ten feet room.

Two chairs stood vacant; Milton sat on one and Mary Lou took the other. No handshakes. No acknowledgment. The two seated guys kept talking among themselves for a minute. Sounded like Italian but might have been Spanish—Mary Lou had no way of knowing.

She remained silent for now, aware there was an unspoken protocol to follow.

"Okay, thanks for agreeing to see us. I appreciate the importance of your time."

"We always have space for our friends. And their colleagues too."

A beady stare at Mary Lou.

"I thought there could be some mutual benefit in us all meeting up. I'll leave you to introduce yourselves."

"My name is Pasquale Bassani and that is introduction enough. Anyone who abuses knowledge of this ends up buried in concrete or stuffed in a sack in the desert."

"Fabio. I help look after Mr. Bassani's business interests."

"Mary Lou Lagotti. I have money to invest in the right project. Thank you for seeing me today."

"That name means nothing to me. What are you to me, Mrs. Lagotti?"

"I'm the answer to your next question. I have significant wealth obtained through illegal channels and I want more of it. Milton told me you were the people to speak to on this. If he was wrong, we can stop this conversation right away and not waste our time."

Both men continued to glare at her and Milton shuffled in his seat.

"That we're in the same room means you've checked me out otherwise you'd be foolish people. And you don't come across to me like mooks. So you should be asking me how we can work together."

Mary Lou fell silent. As much as she wanted to be back in the game, she was no pushover. They needed to understand that from the get-go else no dice.

"Mrs. Lagotti. I mean you no disrespect, but you come here with no track record. All I'm determining is what you have achieved. I am sure there is greatness behind you. As you mention, Milton wouldn't be stupid enough to bring a waster."

"Until now, I have kept my achievements quiet on the west coast. If I tell you, I put my life in danger."

"To be honest, if you don't tell me, your future prospects will be severely curtailed and your two children shall become orphans."

Flat voice. Cold expression. Simple truths. Mary Lou liked his direct approach.

"The First Bank of Boston haul in '68."

Her eyes flit from Pasquale to Fabio and back again.

"Congratulations. That was a million dollar take, was it not?"

"Only if you believed the radio. Nearer to half a mill' dirty. The money's been laundered since then —and is broadly intact."

She watched as Bassani calculated what sum remained in her possession. His eyes widened as he appreciated the potential investment sitting on the other side of the table.

"Thank you, Milton. You can wait outside."

Once the door had closed behind him, Fabio offered Mary Lou a cup of coffee, which she accepted.

"If you want Milton, he'll come out of your end, not ours."

"Understood."

"He will keep the source of your finances with him to his grave. And I'm gonna assume you'd like our business dealings to remain private, which is why I invited him to leave."

"Appreciate it. The fellas lying around the room appear to be okay to stay, apparently."

"If any of these gentlemen make the mistake of opening their mouths, I can assure you, they will lose their tongues."

"Do you have any projects we could work on?"

CHARLIE PENTANGELO HAD put on around ten to fifteen pounds since the day he heard Frank Lagotti Senior had been shot in the face. The two events were not connected, but both were true. Charlie was heavier and the Shylock was dead.

The cream sauces and red wine had flowed well for him as the business interests of the Baninno family improved and increased. Their reach had extended from coast to coast. Back in '68, they had made some initial forays beyond the East Sea Board but in the intervening time, the family had consolidated its hold on the other New York families so much that it needed to expand westward to maintain growth. The mob did not differ from any other conglomerate with a saturated market in one part of the country.

Vegas proved to be a wonderful place. Strong connections with high profile New York performers drew the crowds to the shows and the lure of free money dragged people into the casinos. Never had, so many losers deceived themselves into believing they were winners.

This activity fueled projects further west—along with the power wielded by the New York mob inside Hollywood. Those self-same cabaret performers appeared in the movies and Los Angeles became a location of interest.

The natural consequence of these business considerations was the need to have an increased direct influence in what happened in the City of Angels. There had always been an accommodation between the gangs to the east of Chicago and those to the west. Tithes and appreciation flowed in both directions so everyone was content with the relationship.

By the time a man landed on the Moon the amount of cash generated by Vegas—and its money laundering potential—became an object of direct interest to the Baninno clan. It knew Chicago was too hard a nut to crack but Nevada and beyond was a different game, partly because New York families had been the bedrock of both Vegas and LA in previous generations. Their blood had spilled on those streets.

During the same time, the West Coast mob had ripped itself apart with infighting and an unpleasant decision by some members of the warring families to spill their guts to the Feds. This meant that, despite the tremendous opportunities afforded by having one obscenely rich community and another festooned in poverty, money was tight across what was left of the West Coast families.

By 1971, Nick Lica was barely in charge of the west coast operation amid a string of confessions by mafiosi rats. Beneath him was Joe Dip, the underboss in the City of Angels but there was scarcely a structure beyond them as local hoods kept the numbers racket away from the family's touch. As LA was the movie capital of the world, Joe made a pile of cash out of the porn industry.

Pasquale Bassani reported directly to Dip and maintained his allegiance to this failing empire out of habit rather than any belief about Lica and Dip's ability to steer the family to better times.

"I'm sure we can find some project of ours for you to invest in."

101

"I'M OPEN TO any kind of venture you have in mind."

"If you can't handle yourself in any situation, I'd wonder what you're doing sat here. There are two opportunities to appear recently. One involves brown sugar and the other China white."

"First things first, then."

"There are many the dispossessed and poor living in Los Angeles. For all the obvious reasons, they want to escape from the tedium of their humdrum lives and can't afford to move, get an education or make something of themselves."

"Okay."

"That is where we come in and offer a service to solve their short-term needs. A small bag of heroin enables them to leave their impoverished circumstances for a few hours and it only costs a handful of dollars."

"And how do we make any money if it's all low value?"

"When we ship the material into the US, it is normally ninety per cent pure. That'd kill a bull elephant. So we dilute it to three or five per cent; cut it in with other chemicals like quinine. That multiplies our profit by a factor of twenty, minimum."

Mary Lou smiled. This was quite some business model. Why bother robbing banks when you can rob the poor and ineffectual?

"That means you need somewhere to make the smack cocktail?"

"Yes, that is a cost, but once you are up-and-running with a network of dealers, the money rolls in and the only problem is where to store the green."

"Terrible dilemma to have."

"Right now, there is a factory idle because we need a sizeable amount of cash to buy the first shipment. Within three months, you'd have paid us back and be sitting on a gold mine."

"Pay you for what?"

"The rent of the equipment and manpower. We have a network to sell the material."

"I'd rather you were a business partner than a landlord."

"So be it. Just remember that if we share the profit, then we share the risk."

"I wouldn't have it any other way; it means we must watch each other's backs. If one of us goes down so does the other."

"Understood."

"Tell you what. Why don't we start with a small-scale test? See if we work well together before we get involved in any serious investment. If after a gig either side parts waves then no harm, no foul. We walk away with no malice toward the other party."

"Seems reasonable. Your caution is sensible."

"I'm thinking of a ten grand payment to cover the cost of the rent—just for this first job—of all your resources. And then we split the profit fifty-fifty."

"Mary Lou, a good opening offer but not acceptable. We need eighty per cent. On this job, we take on all the risk. You are merely providing the seed capital."

"My guess is you expect me to run the project and not just cut a check. So there is risk on my shoulders. Besides, without my money, you have no profit and there needs to be an appreciation of these matters. Eighty per cent is not a reasonable figure. I said fifty and I meant it. That is fair and means we can move forward on a similar basis too.

"You know if we are successful, I'll buy the factory and men off you so you'll make your money at the back end. But you will not play me like a sap upfront."

Pasquale and Fabio spoke in hushed tones on the other side of the table. The air was calm and the guys leaning on the walls appeared unconcerned by the discussions taking place before their eyes.

"Your proposal is acceptable."

"Before we seal the deal, tell me about the other opportunity."

"Oh, that is a lot less profitable but much more fun. The high life of the rich and famous in Hollywood is legend. Drugs and alcohol fuel the party atmosphere. The days of Prohibition are well and truly over so we no longer have any interest in that. But as you now know, narcotics attract a very large profit margin."

"Right."

"Cocaine is the substance of choice with the Hollywood set nowadays. In the '60s it was marijuana but a new breed of actor has arrived, wanting something with more of a kick to it. Mellow is out and hyper is in."

"Whatever. There are similar profits to make out of China white in the movie community. Again, funding is the key as we have the connections overseas to get product."

"Why don't we run both opportunities alongside each other?"

"That is entirely possible. Be aware, there is a smaller pool of customers. Even though the product costs more than brown sugar, there is still less actual money to be make out of Hollywood."

"You get to mix with the film stars however."

"Yep. There is that bonus, but it doesn't pay the rent."

"Okay, let us put that thought on hold and focus on heroin."

"I am glad you are prepared to keep your eyes on the prize."

"We are here to make money, not collect autographs. How soon can we start?"

"Depends how long it'll take you to deliver your cash."

"Let's say tomorrow, then."

Pasquale smiled.

"I admire anyone who can lay their hands on ten grand in a day."

"Thank you."

"Half the cash needs to come to us. The other half you use to make an initial purchase with some locals. Once you have the raw product, we manufacture the street bags over the weekend and count the profit before the end of the week."

Fabio went through the details of the job so she was crystal clear what she needed to do. Finally, they shook hands and Mary Lou walked out of the room to start her new life as a heroin dealer.

MILTON LEANED AGAINST the side of his vehicle as Mary Lou returned.

"Everything okay?"

"All is good, thanks."

He slid into the driver's seat and Mary Lou got in on the other side. Out the gates of the parking lot and the car headed back toward civilization.

"You guys work something out?"

"Sure have. You up for working with me on it?"

"Depends what it is. I won't touch child porn but I'm open to almost anything else you got."

"No to child porn? Didn't realize you were a man of principles."

Milton chuckled and Mary Lou smiled, the left corner of her lips curling towards an eye, forming more of a closed-mouth snarl than a positive expression.

"So what is the deal?"

"I'll be looking to use some of your men, if you've any spare. There's a small shipment of heroin needs purchasing, cutting and distributing. Got any expertize in this area?"

"Not directly, no. I've made my money out of the numbers and other gambling pursuits. But I know people who can be very serious minded and handle themselves well if individuals cross the line."

"Good. It's going down this weekend, so I hope you don't have any plans. We'll need heavies for tomorrow when we make the trade and then I'm hiring a lab off Pasquale to cut the smack into five per cent bags. After that, we ship them out and watch the money roll in."

"Tell me the details later and we can figure out how many men we will need."

"I assume this comes with some appreciation from you."

"Of course, Milton. We are not communists. I am sharing the profit with Pasquale so what I give you comes straight from my pocket."

"Spare me the sob story and say me the number."

"Five per cent of the profits and if everything goes well this weekend, I'll add in a one-off brokerage payment too as the introducing agent."

"Is that your best offer?"

"Best and only. If you don't want a piece, then I will hire from Pasquale. All you have to do is supply some fellas and give me some advice along the way because you know the locals. For you, it'll be easy money. I'm the one who'll break into a sweat."

"If it's that great a deal, why offer it to me?"

"Because I am starting out in this town and I want to have friendly faces around when I do business. Someone to watch my back, if you will."

"I can do more than that."

"Don't get any funny ideas, Milton. This is business. If you want anything more from me, it is not for sale. Understood? You've got your girlfriend in LA to look after your dick. Not me."

Silence in the car as Milton mulled over her words. Perhaps she had been too harsh with him, but this was a commercial transaction and Mary Lou didn't want any complications caused by Milton's roving groin. Even if he was interested in her, she flat out did not find him the least bit attractive.

The other thought echoing in her head was that Milton was entirely dispensable after the first haul. He'd given up his connection with no expenditure of money and he was only acting like an employment agency: passing hired hands onto her for a few days paid work. He was not the only source of goons in California.

She figured she was being more than fair: paying him with profit which would far exceed the day rate he might extract from her. That meant she could lean on him and learn how the West Coast mob operated without putting herself as much in the firing line. If the shit hit the fan, Pasquale would look to Milton as the one who introduced her, especially if she was forced to fly the coop.

"No worries, Mary Lou. And no offense intended. Are we okay?"

"Sure are, Milton. All is good. This time next week, we'll be swimming in cash."

"That's the way to drown."

"You could buy Janet a yacht if you wanted to."

"You kidding? Not a word of this to Janet. I keep my business separate from her life. Understood?"

"Fine by me. You organize your world how you want. I meant nothing by it. If you prefer, buy your mistress a sailboat and take the family out for a pizza. For all I care."

Milton laughed and Mary Lou chuckled with him. These men all lived with their double standards and their women did the same. Nobody was honest any more.

"What'll you do with your share of the winnings?"

"Invest it in other opportunities. Stash some away for a rainy day. Might buy a mink coat and something for the twins."

"You sure love your family."

"They're all I got. I've no one to escape from and have an affair with. Nothing personal."

"I love Janet. Really do, but domestic life isn't for everyone and I need other outlets for my… passions. But whatever I do when I go away from her, I always return to Janet. She's my northern star. If it wasn't for her, I'd still be a street punk hustling for quarters."

"My Frank saved me from a life of low-rent alley bootstrappers, but it's just me and the twins left. I gotta do right by them."

"Children are a gift from god."

"They are a gift, certainly."

Mary Lou stared out the window as the smaller houses turned into larger ones. She thought of the night she gave birth to Alice then Frank Jr four minutes later. The agony. And the ecstasy of seeing her charges for the first time.

Milton parked the car outside number twenty.

"Want to come in so we can sort out the details?"

"I'll pop by in two hours. I'm expected home for lunch."

She shrugged and went inside as Milton headed for his fish lunch. Nothing in this world like a good Catholic.

THAT AFTERNOON, SHE phoned Bobby and asked him to come round. He started the conversation after she'd handed over a mug of coffee.

"Is there anything wrong?"

"No, I wanted your advice and some things are best kept off the national phone lines."

"What are you up to?"

"Why do you assume I'm up to something?"

"If you are concerned about a wiretap, you're not baking cookies for the Girl Guides of America."

"You acquainted with a guy goes by the name of Fabio Abate?"

"Do you?"

Another silence.

"That's a yes, then."

"You meet Pasquale too?"

"Sure did."

"Are you about to go into business with them?"

"Planning to."

"You know much about them?"

"Yep. Known them for years."

"Done business with them?"

"Worked with them. Now I'm out of that sort of work, like I told you."

"What did you do?"

"I don't want to talk about it."

"But this is important. Could help me over the next few days—the more I know about them… Can I trust them?"

"They are straight down the line fellas."

"And why did you stop working with them?"

"Number of reasons, nothing specific to them."

"Tired of the life?"

"And some, but we're all weary of something. That's no reason."

"So what was your excuse?"

"Something happened. Totally in my control."

"And completely tragic?"

"You betcha."

"A death?"

"U-huh."

"Won't ask any more."

"Thank you for that."

"All things being equal, would you work with them again?"

"Ye-es. The hesitation in my voice is because of how they behaved at the end."

"Something for me to worry about?"

"Nah. Lightning doesn't strike in the same place twice."

"I am still not getting a great vibe off you."

"No need to worry. Really."

"Okay, but I'm not convinced."

"Would you like me to ride shotgun?"

"What?"

"Be by your side?"

"No thanks. I think I've had more recent experience of shooting someone than you have."

"Maybe so. The offer's there if you change your mind."

Mary Lou liked Bobby, but he came across as quite passive nowadays even if had been a hustler in the past.

"How about Milton?"

"Into anything that'll turn a buck. Like the rest of them."

"Oh?"

"Yeah. I've heard he's quite the reliable type, but expect nothing requiring imagination from him. He knows the numbers racket and moneylending."

"That goes with extortion and violence."

"He's handy with a crowbar and a gun, yes."

"And reliable?"

"You can rely on him to follow the money. If you keep him greased, he'll stay with you until the end of the world."

"And if he sniffs a better offer round the corner?"

"Then you won't see him for dust."

As he walked out, Mary Lou gave him a hug. One day she'd find out who he'd killed to leave the gangster life. But not today. Bobby squeezed her waist and let his hand hang there a while as she stepped away.

"Take good care of yourself, Mary Lou Lagotti. I'd hate for anything to happen to you."

"I'll be fine, Bobby Trevisan."

"Hope you're right."

She closed the door, had dinner with the twins and put them to bed. Cindy had the night off, so she'd stay late the following night. Who knew how long it would take to buy five thousand dollars of brown sugar.

SATURDAY APRIL 10, 1971

102

MILTON DROVE AGAIN with Mary Lou in the front passenger seat. Stephen Franco and Albert Nardi sat behind them, two of Milton's fellas. He assured her they were good guys as he introduced them in a diner on the outskirts of town.

They ate breakfast together—a team-building suggestion from Milton that made sense. Reality was that Stephen and Albert were not the talkative type. As Milton and Mary Lou discussed their plan for the morning's activity, the other two chomped on eggs, toast and coffee.

Neither had a discernible neck and their bodies had been invented for the word 'thickset'. She noticed a bulge in the left-hand side of each of their jackets so she drew comfort from the fact they were both packing a piece. Never walk into a gunfight with a smile and a knife. Not that this should turn into a gun battle. The contact had the heroin and they had the cash. Straight exchange and the four would be out of there before you could count to ten.

That was the intention. Milton preferred to consider what Plan B would look like if things didn't go exactly as intended. His attention to detail echoed Frank's approach to business; he might be a goofball, but she respected Milton for the way he was handling himself this morning. There was more than a fatuous grin and roving dick to the man.

"Albert: whatever happens, you make sure you cover Mary Lou. She is our number one priority."

"Got it."

"And if they are not forthcoming with the merchandise, what'll you do Stephen?"

"Wait on your instructions."

"Correct-o-mundo. Do not decide for yourself to grab the product. Second, do not interfere with any discussion taking place. Finally, do not use your piece unless someone is aiming a barrel at your head or I give you permission."

"Sure thing, boss."

"When we arrive, let me do the talking, okay?"

"Not really. It's my money, my connection and my deal. If they can't speak to me the first day we meet, how are they going to cope with doing business with me in the future?"

"These are old-fashioned men…"

"Who live in the modern world. They like it or lump it, but they must trade with me either way."

Milton was silent and the other two stared blankly, waiting for their next instruction. He sipped his coffee and let the tension subside.

"If you say so. I counsel against it, but it is your party and I am merely a bit player."

Mary Lou nodded to emphasize a decision made but she could see Milton wasn't happy with the outcome. Sometimes being stubborn was not the best way to deal with people.

"I've brought some test equipment which we must use before we accept the shipment. And they are bound to want to count the money. While all this is going on, you two need to keep your eyes open for trouble."

Milton turned to Mary Lou.

"If something goes awry, it's normally when everyone's attention is on checking the goods."

"Have you tested this kind of product before?"

"Yes. Not for a year or so, but I have experience and know what I'm looking for, if that's what you mean."

"It does. What a wide set of business interests you've had."

He smiled in appreciation of her comments and that he couldn't have been very successful in the heroin trade. The profit was too vast compared to the numbers. If it had worked for him, he'd have left small-scale gambling behind.

"Mary Lou, while I'm mucking about with the scales, you must keep your eyes on our hosts, not on me. No matter how fascinating you think I may be, watch them like a hawk, okay?"

"Understood."

"And if the deal goes south, stick your tits out. Might confuse them long enough for us to get the initial shot."

Mary Lou glared at Milton, self-conscious. This was the first day she'd worn jeans and a tee shirt since she'd fled Burbank Airport. After that, she had lived in tie-dyed below-the-knee skirts and dresses. But today, she needed to be ready for action and a skirt wasn't appropriate. The red glow on her cheeks subsided and she took a glug of coffee.

"Just you make sure we're walking out with the right kind of powder, mister. I have no intention of paying five grand for a pile of talc."

"It'll be cool. But if it's not, let's meet up here at three this afternoon and pick over the bones of what went wrong."

Nods all round as they finished their drinks. Mary Lou picked up the check and they split up in their two vehicles.

"How reliable are Albert and Stephen?"

"They've got me out of enough trouble in the past. Got an issue with either of them?"

"Not at all. Just running through everything in my head. I don't know them so that's a concern until I see how they handle themselves. I get you wouldn't bring along a doofus or two to mind the bags, but there's a difference between what you see and what you know."

"Sure. I'd think the same if I was in your sling backs. But they are reliable fellas. Not the brightest, I'll admit, but they have a good nose for situations and respond well to trouble."

"That's what we need."

"Although Albert is prone to shoot first and ask permission afterwards."

"Kidding me?"

"No, each time he's been right, but he generates that split second of panic when everyone thinks they will die, because no one expects him to fire first."

"Something to look forward to."

"We'll be fine. In the general scheme of things, this is a small amount of China white and chump change for our contacts—with all due respect to your hard-earned money."

"None taken."

The rest of the journey took place in silence as Mary Lou stared out the window and watched the world fly past.

NORTH OF THE airport lay a handful of buildings that bled away into the desert. Close to transportation for drug mules and far enough from anywhere citizens might want to go to, which meant the local cops wouldn't bother with the area, not even an occasional drive by. There wasn't sufficient property to be defended to warrant the police time. Perfect.

Milton drove to a building that a realtor would describe as a light industrial workspace. There were two cars parked in front before they arrived.

"Looks like we got company."

"Take everything nice and easy. Let's only bring the money inside when Stephen and Albert get here."

Almost on cue, the two men lurched to a halt next to Milton's vehicle.

"Keep sharp."

Into the building and a hallway leading to a back room—an open space covering most of the first floor. In the corner were spiral stairs heading up to who knows what. There were cardboard boxes and shelving running all along, creating a miniature labyrinth to work around to reach the guys stood at the far end of the room.

Milton raised a hand in recognition as the four picked their way through the controlled chaos of the box-and-shelf maze.

"Nice place you got here, Candido?"

One man nodded to announce himself while the two others remained still. Statues.

"Glad you could make it. Any problems getting here?"

Mary Lou shook her head as a plane roared overhead. No one flinched even though the noise was close to deafening.

"Nice place you got here."

"It'll do, lady."

Alberto and Stephen stood as bookends with Milton and Mary Lou in between. One stranger wore a cream suit, while the three others had jeans and brightly patterned shirts. Straight out of Hawaii.

"We've been informed you have some product you're hoping to put our way."

"Reckon you might be right. You a cop?"

"Nope. You?"

"No."

With formalities over to confirm neither was working for Hoover, they could concentrate on the business at hand.

"How much you looking to pur-chase, mama?"

"We'll get there, my man. No need to rush to the end. First, introduce me to your friends, so we can all know each other better."

He pointed at the other two.

"Silvestre and Barclay. Now we're buddies. Can we get down to business?"

"Sure, man. We can get this done in a matter of minutes."

Mary Lou glanced at Milton, not understanding why he butted into her conversation.

"How much you got?"

"Lady, you have this all upside down. You tell me how much you carrying and I'll say the quantity of product we're prepared to part with."

"Five thousand."

"What the fuck?"

"You heard."

"You dragged us here to buy half a pound? That's not worth switching on the lights."

Why hadn't Milton said something? And what about Pasquale? They were in a dark and dangerous hole, slowly sinking.

"Listen, Candido. There's been a small misunderstanding but nothing we can't sort out."

"Are you fucking with me?"

"No. I was given false information. We can turn this round if we work together."

"Candido, the lady is out of her depth but you and I have a history. You know we can make this good."

Mary Lou shot a fiery stare at Milton, who had undermined her at just the wrong moment. You didn't need to be a psychiatrist to sense trigger fingers were getting itchy. A quick glance at every expression in the room told you everything.

"Stand firm, Alberto. You too, Stephen."

"On it, boss."

"Look, if we talk about ten grand does that buy us a pound of China white?"

"Still hustling us."

"Not at all. Just attempting to get back on an even keel."

"Sounds more like you're trying to run the show."

"Your show and no mistake. If you want to, I'll reach an agreement with you. If not then no harm, no foul and we'll leave you be, straight away."

"No need to go running off, missy."

"None of us are going anywhere, just yet. Depends on the deal you eventually offer me."

"You in charge are you, little lady?"

"Yes. I assume that will not be a problem for you."

"Doesn't have to be. I'll let you know later."

"Waiting on bated breath. So do we have the makings of some accommodation here?"

"Yes, Milton. A pound of raw for twelve thousand."

"That's too rich for our blood."

Mary Lou fumed again at Milton's indiscretion and poor decision making. She did not understand why he thought he should lead the conversation when he was only getting five per cent. The chances of a finder's fee was fast diminishing.

"Then twelve thousand can procure you a pound and a half."

"You weren't listening to Milton. The twelve was too high. We aren't negotiating over the amount it might buy us. In case you forgot, we're here to purchase a pound of your finest."

"No need to get tetchy, mama."

"So how much for a pound?"

103

"TEN GRAND FOR one pound. If you come back with a bigger order, then we'll have more room to maneuver."

Mary Lou knew this was twice the amount Pasquale expected her to spend which meant she was getting fucked by these two strangers. But Milton didn't appear to flinch at the price. So either he had a side arrangement with Fabio and Pasquale or he had set her up to fail. Neither were good news.

On a positive note, she hadn't been stupid enough to only bring the exact amount of cash. Mary Lou thought there might be a better deal on the table if she doubled the quantities so was in a good position to close the transaction Candido proposed.

She opened her money purse and removed ten thousand. One of Candido's guys flipped the lid on a cardboard box and pulled out a bag of white powder. Milton took it and Mary Lou handed over the cash for counting.

He produced some scales and vials of clear chemicals out of his toolkit and kneeled down to test the product. A small quantity of powder weighed out and he added a pipette of liquid onto the spoon. Twenty seconds wait and then he held the cutlery up to the light. It remained transparent.

He scrunched up his face like he didn't understand what was going on. Then he wiped the spoon clean on a cloth and picked out another peck of powder and added a pipette of chemical. Same result: clear liquid.

Milton raised the vial to show Mary Lou and she nodded by reply. Then she looked at Alberto and blinked once to show the seriousness of the situation and to alert him there may be trouble ahead.

"What gives?"

"Huh?"

"You've seen the test result. Twice. What are you trying to pull?"

"Nothing. There's four bags of the China white you asked for and paid for."

"Don't treat me like a fool. That's not heroin and you know it."

She looked around where they were standing and couldn't see her money. They must have stashed it in one of the boxes while Milton was testing the gear. He'd told her to stay sharp and she'd fallen for the oldest trick in the book.

"You have yourselves a problem, but it's easy to remedy. Two options: deliver me a pound of base or return my money."

"Look see, little lady. You got matters all upside down again. Your money's gone—right, Silvestre? —and there's no heroin round these parts for me to offer you. The only thing you and your compadres can do is to walk out and keep going.

"The options you're offering ain't gonna happen, so you gotta decide how you want to end this."

"Listen to me carefully. I do not intend to repeat myself and I need you to be clear I mean what I say."

"I'm hearing you."

"Good. The money or the smack. That's all you got left to choose."

Alberto shifted his stance slightly but everybody else remained perfectly still. Mary Lou eyed Milton, who checked on Stephen. Alberto and Stephen gazed at Candido, Silvestre and the third guy. They soaked in every inch of how they stood and what they did.

Candido took a pack of cigarettes lying on a shelf and lit one, throwing the rest of the packet on the floor. Silvestre, straight and tall like he was somebody, but she knew he was nothing more than a hired hand. A hush descended on the room and, for the first time since their arrival, Mary Lou heard the ticking of a clock.

"Stash or cash. I'll give you five seconds to decide."

Candido blew smoke rings and smiled a cheesy grin, looking to all the world as though he didn't care what she said or did.

"One."

Milton put his drugs paraphernalia back into his toolkit.

"Two."

Stephen and Alberto stood firm.

"Three."

Milton finished clearing his stuff from the floor but hadn't closed his toolkit—a hand drifted near the opening, resting harmlessly. A finger drooped inside.

"Four."

The corner of Silvestre's mouth twitched and a bead of sweat plummeted from his nose onto the floor. Candido stared straight at Mary Lou and Alberto kept staring in front, not even blinking.

"Five."

A SLUG RIPPED through Candido's shoulder causing him to fly sideways with the force of the impact. Mary Lou hit the dirt as Alberto added a bullet to Candido's back.

Milton whipped out a gun from his toolkit and blasted in the general direction of the three men, but not one shot reached human flesh. Stephen stepped aside, behind the corner of a shelf and took aim at Silvestre. A red pool in between his eyes showed the trajectory of Barclay Valdez's slug and Stephen keeled over.

Alberto maintained his shooting rate at Candido and Mary Lou focused her attention on Silvestre, who refused to go down. Milton opened a barrage of fire at Barclay until bloody circles appeared across his torso and he collapsed dead.

That left Silvestre who was scurrying along the floor, trying not to be in anyone's line of sight. A bullet popped into a box and a ball of powder erupted out. Holes plastered the wall and Silvestre cowered round a corner to escape the shower of firepower directed at his body.

Mary Lou aimed square at his chest as the hail of bullets descended around him and pop. He went down as one of her slugs entered his torso and ripped through his heart.

An eerie silence took over the room as Mary Loushe surveyed her people to see who was left alive. Only Stephen had bought it. The rest stood up and headed toward the bodies to ensure they were goners.

They picked up the spare guns and she walked around systematically checking the boxes to find the real China white they'd come for. Alberto recovered her money from a box near Candido's corpse.

After fifteen minutes searching, they had uncovered twenty four bags which Milton confirmed contained heroin and two sacks of more or less flour.

"Six pounds of smack for zero dollars. Nice work if you can get it."

They removed Stephen's body and dumped it in Alberto's car then returned for the money and drugs. If there'd been any gasoline, Mary Lou would have torched the place but there was none.

Instead, they shut the door on the way out and relied on the fact that few would worry about the absence of the inhabitants for quite some time.

Alberto knew to drive to the far side of town—south and still further—and bury Stephen in the desert where no one would find him. Mary Lou and Milton returned to her house, coming in the back way, past the summerhouse. Cindy was playing with the kids in the living room.

While Milton stayed in the indoors out of sight, Mary Lou scurried upstairs and took a shower and changed her clothes. The dirt and dust from their earlier escapade clung to her like a shroud. Then back past the pool.

"You want to freshen up before we shift the gear?"

"Thanks, don't mind if I do."

She stayed with the white while he popped indoors and sorted himself out. Mary Lou took the opportunity to put her money away.

"You ready?"

They walked out the front of the house and transferred the bags into Mary Lou's car—at her insistence. She wasn't sure why the situation had gone so awry, but she was damned certain she hadn't caused it. Until she figured that out, she needed to keep an eye on Milton. And have a conversation with Pasquale too.

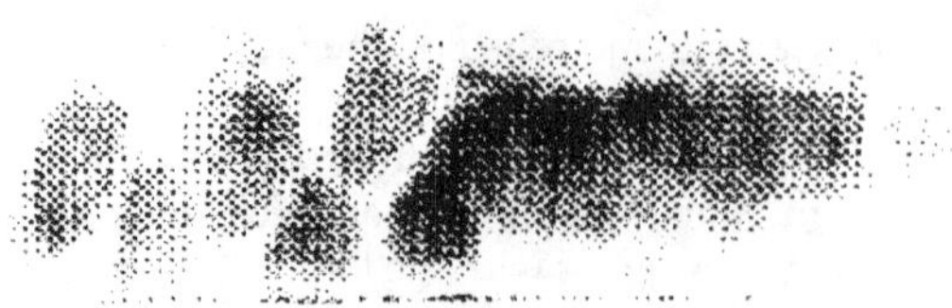

104

BACK IN THE room with Pasquale and Fabio, but this time Mary Lou was not in a good mood. Milton sat next to her and knew she was angry based on the silence in the car on the way over. She hadn't said a word since he came down from the shower in her house.

"What kind of stunt was that to pull?"

"Did you strike a deal?"

"We'll come to that in a minute. Answer my question first."

"You appear quite emotional right now. Do you need a Java to calm down?"

"I'll take the coffee, but you have to explain why you let us walk into a situation where the vendor wanted twice as much as we were prepared to pay. You brokered this deal and it went south almost before I opened my mouth."

Milton nodded agreement, but he couldn't bring himself to look Pasquale in the eye. He shuffled again in his chair as though he hoped somehow to vanish from sight and leave Mary Lou on her own with her anger and Pasquale.

"Mary Lou, I respect what you achieved in the past—back east—but please remember that we judge you on what you do now. And you are not speaking to me in an appropriate manner. I have forgiven you so far, but my patience is wearing thin."

"Listen to me and understand: you set us up this morning and I want you to give me an explanation. If you can't do that, just let me know and I'll be outta here. Along with my six pounds of smack."

"Six?"

"You heard me."

"We can come to that later."

"You betcha."

"Candido and his crew have been a thorn in my side these past few weeks and I was hoping you could sort them out.."

"We sure did. But you could have told me beforehand. I don't mind doing someone else's dirty work. I prefer to be informed in advance."

"Think of it as a small test of your mettle, if you like. For your bank job, you were surrounded by many gang members. We needed to be sure you could handle yourself."

A smirk spread across Fabio's mouth as he glanced at Pasquale every few seconds.

"What's your problem, motherfucker?"

She jabbed a pointing finger in Fabio's direction. He sneered back, not caring what she thought or what she said. The coffees arrived and one of Pasquale's men placed them on the table. This interruption defused the tension but she continued to glare at Fabio as he ignored her and sipped his piping hot drink.

"We appreciate your efforts, Mary Lou. Truly. If you suffered any inconvenience, then we can discuss any necessary compensation."

"A bunch of flowers sent to Stephen's widow would be a good start."

"Just the one fatality?"

"Yes."

"Consider it done. We will look after the family directly. Milton: my condolences to you and those who mourn. He was a solid fella. Rest in peace."

Milton, Pasquale and Fabio made the sign of the cross in front of their upper bodies. Classic Catholic auto-response.

"On the positive side, Stephen was not the only death. Candido and Silvestre will no longer be a problem for you. They breathed their last."

"Good news. That explains the volume of product in your possession. And I assume your stake is intact?"

"Sure is."

"Excellent. Pleased to hear it."

"Not as much as me."

Pasquale allowed himself a brief smile. The tension was diffusing as the two protagonists eased into their conversation.

"Probably not, but they had been costing me plenty—ever since they moved into the area Christmas time."

"And now we have freed you from these concerns."

"More or less."

"How so?"

"Well, as much as Candido was a pain in the ass, he was the front. A guy name of Sancho Mendoza was backing him and will no doubt look to replace the fella with another. Until he does, we take over his territory."

"We?"

"Your hard work from this morning deserves to be rewarded. Assuming you can lay off the six pounds, we can go into partnership on a more extensive basis."

"Partnership?"

"The fifty-fifty deal we agreed when last we met."

"That still alive?"

"Always has been. I enjoy working with professional operators like yourself."

Mary Lou nodded to receive the compliment.

"Once we have the operation up-and-running, we can discuss the financial terms of the partnership. I am expecting to show you appreciation moving forwards, but if this business is as profitable as I believe it is then I should be able to own my own facilities sooner rather than later."

"The future is all to play for. Let us focus on the Mendoza matter and we can deal with the rest afterwards."

"Okay."

"You will need to convince Mendoza to relinquish his control. Either by giving up on the territory or by drawing his last breath."

"How far back does the bad blood between you and Mendoza go?"

"A matter of months. This is business and is nothing personal. I have no desire to see the man dead, but I don't care whether he is alive. What matters to me is that he ceases to impede my business interests."

"Got it. And must I use Milton's firepower or will you be able to offer more tangible support on this occasion?"

"My resources are at your disposal. All you need to do is let Fabio know your needs and he will get it for you. We want you to succeed because your success is our profit too."

"How many men does Mendoza have?"

"Around ten or twenty. They run the north of Palm Springs but there's a sizeable force in LA. That is where I'm keeping my eye on. The local operation is useful to get only in so far as we can leverage it against his main area of control."

Mary Lou contemplated what Pasquale had told her. Chances were he was honest with her and they set her up as a test to see if she could handle herself. And she had passed their exam. But she wondered if she would have been lured into such a stupid situation if Frank had been by her side. In her eagerness to get back into the game, she'd forgotten how easy it was to be suckered into a dumb plan.

"Let's take the fight to Mendoza, Pasquale."

MILTON AND MARY Lou had a bite of lunch in a local restaurant. Nothing fancy: a bowl of pasta and a glass of wine. Simple Sicilian fare.

"Did you know what would go down?"

"Not in the slightest. I was as surprised as you."

"I see. Next time we cut a deal with my money…"

"Yes?"

"When I said to leave me to do the talking: I mean it. You spoke for me back there before we shot them full of holes."

"Did I?"

"Yeah, sure did. If you want to carry on working with me, you need to listen to what I say. And act on it."

"Okay. Understood, I guess."

"Milton, do we have a problem here?"

"What? No. This is the first time I've worked with a woman."

"Get over it. You play straight with me. Don't assume I'm a pushover just because I have no dick between my legs. Then we'll be fine."

Milton ruminated on Mary Lou's words while she enjoyed her fettuccine. She understood her money might give her power but the men around her needed to see beyond her womanhood to bow down to her green.

"Are there any other guys to call on who are reliable like Alberto or Stephen were?"

"One or two I can lay my hands on at short notice."

"That'll be helpful. The size of the pie for this first deal has become a whole load bigger and we need to make sure we secure our investment."

"That's a polite way of putting it."

"Mendoza will come after us—for killing his people and stealing his drugs. Shame we didn't find their cash or we could have lifted that too."

"If they were there, the notes were well hidden."

"Didn't have the luxury of time. Where do you think we should offload the China white?"

"There's a small group of users in Palm Springs which is one reason Candido based himself here. The biggest source of eager customer will be in the LA projects. Watts in the south should contain enough demand for the amount we are seeking to shift."

"And do you have any network to leverage or are we going to go in dry?"

"I shall find out if anyone has any useful connections for us."

"And if not then we can take Pasquale at his word and ask for his help."

"Yep. Let's remember that his help comes with a price tag attached."

"I know but even forty per cent of something big is better than a hundred per cent of nothing."

Milton nodded, realizing Mary Lou's logic was flawless and acknowledging her pragmatism.

"AND WITH SIX pounds, will that impact the price?"

"Only if we dispose of it all on the streets at the same time."

"You saying we should spread the sales over six weeks?"

"It'll keep the price steady, but the longer we are on the streets, the better chance Mendoza has of attacking us."

"Do you think we should dump all the white this week?"

"I'm not suggesting that either. Just we'll make more money if we restrict supply a little. The risk is that this'll give Mendoza more opportunity to get to our men and kill them."

"It's almost all profit though, isn't it?"

"Apart from whatever fee we pay Pasquale: yes, the white cost us nothing but blood."

"And we don't want Mendoza in our face until we are ready to deal with him."

"Not particularly. He has a fierce rep. His name precedes him."

"That doesn't bother me. So some locals have heard of him: big whoop. I've never known of him so he's not that important. And every man can be felled with a single bullet between the eyes."

"Or a kick to the groin."

"You said it."

They both laughed a little, having regained some trust in the aftermath of the morning's events.

"We should flood the market then. We make some money to fund our next deal and Mendoza will find his prices drop too. Double whammy."

"And this time next week, we divide up the spoils."

"He must die or leave the state. Nothing else will be good enough."

"Fighting talk."

"I'm not in this for the good of my health. I want to make money and build something lasting for my children."

"Flood the market this week and fuck Mendoza the next?"

"Pretty much, yes."

"If we're selling small bags by Monday, we'll need quite an operation to refine the heroin over the weekend."

"I'm sure Fabio will oblige us with the facilities. Remember, they get rich when we make money."

"We should still get going."

Milton looked round until he found the eye of a waiter and gave the universal hand gesture of writing on his palm to get the check.

"Taking out Mendoza is no mean feat. He's surrounded himself with major security and even if you get past his goons, the man is built like an ox."

"That may be so, but there is always some way to bring a man down. We need to find his weakness."

"Do you believe you can take over Mendoza's territory, the time it takes most people to get out of bed?"

"I am a determined woman out to protect her children from the evils of the world. Underestimate me at your doom."

"Right, but you didn't answer my question."

They both chuckled and the waiter arrived with the check. Mary Lou dipped into her handbag and pulled out few notes. Milton's eyes widened as he took out his wallet from his pants pocket.

"I'll get this. Think of it as the first costs of my new operation."

"Apart from Stephen's blood."

"Pasquale already said he'd compensate you, so Stephen is taken care of."

Cold. Stark. Mary Lou'd never been so direct before losing Frank. She thought she'd be more sympathetic, but truth was she didn't give a damn. Stephen was expendable and, come to that, so was Milton. The important thing was to know who you care about and who you do not.

"Is that how you treat everyone who dies for you?"

"Stephen died for you, not me. I can't grieve for a person I knew only a few hours and I won't pretend just to help you feel better."

Milton looked at her, wanting to respond but knowing there was no point having a row about the guy. He was dead, they were alive and that was all that mattered. Mary Lou was right, but she didn't need to rub his face in it.

He drove them back to her house and pulled up outside the front door.

"You contact Fabio and get the processing underway. I'll secure my stake money and we can meet in an hour at the Country Club."

"Sounds like a plan."

Mary Lou hopped out the car and gave Milton a quick salute as he drove away. She turned to face the house and noticed the front door was ajar. Strange. She grabbed her gun and pushed the door with her other hand. Something was not right in the state of California.

105

SHE BRACED HERSELF and stood in the hallway. Scanned the stairs: nothing and no one. Deathly silence. Mary Lou's heart rate increased and a dull sickness in her stomach felt like it would erupt out of her mouth. The kitchen door was closed but, as usual, the living room was visible. She edged toward it, gun in hand.

"Cindy? Alice? Frank Jr?"

Nothing but the ticking of the clock on the mantelpiece. An armchair turned on its side and the contents of the coffee table strewn on the floor. Everything else in the room remained resolutely unchanged—as though nothing was wrong at all. The oppressive lack of noise in the building. Mary Lou's breathing stormed into her ears and her heart provided an undertow of rhythm.

The entrance to the conservatory: closed. The kitchen door open. Dining-room door shut. She sidled up, took a deep breath and whipped the wood open and swung her body sideways in case anyone was hiding inside. Just the table, armchairs, sideboard. Nothing out the ordinary—everything in precisely the location as when she'd been in it last night for dinner.

Back to the living room and over to the kitchen. She peered in at the open cupboard doors and chairs lying in a mess on the floor. A chill ran down her spine as Mary Lou noticed the knife block was missing one blade. The hole screamed to her from the other side of the room. Slowly, slowly into the room, she pointed the gun left and right but there was nobody to fire at and her children were nowhere to be seen.

"Alice!"

Silence.

"Frank?"

Nothing.

Through the kitchen and back out to the hallway. Upstairs. First to her bedroom at the front. Immaculate. Everything in its proper place. No one had been here since she left with Milton for lunch. There was nothing to see in the en suite either.

Next, over to the kids' bathroom, which Milton had used. Nothing untoward but he hadn't done a great job of tidying after himself when he left. No biggie.

A creak. Mary Lou stopped in an instant and tensed, ready to pounce on whoever was creeping around the house. She eased onto her front foot to give herself greater stability and the noise recurred. For a moment, she relaxed as she realized the floorboard under her toes caused the noise.

Still holding the gun in one hand and keeping the other on her bag to stop it swinging in her way, Mary Lou popped her head round the three other bedrooms. All the doors were open and half a glance inside showed there was nothing to see—apart from a spare bedroom, Alice's princess-themed palace and Frank's whirlwind debris-littered crash pad.

The only place left was Cindy's attic space. Again, the room might have needed a tidy but there was no one there: not under the bed, not in her wardrobes. Nada.

Mary Lou stopped for a second and tried to concentrate. Perhaps she had overreacted. What if they'd all gone out for a walk and Cindy had just forgotten to shut the front door properly? That didn't explain the upturned furniture. Her paranoia was well-placed.

With nothing else to see, Mary Lou descended to the living room. Her eyes cast round until she remembered she hadn't checked out the conservatory. And it's sliding door was closed, covered by the drapes. She them up so the kids could be in one part of the downstairs and adults could be elsewhere without interfering with each other. Close but separate. Now the blue velvet material of those drapes bore down on her. She was afraid what she would find on the other side.

She pulled the drapes back and leaped into the conservatory where she found: couches, rugs, a box full of toys with its lid shut. But no people.

"Cindy! Frank! Alice!"

Still no reply.

She plopped down onto a couch, looking out at the patio area. The room stuck out so three sides were glass although the far end was covered by drapes. On each side, Mary Lou saw patio furniture and empty space—just as it had been two hours ago when she sat in the summerhouse waiting for Milton. She leaned forward, placed the gun by her feet and rested her elbows on her knees. What to do? Where were they?

This change in body position gave a different angle to her view of the patio and now included a corner of the swimming pool. Mary Lou stared blankly into the abyss of her soul, losing focus on her surroundings. Then she blinked and noticed the pool and the wooden steps leading down into the water with their metal handrail.

She froze at the image before her. While her eyes remained trained outside, she lowered a hand and felt around until her fingers clasped the gun again. Pushed herself up off the couch, grabbed a handful of drapes and yanked them out the way.

The glass doors revealed what she knew was behind them and what she was certain she'd noticed by steps: red. The entire pool was filled with red liquid. Although the shade was quite pale, Mary Lou knew this was the color of diluted blood.

Out onto the patio, gun dangling by her side, she scanned the sides of the pool but no one. In the pool was another story: at the far side, near to the summerhouse, a body floated face down, fully clothed. Mary Lou didn't need to move from her spot to know who it was.

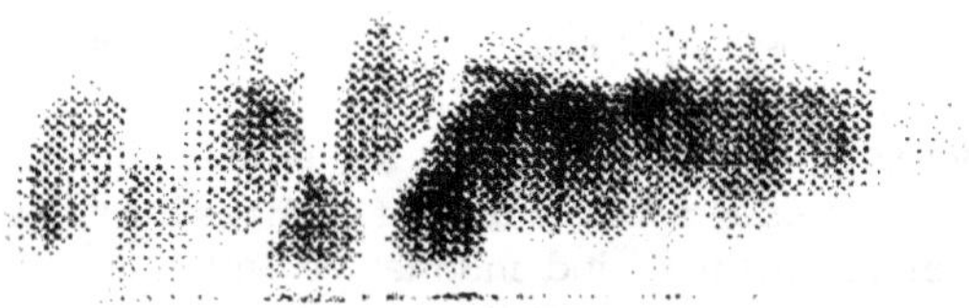

106

CINDY'S ADULT-SIZED corpse floated, bumping the far edge of the pool. As Mary Lou walked round, she raised her gun again in case there was anyone to shoot, but by now she knew the chances were slim to none.

She rolled up her sleeve and grabbed at the body, trying to flip it over. Failed at that, but there had been enough sideways movement for Mary Lou to know Cindy's throat had been slashed. At the bottom middle of the pool, she made out a shiny object glinting in the sunlight, despite the red mist surrounding it. Must be the knife from the kitchen.

Still no sign of the kids. Her only hope lay inside the summerhouse. Mary Lou dried her hands by wiping them on the tiles next to the pool and finished the process by rubbing them on the back of her jeans.

Her bag lay by the conservatory door and she cupped one hand against the glass window of the summerhouse to peep inside, but the sun's reflection prevented her from seeing anything meaningful.

Pulled the door open and shot indoors. A quick look around revealed nothing and the door to the safe room remained stoically locked shut.

She'd lost Alice and little Frank Jr.

First Frank and now the twins. She had nothing. Nothing at all. The absence of her boy and girl twisted her stomach inside out until she felt it spasm violently. The taste of acid hit the back of her throat and she vomited onto the floor.

Still standing, Mary Lou staggered backward and leaned on a chair, not knowing how she would cope. What should she do? Who had taken them and how was she going to get them back?

Her first instinct was to call the police. Not the cops who'd chased her across the width of the country. The local police who would understand a mother's despair and might have already gathered intelligence about their likely whereabouts. They might have been spotted somewhere about town.

Then she slapped her thigh as she perched on the arm of the chair.

"Get a grip, girl!"

Cops were cops wherever they were from. And how exactly did she intend to explain her housekeeper's throat slashed from ear to ear and floating in the pool? Is that what a normal kidnapping involves? Besides, abducting children meant the Feds would be called within the first five seconds. As sure as hell, they'd have a description of her on file. What if McNamara came to investigate? Mary Lou would not be calling the cops. To quash a parking ticket perhaps, but not to get the twins back.

The stench of her own sick lying on the floorboards by her feet made her stomach wretch again. She lurched out the summerhouse. Back onto the patio where she sat down on the ground, back against the summerhouse wall, feet apart, knees up. Mary Lou stared into the empty space between her legs and at the pale crimson expanse of water before her.

Tears squeezed out of both eyes and she let the gun slip onto the floor. Crash. The drops of salty water became a cascade and her shoulders rocked up and down as the sadness engulfed her. Memories of Frank's bloody body flickered across her mind and melded with images of Alice smiling and screaming or Frank Jr scampering and hollering.

Mary Lou allowed herself this silent howl because she felt so powerless. One minute she was having a shower and going off with Milton for lunch, the next her world was turned upside down. Nothing would be the same again. She was angry for allowing herself to believe everything was safe when she'd spent so much of her life waiting for the next time to run, to move on.

Why was she so stupid to think anything was any different, just because she'd wound up in a community on the west coast? Life was filled with broken glass wherever you were and whatever she did.

While she wouldn't get the cops involved, Mary Lou still needed help. She thought about calling Bobby but what was he going to do? One lone over-the-hill gunman? Nah, he wasn't any good. Fabio was probably the only answer available to her although how could she tell whether the west coast mob hadn't had a hand in this? As some way of keeping her in check while she built up their heroin trade?

Strange: there was no ransom note. If you extort somebody, it's best to let them know what they need to do to get their loved ones' safe return. This pointed to the kidnapping not being about money—although she had hardly spent long enough in the house this afternoon to take a call for ransom demands. More time.

If it wasn't a money play, then this was about revenge or power. Mary Lou heard the ringing of the phone. She scrambled to her feet and rushed indoors to the living room and the nearest handset.

"Hello?"

Just as she picked up the receiver, she heard the line go dead. Damn. Goddamn. Was that the kidnappers or Milton or…

She sat on the couch and rocked backwards and forwards trying to get sufficient focus on events to see matters clearly. But every time she tried to think things through, some horrific image flashed across her mind and she had to stop before the pain became excruciating.

Who had taken her children?

THE THREE MOST obvious culprits were the New York mob who finally had caught up with her, Mendoza and the Latino connection or Pasquale and Fabio. The idea it was the west coast mob sounded plain stupid as they had already played their games with her. She'd come good and looked like she would earn them decent bucks, so Mary Lou discounted that option almost immediately.

That left the east coast contingent. If they had come for her, they usually were more direct in their behavior. In their eyes, she'd stolen from step uncle Frank Senior and his loss was shared with them. But their notion of revenge would involve a simple hit on her. There would be no interest in getting involved with her children. A knife in the back or a bullet from a long-range rifle was more likely than a kidnapping and the hassle of dealing with all that before they whacked her.

Mary Lou had heard stories of more complicated tales of revenge. They could have become annoyed the time it had taken for them to find her—they might be vexed at the cost of the resource needed to track her down. If that was the case then maybe they might have operated against type.

The trouble was they would have left a clear message that the twins' disappearance was their handiwork. A note perhaps and, if not, then a phone call with a menacing tone. But nothing? Made the New York contingent unlikely as the perpetrators.

This left Mendoza, who'd have had to act super fast after they did for Candido and Silvestre. Difficult, but not impossible. If it had taken them an hour to find out the white powder was gone and the two men were dead, they could have been round here as soon as spit and carried the twins off before Mary Lou'd had her first mouthful of fettuccine. A cold shiver along her back at the meaning of the words she'd just uttered to herself.

The probability was Mendoza, although why hit someone's family if they'd only made a small gouge into your business? This was not a proportionate response by the man. It also meant she needed to be very careful when dealing with him. He didn't follow the usual rules of the game, which meant he was dangerous and hard to handle.

The other thing was it gave her no better idea where to find Alice and Frank Jr. Even if Mary Lou could get hold of Mendoza, chances were the kids wouldn't be with him. Some hideout, surrounded by a bunch of goons who didn't care if her babies lived or died. At this point, she had to stop thinking for a minute as the ideas rattling around her head were too dark for her to cope with. Terrible images of their tortured limbs permeated the back of her eyelids.

Then the final possibility was plain random: some guys saw the expensive house, the housekeeper and decided Mary Lou was good for a buck or two and tried a kidnap. But again, surely they'd have left a ransom note. Some clue what they wanted and by when it needed to be delivered.

No. Mendoza was the man.

IF MARY LOU was going to do anything, then she needed to deal with Mendoza. She wondered around outside on the patio, trying to remember quite where she left her bag. Truth was she'd kept it near her all this time—a subconscious act. Mary Lou walked a full circuit around the pool. When she arrived back at the corner steps, she noticed the bag in her hand all along. Like an old maid searching for her glasses on her forehead.

Back into the summerhouse and Mary Lou fumbled for the keys to open the hidden door. She put the pile of greens in a locked box and returned it under the floorboard she'd previously jimmied open.

She perched on the arm of one of the summerhouse chairs, getting her head together so she could think straight and figure out the best next step to save her children. With or without Milton, she needed to contact Fabio and get some local help. If Pasquale wanted a real partnership between them, then he should be there for her in her time of need.

Mary Lou returned to the house and stood in the kitchen to dial his number.

"Can I leave a message for Fabio?"

She couldn't decide whether to read too much into his absence. Was he avoiding her or just not in for a million possible legitimate reasons? There was no way to know—not with the information she had right now. The doorbell rang and she automatically headed to the hallway, stopped herself and checked her gun was loaded.

With the pistol hidden from view, Mary Lou opened the door with her left hand to reveal a man dressed in a three-piece striped suit topped with a Fedora.

"Mary Lou Lagotti?"

"Who's asking?"

"Arnold Roach. You owe me money and I'm here to collect. Please take your hand from behind your back. Would be a tremendous shame to kill you after the time I've spent tracking you down."

107

MARY LOU LET her right hand slip to her side so Roach could see her piece.

"You'd better come in."

As she closed the door behind him, Mary Lou noticed a three inch smear of red on the doorjamb. She missed that sign when she first came back from lunch. Was it Cindy's or the children's? Didn't bear thinking about. Besides, there was a mob hitman in her hallway she'd hired two years ago to whack Uncle Frankie.

"As you haven't taken out your gun and shot me between the eyes, I'm guessing killing me is not on your agenda."

"Mary Lou, that all depends on you. Like I said, we had a contract and you only paid me half my fee even though I carried out one hundred per cent of the service."

She craned her head back in the hope the position of her skull would somehow alter her ability to remember whether she'd paid the second installment. Nada. Ran away from California? Check. New life in Canada? Check. Heard the Shylock was six feet under? Nope.

"I appreciate you will not believe this…"

"Try me. You'd be surprised the stories people have spun over the years."

"The hit was aimed at a guy who was financing a robbery I was involved in."

"Mary Lou, I know all about the First Bank of Baltimore heist. You made the news in New York."

"Okay. Well, when the job headed south, ten tons of shit descended and I ended up having to skip the country. I never heard about anything that was happening in Baltimore from the day I turned my back on the place to today."

"U-huh."

"So I never heard you'd carried out the hit."

"I see."

They were standing in the living room by now although neither seemed interested in squishing down into the comfortable couches only feet away.

"Let me ask you a simple question. All I want is some honesty. Can you deliver that for me?"

"Of course, Arnold."

Mary Lou didn't feel right using his first name—a man she hardly knew—but he was pointing a gun at her chest and she had placed hers down on a coffee table as soon as they walked into the room.

He smiled. If she was going to disarm him with familiarity, he could do the same with a look.

"Is the payment available for my second installment?"

"Yes it is."

"Then if you would be so kind as to give me the money, I'll be on my way."

Mary Lou swallowed hard. She had the cash in the summerhouse and it was not a huge amount—certainly not for what it bought her. But she had a nagging doubt at the back of her mind.

"Thing is, Arnold, there's a problem, which I need to tell you about and you'll understand why I am nervous about paying what I owe."

"Oh?"

"Will you be honest with me?"

"I only ever kept my word to you. I intend to continue to do so."

"If I hand over the greens, what's stopping you killing me, anyway?"

Roach laughed and sat down. Mary Lou echoed the action.

"Good question. Usually I don't meet my clients, just their victims, so this isn't a situation I've had to deal with before."

Mary Lou allowed him the time to think as her life was on the line.

"I want to say there's nothing to stop me, but that won't encourage you to hand over the paper. The truth is that I won't kill you because no one has paid me to. I am a businessman and offer a very particular service."

"And if there isn't a fee in it then you don't whack people?"

"Pretty much, yes. I mean, if we were playing poker and you cheated, I'd say there was a justification. On the flip side, if you don't pay up then I will most definitely kill you this afternoon. In my business, I can't afford someone to welch on a deal with me and survive. That is very bad for future earnings."

"I can understand that."

"So you must trust me or you will die. You asked me to kill Lagotti and I did. No question why. Your wish was my command. I played fair and I have been exceedingly patient to wait this long for the second amount."

"I was in Canada…"

"…but you've been back for quite a while, I'd say. Yes?"

"True. A lot has happened since we last spoke."

"I am sure. Time passes quickly when you live our kind of existence: inside a criminal world."

Mary Lou nodded. Even though the man had tracked her down from across the other side of the country—more than the East Coast mob, the cops or the Feds had done—he didn't appear angry.

"I'll get your money."

"I am sure you will, but given you haven't kept your word to me so far, I shall accompany you in case you seek some alternative ending to this conversation."

Roach followed her through the conservatory and out onto the patio. He glanced down at the red water, but said nothing as they entered the summerhouse. Mary Lou unlocked her hidden room.

"I'll need some privacy in there. Look around first if you like, but you can't stand over me while I get your cash."

"So be it. Your personal affairs do not interest me. Only my money. If you come back out of that room without your hands in plain sight, you know what'll happen."

One minute later, Mary Lou walked out with both hands in front so they were visible to Roach before any other part of her body. Open palmed, she gave him the second half of the fee and sat down. This offered Roach an opportunity to count his cash and satisfy himself that all was well.

"Some trouble earlier on?"

Roach pitched his head toward the pool where Cindy's body remained face down. Floating.

"You know anything about it?"

Roach shrugged, lit a cigarette and sat down in a cushioned chair.

"Wanna tell me a story?"

"YEAH, I GOT issues but before I tell you all about it, I need you to tell me how you found me, because…"

"…I'm not the only one looking for you?"

"Something like that."

"I took out Lagotti two weeks after you hit the bank, as agreed."

"We were hoping to launder the money by then but everything went crazy before we even left the vault."

"Uh-huh."

"Then I waited a week for the cash to appear and when it failed to do so, I made enquiries. Took me about twenty minutes before I discovered the extent of my problem."

"Oh?"

"You see, I have a primary client."

"Your fame goes before you."

"Very kind. I don't seek fame, only money. They'll never erect a statue."

"Sure, but in our circles, your name is legend."

"Shame Arnold Roach isn't my real name then."

He smirked, almost appearing to regret the line of work he excelled so well at.

"Let's say that shortly after you fled Baltimore, word was out there was a price on your head."

"Who had issued the order?"

"Does it matter now? Will it make any difference to you?"

"Not really. I'm interested, is all."

"Suffice to say, word came from New York and that meant only one man: Charlie Pentangelo."

"Is his the voice of God?"

"Not quite, but he's only one removed from St Peter for sure."

Mary Lou whistled to show her respect. She never imagined their escapade had been noticed by anyone of importance in the mob. She'd assumed Uncle Frankie had pleaded for help and he'd just leveraged his connections.

"Why were we even on his radar?"

"The size of the haul?"

"Don't believe everything on the radio. They made up that number."

"Quite possibly, but Charlie explained they used that bank as a laundering facility and were not pleased that the person who was supposed to be overseeing the business had skimmed half a million off the top right under their noses."

"Jeez Louise."

"At first, they thought you guys were behind it but a small amount of investigation proved that assumption wrong."

"How so?"

"I terminated the guy that July on a trip to Florida. Anyway, they knew you had lifted the money once the moneylender told them the size of the actual take. To be honest, if you hadn't paid me to plug him, Pentangelo would have done so."

"And you'd got paid either way."

"It is how I make a living. No mess, no fuss, no trace."

Roach's eyes veered toward the pool as if to assure Mary Lou he had nothing to do with the slaughter which took place here earlier. She ignored his gaze—for the moment.

As much as she had to deal, she also needed to be sure she could trust him. Also, she had no idea if anyone had followed him from the east coast and had taken advantage of the man's tenacity to get a bill paid. It might all tie together with whoever stole her children from her.

"We had a lot of heat coming down on us—from all sides."

She felt almost confessional with Roach—partly because of what he knew about her time in Baltimore and partly because of the simple, calm way about him. He might be about to kill her—who knew—but he was respectful to her and for what she had gone through at that fucking bank.

"But that was a long time ago. When did you pick up my trail?"

"In-between jobs, I came over to LA and asked some people a bunch of questions. Didn't take long to figure out you went north. Then three more trips and I tracked you to Clark Park."

"It was you that night?"

"Huh?"

"One night a little over a year after I got to Vancouver. There was a new guy in the neighborhood who sounded like he might be from the mob. So I packed up and left there and then."

"Yes, it was me. I thought I'd found you, but you slipped away. Vancouver is a beautiful city, but Clark Park was a hole. Why d'you stay there? Didn't come across as a good place to bring up young children."

"I thought I'd stick out too much as a foreigner if I splashed out on a fancy pad somewhere real nice."

"Where are the kids, by the way?"

"Not here at the moment."

Mary Lou didn't want to reveal her hand yet, although her voice faltered half-way through the sentence. If she wasn't mistaken, a small bead of liquid rolled out her right eye. Roach didn't appear to notice as he was engrossed by the spectacle of Cindy's corpse bobbing on the pink water.

"We can come back to that later, perhaps."

"That was two years ago—or more. You been tracking me down ever since?"

"Oh no. Nothing personal but I had better things to do with my time. I've been busy, shall we say?"

He took out another cigarette from his pack and lit it with the butt he hadn't quite finished.

"Two months ago, I was in the state and thought I'd see what I could find out. The West Coast fellas had hired my services and I picked up some ideas from them. I thought you'd changed your name again. To be honest, I wasn't expecting you to call yourself a Lagotti."

"Yeah, if I had been on my own, I'd have bought more fake ID and carried on. But I wanted my children to know who they were. And for them to live in America."

"Where did you say the kids were again?"

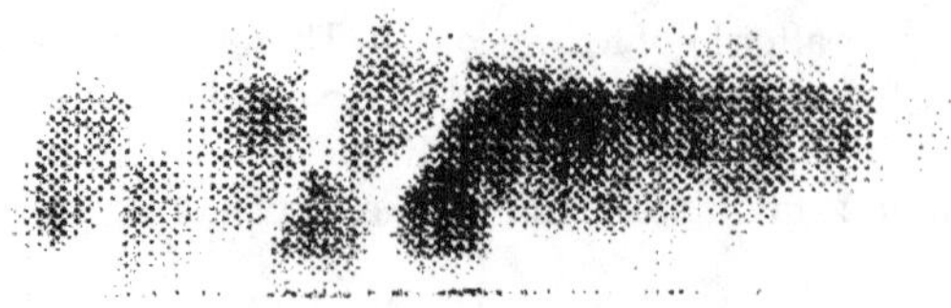

108

CHARLIE PENTANGELO KEPT his black armchair despite all the other changes in the family apartment over the years. He found comfort in the creases which contoured to his body shape. Decades before, the smell of the leather merged with his own natural oils to produce an aroma he could only describe as comforting. The familiarity of the scent enabled him to relax as soon as he sat down—irrespective of the decisions he made or tales of woe that confronted him on an almost daily basis.

In the two years since he'd ordered the hit on Frank Lagotti Senior's killer, Pentangelo had gained more gray—or at least the remaining hair was grayer than before, although the overall quantity had reduced. His patience had diminished in almost direct proportion to his scalp follicles. This was a function of age rather than of his baldness.

Problems he had plenty. Failing to find Lagotti's killer was of little concern anymore. He'd wanted to make a clear statement that people shouldn't go around murdering his men but Lagotti was an unpleasant man. Also, what few assets the guy possessed were picked up within a matter of days and the cash flow continued to roll.

There were bigger Baninno Family problems to resolve that went beyond Lagotti and his now-demised KitKatt Club. Heroin littered the Eastern Seaboard. The tentative approaches by his Sicilian brothers to import opiates proved so profitable that the business line dwarfed the numbers, prostitution and gambling combined. He never thought that day would ever come. The large quantity of low-to-no income individuals addicted to the stuff, and wanting to escape their appalling living conditions, was the cause—public housing had a lot to answer for.

The shift into drug transportation and distribution left some members of the Five Families slow to respond and that created an opportunity which the Baninno clan was happy to seize. With both hands.

As any businessman knows, if your market gets saturated in one place then you need to create a fresh space somewhere else. Baninno saw the way the wind blew—and followed the breeze westwards. At the same time, the upset felt in New York was nothing compared to the fractious relationship between the competing Families in California, who fell apart in the late '60s and no one had recovered their ground since.

With money—and its associated power—from the east coast heroin trade, Baninno made inroads into the West Coast mob. The family funded several ventures and, through indirect means to hide their true intention, supplied narcotics in Los Angeles and the surrounding area—as well as San Francisco.

These thoughts played on Pentangelo's mind because he reported directly to one of Baninno's capos and that meant he stood two rungs below the guy himself. In the last eighteen months, Pentangelo manipulated, murdered and massaged the truth enough to become a right-hand man in the

Baninno Family. And they entrusted him with breaking ground out west—a task at which he proved to be highly successful.

Pentangelo recently finished his lunch—a small piece of veal, potatoes and peas with a decent glass of Chianti—when a call came through informing him that a key Latino business partner lay in the morgue. These things happen; not everyone makes it to the end of the day.

One thing jarred: early reports showed a woman might be at the helm of the attack. Charlie was an old-fashioned Italian American and believed a woman's place was standing by the kitchen sink or languishing in his bed.

As far as he was concerned, it didn't have to be the same woman. But there was only one woman who had crossed his path in business and he assumed she was dead: if she was not, surely someone would have found her and blown her brains out by now. The skirt who robbed the bank with Lagotti's step nephew.

He couldn't be sure it was Mary Lou but his ears pricked up at the news, nonetheless. If she was still alive, she needed to die. A call to Roach was on the cards although he'd issued that decree once before and Roach had not delivered the goods. This in itself was unusual which was why Charlie assumed Mary Lou was already deceased. If Roach had found her, she'd have been dead and he would have collected his fee. You could always rely on Roach.

Charlie's thoughts returned to the news at hand and he flicked through images in his head of potential culprits. The candidates were many and varied, so he couldn't narrow down the suspect list enough to send Roach out to get recompense.

Someone would need to go out there and find out what was going on. Although he didn't want to do so, he knew he'd have to wait until after tomorrow as no good Catholic would want to miss Easter Mass. The problem would take a few days to resolve. In the meantime, he'd place a few calls to see if there was any more information out there. Of one thing he was certain: someone would die for this and there was no way Charlie would accept any loss of territory despite this intrusion into his world.

109

"DID YOU INFORM anyone you'd make another attempt to find me?"

"Oh no. You were one of my freelance contracts. I keep them very separate. My New York boss is aware how I fill my spare time, but never asks me about my outside business. And I'd never tell him."

"Good."

"I didn't do it for you, but for me. If you compartmentalize, you get to lead parallel lives with no wires getting crossed."

"I understand that. I've spent most of the last two years trying to keep my past life clear of my current world. It's worked most of the time."

Roach checked outside again: the corpse had moved about one foot since he cast his eyes in the same direction. His thoughts drifted from his day job to his successful search for Mary Lou.

"You should still take care of yourself."

"What does that mean?"

"Two years ago. They offered me a contract on you, which I passed."

Roach revealed no tell as he lied so gracefully.

"Why? You'd have got paid twice."

"Sure, but if anyone found out, then my reputation'd been in ruins. A week after I terminated Frank Lagotti Senior, you should have paid me or I should have killed you. Neither happened."

Mary Lou stopped to think from Roach's perspective. He was right: her departure and disappearance did nothing for his commercial status.

"Did you hear who picked up my contract?"

"Not at all. No one ever does. These things are always kept secret. Means if they want to whack you, you'll never know when it's coming or who will deliver it."

"Life's tough."

Arnold looked at her, deciding whether Mary Lou was being sarcastic, but concluded she was playing things straight.

"Do you think there's a chance the contract holder has found me?"

"What? Because of the mess in your pool?"

"Yes."

"I doubt it. A hit is clean. If they'd caught up with you, you'd be dead. Unless the contract turned into some revenge shtick, but you're old news. No offense."

"None taken. I want to be old news. Gone and forgotten: that's me. Or at least I was until you appeared at the door."

"I am known for my tenacity."

"And will you be telling your New York pals about me on your return?"

"No. Like I said, I compartmentalize."

"And would you have taken the contract if I hadn't hired you beforehand?"

"And you'd have died a week before you ran away from me."

"Was that when you first found me?"

"Yep. I decided to wait and settle into the Vancouver lifestyle as I wanted a vacation and you were my excuse. When I'm on mob business, I don't hang around."

Roach kept his gray hair short because he was of an age when men's hair didn't pass their ears, even though the new decade had ushered in a world of change since he was a boy.

Between the end of the '60s and today, moon landings had gone from being the most exciting event in the history of mankind to a boring TV experience, needing to be bolstered by scenes of astronauts playing golf. Women were robbing banks and running gangs. His own father would never have believed such things were possible.

"And are all Baninno hitmen as tenacious as you?"

"I must say no, but you'd expect me to say that."

"True. I just want to know if anyone is still after me."

"To be honest, someone holds the paper on you, but the chances are that you could spend decades before they'll be stood next to you in line for the cinema or as you walk across the street. Then you'll look into their eyes for a half second and think nothing more of them. Meanwhile, a minute later, they'll put a slug in the back of your head. Bam!"

"Something to look forward to in my old age."

"Yep."

All during the conversation with Roach, Mary Lou tried to get some sense of the man and the extent to which what he said married up to what was true. She believed him over the contract. The reason she'd hired him in the first place was because of his fantastic reputation: as a hitman but also for his discretion.

No one ever knew if he'd been the guy to off a gang member and that made him special. The younger members of his profession would go to a bar and take bragging rights to get inside a girl's panties or to impress his peers. Not Arnold Roach. He didn't hit and tell.

His comments reinforced her belief that whoever had stolen her children from here was not east coast related. The New York mob might have had a hand in it, but he was right: if they wanted to kill her, they would have done just that and no more. There was no extra money in it for them and no pleasure either.

If he was playing a double-cross on her, he was doing a very good job. She'd shown him where her stash of greens was hidden and he sat down and lit a cigarette. A guy who's being paid to whack you points a gun barrel at your forehead within seconds of that and blows your brains out. He doesn't kidnap your children and pop round for a chat. And Roach hadn't come across as the psychotic type.

"I need your assistance."

"Who d'you want to kill?"

"It's not a murder."

"The body in the pool?"

"Kinda. She was my housekeeper."

"Hard to keep good help nowadays."

"Funny man. It's my babies."

"And?"

"Will you get them back for me?"

"HAVE YOU ANY idea who's taken them?"

"Nope."

"Is there anyone who might wish you harm?"

"Several—and most of my enemies became so today. Those that survived."

Mary Lou's words hung in the air for a second as Roach processed the implications.

"Yes, I can help you although I spend more time killing than saving lives. You understand that, right?"

"I do but you are one of the few people I trust at this point."

He nodded but remained silent. This was her show and she needed to run it.

"So what next?"

"We need to figure out who took them and then we go get them back."

"Who is top of your list?"

"That's my problem. I can't see how the guys I messed with this morning had time to do this by the end of lunch."

"You'd be amazed how quickly well-motivated individuals will act."

"What should we do first?"

"People who kidnap want something and the best way for them to get it is to ask. So you need to stay near the phone."

"Sit here and do nothing, you mean?"

"Waiting is doing something. There are moments to run and minutes to sit. You must bide your time."

"And what will you do? Sit next to me and watch me listen for the ringing of the phone?"

"No. I thought I might hit the streets and see what I can find out."

"You don't even know where to begin."

"On the contrary. Most of the connected guys in this town have been my customers at some point or other. I'll be fine. You must promise me to stay put. The lives of your children may depend on it."

"I get it. Don't worry."

"I'll call you every hour to find out if you've heard anything. So just because the phone rings…"

"…doesn't mean it's bad news. I understand—and thank you."

Mary Lou wrote her number on a small piece of paper and passed it into Arnold's palm. He stood up and left the house. She remained seated in the summerhouse trying to figure out how she would do nothing and not lose her mind.

Cindy couldn't remain face down in the pool forever and Mary Lou knew she couldn't call the cops. As the boys in blue weren't swarming towards the house at the minute, she needed to find some trustworthy people to sort out the mess. Pasquale was her best hope and Fabio had the right contacts.

His voice was clear on the line although she thought she might've heard a small click before Fabio spoke.

"I need a cleaner."

"Is extensive work required?"

"Yes. At my home."

"I'll send someone over shortly. I don't want any information right now but you need to tell me what has occurred. Why not pop over now and by the time you return, everything will be sorted out."

"No can do, I'm afraid. Related to the matter in hand, I need to stay by my phone."

"Expecting an important call?"

"Yes."

"I see."

The phone went dead and Mary Lou wondered if she had given away too much or too little information. She'd find out soon enough. Into her walk-in wardrobe and she chose two revolvers and a shotgun. She pushed the pistols into her waistband—round the back—and left the rifle near her feet. Any unexpected visitors would catch a hail of bullets. No questions asked.

Mary Lou picked herself up and headed into the house to position herself by the phone, but also to have a line of sight both front and rear. She propped the conservatory doors open. By sitting on a corner of the couch, she could turn her head one way to view the swimming pool and turn it the other to see her driveway. A hand rested by the phone and the other nestled between her thighs. It had nowhere else to go.

The abject feeling of powerlessness permeated every pore of her skin and crept into each organ. Mary Lou felt the emptiness of her breath as she exhaled and let tears fall from her cheeks as the possibility of what might happen to Alice and Frank Jr seeped through her consciousness.

Who hated her so much, they'd be prepared to harm two innocent children?

110

TEN MINUTES LATER and a knock on the door. Mary Lou had watched the guy walk up the drive holding a tool bag in his left hand. Fabio must have sent him. In case she was wrong, She grabbed a pistol and hid it behind her back before she greeted her caller.

"Cleaner."

"Come in."

As soon as she could, Mary Lou shut the door behind the guy and replaced the gun in her waistband.

"You were quick."

"Told it was an emergency."

"Like there's no tomorrow."

"I'd better get to work then. Where to?"

She led him through the house until they stood by the far side of the pool. He looked around and dipped his fingers into the water. Removed them and sniffed his fingertips.

"How you want me to deal with the body?"

"Huh?"

"Was it a loved one?"

"No, but show her some respect. At least until you've driven her away."

"Understood. I'll bring in some materials from my truck."

Hands in pockets, the fella padded out and came back five minutes later with a roll of black plastic.

"Need a hand?"

"Best if you leave me to get on with it. I'll call you once the body's out the way."

"Okay."

Mary Lou slipped back into the house unsure what to do next. She returned to the couch and tried not to listen out to the noises confronting her ears from outside. She didn't even know the guy's name. And the thought of what he would end up doing to Cindy churned her stomach, which was already tied in knots with the kids.

She sat by the phone and tried to empty her mind but no can do. Images of Alice and Frank Jr permeated her eyes until she got a headache. Mary Lou popped upstairs to her bathroom cabinet to grab herself some meds to take the pain away. The irony wasn't lost on her that Milton had driven off with enough powder to keep her nullified from life until the day she died.

Her fingers tapped on her knee until the rhythm annoyed her too much. She couldn't think straight with the scraping sounds coming from the pool. Cindy deserved better than this. Her kids needed much better than whatever was happening to them. And here she sat on her ass waiting for a call from the kidnappers or from Roach. Then the phone rang.

"Yes?"

"Any news?"

"Nothing. Fabio sent round his cleaner though."

"That's something, I suppose."

"Anything your end?"

"Nope. I've spoken to a few guys, but no leads yet, although it's early days."

"Keep telling yourself that."

"I know. I'm doing the best I can."

"Sure, but sometimes your best isn't enough, is it?"

"No. It's not."

"Call me in another hour and hopefully one of us will have some news."

"Sure thing."

The line went dead and Mary Lou wondered if Frank Jr was still alive. A shiver ran down her spine and she realized she shouldn't let those kinds of thoughts enter her head. No good would come of it.

"I'm gonna need some help to refill the pool."

She didn't know how long the cleaner had been standing there.

"You catch my conversation?"

"I'm not paid to listen. Just to clean."

She nodded and walked back to the patio. The water was still pink but there was no sign of Cindy. Like she had never been there at all. Mary Lou showed him where the taps were and they watched as the liquid drained away. Then the guy used the steps to reach the floor and applied bleach to every surface he could see. Once done, he hosed down the tiles and she helped him fill the pool again.

"I'd better take all her possessions—unless you're planning on filing a missing persons?"

"Hadn't decided. What you think?"

"You want the cops hanging round here for days asking questions you prefer not to answer?"

She shook her head.

"Then show me her room."

Another twenty minutes and the cleaner was done. Mary Lou remained near the phone as though her proximity would increase the chances of her receiving a call.

"I'm outta here."

"Thanks. What do I owe you?"

"Nothing. It's all taken care of. Including sales tax and tip."

He chuckled.

"I don't even catch your name."

"Good. What you don't know won't kill you."

He tipped his hat and walked out the house, never to be seen again.

MARY LOU SAT on her own until the silence became unbearable and the beating of her heart invaded her brain. The ticking of a clock engulfed the living room and the movie in her head took another turn into an even darker place. Children's limbs and splatters of blood ran through her visual cortex and she screamed, but no one was there to listen. Nobody came to wrap their arms around her to make the pain go away. She was alone.

Mary Lou remained where she sat for a lifetime and then the phone erupted. She grabbed the receiver and listened the voice at the other end.

"Has the cleaner been?"

"And gone."

"Any word?"

"Nada."

"Just a waiting game."

"Sure, I know. But when we find the kids: whoever did this—I want them dead. No questions asked. I don't care who it is or if you're in business with them. Even if it's your mother. She's getting her throat cut all the same."

"Yep."

"There'll be money in it for anyone who can give me the name of who it is and more for the person who kills those fuckers."

"Sure."

"I mean it, Fabio. These are my kids."

"We understand your anger. Honestly. But we also know we have people on the street hunting for your two children and they will find them as soon as they are able—and not a moment before. Until that second, the most you can do is nothing. Sit and wait. It might not be what you want, but it is what you need to do, anyway."

"Feel so helpless."

"You are being strong for your bambinos. When the time is right, you will act—I am certain of that."

"Sure will."

"We understand you have gained a little unofficial help along the way. Are you positive you can trust him?"

"I trust Roach with my life because he hasn't killed me. He is the one man I know feels no ill will toward me. If he did, I'd be floating in the pool by now."

"Not the best testimonial but it must do. I've heard friends say much worse things about each other."

"And we're not friends."

"Not at all. But he's working very hard on your behalf. That's a good worker you've found."

"He found me."

"You're past was bound to catch up with you eventually. The fact he took so long is the miracle, not that he arrived at your doorstep today."

The doorbell rang and Mary Lou jumped out of her seat. She had been so involved in her conversation, she'd stopped looking outside.

"Gotta go. There's someone at the door."

111

MARY LOU PEERED through the fish eye in the door at the unknown arrival. The man standing before her was shaped exactly like Bobby. She smiled and let him in. He pecked her on the cheek on his way into the living room and sat down on a couch.

She followed him inside and slumped next to him. He said nothing and looked at her, waiting.

"Have you heard?"

"About what?"

Mary Lou ran through all that had happened since lunchtime and he remained still, his jaw slowly lowering. By the time she had completed her tale of woe, he was dumbfounded.

"How the hell are you?"

"I don't know, to be honest. All I think about is getting the children back."

He nodded as he tried to imagine what he would do if the positions were reversed. He drew a blank.

"What can I do to help?"

"Unless you plan to magic the kids home, there's zip."

"Is there anywhere I could go which hasn't already been covered?"

"You tell me. I've been stuck on this couch while everyone else is running around town trying to do some good."

"Any word at all?"

"Nothing at all. Nada. Bupkis."

Bobby fell back to silence and stared into the middle distance. Mary Lou couldn't decide if he was recalling some past life moment or if he was having a minor stroke. Neither was helping, and she became impatient.

A tear rolled out the corner of his right eye and landed on his leg. She squeezed his hand, then stopped herself. What was she doing? Shouldn't he be the one consoling her?

"Sorry. Too many bad memories. Stuff from the past, you know?"

"Sure. I just don't need this from you at the minute. In case you've forgotten, some fucker has taken my children and I have no way of getting them back. There's been no call, no note: nothing."

"We'll find them. You can be certain of that."

"No I can't. I mean, thanks for the words of encouragement, but they are useless. If you've not got anything worthwhile to say then keep your mouth shut. You're a lovely man—truly, but I need strong people near me at the minute because I don't know if I have sufficient strength within me to get through this in one piece. Without falling apart."

He nodded as a response and Mary Lou knew that was the best the fella could offer her. Not because he had nothing inside, but because he had spent too many years bottling up all his emotions so he could function in his violent world. The same environment she was now living in. The place where Alice and Frank Jr were in imminent danger and she had no idea where they were or what she could do to save them. Despite knowing these connected guys, they were no good at all to her.

Then a lightbulb went on over her head. If the local hoods didn't know jack then the perpetrators must come from out of town. That didn't give a clue where they may be, but it narrowed down the search for who's behind the outrage. Chances were that Pasquale had figured this out hours ago, but at least Mary Lou had caught up. The single moment of clarity gave her hope. This was the first time since seeing Cindy's body that she felt she might control the world around her. And where there was one drop of vision, others were sure to follow.

She turned her attention back onto Bobby, who remained resolutely silent after his apology and tear. What a waste of humanity that man was proving to be. She wasn't expecting him to save the day, but she believed him had more inside him than this. She appeared to be wrong.

As if to emphasize the quality of his support, he leaned in and give Mary Lou a hug. She let herself remain in his arms and tried to hide within the strength of his touch. He might not have had much to offer, but sometimes little things can count for more than you'd expect. Perhaps Bobby had his uses. She listened to his breathing and noticed the warmth of his chest against her ear. This moment of calm was more than she could have expected when she saw Cindy and discovered the kids were gone.

"Any idea who or why?"

"Only to hurt me. No names yet but they must have come from out of town."

"Why?"

"They aren't known to locals and no one would be dumb enough to kidnap children of a business associate of Pasquale Bassani, would they?"

"Only if their beef was with Bassani and you were a casual bystander."

"Is that likely?"

"Nope. Only happened once I can remember, and the dudes were found four years later in an unmarked grave near the airport."

"Why is it always an airfield?"

"Because the desert was full?"

Mary Lou managed a smile and he allowed himself a minor chuckle.

"Too soon, I know."

"You're okay, Bobby Trevisan."

"Sorry I can't be of any more use. My days of carrying a piece and breaking heads are a long time gone."

"I forgive you—just this once, although by rights I should be angry with you. And I am."

"Times like these, you need people you can trust, like me. Now and forever more. I'm a safer bet than the sun rising in the sky tomorrow."

Mary Lou kept her face touching Bobby's shirt and allowed herself the luxury of doing nothing other than worry about her babies. She had suppressed all the thought that caused the bloody images to pop into her mind, so all she was left with was a terrible sense of anxiety and to exist in a state of fretting. Then the bell jolted her awake.

ARNOLD ROACH STOOD hands in pockets and came into the house with a shrug and a grunt. Mary Lou had hoped deep inside he would deliver for her. The fact he'd tracked her down over all those thousands of miles and the sheer number of years spent on the road doing so. He was the sort of guy who'd be able to find her babies. But she was wrong. He'd given her bupkis.

Roach slumped into the easy chair and let his hands land on the armrests. Mary Lou sat back down next to Bobby. The two men nodded at each other but said nothing, looking into each other's eyes seeking meaning where there was none. She watched them both not speak to each other.

"How's it been out there?"

"Tough. I feel like I've spoken to every hoodlum in town and no one's heard anything about anyone."

"So you've come back with nothing for me. What are you doing here? Why aren't you out there trying to make a difference? Even Bobby wants to do something."

"Doesn't look like he's achieved much so far, apart from warming up the couch."

"That's not the point. You said you'd go out and act for me but you've got nothing. You have failed me, Roach."

The man glared at Bobby whose eyes remained fixed on the ground, embarrassment coursing through his veins. Mary Lou switched her attention between the two, not knowing which way to aim her anger.

"Whoever took your kids is well hidden else I'd have found them."

"Good excuse."

"Don't take your frustration out on me. All I've done today is spare your life and hunt for your children. Once you gave me my money, I could have waltzed outta here without a care in the world. I didn't and now you're giving me shit. Fuck you."

This was stated calmly and free of malice. Stone cold truths expressed with no emotion. Bobby felt Mary Lou bristle in his arms. She sat forward, removing her body from Bobby's touch. Glared at Roach.

"Fuck you too and the horse you rode in on."

Roach was silent, acting as if there was nothing to say. Even though he was right, her frustration with her incapacity to do anything was oozing out of her. She wanted blood and these two men had offered only sympathy and empty words.

"You said you had all these mob connections."

"SureI do, but no one on the West Coast has had anything to do with the kidnapping. I know these guys professionally. They wouldn't bother lying to me because they understand I am only asking for business reasons. If they lie, there are unpleasant consequences."

"You're just full of shit."

"Leave him alone, Mary Lou. It's not his fault. If the attack came from out-of-town then the people he knows will be no good to us. You see that, right?"

"Don't you take his side."

"It's not about sides. It's about the best way to get the kids back."

"Well, you've not exactly been much use to me today either."

"Lash out if you want. Won't change anything though. We are fighting your corner. Despite how you feel, we are on your side. You can rely on us for sure."

"You used to be somebody but now you're a washed-up nothing. Don't go preaching to me, mister."

"Focus your attention on your kids. Not on the men giving you bad news. The important item is that this hasn't come from California. Either it's some local difficulty or, more likely, from Chicago, New York or Baltimore."

"In which case, shouldn't you already have a name and address for me? Those are your towns."

Roach fell silent again, ruminating on her words.

"I've been out west for three weeks. Plenty of time for shit to go down and me not know about it or even hear a whisper."

Mary Lou allowed the heat in her cheeks to dissipate and for a clearer head to resurface on her shoulders. In the pit of her tensed stomach, knowing there was at least an element of truth to what he said. But this was a strange revenge if it came straight from the mob. Perhaps Lagotti Senior was acting from beyond the grave. That cocksucker was a mean hard bastard. Maybe one of his kith and kin was moving in on her.

"Could it be Lagotti's family?"

"Possible, but unlikely. Why move on you now? There have been plenty of opportunities before today."

"What you reckon, Bobby?"

"This doesn't taste of mob, but it is brutal enough. Maybe with some local help who bear a grudge."

"But why my children?"

"It's got your attention, right?"

"Yep."

"There's your answer."

She mulled over the men's statements and considered all the possibilities of their implications.

"I'll give a thousand dollars to anyone who can get my babies back."

"Save your money. We'll do it for free. You need guys you can trust. Your green won't buy you that."

"I know."

She slumped on the couch and let Bobby return his arm around her shoulders. All three sat still for five long minutes while nothing happened. Each of them hoping for the phone to ring or for one of the others to gain some insight. Something. Any idea who had done this and how to organize the safe return of Frank Jr and Alice.

Two figures walked up the driveway and raised Mary Lou's heart. She rushed to the door and let them in.

112

HER TWO BUSINESS partners, Pasquale and Fabio, tipped their hats and came inside. Before they sat down and acknowledge the others in the living room, Mary Lou wanted to know everything.

"What's going on?"

Fabio eyed Pasquale, and they both looked round for somewhere to sit. She noticed their discomfort and dragged two dining chairs over for them. Clearly they didn't like conducting business in a domestic setting.

"None of our associates are involved. We didn't think they were, but we checked to be certain."

"Then we ensured our people put the word on the street that an outrage was going down in our territory which incurred our displeasure."

"A measured tone so our men understand when we are angry and when we are curious."

"You are only curious about who's kidnapped my children, right under your nose?"

Pasquale sighed, so even Bobby and Arnold picked up on the exhalation. The two men shuffled in their seats and pretended to keep an eye on the floor. Catching Pasquale's gaze was unwise. The great man stretched his back upright and stared at Mary Lou with abject disdain. He half closed his eyelids and breathed some more.

"Listen. You have asked us for help and that is what we are offering you. We do this because you are our partner and someone has hurt you. Out of respect, we come to you to discuss the matter further. But remember, if your children live or die doesn't change a thing for me. You will still be expected to deliver on our agreement.

"If you can bring yourself to show a modicum of restraint, I am happy for us to continue to support you in your time of need. Although the hour has stretched into most of the day."

Pasquale allowed himself that moment of light relief and then his earlier demeanor returned to his expression. His body remained tense, back straight in the chair. Fabio let his hands rest on his lap until he moved them to cross his legs, after which he placed one hand on his knee with his other on top, fingers interweaved in between knuckles.

"Sorry. You're just seeing my frustration coming through."

"I understand—apology accepted."

"When we find out where they are, do we have a plan?"

"Not at the moment. A cautious approach is to be recommended."

"I thought we take a dozen of your men and we hit them hard and fast."

"That might work in Baltimore, but we operate differently in California."

"So what do you suggest instead?"

"Mary Lou, the aim will be to retrieve the kids before the shit hits the fan. Not create a fucking bloodbath. Your desire for revenge on the perpetrators of this heinous act is secondary to securing the release of the children."

"I know, but I don't want them to get away either."

"Have no fear: they won't."

"How can you be so certain?"

"Because this is my town. And if someone has come here and terrorized one of my people, then they must answer to me. I will hunt them down and kill them—whatever the outcome here."

Mary Lou found solace in those words and a comfort that was better than the warmth of Bobby's embrace. Revenge is a dish best served rather than thrown into the trash. She would taste that pleasure before all this was over. This knowledge sustained her over the next hour as the four men sat waiting for what she hoped would be a phone call from a stranger.

"I don't think I can sit around here any longer.

"And where do you propose you go?"

"I've been thinking. If it's been out-of-towners then the most obvious culprits who fit that description are the dudes we did for this morning. So I'm going back to their warehouse to see what's up. Better than wearing out the cover on this couch."

"You should stay exactly where you are. It is the best place for you to be—even if it doesn't feel like it is."

"I can't do this any longer. It's doing my melon in."

"Please reconsider. If there is any call from the kidnappers, we need them to know they can negotiate with you. They must feel secure so we get your babies back safe and sound. Unharmed. We need not give them any excuse to behave like the barbarians they are. To take children and kill a housekeeper. What's the world coming to?"

Pasquale was appealing to her maternal instincts and Mary Lou understood what he'd said: every word. But she also knew that too much time had passed and that if they were going to deal, they'd have contacted her by now. From Mary Lou's point of view, although her chest could not take the pain of saying this out loud, her babies were dead. All she had left was the certainty of wishing the guys who'd done it a slow and painful, tortured demise.

"I'm going back to the warehouse. Anyone care to join me?"

None of the men spoke and Pasquale shook his head. The three others understood his instructions and remained stationary. Mary Lou stood up and headed for the door.

"You all sure?"

Passive nodding from Roach and Bobby. Pasquale and Fabio stared blankly out, ignoring her question entirely. She checked her piece was in her waistband, walked out the house and into her car. Gunning the engine, she careered out the drive and off to the airport.

BACK NORTH TO Avant Way, Mary Lou slammed her car left and right until she reached two hundred feet of the warehouse. She hit the brakes like there was no tomorrow and dropped the vehicle into a legal parking space. She padded round the side of her automobile and lit a cigarette to give herself something to do while she checked out the scene before her.

Even though they'd shot off the head of the snake only a few hours earlier, there was a flurry of activity with at least three—no, count 'em—four thickset guys walking in and out as calm as day. Mary Lou noticed the truck pulled up near the entrance and the fact the dudes entered with nothing and came out with a cardboard box to dump in the rear of the pickup.

What she couldn't tell—not without getting back inside the building—was whether the children were being held there too. No one was behaving as though there was anything more than crap to shift, but these goons were so far down the totem pole, they were lucky not to be knee deep in soil.

Mary Lou flicked the butt of her cigarette onto the ground and leaned against the side of her car, hands in pockets. The warmth of her thighs drew the blood back to her fingertips, but she had no reason to be cold as the sun was still shining. Other than the chill of knowing Alice could be screaming as she was being tortured. Or worse. Without a moment's conscious thought, Mary Lou's hand covered the area of her stomach where her tattooed rose lived.

Still the men waltzed in and out, boxes bulking out the back of that truck. She considered making her way to the rear of the building to find some less busy entry point. Mary Lou remembered there had been an outside door found this morning which they hadn't used because they didn't have much time for anything other than basic scavenging.

The row of warehouses were all separated and she saw there was a path running behind them. It was ten feet wide, which meant she'd walk down it with ease, but if anyone was out back, she'd be spotted in an instant. Mary Lou considered the odds, weighing up any other options open to her which didn't involve storming the front with her pistol and rifle. One against at least four? Not great.

Time seemed to drag and no better idea popped into her head. So she checked the position of her revolver and sauntered away from the warehouse so she could nip to the path without being too visible. Three warehouses along, she had a straight line of sight to the heroin hotel. Nothing. She crept forward, making sure she was never more than two feet away from a building wall: this minimized the angle for anyone stood on the rear step as she approached.

By the time she reached the corner of the warehouse, her breathing was in overdrive. She paused and hugged the wall with her back, fingers touching the brickwork. Five minutes rest to turn her lungfuls into silent gasps.

The door was painted dark green and a sign was attached, noting people should keep clear as it was a fire escape. Mary Lou edged nearer until she touched the handle. Then she bristled as she heard a crunch on the path. She looked around and saw Bobby ten feet away, approaching from the other side. Her quizzical expression spoke volumes.

"Wanted to make sure you were okay. Someone needed to watch you back."

"Get the fuck outta here!"

"No can do. You can't do everything by yourself. I can help."

Mary Lou became concerned their whispering might be heard inside and scurried over to stand by Bobby's ear. She flitted her eyes left, then right, and snorted out her words.

"Listen carefully. You are not welcome here. You are not needed here. Your time has long since gone and you are of no use to me."

"You don't want to hear this, but you are wrong. You need me more this minute than at any other point in your life. The guys in there are lowlife pond scum and, whatever they're up to, they'd drop you soon as look at you. And you know that, deep down."

Mary Lou blinked and carried on eyeballing the man. Bobby felt her exhalations hitting his cheek. Sensed how far on the edge she was standing. On the precipice. The question was whether she'd see reason and back down, swallowed pride and all.

"I've got to know if they are in there. They could be on the other side of that wall for all I know."

Mary Lou waved a hand toward the brickwork a few feet away and Bobby's eyes followed the direction of her fingers and darted back to her face.

"If they are, we will find out together. There's five fellas in there minimum."

"I only counted four."

"Five to my certain knowledge. And there could be some who are staying indoors to supervise."

"You suggesting we should leave?"

"No, I'm saying we should think smart. Let's take it slow and find out what we need to—without getting caught."

"How?"

"Put your ear to the door and listen."

Truth was Mary Lou hadn't considered that even for an instant. She did as he suggested, craning into the wooden green slats to get better access to anything going on inside. Three, maybe four, minutes later and she removed her ear from the door.

"Well?"

"They'll be finished in a few minutes. After this morning's activity, they are cleaning the place out and I heard talk of lighting a fire."

"Any need for us to go in?"

"No, Bobby. Frank Jr and Alice aren't in there."

"Shall we go home then?"

Mary Lou nodded and they scurried away, down the path and back onto the road and the parking bays.

"Thank you."

Mary Lou pecked Bobby on the cheek and he smiled. She turned to fumble for her car keys and, before she looked up, Bobby had vanished into the dusk. Perhaps he had been an operator in his day. She got in the car and drove home with no greater knowledge about her kids than when she left. Sometimes men can be right, she sighed to herself.

113

PASQUALE, FABIO AND Arnold were sat where she left them—no clear movement. There were coffee cups on the table to show they had made themselves at home. Mary Lou wondered how comfortable they had become and to what extent they'd taken advantage of her absence to check out the summerhouse or her panties drawer. Neither was positive.

"Any word?"

"Nothing yet. How did you guys get on?"

"They weren't there."

Bobby nodded confirmation but added no noise at all. He let attention remain on Mary Lou, who sat down and resumed her wait. He returned to her side and everyone remained precisely where they had originally landed earlier in the afternoon. She glanced at the clock on the mantlepiece and saw five to midnight. A long day with no sign of ending anytime soon.

Two minutes later, the phone rang. Mary Lou's hand darted over and grabbed the receiver. Bobby made out a muffled male voice, but couldn't discern a word that was said.

"For you."

She passed the phone over to Fabio.

"Yes?… Uh-huh."

More noises until Fabio put the receiver down—and smiled.

"We have a location and eyes on the building."

"How far? Who?"

"Let's talk along the way. It'll take us thirty minutes to get there. Who's coming?"

Pasquale explained he wouldn't be part of the rescue party. He was happy to offer more men if she needed it, but he no longer took part in any operations. No one was surprised about this. He was a made man and, despite Mary Lou's feelings, this was insufficiently big-league for Pasquale to be seen with a gun in his hand.

Roach stood up, removed guns from various holsters and checked the clips. He put them all back and announced he was in.

"Thanks, Arnold."

Fabio was next to bow out, but again there were no gasps of amazement. Men like Fabio do not get their hands dirty saving kidnapped children. That left Bobby and nobody thought he'd be coming along, not even as the chauffeur.

"You stay here, Bobby. You can relay messages to Fabio otherwise we'll be out there on our own."

"Sure thing."

"Where's Milton?"

Come to think of it, where the hell was that man? Mary Lou hadn't seen him since he went off with their score after lunch. Had he run off with the powder or had he gone to ground somewhere? Perhaps he'd been taken too.

"Anyone know how to get in touch with Albert Nardi? We could do with his skills right now, with or without Milton."

"You need any more muscle? A small group is better than an army but only three is not enough, surely?"

"Two more trusted souls would be great."

"Consider it done. I'll send them straight to the venue."

"And where is that, then?"

There was a simple reason nobody had discovered the kids in Palm Springs: they weren't there. If anyone had been sent north to Desert Hot Springs, on the other side of the freeway, they would have found a grassy space to the west near the corner of Pierson Boulevard and Golden Eagle Road. A two story white building in the shape of a cross stood opposite eight storage buildings. Gray concrete and monotone walls. Nothing to look at but plenty to find inside.

The time arrived to get back Mary Lou's babies.

Easter Sunday April 11, 1971

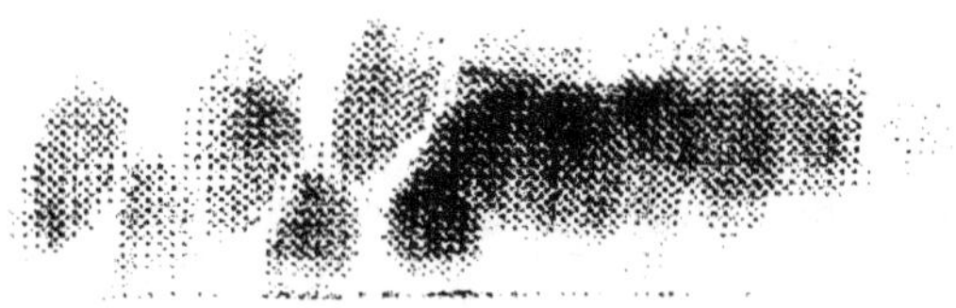

114

THEY CROUCHED BY the white wall of the building on the other side of the road. Mary Lou understood she had to wait for the cavalry to arrive in the form of men in dark suits: Anastasia Serafini and Naldo Pavone. Their introduction was a simple nod and a grunt, and they hunkered down along with the rest.

"We'll split up: Arnold and I will take the front and you two see if you can find an entrance round the back."

"We're looking for kids, right?"

"They are my children, yes. Try to keep people alive until Alice and Frank Jr are found and we are certain they are safe. After that, I don't care if any of them walk out or are carried out in a body bag."

The two newcomers didn't need to be given their instructions twice and vanished into the inky blackness. Roach and Mary Lou waited ten seconds and then headed to the corner of their building to peep round the wall and assess how they'd get to the front without being spotted.

One guy stood by the entrance, hands in pockets. Slouched against the brickwork, he was not expecting any trouble and had lulled himself to a point of distracted boredom. The door was shut behind him. Arnold and Mary Lou stared at the guy for seven, maybe eight, minutes. No one else came in or out: just the dude leaning against the wall waiting for problems to start.

Mary Lou checked her piece yet again, but this time kept it in her hand.

"You keep me covered and I'11 walk straight up to him."

"I could put a slug through his head from here."

"I don't doubt your professional ability, but we need him to land silently."

"Understood. Nothing personal. Use this if you get close enough."

He proffered a small knife he'd hidden up his sleeve. Mary Lou had definitely not noticed it before. Arnold was a consummate assassin. She slid the blade into her back pocket. It was only three inches long so fit snuggly with the handle sticking out, easy to reach.

She walked onto the sidewalk and crossed the street, careful to ensure she appeared from the corner of the road. The warehouse stood resolutely at the end of the row: nowhere to hide. She glanced up and down the street but there was no one visible. When she looked back at the white building, Arnold had blended into the night or he'd moved to a different vantage point. Either way, he was gone.

Her throat was dry and she swallowed to generate some spit. There was a twenty feet path from the sidewalk to the three steps leading to the guy and the entrance door. He had registered her existence and stopped his leaning, although both hands remained in his pockets. She pulled out a cigarette from her bag and pretended to fumble for a box of matches.

"Hey bud!"

She sauntered along the path to give the air of a lone girl needing help. Mary Lou couldn't believe anyone would buy that story, but it was all she had. She tried to squint at his hands to see if he was holding a piece, but the sole street light was behind her and she cast a shadow on the front door. Her outline reduced as she got nearer to the goon. Six feet… five, four, three…

"What you want, missy?"

"Have a light?"

"Wait there."

"Whatever you say, babe."

He scurried down the steps and put a hand into his pants pocket. The knife remained gripped in her palm and she was painfully aware of the beam shining over her shoulder. He squinted and she realized the street light was too bright for him.

"Here you go."

"Thanks, bud."

Mary Lou completed the two feet journey and he flicked the flint wheel of his lighter. It sparked into action and she looked into his dark brown eyes. He cupped the flame and she put a hand to his back. As she leaned in, bending her head sideways as though to take her cigarette to the fire, she plunged the knife into his chest. Mary Lou pushed the blade in as far as it would go using the force of her hand on his back. His eyes widened, shocked by what had just happened. Then she pulled the metal out and shoved it into his throat and tried to wiggle it side to side.

He slumped to the ground, gurgling and clutching his chest and larynx. She bent down and stabbed him in the heart in case the first two hits hadn't been enough to do him in. Then she looked up and down the street: no one had appeared. All was quiet.

Roach came out from out the darkness and they dragged the body along the wall of the warehouse, away from any windows. Before the blood crept over the entire corpse, he checked each pocket in every item of clothing. A wallet, two sets of keys and a packet of cigarettes made up his worldly possessions.

"The light is shining straight at him. We're gonna need to shift his carcass out of here."

"Moving him is more likely to garner unwanted attention than anything else."

Mary Lou thought for a second and nodded consent. Arnold rolled the guy over so he faced the wall and was half-perched between the gray brickwork and the black tarmac. His bleeding front was now hidden from sight and he presented darkened clothing to any casual passerby. Anyone walking up the path to enter the building would know they were staring at a corpse. But who'd be paying a visit at this time of night?

"This way."

Arnold padded up the steps and put an ear to the door. Nothing. He tried one key after another until the lock turned and he could push the door ajar. Mary Lou removed her pistol from her waistband and her stomach knotted. She clenched her piece and followed Roach inside.

THE ENTRANCE OF the warehouse comprised a large area with three doors leading off into the unknown. All remained quiet and Arnold chose one of the three, seemingly at random: left, right or straight ahead.

Once upon a time, this was a reception area but now there was a counter and space for a desk, filing cabinets and the makings of an office, but no furniture or any sign this was used nowadays or that they could expect anyone to appear either.

Back to the second door and Arnold tried the handle. Nothing. He and Mary Lou looked at each other, not understanding what was happening. How could it be locked? She shook her head and in the quietest voice she could muster:

"Let me try."

She gripped the handle until her knuckles were white, and twisted. The door opened just a hairline crack and Mary Lou glanced at Arnold and shrugged. She pushed at the door some more and one eye squinted into the light beyond. There was a staircase in the foreground leading both upstairs and down. Further away was a large room filled with boxes sitting on shelving.

Mary Lou just about made out the silhouette of a man grabbing a cardboard cube and then walking off out of sight. She waited to see if there was any more activity visible, but the guy didn't return. Nor did any of his friends appear. A beat and then they scurried to the stairs.

Arnold looked up and down, but saw jack.

"Where now?"

"Let's finish this floor and only then try somewhere else."

They scooted toward the shelving and found a labyrinth of aisles formed by the boxes. A small army would take at least an hour to check the whole area. There was only the two of them and they didn't have the time. Instead, they stood as still as mannequins and listened hard. If the guy she'd seen was on the floor, his footsteps were too far away to hear.

"Up or down?"

"Up?"

Mary Lou nodded consent and they padded back to the stairs and on to the second floor. The stairwell was industrial in size, so they arrived at the other end of the set of steps, guns pointing into the void. Near the stairs was an entrance comprising clear plastic strips hanging from the ceiling, each four inches wide. While the strips were technically transparent, you could see no detail looking through them. All Mary Lou and Arnold knew for sure was that no one stood immediately the other side. Beyond that was anyone's guess.

Arnold counted down with his fingers—three, two, one—and they both pushed through and stood the other side, arms aiming guns left to right in case trouble was standing, waiting for them. But, again, there was nobody there and nothing much to see. In the far distance, Mary Lou made out the sound of some machinery. She looked askance at Arnold.

"We'd better check it out."

She nodded and they edged their way through the gloom toward the metallic sounds. There were planks of wood and various lumps of debris scattered along their route, but eventually they reached an outside wall and realized they'd missed whatever machine they thought they'd been tracking. They stood a breath apart. Arnold craned his head and pointed to his right. Mary Lou thought for a second and knew he was correct.

Two minutes later, they found a partition wall and the sound was much louder now. Arnold ducked down below the solid lower half of the fake wall, padding along until they reached a swing door. With the most simple of hand gestures, Arnold indicated for Mary Lou to remain where she was.

He let the barrel of his gun peep through the other side, then allowed one eye and his nose to follow. His body vanished for a moment and then it reappeared.

"Nothing doing. It's a packaging plant, but I didn't get a chance to see what's being boxed up. Doesn't matter right now…"

"Because Alice and Frank Jr weren't there."

"Yep."

Back to the stairs and another decision: up again or back down? Up, but this time the floor was emptier than the last, so they returned to the first story and took a moment before hitting the basement. There had been no sign of Anastasia or Naldo. Either they were downstairs or they'd run away before the game got going. Another possibility was that they'd been caught and were spilling their guts as Mary Lou thought this through.

Come to think of it, they hadn't found any rear entrance. Had their men entered via the basement? There had been no shots fired—all was quiet apart from the low level hum emanating from the packing machine. The only thing to do was head to the floor below and everything would become clear.

"Let's get this done."

Like before, they each stood at the far end of a step to give best line of sight on anything about to appear. They edged down until they crouched at the bottom of the stairwell—a concrete floor comprising only a ten by ten feet space and two doors.

Before they could decide what to do, the left-hand door opened and a man walked straight into Arnold.

115

ARNOLD GRABBED THE guy by the throat and swung him round, slamming him into the nearest wall. He used one hand to wrap his fingers around the dude's wrist and smashed it twice against the brickwork until the man's gun fell to the floor. Arnold squeezed until the dude could only just breathe. He spluttered and wheezed, choked spittle landing on Arnold's first finger and thumb.

Mary Lou picked up the revolver from the ground and held it to the guy's temple as Arnold carried on squeezing the life out of his windpipe. His body went limp and he slumped down. Arnold checked his pockets and passed a snub nose over to her. Then a box of slugs appeared out of a jacket pocket. She filled the clip and stuffed it into her waistband—at the front though, as it was quite small and she didn't want to lose it.

"That answers the question which door to try first."

Arnold opened the left one just a crack to have a peep and closed it again, twisting round to face Mary Lou. A deep breath.

"Other side is a large room—more of a workspace, really. I spotted at least four guys hanging around either sat on chairs or leaning on a wall. They look bored like they've been there an eternity, but I couldn't see a reason for them to be huddled so close together. They can't be guarding the floor or they'd be more alert."

"Do you think we should leave them be for now and check out the other route?"

"Reckon so. It's a whole pile of trouble over there."

Arnold's thumb pointed through the left-hand door and they both imagined the first ten to twelve seconds after they popped their heads around to say hi. Instead, Arnold peeped round the right-hand door and reported all was safe. They went through into a corridor which stretched two hundred or more feet ahead. Both sides had office doors running every fifty feet; the top half of each was composed of glass, so they'd need to tread carefully as they made their way along.

Mary Lou was the first to scuttle down the aisle until she reached a door and then she flattened herself against the wall. Arnold stood two feet away from her. She heard his inhalations and imagined the stress he was feeling. A quick nod to acknowledge the next step and she swung round and rolled near the floor, swiftly followed by Arnold. They crouched facing each other to steady their nerves, aware how long the corridor felt.

Arnold pointed at himself to show he wanted to lead and Mary Lou remained stationary to let him pass. Roach stood upright and leaned his head right by the jamb of the next door. A few seconds of intense listening and he walked casually past. He turned round and winked at Mary Lou, who winked back and followed Roach until they arrived at the last door on the right.

This time, Arnold held a palm up to pause Mary Lou's progress. Once he was certain she would not blunder forwards, he placed a solitary finger to his lips. The universal hand gesture meaning 'shut up'. As they stood there, Mary Lou heard the mumbled sounds of a conversation, but she couldn't make out a single word.

Arnold kept his fingers on his lips as he continued to listen intently. His expression gave nothing away though. One long minute and he leaned into Mary Lou's ear.

"There's two, sat talking about all sorts. They are from the east coast and are bitching about being so far from home. No word on where the kids are but Sancho Mendoza is in the building."

"Huh?"

"You heard me right. He's got himself some hired hands."

"From New York? Baltimore? Boston?"

"I don't recognize them, so probably not from the Big Apple. Apart from that, no idea."

"But they didn't have time to come over this afternoon. They must be here on other business."

"And Mendoza has been using them as guards. That's why they aren't happy. Good news is that Alice and Frank Jr are here."

"We need to take them out."

"Leave it to me."

Before Mary Lou could pass any comment, Arnold vanished into the room. Ninety seconds later, he returned. She popped her head around the door and saw the two men lying on the ground, dead. But no sign of any knife wound and no sound from a revolver. Arnold had strangled them both. The most remarkable achievement was to kill the first guy without the other one noticing. Hats off to Arnold.

They scurried to the end of the corridor and held their breath as Mary Lou peeped past the door to see what they were up against. A square reception area with three doors leading off it. The biggest problem were the four fellas standing and sitting round. She had no idea at first glance who or what was behind any of the doors. Arnold pulled out his revolvers.

"Never bring a knife to a gun fight."

He winked and put his blade away into his belt. Mary Lou smiled back at him.

"How do we play this?"

"You take care of the two on the right. I'll handle the others. Anyone left standing: kill them wherever they are."

There was a curled smile around his mouth but Roach's eyes were fixed in a cold, hard glare. This was his business and he knew it well.

"But let's do this clean if we can. The quieter, the better."

She nodded understanding and Arnold pulled out a second gun from his jacket. He mouthed a countdown and slipped through the door without a sound. A solitary crack then a body crumpled to the floor. Mary Lou reached the other side of the door and put a slug in the chest of one of her targets. His body thumped the wall as it took the momentum of the shot and slithered down to the ground. Blood poured from his heart, forming a large puddle on the floor which seeped into the cracks of the tiled surface.

The other target sat at a table, holding playing cards. Must have been enjoying a game of solitaire. By the time he realized what was going down, Mary Lou had got one pace further toward him and aimed at his forehead. A squeeze of the trigger and his head pushed backwards with the force of the bullet that entered his left eye and exited the back of his skull. Red splatter spread across the wall behind him.

Arnold and Mary Lou crouched down and waited for a second. No one appeared from any of the rooms. They scurried over to the corpses and grabbed firearms and bullets aplenty. She was minutes away from finding her babies.

MARY LOU AND Arnold hugged the floor and took stock of their situation. Three rooms led off from the space they were in. Each had a shut door along with a wall comprising a long glass panel running from the ceiling to halfway up. From her position a few inches from the ground, Mary Lou saw heads bobbing in two of the rooms. The third had green Venetian blinds drawn.

Arnold wriggled his fingers to get her attention and showed which room they'd hit next. She blinked her agreement and they rolled over to the first door. Upright but flat against the wall, they could make out three guys inside talking. More hand gestures and nods, then a quick leap up and they were inside, snapping slugs into brains before the saps reacted. He pushed the door shut and they sorted out the corpses, taking more bullets but leaving the guns behind. He closed the blinds to give them a moment's respite.

"How you doing?"

"Just fine. You?"

"Cool bananas."

They put slugs into chambers and edged out the room and took out the second one much like the first. Mary Lou noticed little flecks of red on Arnold's cheeks and shirt. She figured she bore the marks of the blood letting too. The two hunkered over to outside the third room and waited. Arnold pressed an ear to the door while Mary Lou craned to hear any conversation through the glass half-partition. Nothing doing.

In her mind's eye, Mary Lou imagined Frank Jr and Alice sat on the floor playing, while two brutes stood over them. But she knew their situation was far worse than that—in ways she didn't want to consider. There would be only one way to find out and they were seconds from the truth. She breathed deeply twice and swallowed hard. A nod to Arnold, who threw the door open wide, and they shot at every adult they could see.

Four men stood at various locations and a handful of tables and chairs were scattered around. Made no sense: there was no order to the place. Mary Lou remained crouched and took out a black-haired dude who was fumbling for his piece in his jacket. Meanwhile, Arnold made mincemeat of one of the other's brains as pieces of flesh smacked against a far wall.

The other two hit the floor and flung the nearest table over as a barricade. To cause confusion, they hurled two chairs at the open doorway, but neither Arnold nor Mary Lou responded. They tried firing through the furniture but no joy. Arnold scurried into the room until he reached a square-based pillar. Mary Lou covered him during the manouevre with a spray of slugs all over the place. She searched for even a glimmer of the kids, but they didn't seem to be there, goddamnit.

Then all guns stopped firing and everyone took stock, trying to figure out their next move. Arnold and Mary Lou looked at each other and he beckoned her inside. She kept low and made her way to a table, flipping it over before another assault of bullets headed her direction. Then another eerie silence. She was ten feet from Arnold and the fellas were thirty feet behind their upturned table, now gouged with any number of bullet holes. The wood surface was peppered to shit by the slugs, but it must have a metal base beneath or those guys would have met their maker by now.

There was a moment of calm and Mary Lou noticed a door at the other end of the room. In perfect synchrony, Arnold must have spotted the same thing as they both looked at each other, knowing. He slid away from the pillar to create a better line of sight to attack. Arnold turned his head back to Mary Lou and held three fingers up. How had they missed one guy? That wasn't important right now. Despite all his training and deep experience, Arnold blurted out two words.

"Sancho Mendoza."

Mary Lou's eyes widened as that single phrase unlocked all that had befallen her since lunchtime. This had nothing to do with the mob. This was all about the brown powder. If the deal hadn't gone south this morning, none of this would have happened. Mendoza wanted the sweet taste of revenge and the motherfucker who'd stolen her children was a few feet in front of her.

A red veil cast a shadow over her eyes and she ground her molars at the back of her jaw. She raised herself until she saw over her defenses and glimpsed the top of one head. Aimed slow and squeezed the trigger until the recoil sent her arm upwards and a bullet landed in the middle of the guy's skull. A quick duck-down as the survivors responded with their revolvers.

Before they knew what was going on, one of the two made a break for the door three feet behind him. Arnold and Mary Lou peppered the room with gunfire and the last dude behind the table splayed backwards with the force of Arnold's high caliber pistol. The other slammed the door behind him.

"Mendoza!"

They scrambled over to the other side of the room and Mary Lou flung open the door. She saw a leg disappear up a fire escape ladder and then she scanned the room.

"Leave Mendoza to me."

Arnold grabbed the fire escape and Mary Lou stood, guns in both hands, surveying an empty room with one cupboard against a wall and two bodies trussed up lying, one on top of the other, next to the solitary item of office furniture. She didn't need to give them a close inspection to know it was Serafini and Pavone.

Gunfire outside as Arnold gave chase. Complete nothing surrounded Mary Lou. Almost zilch: she noticed the ticking of a clock and swung round to see the circular dial and the blade markings near the edge, counting the seconds until her death.

Then a knocking. From the cupboard. A light tap and not much more than that, but enough to be audible. Mary Lou raised her revolver at the gray object and pulled open one door. Her eyes flitted across the top half as it was lined with empty shelves. The bottom section consumed half the space inside. On the floor sat a bundle of ropes and a gag in each mouth. Their hands and feet were tied, but Mary Lou had found her loves.

Taking the knife from her jeans, she cut through the fibers and undid the knots on the handkerchief gags. Then she held them both as they hugged her back and all three sobbed with happiness.

WHEN THEY ARRIVED home, Bobby opened the door and everyone tumbled inside. The family stood in the hallway in an enormous embrace for a full five minutes. Mary Lou picked up Alice in her arms and Bobby took Frank Jr as they entered the living room. Arnold followed them in, hands deep in pockets.

Once they sat down on the couches, she allowed another tear to roll down her cheek as she pressed Alice against her body. There was a moment when Arnold thought she would never let go, but eventually she scampered off and checked on her brother before returning to her mother and forcing Mary Lou's legs apart so she could loll over one knee.

Ten minutes later, they took the kids off to bed, leaving Arnold to forage for some Scotch and soda. It had been a long night—and an even longer day before. Mary Lou kissed them both as Bobby returned downstairs, but she didn't follow. Instead, she waited until they were both asleep before she dared to leave them.

Back in the living room, the two men had spread themselves out. Each nursed a tumbler containing a yellow-brown liquid and ice. A third glass rested on a coffee table. She picked it up and sat next to Bobby, but she kept her head pointed at Roach.

"Thank you again."

"De nada."

"No, really. You saved my children's lives tonight."

Arnold nodded and smiled in recognition of her words, but he was not comfortable with this kind of attention.

"Let's move on. Mendoza is still out there. We cut off the tail of the worm but the head is alive and well."

"For Mendoza to have acted so quickly, he must have had help."

"East Coast help?"

"That's what it sounded like."

Mary Lou took a sip of her drink and swallowed hard. This wasn't over yet. Not by a long way. If her family was ever to be safe then she would need to finish off Sancho Mendoza but also there had to be a day of reckoning with the men who supported him from New York. The same mob who'd killed her husband and driven her away from the only place she had called home: a dingy one-bedroom apartment in the crappy end of Baltimore.

MONDAY APRIL 12, 1971

116

MARY LOU AWOKE alone in bed, much as she had done ever since Frank lay dying in her arms a lifetime ago. She sat bolt upright and allowed herself a fleeting moment of panic before she remembered where she was and that her babies were safe. Just to make certain, she tiptoed into their room to see them sleeping soundly. A smile and she closed the door behind her.

Bobby was in the spare room and Arnold was downstairs on the couch. The man had quite a snore on him to be so audible from this distance. Proof he lived alone. She returned to her own bedroom and got dressed. Then down to make breakfast.

Eggs, bacon and toast smells roused Arnold and he slunk off the couch, rubbed his eyes of sleep and joined her in the kitchen. Five minutes later, Bobby appeared—the aroma of cooked food had seeped up the stairs but wasn't strong enough to wake the kids, not on this morning. The three sat around the table, quietly chewing and swallowing, lost in their own worlds.

Mary Lou had placed a pot of coffee in the middle of the table and once they had mopped up their crumbs with the crusts of their toast, they filled up their mugs and felt able to talk to each other.

"I'll call the agency and get a housekeeper in fast. This business isn't over."

"First speak with Fabio: if you want Alice and Frank Jr to remain safe, we'll need their help. Two guys in the front, two in the rear and two inside. If Mendoza tries to attack, he'll bring a fucking army."

"Do you think he will?"

"I dunno the fella so I have no clue how hot-tempered he is. Me? I'd exit stage left and come back once the dust had settled. But I'm content serving my revenge stone cold. Others prefer a warmer dish."

At that moment, a scampering of feet and the twins descended on the kitchen. Mary Lou prepared breakfast while Bobby kept them occupied. Arnold remained separate from all this hubbub, somehow able to stay in the room, sat on his chair, while all around domestic normality oozed out of every corner of the surrounding people.

He took a swig of coffee and took a tour of the estate. Out of respect to Mary Lou, he kept his piece in its holster until he was out of sight of the kids. They'd seen enough guns and blood to last them forever and a day.

Forty-five minutes later, a knock on the door and the family's new housekeeper appeared. She looked at least ten years older than Cindy, but had warm eyes. Truth was Mary Lou had explained she was having security issues, so the agency found her somebody who could handle themselves in times of trouble. Within a few days, she could be swapped out for a more playful youngster, if the kids didn't like her. The woman's name was Irma and that was all that mattered.

Alice was especially nervous of this stranger, but Frank Jr warmed to her almost as soon as she'd stepped into the room. He was so much like a puppy dog.

They talked in the kitchen and let Alice see that Irma was part of the extended family. Then Mary Lou suggested they go upstairs to get dressed. The two women and the children left and hit the kids' bedroom. Mary Lou stayed long enough for Irma to take command of the twins and then she made her excuses and returned downstairs.

"All good?"

"Yeah. They'll be fine."

"I'm gonna stick around here today. If you're off taking care of Mendoza, I'll mind the twins."

"Thanks. They need someone they know and can trust. If they are to stay alive, I have to leave them and finish what I started."

Mary Lou popped up to the children and played with them a short while. A simple look in Irma's direction gave all the explanation that was needed. Alice and Frank Jr were excited when their mom told them she was going out for some ice-cream but it might take a while to find. A long hug for each of them and a hushed word with Irma. Mary Lou turned her back on her precious family and left the room.

Arnold had finished his first sweep of the estate when she found him in the summerhouse.

"You ready to hook up with Fabio?"

"I've been waiting all my life for this moment."

They smiled at each other and filled up their pieces with bullets from last night's adventure and from the hidden room's stash. She squeezed Bobby's hand and pecked him on the cheek. Then she and Arnold hopped into her car and sped off to have a private conversation with Fabio.

MARY LOU SAT in Fabio's garden while Arnold stood indoors. She had stopped counting the supporting cast when Fabio started introducing them to her. Each wore the same clothes—white shirt and pants to match the jacket, which contained a concealed weapon. A tie was optional.

A pleasant enough patio area and a gazebo had been erected halfway down the expansive lawn. Fabio's men stood a respectful distance away from him, facing outward in case of trouble. Mary Lou sipped at her coffee and languished in the warm air. To his credit, Fabio was in no hurry and she experienced a peace she thought she'd never know again. He let her completely drain the cup before he got down to business.

"I am glad the unpleasantness with your children has been positively resolved."

"Thank you. May I send a token of appreciation to the widows of your men, who died last night?"

"There is no need, but your respect is well noted."

"To work then: Mendoza is alive and those who backed him remain in operation."

"What are your plans?"

"Roach and I will dispose of Mendoza. There is no question in my mind that mook must die."

"We agree. He crossed a line—no matter what decision you make in business, your family should not bear the physical consequences of your difficulties. Taking your children was an ill-thought through act of a coward."

"But he didn't act alone."

"Very perceptive. No, we don't believe so either."

"You know where the help came from?"

"The east, I'd say."

"Anywhere in particular?"

Fabio's lips curled upward as he witnessed her trying to tease the information out of him. Some things dare not bear uttering.

"Are you aware of the issues faced by the Bassani family these past few years?"

Mary Lou shrugged as she was fairly ignorant of all the goings on. She only knew what she'd picked up from conversations in the Country Club. And there was a lot of rumor masquerading as fact at the nineteenth hole.

"For quite some time, interests back east have conflicted with those on this side of the country. The situation has not been helped by local law enforcement issues."

In the most coded way possible, Fabio affirmed what Mary Lou had heard before: when underboss, Joe Dippolito went down in '69, Bassani took over his rackets. Trouble was that the New York mob needed to extend its tentacles just at the time when Joe Dip was at his weakest. This meant the Pentangelo clan had been nipping at their heels ever since.

That name sent a shudder down Mary Lou's spine. These were the people who'd had the Feds in their pockets and had gunned down Frank.

"Who would have given the order and supplied Mendoza with financing?"

"Charles Pentangelo. Charlie. Leave him to us. Do not go after him."

"He's been trouble to you for three years to my knowledge and you have done nothing about him. You won't change your mind in the next twenty-four hours."

She stared into Fabio's eyes, seeking to instill in him the absolute certainty and clarity that Pentangelo would soon meet his maker.

"He's a made guy and he cannot be touched."

"Even if it frees us from unwarranted attention in the east and delivers us the heroin trade across South LA and Watts?"

"If anything were to befall him, it must not be traced back here. Were that to happen, the kidnapping of Alice and Frank Jr would be the least of your worries. Capiche?"

Mary Lou nodded and checked her cup for coffee but it was long since empty. Only a trickle of dregs at the bottom. The thought of Charlie Pentangelo sucking the barrel of her gun made her smile inside. This was mirrored on her expression as she imagined his gray matter leaving the back of his skull and hitting a wall.

"So we are clear?"

"Like my nail polish."

Fabio frowned in confusion at her words, then looked down at her fingers and understood.

"I have business to attend out of town."

"Just remember you have deliveries to make in California before you go anywhere else."

"I know. And thank you for providing the men to keep my house secure."

"No one should live in fear in their home, should they?"

His comments seemed more labored than Mary Lou might have expected and she stored that thought away for later. She got up and they shook hands. Fabio walked her back to the house and acknowledged Roach with a look. Arnold's reputation stood before him and no words were necessary for this artist.

As they drove back to Bobby and the kids, Arnold refrained from asking a single question about her private conversation. Classy guy.

117

IRMA HAD TAKEN the kids out for an early pizza, so Bobby was resting by the pool. They all sat down and soaked in the late morning rays knowing this moment would surely pass too soon. And they were right.

"First, we take out Mendoza and then Pentangelo."

"Charlie is no an easy hit but at least we know where he is. Mendoza has flown in the wind."

"He won't have gone far. My guess is he's in hiding in LA. And I'd like the opportunity to do more than watch the kids."

"It is an important job."

"Yes, Arnold. But it isn't man's work."

Mary Lou laughed and the two men looked at her.

"Listen to you two. You're assuming a man will do the killing of Sancho Mendoza."

"We are both professionals. Or we were."

Arnold cast a withering eye at Bobby and resumed.

"You've come rather late to this game and are a robber at heart. That's said with all respect due to you. If you don't mind me saying, the Bank of Baltimore heist was nothing short of brilliant."

"Damn straight."

"It is one thing to fire a gun from a hundred feet and hit your mark. That is a world apart from walking up to somebody and putting a bullet in their skull when you can taste the fear in their breath. And do it in such a way you get out of the venue alive."

"Arnold, you're right, but this is a job for a local guy—someone who knows the dives in Watts and can ferret out a dealer who's hit the mattresses."

"Not so fast, old man. You don't need to know every local bar to find a dirty rat. You forget, that's how I earn my crust. I traveled four thousand miles to find Mary Lou. Some sleazebag smack merchant a few miles down the road will be no bother to me at all."

They glared at each other while Mary Lou stared both down. This was not the time for petty squabbles.

"You boys want a drink?"

Shake of heads from both and she continued sipping her coffee.

"The question isn't who will pull the trigger on the mook, but when."

"Today."

Arnold's response began almost before she finished her last syllable. Bobby nodded agreement but remained silent. For a man who wanted to do more then look after the kids, he was doing a great impersonation of chopped liver.

"Can you get the job done by tonight?"

"Yes."

"Good. Bobby, you stay here. As much as you wish to kill someone for me, you are the person I am trusting with my children. I trust Arnold with a slug, but I entrust you with my flesh and blood. And I don't want either of you to let me down."

"I'm here for you."

"I know you are."

She reached out an arm and Bobby took her hand to squeeze it for three long seconds. Then Mary Lou withdrew the limb and he grabbed a gulp from his mug. The seriousness of his situation engulfed him for a moment and he lost focus on the conversation between Mary Lou and Arnold.

CHARLIE PENTANGELO WAS a capo in the New York mob and would have plenty of protection surrounding him every minute of each hour. The trick was to find a crack in this seemingly impenetrable armor. If anyone could figure it out, Arnold Roach was at the top of most people's lists. He held his mug in both hands, repeatedly sipping and swallowing. All the while, staring into the empty pool. The memory of Cindy's corpse floating in the pink sea was just that: a piece of the past. History.

"During the day, there is enough security you'd need either someone on a suicide mission or a Molotov cocktail. Neither option has a great survival rate."

"Especially suicide."

"Most people who throw Molotovs dowse themselves in burning gas."

"Like a Buddhist monk on a 'Nam protest."

"So we should avoid the day, then?"

"Unless you're sitting on a mighty clever idea."

"Only my ass."

"And what about evening?"

"I think we'd have more options. There're the times when his guards change shift. They stand in the hallway, outside his apartment, and get bored. Better still, in the middle of the night, they fall asleep. Protecting Charlie is a dull job. You work your way up as an enforcer to show you can handle yourself in a crisis, but then you hang around doing nothing for weeks at a time, because no one is stupid enough to attack Charlie Pentangelo. Present company excepted. No offense, you understand."

"None taken. Right, Bobby?"

"For sure. Too stupid to care, me."

Arnold blushed, but the grin on Bobby's face belied how he actually felt. Roach was more concerned about Mary Lou's response, because Bobby was just the nurse. Her wink to him gave Arnold the comfort of knowing all was well in the Lagotti household.

"So down the fire escape and hit him while he's asleep?"

"If you've taken out the guys on the roof and have padded down the metal stairs so quietly you haven't woken up the whole neighborhood."

Mary Lou stared at the water in the pool. Arnold sure wasn't making this easy. She'd been certain he'd have had a plan up his sleeve, but they had bupkis.

"What about blowing the place up? Plant a bomb under his bed and be long gone out of town by the time his brains are mixing with the ceiling."

Sigh.

"If we could get inside without being suspicious, then there's just killing his wife at the same time. Neither you nor I care if she lives or dies, but the Pentangelo family will judge it an unnecessarily cruel act to take her out. And then they would come after us. If we can make this a pure business hit, then we might get away with the assault on the capo as a piece of justifiable revenge. He funded an attack on Mary Lou's children, which was so out of line."

"Sounds like you don't think there's a way to get to him."

"I didn't say that, but it won't be easy."

"And we do it, how?"

"Dunno. Blowing him up or shooting him on the sidewalk are not solutions. That I know."

"What's wrong with where he works?"

"It's a mob stronghold. He's not sat in an office dictating memos to some big-tittied secretary, sitting on his knee massaging his… ego."

Mary Lou stiffened on her sunbed and Arnold realized he had gone a pinch too far.

"Sorry."

"De nada. How are we going to kill this motherfucker?"

Everyone remained silent as they mulled over ideas too foolish or insane to voice out loud. Mary Lou went inside after ten minutes to brew more Java. Sitting around was not good for her mental state. She needed action and the closest proxy was the coffee pot.

The problem wasn't how to kill Pentangelo—they would use a bullet or two. The difficulty was getting in and out without being caught. This was a situation more akin to guerilla warfare than an assassination. With this notion as a backdrop, Mary Lou saw she needed to stop thinking like Arnold and Bobby. What would her Frank have done?

He would have got her to turn up in a short skirt and heels and let the goons check her clutch bag. Then when she was alone with Pentangalo, she'd have pulled a piece from beneath her panties and plugged him full of holes. Gun in her bag, she'd walk out, ask the mooks for a light and make sure she pressed herself close just to take their minds off guarding the boss long enough for her to get out of Dodge.

When Mary Lou described the plan to the other two, they nodded, pondered and nodded again. All they had to figure out was where Charlie would be on his own so she could pay him a visit. At home in the evening, at lunch if he didn't go to a restaurant. Even in the mob's headquarters if they came up with a a satisfactory enough excuse for her to be there. The good news was that none of the New York contingent had any idea what Mary Lou looked like. And only a handful, who'd been in the game two years before, had any clue about her past connection to Charlie Pentangelo.

"Let me make a few calls."

Arnold stepped inside to speak to his contacts back east. Fifteen minutes later, he returned with a smile on his face and a fleshed-out plan in his pocket. They ran through it twice, trying to find any holes and to check it out from every angle. Two minor amendments and Mary Lou knew exactly what to do and when to do it.

"Once I've spoken to Milton about the China white, I'll be on my way."

"You need a hand?"

"No thank you. Arnold: you attend to Mendoza. Bobby: keep my babies safe."

They stood up and each hugged the other two. However the dice rolled, nothing would be the same again.

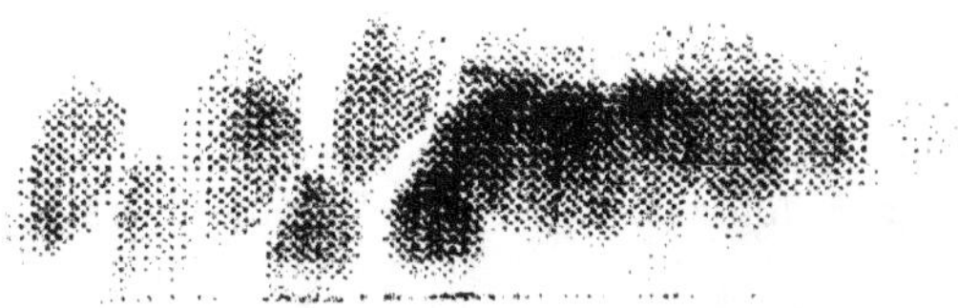

118

MARY LOU DROVE over to the Country Club to find Milton. He'd been missing since he scooted off with her powder, but this was the first opportunity for she to do anything about it. Despite all that had gone down with the twins, she knew deep in her heart she needed to pay her tribute to Pasquale on Friday. So she had to generate some income during the week otherwise Irma would find her employer floating in her own swimming pool, which was not a good look.

Her concern right now wasn't the appreciation, so much as Milton's absence. In the darkest recesses of her mind, a worm burrowed through with the thought he'd absconded with the white—or cut a deal behind her back.

The Country Club was empty—or rather, it was full of people imbibing an early cocktail, but none of them was Milton. The blond hairs at the nape of her neck froze and an icy chill shuddered through her body at the thought of losing all that smack.

Next stop was Milton's house. Janet answered the door in her dressing gown. Mary Lou glanced at her watch and saw it was nearly eleven.

"How are you?"

The woman was frosty—had been ever since Mary Lou talked business with her husband—but there was an extra edge to her voice this morning.

"Just fine, thanks. How's Milton?"

"Fine too."

Terse. Janet's eyes flitted away from the door and to the stairs. Something was amiss in the state of California.

"Am I keeping you from anything?"

"What? No!"

She wrapped her dressing gown tighter round her body, pulling at the belt. Arms folded.

"How's Paulie?"

"Good. At a sleep over with a friend. We should organize a play date with him and the twins."

"He's twice their age…"

"What? Oh yes. Silly me."

Janet wasn't thinking straight and spouting crap.

"Can I come in? I need to talk to Milton about some business."

"Come in? Huh? He's not… It's not convenient."

"Convenient?"

Janet's eyes glanced upstairs again. She gripped the edge of the door firmer than before. Mary Lou noticed the throbbing of a blood vessel on her right temple.

"Is Milton there?"

More discomfort as Janet tied her dressing gown again, only this time she revealed she was naked underneath the silky bed coat. Then Mary Lou woke up and smelled the coffee. Janet had a house guest in her bedroom, no clothes on and Milton wasn't home. When the cat's away…

"No, he's not."

Another furtive glance up the stairs and a shuffling of dressing gown cords.

"Sorry Janet. I didn't realize. Let Milton know I'm looking for him next time you see him."

With a single wink and a dirty grin, Mary Lou turned round and headed back to the car, leaving Janet to slam the door shut and return to her paramour. For a second, Mary Lou wondered who she was fucking. Then she realized she didn't care—unless it interfered with her business interests with Milton.

This left open the question of where the man had gone. Apart from the possibility of having missed him at the clubhouse, she thought she'd try the lab where he should have taken the heroin for processing.

To call the place a laboratory was stretching the meaning of the word—it was a disused factory on the edge of nowhere surrounded by the memory of a Palm Springs long since faded and died. On the corner of Belardo and East Ramon Road, east of the city, the place looked like every other building on the block. Each one was run down to the point of senility and comprised a rusty gate, once imposing doors and brickwork that contained more pockmarks than a teenager's face.

Mary Lou parked round the back and watched as a young dude eyed her vehicle and placed a hand on his concealed weapon. She got out the car and, open palmed, walked toward him. He stared at her as though she was the woman who'd slashed his mother's face.

"Hi. I'm Mary Lou. Is Milton in?"

A flicker of recognition and a terrible quandary: how to figure out if she was telling the truth? His mouth opened, but no words emerged.

"Well boy?"

He stared and caught flies. Mary Lou brushed past him and through the door. What a waste of space. Up some stairs and into the main area. There was a glass room in the middle where the drugs were processed. Scales, bunsen burners, the works. Looked like the biggest science experiment in the world. Mary Lou spotted Milton on the far side and raised an arm to grab his attention.

He smiled and waved back. She held her ground and waited for him to do the right thing and come over. Thirty seconds later and he got the message.

"Good to see you."

"Yeah. Working hard, I see."

"Just trying to make my quota."

"Been here all the time since we split up?"

"More or less. I mean I popped out to get some smokes and a bite to eat. But I slept on a chair in the corner of the office upstairs."

He appeared genuinely confused, unsure of the meaning behind her question. She stared at his expression, trying to read his face and decide whether he'd helped Mendoza at all. There was nothing to suggest he'd double crossed her so she told him about the twins and Cindy.

Milton was devastated and sat down to collect his thoughts. Mary Lou gave him some time to pull his shit back together and briefed him on what she needed over the next couple of days. Bottom line: he must generate and distribute a large quantity of brown sugar by the end of the week.

"Anything else I can do?"

"Just keep these wagons rolling."

"Okay."

"Actually, there's one thing."

"Name it."

"Get rid of the boy on the back door. I never want to see him again. Find someone with some cajones who'll protect my investment."

"You won't see that kid again. Promise."

With business taken care of, she was now free to pursue Charlie Pentangelo to the gates of hell.

MARY LOU PARKED her car around the corner so she wouldn't be seen. She walked to the rear of the house, past the pool and into the summerhouse. As much as she wanted to see the twins she knew there needed to be no witnesses. The last thing she required was Irma to walk in unannounced.

To the back of the hidden room to get her hands on the right snub nose to do the job: as small as possible—given where she'd be hiding it—but with enough punch to take Pentangelo out with one shot. A silencer would make the whole thing quieter, but there was only so much space below her rose.

While she was pondering the matter, the summerhouse door creaked open. She froze. Irma? The kids?

"Is that you, Mary Lou?"

Bobby's voice caused the tension in her shoulders to ebb away. She popped her head out and winked.

"Just grabbing some provisions."

"Make sure the safety's on. That's my best advice."

"Any idea how to muffle the sound?"

Bobby was silent while he thought. He scrunched up his face as he struggled to come up with an answer.

"Not right now. Sorry. Arnold might know, but I'm out of ideas."

"Where's he got to?"

"Already left for his destiny with Mendoza's death."

"Goddamn."

"You'll come up of something. You always do."

"Thanks for the vote of confidence, but this is real serious. I am about to take out a high roller in the New York mob."

Bobby eyed her in silence and nodded. She was right: rubbing out a local heroin dealer wasn't in the same ballpark as whacking Charlie Pentangelo. He walked over and put his arms around her. She responded to the hug allowing her head to lean on his chest for a moment. Then a squeeze and she turned her back to him and rummaged for the perfect killing machine.

Mary Lou heard the door close behind Bobby as he returned to minding her brood. She stared at a .38 and a .22 with no idea how to choose between them. The former would pack more of a punch, but it was a bigger object to shove down her front. Even with the .22, a skimpy G-string was not on the cards as the piece would fall down to her ankles as soon as she moved.

A moment's more thought told her to pick the .38 because she'd need to wear a sanitary napkin to hold the damn thing up no matter what time of the month it was. Did that mean she could afford to bring a silencer too? Mary Lou considered that still a step too far. Where was Roach when you needed him?

ARNOLD REGRETTED HIS decision to save money when he rented his car when he first arrived in California. For five bucks a day more, he could have been sitting in a cooling breeze. Instead, his journey to LA felt like a sauna on wheels. He was roasting and there was still over four hours to go— even if he kept his foot on the gas all the way there. Already he was looking forward to the first stopover.

He wound down his window, but that just let the warm air into the car. Twenty minutes into the journey and his back was sticking to his seat. And there wasn't even any money at the end of this rainbow. Doing a worthy thing was sweaty work. Might be okay for priests but this hired gun wasn't smiling. A bead of salty perspiration dripped over his right eyelid and dropped onto his cheek. This would be a quite a day.

119

MARY LOU DROVE over to Sunrise Way and Park Canyon Drive. Even though the trip lasted a few minutes, the car temperature got comfortable real fast. So by the time she was in a cab heading for the airport, she was cool, calm and collected.

A simple plan: a short hop to LAX and then try to fly nonstop to New York. She brought a fake ID so's she'd have an alibi if one were needed, but tracing her movements across country would be hard as she paid cash all the way.

At Palm Springs Airport, Mary Lou waited in line at the sales desk. She hadn't expected the place to be so busy. Five people stood in front of her and each wanted to tell their life story to the hapless rep on the other side of the counter. Two of the group formed a couple although you couldn't see by their body language. He was the same height as her with matching brown hair. That was all they had in common as their ensuing argument revealed.

They were heading for Miami and he was happy to have a layover in San Francisco, but she was not. Traveling via Los Angeles was her highest priority. As if by magic, Mary Lou hoped he won because she couldn't face another minute of their bickering—especially if she was trapped in a tin can with them.

Ten minutes later and Mary Lou was at the counter discussing options to get to the City of Angels.

"You can catch the 11:10 if you hurry…"

"Or?"

"Or there's the 11:55 nonstop, gets you into LA by 13:05."

The woman watched Mary Lou all the time she stood and considered the choices. She knew what the rep was deciding: does she represent a security risk or does this lone girl simply want a ticket to ride?

"I need to see my boyfriend real soon, you know, but I can't arrive with tousled hair. We haven't seen each other in ages, if ya get me?"

Mary Lou tried to appear embarrassed about the implication of fucking her fictional fella. Her life story revealed, she ducked her eyes downward to show there was more to her relationship with this man than she'd express at a sales counter.

"So what'll it be?"

She popped a finger to the corner of her mouth as if still perplexed by the conundrum.

"I'd better wait. The amount this hairdo cost me, I can't afford to ruin it."

The rep's eyes lifted to the heavens in despair or to glance at the nest on top of Mary Lou's head. Either way, she issued the ticket and Mary Lou jiggled her tush toward the departure gates.

With time to kill, she bought a coffee and sat down at a formica table. After she placed her holdall by her feet, she hugged her drink while keeping her clutch bag on her shoulder. The minute hand on her watch made its way round the dial like a hopped-out hippy. The first announcement from the public address broke Mary Lou's ennui.

She showed her boarding pass to anyone in a uniform who cared to look at it. Despite the hijackings that had taken place the past year or two, American airports had a relaxed attitude to who sat on their planes—even though US aircraft had been attacked. Mary Lou did not complain. This made her life so much easier. To take a pistol on board would be a nightmare if the x-ray security machines were used on everyone and not just with the men who looked like PLO members.

Once she had taken her seat, the plane taxied to the runway within five minutes of her getting comfy. The pilot had a plane to catch. Up in the air, a flick through four pages of the in-house magazine and the descent began.

An uneventful wait at LAX and soon she stood in line to board her LaGuardia flight. Mary Lou had bought two magazines at the news kiosk by the gate and hoped she could use the rest of her time stuck in the plane to relax and to focus her thoughts on any details in her plan she'd missed. The lack of a silencer was near the top of the list—and how to pick the right moment to tackle Pentangelo on his own.

Instead Mary Lou found her choice of a window seat was a poor one. A guy sat next to her who barely fit within the confines of his allotted space and felt the overwhelming urge to express his views to the world, using as loud a voice as humanly possible. She considered elbowing him in the larynx to shut him up, but realized she'd have to mount him to reach past the bulbous fat of his torso.

An hour into the flight and silence reigned—or rather there were silent moments in between his incessant snoring. At least his opinions remained inside him.

Mary Lou allowed her head to relax onto the back rest and she soaked in the calm. With her eyes closed, she contemplated Charlie Pentangelo's last day on Earth. Then darkness engulfed her, and she woke up with a judder and a start two hours later. Jack Blowhard was complaining about the food and his drink. The stewardess did her level best to stay cool under pressure, but Mary Lou could see the woman was about to lose it big time.

The waitress in an airline uniform called over the chief steward and Blowhard heard how his feedback was valued, and as it had been provided, they would take a note for future reference. For now, he needed to shut the fuck up and stop bothering them as they tried to get on with their jobs. Mary Lou paraphrased because, even if Jack wasn't listening, all the other passengers knew exactly what was being said.

As if proof were required that shouting loudly gets yourself heard, Blowhard was offered an upgrade to business class. With more reluctance than you might expect, he accepted the offer with the utmost disregard to anyone's feelings and comfort but his own. Five minutes later, he departed Mary Lou's life forever. She eyed the man sat on the other side of Blowhard, who appeared as relieved as she was to see the whale go.

Three hours later and the wheels touched down at LaGuardia. If Mary Lou had a plan, it was as well laid out as it would ever be.

NEW YORK'S DOMESTIC airport was as dirty and disgusting as Mary Lou remembered. LaGuardia held the unique accolade of being the most ugly monstrosity the Brutalist Movement could create. Like so many air transport facilities around the world, the filth and noise of the establishment attracted the worst elements of society—like flies to a midden.

She had spent too many years living in such surroundings to pay much attention to the lowlife scum swarming around her as she waited for a cab to take her into the city. Pan-handlers, smack-heads and winos vied for the money held by the recently disembarked. They were ignored or shouted at: this was New York City.

"To Wall Street and South."

Manhattan looked beautiful in the moonlight: the lights of the buildings twinkled as the taxi hurled itself over Queensboro Bridge. Mary Lou marveled at the skyscrapers, punching their way into the inky blackness above the Big Apple. Her first sight of the city of her childhood hopes. When she left home, she'd planned to head straight here, but one curve ball after anther sent her on a different path. Now she had arrived in the land of her dreams and it felt good.

The cab reached Manhattan and turned south onto Second Avenue, just past 59th Street. Every block felt as though the taxi moved from one world to another. The ghettos existed cheek by jowl with barely a sheet of cigarette paper between them. Down into single digit streets on the edge of the East Village and over Houston to Chrystie.

"Right on Delancey and left on Varick."

Mary Lou barked out her instruction because Little Italy loomed and she didn't want to take any risks. Better to spend an extra buck or two than get stuck in traffic and while away the minutes staring at Pentangelo's goons. Arnold's detailed mental map of the city was serving her well.

"Head to Liberty and then right onto Pearl. After that, you can go straight there."

"It's your dime, lady."

These were the first words the driver uttered since Mary Lou got in the cab. She was grateful he hadn't told her his life story or shared his world view on aliens or indigents.

When he pulled up at Water and South, Mary Lou rounded the fare up to the next dollar and exited the vehicle. She pretended to search in her clutch bag until the taxi drove off: she didn't want anyone to piece together her movements from airport to her lodgings. She sucked in gas fumes and then turned down Cuylers Alley to reach a quiet unobtrusive hotel.

The Roxboro was a family-owned affair, where decades old grandeur had made room to faded wallpaper, crumbling plasterwork and a musty aroma reminiscent of decay. A place where nobody cared what you did or who you were—provided you didn't trash the joint more than it was already trashed. Mary Lou would do well there.

She paid cash in advance to facilitate a rapid exit the next day and trudged up the stairs to reach her bedroom—that way she had time to check out her emergency exits, although she wasn't worried about hotel fires.

Up in her one room, Mary Lou closed the drapes so no one could see in. She locked the door and placed her pistol on the desk. Two minutes later, the revolver lay in pieces on the guest furniture and was reconstituted back into a deadly weapon in a matter of seconds. Mary Lou knew better than to check it more than once. If everything was fine, messing with the gun would do no good.

She removed her possessions from her bag and hung them up onto one of the two hangers supplied inside the flimsy wardrobe. Then a brief trip out to grab a slice of pizza and a soda then back to her room and a quick shower. Off to sleep with no bed clothes—perhaps she'd packed a bit too lightly. Within a minute, Mary Lou's snoring kicked off, but only the guy next door could hear her heavy breathing as he jerked himself off to what he thought was going on in her chamber.

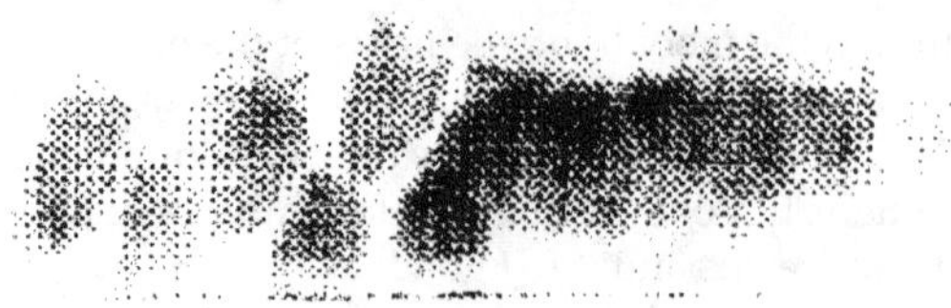

120

WHEN SHE WOKE up, Mary Lou rolled yesterday's clothes into a ball and shoved them into her carry bag. She considered wrapping the piece in the blouse, but decided against it. Life would be hard enough today without having to wrestle a revolver from the armhole of her top. She gritted her teeth and placed the cold steel inside the largest panties she owned, underpinned by a sanitary napkin. Then she slipped on a miniskirt and checked herself in the mirror. For the briefest of moments she convinced herself nobody would see the bulge protruding between her legs. She practiced walking from one side of the room to the other—a John Wayne impersonation playing in her head.

Finally, an uplift bra and a white blouse which was too tight. She had meant to throw it out, but had never got around to doing so. Good job: part of her plan rested on the goons staring more at her legs and boobs than at anything in between.

Down the stairs and out the door. Left out the alley entrance and back onto Wall Street. Everyone was too busy to spot a woman place an item of clothing in every trashcan she passed. May Lou's final deposit: the carry-on bag itself. She had no further use for it and besides, the damn thing would end up being a liability.

Once free of her refuse, Mary Lou headed uptown in case anyone followed her. When she reached William and Pine, she stopped and hailed a cab to Broadway and Broome. Then a walk five blocks east to arrive at the north side of Little Italy. Somewhere south lay her prey.

FIVE BLOCKS WIDE and three down, Little Italy had become the most intense and Sicilian location outside of Europe. Many people had emigrated from the Old Country, but the Sicilian dons were in charge. They were leaders back home and they had brought their power with them in their suitcases. Some were natural-born Americans, but they remained a breed apart: Italianamericans.

When Mary Lou sauntered south of Broome, she entered this foreign land with no passport, no experience of the place before and no knowledge of the local language. Armed with high heels, a short skirt and cleavage, she made her way down Mott Street and endured the catcalls and whistles from the neighborhood chimpanzees. When hands pinched her ass—or worse—she did her best to flick the fingers away with a hand as if they were annoying insects, even though all her instincts told her to stop and knee the fuckers in the balls.

But Mary Lou was not in this ghetto to fight for female emancipation: she was here to free Charlie Pentangelo from his mortal bonds. Instead she walked by the kerb as that meant the men could only attack her from one side—a cute ass wasn't worth getting run over for. Not even hers.

She crossed over Grande and turned right, back a block, until she reached Mulberry, the epicenter of the ghetto. Mary Lou knew that at the other end of this block was Charlie Pentangelo. Or rather, Arnold had told her Pentangelo's business was on the corner of Mulberry and Hester and that was one block away.

When she got within spit of Hester, she ducked into a cafe and ordered a coffee. The waiter leered at her and returned with the drink, using his reappearance as another excuse to stare at her cleavage. Mary Lou ignored his gaze and focused on the job at hand. She positioned herself at a table next to the glass frontage. This gave her an excellent vantage point to survey the street.

For an hour she sat and let the world go by. Couples holding hands wishing their lives away, businessmen pounding the sidewalk as they rushed to make more green. Housewives scooping brown bags in their arms, brimming with provisions. They all hustled past, but no one appeared of any interest to her.

On the other side of the street stood a restaurant and out front were four tables. Three were occupied and she saw a small upside down V-shaped notice at the empty setting. People came and went, but that table remained untouched. This absence was only a happy accident when Mary Lou first sat down, but now the lunch trade began to arrive and there was no obvious reason to hang onto prime real-estate unless it was reserved for someone special.

He arrived at twelve thirty along with two associates. How could she tell? One guy rested his haunches and the others stood, looking away just like guards do. The other clue was that these three fellas wore gray suits with a vest. The only dudes on the street sporting such attire: mob through and through.

She put her coffee back on its saucer and stared. Twenty seconds later and the waiter came forward and leered again.

"Is everything okay?"

Mary Lou nodded and let him beam down at her cleavage some more. His gaze was less important to her at this point than her keeping complete command of the vista before her. She rested her eyes on the main man as he placed his order and a glass of red wine was presented shortly after. Five minutes later and he tucked into what looked like a bowl of fettuccine.

While she froze in her seat, Mary Lou failed to notice a simple fact about the man chowing down on his pasta: his blond mane. Now she stared for an extended period, her attention drifted from his actions to the environment. Something was amiss, but she couldn't say what. Then it struck her—he was far too young to be a capo. And then the hair.

Her eyes flitted from one part of the street to the next as she realized she'd wasted so much time on the wrong person. Pentangelo might have gone straight past her and she wouldn't have seen. Damn. Goddam it!

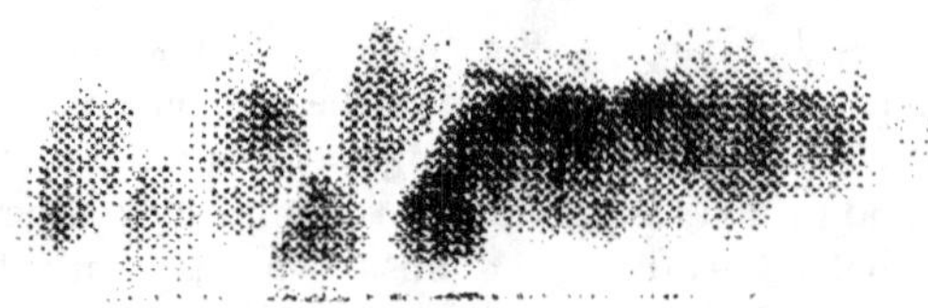

121

THE GRIM REALITY of her ruined time fell on Mary Lou's back and her shoulders slumped.

"You all right? You're looking mighty pale. Sure I can't get you something? Another coffee or a small grappa?"

"Huh? No, I'm fine, thanks. All I need is the check when you have a chance."

Calmness personified, Mary Lou left a five spot and walked out the cafe with one thing on her mind: to find Charlie Pentangelo. She waggled her tush along the sidewalk, hoping her presence as a stranger would be ignored in favor of her physical assets. And she wasn't wrong. The women looked straight through her and the men kept their minds on anything apart from her face—just how she wanted it.

Four storefronts further on Hester, Mary Lou stopped, opened her purse and pulled out a compact mirror and lipstick. For no obvious reason, she stared at her forehead, eyes, cheeks, lips and chin in the circular reflection. Then she put the objects back in her bag and removed a pack of cigarettes and a box of matches. After six, no seven, attempts, she kept the flame alight long enough to ignite the end of her smoke. A deep inhalation and she continued down Hester.

Anyone who knew her in Manhattan would have known what she was really up to. Mary Lou was certain Pentangelo was based within one or two buildings from the corner of Hester and Mulberry— unless Arnold was misinformed. As she'd gone so far west, she reckoned Pentangelo must have been behind her. The mirror proved her right. Like all great capos, he was flanked by two well-dressed goons and sported a gray flannel suit with the jacket nuzzling defiantly around his shoulders.

By messing about with her cigarette, she gave him enough time to overtake her. Then they played cat-and-mouse along the sidewalk as he crossed there and back, grabbing an orange off a stall and talking with a storekeeper a little further on. All the while, his two gorillas stood only three feet away from him.

As she and Arnold thought: there was no way to plug him and flee the scene without getting a slug from one or both heavies. When they walked past, she noticed the bulge in their jacket pockets, reflecting the exact position of their revolvers. They'd be high caliber—massive power to be unleashed with a thunderous clap.

They continued along Hester until Pentangelo headed south onto Baxter. Mary Lou kept walking in case the goons were getting twitchy. When she reached the far side, she turned south remaining on the opposite sidewalk for two hundred feet. The three men stopped and Pentangelo spoke in hushed tones. His mouth was inches from their ears: nobody would hear his instructions other than the intended recipient.

They nodded and one walked back north. The other stayed with Pentangelo as he disappeared into a doorway. Mary Lou wanted to follow straight inside, but she knew she had to deal with the pinstripe gorilla first. There was no point entering the lion's den if an army was about to be brought in behind her.

Instead, she leaned against a building window as if she was feeling faint, but this was New York so nobody came to help. She watched Pinstripe retrace his steps back to the corner and then he stopped, planted his feet into the paving slabs and waited.

He made everybody walk round him—he plain didn't care. And he was sufficiently well known by most locals that they shifted away from him before they needed to. The man's reputation preceded him.

What was he doing? Who was he waiting for? Two minutes later and the mystery was resolved: a woman appeared holding a bunch of flowers—white, purple and an unusual shade of brown. The goon put his hand in his pocket and pulled out a roll of green. Far too big an amount to be carrying on the New York streets but that didn't seem to be bother him. Cash handed over, he took ownership of the blooms and headed into Pentangelo's building.

Mary Lou waited a short while before making any move. The last thing she needed was to go through the front door only to be met by Pentangelo and his gorillas coming straight out. So doing nothing was the best option, but this wasn't one of Mary Lou's strengths. Her desire to get the job done gnawed at her stomach, but she held firm and made sure her feet remained glued to the sidewalk.

She tried counting slowly to ten, but that took only a few seconds. Another cigarette and she let it burn through without one inhalation. That was five minutes clear and she could wait no longer. A uniform cop walked his beat past her and she waited some more for him to make his way down the street. When he was four hundred feet away, she jaywalked over to Pentangelo's entrance.

Now the first decision of significance for the assassination of Charlie Pentangelo. To go in the front or take a different route inside? Every instinct told her to follow the plan and walk straight in, but part of her wanted sneak round the back and get in some other way.

Arnold's words echoed in her head: they won't suspect a pretty broad with a sob story. Anyone else will be met with a hail of bullets. That sealed Mary Lou's fate as she strode to the front door and pushed it aside, entering the foyer in one swift motion. No matter what happened later, there was no turning back.

MARY LOU SQUINTED in the half-light, trying to get a feel for the first floor interior. To her right, immediately next to the entrance, were a row of mailboxes. The lobby was unassuming and small: only twenty feet by twenty. An elevator door, paired brown to match the walls, stood facing her and to the right was a sign showing the stairs.

The elevator system was modeled on an art déco design with a dial containing numbers from one to six and a needle pointing at the digit representing each floor. As Mary Lou examined the dial, she witnessed the arrow leave number four and start its return to one. She braced herself and sprinted for the stairs. No sooner was she hidden behind the stairwell door than the elevator opened to reveal… nobody.

The cockroach by her feet heard Mary Lou exhale and she returned to the lobby. The insect scurried back into a dark hole in the skirting. She stood in front of the open bronze door, sighed and stepped inside. A finger pressed 'four' and the doors slid shut. Several deep gulps of air and she clutched the strap of her bag. The next minute would dictate the shape of the rest of her life.

A whir and a clunk as the machinery weaved its magic spell and hauled Mary Lou up to the fourth floor as she undid another button on her blouse. The box juddered to a halt and screamed open to reveal an ordinary corridor with small apartments scattered behind the row of doors before her. The two gorillas stood either side of a particular doorway and Mary Lou knew she'd found her quarry.

She shimmied over to the nearest gorilla and looked up at him. As she approached, his eyes bore down on her breasts and upper legs and—against her will—a warmth spread across her cheeks. While she was annoyed with herself for reacting that way, she understood how it played well for her conversation with him.

"Excuse me, but I need to speak with Mr. Pentangelo."

"Do you, missy?"

"Yessir. It's on a mighty delicate matter."

Mary Lou sent her eyes downwards and she placed her free hand on her belly, immediately over her rose tattoo. She stroked it twice and left it on her stomach, implying there was something beneath her palm she needed to keep safe.

Now it was the gorilla's turn to change to a shade of red and he looked at his colleague, who'd been stood on the other side of the doorway and had observed everything, but without moving one iota of his body.

"Is he expecting you?"

Mary Lou sashayed over to the other guy and ensured she straightened her back when she halted within two feet of him to afford him the maximum opportunity to eye up her cleavage. The strategy worked because the next four seconds he said nothing and just stared. During this enormous gulf of time, the first gorilla ogled from the side. His gaze burned the sides of her breasts and the point on her thigh where her miniskirt ended. All part of the plan, but it still made her feel dirty, used and then angry—very much not part of the plan. To succeed, she must play the game cool. Cool as an ice cube.

She shifted weight from one foot to the other and that gave both gorillas another opportunity to enjoy the view some more. Mary Lou picked off some imaginary fluff from the gorilla's jacket and smiled at him, feigning nerves.

"Do you think I can see him?"

"You haven't answered our question."

"Huh? What's a girl to do? I'm so confused."

"An appointment. Do you have one?"

Mary Lou detected an edge to his voice, like suspicions were growing inside his pea-sized brain. Stay calm. Stay cold.

"I'm afraid not. You see, I've just received some shocking news and I came straight round to seek help. And justice."

As she uttered the last two words, she put her hand back on her stomach and implied a connection between the baby in her belly and some wrongdoing. Had she drawn enough dots for this lunk to see the implicit picture she painted?

Perhaps her nervousness was conspiring against her, but at that precise moment, Mary Lou noticed a shifting of the steel touching her groin. If that snub nose moved any more then it would land on the floor and she'd be dead in less than three seconds.

Good news was that her genuine anxiety played right into her hand. The two goons huddled and whispered to each other for half a minute.

"Wait here."

The one she had first spoken to took her shoulder and pushed her back to the other side of the corridor. A firm but gentle move. No aggression or anger: she wasn't a perceived threat. The pistol shifted again and some piece of metal cut into her flesh. Mary Lou gritted her teeth and hoped this would all end soon. Like real fast.

The other goon opened the apartment door and slithered inside. She leaned against the wall and pushed one knee in front of the other to appear coquettish and to change position and shift the revolver to a more comfortable location. Mary Lou made sure she didn't make eye contact with the dude. A woman in her state would be too embarrassed to look this guy directly at him.

A painful minute stretched to eternity as they waited in silence for a decision from the high priest inside. Finally, the door opened and the goon slithered back out.

"You're in luck. He'll listen to what you have to say."

"Oh thanks."

"I done nothing, lady. It is the big man eating his lunch, you should thank."

"Now we gotta search you. It's the rules, see?"

A lascivious grin took over the first gorilla's expression as he stepped one pace toward her. Mary Lou knew this moment would come and braced herself for its passing.

Plump fingers fumbled over her sides and lingered on her breasts far too long, but she said and did nothing. Much worse had happened to her in the past and if she survived being frisked, then she'd get to Pentangelo. Those sweaty hands stopped mauling her chest and continued on their journey to her stomach and then made their way to her back. This meant he stepped inches from her face so he could reach and she inhaled his stale breath.

Last, he kneeled down with his head by her groin and patted down her legs. Right one first, working from her foot up past the hem of her skirt. Her muscles tensed slightly and his grin appeared to tighten on his face some more. Five inches further and she knew he'd touch the steel of her piece.

Then the fingers swapped legs and he stroked the inside of her thighs before heading to her left foot. All the while, she said nothing and let him find what little pleasure he could in what Mary Lou hoped would be the final minutes of his life.

"She's clean."

"Not that clean or she wouldn't be seeking a meet with Charlie."

Both men laughed and, for a second, acted as though she wasn't there. Then one opened the door for her and Mary Lou entered the lion's den.

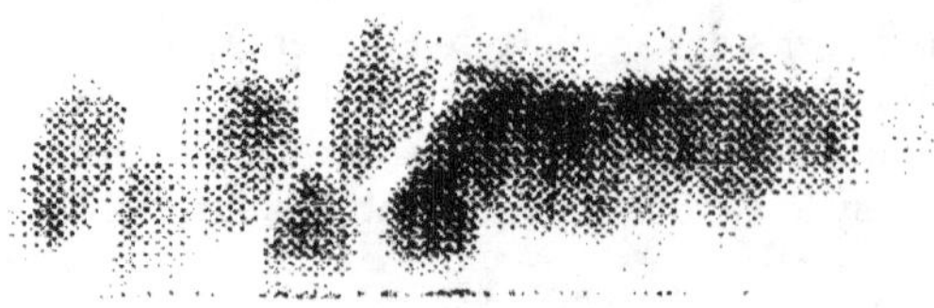

122

ARNOLD STRAPPED HIMSELF into that sweatbox of a car for four more hours. He convinced himself that taking too many breaks would just delay the arrival time, but halfway through and the sweltering heat became too much to bear and he forced the vehicle to park outside a nondescript diner.

There was little to speak of inside either, but Arnold selected a booth underneath a ceiling fan and ordered a jug of water with a glass of ice—and a bite to eat. When the steak and fries arrived, he asked for a coffee too. No matter how hot he felt on the outside, he knew the brew would refresh him. There was nothing like a steaming cup of Java.

He hit the head and walked back to his car, wiped the sweat off the driver's seat and stepped inside. Within seconds he was as drenched as before he entered Dexy's Diner.

"Fucking Californian highways."

Arnold's foot hit the gas and he carried on towards his least favorite city in America. Why LA? It had no heart—there was nowhere you could be in the middle. Just an endless series of ghettos interspersed by nothing. And if that wasn't bad enough: there was Hollywood. The immense wealth surrounded by an ocean of poverty. He was no Communist, but he didn't think people should earn that much money without breaking into a sweat—like he did.

Twenty years before, he'd have been a member of Murder Inc, the mob outfit that resolved all family conflict. They were paid a good wage, but nothing too crazy. As a gun for hire, he commanded an A-list fee for his services—and earned every penny. The reason his clientele kept coming back for more was that he knew how to handle himself in times of trouble and he was a ruthless murderer.

The outskirts of LA came into view and Arnold stopped at a diner. Straight to the washroom to freshen up and a change of shirt from the trunk. Next he headed off to the Watts district in the south and into the center of Mendoza's territory.

He parked in the first lot he came to—the advantage of using a false name on a car rental. If he never saw the damn thing would be a day too soon. Arnold vowed to himself an empty promise: to not be so cheap the next time he drove cross country.

A walk around the nearby blocks revealed the hopelessness of the local youth. They had few options: leave to find their American dream away from their friends or join a gang. Most chose the latter and any who took the first route were long gone.

Inside a dive bar, Arnold hugged a beer and waited. He knew he'd promised Mary Lou to get the job done today, but his vast experience told him it might take several days to find Mendoza. He kept his ears open and his mouth shut, allowing everyone to ignore this stranger in town. The trick was to choose a table near the counter but not to sit on a highchair, because you were bound to steal the silently reserved seat of a local barfly.

Arnold sat, sipped and waited. His patience was rewarded in less than three hours when two dudes grabbed a brew each and talked. As the height of the beer reduced in their glasses, conversation moved onto the day's affairs—instead of pissing and moaning about their women.

"Sancho's got a bee up his ass."

"Any reason?"

"Trouble in Palm Springs."

"What went down?"

"Murder and mayhem from what I've heard. He's on the warpath—demanding heads on plates."

While most would think this chance encounter was way too unlikely to happen within Arnold's earshot, he hadn't picked the venue at random. Roach was well aware the Crew Inn was the Mendoza gang's bar of choice for a late lunchtime drink: he'd dropped a dime when he first reached town. The only thing left to do was to figure out the man's location. Arnold sipped and waited for the golden nugget.

Sure enough, less than one beer later, the men had spilled Mendoza's hole in the ground. Although he was planning to hit the mattresses as soon as he could, he'd done the rounds of his main labs before sending out his goons to wreak merry revenge on Mary Lou and Milton.

Arnold remained in his seat even though he needed no more from the men. He'd learned not to make himself visible when doing nothing could help him vanish into the ether. If no one saw him leave, then chances were that he was never drinking at the Crew Inn at all. Roach spent his life ensuring he had no witnesses to report on his whereabouts to the cops or to the mob. This helped him stay alive despite his vocation.

Fifteen minutes after the two men left, he stood up and exited the bar. It was time to pay Mendoza a little visit.

ARNOLD CHECKED THE address twice and stared at the house in front of him. The right place for sure. He continued past the corner plot to see how many guys were protecting the joint. Two on each side and an unknown number in the backyard. Plus an even bigger quantity inside—they were processing heroin and Mendoza was not a one-man band.

He carried on walking up a block until he figured the goons stopped looking at him. Then he leaned against a tree and took stock of the situation. The chances of Mendoza being indoors were very high. The probability of Roach getting in the building, killing Mendoza and exiting safely was exceedingly low. So he needed to not think about how to get in, but should concentrate on what to do until Mendoza came out.

From his vantage point, Arnold had a good view of the exit routes from the house, so he could react quickly whenever Mendoza appeared. The issue he had now was that an ordinary Joe doesn't hang near a tree for hours in the Watts district of South LA. No civilian would dream of doing something that stupid. He'd need some camouflage if he didn't want to be spotted.

Squatting in a bush was not Arnold's style and he looked round the vicinity for inspiration. While the street was residential, not every house was occupied if the boarded-up windows were anything to go by. Arnold counted buildings and walked away from his tree and went to the back of the houses on the other side of the road to Mendoza's.

A property diagonally opposite the target had windows made of either broken glass or wooden beams. The chances of any legitimate occupiers was low, but he was still careful as he jimmied open the back door using a piece of metal lying in the backyard.

Inside was dark due to the boarded-up windows and Arnold wasn't stupid enough to flip a switch. The art of surveillance was to see but not be seen. To watch and not be noticed. Ideally, you should be able to take a clean shot at a target and get away, but Arnold was less sure this was the right location for the hit itself. He might be completely hidden, but there were a lot of fellas on the other side of the street. All way too close for comfort.

He stumbled his way to the front of the house and struggled to view the staircase well enough to know the upstairs floorboards were safe. Not wishing to take any unnecessary risks, Arnold found his way to a front room with two rectangular windows. One was filled with wood and nails and the other was a gaping hole where glass once lived.

Arnold hunkered down so his head was at the height of the base of the window: his eyes could see out but almost all of his body was hidden by the brick wall. A perfect spot. He glanced at his watch and saw it was nearly two. Chances were Mendoza wouldn't show until evening. Arnold wished he'd eaten something before coming over here. He felt ill-prepared for the afternoon's wait. He cupped his hands and lit a smoke, just as soldiers did in the trenches back in the day.

The second hour was always the easiest, he found. Arnold took a while to get comfortable and not notice the conditions surrounding him. Only then did he occupy the right headspace to last a tedious amount of time.

He twisted his wrist so he could view the face of his watch. Nearly four and nada. Another stare out the window. The goons out front had swapped with fellas from inside about thirty minutes before and that was the only excitement since Arnold had sat down. If this was a normal day's business then Arnold would have contained his impatience. Almost all his working life was spent sitting and doing nothing.

This time things were different: there was no payoff, only revenge. But this wasn't his vengeance— he was merely the agent of death. Arnold knew the real difference was that now he cared. Mendoza deserved to die for kidnapping the twins. Just not right to steal children because a drug meet didn't go his way.

Times were changing—for the worse. He couldn't decide if it was the immense profit that came from the white powder which caused bad decisions or if the caliber of fella was going downhill, anyway. Probably a mix of the two: easy money can be made if you're able to get bankrolled. And a fast buck attracts the wrong dude to the business. It spirals from there, he mused.

As these ideas permeated his thoughts, Arnold continued to stare out the window. The front door opened a crack and three men appeared. Two were dressed like locals but the one in the middle had a three piece suit and wore an air of superiority: Sancho Mendoza—kiddy kidnapper.

Arnold stayed put until he was certain which route they intended to take. Then he slithered out the back and caught up with them, remaining a safe four hundred feet behind at all times. He lost count how many blocks they walked down but he had to catch himself because they stopped. Looked like a restaurant and Mendoza went in, leaving one guy at the front entrance. Arnold guessed the other went to the rear to secure the venue without having to cramp Mendoza's appetite while he ate.

He lit another cigarette and eyeballed the joint before making his move. He walked up to the place and entered, careful not to brush past the goon waiting for Mendoza. For someone whose job was to keep Mendoza out of harm's way, the guy failed at his first opportunity to earn his wages for the day.

Roach, professional assassin, took a table ten feet from him and ordered a steak. He was hungry and after he murdered Mendoza, he'd have no time for food until he had left the city. And he wasn't prepared to wait that long.

123

LINGUINE, POSSIBLY WITH clams, was plonked in front of Mendoza. He tucked his napkin into his shirt collar and stuffed pasta into his mouth. Before Arnold had time to chew more than a handful of bites, Mendoza's bowl was empty and he mopped up any remaining sauce with pieces of bread. He almost looked Italian.

Arnold glared at his steak and raised his gaze to keep watch on Mendoza. A bus boy removed the dish and two minutes later, a waiter delivered a dessert menu, which his prey perused and threw down. He couldn't tell if he would have time to finish his meal or rush out the door with his stomach more or less empty and Mendoza very much alive and back surrounded by his protection detail.

The answer came from a moment's conversation with the waiter and the subsequent delivery of a cup of coffee and some cutlery. Arnold breathed easy and set about attacking the meat waiting under his nose. It was on the chewy side and if he hadn't been working, he'd have sent it back. The fries were okay and the ketchup helped him swallow the gristle served alongside them.

A portion of apple pie with a miniature jug of cream was delivered to Mendoza, who drowned the pastry with the white liquid. Here was a man who did not eat for pleasure, just for fuel. Arnold finished picking at his steak and asked for a coffee and the check. That way he could leave whenever he needed without making a scene or having to rush.

As he sipped the hot colored water, Roach saw Mendoza for what he was: a street punk made good, funded by the mob, but with no style to call his own—another goon in an ill-fitting suit, selling dreams down the river in small packets containing a little brown powder.

The three-piece stood and headed to the back of the restaurant. For a second, Arnold panicked because he thought Mendoza was leaving. A glance at the table showed a bill with no payment. Either he was pulling a fast one—unlikely—or he was about to hit the head.

Arnold got up, making sure he'd left a big enough tip—not so generous for him to be remembered and not so tight to be recalled when the cops came calling. Twenty per cent and not a penny more. He wended his way around and past all the tables until he faced a corridor with a pair of signs: men and women. He opened the right-hand door and stepped inside.

The cramped room comprised a urinal, sinks and a pair of cubicles. Mendoza stood next to another guy at the urinal and both doors to the cubicles were ajar. Arnold waited as though a cubicle was an inappropriate place to take a piss. When the civilian finished, Arnold stepped up, barely two feet away from his target.

He ensured his head remained pointing at the wall in front, but Arnold kept his eyes fixed on Mendoza all the time. The man's hands stayed by his groin until the trickling sound abated, the usual jiggling and Arnold heard the zip go up.

Like every man before him, Mendoza turned his back on Arnold as he vacated his position at the urinal. And that was when Arnold Roach struck.

He used one hand to punch Mendoza in a kidney and the other to grab his mouth and yank the head backward. Mendoza lost his footing for a moment, due to the surprise of the attack, but had the presence of mind—or pure instinct—to reach up and cling onto Roach's arm as it reduced his supply of oxygen.

In response, Roach gave him another punch—this time in the small of his back—before moving the fist to Mendoza's face and pinching his nose. He scrambled with both arms flailing, hoping to catch Arnold out or get some purchase on a limb. Roach held firm and pushed his feet into the tiled floor. Then he raised both hands two inches so Mendoza was forced to go on tiptoe to breathe.

That was Roach's mistake, because Mendoza used the opportunity to kick back with a heel into his leg. Despite himself, Roach released him and Mendoza spun round, fists punching. One thump landed on the side of Roach's head, right by the ear, and he stumbled before regaining his balance. Mendoza ran for the door, aware that help was only a few feet away.

Roach slammed his arm into the back of Mendoza's skull, causing it to ricochet into a cubicle door. The three-piece turned round, blood dripping from his forehead and left cheek. He lunged at Roach, who sidestepped and let him crash to the floor. A swift boot to the groin and Roach picked up Mendoza by the lapels, punched him in the mouth and dragged him to the sinks. With one hand grasping a bunch of hair, Roach pummeled Mendoza's face into a faucet. He screamed briefly but Roach continued until the body fell limp.

He dropped the corpse on the floor, bent down to check the pulse and listened hawk-like for any movement outside. Nothing apart from the clatter of plates and customer conversation.

Roach dragged Mendoza's body into a cubicle, forcing limbs and torso into the narrow confines. He closed the door, allowing the body to fall forward, preventing anyone from discovering the cubicle's dark secret. Roach kicked a hand back under, which was sticking out from the front. He grabbed some towels and attempted to clean up the red mess he'd generated. He checked himself in the bathroom mirror, straightened his tie and tucked his shirt into his pants.

As he made his way through the restaurant, Arnold stopped by Mendoza's table and threw some green down. That way, staff would be even less inclined to go searching as they'd assume he'd paid and went. Or they would hold that belief until someone wanted to have a shit.

He pushed open the front door just as Mendoza's gorilla walked inside. Perhaps his boss had spent longer than normal. Maybe Arnold was paranoid. Either way, he turned left and sauntered down the block, knowing that Sancho Mendoza slept with the fishes.

DOWN THE STREET and Arnold only heard his own footsteps. The echoes engulfed him as he focused on concentrating on not being noticed. Although he had yet to see behind him, Arnold sensed there was something wrong in the state of California.

He pricked up his ears and thought he discerned the clip-clop of leather shoes. Arnold paused, bent down to pretend to tie a shoelace and took a quick look at what was happening. The footsteps had just been a businessman, hot on his heels.

About a block away, Arnold spotted one gorilla hurrying toward him. A second glance revealed the other gorilla four hundred feet behind his colleague. He swallowed hard and picked up the pace, hanging left to cross the street. His jaywalking did nothing and the two fellas kept on coming.

Walking, walking and almost forming a trot, Arnold hurried along the sidewalk, ducking and diving, left and right, hoping to shake his tail. But they remained on his six.

Up ahead, an alleyway and Arnold strode into it and hid behind a municipal dumpster. He squatted and waited, still able to see people passing by the end of the alley. First one gorilla, then ten seconds later, the other fella. He stayed a further twenty seconds, but he had to know if he was free and clear.

Arnold peeked round the corner, gun in hand, but all he saw was a sea formed from the backs of heads. He stood up to get a better view and realized he'd been spotted. The two guys were waiting for him half a block ahead. He reversed into the alley, back pressed against the wall. Think. Think goddamn it!

The alley made an L-shape and the entrance contained the dumpster, some boxes and general waste along with some wooden pallets. He had no idea what was around the corner. Arnold had a handful of seconds to decide and threw himself under the pallets, covering himself with whatever crap he could grab. He lay under there, inhaling the stink, for a lifetime.

After a minute he saw a pair of shoes between the ground and the lowest slat of the pallet lying on top of him. They remained there for four, maybe five, seconds and carried on deeper into the alley. Arnold held his breath and tried to break the laws of Physics by remaining as still as a corpse, while moving his arm to get a clear shot. No can do. By the time his hand was in position, the footwear had gone left and taken their owner further down the alley.

Another minute and no one new had appeared and the first fella hadn't returned. Arnold tried to wait longer, but his overwhelming desire for survival drove him to act. He slithered out from under the pallets. No-show on his man, so he padded over to the corner to see what the dude was up to. Answer: pissing against a wall. Unfortunately for Arnold, he couldn't make it two-for-two as the fella finished before he had a chance to shoot him in the back of the head.

Instead a slug to the heart did the job and the guy crumpled to the ground. He checked the entrance to the alley, but no one was coming. No one had even heard the shot ring out with the din of the traffic. He scurried over to the body, two fingers on the carotid to verify it was a corpse, then he pulled out the wallet and grabbed the green.

Arnold didn't waste time hiding the fella because he wasn't visible from the street anyway. Would take days before even a hobo found the carcass—and by then everyone would know about the hit on Mendoza and do the math.

Back on the main drag, Arnold peered as far ahead as he could, but the other fella was nowhere. Part of him wanted to find and kill the dude and the rest yearned to run away. The chances of the goon remembering his face was low, but non-zero: a decision made. He had to get to the guy before the gorilla got to him—or a payphone.

Arnold figured the best he could do was keep going in the last direction the fella was walking and take it from there—knowing all the while, the guy might jump him at any moment. There's a skill to walking along a sidewalk with the utmost caution while appearing not to have a care in the world. Arnold was a pro.

Three blocks later and the crowd thinned out, giving him a chance to see further ahead. One block up, he recognized the hairstyle of his prey. An increase in pace and he was only two hundred feet behind.

The fella stopped and lit a smoke. Had he made Arnold? Difficult to say. It was a classic move—he'd done it himself that same morning—but the dude might just be a smoker. He pretended to stare at a storefront for five seconds and carried on walking. Without breaking his pace for a moment, he blinked hard because the guy had vanished. Out the blue. Gone. Nada.

He placed a hand on his gun, which he'd put in his pants pocket and took off the safety. He knew the feel of every inch of that piece and achieved the task without blowing his balls clean off. Arnold slowed as he reached the next corner. He headed to the kerb to have the maximum angle as he turned left past the building.

As the new street appeared in his field of vision, so did the fella, who was standing feet apart, gun in hand, aiming directly at him. They both fired at each other at exactly the same time and the guy crashed to his knees. Arnold felt the zing of a bullet and a burning heat in his chest. Then blackout.

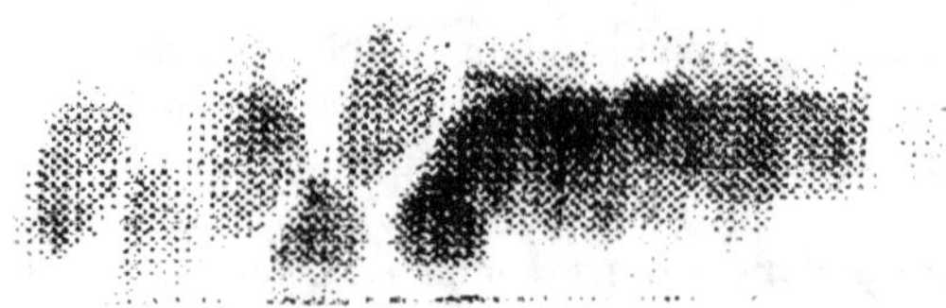

124

AS MARY LOU entered the hallway, she noticed it was festooned with family photographs, young and old, groups and solos. She ignored the blood ties connecting Charles Pentangelo. She didn't care.

A glass door in front of her revealed a mix of colors beyond, but no discernable shapes. She hesitated for a second and pushed it open. The living room contained an array of couches, easy chairs and coffee tables. The red-patterned wallpaper dragged the space down to the size of a postage stamp. At the far end was an eight seat dining table. A man sat with his back to her while the slurping noise of pasta sauce echoed round the apartment. The sound of washing up emanated from a kitchen to the left.

As soundlessly as possible, Mary Lou bent her knees and shoved her hand past her rose and into her panties. Three seconds later, she held her snub nose and had thrown the sanitary napkin to the floor. She flipped off the safety with her thumb. Two hands gripped the gun, arms straight in front as she prepared to take the kill shot.

Pentangelo turned his head ten degrees to the right and she threw both hands behind her back, one finger remaining on the trigger. Without a word, he beckoned her nearer with first and second fingers waving in her direction. The clattering of pans continued in the kitchen and she discerned the sound of running water. A woman's voice hummed to herself.

Keeping her head bowed, she stepped forward until she was ten feet away from the man who ordered the death of her husband and sanctioned her children's kidnapping. Although her overwhelming urge was to fill his brains full of lead, the second part of the plan was for her to escape in one piece.

Mary Lou needed to assess the danger in the kitchen and plug the guy so the gorillas outside didn't suspect a thing. That way, she could walk right past them and vanish on the wide sidewalks of Little Italy.

SHE WAITED TO see what he would do. Without turning his head any further, Pentangelo continued slurping his linguini.

"Come nearer, my dear, so you can tell me your story. My associate tells me you have traveled on a sad path to arrive at my home."

"This is true, Signor Pentangelo."

She let out a tiny sob and ceremonially stepped up a pace, one foot after the other, heels returning next to each other. Second step, then the third. Pentangelo sensed her approach and held out a hand, limp, for her to kiss it—out of respect.

Mary Lou touched the fingers and planted her lips on his cygnet ring. A blood-red ruby set in gold. She thought she would throw up, but she resumed her position, averting her gaze lest the mighty capo incurred any displeasure. The bubbly slurps showed he was relaxed and hungry.

"I met this boy."

"There is always a boy. What is his name and how old is he?"

"Frankie and he's only a few years older than me."

Pentangelo raised an eye to her to gauge her age. This was the first time he'd taken a proper look at her since she'd entered his home. Mary Lou watched his eyes rest on her breasts. This beast of a man was the same as all the others. His brains lived in his dick. He breathed deep gasps of air, and then he resumed his chewing.

"And what happened with this Frankie?"

"We fell in love and he wanted more."

"More?"

"More than I was prepared to give him, at least before we were married."

Pentangelo dropped his fork and spoon into his bowl. Mary Lou tensed, shifting her weight onto the balls of her feet, ready to pounce.

"He dishonored you?"

She let out another sob for an answer to his old-fashioned question. His body was in America but his soul stayed in Sicily.

"Motherfucker."

This word was whispered by one of them, but Mary Lou was unsure if it had been her or him. She could take no chances and knew he had sensed a change in her body language. He swiveled round in his chair just as she took the butt of the pistol and slammed it into the back of his head.

His face hit the pasta bowl, which broke into pieces, and he pushed himself off to snatch at her. Bits of ceramic stuck to his forehead and cheek as he lunged at her, trying to grab at her throat but finding only air. She put the barrel of the snub nose onto Pentangelo's lips, causing him to stop in his tracks. She hissed at him, sulfurous words spat at him, a living embodiment of pure hate.

"My name is Mary Lou Lagotti and you will never forget it. So. Long. As. You. Live."

His eyes remained quizzical and fearful. Then a flicker of recognition and the same orbits widened in understanding and acknowledgement. She pushed the barrel between his teeth and into his mouth. Now he could only breathe through his nose. Small bubbles appeared at his nostrils and she enjoyed hearing him pant his short gasps.

"You finished yet, Charlie?"

A muffled voice from the kitchen. Mary Lou assumed the woman had been a cook, but the familiarity of the question meant she must be his wife.

"Will she come in here?"

Mary Lou's spittle landed on an eyelid, but Pentangelo's expression showed he had no clue. He glanced at the door and back to Mary Lou.

"Don't..."

"I don't care about your wife. If she stays out of my business, I'll stay out of hers."

His widened eyes relaxed slightly and a tear departed his right eye. He gulped. They both heard the squeak of the doorknob as Mary Lou squeezed the trigger. With all the stress of getting into the apartment, she had forgotten about not having a silencer.

Charlie Pentangelo's body flung itself onto the floor, blood splatter landed on the ground before the corpse arrived, and also hit the dining room table and the red wallpaper behind. There was no need for a second shot and Mary Lou knew this before the capo hit the deck. She moved her arm a quarter turn to face the kitchen.

A woman's hand reached out the door and Charlie's wife stood there, staring at his carcass. She pissed herself immediately and remained still, whimpering.

"Go into that kitchen and stay there for ten minutes. If you come out before then, I'll fucking kill you too. Capiche?"

The frightened mass nodded and slunk back, shutting the door behind her and began sobbing as soon as the door shut. She hurried to the hallway and listened for the gorillas. Despite the retort of the revolver, they hadn't moved from their positions. She peeked out the fish eye to make certain: nothing. For the first time since she entered the apartment, Mary Lou heard the radio blasting an opera. How had she not noticed? It didn't matter. What counted was getting out here alive. She checked herself in the mirror and opened the front door.

125

WITH THE REVOLVER in her clutch bag, Mary Lou smiled at the two men, both of whom had their arms crossed and stared at her, eyes darting between her cleavage and thighs. She couldn't help feeling as though they were comparing her skirt before and after, but she convinced herself this was paranoia on her part.

"Everything sorted, little lady?"

Mary Lou glanced downwards as if embarrassed by what had transpired in the apartment.

"Yes, thank you. I'll be able to sleep easy tonight."

"Pentangelo is a miracle worker."

"He sure has set my mind at ease. The man knows how to make a girl smile inside."

"Certainly does."

The speaking gorilla winked at his silent partner, who replied with a dirty grin. Mary Lou stepped over to the elevator and pressed the down button. While she waited, she moved sideways so she could continue to hypnotize the man with her breasts. It worked and the longer she stood there, the more engrossed they became. When the doors eventually opened, the nearest gorilla popped his head inside and selected the lobby for her. He seized the opportunity to place a hand on her ass before removing himself from the elevator.

Using all her self-control, Mary Lou smiled at him as the doors shut and she felt the jolt of the descending mechanism. She stood in the lobby to check it wasn't going straight back up to the gorillas. Then she popped round to the stairwell to listen for footsteps. Silence—apart from the tiny scuttling of cockroaches and other bugs.

Out the front door and a flick of her head backwards. On the street, Mary Lou strode four long blocks west until she reached Mercer and Grand. Then she hopped a cab to Fifth Avenue and scurried into the first women's boutique she found. She grabbed a pair of black slacks and a cream blouse. Brown jacket. All paid with cash.

To not draw attention to herself, she walked north half a block and went into a different shop to try on any random garment. When she left the changing rooms, her old clothes were in the shopping bag. The purchased items were draped on her body. Mary Lou sauntered along one of New York's most famous roads until she reached a trashcan. She threw in her skirt and kept on going. Each trashcan she came across ended up containing an additional object from her bags. After five blocks, the bags were empty and, at the next trashcan, Mary Lou dumped them too.

Another taxi ride took her to Wall Street and she disposed of some pieces of her gun. Two more blocks trudged and Mary Lou got rid of the rest of the revolver. Over Broadway and waited at the corner of Trinity and Rector for a cab to take her to LaGuardia.

She kept her eyes on the road in the hope of willing a taxi to appear, but this was New York and not Hicksville, Tennessee. Before long, the periphery of her vision filled with possible goons. Even though she had been extraordinarily careful, the fear of getting caught hung over her imagination.

"I hope Arnold is doing okay."

A shiver ran down her spine as she imagined Sancho Mendoza still breathing. She twisted her head right, then left. A suit on the other side of the street was looking at her funny. Had he made her? Did she recognize him, even? Don't think so and no—in that order. A woman brushed past her and crossed the road to meet him. Paranoia. Focus on getting a cab.

Half a block south, on her side of the street, a man sauntered toward her. Mary Lou thought something was hickey, but couldn't be sure. As he approached, she noticed a lump in his jacket breast pocket. Four hundred feet… three hundred. He raised his arm and shoved his hand into the bulge. Mary Lou couldn't take the chance and turned around to walk away. Headed west and picked up the pace, ducking into the entrance of an apartment building. He was still behind her. Nearer now, so he'd increased speed too.

She'd been so careful. Where had this fella come from? No time for that. She ran west until she reached the end of the block. Why had she been so stupid to jettison her only gun? As she sprinted round the corner, he was a mere hundred feet behind. Man, that guy can cover the ground.

A taxi was kerb side and an elderly woman closed the door. It flipped its hire light on and Mary Lou leaped inside.

"Drive, goddamn it!"

The cabbie needed no further instructions: this was downtown Manhattan. As they sped away, she watched out of the rear window and saw the guy stop to catch his breath. She blinked and he was gone.

"LaGuardia. Pronto."

The battered vehicle bumped up a gear, snapped into a pothole, and bounced its way to the airport. In the back of the cab, Mary Lou checked herself and applied some lipstick. This part of the journey should be simple, she had thought, but now they could get to her anywhere in the city. They'd acted so fast. Perhaps the wife had rushed out before her time was up.

As soon as she clutched the plane ticket in her hand, Mary Lou ran to the bathroom and hid in a cubicle until the final minute before boarding. When the announcement for the last call came over the public address, she left the safety of her cubicle and joined the throng—careful to remain on the edge of the crowd. Always checking out every face, every person, who looked like they might be on her flight.

Her stress only abated when the pilot instructed the stewardesses to set the doors to automatic. Even then, she clung to the inflight magazine, but didn't read a single word. Twenty minutes in and the only way to gain any peace of mind was to walk up and down the aisles and assess all the passengers. Everyone seemed clean, so she relaxed and tried to get some rest until Palm Springs.

TUESDAY APRIL 13, 1971

126

MARY LOU TURNED the key in the lock and stepped into the hallway. There was an eerie silence and she feared the worst. She glanced at her watch and saw it was nearly midnight. Up the stairs and a check on the twins: both asleep, Frank snored like a state trooper and Alice unconscious while her butt stuck up in the air.

A skip down the stairs and into the living room to find Bobby. No one there. And where was the new housekeeper? Mary Lou couldn't even remember her name. Did that make her a bad parent? Or a busy assassin? Both. The fine distinction was irrelevant, because the woman was nowhere to be found.

Into the conservatory and a view of the pool. Still nothing. She walked out onto the patio and saw Bobby asleep on a chair. She bent down, touched his shoulder and planted a gentle kiss on his forehead. He stirred and, before he got the chance to rearrange himself, Mary Lou blew in his ear and he woke up with a start.

"What the f…"

"All's good. Only me. The kids are crashed out upstairs."

"Jeez. How long you been back?"

"A minute. No more. Everything go okay here? No trouble?"

"No, it's been quiet. Like my conscience."

"Did what's-her-name workout?"

"Irma? Sure. I sent her up for the night once the kids were in bed."

"And they were safe, right?"

"I told you I would look after them."

"But they are my babies."

Bobby laughed.

"Getting older now. Especially Alice. She's middle-aged before her time."

Now it was Mary Lou's turn to smile.

"Yeah, but Frank Jr is still a little boy."

"Little monkey."

Mary Lou chuckled again.

"And he has your laugh. Was good to spend the day with them though. How was your trip?"

"In, shot, out."

"Trouble?"

"Thought I might have been followed to the airport, but all was fine. Well, I was, but I shook my tail."

Bobby nodded in approval.

"Any word from Arnold?"

"Nothing from him, but Fabio called to say Mendoza was confirmed whacked a few hours ago."

"Did he not have anything on Arnold?"

"Nope. So it doesn't look good."

Mary Lou and Bobby were silent, both contained within their own thoughts. Arnold was dead in all but name. She slumped on a chair of her own and let the unspoken truth settle in their stomachs. The ripples in the water picked up as a breeze increased.

Bobby might not have gone out and killed one of her enemies—like Arnold, but he'd done the single thing no other person had ever accomplished: protected her children with the potential to lose his life. Mary Lou opened her eyes and gazed at the man, lying there in front of her. The creases either side of his eyelids and the folds of his pants near his crotch.

She stood up and took him by the hand and led him indoors.

SANCHO MENDOZA'S WIFE, Constanza waited at home for her husband's return. This regular wait was normal as she never knew when, or if, he would show. He never told her the details of his business affairs, but she was smart enough to never ask. Constanza understood her role was to take care of their children and to prepare food for her beloved Sancho.

When one of his underlings came to the door to inform her that Sancho had been gunned down in a restaurant, the best thing for her to do was don black and find a long veil to cover her face.

While he might have been an average lover and rotten husband and father, Sancho had been a great provider and she was a scrupulous saver. There was a sadness welling up her insides, but her eyes flashed dollars. With the amount of green she'd stashed away over the years, her family would be fine for the rest of her life—or so she hoped.

IN CONTRAST, MRS. Pentangelo knew her husband was dead almost before he hit the floor. The noises from the living room were threatening and vicious. The sound of the gun shot still echoed round her skull. She wanted to remember the face of her husband's killer but she had already repressed the shock of the experience out of her mind. An inevitable end given the life Charlie had chosen. By the time she cowered in the kitchen and tried to hang on ten minutes—as instructed by Mary Lou—tears of grief overwhelmed her. Two minutes into the wait, the front door closed and she knew it'd be safe to come out.

As soon as she saw Mary Lou leave the floor using the fish eye, she burst open the door to reveal the carnage inside. Then she sat in an easy chair whimpering while men zoomed in and rushed out again. What happened for the rest of that afternoon didn't matter to her. Everything was as clear as morning: she was the widow of a capo in a New York mob family and she would want for nothing from now until the day she died.

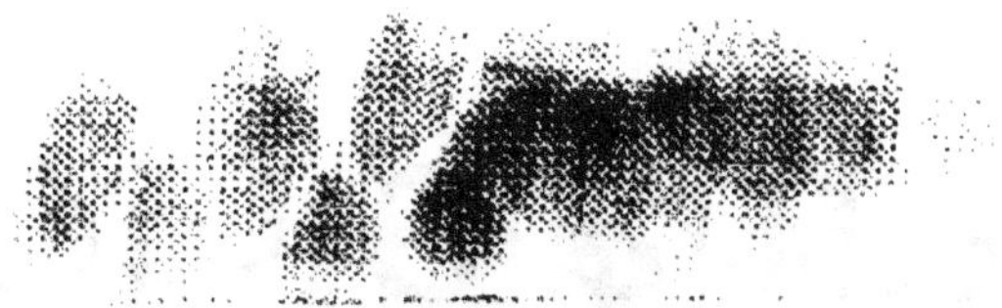

127

MARY LOU STOOD facing Bobby with her back to the bed. She had her family safe, enough money to live out the rest of her days, a man she was prepared to be naked with again. And power that came from the brown powder. She wrapped her hands around Bobby's neck and head. And they kissed. His tongue tasted sweet, and she closed her eyes to capture the moment in her mind.

Then she separated her body from his, unbuttoned her blouse and pulled down her pants. Without a word, she let herself fall back onto the mattress with a coquettish giggle. Bobby smiled, took off his own pants and ripped off his shirt.

He lay on top of her and they kissed some more. Mary Lou's cheeks were warm to the touch, and she thought she might have noticed a tingle at the base of her spine. She placed both hands on Bobby's head and pushed, encouraged and cajoled him downward until his lips were inches below her belly button: right by her rose tattoo. The sensation of his fingers on the inside of her thighs made the tingles shoot up to the nape of her neck.

Images flashed though her mind. Her sweaty body entwined with Frank's until dawn in Miami. Carter tied to her bed in their love nest in Baltimore. Frank lying, head on her lap, as his blood soaked into her skirt by the lockers in Burbank Airport.

Then she snapped open her eyes: Mary Lou told herself to stop living in the past. As that thought flickered in her mind, tingles flowed from her ass to her neck and she allowed herself the luxury of existing in the moment. Of forgetting the pain she'd caused Alice and Frank Jr. Of ignoring the very real possibility the East Coast mob had a hit out on her while she lay on her Palm Springs bed. And pushed away the worries of being part of the mob's heroin trade.

Mary Lou closed her eyes and savored the wet sensation of Bobby's tongue as it followed the path of her rose stem and she gave into the anticipation of pleasure. She giggled again. Mary Lou Lagotti had found peace and her libido was screaming for some action. In a matter of seconds, those tingles of hers became intense. She sucked in a mouthful of air. Let the good times roll.

THE END

Mama's Gone

FEBRUARY 1997

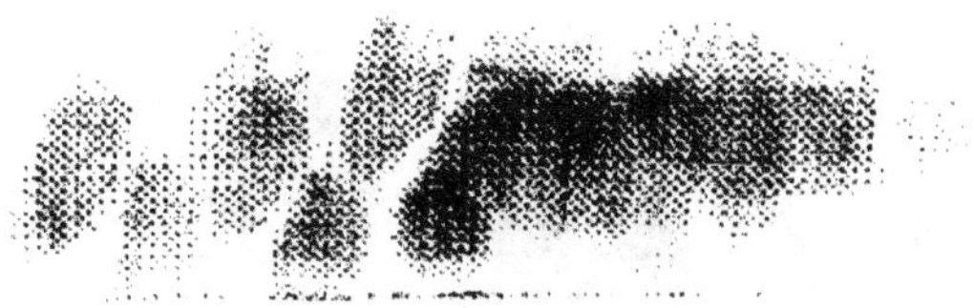

128

ZING. ALICE FIRST heard a whizzing noise and then felt a sharp movement of air—way before she saw anything. And then it was all too late. She turned to her Mama sat to her left as the woman's head hurtled backward. The red circular mess where an eye once was. The blast of brain and skull that splattered the wall. Bobby threw himself toward Mary Lou to protect her from the assault, but there was no point.

He scurried over and lay on his dead wife as Alice hit the deck. Nikolay drew his revolver almost before the bullet flew through Mama, Alice thought. Lara Mikhailov dragged him down to the floor. Nobody in the room was above window height and there had been no fourth shot.

"Anyone else hurt?"

Three shots, one dead. A professional hit for sure. Worthy of the great Arnold Roach, may he rest in peace. Alice held her snub nose ready for action and Bobby cradled Mary Lou in his arms, rocking them side-to-side in the first moments of his grief.

Alice glanced at Bobby and looked at Nikolay. Had his gun been out before the zing? Couldn't be certain of anything right now. Events unfolded around her and she felt completely estranged from them. Despite the body lying near her feet, she didn't believe Mama was dead. She saw it was true, but it meant nothing to her. Like the world stopped still and she carried on breathing—only she continued on the sidelines as everything flowed ever onwards.

Nikolay's bodyguard, Mikhailov edged to a window and cautiously inched her head to spot the sniper. Nada. Nikolay Markov spoke to her but Alice couldn't discern a single word—still trapped in her time-slipped bubble. His mouth moved again but his expression became more aggressive. Angry.

"What just happened?"

"We know nothing of this. My mother's been killed. You think I'd do that? To my Mama?"

Alice found a pistol lying in her hand, which she must have taken out of her handbag. An unconscious action. She glanced round and Bobby had let go of Mary Lou, holding a revolver. Someone would pay for killing her Mama.

129

FATHER CARMOODY BABBLED on and, even though all his words were extolling his Mama's virtues, Frank wanted him to stop. To just shut his pie-hole. He had no right talking about his Mama because he didn't know her. How was anyone taking this man in a frock seriously?

"Mary Lou Lagotti, may she rest in peace, was a mother, a wife, a businesswoman. But above all she was a human being who died in tragic circumstances. She leaves behind two beautiful children—Frank Jr and Alice—as well as Bobby, her dutiful husband."

Mutterings and nods from the congregation echoed the priest's words.

"She joined our community nearly thirty years ago and she quickly became a fabulous contributor to our local charities. As her children got older, and her business activities thrived, Mary Lou grew as a force for good in Palm Springs."

More mutterings and Frank heard his sister sob again. She had done her best to keep it together as the assembled throng entered the building, but now her salty tears were annoying him. Again. He was tired of her and the way she acted as though everything was about her. This was Mama's funeral: not another place for Alice to be the center of attention.

Frank looked round at the sea of strange faces. Who were these people who'd turned up in his Mama's memory? They shouldn't be here. This was a private moment. He didn't want Alice or Bobby there either, but he had no choice. He put up with them because they were family. As for the rest of the congregation? Fuck them and the horse they rode in on.

ALICE HAD NO memory whether it had been yesterday or last week when a person or persons unknown shot her Mama. Everything was a blur. People talking around her, at her, about her. But nothing seemed real. Like a movie playing out in her head—only with actors stood in front of her as the folks she knew—apart from the priest who'd popped out of a hole in the ground almost before Mama stopped breathing.

A gasp of air and another wave of sadness washed over her, engulfing Alice in a deep melancholy. Bobby held her hand but gave her no solace. Nobody could. She wished she had a partner—somebody to be with, who'd hug her and convince her everything would be all right. But she was alone as she stared at the sealed coffin. Although she wanted to confront the reality of her experience, she couldn't bring herself to think about what was in the wooden box. That was a thought too far. Even contemplating the wooden box itself made her want to cry again.

She tried to turn round to see who was here and staring at her, but that required her to let go of Bobby's hand and she didn't have the mental strength for that. Better to ignore the throng behind than lose her lifeline. Her connection with the living.

The priest droned on and each word continued to have no impact on Alice at all. She barely focused on what he was saying, so engrossed in her personal misery.

The sound of glass and the thunk of the bullet whizzing and landing in her darling Mama. Alice was assaulted by another wave of tears.

1973

130

MARY LOU SETTLED into her new role as the business partner of Pasquale and Fabio, representatives of the West Coast mob. The previous year she'd proven her worth taking out a local heroin dealer and also whacking a made man from the East Coast outfit, Charlie Pentangelo.

Now she had full control of the Palm Springs trade, Mary Lou wanted to stretch her reach further than the Watts district of South LA. She recalled one of her earliest conversations with Pasquale and thought today was a good time to mention it. The three were sat in an empty warehouse, all cars parked round the back so any passerby could be forgiven for believing nothing was happening.

"Business is going well, wouldn't you say?"

"Sure. Profits are up and stable."

"I was thinking about Hollywood."

"They make great movies there."

"Last year, you talked about an opportunity we could work on together."

"I did."

Pasquale smiled as he teased Mary Lou. The prospect appealed of being the main supplier of cocaine to the movie moguls and their minions. While it might not generate the sizable profit afforded by selling small bags of brown crystal to the impoverished and desperate in the projects, there was kudos attached. And sideline businesses could arise servicing the needs of the rich and famous, whose tastes and interests were traditionally esoteric and often illegal.

"I'd like to crack open the Beverly Hills safe with you."

"And how do you know I've not pursued this with anyone else?"

"My people have asked around and no one has mentioned your name. So either somebody is dipping their beak in this trough or you are very discrete. I reckon it was worth asking."

Pasquale grinned and glanced at Fabio, who returned the favor.

"Would be great to break ground with you on a new venture."

"Good news. After the first year of operation, we should stick to our fifty-fifty split. On this occasion, I propose funding the start-up out of my end, so I would like sixty per cent of the profit to cover those costs."

Pasquale sat and stared at her for thirty seconds. Then he leaned over and whispered with Fabio awhile. They finished discussions with a mutual nod.

"Mary Lou, you make me laugh. With all due respect, when we first met, you demanded terms because you were putting your sweat on the line. Now you seek an accommodation because you have made money with me and want to protect yourself from unexpected financial downside."

She remained silent because Mary Lou understood she should let Pasquale speak until he was finished before responding. This three-piece suit with olive skin in front of her was one of the most powerful men this side of Vegas.

"And, to be honest, I'd seek the same if I was in your position. Tell you what, I'll lease you back the labs, equipment and people. That way, you make the financial commitment you already seem keen to invest. However, we share the risk because they will be my resources until you pay me off after the first year. That is how I believe partners should behave and it is how I would like you and I to do business, Mrs. Lagotti."

Mary Lou hoped Pasquale would play ball, but she hadn't expected this level of generosity. They shook hands and the deal was sealed. Now she could measure the high currency she held in Pasquale's eyes.

HAVING RETURNED TO her four-bedroom Palm Springs mansion, Mary Lou played with the twins for an hour before she left them with the ever-capable housekeeper Irma and headed to the Country Club. She sat in her usual booth with her back to the wall, so she could survey the entire room with one glance. The red leather furniture was fading but none of the patrons seemed too bothered.

The place prospered because it catered well for its diverse community. There were the ladies who lunched, their men who talked business when they weren't in LA tending to their commercial interests or fucking their mistresses—and the occasional golfer.

Milton Frazzini sat down opposite her just as a waiter delivered her coffee.

"I'll have one of those too, Pete."

The man had been the first to take her criminal talents seriously when she'd hit town after Alice and Frank Jr were born. They'd prospered together—Milton was an effective completer but had a poor track record for succeeding with his own projects. With Mary Lou's brains and his organizational skills, they managed an extensive area of LA's heroin trafficking.

Once Pete left the vicinity, Milton wanted to find out about the morning's conversation.

"We've got the green light to open up Beverly Hills. And the terms are better than I ever expected."

"Hollywood? I thought you had your eye on San Francisco."

"No, you made that suggestion and I nixed it. I've told you before, don't confuse our business with your dick. If you want to visit your latest piece of tail in San Francisco then knock yourself out or tie her up—or whatever. But do it on your own time."

Milton always blushed when Mary Lou talked about his extramarital sex life. Thankfully, this was a rare occasion. It was her job to understand the weaknesses of her key people, so she needed to know what he was up to when he was away from Janet and the boy.

Funny thing was that while Milton was off shtupping his floozy, his wife had something going with a local lad: Pete the waiter. She'd been letting him into her bedroom for over a year now. As a concerned neighbor, Mary Lou kept an eye on the goings and comings of Oakcrest Drive.

"The time isn't right for us to hop over to a strange town. There's plenty of money to make nearer to home. Besides, I thought you might like the Hollywood Hills. It'd give you a tremendous opportunity to mix with all those A-listers."

"Huh?"

"Where there are stars, there are producers. And where there are producers, there are…"

"…girls who'll do anything to get into the movies."

"And that's your kind of girl, Milton."

"I can't help the fact I'm attracted to the desperate and needy type."

"Your words, not mine."

"But you're not disagreeing."

Mary Lou grinned and let out a small laugh which Milton echoed. This would be a fun ride.

MILTON LEFT STILL smiling and Mary Lou waited for Bobby Trevisan to show before ordering any lunch. As if on cue, just as her stomach rumbled, the man walked in and sat down beside her. He squeezed her knee as he kissed her hello.

"Kids okay?"

"Reckon so, but I've been in the summerhouse all morning. No raised voices and no sign of Irma, so all was fine."

Mary Lou gazed round the room and rested a hand on his thigh. They had been together a year and she trusted him with her children's lives. Now she was busting with excitement, but Pete arrived with their menus, so she waited until they'd given their orders.

"We've got a new gig. It's all been arranged with our friend from the Hills."

A euphemism for Pasquale was always best in a public place—even one as private as the Country Club.

"Great! What's the plan?"

"I'll tell you when I have it figured out. Minimum we need is to liaise with Fabio as there's new product to process and locations to scout: we're running the studio snow express."

Bobby smiled and planted a kiss square on her lips. They had been investigating, plotting and planning for this caper over three months, day and night. Finally, it had come good and received Pasquale's blessing.

The incumbent suppliers had grown lazy and relied on the movie producers to supply the dope to the stars, but the studio system was falling apart and a new breed of film maker needed a new type of drug dealer. The Lagottis would go straight to the young brat pack and their enormous propensity to party and imbibe a cocktail of intoxicants. Bobby would resolve any disputes with the old guard using a high caliber revolver. You can take the man out of the mob, but you can't take the mob out of the man.

The Lagottis and Pasquale were as aware as anyone that drugs were just the beginning. The parties needed hosts and Milton was the guy to supply the right quantity of girls, eager to break into showbiz. Those that didn't make it onto a studio lot could be encouraged to deliver a performance or two in the underbelly of Hollywood and its porn palaces. Get the distribution right and even an average hardcore product could generate as much as heroin. No small feat.

BOBBY PLACED A call to Milton after lunch and they met in the summerhouse forty minutes later. The drapes overlooking the pool were drawn for privacy to separate domestic and business life. The fifty-by-twenty-feet space was a mix of comfortable easy chairs, couches and formal working environment. Mary Lou installed a desk near her secured walk-in cupboard and armaments storage. Next year, she told herself she'd install a safe—for the guns and the money. Until then, Mary Lou was the sole owner of the key to her secret wardrobe.

Coffees poured and cigarettes lit, they set about organizing the snow express.

"Fabio's runners will serve us well at the get-go until we've made our own contacts. They'll know the cool places and the most valuable party hosts."

"The next task is to organize the parties. Create some happenings. And that's where you'll come into your own, Milton."

"What do you need me to do?"

"The thing you do best: find some willing girls, who want to hang with the celebrities. And don't mind what they get up to with them when they're there."

Milton's expression was thoughtful for a spell and then his eyes widened as he got the joke. He loved to run call girls because he allowed himself to taste the merchandise which he never did with narcotics. The man lived in a moral sewer, but he had his principles. Whores, booze and gambling were fine but drugs were for the birds.

"Bobby, I want you to keep an eye on our heroin trade. The last thing we need is for that to turn to shit while we're growing new shoots near Burbank."

"Sure. Just don't push me out of the story."

"I won't. Only we mustn't take our eyes off the ball. We'll all share the prizes."

He nodded consent although Mary Lou hadn't asked his permission. This was her show and she was running it. The two had found a way of sharing a bed together while she wore the pants outside the bedroom. It helped that she was a successful bank robber and he was a washed-up mob killer. Both Mary Lou and Bobby had pasts they couldn't forget or escape from—no matter how hard they tried.

"The next week will be crucial. We need to deal firmly with any objections we may encounter. Better to put them in the morgue than leave some hopped-up hippie to complain we're stomping all over his territory."

"I'll take care of incidentals."

Bobby inhaled deeply and stubbed out the remains of his smoke. Despite what he told himself, he still enjoyed killing people and Mary Lou got it. So did Milton, who always showed him the utmost respect—no matter what the circumstances.

"Once we've established a toe-hold, we'll need a couple of girls to keep the good times rolling and to make sure our new friends buy their gear from us."

"It'll be my pleasure to run that end of things."

"Just remember we don't care how much hooch our whores drink or how many lines go up their noses. But their job is to get the guests to purchase our product and to do whatever they are asked. They can't say no to any request, no matter how debauched: church girls travel home in body bags. Capiche?"

"Understood. I've run this racket before. I'll be on top of it all."

"Are there any you won't be road testing?"

Bobby laughed and raised an eyebrow.

"Not unless they're under sixteen. I don't judge our customers but I will not fuck kids."

"A true gentleman."

"Let's get back to business."

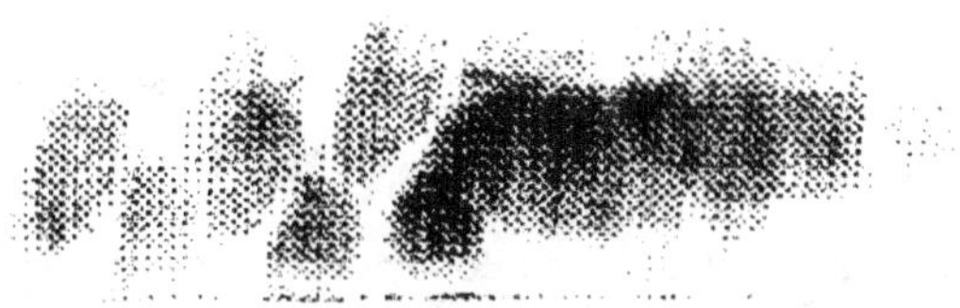

131

FRIDAY WAS THE first chance to put the operation into practice. Fabio's people and product were in the right hands at the correct location as an all-night party was in prospect. Hank Milana was celebrating the wrap on his latest offering: a gritty portrayal of New York street life shot on a back lot in Burbank.

Independently financed, its executive producer had returned to Manhattan, which meant Hank was in charge of the festivities. Lucky for him, Milton was on hand to keep the booze flowing and the lines cut, ready for snorting. He was a natural.

Although Hank balked at the initial price asked for the snow, he relented after two free samples. The deal duly sealed, the guests could enjoy themselves the way only young acting egos can. Milton watched the action from afar—never mix business with pleasure. And despite his base desires and the writhing mass of naked bodies before him, he did not partake.

Don't get high on your own supply, for sure. Don't ball your own ass when someone else is paying the bill. Watch, enjoy and learn what you can about your customer and their friends. That way, there'll always be another party.

He lost track of where his two hostesses had got to about an hour before, but Milton could be sure everything was fine because his eyes never left Hank. And if that man was happy then Milton was happy too. He saw Hank was happy because the artiste was snorting a line off the bare ass sticking up from a couch. The wink was a clue and the bear hug made him certain.

A glance at his watch told Milton it was four in the morning. He yawned and stretched his back to get more comfortable in his chair. With no notice, a woman fell on his lap, rolled off and danced in between his legs. Her groin was at head height and the only thing she wore was a smile. Milton kept his professional cool and tried to look past her rhythmic hips and maintain his vigil on Hank.

Each time he regained a line of sight, she moved so that her pubes were the only things he could see. He placed a palm on each hip to stop her movements, but she misread his actions and pushed herself into his face. This was one horny hippie.

Milton shrugged, stood up and took her by the hand. He walked up to Hank who was lying on a bean bag with someone's lips around his dick.

"Adam, meet Eve."

He positioned the woman so Hank's mouth was six inches below her navel. As he turned back to his chair, Milton saw the two had worked something out.

"The things we do for money…"

DOWN THE ROAD, a month later, Mary Lou and Bobby contemplated the expanse of a faded hotel on Sunset Boulevard. The realtor busied around them so he was desperate to get the property off his books. They did their best to ignore him and concentrate on the potential of the crumbling beauty rusting and aching under their feet.

Mary Lou's idea was simple but brilliant. If you own the venue where the exclusive gatherings take place then you don't have to worry about finding the next party: the soiree comes to you and you control everything that you pay for within a known environment. Besides, spending dough on a heap on Sunset Boulevard could only increase the value of the real-estate. Whatever happens, they win.

Soon they supplied cocaine to four parties a week, although Mary Lou viewed this as just one tip of the snow-capped iceberg. The hotel was big enough for them to run five or six separate events at the same time—but that was way into the future.

For now, they'd renovate the first floor with its ballroom: convert into an amazing party space and a reception area and restaurant, which could become an enormous bar and chill out zone. Security in the grounds and scrutiny of all who entered the Palace would mark out the place as the number primary location for the cognoscente.

Mary Lou gouged the realtor on price and two weeks later, the venue was theirs. One month of intense building activity supervised by Bobby and the former hotel was ready for business. By throwing an incredible quantity of men at the problem, Bobby had fit out the first floor—and converted the second into a series of offices and, what he liked to call, relaxation rooms.

Stood in one of these boudoirs, Mary Lou wondered why he had bothered. He smiled and led her to a clock hanging on the wall.

"Look right in the center of the dial."

His finger pointed to a black piece of glass. She was none the wiser and followed Bobby out of the room, into the corridor.

"Notice anything different from when we were here before?"

"The cockroaches are gone?"

"Yes, but there's something else: the rooms are smaller. Look."

He took her around the rooms, dragging her first to one wall and then off to the adjoining surface in the next chamber. Eventually, she saw it.

"Why have you thickened the walls?"

"To make a hidden corridor. That way we can move around the place without being seen."

"And what's that got to do with the clocks?"

"We've hooked up a cine-camera for each room."

Mary Lou smiled, but let Bobby carry on his explanation.

"We're getting the famous or the nearly famous in our orbit. But in a while, the powerful and the influential will want a piece of our action. Then we might find it useful to have an edge if you see what I mean."

SENATOR TEDDY PRESCOTT enjoyed the high life and the various perks offered him as a representative of the Californian people. He split his time between Washington and Los Angeles. Like so many Americans, movie stars were magical superheroes to him and he grabbed every opportunity to mix in their circles.

As a Republican, he fought a hard campaign on a pro-guns and anti-tax ticket. The right to bear arms against the British without paying for the privilege proved irresistible to voters and he won by a wide margin. This was back in 1970 when Sharon Tate's killers were still unknown and Vietnam continued to rage.

With a beautiful blond wife and two extraordinary children, the Prescotts were a wholesome group, projecting the family values electors liked to see. Five months after they opened the Palace, Milton called Bobby around six in the morning with news about Senator Prescott.

"We have a situation and need you to deal."

"Can it wait a couple of hours?"

"No. You better come over as soon as you've got your pants on."

"Understood."

BOBBY STOOD AT the fisheye lens staring in at the room. He watched and waited, with Milton hovering next to him. After three minutes doing nothing, he stepped out of the hidden corridor and entered the scene of the crime.

"Hello Teddy."

The senator sat on the edge of the bed, a towel covering his lap. Milton made sure no one had offered him any clothes to wear. Best to keep him feeling vulnerable until Bobby arrived.

"Can you remember what happened here?"

His hand indicated the bloody mess lying on the floor on the other side of the bed.

"We were fooling around and everything was fine. I don't…"

Bobby walked round and picked up a beer bottle, holding it upside down, so red dripped off the neck and onto the wooden flooring.

"Looks like you were partying quite hard."

Prescott's eyes glanced at the glass container and tears welled up inside him. Bobby placed the object between Prescott's feet so he couldn't avoid its reality. The blood followed its natural course downwards and dribbled over the whole surface of the glass and onto the floorboards.

Then Bobby returned to the body and kneeled down to study it more closely. The girl lay face up, arms by her ears. Bruises around her neck, shoulders and head. And a tremendous amount of scarlet over her groin. There was no way to tell if she'd been unconscious when she died or whether she had struggled against the monster until the end. All her clothes were strewn over the floor and Teddy's were folded neatly on a pile on a chair. Bobby noticed the mirror and razor blade on the bedside table, but there were almost no crumbs of powder visible.

"She's in quite a mess, Teddy. She disrespect you?"

"No, not at all. Lizzie was a wonderful girl."

"Then what went wrong?"

Prescott looked up at Bobby with a quizzical expression. A shrug and more tears.

"You have nothing to worry about. I am here because I want to help you."

"Thank you."

"We will tidy up this room first after you've gone. It'll be like she never was here. That you were never in her bed and that you two were never together."

Teddy's body juddered as he turned his head to glance at Lizzie one more time. The towel on his lap fell to the ground and Bobby walked away. Once he'd closed the door behind him, he instructed Milton to give him the film from the camera.

"What would you like me to do with Teddy?"

"Set Prescott free and get Fabio's cleaner in as soon as possible."

"Okay."

"And next week, pay Teddy a visit and ask for a donation for the girl's funeral."

"Funeral?"

"I want you to remind him of what happened and that we have not forgotten. There'll be no burial. You know better than that. Dump her body in the desert."

"She'd been with us from the start. Great piece of ass, popular with the clients and sure could get them to pay for snow."

"Thanks for the eulogy. He must be out of here in the next thirty minutes. She needs to be out of here by lunchtime. Discretion is key in these situations right?"

"You betcha. By the time the rest of the guests wake up, this will be just a bad memory for Teddy."

"Damn straight. And sorry if I was grouchy when you called. Don't enjoy being woken up in the middle of the night."

"De nada. I figured some things are more important than sleep."

"Say that again. What was Prescott doing, the fucked-up whack-job?"

"I have told you, Bobby: I do not judge. Some behavior goes on under this roof, you wouldn't believe. The depravity I've seen…"

"I can only imagine—and that's enough for me. You keep the cine-reels, though?"

"Some of them might be sickos, but I'm not stupid. Of course I do."

"Good man."

BOBBY VISITED PRESCOTT at the family home a week before Thanksgiving. The place stood in vast private grounds in Malibu. Tailored lawns and adobe-style buildings. A butler answered the door and led him into the library. He settled into a brown leather chair and made himself comfortable.

When Teddy Prescott entered the room and saw Bobby lounging near his books, he almost popped a blood vessel.

"What are you doing here? Our business was finished a long time ago."

He remained seated and beckoned for Teddy to join him. The man wasn't used to mortals acting this way in his own home.

"I'm pleased to see you again too, Teddy. From what I hear, you haven't fucked any underage girls with any bottles lately. Or hasn't word spread fast enough yet?"

Bobby removed an imaginary piece of fluff from his knee. Mainly to give the senator a minute to collect himself. Prescott slumped on a nearby stool.

"There was no need to send me the film of my actions. I regret what I did in a moment of… passion and I paid handsomely so the child could be taken care of properly."

"Save the protestations for the voters. Or your wife."

Teddy's eyes flitted at the closed library door and back to Bobby.

"I am not here to chat about the past. What's done is done and I'm not in the mood for nostalgia. Let's talk about our future."

"What do you mean?"

"You are a powerful man, an honorable man. A man of influence—in California and other states like, say, Nevada."

"So?"

"My wife and I are about to take over a casino in Las Vegas and we do not want any trouble from the Gaming Commission. You can help us."

The blood drained from Prescott's face and he glanced at the door again.

"Before we talk turkey, why don't you offer me a beer…"

1994

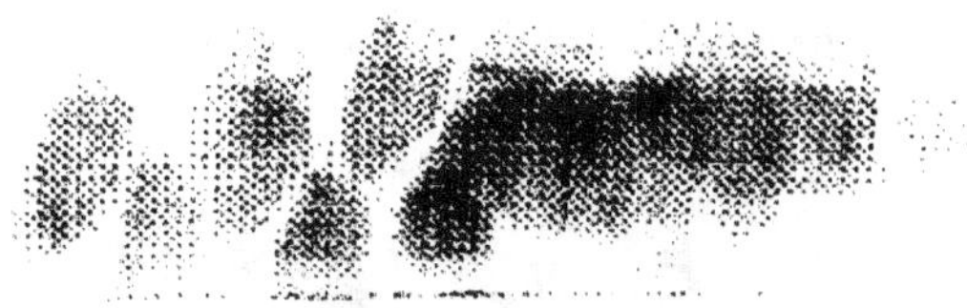

132

THE TWINS CAME home from their very separate schools and OJ Simpson stood trial for murdering his wife. While the latter fact consumed the nation, Mary Lou couldn't wait for her babies to return to the nest.

Bobby drove to collect Alice from Berkeley while Frank made his own way back from San Diego State. The boy only carried a suitcase and a backpack. She filled the car and trailer to the brim. Thanks to good packing by Bobby, there was just sufficient space left for two people to squeeze in between the boxes, bags and cases.

"What have you got in here?"

"My life."

He nodded, shrugged and set off for Palm Springs. On arrival, Alice threw herself into Mary Lou's arms.

"Mama, so good to see you. I've a thousand things to tell you about."

"And it's great to have you back, but Frank's home too. Arrived an hour ago…"

Alice took her attention off her mother's face and glanced round the hallway. A case and backpack lay in a heap near the kitchen door. Her gaze floated into the living room until the sprawling mess of her brother filled her vision. He blinked acknowledgement in her general direction and she offered a half-smile.

Mama led her onto the family couch and continued to hold her hand while Frank carried on with his tales of school. The anecdotes were tedious and, at least twice, Alice reckoned he was making it up as he conjured a mix of urban myths and other people's experiences. She couldn't bring herself to imagine him studying, going to lectures or doing anything which might involve effort. In her head, she'd wondered how the hell he'd graduated at all. At her darkest how, she even thought Mama had paid San Diego State to get him through at all.

At that same dark moment, a flush of pride filled Alice's heart because her degree had been earned through hard work, commitment and deep resolve. And it was a better school too.

She waited patiently until Frank ran out of steam. She knew Mama did not approve of interrupting her firstborn male child. Alice's four extra minutes on this planet counted for nothing.

All this time, Bobby sat silent in an easy chair. He'd been a member of this family for over twenty years, but sometimes he didn't feel a part of it at all. This afternoon was one of those moments. Before Alice could get into the full swing of her story, Irma appeared from the kitchen with a tray piled high with coffee and cookies.

Even though she was only the housekeeper, she kept a special place in her heart for those two bundles of joy. Not that they hadn't caused their poor mother grief over the years, especially the boy. He was a tearaway when he was a teenager—not much better now, only he had more money to get himself out of trouble without Mrs. Lagotti having to step in and save his scrawny ass.

TWO DAYS LATER, Frank grabbed his things, kissed Mama on the forehead and told her he was off to New York for a while. Mary Lou offered to drive him to the airport, but he declined.

"I don't like long goodbyes and you'll cry if you take me there."

After the taxi whisked him away, his mom sobbed. Once her eyes had dried out, she walked through the conservatory and onto the patio. Alice was floating on an air mattress in the middle of the pool, so Mary Lou sat on a sun lounger and watched her darling daughter soak in the rays.

"What are you going to do?"

"Lie here until dinner. Dunno."

"That's not what I meant. Frank's just left."

"He'll be back."

"For New York."

"Oh. That boy sure has a mind of his own."

"Am I going to lose you too?"

"You haven't lost Frank. He just doesn't know how to settle down anywhere."

"And you?"

"I'd like to grab this summer if I can. The next time I have this much vacation will be when I retire."

"Okay darling. You deserve that if nothing else. Then what?"

Alice slipped off her inflatable mattress and swam to the edge nearest to Mary Lou. Then she hauled herself out the pool and sat opposite Mama.

"I want to work with you and Bobby."

Mary Lou stiffened and shuffled on the lounger.

"What do you think we do—apart from making a few investments?"

Alice laughed and wrung the excess water from her below-the-shoulder length hair.

"Investments. Please? Frank and I aren't stupid. All the discrete conversations in the summerhouse. The men in dark suits who go through this place like it's their office. And Milton? Do you know what the kids at Montgomery High used to say about him?"

"Come with me."

They strode past the pool and into the summerhouse where Bobby sat, working at the desk. He swung round at the noise of the door opening.

"Alice wants to work with us."

"Do you have a résumé?"

"Be serious. And she says the kids have known about our business for years."

"And what is it we do, Alice?"

"Heroin and cocaine mainly. At least that's what you guys talked about most before I skipped off to Berkeley."

Mary Lou stared at Bobby with gritted teeth and he looked right back at her.

"Are you a cop?"

"No. What makes you think I might be with law enforcement?"

"You'll understand why later. You're correct, we started with narcotics but we used some of those profits to diversify into… other realms."

"Such as?"

"Prostitution and gambling mainly."

Alice whistled out of respect. She and Frank figured out the drug angle when they snuck up to the summerhouse and eavesdropped on the conversations going on inside the taboo building. But she hadn't realized how busy they'd been while she had been away.

"Like I said: I want to help. I'm smart and I could drive the business forward."

"You've been talking about having someone to assist with logistics. She could start there and we can see how she handles herself."

Bobby nodded. He knew this wasn't a discussion. Mary Lou had decided and this conversation was informational only. He thought it a good idea, but his opinion was not sought. So he didn't offer it. Alice always had a sensible head on her shoulders and was bright as a button. Frank would be a better choice to deal with a Mexican stand-off but he doubted if either had fired a gun in their lives. Mary Lou had wanted them to have a normal childhood and not get involved in their criminal ways. Something had changed her mind, clearly.

FRANK TOOK A limo from LaGuardia to a chichi hotel in SoHo. The decor comprised white walls and floors with every piece of furniture made of transparent plastic. He dropped a C-note on the concierge before he hopped up to his suite so he was guaranteed delivery of a girl and a snort or two of cocaine within an hour of tipping the bellboy.

Having fucked her twice, he got bored with the skirt and sent her packing—with a respectable gratuity because she'd been good while she lasted. That left the rest of the pile of coke for himself and he cut sufficient lines to keep him going until morning.

Once room service had delivered his breakfast, Frank called down to the concierge to arrange for more female companionship. The two hookers kept him amused for the entire afternoon but he got bored again. Up to some designer stores on Fifth Avenue and back to the hotel bar to see if his new threads attracted the right kind of woman: easy to impress with big tits and few opinions of her own. The venue was full of his target market because so many rich, dumb men with high libidos and few social skills inhabited these kinds of drinking holes.

With a credit card, which had never received a single payment from him, Frank soon found himself surrounded by adorable asses. The only question left in his mind was which one to pick for tonight. He felt like going clubbing and didn't want to be let down by a girl with poor rhythm. He chuckled to himself when he realized when he brought her back to his suite he didn't want her to have poor rhythm there either. Fuck-a-doodle-do.

The vintage champagne flowed and the chicks hovered around the rooster. Bubbly conversation continued into the evening as every now and again he popped into the washroom to take another hit of his snow. Each time he walked away from those short skirts, he risked some cock taking over his flock of fuckables.

As predictable as the rising sun, when next Frank returned he found some Latino hunk stood by his ice bucket entertaining his ladies. The guy didn't yield an inch and carried on talking as though Frank wasn't there.

"Hey, bud. You're in the way of my champagne."

"You can take it in a minute when I've finished telling my friends about what went down last week in the studio."

"No one wants to hear. Move on, buddy. I need to get to my drink."

The ice bucket was on the bar and the bartender maintained a watchful eye on its contents—Frank looked after those who looked after Frank. The barkeep listened in to the conversation between the men but said nothing. Just carried on cleaning the whiskey glass in his hand.

The Martini Bar in the Courtney Hotel was renowned for two things. First, as its name suggested, they mixed a mean martini. Second, all the waitresses in the bar wore the same uniform: a light gray one-piece cotton-and-lycra body suit which had long sleeves to cover the servers' arms but no legs. Every crevice of the women's bodies were on view.

Just as he uttered his last words to encourage the Latino to step down, a waitress hustled by and the guy stopped paying attention to Frank and stared at the woman's crotch. There was something about the shape of her thighs and roundness of her ass that made him want to see more. Big mistake.

Frank grabbed Julio's hand that held his champagne glass and twisted it behind him. This caused Julio to turn and face the bar and Frank seized the hair at the back of his head and push his skull down onto the bar. In one smooth action, the barkeeper snatched the ice bucket and its contents off the clear plastic surface a quarter of a second before Julio's forehead smashed down on the unforgiving hardened material.

The women surrounding them screamed and scattered to leave Frank alone to assault Julio further. Red gushed from his head and the bartender leaned forward.

"Mr. Lagotti…"

Frank pushed Julio's skull into the bar more and looked up.

"I think the gentleman has received your message loud and clear. Why not let him go now?"

"Are we through?"

Saliva, blood and a tooth left the mook's mouth and a brief nod showed consent. Frank released him from his grip and pushed his body further down the bar away from his perch.

"How do I look?"

"I'd say you should pop to the bathroom. Looks like you might have a spot or two of dirt on your shirt. By the time you come back, I'll have set up another bottle—on the house. None of the last one was lost, but it may leave an unpleasant taste in the mouth, anyway."

Frank did as he was told and returned with a smile on his face and a white ring around his nostrils. He swigged a glass of champagne and then took stock of the room. A quick check that Julio had left and Frank collected chicks again. Trouble was, his heart was no longer in it and by the time the bottle was empty, Frank decided to leave.

"What entertainment can you offer me this evening?"

"Chilled or high octane?"

"Do I look chilled?"

The concierge smiled and picked up the phone to reserve a table in the VIP area of an '80s Old Skool club night.

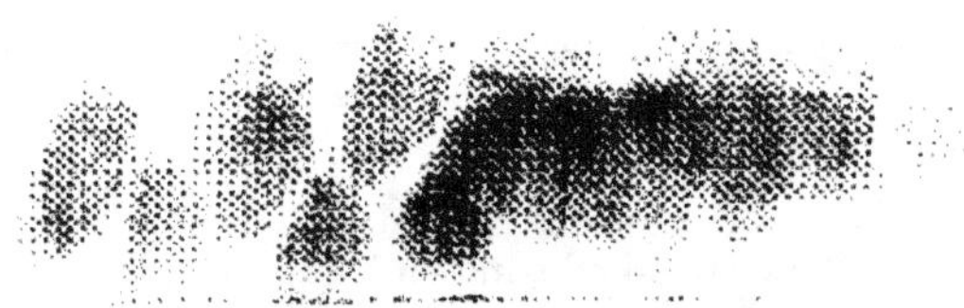

133

THE PHONE CALL came through direct to Mary Lou. Although not inevitable, she couldn't remember a time when Frank hadn't asked for help to get himself out of a hole.

"Hi Mama."

"Hi Frank."

"I'm in a spot of trouble."

"Where are you and what's the problem?"

"They got me on intent to sell."

"Where Frank?"

"Ninth Precinct."

"Manhattan?"

"Yeah. How long since you were arrested?"

"Just got here. They processed me and then I demanded my constitutional phone call."

"Say nothing but be polite. I'll send someone over to sort this out."

"Thanks Mama."

Mary Lou hung up the phone and sighed. That boy never learns. What did I do to deserve him? Then she thought back on her life for a moment, shivered and realized the answer. Dragging herself to the present, she called a New York attorney and briefed Harvey Knight on the situation.

"It's a pain but can you get him out of there today? I don't want Frank spending a night in a police cell."

"Will do. You know the best thing for him might be to find out how the other half live."

"He's my baby."

"Who is old enough to sell narcotics to an undercover cop"

"Just free him and spare me your lectures on child rearing."

"Not a lecture, but the finest legal advice I have ever offered you—the small fortune you've paid to cover the amount of my time I've spent extricating him from law enforcement holding facilities."

The silence on the line meant Harvey's words hit home.

"Get him out, Harvey."

FRANK STARED AT Harvey across a precinct table. As ever with the boy, there was a story and an excuse.

"I was at a party on Avenue A."

"How d'you hear about it?"

"A pickup in my hotel bar… We were all relaxing and laughing and having a good time."

Harvey nodded. He understood what a good time meant to Frank.

"And I was sharing the coke. Everyone was doing a line. Nobody seemed bothered. Then one black bitch asks if I can get some for her. Now I'm always willing to oblige a young lady in distress but I don't know her from jack shit. So I play it cool and tell her I'll help her if she helps me and we leave to find somewhere more congenial to conduct business if you get my drift."

"Was there anywhere to your liking in the apartment?"

"Truth was the only place to be alone was the bathroom. So we go to it and afterwards I ask her how much she wants to buy. With her scrawny ass still sat on my dick she asks for four 8-balls. I tell her I can get that weight to her tomorrow. She pushes to have it there and then, and encourages me by getting on her knees and sucking me off."

"And you relented?"

"Couldn't think of a good reason not to help the skank out. She showed me the green and we hopped over to my hotel. Up in my room, I took out the snow, she had a taste and just before I thought we were done, she pulls a gun and a badge from fuck-knows where and makes me assume the position. I swear thirty seconds later we were joined by the rest of the squad. Was a set up, man."

Harvey's legal pad had filled up with notes.

"Did she instigate the sexual intercourse or did you?"

"Me, but she didn't object."

"And the oral?"

"All her own work. My plan was to ball her back in the hotel."

"And you did not try to ask for money until she mentioned it?"

"Yessir."

"I assume she never spoke of her chosen career."

"It was a party. Who talks about how they earn a living?"

"Interesting they haven't charged you with any sex crimes. Protocol should have stopped her from fucking you. The drugs charges: we can make them go away. A quiet word with the man upstairs if due process can't extinguish their flame. I'm more worried about why you were part of a sting… How long you been in town?"

"Couple of days. No more."

"No disrespect but have you got into any other trouble since you arrived here?"

He stared and struggled to remember. The amount of cocaine coursing through his veins meant his memory was not operating at full speed. Harvey waited. Frank tried to wind back time and listed his activities after landing at the airport: girls, drugs, booze—and not much else. His blank expression spoke volumes.

"Any altercations?"

"Huh?"

"Fights?"

Frank shut his eyes for ten seconds and thought some more. Then his eyes flashed open wide and he smiled.

"Not a fight exactly. I mean, I can handle myself."

He described the hassle with Julio while Harvey continued to take notes. Anyone stood over Harvey's shoulder would have seen he had drawn a perfect cube underneath his legal assessments of Frank's situation. He put his pen down and closed over the pad.

"Frank, sounds like you made a mistake, dear boy. From what you say, I think you had a tussle with a well connected New York family. They have extensive narcotics operations across the Five Boroughs and enough reach to get the cops to set you up. Chances are the woman was theirs and not a real cop. You sure she was black and not Hispanic?"

"Now you ask, dunno. What's the name of the family she's with?"

"Don't worry about that. If I were you, as soon as you're out of here, check out the Courtney and leave town. You do not need the mob breathing down your neck."
"Fuck-a-doodle-do."

DESPITE HIMSELF, FRANK left his hotel and headed off to JFK. He had no idea where to go but he was certain he'd had enough of America. What was the world coming to when you found yourself in jail for banging a girl who wanted some snow? Besides, the Latino had no right to take over his women —and it didn't matter what tribe he came from.

So a trip abroad made sense. At least for a short while. And wouldn't Mama be pleased if he returned with a new business partner? He and Alice figured out all about the narcotics trafficking and Frank reckoned that was something he could turn his hand to as he understood the product intimately —cocaine anyway—and handled himself well when cutting deals. Frank'd got a skank to suck him off for the price of a few 8-balls only last night.

With his limited knowledge of world geography, Frank chose Spain as his destination. It was close to Africa but Europe sounded a lot more civilized. Once he'd wrapped his head around the idea that his dollars were no good to him, he discovered the joys of being an American abroad.

He could be as obnoxious as he wanted, provided he kept a smile on his face because the local muchachos had no idea what he was saying. Frank used as little of his own pesos as possible and slapped all he could on his credit card. Only the small bars and drug dealers demanded cash. After a few weeks, he hopped from Madrid to Barcelona and then onto Seville. Then he bumped into a bunch of kids who were heading to Marbella and he hitched a ride with them.

The days of hardcore Balearic beats had faded, but that didn't mean there was no life left in the clubs. With a different music scene, to the ones he was used to, came a distinctive drug of choice: ecstasy. You would be forgiven for thinking the west coast student communities would have embraced the tablet that made you want to hug anyone who moved. But no. There was more money to be generated from powder than tabs so organized crime wasn't too interested—including the Lagottis.

Frank was in his element though: dancing beyond dawn, off his head on drugs, surrounded by semi-naked women. When he wasn't fooling around with them, he was fucking them and if he wasn't doing either of those two things, then he was asleep. A twenty-four-hour party person.

Three months since he hit the southern coast and all he had to show for the experience was a sore dick and intimate knowledge of every ass in the neighborhood. He woke up one Thursday to find his face by someone's bush. Frank looked around and saw he was in a bedroom but he had no idea where he was or who owned the pubes near his lips.

He gave them a quick lick but was swatted away like his mouth was some kind of fly. His feet were on a pillow and somehow he'd turned round in his sleep. Or they'd both crashed out half way through playing. A dirty grin spread across his face.

Frank was thirsty, so he hauled his carcass off the bed in search of liquid. The studio apartment offered him a sink in the bathroom and another in the kitchenette. There were foul dishes piled high in the kitchen and spent needles lying next to the toilet. He took his chances with the sink faucet and glugged back several handfuls of water.

Then he turned around to check out the devastation from the night before. The girl wore only a blue bra with yellow polka dots and snored loudly. Frank walked over and moved her head so it was resting on the mattress and the noises abated. That helped him think more clearly. Almost before starting, his attention wandered off as he noticed the roundness of her tits peeping out from the sides of the skimpy underwear.

What was he doing? He had told himself he would forge a new connection for Mama but all he'd achieved was a heavy dose of sex, drugs and rock 'n' roll. He needed to get his head in the game. Frank opened the fridge as an auto-response to his stomach rumbling. The girl mumbled something foreign and rolled over face down.

There was nothing to eat except raw vegetables and butter so he gave up on breakfast and turned his attention to the bush on the bed. She was stretched out like a starfish and he scratched his balls for no good reason. He felt his hard-on and decided not to waste it. Frank considered taking her from behind but experience taught him he'd need to wake her up to get an orgasm out of the coupling. Nah, too much effort. Instead he jerked himself off while standing over the girl. A gift of love for when she surfaced.

That night he took the ferry across the Mediterranean Sea and docked in Tangiers. If he couldn't make some solid contacts here, what was the point?

134

IN SEPTEMBER, ALICE and Bobby headed off to Vegas so she could learn about the family business. Running a casino was a huge undertaking and competition was fierce. A decade before, the mob had left the strip, ceding control to the entertainment corporations. Off the main drag was a different story. Footfall might have been lower but gambling margins were sufficiently high to make it a profitable venture. The opportunity to launder cash from their other operations kept motivation up during the occasional month when takings were down.

By Thanksgiving, Bobby allowed Alice to spend two days a week alone at the helm. The initial response from senior staff was disdain thinly disguised as utmost respect. They saw the daughter of the boss dropped on them and what had she done to earn the role—apart from the advantage of nepotism and privilege.

The third week at the Lady Fortune Casino, trouble came knocking at ten at night. Alice was sat in her office to check the day's takings before the evening shift was over. The phone rang and five seconds later, she picked up.

"We have a code blue."

A simple phrase to describe one problem: someone was cheating and the person on the other end of the line was stood on the casino floor.

"Where?"

"The poker tables."

"Down in a minute."

Alice headed straight to the surveillance room where closed-circuit TV monitors were laid out, row upon row. There wasn't an inch of the gaming spaces that didn't have a lens aimed at it. Sat in front of every monitor was a guy staring, watching, waiting for some behavior that was out of the ordinary.

"Talk to me."

"See the john in the blue baseball cap?"

A quick scan of the screen and focussed attention where the finger pointed.

"He has two different signals. A usual tap on the baize and he gets the top of the deck."

"Like everyone else."

"Watch. Once or twice, fingers from his other hand rest on the table and out come cards from the bottom."

Within five minutes, Alice saw for herself.

"How much is he up?"

"Hundred thousand so far."

"Let's keep this civilized. Go down onto the floor and invite him to our VIP room. Offer to help to bring his winnings along. Then meet me in the auto shop. I'll be down in a short while."

Alice walked over to the internal phone fixed to the wall next to the door. She dialed reception.

"Page Naldo Friscelli and tell him there's a car needs fixing."

Bobby had introduced Alice to Friscelli their second day in Vegas. They spent only fifteen minutes together but Bobby assured her she could trust Naldo with her life. He was the quietest, most grounded human she had ever met. Every pore oozed strength. Ten years younger than Bobby but she could tell there was a special bond between the two mobsters. This meant Naldo would be true to his word when he offered her undying allegiance.

As Alice entered the auto shop in the basement of Lady Fortune, she was hit by the stench of motor oil. A wide variety of tools hung on the walls and in the middle was sufficient space for three vehicles to be worked on at the same time. Right now there was a solitary chair and one man wearing a blue baseball cap, sweating profusely.

Alice walked toward him and everyone heard the clink of her heels on the tiled floor. She stopped four feet away from the john, forcing him to look up at her.

"How much has he won so far?"

"Hundred and fifty grand by the time we got to him."

"The dealer?"

"On her rest break."

"You've been a lucky man today, haven't you?"

Alice hadn't moved her head from staring at the guy during this conversation, but her change of tone showed who she was now talking to. He nodded in reply and swallowed hard.

"Get this lucky guy a glass of water. He can hardly speak with all his good fortune."

Beat.

"We like winners at the Lady Fortune. It shows our customers that anyone can succeed. Young or old, rich or poor. It's the American dream."

Alice circled round the chair, returning to her initial position. Even more sweat as she kicked the leg of his seat.

"But casinos only thrive if they are fair to everybody and everyone plays fair… Did you play fair?"

His eyes, filled with fear, widened further than either of them thought possible. Naldo stood by the entrance, a position he'd held since Alice entered the room.

"What did you say? I can't hear you. Did you play fair?"

Another hard swallow but no sound came out of his mouth. He glanced at Naldo and back to Alice.

"See, we've been watching you and know you haven't been playing by the rules. So we know what you've done. The question is whether you are man enough to admit it. That will determine what happens next."

"How long you know the dealer?"

"Four years."

"How long you been coming here?"

"A week."

"How much you made in total?"

"Nearly a million."

"Congratulations. The smart thing was not to take too much on any particular day. The dumb thing was to continue coming back."

"I figured little and often would keep us under the wire."

Alice nodded and patted the john on the knee. Then she idled over to Naldo.

"I don't want to see his face in Vegas again. Same for the dealer. And give a five thousand bonus to the guy who spotted them. Then I'll fire his ass because he took too long to do it."

Naldo nodded and Alice left the room without looking back. That afternoon, he drove to the desert with a spade. His trunk was empty when he returned.

VEGAS WAS AN unreal town at the best of times and Christmas time doubled the insanity of the place. Like a bad smell on the sole of her sneakers, Frank appeared at the Lady Fortune in early December.

"Mama told me to come and help you over the vacation season. So here I am!"

"She never mentioned it. What makes you think I need you?"

"Hey, don't give me that sisterly look. I'm here because Mama asked me. If you've got nothing for me to do then I'll hang for a while and head off in January. No big deal."

"Is Bobby aware you're here?"

"How the fuck would I know? I can't read minds."

Alice gazed at the bedraggled heap of a brother stood in her office and sighed.

"Listen bro'. I've got things covered. Nothing personal but we don't need your… talents… here. Stick around for sure but keep clear of the cops. And that's real important in the casino: any issues and we lose this license to print money. Do not fuck this up. We can give you some chips if you want to chance your luck—only we get them back out of your winnings. If you have any."

"Don't mind if I do. Can you comp me a suite too?"

"A room, not a suite. They're for the high rollers. Not lifelong losers."

A smile crept across Alice's face as she enjoyed the moment. Frank appeared untouched by her putdown.

WHEN FRANK AND Alice weren't competing, the twins got on fine. With party season in full swing, she introduced her brother to the few friends she'd made since hitting town and he returned the compliment by getting them invites to the coolest gatherings in the city.

Their first joint attendance was in a penthouse owned by a dude Frank met the night before in a champagne bar. When the twins arrived, Alice surveyed the scene in the living room and didn't want him to leave her hip. So many people and such a buzz. It was overwhelming, but not for Frank who thrived in this atmosphere. Almost before she'd exhaled, he blazed a trail straight to the makeshift bar on the far end of the room, introducing himself to what he hoped would be his first liaison.

Alice stood transfixed, trying to decide where to go. While Frank's degree was a miracle, Alice earned hers by studying every night when she wasn't working to pay her way. Mama had helped, for sure, but she didn't believe her college place was a right just because she wanted it. This meant she spent scant time at frat houses or sorority parties with commensurate fewer social skills than her younger brother.

"Overwhelming. Isn't it?"

Alice's head nodded in agreement before she had a chance to see who she was talking to. Tall, dark hair and cute lips. The guy's body was well-toned beneath his blue designer suit and Alice smiled at him.

"Shall we get a drink? I'm Tom."

Without another word, he held her by the hand and they zigzagged over to the bar where he ordered a martini for himself.

"Cosmo, please."

She reckoned he was only ten years her senior and conversation flowed into the night with a healthy mix of dancing and smooching to while away a few hours. Before long, they were leaving the apartment block.

"Fancy a nightcap?"

ALICE AWOKE WONDERING what she was doing beneath silk sheets. Then she recalled the two hours between leaving the party and falling asleep. Tom had been much the same as the other men she'd slept with. She didn't hold it against him as she hadn't experienced an orgasm with them either. Alice was thinking sex was overrated for women, despite what the glossy magazines said.

The guy was still asleep, out for the count. Something about the feel of the sheets on her skin made Alice stop for a second and enjoy the sensation over every part of her body the silk touched. Her stomach, breasts, a knee and crotch. She turned to look at Tom again to make sure he was definitely sleeping.

She moved her hand down between her thighs and did to herself what he failed to deliver. Then she scooted out of bed, grabbed her clothes and went home to shower and change for work.

THE NEXT EVENING, Alice and Frank entered a different apartment but she couldn't say if she was staring at the same people. Plucking up more confidence than the night before, she wended her way round the chatting drinkers hoping to make eye contact with someone long enough to start a conversation. She also was on the lookout in case Tom was here.

A red dress caught her attention which was attached to a smile.

"Just got here?"

"Uh-huh. I'm Alice."

"Samantha, although everyone calls me Sam. I don't know why I introduce myself as Samantha because I prefer Sam too."

The entire sentence came out in one nervous breath and ended in an embarrassed giggle.

"What does a girl have to do to get a drink at this party?"

Sam took Alice to the bar and they both ordered cosmos. She enjoyed watching the woman sashay her way over to a space near the balcony. They peered outside, but it was too cold for anyone to want to stand out there. The red plunge dress swooped down at the front and almost was open to Sam's navel, so Alice thought. Her eyes lingered on the sight longer than politeness allowed.

Conversation and cosmos flowed through the evening and Alice couldn't help feel jealous every time Sam received attention from the many male suitors. Even Frank flitted by at one point. As guests left, Alice touched Sam on the arm and suggested: "Fancy a glass of wine back at mine?"

"I thought you'd never ask."

SAM'S RED DRESS lay underneath her panties on the floor of Alice's bedroom. When the older twin woke up, she realized what she'd known for many years, but had refused to acknowledge: dicks didn't do it for her. She rolled over to face Sam and stroked her stomach just enough to rouse her from her slumber. A sleepy smile in response and Alice leaned in to kiss her newfound lover.

They met up every night for the next week but Alice ensured she kept her word to Frank and they both accompanied him to the slew of parties he'd gained invites to. She understood her brother believed his chances with women improved if they saw him entering the party with girls who were obviously friends. Softened his image and made him a safer prospect.

The bubble burst on Alice's Saturday night when the phone rang two minutes after Sam went down on her. Three in the morning, according to her watch.

"Yes?"

"Hi. I need your help."

"You sure pick the worst of times, don't you?"

Alice picked up the call only because it might have been the casino needing her urgent attention. A brother bleating was a different story altogether. She positioned herself with her back leaning against the head board and her legs apart, knees up. Sam took the hint and carried on where she left off.

"Huh?"

"What's the matter, little boy? It's the middle of the night and you've woken me up."

"I wouldn't want you to panic or anything but I'm in a lovely home with a revolver pointing at my head. Turns out the woman I met at the party earlier has a husband."

"And he is the one with the gun?"

"Yep. He's a reasonable guy. If we wire him compensation, he won't shoot me in the balls."

As soon as Alice talked about firearms, Sam stopped her stroking and scurried to the bathroom. Some family conversations best stayed private. Alice watched her leave the room with lust and disappointment that their fun was over.

"Answer me straight, okay?"

"Yep."

"Do you believe him?"

"Yes."

"Any other option for you to get out alive?"

"No."

"How much?"

Alice heard a muffled voice in the background name a six-figure sum.

"Tell him I'll wire it over as soon as the banks open."

"But it's Saturday, sis'."

She grinned at the fact that the time with Sam had made her forget the day of the week. And at the fear in Frank's tone.

"Don't think you can charm your way with the couple until Monday morning?"

"No."

The husband's voice got louder.

"Only joking. I'll send Naldo over with the money. He'll be with you in less than an hour. The man will resolve the issue. He always does."

"Thanks. Is this guy reliable?"

"He'll follow my instructions to the letter."

An audible sigh and Frank's relief was palpable.

"We can talk about how you got yourself in this situation in the office, young man. Swing by—sober—in the afternoon."

"Sure thing. And thanks again."

One phone call to Frescetti and he agreed to take care of everything. Alice lay there and grabbed a pillow to inhale Sam's scent. Her fragrance filled Alice with butterflies.

"Come out, come out, wherever you are!"

The bathroom door opened a crack to reveal a hand and half a head.

"Is it safe?"

"Always is, my darling."

"I don't like guns. They scare me."

She pouted and leaned back on the en-suite door to close it. Alice beckoned her over with a first finger and Sam lay on top of her, between her legs. They hugged for five, maybe ten, minutes until the tension left Sam's body. Then Alice giggled, placed both hands on the top of Sam's head and pushed down until her tongue resumed its earlier work.

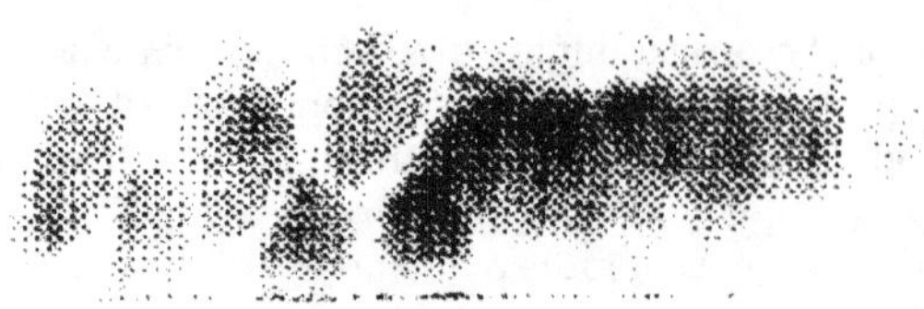

135

NEW YEAR'S DAY approached and Frank still hadn't left. Alice didn't mind as much as she thought she would, but on one of Bobby's occasional trips to town, he could see she was happy. Hence more relaxed about her annoying baby brother.

"You met someone?"

"What makes you say that?"

"No reason. There's a glint in your eyes or am I mistaken?"

"Don't know what you mean."

Alice pursed her lips and waited for a second to produce a dramatic pause. Bobby waited for the payoff.

"Sam."

"And when will you take Sam home to meet your mother?"

"We met at a Christmas party, so it's way too quick for anything as serious as that. Too soon for you too—before you ask."

"Shame. Anyone who can put a smile on your face is always worth meeting."

"Leave things be for now."

"Back to business then. We have been encountering resistance in LA and have traced the cause to a neighbor of yours."

"How so?"

"The beneficial owners of the Ace of Spades are chiseling into our heroin trade. There have been skirmishes but nothing heavy yet. I'm making you aware because these matters can blow up in your face mighty fast."

"Are you concerned enough to want to stick around?"

"Concerned enough to fly over but you kids must stand on your own two feet. And you stopped clinging to your mom's apron strings years ago."

"Seen Frank this trip?"

"Landed and came straight here. Besides it's before lunch so what're the chances of the boy being awake?"

Alice laughed and Bobby smiled. Now they worked together, he was far more open about his opinions about business or the family. Her memories growing up were of Bobby being the most taciturn human she'd ever come across. Maybe he chose the time and place to mouth off. Pas devant les enfants.

Bobby stayed in Vegas long enough to share a cocktail with Frank but left before any heavy session could get going. This made Alice less secure as she felt as though Bobby rushed back to circle the wagons. She canceled leave for all security guards and put them on alert for any potential crisis.

Half an hour after Bobby departed she got Naldo to bring Frank up to her office before he was too wasted.

"Did he mention something to you?"

"Nah, chewed the fat then hopped back to Palm Springs."

"There could be problems about to hit us. Until it's over, stay in the casino. Get the concierge to order in what you want, but don't leave the building."

Frank sat straight in the chair. A serious expression ripped across his face in a way Alice had never seen before.

"How bad?"

"Not sure but important enough for Bobby to take a day trip. There's shit going down at home too so we need to be careful."

"You might not believe me but I want to help. Tell me what and I'll do it."

"Forgive me, Frank if I don't jump up and down with glee. Your track record involves snorting and whoring. Neither of these qualities are in high demand right now."

"Give me a chance. That's all I ask."

"I will bear you in mind if the opportunity arises. In the meantime, stay sober and make yourself useful helping Naldo and his crew. Follow his instructions to the letter then who knows what'll happen."

THE ATTACK CAME the following day when an armored van left the Lady Fortune on time laden with used notes. Bad news was: it never reached the bank. The Lagottis had been robbed of a little over three million—or a week's take.

"Make enquiries. We need to know who did it, who is holding our money and where it is held. No actions, no reprisals against any suspects. We stay calm and serve our revenge like a fine white wine."

"Smash the neck and gouge their faces out?"

"No, Frank. Cold. We serve it cold once we find out everyone involved along the trail. If we act too early then the other perpetrators will fly to the four corners of the country."

Her brother nodded consent but Alice was not convinced. She gave Naldo a look as if to instruct him to keep special close to the boy.

"This doesn't mean we should appear to sit idly by. Can we please hire out-of-town experts to set a fire in the basement of the Ace of Spades? Nothing to destroy the building but enough to cause a modicum of chaos and a lot of inconvenience."

Her other thought was that if the money was still inside, they'd have to keep it safe and move it immediately. It's much easier to follow three million dollars in one vehicle than chase down batches of fifty thousand—or worse.

TWO DAYS LATER and Alice entered the auto shop to see Frank pounding a man's head to a pulp with his fists. Blood splatter and teeth littered the floor. Naldo looked on but did nothing. Three others in his crew sat around sipping beer.

"Stop this frat meeting right now."

Frank held his arm back but did not land another blow. Naldo passed him a towel and he tried to clean up the guy's face.

"I thought my instructions were clear. And I expected better of you."

A dagger-eye glare at Naldo. Then Alice strode in to take her place next to Frank. She looked down at the man: hands and ankles bound with electrical cable. An oily rag stuffed into his mouth with tape stuck over it. His nose the only outlet for his noisy breathing. Despite the violence meted out, he was calm. Alice thought he'd be hyperventilating, but no. Naldo had the measure of him. The punches were just to keep his mind occupied until she arrived and squatted down so her head was the same level as her captor.

"I want you to listen carefully when I say these things to you."

The guy stared straight at her with hate burrowing into her skull. Then he blinked and the edge to his manner abated. He maintained eye contact and his breathing rate increased a touch.

"You are here because your father and the rest of your family stole from us. This is not acceptable. The good news is that we have recovered our money and each of the individuals involved in the theft have been liquidated.

"Before they died, each of them confessed to their part of the crime. You need not worry on that account because we all know you did not commit the robbery. And we will not torture you into confessing to something you did not do. We're not the Feds, after all."

They all laughed and Alice discerned the corners of his mouth turning upward too.

"That's the good news: the money is back where it belongs. You, my friend, are our reparations. You represent the compensation we are owed for the inconvenience and upset caused by your father—and his kith and kin. We mean you no ill will."

Alice touched the guy's arm to show she understood his concerns and his breathing returned to its earlier pace. She stood up and walked over to Naldo who rummaged in his pockets and then resumed his original stance. She sauntered back and mopped the bloody forehead with Friscetti's handkerchief. Then she slid the material over his cheeks and soaked up the red still dripping off his chin.

A quick pull and she ripped away the tape over his mouth. The guy spat the rag out and took in mouthfuls of clean air. Alice dropped the reddened cloth onto the floor and clicked her fingers until someone passed her a beer. She let a few drops land on the guy's lips to moisten them and held the bottle so he could take two, no three, long glugs.

Alice took the drink away to give the son of the Huang family a chance to catch his breath. Then she switched the bottle for the revolver she'd kept in her other hand, pushed it in his mouth and squeezed the trigger. His brains flew out the back of his skull and Frank jumped with a start.

She put another slug in his heart and fired a third shot into his groin. Alice flipped the safety on and placed the gun on top of the bloody handkerchief. Perhaps for the first time in his life, Naldo smiled. His student learned fast.

As she walked out, she turned her head in Frank's direction.

"That's revenge served cold."

She strode back to her office and hopped into the shower—the facilities were extensive but not surprising as she worked and lived in a hotel. A call to Mama to let her know everything was under control, then home time.

Alice stayed in a suite on the twentieth floor so her commute was minimal. Sam cooked two bowls of stir-fried chicken with noodles. They sat on opposite sides of the dining room table, which felt like they were an ocean apart. She reached out to touch Sam's hand in between mouthfuls.

"What's wrong dear?"

"Nothing really. The food tastes great… I'm not that hungry, is all."

"Thanks but there's something up with you."

"Work. It'll be fine. Right now I'd like you to take me to bed and hold me."

Hand in hand, they scurried into the bedroom and slipped under the sheets. Alice nestled in between Sam's breasts and tried to exorcize the image of her first kill out of her head. The softness of Sam's skin comforted little that evening but Alice inhaled her fragrance and the demons floated away by the time they were both asleep in each other's warm embrace.

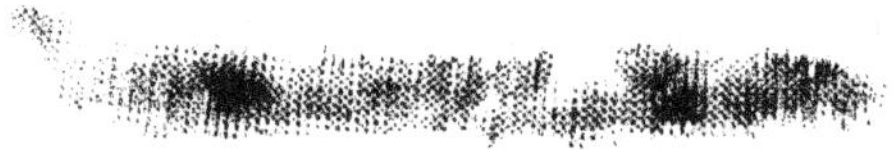

SHUN HUANG SAT on the other side of the table to Mary Lou in a nondescript meeting room in an anonymous hotel chain in the heart of Los Angeles. Also present was Bobby, Shun's brother and a bodyguard each. There was no need for the muscle for either group because no one would be stupid enough to attack these two bosses in the middle of peace talks.

"We have come here today to end the difficulties between our families. Both have suffered loss…"

"Some more than others."

"…but the important thing is for us to draw a line under all the unpleasantness and to move forward."

Mary Lou had spent a week of shuttle diplomacy to get Shun in the same room. The intermediary they'd used had convinced him the war must end and that Mary Lou was open to compromise. Word on the street was she'd ordered Shun's head on a platter—the work begun by Alice was to end with Mary Lou. The truth was Mary Lou didn't care whether Shun lived. She wanted him to stop muscling in on her drugs supply lines. Every day she wasted fighting him was more time when earnings were down.

"We are here to prevent more blood being shed. One of my sons died because of our differences."

"That is a lamentable state of affairs and I am truly sorry for your loss. If we reach an agreement today, I guarantee no member of your family'll die at our hands."

"Your word is important here because it is all you have. Without power or wealth, we are alone before our gods with only what we say to keep us on a true path."

"You have my word. But in exchange, I need to know you will cease your encroachment into my territories. You have carved out a niche for yourself here in LA at our expense and attacked my property in Las Vegas. You must put an end to both matters."

"My son paid the ultimate price for our actions in Vegas. Now I am left only with daughters. Your business operations and your children will be safe there—from our involvement."

"And what about LA?"

"We need to earn a living and our access to Chinese sources means our product is much cheaper than yours. I'm talking opiates here. Let me be clear: we are not departing the city just because we are inconvenient to you."

"I understand and respect that. Your family has done well in a short space of time. At our expense though."

Mary Lou stared at Shun while they spoke but Bobby made sure he was on top of the entire roomful of people. They had talked through their game plan for the meeting into the small hours sat in the summerhouse and then later in bed. Bobby had been told that Shun's brother wanted blood revenge and had been put in his place by Shun. The man might be a grieving father, but he was a smart businessman first.

"Yours is the biggest heroin operation in California. We were bound to nibble at the crumbs on your plate."

"What I propose is a way for you to consume a three course meal."

"I am here to listen."

"Build up your business by all means. If you open up territories we are not yet covering, then we can support you with the resources we have available. For that we receive twenty per cent of your turnover. In areas of ours which you now occupy I must ask you to share more of your good fortune because it has been gained off the back of twenty years hard work on our part. In these places, we will get fifty cents on the dollar."

Shun stared at Mary Lou for fifteen seconds and then leaned over and whispered to his brother, cupping his hand in front of his mouth to hide the movement of his lips. Mary Lou didn't bother to even strain to eavesdrop. She knew their plan and how she would respond no matter what he said. Bobby continued to survey the room.

"What would these resources be?"

"People, guns, processing labs. I could even get you some office space if you wanted."

This last comment raised a brief smile on Shun's face. He resumed his whispering and Mary Lou went on staring. As their conversation appeared to carry on for a while, she stood up and walked over to the coffee pot to get a second cup. By the time the mug was empty, Shun and his brother had finished their dialog.

"Under the circumstances, we are open to sealing a deal but the price you ask is too rich for us… Ten and thirty per cent."

Mary Lou picked up her coffee and pretending to take the last sip from it. She opened her clutch bag and applied lipstick using a makeup mirror. She saw the impatience in Shun's eyes.

"Twenty and fifty. Your family remains safe and we do great business together. And we both get to dip our beaks in the trough."

"Twenty and forty?"

Shun knew the money was to be made from South LA and other Lagotti territory. New areas would be harder to capture and he wanted an easy life. He was too old to spend a year or two fighting his way across LA, block by block.

"Fifteen and fifty. Take it or leave it."

Mary Lou placed the lipstick in her bag and waited for the whispering to subside.

"We agree."

"And five per cent ownership of the Ace of Spades."

The brother's blood vessels nearly burst out his temples but Shun showed restraint. He looked at his brother and stared at Mary Lou.

"Done."

The tension at the table dissipated with nods from all concerned and Shun walked round to Mary Lou so they could shake on the deal. With business settled, there was nothing more to say and everybody left. Bobby held back briefly to let the meeting room manager know they were done—and settle the check. Before they strolled out the lobby, Mary Lou told him to wait while she headed off to use a hotel phone.

"Just called off the hit on Shun and his brother."

Bobby smiled. They had taken the time to cover every eventuality. Cutting the head off the snake was one of many options they'd considered.

1995

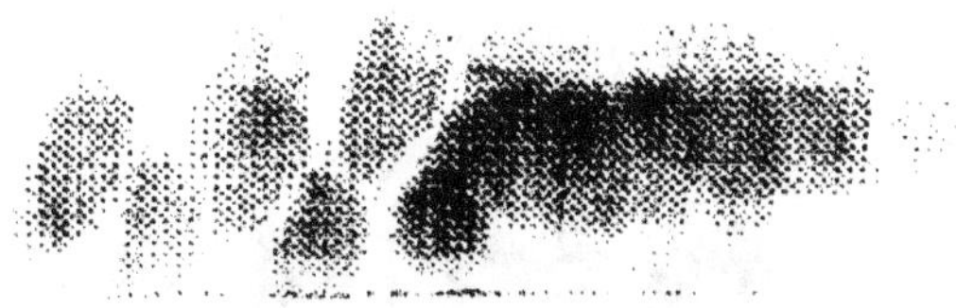

136

"YOU'VE DONE WELL here. Revenue is up and the place is running nice and smooth. You should come back to Palm Springs."

Bobby and Alice sat in her office in the early evening. She'd enjoyed being at the helm of Lady Fortune and had forged a comfortable life. Sam visited from Boston most weekends which meant Alice could concentrate on work but still fall into the arms of someone she cared about. And the sex was good too. Would she be able to recreate all that under the watchful eye of her mother? Besides, running a casino was fun and when there was an occasional spot of bother, she had shown herself she could handle it.

"Vegas is more my town. The bright lights. The buzz when you hit the streets. You can taste it. There's green coming out of every manhole cover. This is a moneymaking wet dream of a city."

They lounged on the couches Alice had introduced to the vast expanse of the office almost as soon as she'd moved in. Bobby missed a trick—she encouraged people to stick around and have informal conversations so they'd reveal more of what they were thinking. Alice was so much more than a black designer pants suit and red lipstick. That was all Frank saw—on one of the rare moments he was sober.

"It's a great town for sure and you can always visit it. No one's saying you should never come back. But you need to listen to me. Your mother and I would like you on the west coast. We have some issues in California and you and your brains must be here to sort things out."

"Mama wants me to return?"

"Yes. You can live in LA if you don't want to hang in sleepy Palm Springs."

"She asked for me? Not Frank?"

Thoughts of Valentine's Day holed up in the suite with Sam were evicted from her mind.

"I'm in. Let me know when I need to move. And you're right, I can't stay cooped up in Palm Springs."

"Until you get yourself sorted, you could use the top floor of the Palace."

"Who'll take over at this end?"

"No one could replace you, dear."

"Okay…"

"I'll go back to keeping an eye on things. We'll bring in a manager. And before that Frank can earn a day's wages."

"Don't spend too long in between trips if you want the place to be still standing."

Bobby issued another smile. She much preferred the adult relationship she had with him.

"And Naldo comes with me."

"Naturally. I wouldn't have hooked you two up if I thought you'd separate so easy."

Alice smiled now, realizing how important Friscetti was in her newfound world and the trust he'd been given to mind Alice Lagotti, daughter of Mary Lou.

THEY SAT AROUND the pool in the afternoon, tumblers of whiskey in their hands. In the five days since Alice returned to California, she had spent the first day unpacking. The thought of living in the Palace long-term was too weird to handle, even though she'd lived above a casino and hotel for months. Somehow that felt normal whereas in her childhood, it was somewhere to visit for sure, but Mary Lou never allowed the twins the run of the joint. There was something taboo in the woodwork.

As an adult she got the fact it was a glorified whorehouse and cocaine dispensary although nowadays the selection of narcotics was far wider than that. The prostitution continued, but the parties were drying up. New Hollywood wanted different nighttime escapes and shipping in younger girls wasn't the answer. Frank would be in his element though he'd fuck his way through the profits in his first week.

Then she flew Sam over and they pretended to be tourists around Beverly Hills, much as her mother had done decades earlier when Alice could barely walk. Days of sightseeing and nights of naked bliss. Sam was proving to be an essential part of her life.

"Would you think about moving west at some point?"

The question came out of the blue in the middle of horsing around on a couch in the living room. They both had their hands up each other's skirts while they watched a movie.

"Maybe. I'm doing well in Boston and my company only has a small practice out here. It would be like a demotion."

She was an account exec at a media and marketing firm: she needed to be where the clients were. Sam's finger continued its massage, having stopped for a moment.

"I'm not saying no, dear. Just it'd be a big move for me and, well, we've only been going out three months…"

Sam was right: Alice was moving way too fast. There would be time enough. Instead, she should lose herself in the moments they had together here and now. She closed her eyes and focused on Sam's first finger. When she opened her eyelids, she was back sitting with Mama and Bobby on a lounger by the pool.

"Palm Springs is quiet in the Winter."

"Gets cold at night though."

"Sure, but I'd forgotten how restful the town is."

"That's not Palm Springs—it's 20 Oakcrest Drive."

"Yeah. Only have happy memories of this place."

"What about Cindy?"

"Who?"

"A family friend, you might say. But it doesn't matter. You don't remember her and she's long since gone."

They each took a sip of their drinks, almost in unison.

"Tell me: why am I back on the west coast? Can't be to have another drinking buddy."

"Huang was a red flag to me. I know we have resolved them as a problem…"

"In the short-term."

"…but they represent a bigger threat to our organization."

"How so?"

"Entry into narcotics is getting easier by the day. Any fool with a bag of pills and some foot soldiers can take over a handful of blocks. Before you know it has happened, they control a district and you're fighting to retrieve what's yours. Doesn't mean we shouldn't fight for every inch we own, but as the struggle gets harder, more gangs will appear and it won't be like the good old days when five Families ran the country. We must deal with each bunch of sniveling upstarts one-by-one."

"So we must find additional ways of earning money before it gets taken away by the Feds. They are proving way too successful at getting stool pigeons to squawk."

"And what have you come up with?"

"Us? Nothing. We've been around too long. We need someone new to the game to introduce a touch of zing."

"Get Irma to mix me a cosmo. It'll be a very long night."

ALICE LEFT OAKCREST at six in the morning. By midnight the cosmos weren't cutting it for her so she moved over to vodka tonics. This made her chatty and giggly but nothing more. Mama and Bobby gave up by two because her conversation was slurring too much for anything to make any sense. So she flipped around the cable channels in search of inspiration. Three hours later, Irma came downstairs to find Alice dribbling on an armchair and called her a taxi.

When she woke up in the Palace, her eyes widened like a spark had been lit inside her. She rummaged round the apartment until she found a phone and dialed as shakily as her still-drunk finger would allow.

"Mama, I've got it. We'll reinvent the numbers racket."

"Don't say another word. Go back to bed—you've only had an hour's sleep—and come over this afternoon to talk this through."

The line went dead and Alice checked her watch. Mama was right. She got out of her clothes and sloped under the covers. Within two minutes of closing her eyes, she was sleeping like a baby, albeit a loud snoring infant that reeked of booze.

"YOU CAN BET your bottom dollar that everyone loves to gamble."

Mary Lou and Bobby sat in the summerhouse while Alice paced up and down taking occasional sips from her orange juice.

"The Lady Fortune proves it's true. Hell, Las Vegas shows I'm right. Americans will bet on anything. That's why before the war, they'd even bet on a number. That was all the numbers game was."

"Yes, but you know they rigged it?"

"Of course. Arnold Rothstein was behind all that, yeah?"

"Love the history lesson. This trip down memory lane is fabulous but..."

"Don't you see? Haven't you been watching the news?"

Bobby and Mary Lou looked blankly at each other. Had they been so caught up in their own little world to have missed a life-changing event? Alice waited as patiently as she was able for the penny to drop. When the two turned back to stare at her eager for a clue, she realized she'd have to wait until hell froze over before any flicker of recognition from her audience.

"California State is starting a lottery. Ordinary Joes will slap greens down on the counter of their local convenience store hoping to win millions. Instead of a shady dude writing their lucky number in a ledger, they'll walk round with a shiny piece of paper printed by us with the digits neatly circled."

The expressions remained the same: abject incomprehension why Alice was so excited.

"There's a load of security around manufacturing the tickets but the store owners won't care if the pieces of card are legitimate or not. They get paid by the Joes. Having real-looking lottery cards would be fantastic and we must have sufficient cash to grease enough palms in the right places. It'll be like we're printing our own money, only we do it through a network of retailers."

Everyone was quiet for a spell until Mary Lou punctured the silence.

"What if someone wins using one of our tickets?"

"Either the fake is good in which case the Joe gets his cash. Or it's not and the storekeeper takes the heat."

"And then word goes round they bought the cards from us and…"

"…and nothing. I'm talking about looking and acting like a wholesaler here. They won't know the difference. We charge the same as the real guys only our costs are lower because we're not using high tech printing presses or having to pay union rates."

"It's so simple, why didn't we think of it?"

"You've been doing this too long and don't drink enough cosmos."

"She has a point."

"About the cosmos anyway."

For the first time since entering the room, Alice slumped down on an easy chair. She drained her juice and slammed the glass down on a nearby table.

"Oops, misjudged the height of that."

Mama sent Bobby to the kitchen for a refill for Alice and a large pot of coffee.

"And cookies."

When both he and Irma returned with a bountiful supplier of drinks and munch, they worked through the fine detail. Planning a successful new venture was down to the small print. Alice's big picture made perfect sense but the little gotcha details would send them to jail.

Four hours and two plates of cookies later, they thought the master plan was one hundred per cent bullet proof.

"Let's sleep on it and go through everything again tomorrow. Do you want to stay for dinner?"

"No, I've got stuff to do. Thanks Mama."

"It'll only be a bowl of pasta."

"I mean for wanting me to be in on this with you."

"Silly. Apart from Bobby who else could I turn to in my hour of need?"

Alice shrugged then kissed her mother on the cheek before she left. Mama could have called Frank. That was the answer to Mary Lou's question that Alice didn't want to hear. And Mama hadn't said.

At home, Alice stepped out of her jeans-blouse combo and went back to bed. She so needed more sleep. Before she allowed herself to close her eyes, she put a call through to Sam.

"I've missed you."

"Me too."

"Would you like me to hop over to Boston this weekend instead of making you fly over here?"

"No. My house share isn't as cozy—or private—as your penthouse. Besides, I get a chance of glimpsing a cavorting A-lister at yours."

"That's the nicest way anyone's said you live over a whorehouse I've ever heard."

"I know you're embarrassed about it, but I think it's hot. All those people naked beneath us humping away—it's bestial."

"Tell me, what are you wearing right now…"

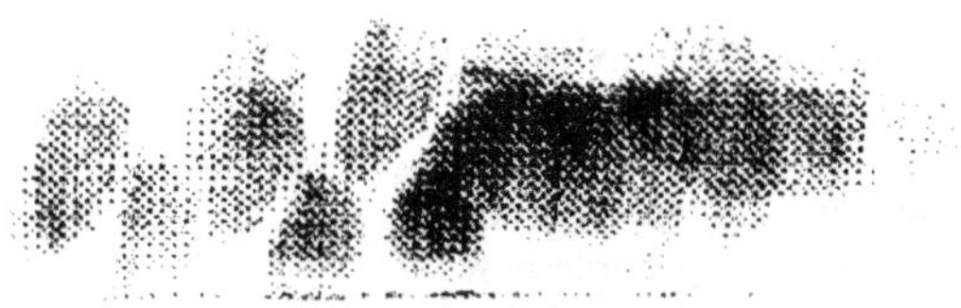

137

ONE INDUSTRIAL PARK is much like the next. Vast buildings made of concrete with no attempt by the architect to inject any beauty in the affair. Once constructed the block is surrounded by a car lot big enough to house the vehicles of all the poor saps working inside the gray walls.

The only planning that takes place is to ensure all the roads are straight—to maximize real-estate usage within each plot. No spare land is wasted on making space for a tree or even a small shrub. Nothing to make a human feel alive.

Another touch to alienate the worker ants is to encase the entire experience in barbed-wire fencing. Keeps uninvited guests out and prevents workers from escaping.

Such an enterprise was the Bakersfield Industrial Park, situated as its branding hinted at the intersection of the two highways where a community had grown called… Bakersfield. The park lay at the dirtier end of the tracks where no one wanted to live but when you lived in a nowhere town, you took any job under any circumstances that was going. This provided the best explanation why anyone worked at the concrete block with the name Bakersfield Printing on the awning nailed to the right of the main entrance.

Monroe Linwood spent twelve years at the plant before he met anybody associated with the Lagotti family. He was yet another guy propped up at the bar or playing the odd game of poker with the boys on a Thursday night. The first thing that made him unusual was the clever way he'd got all the local loan sharks to hold markers on him. Cards were not his passion but baseball kept him alive despite the anchors weighing him down like his dutiful wife and four adoring children.

A hop, skip and a jump later and Mary Lou held those markers and could make Monroe an offer, much as her step uncle had done decades before. Only on this occasion she wasn't intending to rob a bank.

"Thank you for taking the time to see me."

Monroe, Mary Lou and Alice sat around a motel room bed while Bobby and Naldo stood near the door. The place was packed and Monroe was nervous.

"SO'S WE'RE CLEAR: you owe me a lot of money. All the debt you have amassed with local operators has been bought up by me. This means I've paid off all your debt."

"Thank you ma'am."

"You are most welcome. That was your good news for the day. Now you need to come to terms knowing that every red cent you owe to me."

Monroe gulped because what Mary Lou said scared him and everyone staring at him had made him feel nervous from the moment he entered the motel.

"Do you know how much you have gambled away?"

He shook his head. If Monroe knew the amount, he wasn't going to utter it here. This woman knew the big number.

"Over one hundred and twenty thousand dollars plus chump change. Out of interest, do you have that sort of money to repay me?"

Another shake of the head.

"I thought not because if you did, I'd have expected you to pay some of it back to open a line of credit… Do you have a life insurance policy by any chance?"

"No ma'am."

"So you're not even worth anything dead to me."

Monroe's eyes lifted from the floor and opened wide in Mary Lou's direction. She let the idea of his death hang in the air for five seconds until the notion ran out of energy and landed on the carpet, soaking into the stained geometric pattern.

Mary Lou turned to Alice and Monroe shifted his attention accordingly. Alice's soft voice forced Monroe to strain to hear her words.

"Do you have fifty bucks spare each month?"

"Huh? No, ma'am."

"You see, if you paid fifty dollars a month, it would take you two hundred years to pay me back. And you can't even offer that much."

A tear departed Monroe's left eye and traveled down his cheek to drop onto the carpet and join the idea of his death.

"I sure am in a fine predicament and no mistake."

Alice offered him a cigarette from her pack. With a shaking hand, he removed one and put it between his lips. By instinct, he fumbled for a box of matches in his pants pocket, but found diddly squat. She picked up her lighter from the bed, flicked it on with her thumb and held the flame near the end of his smoke. Monroe inhaled and the tobacco caught fire.

"You have a way of sorting out this mess you've got yourself into. You must listen to what I have to say and decide what you will do."

She outlined the plan for Monroe to use his access to the printing shop to borrow a template for the State lottery cards just for one night. He had to walk out to his car with it and drive home on a particular day. Then not lock the automobile overnight, return to work the next day and return the plates.

"Do you understand what we expect you to do?"

"Yes I do."

"Will you help us and clear off your debts for the sake of less than an hour's effort?"

"Well ma'am. You've told me you won't kill me and what you're asking is mighty dangerous. One hour or no. So why don't we agree that I never place a bet again and leave it at that?"

Mary Lou responded without hesitation.

"You are worth nothing to us dead and maybe your family will shed a tear. But I promise you this: if you choose not to help then one by one your children and your wife will find out the many miserable ways to die. And I guarantee you will shed a tear because their deaths will be on your hands. Each and every one."

The guy swallowed hard, took a long drag on his cigarette and stubbed it out in the ashtray lying on the bed. Then he wiped his nose on his sleeve, cleared his throat and spoke with all that his dignity would muster—which wasn't much.

"Let me know when you want us to rip off the California State lottery."

138

ALICE AND BOBBY were working together just like the first week at the Lady Fortune, only this time she wasn't so green around the gills. She was pleased Mama was entrusting her with the project and happy to be collaborating instead of running it all herself. It was good to have a trusted soul with whom to bounce ideas.

The lottery wouldn't launch until much later in the year which meant they had enough time to get everything ready. The biggest hurdles were to prepare the printing presses and to pull together a team of hustlers.

Alice scouted suitable locations to print vast quantities of fake lottery tickets and Bobby used his connections to find guys who could persuade without breaking bones. Any fool can threaten a storekeeper with a gun. It took brains to achieve the same wearing only a smile—and a three-piece suit.

While she traveled around the state, Alice also checked out various towns to live in. Sam might enjoy the sizzle of living in the Palace, but Alice thought she'd find more comfortable surroundings: Sunset Boulevard had seen better days. When she looked at Malibu for light industrial parks, she headed into the center of town to see if there were any condos of interest.

After two weeks on the road, she and Bobby met up in the summerhouse. Mary Lou sat in on the conversation so she could keep abreast of how things were progressing.

"The crew is forming slowly. Too many guys only know how to crack heads."

"I blame the violence on TV and video games."

"Hilarious. Is there anywhere to print the tickets?"

"Agoura Hills. It's on a main road route for our trucks—you have trucks, right? I could oversee the operation easily from Malibu, the other side of the Santa Monica Mountains."

"Say what?"

"I'm thinking of moving there."

"Let's come to that later. My memory of the place was that it's a sleepy hick town."

"Hick town? Yes. Sleepy? Not so much. Perhaps when you were a boy but I don't remember the moon landings, so who am I to say?"

Alice winked at Bobby, who smiled back.

"There's an industrial park away from the residential area. It's not exactly built up near there for sure, but its main street has a certain buzz about it. I mean a bunch of fellas wouldn't stand out in the local diner. They are enough out-of-towners waltzing around for them to pay no nevermind."

"Security?"

"Usual deal. We'd have to make our own inside any building so we didn't draw attention to ourselves on the street. If you want no one within a thousand feet, then we could buy farmland and station rancheros at the gate."

"Good work darling. Why don't you show me and Bobby the sights of Agoura Hills tomorrow and we can run with it or rule it out?"

"Okay, Mama."

"That's settled. Now tell me about Malibu."

"It's a cool place to hang out and it'd be somewhere I could call my own."

"Don't you enjoy living rent free?"

"Of course it's been lovely and I am truly grateful. Only…"

"…you don't want to hang onto your mother's apron strings forever."

"Right. And as fabulous as being on top of a cathouse is…"

"…you've had enough consorting with prostitutes on your doorstep. I understand. You realize we can't protect you as well outside our premises."

"True, but I'm sure Naldo will put together a crack protection detail."

"Sure, but at your expense as you are choosing to create the complication."

"Understood. And it's not a problem. It is an opportunity for me to have my own bricks and mortar."

AFTER THE FAMILY trip to Agoura Hills, Mary Lou signed off the venue. Then they popped by Malibu so Alice could show them the real-estate she was seeking. Nothing much in the scheme of things: beach-side residence with a pool, an untold number of bedrooms and sufficient space for live-in help.

Like she was reconstructing her childhood but relocating it for a sea view. With her success at the Lady Fortune behind her, Alice could afford to pay for this indulgence. Mary Lou and Bobby agreed to support her fulfill her dream. She might have run a casino but she'd never had the pleasure of dealing with realtors before.

That night, Alice returned to the Palace and found Frank in the main lobby. Up in the penthouse, she offered him a glass of champagne.

"Mighty kind, sis'."

"You're lucky to catch me in. I've been on the road these past few weeks."

"So I hear."

"Oh? Keeping tabs on me?"

"Nah. I spoke with Mama a day or two ago. That's all."

Although the pair were far from friends nowadays, Alice was pleased to see her brother. He reminded her of times gone by. Of messing around in the Oakdrive pool and playing in the park. The time before High School and the death rattle of puberty when the twins found they'd lost whatever special connection had been hard-wired into them at birth.

Deep down, Alice knew this pit of nostalgia was a displacement emotion for Sam. But warmish feelings about Frank were the best she had in the absence of her girlfriend in her bed.

"Anything in particular bring you to LA? I thought you had a casino to run now I'm not in Vegas to look after it."

She couldn't resist turning the knife in his side—it came so naturally to her as a reaction.

"Don't be like that, sis'. The Lady Fortune isn't much fun without you hanging around. So I was wondering if there was anything you were up to that I could help."

"Nope. I'm good thanks."

"Word on the street is that you're setting up a nice lottery scam. Certain I can't dip my beak?"

"Absolutely sure. And you mean Mama told you what we are planning, right?"

"Yeah, just messing with you. I'd love to be in on any new deal going down. For once I want to build something that the family can be proud of. Contribute. You know?"

"Yep, Frank but this isn't your party. You must find some other thing. Possibly elsewhere."

"Understood. Haven't been to the east coast for ages. Maybe I should try there."

"And I'll tell Bobby not to expect you back in my old office any time soon."

Alice let him stay in one of the guest rooms overnight. When she came home the following evening, he had vanished and left a note on the dining room table: "Gone fishing. F xxx"

MONROE TRAVELED TO work every weekday without fail. Even when his back played up, he appeared at the gates ready, willing and able. In the past, he might have sloped off to watch a baseball game or to try his hand at poker, but now he was a model, but nervous, citizen. His wife Laura noticed the difference within days and the kids enjoyed having their dad around to play with. This halcyon calm and joy persisted until June when the smile was wiped off his face one crisp morning.

He'd backed out the drive and was about to slam on the gas when he saw a dude a little ways down the street waving at him. The guy half stood under a tree and Monroe was lucky to spot him. He coasted toward the fella and wound down his window.

"Can I help you, bud?"

"Sure. You remember your agreement?"

"Huh?"

"The motel…"

A blank expression held for three seconds and then wide-eyed recognition of the name and his compact with the devil in a designer pants suit wearing red lipstick.

"Today you keep your word. Do what you must do at work and leave the item under the driver's seat."

"Don't lock up tonight, right?"

"You said it, friend. Do that and we won't see each other again."

"What if I can't get to the templates or they've put on extra security?"

"Then figure it out or we'll meet again. Look stay calm and think on your feet. Besides, any real problems and you can leave a note in the car instead. We'd rather wait one more day and obtain the item than you fuck things up for everyone. Capiche?"

IN HINDSIGHT, MONROE realized it was the easiest way to earn a hundred and twenty thousand dollars. How he sneaked out with the plates defied belief. His security pass gave him all points access and because they'd been printing cards since Easter, everyone had grown complacent. There were no checks, no metal detectors. Nothing his imagination had conjured up on his route into work.

When he got home, he parked frontwards in the drive as usual. The only difference was that he didn't turn the key in the lock before coming inside. The following morning the plate was where he'd left it but with an envelope containing a stack of bills.

He stuffed the greenbacks into his pocket and replaced the template early in his shift. They hadn't mentioned any payment on top of clearing the debt. Mighty stand up that Lagotti girl. The doofus used the cash as a massive beer and betting fund. The local bar had never known such trade and relations with his wife took a predictable drunken downhill slide.

Pumped with arrogance fueled by the ten grand donated by the Lagottis, Monroe shared his views on women, gambling and work to any barfly in his vicinity. This made him unpleasant but of no consequence to anyone. When his friends tired of his endless tirades, he needed more interesting stories to spice up their interest.

"Don't buy a Scratcher in November. I betcha there'll be fakes flooding the market before you can sneeze."

That Tuesday evening sealed his fate because two days later, he was visited at work by the local law enforcement. Monroe joined them for an interview at the sheriff's office and discovered the pleasure of an overnight rest in one of their cells.

Despite the genuine fear for his family's safety, Monroe spilled his guts to the detective because the secret burned him up inside. Anyway, they'd promised him that if he did the right thing, they wouldn't touch Laura and the kids. They had kept their word so far. Been stand up guys. And he had done what they asked—to the letter.

ALICE PICKED UP the phone, listened to the news from the other end of the line. Her face remained impassive and all Sam could do was know it was work and something serious had come up. She knew better than to stick around and popped back inside Alice's Malibu beach-side retreat and fixed herself another drink.

"He's been arrested for sure? Not just a person of interest?"

"Correct. From what I understand, he's given them a full and frank statement. During Prohibition, they'd say he sang like a canary."

"Have you seen the cop's report?"

"Not yet. Hope to do so tomorrow."

"Are they going to indict and how much has he provided about the people in the motel meeting?"

"Yes and don't know at this point. My contact said the confession was full and frank but he gave no details."

Alice sighed: she didn't need these kinds of problems screwing with them. Mama would not be pleased. She should deal fast because nothing gets better unless you make it so. To pretend Monroe hadn't squawked was plain stupid. What's done was done and she needed to put it right as quick as possible.

Sam wandered onto the balcony to see if Alice was finished with work and they could get back to staring at the stars and fooling around.

"Okay. Keep me informed as and when. Bye."

She stood next to Alice and placed a palm on Alice's cheek.

"Are you done?"

"Not quite. One more call and I'll be all yours. Won't take long."

Alice squeezed Sam's butt before patting it to encourage it to turn away and go inside. To reinforce the idea, she passed Sam her empty glass.

"Be a dear and mix me another cosmo."

Alice blew her a kiss and she padded to the cocktail shaker, ice bucket and assorted bottles in the living room. Meantime, Alice dialed a number she knew by heart.

"I've got an urgent job for you and nobody else. Monroe Linwood is breathing and helping the police with their investigation. Let me know when the cops find he's accidentally died in their facilities."

"And the family."

"Leave them be for now. They've suffered enough living with the motherfucker all these years. My contact is finding out what the police found out and he'll tell us whether Mrs. Linwood knows anything. If she does, she'll decide to hang herself with the shame and the grief. Okay, Naldo?"

Before breakfast was served, Monroe choked himself on shards of the sheeting from his bed.

ALICE SAT BOLT upright with a judder and saw Bobby's hand in hers. The priest droned on. She recalled the cold blast of air as the bullet flew into the room. The incomprehension of the meaning of the breeze. Then the sound of the shot and the gentle splatter of liquid on her face.

All she could do was close her eyes and squeeze Bobby's hand tight. The inner yell of pain consumed her again and she escaped from the present by thinking about the past.

139

FRANK CHOSE NOT to head to New York after the trouble he got in there last visit. He had no desire to spend time behind bars again even if it was only a few hours. So he tried to imagine where he could go to chase tail and party hard.

A lascivious grin crossed his face as he remembered a town where three quarters of the population were students: Boston. Term time the place was awash with willing ass and out of season there was still more than enough to go round—if you had green in your wallet and snow in your pocket. You could fuck anything you wanted with that potent mix about your person.

At Logan, he told himself he'd keep his word to Alice and find a business opportunity to exploit. First, he needed to get a place to stay and free his mind from the grind of running that casino. He took a taxi to the Boston Merit Hotel and settled into a suite at the five star establishment. His bottomless pit of a credit card funded by his mom delivered the finest of room service meals before he sauntered out of the lobby that evening in search of female companionship.

Frank considered himself to be showing high moral fiber by wanting to go to a nightclub and buy tonight's pussy with cocktails and cocaine. In the past he'd have had a word with the concierge and stayed in his room. So he sat in the VIP area of a heaving club trying to pick out someone to impress.

The choice was phenomenal and Frank couldn't decide which way to look first. The problem would separate the contenders from the crowd. He left the safety of the VIPs and hit the bar. A group of five girls stood nearby and four of them he'd happily fuck. The fifth one had hair too short, so Frank'd let her suck him off if he had to. He ordered a bottle of vintage champagne, which caught their attention due to the flurry of activity associated with delivering and opening it. As planned.

"Would you like a glass? Sharing is caring."

The prospect of free booze could not be turned away and they eagerly agreed. Forty minutes later and they were dancing. Another quarter of an hour and they sat at his table in the VIP section. Conversation giggled, twisted and flowed until he decided it was time to find out who really wanted to party.

"Anyone fancy a little something to perk you up?"

Only Eileen was interested, who was Frank's favorite on account of her hot pants, round tits and hair down to her nipples, so he imagined. He ordered the others another bottle of champagne to keep them warmed up and led her away by the hand. Two Jacksons got the attendant to let them into a cubicle in the women's bathroom.

A kiss and a squeeze, then he put his finger to his lips and Eileen watched him cut a line and snort it up his left nostril. Then he set up a second and offered it to her. She nodded and held her hair in one hand and sniffed away. Frank smiled and they kissed some more. Then he pushed her downward until she was crouching below him. She looked up at him, grinned and undid his pants. This Ivy League beauty understood the meaning of a fair trade.

She stayed with him for twenty-four hours and then he got bored with her and the two friends who tagged along. The three enjoyed his snow and he pleasured himself inside all of them. The great thing about money is that everyone wants to taste it but even he understood pretty ass followed his green, not him, and the fun eventually faded and died.

A WEEK LATER and student tail stopped interesting Frank. There was too much chase involved with an educated female, besides which he was noticing a burning session when he took a piss. Antibiotics and abstinence were the orders from the hotel doc and that made sense.

This created a problem: he could spend his daytime looking for business opportunities, but what about the long nights? The answer came to him as he sped across town in a taxi—Chinatown. The handful of blocks known as the epicenter of Asian culture was not Frank's chief concern. It was the opium dens.

While his family had built its second fortune out of heroin, he hadn't considered the poppy seed as anything relevant to him, but his first foray with opiates in Morocco showed him how wrong he could be. The warmth inside was incomparable—like being blown by a thousand vestal virgins. Only better.

After a week, during which he hardly left his crib, the madam told him he had to go. His money had run out and his credit card was not accepted in this cash-only business establishment. At the hotel, he made his way up to his suite and phoned Palm Springs.

"Mama. I love you very much and I need your help."

"What is it now dear? Money or a lawyer?"

"Mama. I'll pay you back this time I swear."

"Do not make promises you have no intention of keeping. You are nothing without your word. How's Boston?"

"You having me followed?"

"Who do you think pays your credit card each month? Don't be silly."

"It's a great town and I got connections who can help with our business. Only…"

"…you need more green before you can close the deal."

"Speculate to accumulate, you told me."

"Throw my words back at me. Nice. So I'll do the same to you. I've said this before but today I mean it. If you're a man, you'll keep your promise. This is the last time you get any money from me. Just don't tell your sister. And you will pay it or I shall treat you like any other debtor. Capiche?"

Frank had no desire to sleep with the fishes and, perhaps for the first moment in his adult life, he told the truth.

"You have my word, Mama."

"I'll wire over the cash later today. Family discount: you get twelve months to return the capital and a tithe in interest."

FRANK'S TIME PARTYING in Spain had not been a total waste as he'd had the smarts to take the ferry to Morocco and investigate what the country had to offer. Local hashish was supplemented with opiates from Afganistan although sometimes it came from as far away as China.

He hadn't contacted the upper echelons of the trade but he knew well connected guys who'd deliver him a couple of kilos of product should he so desire. And they were keen to supply into the US as any entrepreneur would.

This created Frank's chance to take Mama's scratch and morph it into gold. He might have been to college but deep down he was a punk and he only took two days to assemble a motley bunch to push his wares onto the streets of Boston. While they sold bags of crystal on street corners, he looked to gain a foothold in the opium dens themselves.

During the first month, his crew sucked in several beatings as existing suppliers flexed muscles to show the new kid on the block not to fuck with them. But they hadn't met Frank before or knew what he was capable of. The boy had a spine of reinforced steel and he refused to back down. If some thug put one of his in hospital, he went out to find the guy and slit his throat personally. He never bothered checking whether the corpse made it to the morgue.

The second month was easier. His street team had found a groove and had elbowed itself into four blocks of turf to make a living. Wasn't much, but it was a good start and offered Frank his first scent of income in his life.

He felt positive about earning money for himself and this fed his desire for more. With a spark lit within, he found the grit to focus on securing an opium den. Like all narcotics businesses, they faced two main risks: hassle from the cops and supply drying up. Police were paid off to turn a blind eye to all but the most obvious indiscretions.

The owners of the dens usually were not the drug runners themselves. For reasons of tradition these were viewed as separate specialist tasks, but Frank didn't see it that way. He got himself basement rooms and decked them out ready for some johns. Via his street crew, he found a madam to run the place and some Chinese dudes to keep the peace. With payments to the Police Benevolence Fund, he was set to go.

The boy figured he didn't need to take over anybody else's shack because there was plenty of old men wanting to toke on a pipe. Why go to the effort of slamming heads together when you could start operations with no one noticing or giving you a hard time?

By June, Frank had three locations owned and two others supplied by his crew. Cash rolled in and he paid back half what he owed to Mama as a sign of goodwill and to show her he was making good on his promise. Besides, he knew soon he'd be asking his mother for a favor that didn't involve money.

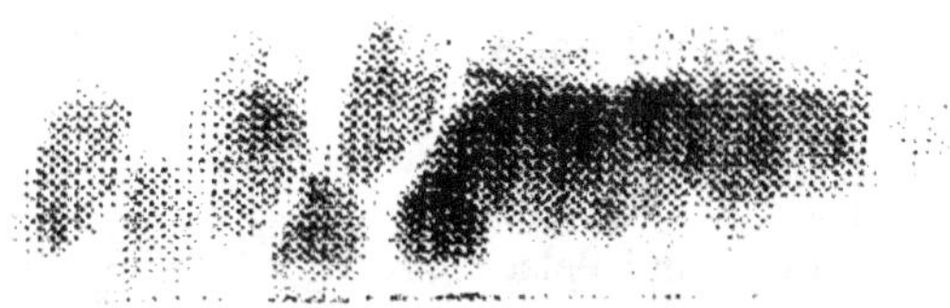

140

FRANK BELIEVED IN thinking big. The money from opiates would flow freely and coagulate in his pocket. But it wasn't enough. The most important thing to him was to be more successful than Alice. The cash coming out of Chinatown was a good start, but nothing greater than that. She took over a casino, so he needed to set up a gaming house from the get-go to show Mama how much better he was than the girl.

From where he stood in the reception area of one of his opium dens, there was a world of possibility opening up to him but it would not be in Boston. Betting on the east coast centered in Atlantic City so that would be his destination. He spent days treading the boardwalk in AC to find just the right establishment.

Any place whose name he recognized was of no use to him. Frank needed somewhere that attracted customers but wasn't too good at its job. That meant the management would be weak and ripe for a discreet takeover. He discovered his quest one block up on South Michigan Avenue where he came across a broken sign announcing the Lucky Nugget.

When he walked into the joint, he saw enough johns at the slot machines to believe the place wasn't too far from the main drag. Then he stood and watched roulette tables, poker and blackjack. There was craps going on at the other side of the room but Frank didn't have a nose for dice.

Card games interested him more because there was a skill in finessing your hand. The spin of a wheel or the flip of a numbered cube only required you to calculate the odds. An ordinary pack of playing cards held an infinite set of possibilities to be manipulated by a knowing expert.

Within thirty minutes of standing in the room Frank spotted four examples of card sharps at work. The owners were hemorrhaging money to cheats and their own stupidity. He looked round the ceiling to see how many cameras were operating, but either they were exceptionally well hidden or there were none; probably the latter.

Then he exchanged some chips—enough to get him invited to the VIP room on the second floor. A champagne bar at one end and a comfortable mix of different tables for the high rolling aficionado. Frank noted how the only women were dealers. If he ran the joint, he'd turn this area into a lap dancing club. Men don't just want to gamble their lives away, he mused.

A glass of complimentary sparkling wine inside him and he killed an hour at a poker table. The dealer had fascinating long bright pink nails which took his mind off the game. Or at least they would have done so had he not spent so much time staring at her fulsome cleavage.

Despite his preoccupation with her breasts, Frank stood five thousand dollars better off and gave her a purple chip as a tip which he dropped in between her tits. He cashed in his winnings and left the joint.

The next morning, Harvey Knight took Frank's call wondering which precinct he'd be heading to shortly.

"No, it's nothing like that. I want your advice on buying a casino."

"Is this booze talking, or worse?"

"No man. I'm deadly serious. I've found a place in Atlantic City but I need your help to buy it. Shall we meet up and talk things through?"

"That where you're based now?"

"Will be but nowadays I have business interests in Boston. If we pull this off, I'll move over here for sure."

"Can you get to my office for tomorrow afternoon?"

"Yep."

"See you then. Stay on the line and my secretary'll finalize the details."

"DOES MARY LOU know what you're up to?"

"Not right now but I wanted to be better informed before I speak to her."

"Good decision. Tell me what you expect out of the deal and then we can work out the best route to get you there."

Frank explained his idea to run the place but to own the joint too because that's where the real money was made. He didn't want a salary—he wanted income with capital growth. Harvey listened and sipped his coffee. This boy impressed him and was so much more of a man since they last met.

"Thing is, I'll need my name on the game license, but my past doesn't make me first choice, does it?"

"You are right. If the owners want to sell and you agree terms, the gaming license could prove sticky. But you are also correct in thinking your mother can help. When you speak with her, remind her it'll be worth dropping a dime to Teddy."

"Who?"

"Teddy. You don't need to know any more about him at this point."

"And financing? I've got some scratch but it won't be enough."

"How much?"

"Low seven figures."

"Congratulations. Last time we met, you didn't have a cent to call your own and I'd have bet on you floating down the Hudson before the month was out."

"Thanks, I guess."

"Don't take it the wrong way. You've done well. That's a positive and I'm recognizing that in you. If you were still the same mook cracking heads in five-star hotels, then you wouldn't be in this room today."

Frank nodded and thought how far he had come since then.

"If you think it'll help, why don't we phone Mary Lou now so she can tell you're serious."

"How does the call do that?"

"My meter's been running the minute you sat down. The cost of a long distance conversation is the least of your worries."

Harvey beamed at him because the joke was very much on him—but it was at his expense and one he could afford.

"Hi Mary Lou. How's tricks? You will never guess who I've got in my office…"

AFTER FRANK BROUGHT along three members of his crew, the owners of the Lucky Nugget decided staying alive was a higher priority than owning the casino. They exited their family business as quickly as they could so he bought the joint for next to nothing. Teddy Prescott pressed some flesh and the gaming license was safe when the Gaming Board met.

"Nice guy, Teddy."

"Yeah. You should have a beer with him sometime."

Frank couldn't tell if Bobby was serious, but he didn't care because the place was his. First order of business was to hire some watchers to keep an eye on the tables. With security sorted out, he set about being creative with the second floor.

The previous owners tried to attract wealthier individuals with limited success. The place wasn't upmarket enough for real high rollers and it suffered from being a block from the boardwalk where the serious action happened.

Frank understood what johns wanted in life: to bet a little, drink a little and to chase tail a lot—or as much as they could get away with if they were married. The Lucky Nugget would deliver all that an American male in AC could afford.

He was also sufficiently self-aware to understand the last person to run the joint on a day-to-day basis was him. He hated paperwork and was still learning how to keep people onside. His small team in Boston was one thing but a hundred or more in AC? You gotta be kidding. Leonida Acerbi came highly recommended by Mama who had hired him to manage the Lady Fortune four years ago.

"Personal circumstances prevented him from staying with us longer, but he was a great guy. Kept everyone in line. Motivated the dealers to keep the johns playing. Good fella all round."

"Spill. If he will work for me I need to know all about him."

"He left Vegas in a hurry. For reasons I never understood, Leonida started a relationship with the daughter of the Las Vegas sheriff."

"Straight out of a Roy Rogers movie."

"Don't get cute. The old man found out and wasn't happy about the situation. The next day when I heard, I didn't crack open the champagne either. Sheriff Redneck only discovered anything because his fair maiden confessed she was pregnant and Leonida skipped the state line the same afternoon."

"Wow."

"Turns out the reason she told her pop was because she couldn't figure out whose it was. She'd been spreading her legs for several guys all at the same time."

"And you still trust Leonida?"

"His judgment with women is flawed, but he knows casinos. And he didn't spill a single word about our operations to the girl."

"How can you be so sure?"

"First, we had no trouble afterwards. Second, we interrogated him when we caught up with him the following week."

NATURALLY LEONIDA WAS worth his weight in gold and drove the Lucky Nugget into a healthy profit within weeks of his arrival. Frank offered him one piece of advice before he started.

"Keep your dick to yourself. Do not go chasing ass in AC without checking out her family history first, you get me?"

"You don't have to worry about that. I'm a changed man—I got married to a stripper and have plenty of action at home, thank you."

Frank chose not to apply the same rule to his own sexual encounters. A pile of lap dancers within easy reach was too much of a temptation for him. Once the club was running efficiently—and it only took four weeks from launch, he spent an unhealthy amount of time on the second floor. The way he viewed it: he was paying the girls to show their tits and asses anyway, so he might as well enjoy the product.

After two nights, he decided that watching was for chumps and he bought a few hours with some of the prettier skanks. He saw how desperate they were for green and that they'd agree to anything he suggested if the price was right. He'd get them stoned to within a wisp of consciousness and then fuck them any which way he could conceive.

"Frank, leave the girls alone."

"I pay them. I tip them. The Nugget gets its fair share of the profit."

"Let's set aside the fact you're getting high on your own supply of women."

"Nicely put."

"Once you've spat them out, the whores are in such a bad state, they take a day or two to recover—and during that time they're not earning. I hate to say this to you, but…"

Frank gritted his jaw.

"…you're pissing on your own porch and it must end."

Leonida paused and let his words sink in. This could put his job—or even his life—in jeopardy, but the consequences of saying nothing were worse. If Mary Lou found out he'd not tried to stop Frank sabotaging his own joint, she would issue the hit on him there and then. No questions asked.

"Why not take a break from the Nugget and spend time in Boston? I'll look after everything here while you build up your business interests there. Or remind yourself what educated ass tastes like. When you come back, you can play on the first floor again."

"But not on the second?"

"No, Frank. We were making a lot of money there until you went through all the girls. To be honest, most of them will leave if we're not careful and word on the street is that someone'll die soon the way you treat them. I'm not judging, but I am trying to run your business."

Frank shook Leonida by the hand and gave him a brief hug.

"Thank you—for your honesty. Takes a brave man to say what you did."

"Just looking out for your best interests."

"I respect that. Book me a flight to Boston tomorrow. Looks like AC needs a break from me."

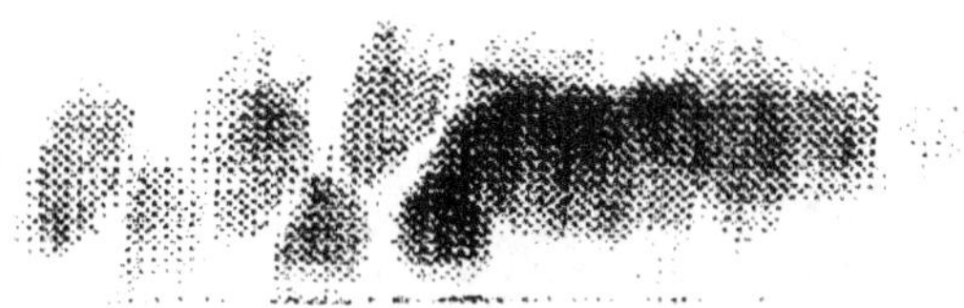

141

SOME WOULD SAY they had an idyllic life together. Mary Lou and Bobby split their time between home in Palm Springs and the hustle of the Palace in the crumbling facade known as Sunset Boulevard. It was like the inhabitants of Los Angeles had watched the film and lived its dream.

"I don't know what Alice was complaining about. This apartment is lovely."

"Until you step outside. Then you are surrounded by all the girls from Partytown USA."

"We might be married but you're telling me you have a problem going down an elevator with a bunch of drugged-up semi-naked hookers?"

"Me? No. I've always admired the female form in all its glorious varieties."

Bobby leaned over in bed and kissed Mary Lou on the cheek while stroking the tattooed rose beneath her navel.

"Just Alice isn't a middle-aged guy. She might have a different perspective."

"Kids of today: ungrateful. Pure and simple. When I was her age, I lived in a two-room apartment the size of a nickel. And was happy to be with a man who could afford the rent."

"Well, she's not with someone and was brought up in much better circumstances."

"I know but…"

The thought ebbed away as Bobby's hand left her stomach and went to find some other fun. A giggle and two deep sighs from Mary Lou showed it had succeeded.

NEXT DAY IN the summerhouse, they talked about business and the difficult trading conditions.

"Trouble is: the days of receiving protection from the mob have long since passed. I can't remember when we saw Pasquale or Fabio last."

"I heard they retired to Florida."

"No kidding. I thought both would die in California."

"Maybe they will, but they're enjoying games of penuchle with their old comrades in arms. Miami-Dade County is where capos go to rest."

"I've still got one or two more projects before I hang up my hat."

"You've plenty of successful years in you yet."

"Tell me about it. I'm finding new ideas hard to come by—Alice will save our bacon."

"And without a mob behind us, every muchacho for miles comes biting at our ankles."

"They don't play by the rules either. Instead of taking out a street dealer, they whack the boss. What kind of way is that to live?"

"If the rats and cockroaches won't get you, then your own fellas will. The Feds have been far too good at getting stool pigeons to blab."

"And once they start, you can only stop them with a bullet."

"Sometimes I wonder why we bother having a house phone."

"We never have a conversation on it in case the FBI has it tapped."

"Worthless piece of junk."

Mary Lou was right to be cautious. Too many fellas who'd built up worthwhile operations served life sentences thanks to the testimony of those they thought they could trust. The Feds had turned underlings against capos and capos against bosses.

While she and Bobby had never risen through the ranks—they were so far from thoroughbred Italian—they had created a sizeable organization. Not having to pay their tithe helped the bank balance, but they spent considerably more than ten per cent on security for their empire.

Without the safety net of the mob, finding a reliable partner was hard. Ventures popped up and fell apart all too easily as mistrust or deceit revealed itself. Narcotics was fraught with danger.

Drugs had been the most profitable part of the business for years, but was populated with the most unstable and untrustworthy characters. This meant pieces of the jigsaw would break apart with a moment's notice as someone was taken in for questioning or got plain greedy. Mary Lou and Bobby spent a disproportionate amount of their time keeping all those plates juggling in the air. It was tiring and they both knew they were too old for that caper.

In Mary Lou's head, Frank was the perfect guy to manage the narcotics operations, but she needed to wait for him to grow up more before she could let him take over the reins. Alice had the temperament to flourish with all the other parts of the business. She had every faith Bobby and Alice would run things very well. Gambling, prostitution and their other rackets would thrive under her stewardship.

But Mary Lou wasn't ready to give up and head over to Boca Raton just yet. Knowing the lottery gig would succeed was the first step and figuring out how to replace narcotics revenue with something safer was the second. After that, she'd have to see. Besides, she didn't want to hand over a doomed business to Frank. Perhaps he could make it thrive. He had street smarts and had a better idea than Alice of how the ordinary Joe thinks.

BACK IN THE Palace, Mary Lou and Bobby took advantage of what the city offered. They checked out a show and dined in some of the most pretentious restaurants on the west coast. The money continued to roll in and Frank's call about the Lucky Nugget made Mary Lou think her son was finally growing up. Even Bobby had to admit the guy was something.

"I'm surprised to hear myself say this, but the boy has done right by you for once. He has actually given you some of your cash back."

"Half of our money."

"And not only does he look like paying the rest but he's got sufficient surplus to fund the purchase of his own casino."

"Wonders will never cease."

"And some. I bet it'll put Alice's nose out of joint."

"I haven't told her yet. She needs to have total focus on the lottery gig. That's big news for us too."

"For sure. More states'll legalize gambling because they are desperate for money. What Alice is doing in California, we can replicate across the country. Frank opening up an opium line on the east coast is our first narcotics venture on the Eastern Seaboard. Your children are something else."

Mary Lou grinned from ear to ear.

"I know. I'm very proud of them."

Then she burrowed under the sheets until Bobby's breathing became deep and rhythmic.

MONROE LINWOOD WEIGHED on Mary Lou's mind. While she was pleased with the way Alice handled herself at the situation they'd got to within a few hours of a knock on the door and a troop of Feds tipping hats and thrusting a search warrant in her hand. Too close for comfort.

There was only one thing to do: a top-to-bottom security check on everyone in the organization. And no exceptions. They'd begin with narcotics, the weakest area, and move on to prostitution later. Mary Lou sent Bobby on the road to interview anyone peddling, manufacturing or managing the various operations along the Californian coast.

Nothing. Their call girl rings were a mix of high-class hookers in a place like the Palace through to much cheaper options for the working man, who'd rub their tits for twenty bucks and the promise of a shot of tequila.

The locations were diverse and diffuse. In LA, the model created on Sunset Boulevard was replicated although renting apartments in a cheap condo served a cost-effective means of delivering the girls to the johns. This required someone to run each apartment or an entire block for those with the right skill set.

Bobby began in the Palace because he had a soft bed to sleep in overnight. As he expected, everyone was clean. When he moved away from the confines of Beverly Hills, the story changed. He found apartments run by a dude called Coby Ingham.

They hadn't met before and Coby had a self possession Bobby hadn't come across for quite some time. Almost like the guy felt protected by an unseen hand and wasn't the least bit bothered about his line of questions. If that hand was cloaked in an FBI leather glove then they were in trouble.

Bobby called Naldo as he was round the corner looking after Alice. Within an hour, Coby was bundled into the rear of a van and taken to a special location out in the desert. A person could scream until their lungs burst out their mouths, but no one would hear them call. This place was remote as hell.

By the time Bobby and Mary Lou arrived on the scene, Naldo had the guy tied up with electrical tape—wrists and ankles—with a hood over his head. The shack was replete with shelving attached to two of the walls. On the shelves were the full gamut of DIY tools that looked as though an electrician, carpenter and plumber had stowed away all the equipment they might ever need.

When the couple walked in, Naldo nodded at them and pointed at the hooded figure in the middle of the room. His wobbly chair only added to the sense of foreboding Coby felt. Mary Lou grabbed a stool and positioned herself in the far corner so she could observe proceedings. Bobby dragged a small wooden table and stopped when he'd placed it in front of Coby. He sat down opposite him and gave a hand gesture for Naldo to remove the hood.

As soon as the material was off his head, Coby blinked four or five times and tried to get the measure of the room. Before he had time to focus on any individual, Bobby slammed his fist down on the table to attract Coby's attention. He was startled and gave a little jump. Other than that, he stayed cool.

"How long you been running the girls in your apartment block?"

"Dunno. Two, three years. I don't know why you're treating me this way. I've always delivered on my numbers."

"This isn't about money."

Coby stared right though Bobby, trying to figure out what gives. He looked askance at Naldo and then he noticed Mary Lou. Neither gave anything away and both turned their heads toward Bobby. Coby refocused on the man sat opposite.

"What is it about?"

"You, Coby. This is about you."

"Huh?"

"Let's start with the basics, shall we? Are you a cop?"

"No."

"Are you a member of any law enforcement agency?"

"No."

"Are you working with any law enforcement agency, local or federal?"

"No. Look, whatever you think I've done, you're wrong. I wake up, I check the girls are fucking the johns, I sort out any problems. I sleep. That's my life. Period."

"Coby, you are too generous. You must spend some time outside your rat hole. I mean, how d'you eat? Do you have a girlfriend? You go to the movies occasionally."

"Of course I eat. And I've got a steady."

"Right. So don't tell me all you do is work because that's not true."

A stone cold stare boring into Coby's soul.

"Only speak the truth in this room, understand? You lie, you die."

Coby's eyes widened. If the circumstances of his arrival hadn't rattled him, then Bobby's words sure did the trick.

THREE HOURS LATER and Coby was singing like there was no tomorrow. Bobby accused him of skimming the proceeds of the block. He admitted to it. Was he feeding information to the cops? Yep. To the Feds? Sure. The fact he had electrodes attached to his balls might count as coercion in a court of law, but the shack was not a duly constituted venue exactly.

All the while, Mary Lou sat impassively watching Coby while Naldo earned his bonus. Red trickled out of Coby's right cheek where Naldo had made an early incision. His wailing was too loud and Naldo moved on to a different body part. No one wanted a headache from all that noise. A fingertip lay on the floor in a large pool of blood. Naldo had strapped each wrist to the armrests of the chair before he got the shears out.

When Coby regained consciousness, they gave him a glass of water and took out the electrical equipment. He admitted everything: the Feds, the skimming. Everything. Bobby reckoned he'd have sung to the assassination of Abraham Lincoln if he was given the chance but Mary Lou interceded.

"Let's finish up, gentlemen."

Coby dribbled toward Bobby, who thought he discerned a smile of sheer relief. Unfortunately he misunderstood Mary Lou's instructions. Naldo kicked the chair over, whipped out a pistol and shot him once in the head and once in the heart.

"Now we know."

Bobby wasn't so sure. He felt Coby was hiding something but by the end the guy was singing to every suggestion put in front of him. Naldo and he were an excellent team at extracting information from people but this didn't sit right. As a mark of respect to Naldo, Bobby helped him destroy the body and clean up the shack ready for their next visit—whenever that would be.

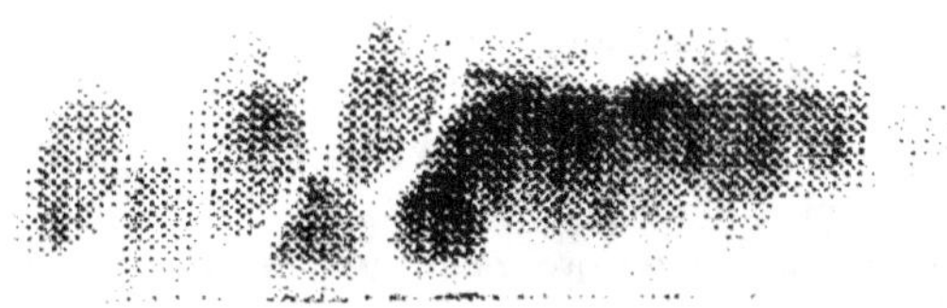

142

COBY WEIGHED ON Bobby's mind. Not so much his death—that had been almost inevitable the moment Naldo dragged his sorry ass into their desert hideaway. Bobby kept playing back the confession in his head. Over the years many men had admitted all sorts of misdeeds to him. Mainly they told the truth and occasionally they would lie. Or rather, they might utter an untruth at the start, but Naldo's persuasive techniques encouraged them to change their story—at least by the time a pair of pliers or a scalpel had been applied.

A few brave men lasted a little longer but not much more. Coby had been different. He'd fixed on claiming his innocence and only broke down just before his end. His behavior wasn't consistent with his words. Bobby feared they had made a mistake although Mary Lou was satisfied: she'd found her canary.

The guy had something to hide but maybe it had nothing to do with Feds. What if his only sin had been to shtupp the odd girl in his block? Or even every one of them. Might he have held back that information thinking it would be better to admit to that than have his dragon-wife find out.

The only promise Bobby had made was that lying would get him killed. If Coby thought he was giving up a story Bobby wanted to believe then it wouldn't have appeared as a lie and Coby'd have survived. Only Bobby didn't tell him the truth. A tangled web.

WHEN HE NEXT met up with Alice in her Malibu apartment, Bobby voiced his concerns.

"You got to be kidding, right?"

"No."

"You reckon you coerced a confession out this guy."

"I'm saying I am not sure if we did. Mary Lou called a halt to the proceedings a little early for my taste."

"And despite that, you sat there and did nothing."

"Hey wait a second. She issued an order and Naldo executed it immediately after. There was no chance to think and intervene."

Alice remained silent, ruminating on Bobby's response. She respected that he was an arch interrogator, but her mother wasn't prone to errors of judgment. She'd never seen Mama do that.

"When was the last time you can remember Mama making this kind of mistake?"

"Never. That's why we are having this conversation."

"Have you asked Naldo?"

"No way. He is loyal to both Mary Lou and I. So he'd just be hopelessly conflicted."

"He's never expressed an opinion to me."

"The man watches and waits. He follows orders. It's what he does. But he has his own mind and expresses his views when he thinks it appropriate."

"Old school."

"All the way back to the Sicilian hilltop village where he was born."

"And such a charmer."

"Yeah, he doesn't believe in getting too close to a woman in case he has to bury her in the desert."

Alice's jaw dropped.

"Joke. He's been married, but she died. Long time ago and, let's be honest, in his line of work it's hard to find the right person."

Alice laughed and they both turned their heads to the sound of the front door opening.

"Talking of which, let me introduce you to Sam."

"Hi."

Bobby put his poker face on and they shook hands.

"Hi. Pleased to meet you. I'll be back in a moment."

Sam kept the shopping bags in her hand and scooted off to the bedroom. Bobby's head followed her as she departed the living room. Once she'd gone, he allowed a smirk to take over his expression.

"What?"

"Sam?"

"Yes. That's Sam."

"Samantha."

"That's what I'm telling you. For a smart man, you can be quite dense sometimes."

"And you can be quite misleading. You never mentioned Sam was…"

"…someone I really care about? Oh, I did."

"Don't be coy. We didn't you tell us about your… lifestyle?"

"Because I didn't want to have this conversation. And it's not a lifestyle choice: this is who I am."

Sam was as good as her word and came back into the living room.

"Shall I open a bottle of wine or do you have more business to discuss?"

"Business? I'm family."

"A family business."

She wandered off into the kitchen to grab something red and Alice joined her to help with glasses. Upon their return, Bobby had moved himself from the breakfast table onto a couch.

"To the two of you."

Raised glasses all round, a clink and finally a sip of a Californian grape.

"What line of work are you in?"

"Marketing. I'm at a large agency in Boston. We handle lots of the household brands."

"And you do…?"

"I am an account director."

"Not being funny but I have no idea what that means."

Sam spent ten minutes explaining the difference between sales and marketing. Then another five describing the structure of agencies.

All the while, Alice looked on, enjoying the view as her favorite people talked to each other, nodding and laughing along the way. Sam sat next to Alice on a two-seater opposite Bobby. As their chatting continued, Bobby noticed the tension in Alice's shoulders subside and by the time the corporate lecture was over, Alice had placed a palm on Sam's lap. Sweet.

"Enough about me. Alice runs the family show. What do you do?"

"Does she? I just help if I'm needed."

"Oh gosh. I never said I was in charge, Sam."

She squeezed Alice's hand.

"No honey, but you must be fairly important to spend so much time on it."

"Alice is being modest: she's up there. We don't know what we'd do without her."

"Yeah? Did Mama say that?"

"Sure did."

Alice glowed and Sam gave her a showy kiss on the lips.

"My businesswoman of the year."

"You two hungry because I'm starved. Choose somewhere nice to eat round here. My treat."

That night in bed, Alice pondered over Bobby's reaction to Sam. He was probably out of his comfort zone hanging with a couple of lesbians, but he had handled himself well and appeared glad that she was happy. He was a cool dude.

"I'VE HEARD OF this guy in Silicon Valley."

"Great. Why don't we invite him over for dinner?"

Mary Lou and Bobby lay by the pool next to the summerhouse. He'd been back from Malibu about a week but had decided not to voice his concerns about Coby. Alice was right. They both had a good nose for trouble and he had confessed. Let that be an end to it. Wrapped up in his own thoughts as he had been these past seven days, Bobby forgot to tell Mary Lou about Sam. She knew her daughter had met someone—but was unaware of the precise details.

He had known his wife over twenty years but, even if he'd had a clear head, Bobby wouldn't have an idea how to explain Alice was a dyke. He wasn't especially prejudiced himself but Mary Lou came from the deep South and they have different rules down there. Like hanging blacks and burning crosses.

Mary Lou sighed, dragging Bobby's attention back to reality.

"This is serious. I've got an idea to make some significant money."

"Does it involve narcotics?"

"Not at all."

"Talk to me, babe."

Mary Lou outlined the scheme she had in mind. The guy she'd been introduced to, while Bobby was lying by the beach, had access to high-tech equipment—computers, circuit boards and so on. They had contracts to make precision instruments for the Pentagon. This is when the dude should have kept his mouth shut but Mary Lou used her powers of persuasion to keep him blabbing away.

Two options opened up to them. They could invest in the stock and use their inside knowledge to know when to sell or buy a bigger stake. Alternatively, they supply the instruments under George's supervision and get a direct line into the US government.

Bobby loved the vision, and making a dollar out of insider trading sounded fun, but he knew from her tone that Mary Lou was interested in fighter jet instrumentation. He was far from convinced. The idea a company controlled by a Lagotti would win and keep a defense contract was absurd, crazy even.

"Give me his details and Naldo and I can have a sniff around. See if he's legit."

"Feels good."

"Yeah, but to be honest I'm not too sure. Doesn't sit right in my gut."

"It's the future, Bobby."

GEORGE LIM APPEARED to be a stand up fella. A house out in the valley and recently married to a local girl. He was a natural born American and his parents had emigrated from Taiwan before he was even a twinkle in his father's eye.

Neither Bobby nor Naldo could unearth any vices to slow the dude down. Didn't gamble, smoke or drink. And didn't fool around with other women. From what they could tell, he lived to work and was one hundred per cent dedicated to the business. The company specialized in jet fighter kit. Details of what the place did went way over their heads, but George had told Mary Lou the truth.

"If he's got such a straight back, why is he prepared to play such a curve ball?"

"Dunno boss. At least, not yet."

They expanded their search to find his angle but there was nothing on him. Naldo focused on the wife while Bobby worked on the rest of the family. Then everything became crystal clear. Mrs. Lim was a bookkeeper and beyond reproach. She serviced several local small firms and that was all. And she wasn't pregnant even though they were trying.

Papa Lim told a different story—he created George's desire to walk on the wild side. The man was ill. His pancreas was failing him. Kidneys too. With no intervention, he'd be dead in three months, six if he was lucky. He came from the old country and hadn't invested in medical insurance and was up shit creek without a paddle—to coin a surgical phrase. So George wanted cash—and fast.

The scale of the surgery was way beyond anything a personal loan might deliver. He was smart enough to realize he needed access to dirty money. At heart, the guy was a square which was why Bobby didn't trust him.

"Once his dad is all fixed up, he will have no use for us and no desire to keep playing our game."

"Perhaps, but when he's swum with the sharks, he must meet any obligations he has to me."

"You're relying on his good nature to ensure he stays on the wrong side of the tracks."

"These kinds of opportunity come along once in a lifetime."

"Not sure about that. This gift horse relies on a straight fella. I don't think we should hang our colors to this mast."

"I disagree. There's a ton of money for very little effort. What's not to like?"

"Do me a favor. If you have to see this thing through, do everything through intermediaries. Never meet him. Never let him hear your name. I've got a bad vibe—really do."

"Promise."

"For real?"

"Cross my heart and hope to die."

THE FIRST OCCASION internal compliance checked on George, he folded faster than someone holding a pair of twos. Mary Lou hadn't even had time to release any funds to him. So there was no crime to confess apart from conspiracy and the guilt was too much for his carcass to bear. Word reached Bobby that George was discussing their plans to the local cops but because the Pentagon was indirectly involved, the whole operation was about to go sky high.

A single call to Naldo nullified their risk and George met with an auto accident that night. The boys in blue had sent him home and arranged another interview the following day when the Feds would swing by. He never made it—nor did his dad who died two months later, around the same time Mrs. Lim found out she was pregnant.

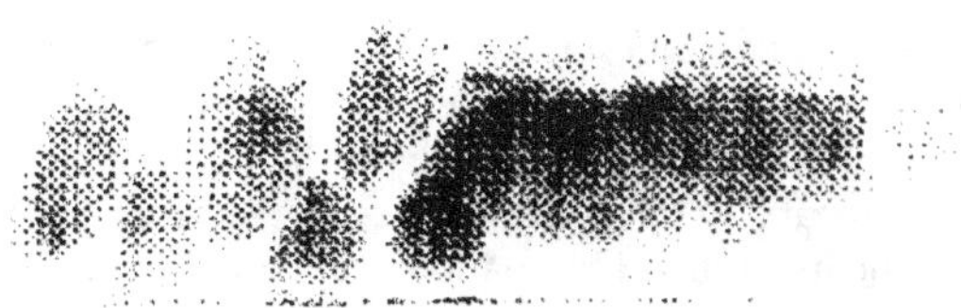

143

"WELL, IT'S A pleasure to meet you."

"And for me too. Alice has told me so much about you."

Mary Lou and Sam shook hands and everyone moved into the living room to sit down, leaving overnight bags in the hall. Drinks were offered and dispensed. Then that small awkward pause when no one quite knows which topic of conversation to kick off.

"This looks a lovely place you guys have got here."

"Thank you. Bobby: why don't you give Samantha a tour?"

He stood up, grabbed his whiskey and the two headed to the conservatory and then the pool. Alice and Mary Lou stayed where they sat. In silence.

"What have I done wrong?"

"You've disappointed me, darling. Why didn't you mention Sam was…"

"…a woman?"

"Yes, was it so hard for you to tell me you're gay?"

"I was scared of what you might think of me."

Mary Lou laughed. She was a child before the Sixties. Why would she be that prejudiced?

"Provided you are happy, that's all I care about."

"So how have I disappointed?"

"You should have just said. Passive aggressive doesn't suit you and it's not how I brought you up to be."

A tear rolled down Alice's cheek which she quickly smeared away. How could she have misjudged Mama so badly? And now she hurt inside and had the childish impulse to run over to get a hug, so everything would be okay. Only it wasn't.

"I didn't know how you'd react. It's not something we've ever talked about. I'm sorry but I could not conceive of the right words. Showing you seemed the only way."

"It must have been difficult living that lie—I get it but I am your mama and you can always rely on me. You don't hold on to my apron strings but you may still receive help from me. It's not a sign of weakness."

Bobby and Sam sauntered through the room and into the kitchen before heading upstairs.

"I just want to stand on my own two feet and be the best person I can be."

"You are a Californian, I'll give you that. Your mother is always here for you in rain or shine. You shoulda said, is all."

"I'm sorry. Forgive me?"

"Of course darling. I love you."

Sam sat back next to Alice, who kept her hands to herself and looked as though she wanted to curl into a tiny ball. Sam dangled an arm on Alice's leg as she leaned forward to grab her drink. Bobby watched Mary Lou as she saw the hand rest on her daughter's body. He noticed his wife's spine stiffen momentarily and he wondered what had been said between them to make Alice's eyes red. Sam must have spotted this too because she maintained her hand on the thigh after she returned with her vodka tonic.

THE TENSION IN the room dissipated once everybody sat down to eat. Irma had cooked up a storm and by the time she'd served coffees, everyone was full. Alice and Sam cleared the plates after each course as dutiful children do.

"How do you find Boston? My son, Frank spends a lot of his life out there."

"It's a lovely chilled town. The people are friendly unlike New York, but they've still got some drive to them."

"And it isn't a retirement village like Palm Springs."

"Mama, there are folk my age living here only they don't mix in your circles."

"The only real downside is there are far too many students."

Alice laughed.

"It wasn't so long ago that we were at college."

"Yes, but we're not there now, thank goodness."

All four chuckled at that and conversation continued for another hour. Then Mary Lou saw the clock on the mantelpiece and shuffled forward on the couch, play-slapping Bobby on the knee.

"It's way past our bedtime, but you stay up as long as you want."

"Thanks Mama."

Goodnight kisses ensued and once all permutations had been covered, Mary Lou and Bobby headed upstairs.

"WHAT DO YOU make of Sam?"

"She seems a nice girl."

"Nice enough for Alice?"

"No one will ever be good enough for my daughter. Not in my eyes at least."

"It's a mother-child thing. I get that. But ignoring the inevitable impossibility of her meeting your high expectations… what do you think of her?"

"She makes her happy. Did you see the glow in her cheeks each time Sam touched her?"

"I did. They're a good couple. But you didn't answer my question."

"Ask me again in the morning. There's something I can't quite put my finger on. Let me sleep on it."

DOWNSTAIRS ALICE AND Sam had moved onto the patio as it was such a beautiful night. The moon shone brightly and the air was calm. They shared a sun lounger and cuddled in the darkness.

"Your folks are good people. I like them."

"Yeah? I've known Bobby all my life so I don't know any different and my mother is my mother, if you see what I mean."

"Sure do."

They both were mesmerized by the moonlight on the ripples in the pool and drifted into silence. Alice stroked Sam's thigh in response to her squeezing of a breast.

"You're very forward for a girl from Boston…"

They kissed and then Alice stood up, stripped down to her underwear and removed Sam's clothing. Then she walked to the edge of the pool and jumped in, swiftly followed by her girlfriend. The two splashed about for a while until they wound up in the shallow end and Alice took off Sam's bra and then her own. More kissing and hands meandering over each other's bodies.

"Shouldn't we go upstairs? Your parents are the other side of that balcony, aren't they?"

Alice slipped her hand inside Sam's panties.

"More time here won't hurt if you're not too loud. Then you can take me to our room and fuck me there too."

MARY LOU AWOKE late next morning. Her ability to get to sleep was hampered by the sounds of her daughter frolicking in the pool with Sam. She preferred not to imagine quite what frolics occurred and kept her mind focused on the euphemism. Like every mother, she was protective of her daughter's groin and its sexual activity—gay, straight or bi.

Now she was conscious, she had another chance to replay her thoughts about that woman. Sam had said the only downside of Boston were student numbers. That did not sound right. Surely, the biggest issue was that she was thousands of miles from Alice. Perhaps Sam didn't wish to state her undying love for her daughter—because she wouldn't have meant it or it would have been too embarrassing. But she had the opportunity to make some polite statement about wanting to be together.

This made Mary Lou want to find out why Sam was holding back. Even if Alice was living in the moment and enjoying the best ride of her young life, Mary Lou needed more. That girl was hiding something from them.

Alice hadn't been forthcoming with her about her sexuality, but she'd assured her mama that she and Sam could talk openly together. For instance, Alice wanted Sam to relocate to California but she was tied to her job. Alice knew they were far too early in the relationship for her to make that kind of demand on Sam.

By the same token, Sam resented the time Alice spent working in the family business. She didn't know precisely what any of it was—Alice made sure of that—but she could tell it wasn't all on the level. A casino manager doesn't pick up sticks and leave to live above a bordello just because her Mama asked.

And if the emotions at the heart of the relationship were sound then what was Sam thinking but not saying? What was her secret? Alice was convinced Sam had genuine feelings for her, so what could she be hiding? Something about herself or what she got up to in Boston. By Alice's own account, they'd met in the most random of circumstances and it had taken Sam ages to talk about where she came from.

Perhaps, she had trust issues or her background was so shady she refused to tell a woman she was prepared to travel across country to be with—and who might be involved in criminal operations. That limited the gene pool of possibility to a handful of ideas. If Sam was a criminal then Alice's family situation would not be an issue. But if she was at the other end of the honesty spectrum, then that'd make perfect sense.

With all the problems Mary Lou'd had with people squealing, she hadn't looked closer to home. And once this idea arrived inside her head, she couldn't shake it: Sam was a stool pigeon and had finagled her way into Alice's heart to be a mole for the Feds.

MARY LOU NUDGED Bobby awake. He grunted and tried to roll back to sleep, but she shook his arm until he got the message it was time to talk. She explained what had been running through her head and waited for a response. Bobby plumped up pillows and busied himself to gain more valuable minutes to consider her words and wake up more before speaking.

"I don't see it. They're a lovely couple: the way they preen each other is adorable. When Alice speaks, Sam is captivated by her voice. It might not be love—who are we to say—but it is a mighty strong lust for sure. She cannot fake that."

"You must admit it's weird: 'the only downside is students'. Come on, that's not normal. She's hiding something and she can't be trusted."

"Alice has been careful not to let Sam eavesdrop on any business conversations. That is one of the few causes of tension between them."

"Because the woman wants to find out what we're up to."

"Because she wants more attention paid to her than Alice gives. Bit childish but not sinister."

Mary Lou crossed her arms and sulked. She didn't understand why Bobby couldn't view things as she did. He was blind sometimes. Almost like he could see no wrong in people or he had a soft spot for young beautiful women. Men were useless.

"How can you be so sure? Nothing she has done since she arrived in this house today signals you're right. All we've seen is she's a cute ass from Boston… I bumped into them in Malibu too."

"What? Why's this the first I'm hearing about it?"

"I forgot it had happened after I returned. Besides it was only a few hours. I popped by, we ate and I left. Finito."

"What the…"

"Don't give me a hard time over this. Was just after the Coby Ingham thing and as you know, it took me a while to get my head straight after that one."

"And here we are again deciding whether we have another stool pigeon."

Bobby was silent. He had no idea why he hadn't mentioned the dinner to Mary Lou. Probably because he reckoned it only right that she should meet Sam before he did. If he'd been playing his A game, he would have said. Hey, life's a bitch and then you die.

"When I met her before, she gave me chapter and verse on the marketing industry. Could have been well-researched patter, but it didn't feel like it. She cared too much for it to have been a rehearsed speech.

""Unless she's a good actress and practiced the spiel."

"True, but that doesn't change how I felt—or the time Alice has spent with her and not suspected a thing."

"How were you when you discovered muff? You reckon Alice was any different?"

"Harsh, Mary Lou."

"Perhaps. No matter what you say, I can't trust her."

"Fine. She's not getting access to anything important—apart from the hand of the fair maiden Alice."

"It's not her hand that either of us are considering right now. And that's doubly worse for you, dirty old man."

The noise from the girls' bedroom picked up again at that precise second. Mary Lou and Bobby looked at each other and laughed.

"Full of energy, those youngsters."

"Let's see if we can beat them at their own game."

They buried themselves under the covers and tried to find new ways to make the other breathe more deeply than they'd ever done before.

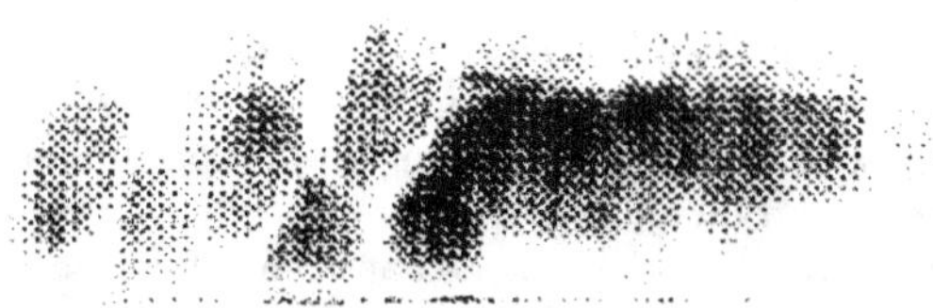

144

ALICE DROVE SAM around Palm Springs in her soft top sports car. She pointed out its sights—few as they were—and stopped outside Montgomery High.

"Best days of your life?"

"Nah. Loved the classes, but I was never one of the popular kids. Tried to keep myself to myself, but with Frank in the same place, it was hard to hide for very long."

"Geek girl?"

"Yep. If Frank hadn't been my brother, I'd have had on okay time."

"Did he seek the limelight and drag you along too?"

"Er no. He played the fool, got into heaps of trouble. Teachers somehow expected me to be responsible for his nefarious activities. Kids thought I was cut from the same cloth as him because we are twins. He believed every day was party time. Still does."

"Pain in the neck but fun to be around."

"That's Frank, through and through."

"Any happy memories at all?"

"Prom night. Peter Hatheway gave me a corsage and picked me up in a stretch limo. We danced and drank the fruit punch laced with hooch. He took me by the hand and we went round the back of the buildings and out onto the running track. Lost my cherry on the pole vault mattress. Biggest bounciest bed I've ever been on."

"Was the sex any good?"

"Not for me. First time anyone gave me an orgasm was you. Before that, I was flying solo."

They kissed to reinforce the special bond Alice felt for Sam.

"How about you? Any man been worth it for you?"

"One or two, but that doesn't matter because I'm with you now."

Alice squinted at her, not knowing what to make of that last comment. Against her better judgment, she let it alone. This was neither the time nor the place.

"Hungry?"

"Ravenous. Where do people go to eat in this town?"

THE WOMEN SAT down at a circular booth in the Palm Springs Country Club. By association, Alice was known there although she hadn't visited the venue for a while. The red leather seating was threadbare when her mother first came there in the Seventies and nothing much had changed—the menu had been reprinted. The restaurant and bar continued to have a mixed clientele: it was the golf course's nineteenth hole, there were ladies that lunched and a meeting room for local businessmen. Nowadays, it had gained a reputation as a cool drinking spot for the children of the wealthier members of the community.

Alice ordered linguini with clams in a white wine sauce and Sam tried the steak. Their cosmos arrived and they clinked their glasses to toast their first drink of the day. As expected, the food tasted wonderful. The decor was shabby chic, but the proprietor cared about his guests' palates.

Once their plates were empty, they ordered more cocktails. Before the waiter returned, a pair of dudes came by and introduced themselves as Brad and Martin. They chatted for a minute or two.

"Mind if we sit down?"

"By all means."

Alice and Sam glanced at each other. The way the boys behaved, they clearly were something in this town—or thought they were. Both were clean shaven and wore designer casual wear, so they had money if nothing else. Alice leaned over and whispered in Sam's ear.

"How much do you think we can scalp them for?"

"Few hundred. Whoever screws them over the most: loser buys dinner."

A nod and they switched on their smiles.

"Shouldn't you boys be out working? In a supermarket or however you earn your living."

"We have investments that do the work for us. Let the chumps toil—we prefer to play."

"What's your handicap?"

"Huh?"

Sam sighed disdainfully and pointed at the eighteenth green outside.

"Oh, golf. Not my idea of a game: chasing after a ball you're always hitting away from you. Makes no sense."

Alice laughed at Martin's comment. Bobby said the same thing, but it didn't stop him from teeing off every week.

"You enjoy games, Brad?"

"Sure do. I'm a gambling man so I prefer the odds stacked in my favor, but any card game floats my boat."

"Me too. There's nothing like the thrill of taking a leap into the unknown."

The waiter arrived with the cosmos and Brad put green on the table for payment. The attendant looked at Alice and she nodded consent, so he picked up the cash and walked away.

"Thanks for the drink, Brad."

"My pleasure."

"If you don't play golf Martin, how do you spend the hours between waking up and falling asleep?"

"I keep myself busy: hosting pool parties, hanging with beautiful people—like yourselves."

Sam and Alice smiled and fluttered their eyelids. These saps were one hundred per cent ego with no space for anything else.

"Haven't been to a pool party in years…"

Martin heard Alice's cooing and got the hint.

"Fancy coming over now? I can make some calls and get the gang over later."

ALICE AND SAM stood opposite Brad and Martin with martinis all round. Martin had made a big deal about how to concoct the perfect vodka martini, so he'd set himself up to fail. The cocktails only disappointed but the women weren't here to critique his bar tending skills. Alice had parked her soft top at the front of the house next to Martin's Italian beast of a sports car.

"Here's to partying on down."

"I'll get some music going."

Once Martin returned, electronic beats poured out of the PA pumping onto the poolside veranda. All four tapped their toes and a minute later, the boys had grabbed the girls by the hand and encouraged them to dance. Five or six tracks on—who was counting?—and slower rhythms hit the air and the couples paired off for more intimate moments.

Alice wasn't too happy with Martin's octopus hands but when she glanced over to the other couple, Sam didn't appear to be annoyed that Brad's fingers were clamped to her ass, squeezing her like a used sponge. To her surprise, Alice minded though. The point of being here was to rob the overgrown kids and her jealousy spurred her on to go for broke.

As Martin kissed her on the neck, she undid his shirt and put a hand on his belt buckle. Sam saw what Alice was up to and followed suit. Neither of the boys objected and their egos bloated a little more than was usual as the women undressed them down to their shorts.

"Your turn, but don't get fresh. I'm keeping my undies on… for now."

The warmth of Alice's whisper against Martin's earlobe was more than enough to make him follow her orders to the letter. Brad copied his friend with a similar warning from Sam, who then walked him over to the base of the diving board. She sat down, legs apart, and reeled him in toward her until she wrapped her thighs around him. Christmas was coming early for Brad it seemed.

Martin stepped forward, within an inch of Alice, who embraced him again and shoved a hand down his shorts to maintain his interest. She twisted the two of them round so she could see the diving board and monitor what was happening with her Sam. The sight of Brad's pure white ass nestling above the waistband of his bermudas told her he was at the same level of excitement as Martin.

The women winked at each other and made their move.

"Let's get naked and then we can fuck in the pool."

Martin nodded and whipped off his shorts then called over to his friend while Alice slowly undid her navy and white striped bra.

"Come on guys! Get with the program."

Brad kept a hand on Sam's breast as he looked around, assessed the situation and grinned.

"You up for some more fun?"

"The sooner you stop talking, the quicker we'll be fucking."

His smile was so broad, Sam saw his teeth. Her bra was already on the floor. She took her time, putting her hands on her hips to avoid undressing further. Five seconds later, Brad and Martin were in the water with their hard-ons. Alice and Sam reacted fast by grabbing the guys' clothes and throwing their own back on before the guys could do anything.

Alice palmed Martin's car keys he'd dropped on a patio table and turned to face the pool.

"Sorry boys, changed our minds now we've seen your equipment."

Sam laughed to emphasize the point. Then they both dashed to Alice's soft top.

"Take my keys and follow me. Don't ask questions: there's no time."

As she spoke, she looked back and saw Brad and Martin heading toward them. Neither man was in a particular hurry so they didn't know about the car. Sam appeared flustered but hopped into the driver's seat nonetheless. Alice unlocked Martin's vehicle and they sped off, leaving him to swear at them in the distance.

Alice kept a steady pace below the speed limit until they arrived at the airport parking lot. She drove to what she hoped was its furthest corner and carefully parked. Sam sidled over and let Alice take over the wheel.

"That was hot."

"They deserved it."

"I could become used to the criminal life."

"Stick to grand theft auto and you'll be fine."

"You'd better get me home fast before this buzz goes away. I don't want to use a drop of this rush on anyone but you."

"Why wait? There's an airport motel coming up just about… now."

AN HOUR LATER they left the motel and headed back to Mama's to pack. In the coolish light of the early evening, Alice reckoned not being in Palm Springs would be a good idea. Martin would be unlikely to want to tell the cops he got stiffed by two out-of-town broads, but he'd have to report his car stolen to have any hope of getting it returned. Alice had wiped her prints off every surface just to be sure. The vehicle retailed at north of a quarter of a million and Sam pointed out it might have a tracker so he had no need of police help. She was probably right.

"I stole the car so you are definitely buying dinner when we get home."

"Worth every penny."

Alice hugged Bobby and kissed her Mama goodbye while Sam stood patiently by. Handshakes and adios for her, then into the soft top and away. On the way back, Sam mused about their trip.

"I like your folks. They come across as warm and welcoming."

"Bobby is a good man. Says little, but he watches and learns."

"He's always been chatty with me."

"The man can be charming too."

"Switches it on for the ladies, does he?"

"A man with a dark past from what I see, but neither Mama nor Bobby have ever told me what he got up to before they hooked up."

"Sordid and dirty—all free love and squirming naked bodies?"

"Bobby? I don't think so. More likely to be a tragic death and unconsummated passion."

"Shame. I was hoping for a tale of bondage and a secret dungeon where he tortured leather-clad souls within an inch of their sexual deaths."

"You lost me at bondage… I need to decide where you'll take me for my prize."

"Almost forgot about that. When will we get in?"

Alice glanced at the clock on the dashboard and added numbers up in her head.

"Nine at the latest."

"Do you mind if we stay in tonight? We'll have more time to think of somewhere real special for your prize. Besides… I've got some other ideas about how we could spend the evening instead of sat in a restaurant."

Alice needed no further explanation as Sam reached over and placed a left hand on her crotch.

"Take away pizza will do just fine."

She parted her legs slightly and pressed down on the gas pedal.

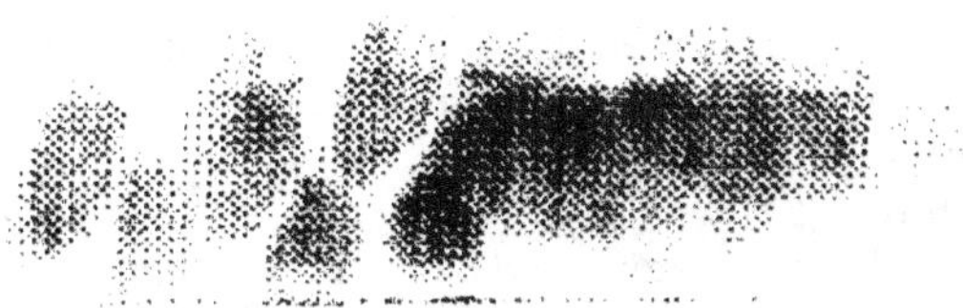

145

MARY LOU AND Bobby decided they needed to find more opportunities to sidestep the heroin racket. And as much as they wanted to stay local, they knew there was money to be made outside LA. They were not turning their backs on the City of Angels as spreading their wings.

She'd had her eye in San Francisco for some time. The place had never been under mob control and as a small operation, Mary Lou thought they could make their mark quickly given the muscle they'd bring.

With November fast approaching, Bobby wanted to get lottery card production up-and-running although Alice preferred to supervise that end of things. Logistics resolved that argument in Alice's favor: it was cheaper and quicker to truck over the fake cards than build a new plant.

A fresh batch of sales representatives were hired and cash poured in, just as it had in LA. The state's finances might be in disarray but Mary Lou and Bobby were almost literally printing money in Bakersfield. The sudden influx of green made her want more out of San Francisco.

"What else would be easy to set up?"

"Girls… and boys for that matter."

"It's not a gay city—just has a gay area."

"Anyway. The answer to your question is sex. Let's ship in some girls from our LA clubs to begin with until we can recruit local bait. If we use the gentle art of firm persuasion, we could run three lap dancing bars before the weekend."

Bobby and his enforcement crew spent two days driving round town to locate suitable venues. He was searching for the rare combination of relative success and weak management. If you possess a knowing eye and are prepared to sit in enough dive bars, then you can find almost anything. His gang were under strict instructions to drop a few notes on the girls but not lose sight of the prize: to check out security arrangements and how much muscle was hiding behind closed doors. He told them he'd let them have a weekend pass with any of the floozies they wanted once the Lagottis were running the joints.

Three locations were selected and his crew split up and attacked each at the same time. Existing management was offered a cash payment to leave that night. Given the size of the offer, two accepted in an instant and walked out immediately with a brief case crammed with money. The third venue contained a more reluctant host.

His perspective was that he'd built the Booty Bar from nothing and a bunch of out-of-towners would not get him to shift just because they asked.

"I understand you have not planned to exit this establishment but I can assure you, it would be left in safe hands."

"You don't appear to be listening too well. The place is not up for sale."

"We have offered you money, which you have rejected. I heard you say that clearly. So I won't embarrass you by making the offer twice."

"Finally, you get the picture."

Bobby laughed. This small-time operator stood before him thought he'd walk away with his tail between his legs.

"The best thing I can suggest you do now is to give me the Booty Bar as a gift—man to man. And because I am a businessman at heart, I shall find other ways than cash to show my appreciation."

It was Anton Markov's turn to laugh.

"You been smoking the whacky baccy before you came in here or the sight of all that pussy outside has made you crazy. Watch my lips: I am not giving you the joint and I'll not sell it to you."

"That's a shame. Is that your final word on the matter?"

"You bet your last fucking dollar it is."

Bobby smiled and put his hands in his pants pockets as he turned to face Naldo.

"The guy thinks I'm a comedian. But if he won't sell and will not give the place a way, what can we do?"

Naldo lunged forward at Markov and thrust a knife straight into his heart. A violent deep incision and Markov hit the floor. One minute he's talking business, the next blood is pouring out of his mouth and onto the carpet.

"We kill you, motherfucker. That's what we'll do."

Naldo started cleaning up almost the instant he had rested Markov's head on the ground. Bobby watched him for five seconds and then looked at the other two fellas he'd brought with.

"Make yourselves useful, eh?"

BOBBY LIKED THE layout of the Booty Bar with private dancing rooms close to the stage and the bar at the rear of the auditorium. Whoever they installed here to run the joint would have a great line of sight over the whole proceedings. And an office behind the bar so you'd never be too far from the action.

When the last john left the building at six in the morning, Bobby locked the doors and explained to the hapless workers they had options. Stay and work for him or fuck off with no hard feelings and today's wages. Everyone stuck around, which was no surprise as two of them had seen Markov being dragged out the back and dumped in the trunk of Naldo's car. Word had got out about their erstwhile employer before Bobby had a chance to talk to them.

He gave everyone a bonus to keep them sweet and then sent everybody home so his crew could comb through the place to make sure there were no complications. They looked out for any unopened safes and ensured there weren't any others hiding in the shadows, too scared to confront the new owners.

No Markov minions but two ledgers and one safe. Bobby had low expectations about its contents as the box was small and found at the bottom of a cupboard. They dumped it all in his car and he drove off to apply his skills to crack it open. Naldo made yet another trip into the desert to offload Anton Markov, onetime owner of the Booty Bar.

MARY LOU MIGHT have harbored the belief that San Francisco was a chilled out town but no one had explained this to its more recent arrivals. When the Italian mob's control over organized crime wavered in the 1990s, other groups leaped on the opportunity to take over. Many of these people came over from the newly independent states of the former Soviet Union—and from Russia itself.

Their background in abject hardship under the yoke of Communist oppression set them up to be ruthless dictators in charge of their own gangs. This made the Markovs no different from hundreds of families who entered the country illegally to seek their fortunes, having created seed capital from the black market back home.

If Mary Lou had known the specific history of the Markov clan, she would have advised Bobby to tread carefully around Anton instead of whacking him during their first argument. As night follows day, the Markovs moved with tremendous speed after Anton's death.

Two nights later, smoke was seen coming out from under one of the private rooms of the Booty Bar. Within a quarter of an hour, flames licked the stage and only five minutes after that, the second floor collapsed on top of the auditorium. Everyone escaped unharmed but the unflinching revenge sent a clear message to Bobby. They sure had picked on the wrong person to chisel out of a bar.

Mary Lou took the news badly while Bobby thought having control of two out of the three venues was good work. She believed the Markovs had taken a diabolical liberty by destroying her property. The fact it had been theirs forty-eight hours before was irrelevant to her. Everyone needed to see you don't mess with the Lagotti family—otherwise any upstart with a shotgun could come calling. Her reaction was simple.

"Find out who did this to me and kill them."

"We took the fight to them by shooting one of theirs."

"And we will finish this by putting more of them in the morgue."

"I'm not sure we should escalate this. Both sides could put each other's actions down as an unfortunate incident but a fair trade. If we retaliate now, then they'll come back and hit us harder. It's inevitable because that is exactly how we would respond."

"I don't give a shit how many bodies pile up, we must be seen to be stronger than them. Else we'll lose leverage everywhere."

"Sure thing babe, but we are weak over in San Francisco. Our power base is in LA not along the coast. Do you think we should divert resources away from making good money just to show a bunch of Russkies we mean business?"

"Damn straight. We can't let them come over here and walk all over us. If they do that, within three years they'll have everything and you and I will be six feet under."

Bobby sat pondering Mary Lou's words and mulled over his own concerns. She had more energy than he had. And his crew were most likely to wind up dead. He hated organizing funerals and dealing with crying, resentful widows. But taking it all into account, Mary Lou was right. Yesterday it was the Booty Bar and tomorrow it would be gaming, the rest of the girls and then the narcotics operations. They needed to destroy the parasite before it throttled its host.

THE MARKOV FAMILY occupied the Tenderloin district on McAllister and Larkin. Generations of impoverished inhabitants had lived and died on the same streets as these stocky Russian gangsters, who landed on the west coast and sustained themselves through a highly effective protection racket which blossomed into prostitution in all its guises.

Their girls were streetwalkers in the main run by a bunch of punks and a network of pimps. The Booty Bar had been a rare attempt at refinement because the senior family members understood the importance of rising out of the criminal primordial ooze. They needed ways to make more money and controlling a legal venue gave them the opportunity to hire out skanks at a much higher rate. While a cathouse would have boosted revenues, the Booty Bar delivered greater respectability too. Besides you could legally comp a cop a short private dance but lending them a hooker for half an hour was a whole different ball game.

Hence the vicious response. Anton may have been stubborn, but he was in charge of the only shred of legal activity operated by the Markovs. They could not let the affront to their reputation go unchallenged.

BOBBY AND HIS crew—Naldo and three trusted associates—began by cutting girls on the street. This was simple and sent out a clear statement: if you hit our revenues by burning down our building then we will scar your product. Only the sickest of the sick wants to fuck disfigured hookers.

The Markovs replied by attacking the other two bars under Lagotti control: the Red Stocking and the Dahlia. On this occasion, no matches were applied to the situation. Instead goons were despatched to threaten the staff—girls, bartenders, the lot. The following day, everyone was too scared to enter the premises. Mary Lou sent guys and whores in from LA but they received the same clear message.

On the night of Christmas Eve, Mary Lou ordered her fellas to slash throats and less than a week later, the body count had reached double digits on both sides.

"This madness has to stop. This war of attrition is hurting all of us with no sign of letting up. We've lost good people and for what? A stake in the ground and a chance to sell the sight of an ass a few miles further north."

"Organize a conference. We can afford to allow ourselves a graceful defeat on the prostitution because the lottery cards are going gangbusters."

146

MARY LOU REFUSED to come to the meet and insisted Bobby go instead. He knew this was a mistake but her mind was made up. A seedy hotel conference space with a view of a car lot—if you bothered to look outside. Naldo frisked the Markov attendees and one of their goons checked they weren't packing pieces. Everyone was clean.

The room had capacity for six chairs and a rectangular table which was exactly what was required. Bobby sat with Naldo to his right and Ernie Santo, a third generation American who'd worked alongside Naldo for years. Solid, reliable but occasionally prone to chatter. On the other side of the oak veneer was Nikolay Markov and two guys who were estranged from their clothes. It looked as though this was the first time either had worn a jacket. However, Bobby understood these individuals will have been the ones who torched the Booty Bar and murdered his people. They might seem like redneck hicks but he knew better than to underestimate them.

"You have encroached on our territory and performed horrific acts on our property."

"Let's be honest with each other Nikolay, both sides have deployed knives and guns causing pain and misery. Nobody is innocent here."

Bobby paused and stared at the three sitting opposite. There was no way Markov could seize the moral high ground.

"The point is, we're sat here today to put an end to the bloodshed so we can all go back to work."

"Agreed. But we must take into account you killed my nephew Anton."

"There is no need to bring out a roster for the dead but I acknowledge the death of your family member and I am sorry for your loss."

"Thank you. He was a stubborn cocksucker, but he was my sister's stubborn cocksucker. I hope you understand."

"I do. This is my proposal: we cease our efforts this year to stretch our wings in San Francisco's prostitution market. You stop attacking my people and we'll not muscle into any lap dancing clubs or hooker networks, whether owned by you or not."

"I see."

"By now, you should have done your homework and found out who we are and the reach we have in California and Nevada. We do not intend to stand still despite our… local difficulties here. You have shown yourselves to be formidable fighters and we respect that."

"You are right to give up on pussy in this town. This time next year, I shall be the only man selling ass on these streets and you won't get in my way. But you have forgotten about Anton."

"Direct compensation will be difficult because I've already just given up rights to prostitution and also because Anton had a simple choice and he picked foolishly. No disrespect to you or your sister."

"The boy was not the sharpest tool in the box. What are you suggesting?"

"A business relationship with us. To keep the girls on the streets or pumping those poles while they lap dance, I imagine you ply them with narcotics. We would like to supply them to you. This will be at a lower price than you pay now and of a higher quality, not that it matters to you. The compensation is the amount of green you save. Tell your sister whatever you want but that's the most Anton's life is worth."

The corners of Nikolay's mouth raised upward in the best imitation of a smile he could muster.

"Drugged up and fucked up—that's how we like them."

"Are we agreed?"

"Sure, why not? If it doesn't work out, I will go to a different supplier and then find and kill you for betraying our agreement."

Nikolay stared through Bobby who grit his teeth and inhaled deeply. Now was not the time to rise to this Russian's bait. They both knew the Lagottis were getting a beating. Only Nikolay wouldn't let Bobby off the hook.

"Oh, and one last thing. We shall relinquish immediate control of the Dahlia to you but keep the Red Stocking. Naturally you will supply all the girls to the club for a fee and a month ago you didn't have the Dahlia in your operation so that is a gift from us to you."

"Very well. At least I'll know where to find you. Our commission is sixty cents on the dollar—of the profit."

"Let's not get greedy so close to the end of our discussions. You can have fifty per cent of all revenues from the girls but not a penny more. Anything else we wring out the johns is our affair."

Bobby sat back in his chair and noticed Naldo place both hands on his lap. The man was ready to pounce because this was the moment when the deal all came together or fell apart into violence. Bobby had ceded ground until his final push and Nikolay might not fall for the ruse.

"This is acceptable."

Nikolay leaned across the table to shake Bobby's hand and the two smiled. He knew better than to trust the Russki but he'd stopped the bloodshed—for now. And they had a new customer for their brown sugar.

As they walked out onto the car lot, a gust of wind hit them all in the face like they'd been slapped back into reality. Far in the distance someone was playing carols. The sound of sleigh bells permeated Bobby's consciousness and he remembered what time of year it was.

"Merry Christmas to you and yours."

"Huh? Oh yes. Season's greetings."

They stood facing each other for a second until another blast of wind cut through them. Bobby nodded, slapped his hands together in a failed attempt to improve blood flow to his fingers and walked away. Naldo waited a short while to watch the Markovs depart.

"We should have killed them while we had the chance."

Bobby glared at Naldo's rare intrusion into family decision making.

"We'll make money out of them and no one has to die over the vacation. Besides, we only promised to stay out of prostitution for a year. The man has dreams but at heart he's a street fighter and they get toppled by the next guy with a bigger baseball bat."

SAM SPENT CHRISTMAS Day at Alice's, watching the sea beat against the beach although they popped over to a restaurant for a five course lunch. She enjoyed her time with Alice but the initial buzz had worn off. Separated by thousands of miles, the relationship needed a kick up its ass. Because they only saw each other one or two weekends a month, they both made sure there were no arguments or any reason to spoil the experience when they were together. That also meant all their different expectations and opinions remained unresolved.

Alice was besotted with her, but Sam could no longer tell herself she reciprocated. The sex was still good and the presents lavished on her were not to be sneezed at. All the same, she was bored but didn't have the energy to end it.

Christmas Day was a perfect example of what was wrong. Each individual moment was wonderful whether eating the most perfectly cooked turkey in the world, sitting watching the sun set over the Pacific Ocean or clinging to the headboard of Alice's four poster bed. But they added up to nothing. They would never be a normal couple and when they talked about the future, they were kidding themselves.

So Sam sowed the seeds of her departure before she even arrived, blaming a work party for her need to return to the east coast. The sadness on Alice's face almost made her cry but Sam tried her damndest to ensure Alice had the best Christmas away from her Mama she'd ever had. If not the finest then filled with the most sex.

AS SOON AS the plane landed at Logan, Sam felt a tremendous weight lift from her shoulders. She scurried back to her apartment, cracked open a bottle of wine and got merrily drunk watching TV reruns until she gurgled asleep in the late evening.

The next day, she opened her address book and investigated the party scene in her home town. With only three days before New Year the last thing she needed was to spend the upcoming nights alone. Good news: she was in luck. Every night had something to offer until the clock struck midnight on Sunday, December 31.

Thursday evening was a washout. Sam found herself cornered by a rich doofus who was more interested in his opinions than hers but that didn't stop her taking him home. His punishment for the tedium inflicted on her was to hail a cab on the street at four in the morning when she decided he wasn't going to be any more use to her in bed.

Having secured two days vacation time, Sam headed to the gym on Friday afternoon and dolled herself up. She wouldn't make the same mistake tonight. Kickass: that was her new motto.

The party venue was a penthouse overlooking State Street and, given the height of the apartment block, looked like it had a great view of the bay. Sam mingled, chatted with a few interesting people and was considering leaving to find action elsewhere when she sauntered to the makeshift bar for one last drink.

"Champagne?"

"Why the hell not?"

"I've yet to come up with a good reason myself."

"In that case, let's see what happens. What's the worst, right?"

Sam clinked glasses with the guy who was very self-assured but wasn't trying to take over the conversation.

"You local or breezing through town for the festive season?"

"Grew up in New Jersey but I've been living here since I left college."

"Study here?"

"Used to."

"Bright girl. And smart enough to stay in this beautiful city."

"And you?"

"I split my time between here and my other ventures on the east coast."

"Entrepreneur?"

"Do my best. Business is never easy…"

"…but you're doing well to afford that suit."

Sam reached out to feel the material of the jacket and the guy smiled and seemed to puff his chest as she did it. Having fingered the schmatta, Sam pressed down the lapel so it was flat again and gave herself the opportunity to lay her palm on his upper torso above his heart ever so slightly longer than was proper.

They continued to talk and she moved onto a cosmo or two, a habit she'd acquired from Alice. The guy took Sam's glass and placed it on a nearby table. He put his hand on hers and led her to the dance floor where a DJ was cranking out the tunes. He had some good moves but focused on dancing with her rather than impressing her. The same couldn't be said for most of the others hovering near her like flies buzzing around a picnic hamper.

When the beats slowed down and half the people sloped off to drink a little more, he got intimate without getting fresh. For Sam that meant she was happy for him to kiss her neck and put his hand on her ass but he didn't rearrange her panties. What a gentleman.

"Would you mind if we found somewhere quieter?"

"Good plan. Like to come back to mine for a Java?"

"Your place sounds fine. Okay if I bring some party powder to help with the… coffee?"

"Nice idea. I'm Sam Wray."

"Frank Lagotti."

SAM AWOKE FACE up from the brink of a horny dream to find her feet on the pillows and Frank's head between her thighs. She stretched her arms and arched her back. In the corner of her eye she saw two lines of white on the bedside table.

Although she needed a hit to kick-start the day, there was no way she wanted to interrupt Frank who was hard at work creating ripples of tingles throughout her body—emanating from her groin but spreading to her toes, her fingers. Even her eyelids felt more alive.

Later they snaffled up the remaining coke and spent the rest of the day naked and sweaty. The simple act of having Alice's twin in bed with her turned Sam on. The rush was immense.

"So am I better than Alice?"

"If I thought you'd compare yourself to her, I'd never have mentioned it."

"Don't lie. Must be freaking awesome to have a brother and a sister."

"Has its moments, for sure."

Sam didn't want to get bogged down by thoughts of Alice and her delectable body. She was having fun and wanted more.

"Are we going out tonight or shall we party at home?"

"No need to decide. You throw a dress on and we'll hang out with some people I've met and if everything's cool, we can invite them here—or to mine—to carry on the entertaining until the sun rises again."

Sam rolled on top of Frank, rocking forward and back until his breathing changed rhythm.

"Sure thing honey—only not just yet, eh?"

1996

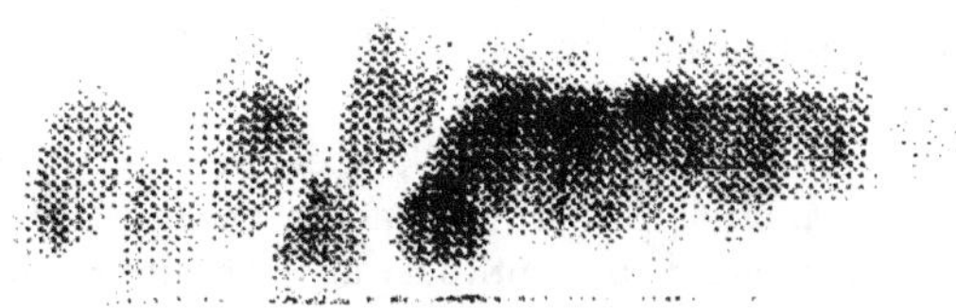

147

THE PREVIOUS YEAR ended with Indiana's decision to reintroduce a handful of riverboat casinos. One of the earliest licenses to be granted was run from Chicago, out of East Dubuque and Mary Lou saw this loosening up of gambling laws as a natural extension of their existing casino operations. All she needed to do was convince the Gaming Commission that Alice was an appropriate person to own the vessel.

"Another day, another license to be bought."

"How is Teddy Prescott?"

"Been better. He had a heartache three months ago and there's talk he'll step down soon."

"We should have a conversation before he does anything rash."

"I'm sure he will be pleased to see you. Always has been in the past."

"Send my regards."

Bobby flew out to Prescott's mansion the following day. The butler answered the door and showed him to the library. This room with its musty books felt like a home from home although Bobby had only visited Prescott a handful of times. Unlike every previous occasion Hannah Prescott appeared in the doorway in place of her husband. Bobby stood up from the insanely luxurious armchair and took the five steps forward to introduce himself and to shake her hand. Hannah kept her arms by her side and her expression reflected her disgust for him. Teddy had briefed her.

"Mr. Trevestan, I am so sorry you have had a wasted journey."

"Call me Bobby. How is Teddy?"

"Far too ill to receive visitors, I'm afraid."

"So he knows I am here then? Or have you reached that decision on his behalf?"

"Mr. Trevestan..."

"... Bobby..."

"... my husband has made me only too aware of you. He asked me to convey his apologies but you will not be seeing him today."

Bobby stared into the eyes of this shrewish woman. Chances were she was just trying to protect the senator from the myriad strangers who spend their lives lobbying politicians.

"Has Teddy told you how he and I first met?"

"No, he hasn't mentioned..."

"... then you can't possibly expect me to believe Teddy won't see me. So either you have decided for yourself or he isn't here anywhere. Which is it, Hannah?"

Bobby's expression gained the edge of a grimace and he moved a step forward to enter her personal space.

"Fellows like you do not intimidate me. You think you can walk into people's homes and order them about, but you are wrong."

"And women like you believe you can boss men like me around and we'll do what you say. You are making a very poor mistake. I could help your husband get the finest medical treatment, for example. I am able to protect him, you and your entire family from life's misfortunes."

"Don't threaten me, Trevisan."

"Lady, this is no threat. Answer my question: is Teddy in this joint?"

Hannah looked at Bobby's eyes and her cheeks flushed red.

"Yes he is, but he's too tired for visitors. He asked me to send you away as he doesn't have the energy to see anyone nowadays."

"He'll see me. Now."

Mrs. Prescott nodded and walked out of the room at such a pace that Bobby could easily follow her up the stairs, along the landing and into a large bedroom. Hannah pulled up a chair near the bed and Bobby sat down facing the tired man lying under the sheets. Without turning around, Bobby issued a clear instruction:

"Shut the door on your way out."

Hannah parted her lips as if she planned on replying but closed her mouth and left.

BOBBY RELAXED BACK in his seat and watched Teddy Prescott wheeze in front of him. The heart attack had knocked him sideways.

"Hi Teddy. Good to see you."

"Seen better days."

"That may be so, but you've got some great years ahead of you still."

"Not sure about that from what the doctors have told me."

"Ah, their job is to make money out of you being ill. They want to keep you down. You will bounce back from this. Just focus on building up your strength and you'll be in the Palace humping your way through our girls like there's no tomorrow."

"There may be no tomorrow for me. That's my point."

Bobby watched this old man's face. He had a real fear he was on his last legs.

"I hope you're wrong, Teddy - for your sake and mine."

"You always want something but this time I'm far too gone to do your bidding."

"You're still here, Teddy. And this isn't about you. It's about your darling Hannah."

"Leave her out of this."

"I can't ignore her when you sent her down to meet me instead of calling me up here to speak to you, my friend."

Prescott began to cough, caused by the tightness in his chest: the stress of seeing Bobby.

"Do you fancy a beer? I think I do. Shall I find Hannah and ask her for one?"

Beat.

"Did you ever tell her?"

Teddy's pale complexion gained a reddish hue.

"Thought not. I mean, how can a man explain to his wife he raped an underage prostitute to death with a glass bottle? Fucked if I know how to start that conversation, but that's what you'll be doing soon unless you listen carefully to what I need you to do, you shit bag."

A pause as Bobby crossed his legs and picked off a piece of white fluff from Prescott's sheets.

"It's your reputation on the line, not mine. In five minutes time I can tell Hannah what you did and then you'll be dying and divorced. Well, what's it to be?"

"What do you want me to do?"

"I brought a letter with me today and you will sign it to recommend Alice Lagotti as a fine upstanding member of the community to the Gaming Commission. The family wants to run a riverboat casino."

Bobby pulled out the typewritten sheet from his inside jacket pocket and fumbled around until he found a pen. Teddy took it and Bobby held the paper so he could write a wobbly signature.

"Thank you for your cooperation. As ever, we appreciate the assistance you've provided over the years."

"This was the last time. I can't..."

"Don't be ridiculous, Teddy. You can - and you will. We ask little but, as you know, sometimes we need an accommodation. Besides, mark my words, you'll be out of this bed soon enough. I made this offer to Hannah but I'm making a promise to you. I shall arrange for one of our doctors to pay you a visit."

"Please don't..."

Bobby stood up, put the letter in his pocket and patted Prescott on the shoulder. He might never have liked the senator but Teddy had always come good for them and he looked pitiful right now. Worth showering a few thousand dollars on the old goat if only to make Bobby feel better on the off chance he had to call again.

ALICE ENJOYED SPENDING time with Mama especially as she had been entrusted to kick off another key project for the family. East Dubuque nestled just south of the state border with Wisconsin and on the opposite side of the Mississippi to its bigger brother, Dubuque in Iowa. To describe the town as small would be an understatement but Mary Lou wasn't shacked up in the East Dubuque Regal to settle down and make a home for herself.

She and Alice only needed to spend a few days here to set up a boilerplate legal entity and to ensure Alice met the residency requirements laid out in the statutes to secure the casino license.

"We'll have to stay past the weekend, won't we?"

"Looks like it right now. Can't be helped. People don't move fast in these hick towns—and we're from California."

"I know, but this is the first place I've been where I feel bigger than it."

Mary Lou smiled: she'd raised herself a city chick.

"It'll grow if we have anything to do with it."

"Saturday, shall we visit Chicago for some shopping?"

"Spoken like a true Al Capone."

"A girl has to have fun sometimes. All work and no play..."

"...makes Jill a rich woman. I'm teasing. Chicago is a great idea—unless you'd rather meet up with Sam instead of hanging out with your old mom."

"You're not old. Anyway, I told Sam I'd be busy the next few weeks so she wouldn't think I was ignoring her. The family business comes first."

"It'll take two hours to drive over there, less if I'm behind the wheel so why don't we stay overnight?"

Alice clapped her hands with glee like a little girl and gave Mama an enormous hug.

"That'd be great. Just like we used to pop over to LA when I was a kid."

"Only one difference, darling."

"Huh?"

"This time you're paying."

SIXTY YEARS BEFORE, Chicago had been at the epicenter of mob activity thanks to its location smack in the middle of the country's waterways for transportation and to the pliability of its local law enforcement officers. That was then. Now the organized crime syndicates were no more and anyone could walk the streets safely without the grinding fear of being shot—unless you were black and poor of course.

Mary Lou and Alice checked into their hotel and sat in the bar contemplating where to eat dinner. Alice thumbed through the local newspaper while Mary Lou went to a phone to speak with Bobby. When she returned five minutes later, concern was written all over her face. Alice's back stiffened as she braced herself.

"What's happened?"

"I've got to go."

"Where?"

"Atlantic City."

With those two words, Alice's heart sank because it meant only one thing: Mama needed to bail out Frank. Mary Lou saw Alice's expression shift from excitement to misery.

"He needs me so I have to help."

"And how old does he have to be before you let him stand or fall by himself?"

"Probably never: he's my son and I love him so I must care for him. Just as I love you and want to look after you."

Alice glared and sulked, hiding her head behind her paper. This was not the weekend she'd wanted. Frank always got in the way.

"This isn't a debate. I'll book a flight now. Would be great if you'd drive me to O'Hare but I'll take a taxi if you won't."

"Don't be like that, Mama. I'll drive you for sure. I'm disappointed. That's all."

Each word was true—Alice was saddened but not at the prospect of losing a weekend's shopping because retail therapy could wait. It was her mother and her blinkered attitude to Frank. That was disappointing her because it never seemed to change. The boy snapped his fingers and Mama came running. Every single time.

FRANK FACED DISAPPOINTMENT of his own but this was business and not personal. Leonida had vanished and so had a cool half a million in cash from the Lucky Nugget safe. The two events were connected because it was too much of a coincidence and a member of the reception staff saw Leonida leave with a case in his hard. Frank might not have been Philip Marlowe, but he was no schnook.

His gut told him to track the motherfucker down and slice his skin off while his head said he should focus on the business and not let the red mist take over. In the short-term his head won and he called Palm Springs only to hear Mama was somewhere in Illinois with the golden girl, Alice.

A fresh layer of anger descended on his shoulders and he vowed to find Leonida and settle matters the old-fashioned way. Two hours later, three men burst into Leonida's hotel room. The guy hid in plain sight in AC instead of fleeing town at the earliest opportunity. All wore plastic masks but only one spoke to the prostitute sitting astride Leonida.

"Put your clothes on: the party's over."

As the whore scuttled off Leonida's body, he stretched his hand to the bedside table. Three revolvers aimed at his head.

"Don't do it. Not even to get your piece."

"I was going to pay her."

"No need to bother. My treat."

The girl just finished putting on her dress and Frank pointed at her panties lying on the floor. She nodded, put them on as quickly as she physically could and looked round the room.

"Got everything?"

A nod. She tried her best not to make eye contact.

"How much does he owe you?"

"Thirty plus tip. No offense."

"None taken. We all have to earn a living."

Frank pulled out a thick roll of bills from his pants pocket and held out a C-note.

"Now beat it. And remember you were never here."

As the girl took the bill, Frank squeezed her ass under that short dress with enough venom for her to know he wasn't fucking about. The masks and the guns were sufficient reminder however, so she knew it was a just a cheap grope. Under the circumstances, she let it ride and scurried out the room.

By the time Mary Lou arrived that evening, Leonida had three fewer fingers as Frank was no expert in torture. They were holed up on the third floor of the Nugget which Frank had never bothered to renovate. Leonida was tied to a chair in an otherwise empty room. The two windows had one shutter ajar and a bare bulb was on, hanging in the middle of the ceiling.

Frank's problem was simple: how to get Leonida to say where he'd stashed the money. While the guy was willing to talk, he reckoned he was a dead man so had no motivation to spill his guts.

Mary Lou stood in the corner watching proceedings as she did when rats were being tortured. Her son was doing his best but all he was achieving was causing the dude pain. She beckoned Frank to stop for a moment and he walked over to her with Leonida's blood dripping from his knuckles.

"Carry on like this and he'll be dead but you'll be no closer to our money. What leverage do we have?"

Frank shrugged. His plan relied on hurting the guy until he squealed, which plainly wasn't working. Mary Lou sauntered toward Leonida, circling him before stopping in front of him. She leaned forward and raised his head by gently moving his chin.

"How did it come to this? You are not looking in good shape. I hope you understand unless you tell us what we want to know, my son will continue to beat on you until you are dead. That could take a minute, an hour or a day. Or longer. If I make a phone call, I could get someone who could kill you over the course of a week… or more."

She bent down until her lips were next to his right ear.

"A week or longer: imagine that."

Leonida strained to look at Mary Lou's face but she had to stand up before he could check out her expression. When their eyes locked, he thought through the reality of her words. He swallowed hard. Mary Lou stood and waited.

"The key in my jacket opens a locker at the station. The money's in there."

"If I send someone over and the green isn't there, do you understand I'll make that phone call?"

"It's there. I promise."

One of Frank's goons rummaged through pockets until he found the key. Then with a nod to Mary Lou he left the room. Mary Lou pulled a gun from her waistband and shot Leonida in the head.

"Clean up this mess, Frank. And then find out how you missed that key. Now, take me somewhere decent to stay for tonight. Tomorrow I want to get back to your sister."

148

DESPITE HIS ILL-health, Teddy Prescott came through for Bobby yet again and soon Alice's name was added to the roster of legitimate gaming professionals. Work began in earnest. A vessel had been located, bought and renovations were in motion. The infrastructure was only half the story because a casino was successful if you used the right people and that was proving to be harder than they'd imagined.

The riverboat's route would take it on a loop between Davenport near Iowa City and Fort Madison further south. Every two-bit outfit on both sides of the Mississippi wanted to get in on the action but there simply wasn't room to fit all those beaks in the trough. Instead, Alice found hiring dealers, watchers and counters too difficult.

"Everyone we approach is in somebody's pocket—it's ridiculous. We can't trust anyone because they owe somebody else a tithe."

"And we don't have this problem with the Lady Fortune?"

"Hell no."

"That's the answer: bring in the best we have from Vegas to do a stint afloat and every outfit will see they've got no way to earn off us. They'll back off and if there's anyone worth hiring, then we can afford to pay them a premium. At least while the dust settles on the venture."

Alice understood the riverboat, which they'd christened the Queen of Sheba for no good reason Alice could fathom, would draw gamblers away from local games but their real market was tourists and high rollers. None of the penny ante hustlers nearby would lose out of the big money because neither group frequented their dive bars now.

Her other thought—and natural response which she hadn't acted on yet—was to break a few heads so the various gangs who were buzzing around their ears would receive a clear message to stay out of their way. Alice knew her Mama would want a more subtle approach. Mary Lou preferred to give everybody a chance to do the right thing. If they made a poor choice, a ton of shit would descend on them, but they had an opportunity to succeed upfront.

With the Queen of Sheba fresh out of the dry dock, they sailed the steamer up and down the mighty Mississippi as a pre-launch for the casino. A special guest list was operating where you only got on board if you were a Vegas regular or local dignitary.

Like all Lagotti venues, cameras operated in every room. Technology had moved on from the early days of the Palace and video replaced the need to pick up the film from each device. Instead surveillance was set up to catch thieves and blackmail the rich and powerful.

The launch showed the debauchery of the average joe and revealed a few minor glitches in their security. With one round trip under their belts, the rest would be a walk in the park.

THE WINDY CITY offered Mary Lou opportunities way beyond riverboat gambling and with the mob receded into the distance, there was every reason to exploit them as much as possible. In reality, the lack of any organized approach to criminal activity created a hole into which she happily jumped in.

The sheer size of Chicago as a major city meant there were millions of worker bees and the onslaught of the Reagan years had left them with fewer rights and a much quieter voice. There remained unions representing the case for labor over capital, but they had a smaller number of supporters than in the good old days. Mary Lou figured they needed an edge and she'd be happy to supply it.

Union membership was still strong among government workers like teachers and fire fighters although they weren't militant because of their sense of vocation. The same couldn't be said of the private sector and that is where Mary Lou focused her efforts.

The Roofers and Bricklayers Union represented those in the building profession and Mary Lou reckoned they'd want to ensure they had continuity of employment. With the large volume of skyscrapers still ripping through the horizon, there was a huge amount of money to be made from the inherent conflict between big business and the contractors they hired.

"So let me get this straight: you want my members to pay you out of their hard-earned wages in case the bosses turn violent. And that is something that hasn't happened in Chicago since before the Korean War."

"That is correct."

Mary Lou sat with Jerred Dudley in the headquarters of the Roofers and Bricklayers Union building. The irony was not lost on her that the joint was a decrepit mess but it was no worse than she had been expecting.

"That's not much of a proposal now is it?"

"You see Jerred. That depends on your perspective. If all you ever do is to look back over your shoulder at the lessons of the past, it doesn't come across as an interesting proposition. But if you're the man who has his eyes set on the future, that's a different matter."

"And I suppose you think I'm that sort of guy?"

"Naturally. I need not remind you of the brute economics facing your men. Big corporations spend millions to vie with each other to build the tallest, the fanciest skyscrapers in the world. They rely on hiring locals to do all the hard work. Only trouble is that union rates of pay cut into their profit and they are tempted to bring in outside agencies."

"We make our contributions so those kind of problems don't arise."

"Haven't happened in the past. Sometimes bribes are not enough."

"Listen lady, we do not get involved in bribery. We pay into an arbitration service so industrial action is minimized."

"You must consider what happens if that fails. Four major projects are about to break ground in the next six months and your members need to be on site for all of them."

"I am aware, but I don't see why you are bothering me with this."

"Because Jerred, I have it on good authority that you will face this problem very soon."

Dudley laughed and allowed himself to wallow in his perceived joke. All the while, Mary Lou sat and stared at him. Motionless.

"I suppose you want me to believe you can save us from an event that isn't likely to happen."

"Oh, it will."

"Tell you what: come back when we actually have a problem and if you fix it, we'll have another conversation. Until then, you're wasting my time."

A DROP OF blood splatted on Alice's cheek after the sharp blast of air flashed past. Nikolay slammed to the ground almost before the slug had landed in Mama's body. As though he knew it was coming. The tear that fell out of Bobby's eye and deposited itself on Mama's chin.

Total disorientation. No sooner had Alice hit the floor, she lost track of which direction she was facing. Her entire focus was on Bobby holding Mama. Her red pool growing and pouring down her body and over Bobby too.

Alice looked down at his hand and they were still listening to the sermon. The constant monotone was hard to follow. She wished the priest would shut up. A brief twist of her head revealed Frank sat on Bobby's other side.

He was bowed and his hands gripped his knees like they were about to fall off. Alice had no idea quite how he was coping—they'd hardly spoken since the day Mama died. His knuckles were white. Not going well.

Alice swallowed and blinked. Then she was back on the Queen of Sheba.

149

THAT WEEKEND, BACK in the summerhouse, Mary Lou, Bobby and Alice mulled over the week's events.

"We can nix any plans for labor racketeering. Illinois is dead to us. The lack of organized crime has turned the town soft. The unions have figured out how to get on with management so we have no leverage."

"How many did you hit?"

"Double digits: builders, carpenters, road repairers, duct repairs, refuse collectors and so on. I've tried them all and got nowhere. It's time to leave Illinois."

"Apart from the Queen of Sheba, of course."

"We need to get out—there's nothing here for us."

"Gambling. That's working really well. We might not be at full pelt yet but we're in profit and set to do even better this year and next."

"Bobby's right. And I know we can build on the work we've previously done. We should not walk away at this point."

"There's a time to stay and a moment to go. And now we should say goodbye to the Land of Lincoln."

"Why not sleep on this? The revenue from the riverboat has been good for us already. We shouldn't throw the baby out with the bath water."

Alice nodded to reinforce Bobby's concerns. Her eyes flitted from him over to Mama and back again. All her hard work was about to be poured down the drain by her mother. It made no sense but what flashed across her mind was how the decision was so irrational.

"We're leaving Illinois and there's nothing more to say."

Alice walked out the room and headed into the kitchen for more coffee. As she returned, she found Bobby sat on a lounger with a cigar in one hand.

"Did you storm out or were you thirsty?"

"BOTH. DO YOU know what happened in there?"

"Not too sure. Mary Lou hadn't talked about this. I can see why the labor racket is not for us. But the Queen of Sheba is set to rake in a lot of cash."

"Yep."

They were silent for a spell and the only sounds came from Mary Lou inside the summerhouse.

"What'll we do?"

"Keep the place running—at least for a while. Mama has had a series of knockbacks and that has clouded her judgment. Give her time for the dust to settle."

"How long is she going to need? I mean I can't sit here for a week and wait for her to see sense."

"If you go back tomorrow, I can handle the situation here."

"You intend to deal with Mama?"

Alice allowed an enormous laugh to erupt out of her mouth—so much so, her hand was forced to quickly muffle the noise. They both turned their heads to check on the summerhouse door but it remained firmly shut. Bobby smiled.

"She's a force to be reckoned with, but she has been known to listen to me."

Alice raised one eyebrow in disbelief as a response.

"No, really. But I don't have those kinds of conversation in public."

"That's your idea of pillow talk, I suppose?"

"Do not get fresh, young lady. In private, away from people, is all I meant."

ALICE AND BOBBY sat down with Mary Lou, who had been sitting at the desk making lists. Once she noticed their return, she stood up and joined them on the more comfortable seating.

"Is there anything else for us to discuss?"

"Alice will go back to the Queen of Sheba tomorrow and begin the wind down. I'm sure we can find someone to buy the license pretty quick."

"No more boat trips, you understand darling? We are quitting Illinois as of this minute."

"Yes, Mama."

A glance to Bobby. Alice was far from happy lying to her mother but they couldn't afford to stop the riverboat operation now. The payoff for all their hard work would land in their laps over the course of the next twelve months.

"Good girl. I can always rely on my Alice."

Mama hadn't spoken those words to her daughter since before she was in High School. She almost felt like a child again. This perspective repeated itself that night when Alice stayed over in her old bedroom. She was so unnerved that when she woke up in the darkness just after midnight, she crept downstairs and crashed out on one of the living room couches.

Before the rest of the house surfaced, Alice got up and headed back.

BOBBY RECKONED HE awoke first but Mary Lou was already staring at him. He rolled over and they hugged.

"I think I heard Alice's convertible roar into action a few minutes ago."

"Me too. I wonder why she's off in such a hurry. She could have waited for us to have breakfast together."

"Perhaps she wants to beat the worst of the traffic."

"Even so."

She nuzzled in and they hugged some more.

"Do you still feel the same way about Illinois this morning?"

"Yes, babe."

"Because I'm not so convinced."

"Oh? The Queen of Sheba will make us a lot of money over the next two or three years."

Bobby was puzzled because Mary Lou had made a complete turnaround since last night.

"Keep the riverboat?"

"Sure thing. Why not? You think we should ditch it? To be honest, Alice has done another fantastic job and we should let her carry on. It's right for her and good for us."

"I agree."

"I thought you just said the opposite. You really should decide what you believe and stick to it, babe."

Bobby continued the hug which turned into kissing and before long, neither were focused on the Prairie State.

ST THERESA CHURCH stood on East Ramon and South Farrell Drive. A new build from the 1940s, it didn't come across as a bastion of the Holy Roman Empire from the outside. The modern facade hid the grim reality of the Christian temple. As you walked through the entrance, you were greeted by row upon row of wooden benches facing away from you and positioned so the altar was the main attraction. Halfway along on the left was a large cupboard with two doors, one at each end.

Without giving it a moment's attention, Mary Lou headed straight for the confessional and entered on the right-hand side. The space was poorly lit and a small window slid open once she'd closed the door behind her. She kneeled down because there was a cushion on the floor and no chair.

"May God, who has enlightened every heart, help you know your sins and trust in his mercy."

"I haven't been to a church or spoken to a priest since I was fifteen years old, but I want to speak with one now."

"My child: this is a confessional. I am happy to spend time and discuss what troubles you, but unless you wish to confess your sins to me, then we must go somewhere else."

"Then what are we waiting for?"

Mary Lou followed Father Ardal Carmoody past the altar to a door on the other side of the church, which she hadn't noticed when she first arrived. The priest led her down a short corridor and into his office, indicating for her to sit down while Carmoody walked around to sit at his desk.

"So what's troubling you, my dear?"

"HOW'S THE WORLD of Mark Twain?"

Bobby and Alice sat in her South Dubuque office overlooking the harbor. It wasn't her favorite place, but it was functional. Tables, chairs, window, filing cabinets—without the luxuries she'd enjoyed at the Lady Fortune. The town lacked the charm of Las Vegas too—or rather it had none of the razzmatazz.

"Same old. We need new ways to squeeze the green out of the tourists. The high rollers seem to enjoy not being stuck inside a darkened hall."

"Nice to hear we're doing something right. But you didn't ask me to visit this backwater to give me good news."

Alice took a sip from her coffee and swallowed as though the liquid contained razor blades.

"How's Mama, would you say?"

"Fine. She is concerned we still have too much exposure in narcotics but apart from that, she's okay."

"I'm not talking about business. Is she in a good shape?"

Silence. Bobby ground his molars and stared at Alice, making no sign of answering. He glugged some of his coffee down and Alice felt as though he didn't take his eyes off her for a second.

"Why d'you ask?"

"Have you forgotten what happened with Mama just the other week?"

"Are you still thinking about that?"

"Of course, aren't you?"

"She was tired—not thinking straight."

"I'm not sure that's all it was. I mean: the next day you said she acted like the night before never happened."

"Lack of energy—no more and no less. I spend way more time with her than you do so I know what I'm talking about."

"I am concerned, Bobby. Mama never gets anything as wrong as she did then—as though she was a different person."

"Don't worry, it's all fine. Only low blood sugar."

Alice shook her head but failed to respond. She couldn't understand how Bobby wasn't able to see what she could. Mama was not the same, but she had no idea what was up.

"You don't sound certain. Think for a minute. Is there anything you can think of?"

"Tiredness is all."

"Then give her a vacation. If you're right, take her away for some R&R. Then she'll come back and be completely better."

Bobby picked at a piece of fluff on his sleeve while Alice watched and tried not to fume. Her concerns were genuine and he appeared to ignore them completely. In reality, he had noticed his Mary Lou had behaved a little strangely. She would vanish for hours at a time and not say where she'd been. More than that, she acted as though she hadn't been anywhere even though he knew she hadn't been at home.

He considered tailing her but decided against it: whatever she was doing was none of his business. Unless she had started an affair which was unlikely because he was still getting action in the bedroom. A vacation might clear the air.

150

MIAMI SURE WAS a crazy town—the mix of people and the Latino beats conspired to produce a city teetering on the edge of excitement every day of the week. Boca Raton was where gangsters went to die and Miami was the place for those who chose to live.

Their seafront hotel was close enough to the action on Ocean Drive to be fun, but the Jackson Hotel had sufficient stars on its hoardings to ensure the hardcore party animals stayed away. Mary Lou and Bobby sat at a table in the patio restaurant watching the world walk past. They held hands all the while and pointed out to each other amusing sights: rollerbladers with neon pink thongs and their miniature pooches, bowling ball shaped men sweating into white linen suits, wrinkled hags wearing leopard-print butt-length dresses. The freak show that was Miami Beach.

"I'm glad you talked me into this."

"We both deserved a break. It's been a tough few months."

"I'd forgotten how much I love this town."

"Didn't know you'd been here before."

"A lifetime ago. Before we met."

"I see. Were you with Frank?"

"He wasn't born then."

"I meant his father."

FRANK LAGOTTI FOLLOWED Mary Lou into a boutique of Collins Avenue filled with chichi beachwear. She grabbed six or eight different bikinis of varying styles, colors and patterns. After what felt like an interminable amount of time, she reappeared from the charging rooms with a red and white striped bikini which looked the same as all the others to him. She kissed him as they left the store.

"I've never had anything as pretty as this in my life. Thank you."

"De nada."

She planted another kiss on him, only this time fully on the mouth. He tasted warm and she melted as his fingers ran down her spine, finishing with a squeeze of her ass. Her silver boutique bag in one hand and her man in the other, Mary Lou headed back to their small hotel and into their room to change into the new purchase.

They had fresh white linen on the bed—the maid had got in early—and the headboard was pastel blue to match the nautical theme of the rest of the furniture. Frank pulled out his swimming trunks from a drawer and Mary Lou unwrapped her bikini from its tissue paper and placed both items gingerly on the covers of the bed.

Without saying a word, but in perfect synchrony, they both chucked their clothes on the floor and stood, soaking in the sight of the other's body. Mary Lou walked round to give Frank a kiss while he wrapped his arms round her torso, one hand massaging her right breast. Tingles flashed along her spine and she leaned into him to feel him against her skin.

"I MEANT HIS father"

"Huh?"

Mary Lou was confused. She looked around and saw Bobby but only a minute ago she'd been with Frank, the man who'd given her the twins. She clung to her chair and hoped the world would right itself soon. Bobby sensed her distress as she dug her nails into his hand and decided to just remain calm and let her ride out the storm in her mind. She knew she was in Miami and she closed her eyes for a second…

Frank made Mary Lou stand up and she felt his groin pressing against her rose tattoo. A tingle sprung from her crotch as his fingers investigated her body. Despite the problems with the First Bank of Baltimore, they were in a wonderful place together. Like they were inseparable and perfectly attuned to each other. Bound by more than the sweat caused by the intensity of their sex and the heat of the night.

On the second day of their trip, they hung out the 'Do Not Disturb' sign on their room door and occupied the morning naked, in bed and happy. Perhaps for the first time in Mary Lou's life. Then they hit the beach before lunch and spent the early afternoon people watching in a cafe. When they packed, Mary Lou put her new bikini back in its wrapping and into its silver store bag before depositing it into her luggage. On the plane, she nestled on Frank's shoulder and fell asleep, content from the forty-eight hour sojourn.

MARY LOU OPENED her eyes with a jolt and saw Bobby sat next to her on the Jackson patio. More disorientation. A sip of coffee helped to give her focus and she recalled the reason for being in Miami.

"I'm glad you talked me into this."

"Tough few months, huh?"

"Sure have been. At least the boy is getting a grip on himself. And Alice is doing fine—a real treasure."

"One smart cookie, that girl."

"Always was. She'd let Frank run and wade through the swamp and then glide around the dirt to avoid the shit."

"Self-reliant too. Very mature head on those shoulders."

"Knows what she wants and ruthless when she needs to be."

"Have you come to terms about her… lifestyle?"

"I've never had a problem with Alice being gay—I just don't like passive-aggressive bullshit. That's a totally different ball game and I won't stand for it. Never have and I'm not gonna start now."

Bobby stroked her hand with his thumb. Mary Lou was a fabulous woman and he was a lucky man to exist in her orbit. He turned to soak in her beauty with the sunset in the background and realized he'd forgotten how much he was physically attracted to her.

"Shall we return to the room?"

"I'm good here enjoying the view."

"What if we go up and fuck until it's time to eat?"
Mary Lou released his hand and stood up.
"Should have said. Come on then."

DESPITE BOBBY'S CLAIM that all Mama needed was a week's R&R, Alice was not satisfied. So she took a plane to visit her brother in AC. This was her first trip to the Lucky Nugget and she tried her best not to be disappointed—or at least not show it.

Before the end of their teenage years, the twins learned not to spend too much time alone together because arguments always followed. There was something in their chemistry that caused explosions. As adults, their lives had separated and their different paths enabled each to avoid the other at almost every turn.

The appearance of his sister at the casino was a genuine surprise for Frank. Since Leonida's untimely departure, he had not yet hired a replacement. There had been several excellent candidates, but Bobby had gained trust issues and couldn't bring himself to let anyone inside his circle.

The impact of his indecision was simple: Frank was working harder than he'd ever done before in his life—and he was stressed. Then Alice appeared at reception seeking an appointment with Mr. Lagotti.

"Hello stranger."

"Hi, Frank."

"What brings you to this side of the country? I hope you're not here to offer me advice because I really don't have time to listen to your anecdotes about management acumen."

"Hadn't crossed my mind. You got problems? I'm here about Mama, not the family business."

"Yeah I had local difficulties. Hasn't Mama mentioned the trouble with Leonida?"

"Who?"

"Leonida Acerbi, my casino manager. We had to… let him go after we found his fingers were getting too sticky for his own good."

"And your problem is…?"

"I can't find anyone to replace him and it will send me to an early grave."

Alice chuckled at the thought of Frank pulling his finger out and grafting instead of fucking his way through life. Any sympathy in her bones for his situation ebbed away, but she tried not to show it as she was here to seek his help—for the first time since she was sixteen.

IN THE CONFINES of his office, Alice felt better able to talk to Frank without the constant desire to bait him. He might be snowed under by the responsibilities of leadership, but she saw a glint in his eyes—almost a glow—that made her think he was evolving as a human being in front of her. Maybe he enjoyed bossing people around.

"What's the matter, sis'?"

"Something's not right with Mama, but I can't put my finger on it."

"And does Bobby share your view?"

"No. He reckons she's tired and nothing more. That's why they've gone off to Florida this week. What about you?"

"Me? Nothing. She looked okay last time I saw her. In fact, she seemed more than fine under the circumstances."

"Your personnel issues."

"Uh-huh."

Alice wondered how reliable Frank's opinion was to her. In the past he'd shown himself to be one of the most inept and useless people she'd ever had the misfortune of knowing. Yet Mama had set him up to run a casino just like Alice. The woman had a deeper insight than Alice, for sure. Perhaps it was all in her head and she was worrying over nothing. To shut down the Queen of Sheba wasn't fantasy—it nearly became a reality.

"The thing is that some of Mama's decisions have been…"

She could not bring herself to say what was lingering at the back of her mind. Dare not utter those negative thoughts out loud.

"…ill-advised."

Frank tilted his head to one side, not sure of what to make of Alice and her concerns. He figured she must be serious otherwise she'd never have wasted her valuable time on him, but she had nothing specific to offer. Women's intuition didn't cut it with him.

"How so?"

"She wanted to shut down the Queen of Sheba because she hadn't been able to gouge any of the Chicago unions."

"And you'd have been left running the bathtub with no baby."

"This isn't about me: it's Mama we should focus on."

FRANK COULDN'T HELP himself and he let out a guffaw. Alice's concerns for Mama just boiled down to fear of appearing to fail. Like everything in Alice's life. He had almost believed her but luckily he caught himself in time.

"Alice, listen to yourself. It's not Mama that needs help: it is you. Can't you see Mama's doing what's best for the family? If a casino has to be abandoned, then so be it. Same for me here. She and Bobby have big plans and we have to accept they aren't showing us the entire picture. Not right now, anyway."

"Bobby agreed with me on this. He thought she was wrong too—only he let things blow over and Mama changed her mind. But that didn't stop us losing a million dollar a month profit from the riverboat operation. Just because she was snubbed."

Frank couldn't conceive of his Mama not making the right decision first time. So Alice and Bobby must have misunderstood. Or something. The grim possibility that Mama was wrong would not get a firm purchase in his head. There was no way he could survive without her being there for him. This was not the point for him to lose her.

"Mama's fine and you are losing your mind. I might have done too many lines of coke in my life but you are the one who's paranoid. You should listen to yourself. Mama says something you don't like the sound of because it hits your operation in the belly, next you're traveling round the country announcing our Mama is a psycho."

"That's not what I said."

"The only time you had a problem was when she threatened the Queen of Sheba. Admit it, sis'. You're afraid Mama's gonna take your favorite ball off you and lock it in the summerhouse cupboard."

"Fuck you."

"And the horse you rode in on."

Alice stood up and stormed out of the office, out of the Lucky Nugget and straight to the airport. Having calmed down, she thought about hopping over to Sam as Boston was so close. She wanted to spend the night in her lover's arms but when she rang, there was no reply and Alice didn't have the stomach for more disappointment today: she wasn't in the mood. On the flight back, she shut her eyes and dreamed of Sam's body and all its crevices.

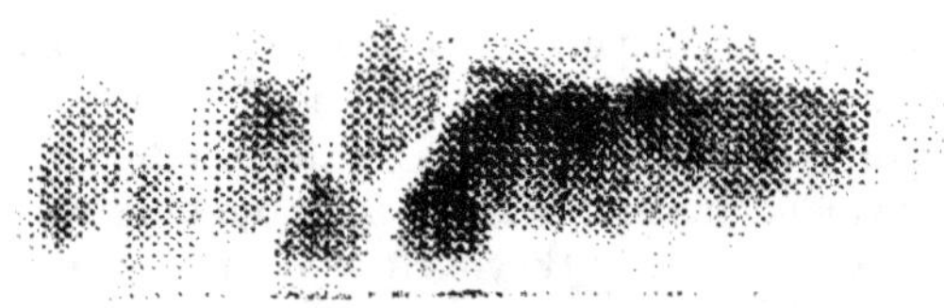

151

MARY LOU AND Bobby lay in their Jackson Hotel bed and watched the evening transform into night. Tired and a little sticky around the thighs, Mary Lou's head rested on Bobby's chest as they both watched stars appear and twinkle in the sky. Her hand stroked his kneecap while several of his fingers supported one of her breasts.

"First San Francisco and then Chicago. It's not easy anymore."

"It'll all be fine. Some you win, some you lose."

"Seems like we're losing a few in a row."

"You worry too much, Bobby. Next year we'll take San Francisco. The Russians have bought themselves a small amount of time to make hay. And as for Chicago, I never thought we'd wrap up that parcel. It was worth a trip and a few days in a hotel but we both knew we weren't serious otherwise we would have gone over there with a large crew and spilled enough blood until everyone saw sense."

"Maybe so… I spoke with Milton. The Palace didn't make money last month. First time ever. He reckoned the Hollywood johns aren't coming to the parties. There's fresh competition from gangs offering cheaper pills and underage thrills."

"That man has been blaming someone else for his own failure to run his business for twenty-five years to my certain knowledge."

"You may well be right but that doesn't mean there aren't fellas nipping at our ankles. They are real and we need to deal."

DEAL. MARY LOU'S mind flitted back to the moment she and Frank Lagotti were escaping cross-country from Baltimore and made some money in Vegas. She had no clue how to play poker but he knew it all. He held the cards in his palm like a pro and threw them down so they rotated a full circle before landing perfectly for the dealer to read them.

She admired the skills he'd built up to do it, learned in the joint during his interminable incarcerations. As they fled to California, Frank never missed a step no matter what problem they had to face. His mind raced to get past the hurdle before him. Never over—always around.

Once they got a hundred bucks together in clean bills, they hightailed it out the casino. Seconds away from being caught by the mob, the cops and the Feds. Mary Lou felt so alive: never knowing if that breath would be her last.

Like the day when she and Frank argued on the way back from a gang meet before the heist. This was at a time before they knew they could trust each other. He blamed her for sleeping with the bank rat, Carter and she accused Frank of fucking men in jail. The hate and pain in his eyes as the words left her lips. One drop of his spittle landed on her cheek and she thought he would kill her with his bare hands as soon as the jalopy screeched to a halt. They were alive in that casino though. And in love by then. What was its name?

Doesn't matter. When they walked around town and thought they were being followed by a mob guy. Frank had the brains to get them to hide in a lingerie store and the fella was too embarrassed to follow them in. She grabbed a beautiful bra-and-panties set to pretend to try on but Frank wouldn't let her keep it as they ran out the rear entrance.

"We're bank robbers, not thieves."

"Aw, but I like it, Frank."

"AW, DON'T STOP. I like it, Frank."

"Huh?"

Bobby's hand was now massaging her breast. This was in direct response to Mary Lou's hand moving up from his knee and somehow reached his groin, which she had been stroking absentmindedly for the last five minutes.

"Don't stop, Frank."

He could see Mary Lou's eyes were shut as his palm moved toward her rose, but he couldn't quite reach without moving them both. Bobby considered his options and then placed a hand under her head and replaced his body with three pillows. That freed him up to lick her torso and make his way down to her belly button, and then her tattoo. All the while, her eyes stayed shut.

"Don't stop…"

Still Mary Lou's eyes remained closed and Bobby hoped and imagined the pleasure she was experiencing. The odd judder of her thighs gave him a positive vibe. As her breathing intensified, Bobby noticed the perspiration on her stomach. Then, as he looked up her body and watched her torso heaving with the need to gather oxygen, for a moment one eye opened and cast about until it locked onto the sight of his head.

A scream and Bobby stopped in an instant, not knowing how he'd hurt her. Mary Lou kicked him in the face as she scurried to the other side of the bed, rolled off and grabbed a pistol resting in her clutch bag lying on the floor. A second later, the safety was off and she aimed her piece directly at Bobby's heart.

"Who the fuck are you?"

"I'm Bobby."

"Frank?"

"Bobby."

Calm voice. No motion to his body. Both hands visible. Staring straight into her eyes. Into her soul.

"Where's my Frank?"

"He's dead. Do you remember? He died before you met me. I am Bobby Trevisan."

She slumped onto the floor, sobbing. He walked round and removed her finger from the trigger. Then he sat next to her, holding and comforting the woman he loved until the tears subsided.

BOBBY HADN'T SPOKEN again about the incident in Miami and Mary Lou hardly noticed it had occurred by the time she'd got herself back together. The rest of the vacation passed with nothing happening of any significance. Cocktails, sun, sex and lying by the rooftop pool of the Jackson. These were the tropes of their Florida experience—and retail therapy.

When they returned, Bobby suggested he should hustle a little more and let her hang in the summerhouse and enjoy the weather. Mary Lou admitted to herself she didn't have the energy she once had and was happy to take advantage of Bobby's generosity—if only for a short while.

She spent the mornings in the conservatory and Irma made sure she ate a healthy lunch with a dose of coffee. Then a sun lounger in the afternoon. When Bobby appeared in the evening, Mary Lou had invested in a nap.

Three weeks into this new relaxed lifestyle, Mary Lou lay on a recliner around two and thought how she missed Bobby and wanted to see him. But he was out of reach. She ached for Bobby the same way she yearned for Frank each time he was in jail.

THE LAST STRETCH when he was in the Baltimore Penitentiary was the worst. Frank's Shylock step uncle kept Mary Lou in clover but that didn't help her fill up the days. Endless hours strolling around shitty areas of Baltimore waiting for the next visit. The green was enough to get by on, but not to afford any luxuries. She'd scrimp and save just to smuggle in extra smokes for Frank.

He was the only one in the gang to do any time for the previous robbery. Kid stuff: a supermarket heist gone wrong. Word on the street was that Frank's buddy, Louis had squealed to the cops who were lying in wait when the fellas exited the store. As soon as Frank was out on bail, Louis took an express descent down the outside of a building and Frank never spoke of him again.

Mary Lou never liked Louis anyway: the first night they met at one of the many parties in the neighborhood, Frank introduced her to him. Thirty minutes later, the guy had his hand on a place not even Frank's fingers ventured for several years. From that moment on, she never allowed herself to be on her own with Louis. She loved Frank dearly by the end, but his friends and family sucked elephant cocks.

Those three summers Frank was away stretched to eternity. Mary Lou was young and had needs of her own. She wasn't ready to be a gangster's moll and yearned to do more than sit at home and wait for her man's return. She dated occasionally but never someone from the neighborhood. If word got back to the Shylock that she was fucking around then she'd have been on a one-way trip to oblivion.

The sex meant nothing, but it relieved the boredom and it took her out of that tiny apartment. All she did was spend a few brief hours in someone else's cramped home with her legs apart and the tingles flowing if she was lucky. Most of the time she'd jump into the shower as soon as she returned to wash away the dried spunk and a sense of being dirty generated by the couplings. No matter who was trying to make her orgasm, she felt so painfully alone.

She spent the last six months with an S&M freak hoping the different experience might help her feel something but handcuffs and nipple clamps left her sore and just as empty as any other way of fucking she tried during those long years away from Frank.

The only solace she found was watching the late evening chat show with a bowl of cereal for company. Vodka instead of milk and the constant sound of crunching inside her skull to mask the canned laughter from the TV.

THE FIRST NIGHT Frank was out of jail, Mary Lou had tried to be as understanding as she could. It had been years since he'd been with a woman and her expectations had been low, even though she longed to be intimate with the man. After he had fallen asleep and she'd finished herself off, Mary Lou went into the bathroom to take stock. She stared at herself in the mirror, assessing every blemish of her skin and freckle on her face.

At some point, she poked at her breasts as though they were bearing the weight of her ennui. Then her attention returned to her nose and she leaned in to get the best look. The coldness of the basin dug itself in against her rose as she moved her head one way, then the other, to assess the damage done despite the paucity of her years on this planet.

Every so often, she heard Frank talk to himself as he slept and an occasional vehicle zoomed past. This was the last time she would be by herself. Her moments of solitude were over now he had returned.

Mary Lou pulled down the lower lids of her eyes and let the skin flip back into place. A childish game she repeated two more times. Then she blinked to get her sight to return to normal.

She opened her eyes and knew exactly where she was: Oakcrest Drive. The crow's feet in the corners were a clear demonstration of how much time she had allowed to pass in her life. Mary Lou knew she had to stop this malaise. She couldn't waste her days away again like she did waiting for Frank to serve his debt to society.

On vacation, Bobby had been right: there had been too many losses of late and the moment for action had arrived. They needed to bring the fight to San Francisco.

152

MARY LOU WOULD not sit around and let herself get cornered like happened with Frank when they were fleeing the heist. If she'd learned anything from the time spent in Burbank Airport, it was to watch your back and come out fighting. They were out to beat her and so were the Russians in San Francisco. She could kneel on the ground next to the lockers, pinned down by gunfire from the hoods, or she could pick up Frank's piece and shoot her way to freedom.

We must obliterate the Markov scum from this world and that is what she would do. To put this plan into practice, she needed some high class muscle, so she asked Milton for his help.

"Thanks for dropping a dime. We don't speak nearly as much as we used to."

"I need your help in a matter I wish to resolve. Can I count on you?"

"With my life, you know that. What do you need?"

She outlined her idea and Milton listened intently. When she finished, he whistled allowing his exhalation to form into a single note. He hadn't heard anything as bold for many years. Respect to the woman.

THE NEXT DAY, Mary Lou drove over to LA to speak with Milton in person. The Palace had faded over time, the paintwork was chipped, plasterwork crumbling, but Mary Lou didn't notice as she walked along the corridors to Milton's office. Like every other operation the man had ever touched, he had let it turn to shit. The only difference with the Palace's call girl racket was that it took twenty long years instead of Milton's usual six months to fuck it up.

"Thanks for the opportunity. I doubt if you realize how good it is to be working with you again. I've missed being so close to the action."

"Don't know what you're talking about. Let's get down to business, shall we?"

"Sure, I'm listening."

"You need to source at least ten reliable men."

"I'll need a short while as I am not in that line at the moment, but it can be done. Just a function of time and money."

"Once we've all met up to go through the details, then we'll take the place when it's full."

"When all the Markovs are in one building?"

"Yes, that's what I said."

"How many vehicles do you want for the hit? Everyone in their own or as few as possible for a fast getaway?"

"There's no point doing it if we can't get safely away."

"Right…"

Milton tilted his head and looked at Mary Lou. He couldn't decide if his hesitation was caused by not concentrating on what Mary Lou had just said or if there was a disconnect between her words now and what she'd told him on the phone yesterday.

"You got a problem with this?"

"Not at all. I won't lose any sleep over a few dead Russians. From what little Bobby mentioned to me, sounds like it's payback time."

"Shoot 'em in the knee and get the hell out of Dodge."

"Knee? I thought we're killing them."

"Yep."

"Murder, not maim."

"Homicide is the name of the game."

"Good. You lost me there for a second."

"We send one fella in early to stake the place out and then the rest of the crew swoops in, does the job and gets out before any law enforcement can grab us."

"Shall we use Naldo?"

"Whoever you think is best. There'll be big bonuses for everyone when we get back."

"I'd advise you and Bobby to stay at home—or rather book and go to a restaurant that night. You must have a watertight alibi."

"Bobby?"

Mary Lou looked straight at Milton, who returned the gesture. There was his confusion coming right at him again.

"You don't want him there, do you?"

"Use the best you can get."

"And Bobby?"

"You decide—I told you."

Milton's mouth went dry as a sense of anxiety welled up inside. Was this an elaborate ruse by her to put Bobby in the line of fire? More likely he was being oversensitive and needed to keep his head in the game, but his instinct to double-check with the man might place a target on his skull.

Over the years, Mary Lou handled treachery the way a surgeon dealt with a malignant tumor. She smiled at him and relaxed back into her chair as though the main order of business had been taken care of.

"How's the Palace doing?"

"So-so. The Hollywood parties are fewer: the stars prefer a more private space for their booze, narcotics and fucking nowadays. It's the control of the studios: they want their product to be wholesome and clean. But our regulars still pass through although the cops are getting harder to pay off because we look more like a cathouse than somewhere for the rich and powerful to come. And play."

"Times are tough, Milton. Every year, it gets more difficult to make money out of the things on which we could always rely: prostitution, narcotics. Even gambling."

"For real? I thought the casinos were doing great guns."

"They are today, but look what's happened in Vegas. Entertainment companies now own mob venues. Crazy. And the only reason gaming has been permitted outside Vegas is so states can get their grubby hands on hard-working people's money. So that means they'll over-regulate the fuck out of it and we'll be pushed to one side. Not today or tomorrow, but eventually."

ELEVEN MEN AND a solitary woman sat in a large disused room at the top of the Palace. Mary Lou, Milton, Naldo and nine other guys who you'd be a fool to mess with even on a bright day in the middle of summer. Each had found a chair and they'd formed a loose circle like they were attending a group therapy session.

Milton made some cursory introductions so everyone more or less knew each other. Most of the crew had worked with at least some others before but in the heat of the moment, it paid to know who your friends were.

"When we go in, we enter hard. The best we can hope is that they aren't expecting us. Once the first shot rings out then they'll draw their guns and fire back. We need to be slick, fast and ruthless. If we leave one Markov alive, they will come and destroy us."

The men murmured to each other—not because the job was too difficult but because their adrenalin was already pumping and they weren't even in the right city yet. Mary Lou ran through the family tree and took pains to make it clear she wanted them to identify each body so she could keep an accurate tally of who they still had to whack.

"Is there anything you want to add, Milton?"

"Not really. You covered the important points."

He glanced at his watch and a bead of sweat dropped onto his wrist. Then his eyes darted to the corridor and flitted back to Mary Lou. Almost on cue, the door opened and Bobby walked in and the entire room fell to an eerie hush.

"What're we doing here, people?"

"I've instigated an operation to clear up the Markov problem."

He nodded and took her off to one side so they wouldn't have to talk in front of the fellas.

"What are you doing?"

"Cutting out a tumor."

"We have a peace agreement with them. We shouldn't move on them unless they become an irritant or they break their word."

"They can't be trusted and we need to preempt their inevitable attack."

"No, it is to our advantage to get them to build on their San Francisco empire. That way, when we take over, we'll have something significant to own."

Bobby turned round to face the guys.

"Thanks for coming but there's been a change of plan. You can step down for now. Of course, we will cover your costs with a bonus for any inconvenience. Milton, will you get things organized?"

"Sure, Bobby. Always happy to help."

Mary Lou fumed where she stood. Arms folded, she said nothing and couldn't understand why Bobby was treating her this way. The betrayal of it all. In contrast, he could not wrap his head around why she believed now was the time to take out the Markovs. They didn't utter a single word to each other all the miles back to Palm Springs.

The next day Mary Lou woke up as though nothing had happened, but Bobby knew and remembered.

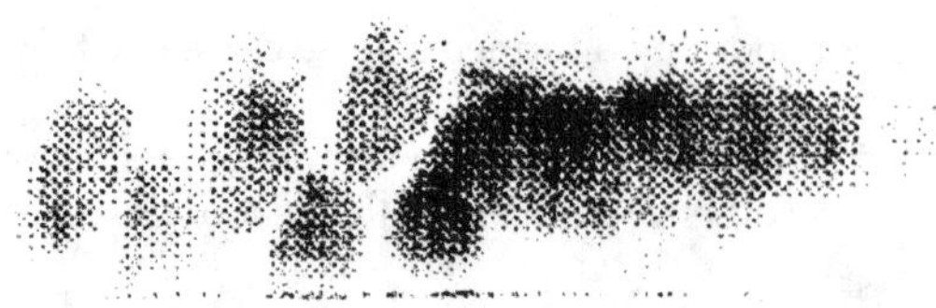

153

BOBBY POPPED OVER to Alice's apartment rather than spend time in her cramped and crummy office. A heap of Chinese food had just arrived and they spread all the boxes out on the dining room table.

"I think we've over ordered."

"You reckon?"

They sat down and pecked at the noodles, chicken, veg and rice until they thought they would burst. Half the meal remained untouched: Alice's prediction was right. Then she poured two more beers and they moved over to the couches to settle in for the evening.

"We nearly went to war a few days ago."

"What was the Bay of Pigs moment?"

"Don't joke. We were damn close. For reasons that escape me, she wanted to take absolute revenge on the Markovs."

"From San Francisco?"

"The same. She got Milton to put a crew together for a St Valentine's Day massacre. Good news is that even Milton, who's as craven as hell, knew it was wrong and dropped me a dime."

Alice sat and stared, mind racing, trying to process the implications of what Bobby just uttered. She had never heard of Mama be countermanded before. The idea of Milton and Bobby conspiring against Mama was shocking. The fact they felt they needed to do that was jaw-dropping.

"We walked onto their turf and tried to muscle them out, right?"

"More or less. There were poor choices on both sides which led to the bad blood. Didn't take long to resolve, which shows it wasn't that big a deal."

Alice accepted what he said but his response showed there were other situations not yet mentioned. Once he'd filled in the gaps, Alice had her head in her hands.

"This is the end."

He raised his eyebrows and sipped his beer.

"Not for a long time, but we need to make changes. Mary Lou needs more of a rear seat role—whether or not she wants it."

"You're not talking about ousting her."

"Encourage her to choose a more consultative position."

"Get her to step down, you mean."

Alice's words hung in the air and the two soaked in the idea that someone else must take over. Neither wanted to engage with what that meant or talk about what was to happen later. They sidestepped the whole topic for ten minutes as they lapsed back into general conversation.

ALICE SPENT THE next day ruminating on her chat with Bobby. They had discussed whether Bobby should run the business but he was insistent that he was not up for the job, claiming age and not wanting to tread on Mary Lou's toes. He was careful not to express an opinion who it should be even though there were only two contenders.

Did his silence on the matter imply he was in favor of Frank? Bobby rarely had any desire to stand in the center of a family squabble. He always ensured he was in a different room whenever the twins argued as kids. This left Alice with a simple thought: how could she make her mark as the leader of the new family? She didn't entertain the notion Frank should run the show for even a second.

Her analysis was quick and honest: Mama had worked out they needed to diversify and expand. The best way to grow was to form an alliance with another gang. A partnership forged out of strength would last the test of time because both parties would gain something significant from the other. The Lagotti family had large multi-state gaming and narcotics operations, and owned a string of call girl rings. They even had some stretch on the east coast and had the occasional Senator in their back pocket. These were assets other gangs would dream of having.

Alice knew the family's weaknesses too. They had insufficient hired hands to attack new territories: San Francisco showed that to be all too painfully true. And they'd been stumbling around desperate to find the Next Big Thing they could seize for their own but nothing had appeared on the horizon.

Another issue was that their call girl operation hadn't moved with the times or expanded for as long as Alice could remember. Milton might be an old associate of Mama's but hadn't been pulling his weight. The Palace had always been a disgusting venue, but it was poorly managed too. Even Frank had worked out to split the Nugget into gambling and lap dancing.

When Milton saw the parties were going off the boil, he should have converted the first floor into something else: pole dancing for sure, but a gentleman's club, maybe, to attract a better quality of john who'd pay for a cocktail with a whore on his knee, before he walking upstairs to pop a pill and fuck her.

No matter. What they needed to do was find a partner: one who had muscle but little reach. Someone with the desire to grow but would cooperate and not just screw them over. Somebody with imagination. The interesting thing about the Markovs was that Nikolay still came to the table even though a nephew lay in the morgue. That showed he was serious about his business and believed the Lagottis could do him harm if the fighting had continued. These traits were what she was looking for although Alice was aware that many would see him as an enemy.

ALICE REACHED OUT to Nikolay Markov, who agreed to meet for a coffee. He was surprised to receive a phone call from the Lagotti girl and was intrigued to know what she had to say. Her mother and stepfather had acted like mooks a few months ago but it never hurt to talk. Nikolay might have been aggressive when negotiating with Mary Lou and Bobby, but despite appearances his ego was under control.

"Thank you for agreeing to meet up."

"I was surprised you called. Does your mother know what you are up to?"

"I'm not up to anything. The last occasion you met with members of my family, matters came to a head somewhat violently. Now the dust has settled, I thought we should at least have a conversation or two. There is an agreement operating in San Francisco."

"The truce is holding—for the moment. What makes you think there is anything to discuss?"

"Our shared operations in…"

Alice stumbled over the venue's name.

"…the Red Stocking. You should do your homework better."

"The name is less important than the fact that profits are up ever since we worked together."

"True. We have all benefitted in the short-term. Doesn't mean the place will make money in a year or two."

"But I'd like to think if revenues were to go south, we'd either figure out how to fix matters or use our brains and shut it down."

Nikolay stirred the sugar he'd dropped into his coffee. His eyes focused on his cup and then he stared at Alice without responding. He was keeping his cards close to his chest, but she expected him to play things cautiously.

"I heard your men were fierce fighters. They handled themselves very effectively against us."

"Your people are Americans. They have grown soft over the generations since they stepped off the boats from Italy. My guys are fresh arrivals with the blood of Cossacks coursing through their veins. They are tough; if they show any weakness, then I kill them."

A HOLLOW CACKLE erupted from Nikolay and Alice did her best to echo his extraordinary good humor but all she could manage was the smallest of grimaces.

"Once you've been in this country a while, you learn that sometimes it is who you know that counts and not what caliber pistol you're holding."

"There are stories that you hold politicians in your pockets and I offer the utmost respect to you if those tall tales are true."

Now it was Alice's turn to stir her cup and stare at Nikolay. That was his first positive statement about her family the man had ever uttered. Almost as if he knew the direction she was taking the conversation and wanted to hustle her to the end point.

"Work with people and you build up relationships that can last for decades."

"Your mother's achievements are well known. If we hadn't got off on such sour terms, I would have had the chance to find out more about her. These are the difficulties you face when blood is shed— not that my nephew was worth jack shit. I was concerned about the principle, not that sniveling piece of garbage. He came from my sister's loins, not mine."

Alice perceived a judder run along Nikolay's body as he mentioned his sibling. She almost felt a connection with him at that moment, but wondered if she had merely projected her own thoughts onto his actions.

"Family life isn't always a bed of roses."

"Tell me about it."

Nikolay checked the time on his watch.

"This has been a most pleasant exchange, but unless there is something specific to discuss, then I need to make a move."

"I wanted to hear your thoughts on us working more closely together. Our tribes would benefit."

"You and I?"

"Our families."

She knew he'd only asked her that to rattle her and she'd almost fallen for his ruse, but she was a smart cookie.

"If there are particular opportunities, then I am happy to consider them, but on similar terms to the Red Stocking."

"That deal was agreed to create a ceasefire. What I'm suggesting is a long-term partnership so we would split profits equally and fairly. That stops resentments building up, which lead to perceived sleights and loss of life. Successful businesses should be about making money, not killing people."

"I understand you might not want the Stocking as a basis for future considerations, but one thing is not negotiable: I would always be in charge. No woman has ever told me what to do and it ain't gonna happen now."

ALICE CONTINUED TO mull over each of Nikolay's words two days later when Sam made a rare appearance on the west coast. Despite telling herself how much she needed Sam in her life, Alice hadn't noticed her absence as she thought she would. There was only that time when Mama cracked before her eyes that Alice yearned for her lover.

In bed entwined with Sam's body, Alice wondered the extent she could trust Nikolay and whether a man—like Bobby, say—might thrash out a better deal, just to play off Nikolay's prejudices. Also, she needed to work out what he would need to be offered to give up control over any new operation.

Her musings were interrupted by Sam's fingers and tongue which were busy toying with her erogenous zones. She relaxed into the experience and spent the next hour fondling and fucking until both she and Sam were exhausted. With her head still within licking distance of Sam, Alice asked herself what other options did she have? Bobby was too old, Frank was too much and Milton was too incompetent.

"If you will hang around down there, do something useful, dear."

Sam's admonishment shook Alice back to reality. The Markov dynasty must wait at least until the morning. While Sam was in her bed, she should make best use of that succulent body. Thirty minutes later, she was asleep while Alice carried on ruminating on Nikolay Markov.

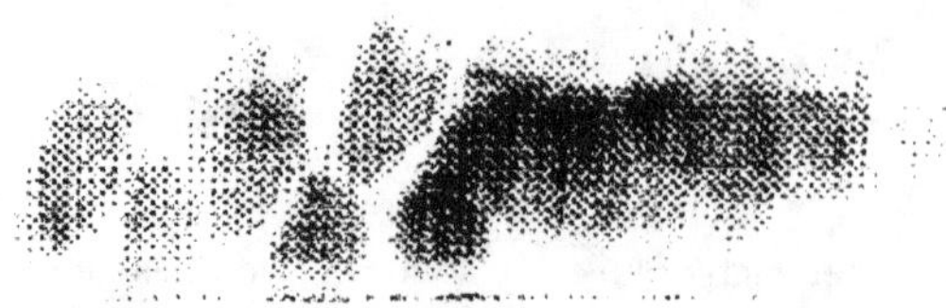

154

ALICE AWOKE WITH the shock of finding Sam between her legs and the pleasure of all that implied. Later, Alice got out of bed to make them both a coffee. Sam stepped onto the balcony and had a smoke. When Alice returned, she popped the coffees down and lingered on Sam's silhouette. That woman still turned her on and her stomach butterflies flew around in a circle while she gazed at the beauty in front of her. She soaked in that long back and visible spine, those calves and up to Sam's curvy ass.

Sam looked over her shoulder and saw Alice staring. In response, she sashayed into the bedroom like a catwalk model, hands on hips, walked up to Alice and planted a kiss on her lips. Their bodies were so close, Alice imagined she could feel every part of Sam's body against hers. Every touch. Ev-e-ry hair.

They returned to bed and fooled around until the coffees went cold. Then they fooled around some more.

"I gotta run."

"Huh? Weren't you staying until tomorrow morning?"

"No can do, honey. I've got to go into work this weekend. I'm sure I told you. There's a major client meeting on Monday and a heap of preparation to do."

"You never said…"

Alice saw zero point in hiding her disappointment because she wanted to be with Sam and when they met, she didn't get the vibe her feelings were reciprocated. Sure, Sam flew across the country to see her but she always seemed to itch to go home. This morning was a typical example.

"Do you enjoy being with me?"

"Don't start this again, honey."

"But do you, because I love the time we spend together."

"Good times, yeah."

"Only good. Nothing more?"

"I've told you repeatedly, it's great with you but the rest of my life is in Boston."

"The company is headquartered there so you need to be in the center of things. I get all that, but what if I set you up with your own practise here?"

"In Malibu?"

"Anywhere in California. San Francisco, LA. You tell me."

Sam stopped stuffing her possessions into her travel bag.

"You'd be willing to do that for me?"

"So we could be together… more."

"Are there strings attached? Sounds as though you would only support my business if I carried on sleeping with you. Makes me sound like you want to be my pimp."

"What? No. I mean that if your work is the only barrier to being together, I can sort that out. A business deal is just that: business. What you and I have outside the office would be separate. Do I wish us to get even closer now? Yes. Will living on the same side of the country help? Yes it should. Do you want to do that? I have no idea."

Sam sat on the bed and held Alice's hand.

"That's a fabulous offer, honey. Really. But I need to go away and think about it. You see, the truth is I don't know how I feel about any of this. I love our being together. The sex is amazing and you are truly great company but I have no idea what I want of my life. Until then I can't answer your questions because I just don't know any answers."

"I understand but I still must know. Take your time, but if you don't want us to carry on, be honest and say so. Do not leave me hanging."

A tear dripped out of Alice's left eye and splashed onto Sam's hand. They hugged until the redness around Alice's pupils had faded. After, they lay down and fucked again. When Alice was resting, eyelids closed, Sam kissed her again and slunk out of the apartment.

ALICE STAYED IN bed the rest of the morning. She spent the first hour replaying her conversation with Sam. By the end of that time she had no greater insight into what Sam wanted or would do than when she started analyzing the thing to death. So she moved onto Nikolay Markov.

He was open to some form of alliance but he couldn't bring himself to cut a sensible deal with a woman. Yet. Alice needed to create the opportunity for him to work with her so he could judge her based on her deeds and not his prejudices. The trick would be to find something he wanted which would be an easy give-up for him so she could get her foot in the door. One thing was certain: nothing about the Red Stocking arrangement should be on the table.

ANOTHER DAY, ANOTHER cup of coffee. Alice and Nikolay sipped and covered as much small talk they could both stomach. Alice kicked off proceedings by thanking him for meeting up again. She knew how to manipulate male egos.

"I've been thinking about our last chat and have a suggestion I'm hoping you'll find of interest."

"There had to be some proposal otherwise why meet up. Unless you wanted an excuse to see me again."

"That's right. But as we're here, I'll explain about my idea, anyway."

Nikolay half-smiled and sat forward in his seat.

"We discussed how your men are so effective and I was wondering if you'd be interested in a simple trade. Six of your fellas for either hard cash or narcotics."

"I don't need your drugs."

"Our product is cheaper and better quality, but that's your choice. How about the green?"

"My men aren't cattle to be bought and sold."

"Nope. They provide a useful service and I am proposing to pay you for them to render that to me. With one addition: I provide you with an extra amount upfront so that if things work out, after twelve months they move over to my wage bill. If it doesn't pan out, no harm, no foul and you pocket the money I've already given you. The end."

"I underestimated you, young lady."

"You're not the first."

ALICE STAYED OVERNIGHT in Fog City as she'd agreed to continue the discussion with Nikolay the following evening over dinner. He picked an ordinary looking pasta joint in the Tenderloin district, near to the Red Stocking. She arrived in the neighborhood sixty minutes early because the venue was in the heart of his territory and she wanted check the area out. She had no desire to let herself get kidnapped —or worse.

There was nothing out of the ordinary about the restaurant, the surrounding buildings or any of the people who came and left in the thirty minutes before their scheduled appointment. Nikolay arrived a little over fifteen minutes early while Alice made him wait until the allotted hour.

As she headed for their table, Nikolay stood up and Alice offered her hand which he took and leaned in to kiss her on both cheeks, European style. The Old Country remained inside him despite being so many miles away. He pulled the chair out for her to sit down—ever the gentleman and quite the reversal of his gruff exterior the previous day.

They ordered food and light conversation ensued. Nikolay came across as an earnest figure surrounded by hordes who wanted to knock him off his perch. His situation wasn't that much different from the Lagottis. Only he had a Russian accent and Mama had a Southern drawl, even after all these years away from the Confederacy.

DESSERT WAS SERVED and all she had achieved was to massage Nikolay's ego and in return he'd paid her several compliments about her dress, her hair and other aspects of her appearance. Business hadn't been mentioned and Alice was getting impatient.

"Have you considered my proposal?"

"Yes I have. While the terms are well structured, I wonder why you have need of Russian muscle. What ruse are you planning that you wish to exclude me from?"

"Good question, Nikolay. It's thinking like that which makes you an attractive business partner."

"And?"

"You want me to lift my skirt before you've said whether you're in the game. That's not how I operate. Show me you choose to work with me and we can share in the profit together. If you don't pay into the ante, you have no right to look at my cards."

"You can have six of my men for a year. That is not a problem. Give them fifty per cent more than I do and you buy their loyalty for every minute the money lasts. An upfront consideration of twenty thousand will be sufficient."

"Even though I am saving you much more than that in wages alone, I accept those terms as a sign of good faith."

"Agreed. Now tell me your plans."

"I am looking for some enforcers because it is time to break new ground. Our gambling operations stretch across California, Illinois, Nevada, New Jersey and Massachusetts. I want to use these locations to move into neighborhood prostitution and labor racketeering if possible. We would need to seize opportunities on a case-by-case basis and have fellas who can handle themselves for that. Ours are great but it never hurts to hold more baseball bats than the other guy."

"I would love to have a piece of that action."

"For a price. Your strength lies in your ability to find tough men, but my understanding is that your reach doesn't stretch much beyond the Tenderloin. A statement of fact and not a criticism."

"No offense taken—yet."

"Seems to me if we are a good fit together, success will follow for both of us."

DESPITE HER PROTESTATIONS, Nikolay insisted on driving Alice back to her hotel—or rather his driver took them both. When the limo pulled in, they carried on talking until Alice thought it only polite to suggest they continued the conversation over a an aperitif. Nikolay agreed in an instant.

"What would you like?"

"I insist. Let me buy you a drink."

"Very kind. A cosmo is always welcome."

Nikolay ordered the cocktail and a vodka tonic for himself. Once the drinks arrived, they moved to a table which had more comfortable seating and gave Alice a view of the bar area leading to the hotel lobby.

"You reckon we can pull this off?"

"With my brains and your brawn, we'll rule the world."

"Your beauty and my experience, you mean."

Nikolay squeezed Alice's knee under the table but removed it back onto his lap. A momentary invasion of her personal space, which raised a red flag in her head. For the rest of their time in the bar he did nothing else inappropriate and Alice relaxed again.

"It's been a great evening. And I reckon we've made a lot of progress."

"Certainly. Looks like we are a good fit as you were saying earlier."

They were in the lobby by now so Alice halted. Nikolay stopped too but gave no sign he was ready to leave the hotel. She tried to think how to call it a night.

"Let's call it a night."

Sometimes go with the obvious.

"The least I can do is to walk you to your door."

"There is no need."

"I insist."

Alice shook her head, shrugged and headed to the elevator, accompanied by Nikolay. At her door, she unlocked it and turned round. Nikolay pushed past her and strolled in. She sighed and followed.

"Now you've seen me in, it's time for you to go."

Nikolay walked up to her and picked off a piece of fluff from the front of her dress, just above her breast. She swallowed hard, grasped his hand and put it by his side.

"Don't be like that. I thought we were getting on fine."

"We have been: so far, but you're overstepping the mark."

"No I haven't."

With those words, Nikolay grabbed the front of Alice's dress and ripped it apart so the material above her waist fell away. Standing semi-naked, her knee instinctively traveled straight up to smash against his groin. Nikolay hit the ground clutching himself as Alice towered over him.

"If you think I'd want your dick anywhere near me, you are delusional. Now get the fuck out of my room, little man, before I cut it off."

January 1997

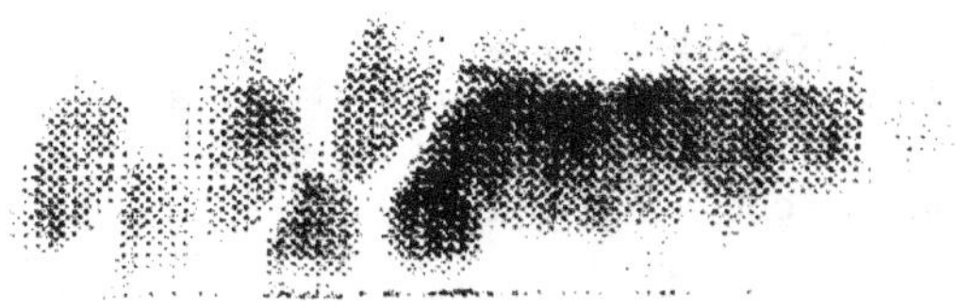

155

NIKOLAY'S RESPONSE WAS more subtle than Alice could ever have imagined. Instead of coming back that night and slicing her open with a bolo knife, he put the squeeze on the Red Stocking and anyone associated with it. Bobby then instructed Naldo to pay a visit to the Bay City to find out why the Markov clan was getting fresh. He returned with bupkis so Bobby told him to take a bite out of their territory.

The next day, Naldo visited the B-Bang, a lap dancing club on the edge of the Tenderloin. There was nothing to distinguish it from any of the other clubs on the same drag once you got inside. The exterior comprised an ordinary facade with a ten feet high neon sign perched on the roof of the low-rise building. The lights depicted an animation showing blue panties lowering to reveal a red pubic triangle. No one could claim they didn't know what to expect when they walked through the door.

Naldo scooted round the rear of the club and found a yard filled with garbage and three girls, coats over their shoulders, sat having a smoke before returning to the drudge of their work. In the meantime, they gossiped and laughed, ignoring the slight chill of the night. Naldo opened the metal gate and stepped inside. One girl, wearing yellow and black, noticed his arrival.

"Beat it, bud. This is for staff only."

He ignored her instruction and ambled toward her.

"Go round the front if you want to watch. This area ain't for the likes of you."

Naldo nodded but continued his journey to the girl, both hands in his jacket pockets. The other two stood up and formed an approximate line either side of Yellow-and-Black. He stopped when he was four feet away from the nearest skirt. None of them were over sixteen and Naldo closed his eyes for half a second.

"If you don't get out, I'm gonna call the manager."

As he opened his eyes, his right hand whipped out of his pocket to reveal a three-inch blade and he swiped at Yellow-and-Black's face. A line of red appeared below her left eye and she screamed, clutching the side of her head. Naldo stepped a pace forward and swung at the other two. By the time his arm returned to rest by his hip, all three were cut and screaming. One headed to the backdoor and Naldo turned round, out the yard and vanished into the night. Although they didn't realize it, they were lucky. Under any other circumstances, Naldo would have slit their throats, but he was following strict instructions: give Markov a warning not an all-out assault.

The moment Bobby ordered the attack on the B-Bang, he knew his people in the Red Stocking were at risk. Sure enough, an hour after Naldo left the yard, a firebomb hit the front of the building. Then things got nasty and the field of battle spread way beyond the confines of the San Francisco city line.

Within a week, blood was spilled on both sides and operations halted or destroyed. What nobody in the Lagotti family factored into consideration was that Nikolay Markov was Russian. That meant he had connections far beyond his immediate reach in the Tenderloin in SF. And the fellas he knew had almost unlimited resources and not one inch of sentiment in their bodies.

MILTON SPENT ANOTHER night sleeping in a fuck-room in the Palace. Ever since the Markov trouble had spilled outside SF, his time had been occupied inside the Lagotti fortress, protected by extra armed guards, to keep him safe. Six men in three shifts were stationed at his family's home in Palm Springs and that made him feel better. He had been around the block long enough to remember the twins' kidnapping.

The one thing he missed was Elsie, with whom he'd been having regular encounters for the past two years. He spotted her the day she started at the Palace: he was down in the reception area when she walked in and lit up the room for him. Before she got the chance to earn any money, he put her on his personal payroll and bought her clothes, trinkets and her own apartment.

A week without Elsie felt like a lifetime and that was too long for Milton. At first, he hadn't wanted her anywhere near the Palace because it might be too dangerous, but seven days later and his opinion had shifted.

"Baby. Pack yourself a bag and get your tail over to the Palace. Papa wants to have fun and he's been missing your loving."

"I'll be right over. See you in thirty."

Forty-five minutes later Elsie had yet to appear, but Milton accepted that LA traffic was shit any time of the day or night. After an hour, he started pacing and tried to take his mind off the wait by watching footage from the peephole cameras. When ninety minutes had passed, he began to fret and two hours since the phone call, Milton flipped his lid, hopped in his car and headed over to Elsie's apartment.

When he got there, the entrance was an inch ajar. He pulled out his pistol and pushed the door open and walked inside, eyes darting left and right. Something was wrong. Intruders maybe. Through the hall and into the living room. The answer lay in a large pool of red on the rug by the couch: Elsie was naked and knife wounds punctured her torso, her legs, her groin.

Milton squatted and threw up. Once he'd pulled himself back together, he thought he heard a creak from the master bedroom. He took two deep breaths, crept to the door and listened. Definitely a noise. He kicked the door open and pointed his gun forwards. A flash and a bang and everything turned black.

ALICE, BOBBY AND May Lou were in the summerhouse and ten men surrounded the perimeter, some with sniper rifles hidden in crow's nests in the trees. Irma popped her head round the door after knocking and said there was someone on the phone. She thought it might be Naldo, but as ever she hadn't asked. What she didn't know couldn't kill her. Bobby walked back to the house to take the call. When he returned two minutes later, he was ashen.

"They've killed Milton. Put a bullet in his brains and dumped his body on the sidewalk outside the Palace."

Alice's jaw dropped and Mary Lou looked on, stone-faced.

"IT'S TIME FOR you to come home, son."

"I'm fine, Mama. Why d'you need me on the other side of the country?"

"We have issues and I require you by my side."

Frank lay in bed with one hand on his girlfriend's stomach and toyed with her belly button as he spoke. For Mama to place the call meant some heavy shit was going down. And the lack of information she was offering showed him she was concerned about ears on the line.

"I'll get over as soon as I can."

Frank put the phone down and sent his fingers below the belly button.

"Come on, you and I are off on a little trip."

"I don't think that's a good idea."

"Nah, it'll be fine. My family is very accommodating of strangers. And you're not that strange at all."

"Even so, I should stay here."

"Nope. If what might have gone down has happened, you won't be safe. I won't be able to protect you."

"Just remember I told you I shouldn't come along."

"Duly noted. Now put your panties on so we can get going."

She giggled then wriggled into her skirt, ignoring Frank's underwear instruction. He smiled and licked his lips.

"Dirty minx."

FRANK AND HIS girlfriend arrived in Palm Springs and headed straight to Oakcrest Drive. Into the house and up to his old room, which was now a spare bedroom after all this time. They unpacked and lay on the bed for half an hour.

Eventually Frank had enough and went downstairs.

"I've got a headache. I'll be down later."

Frank shrugged and made his way downstairs. Empty. So he walked through the conservatory, out past the pool and into the summerhouse. Bobby and Mama sat talking and they both smiled at his arrival. She ran over, gave him a hug and tiptoed to kiss him on the forehead.

He suffered in silence—a grown man treated like a child—but when she messed with his hair, he brushed her away. Mary Lou laughed at him and sat back down. Frank slumped down on his own in an armchair to prevent further maternal attacks on his dignity.

"Where's Alice? I thought all ships were coming into the harbor."

"She'll be along later. Right now she's under Naldo's protection in a safe house."

"Why does she get special treatment? Can't she look after herself?"

"More than you'll ever know. We thought it best for her not to stay in her apartment as it's difficult to defend from attack."

"Are we on some kind of lockdown?"

Bobby glanced at Mary Lou who stared at Frank. Neither of them felt the need to respond to him and he waited to find the answers to his questions.

"Was the flight okay?"

"Yeah, we had a smooth run and thanks for sending a car to pick us up."

"De nada. We?"

"Yes, I brought someone with me. If lives are going to be threatened, I want to know she was safe too."

"Who?"

"My girlfriend. She's taking a rest right now but you'll meet her later."

"Does she have a name?"

"Sammy. I think I might be serious about her, but before you get too excited, it is still early days, so don't freak her out."

"Bravo, boy. And well done to Sammy: the first woman ever to tame our little boy."

"Leave me alone. All I ask is that you're nice to her and try not to make fools of yourselves around her."

"We know how to behave. The question is whether you can keep it in your pants until you guys are in the privacy of your room."

"Are you ever going to let that go? I was eighteen and you weren't supposed to be back until the following day. Jeez."

"Both of you: stand down. We are facing a dangerous situation and the last thing we need is to lose focus and fight among ourselves. Please, people."

AS IF ON cue, in came Alice with Naldo in tow. When he saw the whole clan was here, he nodded to Bobby and shut the summerhouse door behind him as he left. The man knew not to intrude on family business.

Hugs for her Mama and Bobby, then Alice sat down next to Mama, a single glance at Frank, only acknowledgement of his existence she could muster.

"Is someone going to tell me what this is all about?"

"The Markov clan has attacked a number of our west coast operations. Meth labs, heroin labs, prostitution. They've hit the casinos, but so far they haven't damaged the Queen of Sheba or Bakersfield Printing. We have to assume it is only a matter of time though."

"And we've just sat back and taken this insult?"

"Not at all. Under Naldo's stewardship, we have brought their call girl operation to its knees and cut their supply lines for cocaine, ecstasy, opium and meths. Blood has been shed: us and them."

"So why am I hearing about this only now?"

"This may have been a disturbance to business, but we thought it was relatively contained. Until last night. They shot Milton in the face and cut off his dick. Stuffed it in his mouth and dumped his body on Sunset Boulevard."

Frank fumed and Bobby was certain he saw steam seeping out of his ears. Alice inhaled deeply on her cigarette as she tried to keep it together, despite Milton's loss.

"What are we waiting for? Let's get all our men over to San Francisco and kill the motherfuckers."

156

"BEFORE WE RUSH over to San Francisco, we need to have a plan—and know it'll succeed."

"Kill them. Kill them all."

"Not helpful, Frank. We've tried direct violence and harassment and it hasn't worked. We have to find a different solution to this problem."

He sat back in his chair and sulked. No one was listening to what he had to say. Nothing in this family ever changed. Here he was skulking around his Mama's house when he was making real money out east and nobody seemed able to recognize he'd done it alone.

"Is there anyone who might intercede on our behalf?"

"Pasquale has been out of the game too long. He's the only made man I've ever known and trusted. Beyond him, we are on our own."

"There's only one Nikolay Markov and three of us."

"Four," chimed in Mary Lou.

"Sorry, four of us. Let's call a peace conference and kill the fucker."

"Let it go. We need a solution the whole Markov family will stand behind and mass murder is not the answer."

If Frank had bothered to listen, he would have detected a definite edge to Bobby's voice. The man was tired of Frank's unhelpful repetitions. As for Alice's scowls, Frank always discounted her disapproving expressions.

The only person whose opinion mattered to him was Mama and she remained perfectly calm. Totally still—like these discussions didn't matter in the grand scheme of things. That response gave Frank the strength to believe she was on his side. Why else had she dragged him across the country? His methods were direct and blood-soaked. She'd have nixed his idea if she really wanted to silence him.

ONE LONG HOUR with everyone circling round the same problem and offering no useful fix, Irma popped in to warn them food was to be served in a handful of minutes. Frank left the summerhouse and inhaled fresh air. His family was doing his head in—how much more he could take? Sammy was still asleep when he got back into the room, so he blew in her ear to rouse her. First she flicked at her earlobe as though a fly was annoying her but persistence paid off and a minute later, she opened an eye.

"Time to eat."

She tried to generate a half-smile but failed and only transformed her expression into a grimace. A sinking feeling hit the pit of her stomach. This meal would be painful, but she'd known this day would come and had done nothing to prepare herself or Frank for its arrival.

"I need to change first."

"Well, get a move on then," he said as he placed his hands in her panties."

She squirmed as Frank fooled around and gasped when matters got more serious.

"Now we can eat, right?"

She nodded and slipped into a blue dress while he did up his pants. Sammy held his hand as they left the bedroom, which he mistook for affection. Fear of meeting Alice was the real cause.

FRANK AND SAM walked into the living room and Alice's jaw opened wide. Bobby's eyes darted between Sam and Alice, while Mary Lou watched benignly.

"Good to meet you, dear."

Sam's mouth twitched a smile as she had no idea what to do next. His mom hadn't remembered her but Alice sure as hell had.

"Hi all. How are you doing?"

Frank appeared to not notice the confusion and embarrassment on everybody else's faces. Then he blinked and realized he'd stepped into the middle of a Noel Coward play. Mumbled responses to Sam's question ensued as Bobby, at least, tried to salvage the moment and steer everyone well enough to sit down to eat.

The silence was broken by Irma who took them into the dining room to serve their meal. Bobby and Mary Lou at each end of the table with Alice sat opposite Sam and Frank. A pleasant family meal. The knives were needed more to cut the tension than the veal which was tender and flavorsome.

Alice trawled the food around her plate. When Sam first walked into the room, as Alice exhaled, a wave of anger overtook her body and she wanted to grab a gun and shoot Sam through the head. Then she inhaled and withdrew from the world, wanting to curl into a little ball and vanish into nothing.

Now she glared at Sam, occasionally scooping a mouthful of veal or potato. Mary Lou ate her meal in silence, focused on her delightful food and not experiencing the same emotional fallout as the rest of the table. Bobby knew better than to stand in the way of the twins, their lover and their mother.

Almost the minute Irma cleared the plates away, Sam declared she was going up to bed. Frank shrugged and, given the lack of joy in the room, followed soon after. Alice listened as his footsteps announced his arrival on the second floor.

"Why didn't you tell me?"

"He called her Sammy and she hid in their bedroom until just before dinner. I found out the same instant as you."

"Fucking whore."

Neither disagreed but Mary Lou remained resolutely silent. Bobby opened his arms and Alice walked towards him and accepted the hug. All three sat down in the living room and attacked a bottle of Scotch. Two hours later, Alice crashed out on the couch: she couldn't face being only a wall's width from the rutting couple.

"We still a need plan."

"Kill the bitch."

"Not what I meant…"

FRANK TUCKED INTO his pancakes with gusto while the rest of the family was subdued. He and Sam had a long conversation the night before when she explained to him what he was too emotionally illiterate to comprehend for himself and now he understood why everyone was acting so strange. The man remained untouched by everybody else's emotional fallout, but Sam made him promise not to lay into Alice—for her sake and a quiet life.

His response was to fill his face with food because he couldn't be sure anything apart from barbs would come out of his mouth if he spoke. Sam pecked at her maple syrup soaked circles but could only meet Alice's gaze once or twice.

Alice's sense of loss stayed with her from the moment she woke up but she recognized nothing and nobody would make her feel better—in the short term. She wasn't hungry but despite this, she made sure she ate some of Irma's cooking and instigated a tiny amount of small talk. The silence was too oppressive and centered on her.

"These are so good."

"Irma's done a fabulous job."

"Yep."

"Anyone had fresh thoughts about the Markov problem?"

"You won't hear me say this again in my lifetime, but Frank might be correct."

"Thanks sis'."

"Hold back the hugs: you didn't let me finish."

"You could be right that direct intervention is the answer. But you're probably thinking about rushing in with a crew and committing merry mayhem."

"Pretty much. Go in, kill 'em, escape."

"That is the opposite of what's to be done. We need to cut off the head of the snake and leave the body alone."

All silverware was placed on plates as Alice grabbed everybody's attention.

"What are you thinking?"

"One person—not a crew—go to the Markovs and once they are facing Nikolay, a bullet to the head solves all our difficulties. The rest of his family and fellas will fold immediately."

"And who should get this assignment?"

"Nothing personal Sam, but perhaps we should carry on this conversation in the summerhouse."

"It's okay, sis'. Sam knows about my business."

"And about ours too?"

"No, Alice. Just Frank's world. He let me in."

A glare for a response and Alice stood up.

"You coming? We've already said too much in front of her."

The ease with which they'd moved from breakfast to assassination showed how Sam had entered their circle of trust by stealth. Now she had enough to run to the Feds and pocket herself a healthy reward. Bobby thought for half a second and stood up, which encouraged Mary Lou and Frank to follow.

ENSCONCED IN THE safety of the poolside building, Alice was more relaxed.

"So who should go on the mission? Can't be me because Markov won't believe I have any interest in him or his family. Mama and Bobby aren't believable either."

They all did the Math and that left only one person.

"You looking at me?"

"I don't see anyone else here."

"Got to be kidding. I want Nikolay Markov dead but only if I am still alive. I'm not volunteering for a suicide mission."

Alice's eyebrows raised themselves up on their haunches and she smiled.

"I thought you wanted to kill them all."

"Not at any cost."

"Good to come home to a warm bed, huh?"

"Does my sleeping with Sammy bother you?"

"Children!"

Mary Lou bellowed across the room at the squabbling twins. The effect was instant silence and sheepish looks.

"Sorry, Mama."

"If you're not willing to go, who should we use instead?"

"Someone from out of town."

"We could get Naldo to recommend a shooter. He's seen some action in his day."

"Sure has. They need to be beyond reliable. That's the trouble with strangers: how can we trust them? With all due respect to any suggestion from Naldo."

"Is there any chance of finding Markov alone long enough to hit him and get away?"

"Naldo already checked that out. He's always with somebody by day or has armed guards surround him at night. There's too much firepower near him."

"Sniper?"

"That's a possibility. A rifle trained on his bedroom window might work but he keeps the blinds shut at all times so basic aiming would be tricky."

"We're getting nowhere with is. All we've figured out for sure is we want Nikolay Markov dead."

"A BOMB? INSTEAD of a focused strike, perhaps we should blast the fuck out of an entire building."

"Family home?"

"It is one thing to hit Nikolay with an incendiary device. It's another to murder his wife and children."

"Okay. His kids don't go with him to work, right?"

"True but he doesn't even have an office. He travels round, visiting his venues collecting his tribute. The guy is shrewd: can't fault him for that."

"Sniper in a helicopter?"

"This isn't the movies. Let's not clutch at straws."

"Feels like that's all we've got."

The three continued to chew the fat until lunch but were no nearer to any useful conclusion. Sam joined them to eat and in the afternoon, she and Frank left the compound. Alice stayed with Mama and Bobby, which was enjoyable but delivered no plan.

"Maybe killing him isn't the answer."

157

ALICE AND BOBBY sat in the summerhouse. It was the wrong half of the year to sit outside although the temperature wasn't that cold. Another Californian Winter's day. Mostly, they were silent in their own worlds but now and then, they'd glance at each other or mumble a few words. Bobby hid behind a newspaper and Alice didn't pretend: she was plain sitting doing nothing in particular.

Or rather, she was using the time to focus on Nikolay Markov. Until the moment when his dick took over from his brain, Nikolay appeared to be open to working together—unless the entire evening was a ruse to get inside her panties. If she set aside the fear and humiliation he'd reaped upon her, the Markov clan was a great fit. Alice did her level best to compartmentalize business from her personal experience of the man. Each family had different but complementary strengths which would support the other's weaknesses. A marriage made not so much in heaven but a lap dancing club in the Tenderloin.

Perhaps the trick was to appeal to his wallet or his ego. Puff him up and take the sting out of his tail. Once everyone and everything had calmed down, either he'd see the sense in the deal or she'd slice him open from throat to groin at some later date.

"We should make a peace instead of killing Markov."

"Do you not think we're beyond that now?"

"Not necessarily. Whether we want to admit it, we need them—or some outfit like them."

"You might be right but that's not what I meant."

"Huh?"

"We have killed his family. He's murdered Milton and we've both lost fellas too. I'd suggest relationships are founded on trust and we're living through a fundamental breakdown in that ingredient."

"Only if we let go of hope."

"You can take the girl out of California…"

"…but you can't take California out of me."

"Your optimism is astounding."

"You need faith that change is possible if you're to succeed. And sometimes that involves finding the good in people. Even someone like Nikolay, who is a cockroach. If I could stamp on him and destroy him then I would, but we can't see how to rid ourselves of the Markov infestation. That means we have to accept they'll be around and learn to live with them."

"Was that a long speech to say: if you can't beat them, join them?"

"Pretty much, yeah."

"BOBBY SAID YOU'VE come up with an idea."

"Yes, but I'm not sure how you'll respond."

"Won't know until you tell me."

Bobby sat still and let the women continue their conversation without interruption.

"If we can't assassinate Nikolay Markov then we need to join forces with him. There's no other way a neutralize him as a threat."

"Sounds the exact opposite of what we should do. How can we trust a man like that?"

"I'm not saying we do. Just that it'll be the easiest route to stop the war. If the killing reduces, we have a better chance of making money and surviving until Easter."

"Sure would be great to find some calm. All this hostility isn't good for the soul."

"Right. The man is too difficult to destroy at the moment, but that will change once we get him to lower his guard. To do that, we must build a peace with him. Create a joint operation to work on together and then make a move."

"That's fine but I would need to be top dog. He would report to me on this project."

"I can't guarantee that'd happen Mama. Besides, the endgame is his removal. If he rules the roost, that would just put him in the place we require for him even faster."

"I couldn't take orders from that man. Milton's in his grave because of him."

"It wouldn't matter. Within a month, he'd have called off his hounds and then we deal with him."

Bobby stood up and headed for the door. With a hand on the handle, he turned around.

"Alice is right. To get Markov into the morgue requires us to put him on ice first. Until that point, we suck in any discomfort."

He didn't wait for any reply and walked out.

MARY LOU STARED at the closed door and Alice wondered if she was in a trance. Then she blinked and mentally returned to the room. Mama smiled quietly to herself and turned her attention to Alice.

"You met up with him."

"What?"

"Nikolay. You had a meal with Markov. What happened that meant you wouldn't tell me you'd even seen him?"

"Don't want to talk about it. I made a mistake."

"One that's cost us several good men. From what I've been told, all this maelstrom of blood letting started shortly after you broke bread with him."

"I am all too aware."

"And the fact you kept it from me means either you're about to turn traitor, he did something wrong or you behaved inappropriately. Which was it?"

"I'm no traitor, Mama."

"Sure, dear. You wouldn't be the first woman in this family to have had to fend off sexual advances from a man."

Tears ran down Alice's cheeks and they hugged, but Alice refused to go into any details about what went down in her hotel bedroom and Mama didn't elaborate on what had happened to her when she visited Uncle Frankie and he laid his hands on her.

FRANK HAD NEVER been to San Francisco. When he arrived, he was not disappointed and he was not alone: Isaak Vasilev sat next to him on the plane. When he realized a firm hand was required and a violent disposition, Isaak was the first person who popped into his head.

They had met when Frank had got into a spot of bother in Morocco shortly after leaving school. The local dealers weren't impressed with Frank's attempts to introduce a little healthy American-style competition to their country. Isaak appreciated Frank's entrepreneurial efforts and applied a knife and a gun to the problem. They had kept in touch ever since and when Isaak moved to the States, Frank ensured he found the man work that suited his talents for murder and mayhem.

Over the course of a week, Frank and Isaak made inroads into the Markov empire. First, they unearthed a meth lab which supplied Nikolay and sent Molotov cocktails into the building. The next day on the other side of the bay, they did the same to a crack house.

Isaak paid a visit to the Red Stocking and sliced himself some whore faces so they hit the Markov cash flow very rapidly and without getting spotted. By the third sunrise, the Markovs noticed Frank's antics. The good news was that they were like a needle in a haystack to find. Two men in a city of millions gave them the best odds to survive.

BY FLYING UNDER the radar, Frank was having a low-level impact but his activities were far from a game changer. His family would learn to trust him if he showed them he knew what he was doing. So the next logical thing to do was to build an operation in SF, something no Lagotti had achieved.

A narcotics play would take too much time to prepare, but a brothel would do the trick and only required rent to be paid upfront and girls would earn that night. Twenty-four hours later and Frank held the keys in his hand to an undesirable residence on the edge of the Tenderloin as far away from any Markov establishment they knew about.

While Isaak set about organizing rudimentary furniture for each bedroom, Frank hit the bus station to grab fresh tail among the new arrivals to the city. A rental car took the hapless ladies to the house and Frank gave his employees a full staff induction. He showed them the bathroom and explained how they kept their tips but the first thirty dollars from each john belonged to him. Any trouble, they screamed and Isaak would sort the dude out.

The next day, Isaak added partitioning in the larger upstairs rooms and Frank returned to the bus station for more ass. Without Nikolay noticing, Frank had kicked off a San Francisco operation by slowly boiling the frog. Slamming into an existing deal would never work, Frank reckoned.

He stayed in the area to get to know the locals and to hire a timekeeper and troubleshooter. As fabulous as the cathouse was, Frank had other plans for his time which didn't involve fucking. He smiled at that idea: he never imagined such a statement might ever be true. Besides, when he got home, he'd have Sammy in his bed and what she could do with her body was worth waiting for.

158

PASQUALE BASSANI WAS an old man, who enjoyed nothing more than sipping coffee at a cafe, a casual round of golf when he had the energy and quiet conversation with his family and friends. Florida was the perfect state to retire in because its weather was fine and the stresses of his former life were far away. There had been a long tradition of gangsters staying in Miami-Dade dating back to Al Capone so Pasquale was in good company.

When he retired to the Sunshine State, Pasquale sold up all his investments in the various illicit assets which he owned and ensured everyone knew it. He'd heard too many stories of revenge being taken on the older generation because they were sitting ducks.

Visitors were welcome but Pasquale had no desire to be dragged into the problems of today. The mob world was behind him and he lived with the riches that life had generated for him. So when Bobby called to ask his advice, Pasquale was cautious. Not out of any distrust of Bobby: he and Mary Lou had been doing business together since the early '70s.

He didn't want his words to cause someone to be killed and a misguided relative take retaliatory action against him. Pasquale had survived way too much to be whacked by a teenager with a gun and a point to prove. No one would make their bones by sending him to the morgue.

Bobby and Pasquale sat on his patio and sipped a glass of red wine each.

"Thank you for allowing me to come here to speak with you."

"Most welcome. How is Mary Lou?"

"Fine. She sends her regards."

"Strange that she is not here in person. Matters are so difficult you need to see an old wizened fool like myself, yet Mary Lou stays at home. Talk to me, Bobby Trevisan."

"We are in a dangerous situation and I am seeking your advice. We have no idea what to do."

"Go on."

Bobby explained the Markov war and outlined the issues with Mary Lou's decision making. Once he had finished, the old boss took small sips from his wine glass and contemplated the problem in silence. Bobby knew his job was to not speak and give Pasquale the time to think things through. Five long minutes later, the man cleared his throat and had another sip to moisten his tonsils.

"Forgive me. My medication gives me a dry cough. It's for my blood pressure, so the doc says, but I'm the most relaxed I've been since the day I was born."

Pasquale slipped into silence and pondered more. And Bobby waited—politely and with the utmost respect for this once-powerful old man.

BOBBY DID HIS best not to hold his breath or tap his fingers with impatience. Pasquale had been the firm hand supporting their efforts through thick and thin. He had been there in the early days and gave Mary Lou her big break when she first drifted into town. Five years earlier, the fella had been the only person to try to save his children. He was solid as a rock and deserved the time to think. No matter how long that took.

"You have exhausted your options through violence, you say."

"The Markov men are real tough and whenever we cut one down, another appears in his place. It's like they're lining up in Russia waiting to join the fight over here."

"They probably are. The break up of the Soviet Union strengthened the Russian mob. Khrushchev never allowed crime families to get too strong. With freedom comes chaos."

"Khrushchev?"

"Whoever. My point is the same and I hope well taken."

"Yes, Pasquale."

"As far as I can see, you have two options. First, find reinforcements and destroy these foreigners. Second, make your peace with them and merge your activities. Half of a large pizza is better than all of a child's portion."

"Where would these extra men come from?"

"Is there anyone else who has a beef with these guys?"

"I don't know."

"Worth finding out then, wouldn't you say?"

A nod. Bobby was embarrassed that none of them had thought of that. They were too close to the trees to see straight through the forest.

"And is a merger the only other option you can see for us?"

"On what you've told me: yes. From what I hear, it's the way of the world. We have always had to adapt to survive. Shed your old skin to let your new one come alive."

"Doesn't that make us a bunch of snakes?"

"And what of it? When the mammals are long gone from this stinking planet, we'll be left with the reptiles and the insects. Serpents and cockroaches will rule the Earth, my friend. Rejoice that you are a snake and not a disgusting roach."

Pasquale knocked back the dregs from his glass and got Bobby to refill it. After he put the bottle down, he mulled over Pasquale's words, sifting through his prejudices to find out if he could deal with the consequences of working with Nikolay. The options: do that or die. Not much of a choice.

He spent another thirty minutes with Pasquale talking about the good old days with both catching up on who had died in the other's circle—Fabio was one of the many names. Then he thanked the great man and took his leave. Pasquale occupied the rest of the afternoon reminding himself of happier times when the Feds didn't have wiretaps and could barely match fingerprints.

WHEN BOBBY ARRIVED home, Mary Lou was already asleep, so he waited until morning to tell her what Pasquale had recommended. As ever, they sat in the summerhouse to talk business, having used breakfast for couples conversation.

"First the good news: Pasquale is doing fine, living out his days in the Miami burbs. The rest is less positive."

"Spill."

"He says we should stop the war before it gets out of hand. Either we find a group with aligned interest in the destruction of Nikolay Markov or we reconcile our differences and learn how to work together."

"Peace is not an option."

"Only if we ignore it and Pasquale was very clear. We need to give peace a chance."

Mary Lou sat and thought. Then she shook her head.

"I can't do that. What Markov has done is not forgivable and needs to be punished. Milton is dead because of him. The guy might not have been the brightest spark in the fire, but he was decent to his wife and to his mistresses. And that should count for something."

"It does, but some things you have to suck in and that's one of them. I'm not saying we ignore what he did to Milton, just that we don't have to act now. His revenge can be served cold—later this year or the next: whichever is more convenient for us. Today we need to make money and spill less blood."

BOBBY COULDN'T TELL if Mary Lou was thinking, sulking or both. He could not read the taciturn puffing of her cigarette. All he knew was her silence. When she stubbed out the remains, he received her response.

"We can win the fight if we carry on and don't give up hope. Look what Frank has achieved in only a handful of days. He and his sidekick have thrown sand in Nikolay's face and set up a cathouse under his nose. That proves we should attack Markov and grow our business interests without the need to sit down and talk. Let alone share the profit from our hard work."

"Short-term gains. Two guys on their own? Of course, they can make early inroads. Will the story be the same in a month? Nah. The whorehouse'll be shut down and the girls'll have their throats cut. And we shouldn't wait four weeks just for me to be proved right. Me, Alice and Pasquale. We've all reached the same conclusion. It is time for a peace conference."

"Frank is leading the way. If we each set up a small group and chip away at their businesses, in a few weeks we'll be in a very different situation. We will starve them of money. Without that, they are nothing."

"Aren't you forgetting their connections?"

"Huh?"

"In Russia."

"Russia ain't America. Fuck his Russki paymasters."

"They have deep pockets and an army waiting to ship overseas. We mustn't underestimate them simply because they don't speak our language."

"A bunch of chimpanzees in suits. I'm not underestimating them: merely discounting them instead. They are thugs and no more. If we want, we can hire our own ape army, but the better approach is to destroy them slowly while generating cash. That's more than they are able to do. Frank has cut off narcotics supply lines already. Every day they lose money, the weaker they become. In less than a month they'll have nothing. Nada. And then we move on Nikolay Markov."

MARY LOU COULD be stubborn, but Bobby felt there was something more at work here. Yes, she was digging in her heels, but her argument was based on Frank's minor success and ignored what had gone on before. As though it had never happened. As if she couldn't remember that it had occurred. He shook his head. His desire to remain loyal to her pulled him in one direction and his mind tugged him in another.

He could not deal with the thought he needed to countermand her plan—again. Perhaps he wasn't strong enough, grown weak after years of easy street. Also, this was the first instance in over a year that he could remember when Mary Lou had passion, fire in her belly. That had to count for something. She was so sure of herself—in a way he hadn't seen for a very long time. Like these dark times were bringing out the best in her.

The last thing he should do is rain on her parade. Now was the moment for the whole family to come together as one, including him. For richer or poorer, better or worse. His job was to stick by Mary Lou and support her. This was her show and, despite his misgivings, she gave the orders and her position was clear.

159

CRIMINAL ACTIVITY IS cyclical like so many businesses which is why Frank worked his girls hard during the weekend and came home to visit Mama on Tuesday. Sammy had returned to Boston but his mind was not focused on her ass despite what she might hope. Unlike Alice, his desire for her was entirely physical and he was too tired to fool around.

He rested in the conservatory after a hearty Irma-fueled breakfast and waited for his Mama to appear. Bobby had left the house at the crack of dawn and the place was silent, apart from Irma's hustle and bustle, which Frank plain ignored. When Mary Lou appeared, she still looked tired and he gave her the time to revive before talking shop.

"How's it been back here?"

"Difficult. The Markovs continue to hit us hard: attacking our labs and they once tried to take our trucks coming out of Bakersfield."

"But we stopped them?"

"Yes, for the past two weeks, armed guards rode in the cabins so the Markov goons were met with a hail of bullets. Didn't come back the following day—the ones who survived."

"There's nothing like a steel toecap in your face to focus your mind."

"Amen to that."

"Huh?"

"What?"

They looked quizzically at each other, neither understanding the other's response. Frank shook himself out of the conundrum first.

"I have applied the same strategy in SF and set up two whorehouses along the way using fresh girls. If we work to the side of their operation, we can eat away at their territory and fight them at the same time."

"That's what I've been telling Bobby and Alice but they won't listen."

"I hear you loud and clear, Mama. The business is safe with me."

"I know, dear and I won't forget what you've done. Never you mind."

Frank glowed inside. So much of his life had been spent being bailed out or disappointing his mom, he'd forgotten how warm positive words could feel.

"And now we must step up our campaign and you've shown me you are the one I can rely on."

"What do you want me to do, Mama?"

"It is time to chew through the heart of their operations: prostitution. You have started well but we need to knock out their lap dancing venues and cathouses. If we succeed, all that'll be left of any substance will be narcotics and you've already started to nix those supply lines."

"Hit them hard."

"Without restraint. Either destroy the buildings or take out the resources."

"You mean kill the fellas running the joints."

"The goons. The girls. If we leave the johns alone, then the cops won't touch us: we'll be doing their job for them."

FRANK RETURNED TO the Bay City and followed Mama's orders. Isaak continued to lay waste to the Markov whores. While Naldo had used a knife, Isaak waded in with automatic weapons and a total disregard for human life, but he always attacked the staff rooms or hit the place after hours. Mama had been clear about that and it made perfect sense.

The San Francisco Police Department didn't know what to do with itself. Local precincts were reporting mass murder one day followed by a total lack of low-level crime the next. The only people who were disappointed were the men hoping for an easy fuck on the way home from work or after sinking a beer or two. They were forced to put more effort into their illicit carnal desires.

Isaak continued his reign of terror until the Tenderloin was free of brothels. Even the independent operators got the message and went on unexpected vacations. What's the point of running a joint, if at the end of the night you're face down in a pool of your own blood and excrement?

THE MARKOV RESPONSE was predictable—much as Bobby and Alice had said. Nikolay put his best fellas on to track down Frank and Isaak. In the absence of any success, all the people found in a Lagotti venue were shot. The two guys went into hiding outside the Tenderloin but soon Frank realized the jig was up.

Not enough guns to finish Markov and insufficient men to maintain control of the new territory they'd won. Their early gains had turned into a series of losses and the splatter of human remains lay all over the streets. Isaak waited until after dusk, stole a car and the pair got the fuck out of Dodge.

OVER THE WEEKEND, Mary Lou flew down to Miami for a break. Bobby stayed at home because he didn't want a vacation while chaos loomed all around. He sent Naldo with her to watch her back.

On Saturday morning, word reached Bobby that two meth labs in the depths of LA had gone up in smoke overnight. That afternoon, the Markovs attacked their main narcotics processing lab. Fifteen pounds of uncut heroin and ten pounds of cocaine had been stolen and everyone in the building had been whacked.

Bobby tried to contact Mary Lou, but she wasn't in her room to answer the phone. Nor was Naldo. Under ordinary circumstances, Bobby wouldn't have been concerned, but this hit was the kind of incident he had feared would happen and there was no way to protect Mary Lou. In the early evening, he got through to Naldo.

"There's been action. Check out of the hotel and find somewhere quiet to stay tonight. Tell her to come home tomorrow. Let her know supply lines have been hit and that I am insisting. She should understand what that means."

While the tentacles of the Feds had yet to reach their corner of Palm Springs, Bobby used caution when on a public line. He and Mary Lou had agreed to insist on something only if it was a matter of life or death. No questions asked. And for Bobby, this was one of those times.

He briefed the guards in the house to expect trouble and he told Alice what had happened.

"Do you think we'll get through this?"

"For sure. Your mom and I have dealt with worse in our time. If we remain sensible and do nothing stupid then we will nail Nikolay Markov."

"Has anyone explained that plan to Frank?"

"I'm having a Scotch. You want something?"

"Too early for me."

Bobby poured two fingers into a tumbler and added four cubes of ice. Then he raised his glass like he was giving a toast.

"Here's looking at you, kid."

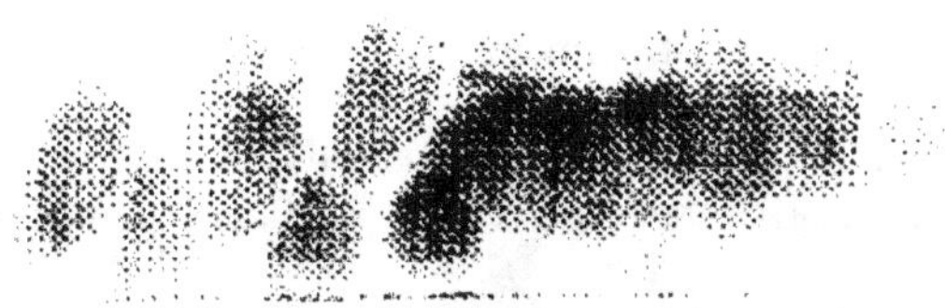

160

BOBBY AND MARY Lou sat on the summerhouse couch with Alice and Frank in separate armchairs. The events of the past week had permeated through all of them. The stress caused by being at war had taken its toll. Everyone looked fraught even Mary Lou, fresh from her weekend in the sun.

"Let's get started. What's the latest?"

"Same as the whole of the month: we've been hit hard in Los Angeles and surrounding areas. Narcotics, prostitution. There has been some disruption to our gambling operations too. Revenue is down and so are the number of live bodies on the payroll."

"In return, we have disrupted or decimated Markov whorehouses in San Francisco. We've hit their heroin supply and destroyed their pussy product."

"Nicely put, Frank."

"Get over yourself, sis'. We are hurting them. Causing them grief."

"In summary then, they're bleeding us dry on the west coast but there's been zero impact on Las Vegas, Chicago, Boston or Atlantic City."

"'Yet' is the key word here. The longer this goes on, the greater the chance they will expand their horizons. Once Nikolay escalates his actions, it'll be a matter of days before the casinos fall. He can call on an enormous number of men and we won't be able to defend ourselves."

"The good thing about the Lucky Lady is that it is in the middle of the city and local police will not be happy with anyone who disrupts the tourist trade."

"Same for AC."

"The Queen of Sheba is vulnerable: it's a boat on a river."

"Can we find reinforcements to last this month?"

"I'd love to say yes, but I have no idea where to get the right guys. Our best are six feet under and the rest heard what happens when you work for us."

Bobby's hand made a fast swooping gesture across his throat to emphasize his statement. Mary Lou stared, an impassive rock. Frank and Alice nodded or shook their heads depending on the point being expressed. They both sat on the edge of their seats—fresh to the experience of a war cabinet.

"And what are we to do?"

MARY LOU SPOKE for the first time since opening the meeting.

"We must assassinate the Russian. With him gone, all our problems dissolve like sugar in a hot cup of coffee."

"That is not an option: we have been through this before."

"No, we need to cut off the head of the snake. His men will fall in line when he's lying bleeding in the dirt."

"There are no opportunities for this tp happen, Mary Lou. We've ruled out a sniper, a bomb and a good old-fashioned drive-by shooting. No one can get close enough to Nikolay to slit his throat or plant a slug in his heart."

"We need to reach an accommodation, Mama, to take us to a new normal."

Frank snorted, his derision visible on his expression.

"Death is the end of all things. We just carry on what we're doing—only more so. We have casino money rolling in to support us but he does not. Another week, maybe a month. The longer we can last, the sooner his power will be lost. He might enjoy contacts back in Russia, but he is living in the US of A. And that is where he must die."

"Brave words little brother, but saying it doesn't make it so. Yes, we have the money to keep going but not the men. That's what we repeatedly say and no one seems to disagree. Our best are dead and what remains: they are scared and they should be. I know I'm scared. Everyone in this room should be —we are living in fucking dangerous times."

"DARLING, IS YOUR primary objection our lack of fellas?"

"It's up there, Mama. I can't see how to win in a fight when the ring is empty."

"Bobby, that's your issue too?"

"To carry on we need solid guys we can rely on when we turn up the heat."

"So why don't I get us some gold plate muchachos?"

"How're you going to do that?"

"Do you agree if I succeed that we continue with my plan?"

"I guess so. I mean, with enough guns we could pull him apart, I suppose."

Bobby shrugged. He wasn't happy because there was more to killing Nikolay than having a posse of lethal weapons. But it would help. His biggest problem right now was that he couldn't think of a good reason to disagree. If they hit Nikolay all guns blazing, he'd be dead before morning. Fog City would be theirs.

"So that's settled then. I'll go first thing tomorrow and by the end of the week, Nikolay Markov will lie in a body bag.

MARY LOU'S TRIP to New York passed smoothly enough, although her impatience to arrive nearly got the better of her. On the plane, she thought back to the day she took the same flight and assassinated Charlie Pentangelo, capo to the Baninno Family. Their empire had crumbled now and there were few left alive to remember Charlie or recall what he looked like—let alone ponder on what he achieved.

She had spent her time in Manhattan in a perpetual state of fear, afraid of every guy in a three-piece suit who glanced in her general direction. Even the ticket purchase at Palm Springs had felt like agony. Mary Lou recalled fleeing the scene of her crime and being chased across town by Charlie's goons. Such relief at finding a yellow vehicle. That moment when she got in the taxi and they drove to LaGuardia.

And here she stood in the same airport waiting in line to go into the city. This time there was no plan to hide a piece by her crotch and no need to carry any heat. Mary Lou was here to talk—and nothing else.

Just as the Bannino clan's power had waned, so too with most of the five Families that controlled New York since the days of the Big Bankroll. Organized crime in the east coast had followed a similar path to the mobs out west. As the Feds were given a mandate to attack the mob, guys ratted out their compadres and people lost their grip on the rackets under their control.

The operations didn't die on the vine. Instead other gangs took them over with an ancestry that couldn't be traced to anywhere even close to Sicily: the Latinos, Chinese, Russians, Ukrainians and many other nationalities too. A great big racial melting pot of extortion, gun running, drug supply, labor racketeering—and the list went on.

Despite all these changes to the criminal fabric of the Five Boroughs, one group had survived and still dipped their beak into several troughs: the Gagliardi family, with Fiorino at its helm. The man had survived assassination attempts and the encroachment on his territory of just about every gang the country had to offer. He continued to rule his piece of Manhattan and New Jersey with an iron fist.

Decades ago, the seat of his power would have been a swanky five-star hotel overlooking Central Park. That was then and this was now. Mary Lou and Fiorino sat at the back of a restaurant on Mulberry. He had agreed to see her out of respect for Pasquale, but her reputation did her no harm, although the most famous of her exploits deserving the great man's attention was twenty years old.

THEY ATE LINGUINI with clams and drank a glass of red wine each. By the time Fiorino mopped up his sauce with a piece of bread, Mary Lou had tired of small talk and wanted to get down to the reason for her visit.

"I'm glad to hear business is good for you."

"It's not like how it was, nothing is nowadays, but we survive."

"And how is recruitment?"

"That is never easy. The youngsters want fast money and no graft. Something for zip. This is the problem in the world we live in. No one is prepared to wait for success. Everything must happen now."

"We face similar difficulties, but on a much smaller scale."

"Don't do yourself down. I understand you maintain controlling interests in at least two casinos. That's no small boast for a woman to make."

"Thank you. Sometimes it's who you know that counts."

"Influence is a marvelous thing. How we get things done—with a little help from our friends."

"Pasquale recommended I speak with you on a delicate matter where friends on the west coast are proving hard to find."

"I'm listening. As lovely as it is to break bread with you, I assumed Pasquale was not introducing me to a tourist."

"No, I've been here before."

Mary Lou's eyes glanced toward the front of the restaurant and onwards where she sat, all those years ago, to stalk Pentangelo before whacking him. Fiorino's eyelids closed and Mary Lou noticed him clench his jaw. While he admired her guts, perhaps he hadn't approved of her taking out a capo back when time had roman numerals.

"I am very aware of that."

"THE BOTTOM LINE is that we are experiencing some local difficulty in California and need access to some solid fellas for a week or two. Maybe three."

"And how many are we discussing here?"

"Ten would be good, twenty better and thirty would be best. The more we have, the sooner we can get matters settled and your people returned to you."

"How very gracious. What difficulties are you facing?"

Mary Lou outlined the situation in San Francisco and how it was now spilling over into LA. She described their efforts to date and how they were falling short due to the lack of competent bodies.

"I understand your problem, but thirty men is a small army and I don't want them killed or arrested. What guarantees can you offer me?"

"Fiorino, if this was a walk in the park, I wouldn't fly across the country to meet with you. We both know that some of those guys will not survive. What I wish to do is to reach an arrangement with you so that your loss is mitigated and I can show my appreciation for your support."

"This isn't about the money. It's about the people. We already agreed that good youngsters are hard to find and you are asking me to hand over thirty and expect to lose some in less than a week. In a war not of my making and in which I have no vested interest for the success of your venture."

"If you help me now, I could offer you a piece of a casino, for example. Your kind indulgence in this matter need not be paid back with a case of bills. If you are willing, I am flexible in how I show my appreciation."

"I know, but I still don't like the thought of losing good men and I wouldn't insult you by sending you greenhorns. Go back to California and let me think on this some more."

"I could stay in the city and we could speak further, if you liked."

"I'd like you to return to Palm Springs and leave me to consider my position."

Mary Lou nodded, stood up and kissed his proffered hand. Old school mafia. Then she left the restaurant and grabbed a cab to LaGuardia and home.

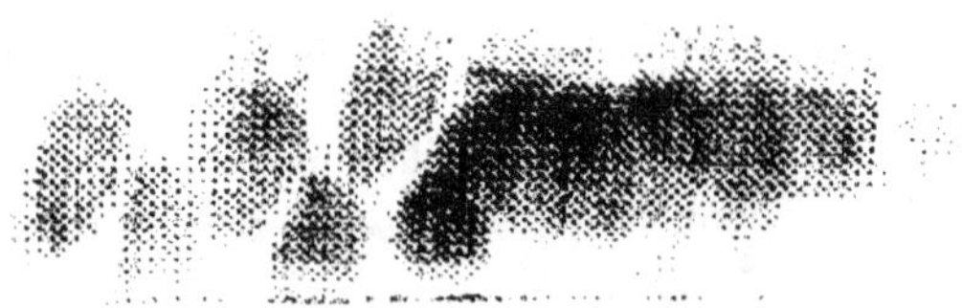

161

TWO DAYS AFTER Mary Lou got back, there was a knock on the door and Irma led the gentleman into the living room. Then she popped into the summerhouse to let Bobby and Mary Lou know they had a visitor.

"Would you like a coffee?"

"No, thank you. I'm not expecting to be here long enough to drink it."

"Then let's not detain you any longer than you need."

Bobby saw Mary Lou bristling and hoped she would remember who had sent Vito to their door.

"Mr. Gagliardi sends his regards and asked me to speak with you directly. He didn't want me to leave a message or note. He believes people he respects should hear news firsthand."

"Do thank him for his courteous behavior."

"Actually, I have changed my mind: a coffee would be most welcome."

Bobby and Mary Lou glanced at each other and summoned Irma to issue instructions. A quick conversation meant bad news, but if the guy was settling in for a drink, perhaps things were looking up. Vito said nothing until Irma reappeared with his mug.

"Mr. Gagliardi thanks you for making the journey to see him in person. This impressed him greatly as a mark of respect, dear lady."

Mary Lou smiled and waited. Bobby sat back in his seat, letting the experience wash over him until he knew whether to be happy or sad.

"He also was touched with your honest assessment of your situation and the way you conveyed that to him. Without gilding the lily, so to speak."

More smiling. More waiting. If you removed the yada-yada, you were left with nada so far. Why the build up? Can't he get to the punchline?

"You requested the loan of up to thirty men and Mr. Gagliardi is forced to decline."

Mary Lou stopped listening. Nothing Vito was going to say would improve her situation, so there was no point. Bobby was concerned to understand why because Mary Lou seemed optimistic when she came back.

"There are two issues he wishes to draw to your attention. First, your predicament is a problem of your own making. As he understands the situation, your bellicose approach infuriated the other party and after you reached a very reasonable settlement, you chiseled away at their territory."

Bobby felt a sickness in the pit of his stomach. Frank's exploits had been visible from New York and they were paying for the consequences of his actions.

"We could put aside the cause of your problems under the right circumstances. But second, the interests of the Gagliardi and Lagotti families are not aligned. Certain business activities have been hindered by your ongoing disagreement with Markov and we need this interference in our revenue generation to end."

Vito consumed some coffee. It felt as though he hadn't taken a breath since he told them how Gagliardi wasn't going to help. The feeling in Bobby's stomach got worse and his gastric wall tightened.

MARY LOU STARED out of the window as she saw no reason to hide her disinterest in what this olive-skinned excuse for a man had to say.

"Mrs. Lagotti: you have been given one week to resolve your local difficulties with Nikolay Markov. If you do not do so, your husband'll have need of an undertaker or a search party. Either way, you will be dead."

She tried to control her breathing as the air filled with the threat to her life.

"My apologies for being blunt but I want to be certain you understand your situation. Mr. Gagliardi is more than happy to forge a relationship with you should you vanquish your foe. What concerns him most is that no business is being conducted while you two slug it out. There is no personal animosity in anything I have said and I hope you appreciate that."

Vito stood up: clearly this was not a debate. He'd conveyed what Gagliardi had instructed and now he needed to leave.

"Can we call you a taxi?"

"Most kind."

Bobby popped his head into the kitchen to speak with Irma and by the time he got back, Vito was standing on his own. The clang of the patio door told him Mary Lou had given up on social niceties with this prick. He had just threatened her life, but he represented one of the most powerful gang bosses in America.

"Forgive my wife. She doesn't like hearing bad news, but obviously we recognize Mr. Gagliardi's respect to send you all this distance for such a short but clear message."

"It's what I do. Pass on decisions whichever way the coin lands."

"I understand. I used to be in the outfit."

"Fine. When she calms down, let her know the clock is ticking. We need this resolved in seven days or less, one way or another. Between you and me, I think Gagliardi would rather work with you but the Russian has the network and we have the product. It's a marriage of convenience and no more, but it needs peace to thrive. Capiche?"

"Got it."

BOBBY WALKED THROUGH the conservatory and out onto the patio to find Mary Lou in the summerhouse. He sat down and explained all that Vito had said and threatened.

"The mob will put a hit out on you in a week if we don't get matters sorted with Nikolay Markov."

Her jaw sunk to the floor and the blood drained from her cheeks.

"Is there no leeway?"

"None. We must end this nonsense now."

Mary Lou rummaged around for a cigarette but her hands were shaking and she couldn't get her lighter to work. Bobby bent over and lit one for her.

"A hit on me."

He nodded as she inhaled on her smoke, letting a plume of exhalation form a cloud in front of her face.

"Good news is that if we succeed against Markov, we have a guaranteed deal with Gagliardi."

"For what?"

"Vito was willfully vague, but they way he talked made it sound like narcotics. Don't know for sure."

"Perhaps they have a new pipeline into the east or from Colombia."

"…A hit."

Mary Lou's attention drifted in and out of focus until Bobby was no longer certain she was taking in anything he was saying.

THE DEATH OF Charlie Pentangelo was a pivotal moment after Mary Lou's twins were kidnapped and then rescued. But the speed with which his body was discovered and she was chased across the city startled her. It had always been a dangerous mission but her single-minded desire to kill the man, who'd caused her so much pain, had kept her focused on the act of assassination. The minute his corpse hit the ground, Mary Lou woke from her death-trance and smelled the coffee.

The thought of the mob giving her seven days before a hit sent her into a flat-spin panic. There was only one intelligent action for her to take: flee. She went into the conservatory and Bobby wasn't there. Into the living room and she heard a clattering in the kitchen. Without making a sound, Mary Lou grabbed her bag, hopped into her car and sped away, acknowledging her protective detail at the entrance to the property before bursting onto the road—and out of town.

Ten minutes later, Bobby came downstairs and tried to locate Mary Lou. Irma hadn't seen her for a while either. A quick conversation with the fellas outside revealed what had happened. Alice returned from the Country Club with Naldo in tow after an hour and Bobby filled her in on the day's events.

"We need to find Mama."

"She's in the wind for now."

They sent word out to their guys in Palm Springs to report back if they saw her. After a further hour there were no reports and Alice was worried.

"Where do you think she has gone?"

"No idea. She didn't pack: she just ran away. Could be anywhere, but we'll find her. We might have hit the mattresses but we've eyes and ears all over town and across the state. She'll be okay."

"I hope you're right."

TWENTY-FOUR HOURS later and they still hadn't found Mama. If she was holed up somewhere in Palm Springs, Bobby reckoned she'd have turned up by now. This meant she was further afield and therefore going to be harder to find: where would be the first place she'd go? No one was too sure.

With Naldo watching their backs, Bobby and Alice began a road trip while Frank carried on his San Francisco exploits oblivious to the misery in his family. They kept him out of the loop because he had enough to worry about on the front line against Markov. Truth was, telling him didn't even flash across either of their minds. Frank had spent so many years apart from the rest, they forgot he was a member of the family.

As Alice had set up a crib in Bakersfield, they tried the printers first but Mary Lou hadn't surfaced there at all. Then off to Malibu in case she'd visit Alice's home but again they drew a blank.

"The Palace has a suite. We should try there next."

THREE HOURS LATER, they pulled into the Palace and headed inside. It was quiet. Four hookers hung near the reception in the hope of a john while the second floor was devoid of human life. Up to the penthouse in search of Mama. The living room was empty but there were crockery and utensils out. The manager said no one had been up there since Milton was killed, apart from the cleaning service.

Alice and Bobby checked the bedrooms and Naldo stayed near the entrance, always alert to external danger. Bobby heard Alice scream and rushed in to see what she had found, passing Naldo who had already drawn his weapon.

"Wait here."

Bobby feared the worst and steeled himself to find her corpse. When he ran through the doorway, Mary Lou was huddled on the bed, naked, and mumbling to herself. He couldn't tell how long she had been there, but the chances were she'd come straight here, judging by the acrid stench in the room and the mess on the floor.

Alice backed away unable to deal with the state of her mother. This once great strong woman reduced to a ball of humanity on a bed. Bobby felt the pain of seeing his lover, friend and confidante at an all-time low. And it was his job to look after her: in sickness and in health.

He held Mary Lou in his arms until her mutterings ceased and she looked at him and smiled.

"I'm glad you're here. I got lost and didn't know where you were. I was scared."

"Sure but we're here now."

"We?"

"Alice is with me."

"Alice?"

"Yes, see?"

Mary Lou peered over Bobby's shoulder at her daughter and Alice raised a smile from beneath her tears. Mama smiled back.

"We don't live here. I'll help you get yourself sorted out and then we'll take a ride home."

"That'd be nice. I'd like to eat first though."

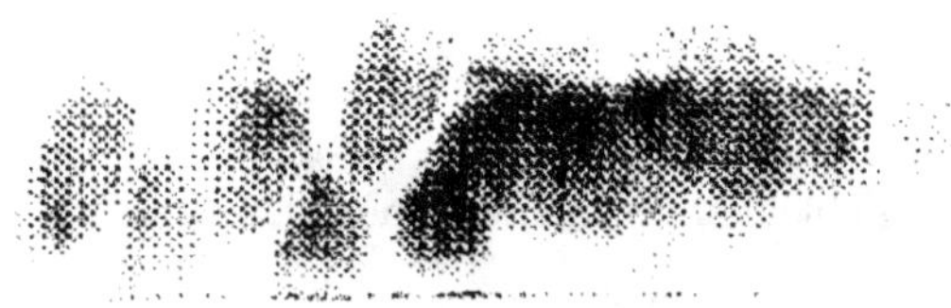

162

THE JOURNEY FROM the Palace was filled with silence in between awkward pauses. Alice was beside herself, unsure how to respond to her mother who appeared unaware anything unusual might have happened. Naldo drove with Bobby in the front passenger seat, leaving the women in the back.

"Would you like us to stop at a diner so you can have a break?"

"Not at all, dear. There's no need to fuss—I'm fine."

"Do you remember why you went to the Palace?"

"Did I? Don't think I did, dear. You might be mistaken about that."

"Leave it, Alice. We won't get very far asking her those sort of questions."

She stared out the window and held Mama's hand. It felt feeble like a child's and Alice wondered how she had become an adult. Didn't seem right. Not at all. The view from the freeway was pure tedium, but it gave her the opportunity to run through what had happened to Mama.

The woman was confused—far more so than Alice had ever imagined possible. To not know of your whereabouts or how you got there... A stream of tears left her eyes as the impact of the meaning of that hit home. But Mama wasn't old. That kind of senile confusion was reserved for much older people. Try telling that to Mama's addled mind.

Forty minutes later, Naldo pulled off the road and stopped at a diner. Despite her protestations, Mary Lou chowed down on a burger and fries while the other three had coffee and cake.

"My Frank and I spent one summer eating in diners. Lots of burgers, gallons of soda. They were good times."

Bobby eyed Alice who looked back at him and glanced at her mother.

"Weren't you fleeing the scene?"

"I guess so, yes. But they were happy days before the darkness set in."

"Darkness?"

"When I was on my own and you kids were born. Canada was a lonely time for me."

"We were babies, right?"

"Little ones. Babes in arms. Cute."

Alice smiled at the idea of being small and cuddled by Mama. Comfort from invented memories. Then the reality of the current situation slammed into her head and another tear rolled down her cheek.

WHEN THEY ARRIVED back at Oakcrest Drive, the family sat down in the living room and Naldo remained on duty outside, the Markov threat ever present. He was as constant as the Northern Star. Inside, Mary Lou announced she was going upstairs for a rest, maybe to take a nap. This left Alice alone with Bobby and the unspoken problem of her mother's mental health. Until Bobby punctured the silence.

"We can't leave her by herself anymore. She's run off once which means she could do it again."

"You're talking about keeping her prisoner."

"No. Just that we need to get a companion for her otherwise you or I will have to stay with her the whole time. And that's not practical."

"A companion? You make her sound like an old maid."

"Someone with medical training who can keep an eye on her and help tend to her needs, health-wise."

"You mean if she loses her mind again."

"She got confused and forgot where she was, but most of the time she is lucid and functions brilliantly. Be careful to remember she is still your mom and deserves your respect."

"Don't talk like that. I am aware exactly who she is. This isn't easy for me. I know I questioned her decision-making because I disagreed with her conclusions. The idea that was the start of something else plain hurts right now because we've done nothing to help her. We focused on ourselves. Never considered that she might have been hurting."

Bobby fumbled around with a cigar and lighter to take his mind off Alice's insights. He poked three holes in one end but the flint wouldn't spark even after six attempts. Alice walked over, sat beside him and used hers instead.

"We have to work with each other on this. We are both in pain now, but we have to acknowledge we will be stronger together than if we lash out at the other."

"This is a shit sandwich, for sure."

"And you're right. We need a nurse so if she goes off the rails, there's someone there to catch her who is experienced in these things."

"In the meantime, I'll get Naldo to call in one of his most trusted guys, who can be a bodyguard until we find someone better qualified. As much as I'd like Naldo to do the job, we need his talents elsewhere at the minute. We are at war with Nikolay Markov and must put that to bed."

"And soon, otherwise Mama's forgetfulness will be the least of our problems."

Bobby puffed on his stogie and let himself vanish in the moment. Alice watched him and tried to find solace in that they'd reached a decision and from now on, at least, Mama would remain safe.

The other reason Bobby stayed with his cigar was that the next thing he would have to do would be to go upstairs and explain to Mary Lou she needed a bodyguard and had to give up her car keys. This was not a conversation he wanted to have, but he understood Alice should be left out of it so there was only one bad cop in town. Even though he didn't want it to be him.

"SHE'S ASLEEP AGAIN."

"Did you tell her about the companion?"

"Yeah. She is not happy because she can't see it's necessary. To her, there are blanks in her life: she is unaware of what is going on."

"That's a blessing. Knowing you were losing your memory would be far worse."

"Devastating for Mary Lou, for sure, but easier for us because we could talk to her about it and she might see the sense in what we say. As it is, she believes we're crazy and over-obsessed."

"She won't like the next thing we have to do, will she?"

"What's that?"

"She can't be head of the family any more."

Bobby looked at his lap and his shoulders drooped. Alice was right, but he didn't want to deal. This was the woman he'd spent twenty-five years living with, loving and who had turned his dismal life around. Now he needed to be her rock as she had been for him. And it hurt.

"I suppose so."

"S'pose? We have seen the choices she's made and the consequences of her actions. We cannot allow her to keep control. Mama must pass the responsibility over to someone else—or more than one of us. I don't want you to see this is some kind of power grab by me. All I'm asking is to make sensible decisions that'll mean we survive this week and have sound leadership after that. Who does it is less important right now than the fact it needs to be done."

"AND HOW DO you propose we get Mary Lou to step down?"

Alice sighed, the air in her lungs escaping from the truths she was about to utter.

"She won't volunteer because she isn't sufficiently aware of what is going on. So we need to agree which of us heads up the organization and let her think what she likes in her more lucid moments. In reality, she is the best consigliere this family could have—no disrespect, Bobby."

"So we sideline her."

"We have little choice that I can see. Mama wants to lead us into a bloody suicide mission against Markov and the mob will kill her in a matter of days if she fails. Now is the time for action. We leave our regrets for another day."

"But I still don't like to hear you say those things. You're braver than me."

Bobby glanced up at Alice who was wiping a tear away from her left eye. No one was in a good place right now. To confront the reality of Mary Lou's difficulties took every fiber of strength and resilience in his body. Alice needed him to be stronger than he felt because she was correct. They had to be there for each other if they were to survive.

"WE CAN'T DO this alone."

"What do you mean?"

"We must include Frank. If we don't get him involved, he won't understand what's going on with Mary Lou. We'd look like we were plotting a coup against your mom instead of saving her life."

"Agreed."

"Also, if you mean what you say, we could end up deciding he is the best person to lead the family."

"That is possible. But I'm telling you I wouldn't be happy about it."

"That's a discussion for another time. First, we need to get him here and away from his jaunt in San Francisco. Next, we agree on what to do to save Mary Lou's life. Succession can wait until the weekend."

Bobby winked because of the absurdity of what he'd just said. The idea such momentous events were occurring right here, right now and not in several decades time seemed ridiculous to him. This was never meant to happen. Bobby always banked on him being long dead before anything happened to his Mary Lou.

Alice's stomach was constricted to the point of agony. The dull ache in the rest of her body had conspired to a position in her belly that made a pure pinpoint of pain. She wanted to cry and never stop but she needed to hold it together. The tears wouldn't help Bobby, who must hurt too, and she didn't want to show him weakness because she was damn sure she should be the head of the family.

Now was not the time to throw her name into the ring but the idea lingered just as the emotional impact of Mama's situation rattled around her ribcage. The funny thing was it was easier to think about that than focus on Mama's mental state, even though it was the task at hand. Was she so wrapped up in herself or was it a displacement activity to avoid the awful truth she could barely bring herself to say in her head, let alone out loud?

"Let's send word to Frank it's time for a family conference."

"Tonight. We can't afford to wait. He needs to haul ass."

"I'll put Naldo on it. Worst case, he drives over to SF and brings him back."

"Might need a conversation with you—not from me."

"We'll see what happens. Either way, we need to get matters settled before we go to sleep tonight. The clock is ticking on Mary Lou's life."

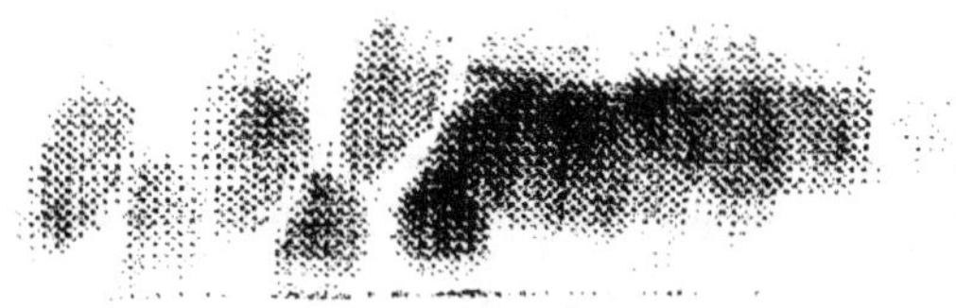

163

NALDO RETURNED FROM San Francisco with Frank in the passenger seat, not impressed with being instructed to come to Palm Springs. Again. To be dragged back by Friscetti was the icing on the cake. He was not in a good humor by the time he arrived and wanted everyone to know about it.

With Mary Lou resting, the other two were in the conservatory waiting for his arrival. The edges of Alice's eyes were red and Bobby sniffed more than usual. There had been raw emotions in the house earlier and even Frank could sense the stress oozing out of the others.

"I'm here. Where's Mama?"

"Upstairs. She's asleep."

"So we must wait for her before this urgent meeting can take place."

"Not really. We three need to talk—thanks for coming back so quickly."

"Naldo was quite insistent for a goon."

"He's more than a hired hand to us as you know, but that's not important right now. We must stay focused."

"On what?"

"Mama got lost yesterday. Plain vanished and wound up in the Palace, not able to explain or remember how she arrived there."

Frank listened but his expression implied he didn't believe what he heard.

"But you found her and all's good. I still don't see what I'm doing here and why you are in a blind panic."

Bobby told Frank about Mary Lou's visit to Little Italy and the clear and present danger provided by Vito. Two minutes later and Frank understood why he'd been driven back to Oakcrest Drive. Alice remained silent because of how incendiary their conversations could be.

"So we must finish our business with Markov in the next couple of days."

"Yes, in such a way that we're alive at the end."

"I return to Bay City and execute the fucker."

"That is still not viable. We need to agree a plan that'll work—guaranteed."

"Nikolay's death resolves the problem."

"It would if we could kill him, but there is no meaningful way to be sure he will die."

"As much as you want to assassinate him, now is not the time. Once we get over this hump, we can pick our moment and skin him alive if we choose. The war must end for certain in the next couple of days or Mama dies."

Frank stared at Alice and tried to process the notion they were going to allow Markov to breathe longer than he wanted.

"And that is the second item on the agenda. The first thing we have to deal with is the best way to get Mary Lou to step down as head of the family."

"You have to be fucking joking."

"If only. She is not in a fit state to do the job anymore. We need to be strong for her and help her move on to be our consigliere."

Alice and Bobby said nothing more as Frank's eyes flitted left and right as he tried to make sense of what he was hearing. His first instinct was to strike out and punch the wall, hit Bobby or slap Alice, but he was aware enough to know that none of these options would get him anywhere. Denial seemed an excellent choice but an hour later Frank continued to receive the same message and it wasn't shifting. His views would need to change instead.

"HOW ARE WE doing this?"

"With respect to your Mama and as smooth a transition as possible."

"Sure. I meant who will take over?"

"Doesn't have to be one person."

"Yes it does, sis'. No organization can be run by a committee. Nothing'll get agreed."

"If all three of us had a vote, then that would work fine."

"Apart from the fact that you two would always vote against me."

"Not necessarily, Frank. But we're getting ahead of ourselves. The question isn't about who should take over leading the family. I'll say it again: how can we get Mary Lou to step down, because I don't want to force her out—unless we have no other option."

"I WILL NOT be the one to push her off her perch. That's plain wrong. Our Mama deserves better than that."

"She does but we don't have the time to wait for her to agree. She doesn't think there is a problem—though we three know there is. We owe her—and all she's built up over these years—to do what's best for the family even if it's not in her short-term interests."

"Fine words sis', but it doesn't wash. I won't usurp our mother."

"If you don't, then I will. You kids might feel yourselves conflicted but I must do the right thing. I might not like it but there's more at stake than my feelings or your Mama's ego—as much as that pains me to say it."

Frank stood up, cheeks all red, and Bobby got out of his chair to square off against him.

"Cool it, guys. Stop acting like a pair of silver-backed gorillas."

The two men were ten feet apart, separated by potted plants and occasional tables.

"No one's pushing my Mama off the mercy seat."

Frank pulled out a revolver from behind his back and within an instant, Bobby aimed his piece directly at Frank's heart. Alice watched the two for a second and grabbed her snub nose out of her bag. She stepped backwards one pace, both hands gripping her gun first pointing at Frank then switching to Bobby, repeatedly.

"We all need to put our weapons down or someone will get hurt."

That was when a bullet blazed through the conservatory followed by a shower of other slugs coursing into every surface in the room.

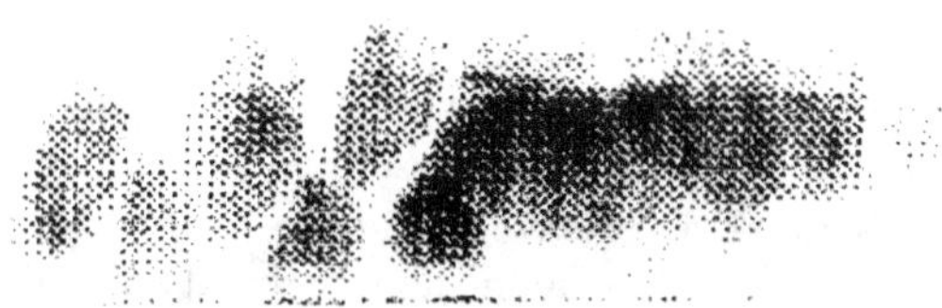

164

ALL THREE SLAMMED to the floor and elbowed their way near to some furniture.

"Where's it coming from?"

"Outside somewhere. I've got no fix on it. Have you?"

"Nope. No idea. How the fuck did they get close enough to make the hit?"

"What about our men?"

The answer arrived as soon as the question left Frank's lips. The sound of a separate wave of bullets from a different distance punctured the drone of the original onslaught. And still they were pinned to the floor with no way to fight back.

The glass in all the windows had all but shattered and bullet holes littered the walls. A woman screamed. Alice couldn't tell if it was Irma in the kitchen or Mama upstairs. The sheer volume of the gunfire made any analysis impossible. Bobby turned his face to look outside and, with a trained professional's eye, he reached a simple conclusion.

"Far end of the backyard at the tree line. Three maybe four shooters. Automatic rifles. Don't waste your bullets even if you've got a clean shot: they are not nearly close enough to take out."

Alice blinked and watched Frank grip his pistol more tightly as though paralyzed with anger at not being able to deliver immediate and bloody revenge.

"Just stay down for now. Either they leave of their own accord or our fellas will deal with them."

"How much armory did they bring with them?"

"Enough to piss me off. If this is an assassination attempt, they fired way too early. Means somebody only wants to scare us."

"Well it's fucking working."

And still the slugs landed inside the conservatory. Bobby had maneuvered himself by a piece of solid wall either side of two broken windows. From there he'd occasionally pop his head far enough out to get a glimpse of the world beyond the summerhouse. But he only gave himself half a second otherwise it would have been his last.

The twins sucked the tiled floor as though there was no tomorrow. Even Frank, despite his bravado, had the smarts not to raise his head too high, let alone try to fire back. He might be an arrogant son of a bitch but he wasn't stupid and understood that Bobby knew his way around situations like this. Frank, on the other hand, was a novice.

ANOTHER MINUTE AND everything fell silent inside but there was still the noise of shots in the backyard.

"Stay down. Nobody moves until I give the word."

Alice intended to spend the rest of her life on the floor and had no intention of being the first up. Frank considered sitting up and firing two rounds but heeded Bobby's advice.

Thirty seconds later and no more shots or sounds until sirens appeared in the distance.

"The local cops took their time. Isn't the captain on our payroll."

"He was."

"Not any more it would seem."

A shout came from the gloom. Naldo informed them that three of the four assailants were dead and a fourth was in the wind.

"How many of ours?"

"Two deceased, one injured. The cops will be here any minute and we've got weapons we need to hide."

"Keep doing what you are doing. You're a life saver."

"Prego."

Bobby indicated it was okay to breathe again. Frank went to see if Irma had been hit and Alice ran upstairs to check on Mama. She was hiding under the bed, sobbing.

"It's all over, Mama. We're all safe."

"The mob's come to kill me."

"We've no idea who's responsible right now. Could be New York but I am not sure that makes sense. Why warn you and then go back on their word?"

"They have done much worse, dear."

"I'm certain."

Alice helped Mary Lou scurry out from her hiding place and brushed her clothes with her hand to make her look less bedraggled.

"We need to get you a bodyguard."

"Definitely. They've failed once and they're sure to try again."

THE COPS CAME into the house and spent the rest of the night bagging and tagging corpses, taking statements and following procedures that made them a general nuisance. The lieutenant in charge of the investigation knew the score: complete the paperwork fast and get out of the residence quick. As he was leaving, Bobby shook his hand and planted five C-notes in the guy's palm. They'd wait until Bobby gave the go-ahead before they identified bodies or poking their noses into Lagotti family business.

Once the uniforms and detectives had departed, Bobby put Mary Lou back to bed. Then he locked the door between the conservatory and living room. Naldo had already doubled the guard on the perimeter as soon as the police had finished interviewing him. For a man in the middle of all that gunfire, he sure saw and heard nothing.

"Who did it? Anyone got any ideas?"

"Mama said it was New York but why would they?"

"Perhaps Markov. Or somebody else trying to move in on us. There's been heat in Chicago, Las Vegas and Boston recently. Some bright spark might have thought to attack the family while our attention was on Markov."

"True. Does Markov have the balls to lay on tonight's treat?"

"Yes. That man's ego is limitless and he has the resources to pull it off."

"Doesn't answer how the hell they got so close. Like one of ours turned rat."

"If we have a traitor in our midst, Naldo will find them, extract all the information we need from them and dispose of the body afterwards."

THE CRACK OF the gun sent Alice spinning, just as the speck of Mama's blood landed on her cheek.

Ten minutes later after the initial Sturm und Drang was over, Alice's stomach felt heavy like a a burden had been added to her body. And she experienced that weight as a dull ache masquerading as an unvoiced roar. As though a fractured yell was about to erupt from deep inside her. Only she knew that she would not—or could not—release that primal scream. It was bound, coiled inside. A cobra that would never leap on its prey. An agony that would never fade.

Ten hours later and the initial shock had abated and that first pang of hurt was less intense. Still noticeably there inside her, but now Alice could walk around without experiencing the jagged edges of her sorrow. She sat in the church listening to the priest eulogizing over her Mama. The ground glass of her sadness eked into every pore and the abject misery of her world permeated all her being.

FEBRUARY 1997

165

NEXT MORNING, MARY Lou padded downstairs with one thought rattling in her head.

"Whoever attacked us last night must die."

Bobby, Alice and Frank all nodded agreement at the sentiment but knew there was no action to be taken at present because they still had no clue who'd done it. Naldo said the hit men were from out of town and he'd never seen than before. That almost ruled out New York because Naldo remained connected to the fellas back east.

"When we find out who it is, then they'll get theirs."

"Must be the Russian. Let's kill the Russian."

"We've been over this, Mama. The guy can't be whacked that easily. Frank's spent a week in the same city as that mook and the fella still breathes. Do you think your son would have let him live if he'd had the opportunity of killing him?"

"I see. Why didn't you kill him, Frank?"

"Too closely guarded and by fierce dudes too. Mean fuckers and professional: knew what they were doing."

"If Frank can't take him out, who are we going to get to do the job?"

Alice and Bobby glanced at each other like they were living through their own Groundhog Day. Frank witnessed for himself Mama's grasp of the complex situation they found themselves in. Mary Lou could not see what all the fuss was about. It was as plain as the nose on her face that the what's-his-name Russian must die.

"WE MUST END the war, Mama. So that means we need to make a truce instead."

"Peace? I thought you said we finish the war. And you do that by fighting harder than the other side."

"Not always. We will win against Nikolay Markov by beating him to the punch. If we negotiate the peace well, we get better access to his territories."

"And lull him into a false security so we can whack him at our leisure later on."

"That's my boy. Let's snare us a Russki."

"But first sit down and agree a deal. That'll get the outfit off your back and we all breathe safer then."

"The mob: I've tangled with them before."

After an hour, the family got Mary Lou to focus more on a peace accord and less on whacking Nikolay.

"Let's send Naldo over with a message we want the violence to end and to sit down and talk terms —again."

"Good idea, Mama."

NALDO HAD GROWN tired of the constant trips to Fog City: too many hills and no one knew how to cook a bowl of pasta properly. Always soggy, never al dente. The first order of business was to speak with Isaak Vasilev and keep him in the loop. If Vasilev was as good as Frank claimed, he would know Naldo was in dialog with Markov and might draw the wrong conclusion.

Isaak was a shrewd one and, while the conversation was cold, he offered Naldo only professional courtesy and respect. Naldo didn't trust the fella's heritage, but they were both key participants in the lives of the rival twins. For him that meant they should follow the hierarchy but could still work well together for the greater good. Isaak appeared to treat his allegiance to Frank as all-encompassing. Perhaps Naldo took the same attitude when he was Isaak's age. Now, even Naldo had gained a sense of realpolitik and understood it was better to get along with people than create unnecessary enemies when all he wanted to do was kill for a living and protect those under his care.

With Isaak onside, they figured out the best way to send a message to Markov was to have a quiet word with Lara Mikhailov, one of Nikolay's associates who had performed her fair share of murder and mayhem these past weeks. Naldo visited her that lunchtime while Isaak lay outside on the opposite roof training a rifle sight at her head.

"FORGIVE THE INTRUSION on your meal, but I need to speak with you on a most urgent matter."

Mikhailov looked up from her newspaper, eyes flitting sideways seeking potential danger.

"Do not be concerned. I am here for a conversation with you and nothing more. If you think about it, were I to want you dead then you'd be slumped over your brisket by now. May I sit down?"

"For sure. And what's to stop me shooting you? I don't like strangers coming up and disturbing my lunch."

"Apart from the fact we are surrounded by witnesses and a sniper's aiming at your head as we speak? Nothing, but you wouldn't hear the message I wish to impart to you from Mary Lou Lagotti."

The name got Mikhailov's attention more than any of Naldo's other words and she put her silverware down to listen.

"We want to arrange a meet-up. We are all losing money and burying good people. Neither is great for business, so it should stop. The fighting must end and we need to agree the peace."

"How do I know I can trust you?"

"You don't, but a single hand gesture on my part or any outward sign of menace on yours and you will be dead. The fact I haven't instigated your killing should show our good faith. If I wanted to carry on with our war, then I should kill you. Right here, right now."

Naldo stared into her beady blue eyes and Mikhailov glared back. Four intimate seconds later and she blinked and relaxed her upper body.

"Suppose I take you at your word, what are you proposing?"

"ALL WE NEED is to agree a neutral venue and that the aim of the talks is to find an acceptable peace. A hotel in the tourist district or on the edge of town would suit us fine. Just not in the Tenderloin."

"And would reparations for past conduct be on the table?"

"As much as it needed to be to agree a peace. Remember, there has been loss on both sides so we shouldn't fixate on monetizing our corpses."

"You have the blood of my friends on your hands."

"I am sure we do and your fingers reek of the guts of our fallen. But we still want a truce and to get back to earning money."

A waiter arrived and Naldo ordered an espresso. Mikhailov continued her chewing, occasionally taking a sip from her glass of water—although Naldo couldn't be sure it wasn't vodka.

"And why now do you come here with your white flag and a promise of a bright tomorrow? What has changed since last week?"

"We have lost enough money and want the pipe to flow again."

"Nothing to do with any trouble in Palm Springs you had? We heard about the attack on the Lagotti house. Sorry business, hitting a person's home. Did anyone get hurt?"

"The housekeeper needed stitches and the morgue received three visitors. Was your hand in that?"

"No. If I had then the four Lagotti family members would be dead and not seeking peace."

Naldo scratched his chin and Mikhailov raised her eyebrows and widened her eyes as if to prepare for her imminent assassination at the hands of Isaak's sniper rifle. Naldo smiled.

"Don't be alarmed. Sometimes an itch is all that irritates me… Let's be clear: you and I are cut from the same cloth. We are professional people who can sniff bullshit a mile away because our lives usually depend on it. You could have killed me the minute I walked up to your table with the piece resting on your lap. My sniper could have taken you out any second after that, but we haven't because we understand there is time for action and a moment to listen. Make no mistake: tell Nikolay Markov to agree to sit down and thrash out a mutually agreeable truce. Both sides must earn money."

Naldo stood up and placed enough green to cover the cost of his espresso and her meal, including tip. Then he headed for the door and walked down the street. Isaak maintained position with Mikhailov in his sights for more than a minute as she continued eating her lunch.

He considered squeezing the trigger but thought better of it: Frank would not have been happy. Isaak dismantled the rifle and returned it to its case. Then he hopped over the top of two roofs and scuttled down a fire escape.

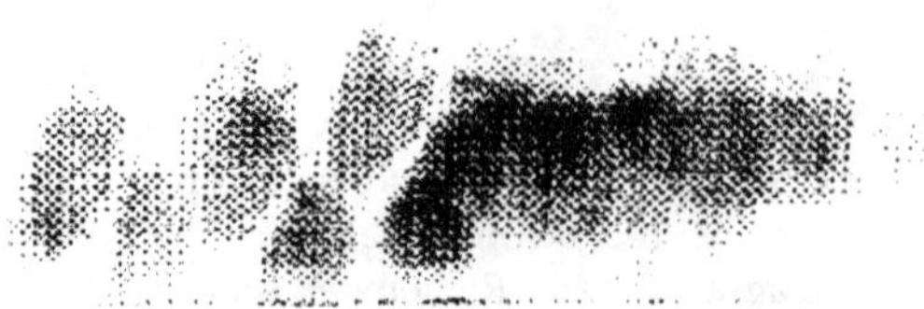

166

MARY LOU SAT on a sun lounger staring out at the pool. The rest of the family were in the summerhouse planning the strategy for the peace conference. They didn't want her there: every time she made any suggestion, someone would shoot her down. What was the point? Besides, the fastest solution to their war with Markov was a single bullet. That much was clear.

Her only problem was to find a person who'd be willing to act as Markov's executioner. The fear behind her daughter's eyes when Alice came back from secretly meeting him was sufficient justification for his death in Mary Lou's mind. Add in the current difficulties and she saw no reason to sit down and talk with that mook.

Naldo and Isaak stood outside the summerhouse door, guarding the occupants while keeping a surreptitious eye on Mary Lou, who would glance up at them now and again. She was still getting used to the permanent bodyguard assigned to her. At the height of her power, she'd protected herself and not relied on anybody else. She didn't see herself as old, but she recognized she wasn't as fast as twenty years before.

The back of her throat was dry, so she got up, but instead of heading to the kitchen, she wandered over to Isaak.

"I need some help indoors. Can you come with me please?"

Isaak looked to Naldo who returned the glance but had nothing to say for himself. So Isaak followed Mary Lou through the conservatory, up the stairs and into her bedroom. He still had no idea what he was doing there.

MARY LOU SAT on the edge of the bed after Isaak closed the door. He stiffened, uncertain of where this situation was heading. She smiled a warm curl of lips and beckoned for him to sit on the stool by the vanity mirror. Isaak relaxed and slumped down.

"There is something I would like you to do for me."

"Tell me and it is done."

"Thank you, but wait until I say what I want before you agree: go back to San Francisco tonight and kill Nikolay Markov. A knife in the chest, a bullet through his brains or a bomb under his car. It doesn't matter how you do it but that fucker must not be breathing in the morning."

Isaak shuffled on his seat, knowing this was the exact opposite of what the rest of her family wanted. But she was the head of the outfit. He couldn't think straight and played it cool to figure things out later.

"Can I enlist any help?"

"No one who's connected to the Lagottis, but if you need a local hand, knock yourself out. The important thing is that Markov must die and the only two people to know who did it are sat in this room right now."

Mary Lou glared at Isaak to impress on him the severity of her requirements and the significance of their secrecy. He shuffled again and averted his gaze from Mary Lou's stare. Fucked if he did. Fucked if he didn't. At this rate, Isaak wouldn't be alive after St Valentine's day.

"AND THIS CAN'T wait until the peace conference, with respect?"

"You mean, it'd be easier to hit a few at the same time?"

"It would make a bigger statement if it happened in public, so to speak."

"Interesting…"

Mary Lou brooded on Isaak's idea, giving it the full focus of her mind, even though he'd only said it to buy himself some much needed space to think. He was surprised she'd given it the time of day.

"You'll be in the protection detail at the meet-up, won't you?"

"I'd expect so. I mean, nothing's been decided yet, but…"

"That settles it. Once the meeting is over, you attack Markov before he leaves the room. He mustn't get out alive. And this has the added advantage that I watch him die with my own eyes."

"We'll all be frisked so I won't be carrying a rod."

"You will know the venue in good time and can make the arrangements. I'll leave you to figure out the details."

Mary Lou got off the bed and held open the door. Isaak took three or four seconds to get the hint, then he sprang up and walked out to resume his position outside the summerhouse door.

"What she want?"

"To find out if I thought a sniper could have a line of sight into her bedroom window."

"And?"

"I told her the answer was no."

"Took you long enough."

"I know you don't need or want to hear this but my grandfather said something to me on his deathbed and I'd like to share it with you."

"What was that, then?"

"Don't fuck your boss's mom."

"Wise guy, your grandfather."

"He was in an outfit."

They both smiled, wallowing in their own wit, but Isaak didn't know which way to turn. Somehow he was being set up by Mary Lou, the butt of someone's lethal joke, and there was no way out of it.

TWO HOURS LATER as the sun set, Bobby, Alice and Frank came out of the summerhouse to grab some fresh air and to clear their heads. Planning was a tiring business. Bobby sauntered into the main house and Alice plonked herself down onto a sun lounger, then lit a cigarette.

Frank paced up and down beside the pool, taking quick puffs from his smoke. Naldo and Isaak remained tethered to their posts, but when Frank stormed inside, Isaak followed him in. Naldo stood impervious to the goings on around him—or so it appeared.

In reality, little happened within his sight that wasn't noted and logged for later use. And because he stayed calm, foolish people would forget he was even there. So when Isaak popped into the building behind Frank, Naldo noticed and recorded that fact in his brain. He had no idea if it was a significant action, but if it was, then he had witnessed it and would inform somebody.

Alice continued on the sun lounger and smiled as she caught Naldo's eye. Both she and Bobby acknowledged his presence whereas almost everybody else acted like he wasn't there. Denied his sheer humanity—even Mary Lou treated him as though he was chopped liver. And they had known each other for a lifetime. Naldo had always given her the excuse that she was too important for him to expect her to treat him kindly, but after this many years, that had worn thin.

BY THE TIME Isaak caught up with Frank, he was four paces away from the bathroom. Frank looked askance at Isaak who indicated nothing was as urgent as Frank's immediate biological needs. When he came out a few minutes later, Isaak was still there, waiting and delivering his words in a hushed tone.

"I need to speak to you as a matter of supreme urgency."

Frank dried his hands on the back of his pants and ushered Isaak into his room. With the door shut, Isaak spoke his mind.

"Mary Lou intends to have Nikolay Markov killed at the end of the peace conference."

Frank eyed him suspiciously as though Isaak had spoken in Classical Armenian. He lit another in a chain of cigarettes and continued to stare at Isaak.

"How do you know?"

"Because Mary Lou asked me to do the killing. And now I'm telling you because I understand that is not the course of action that has been agreed by you and the others in your family. I am in an impossible state. If I don't follow Mary Lou's instructions, she will have me killed. If I carry out what she asks, you, Alice or Bobby will kill me for breaking the peace agreement. On that basis, I am letting you know of my situation and seek your advice how you want me to proceed."

Frank let out a slow whistle and considered matters for a moment.

"SHE WANTED ME to go to San Francisco tonight and whack him but I got her to delay the timing of the hit because if I had not then Markov would be dead by now and your plans would have been in tatters."

"But at the peace conference?"

"It was the first thing I thought of that she might have agreed to. But it won't happen, right?"

"Correct: you are not to hit Nikolay Markov—or any other member of his family without my personal authorization."

"Understood. Will you tell Mary Lou the hit is off because it's not my place?"

"Okay, Isaak. Leave that part to me. You go back to your business and everything will be fine. I'm glad you came and told me: you did the right thing even if you feel as though you've ratted out Mama. You have not at all."

"Thank you for saying so, but it doesn't sit well with me. She is the boss after all."

"You follow the orders you are given, but you are no fool and have shown you have commonsense. That is nothing to apologize for. Go back downstairs and I'll pop down shortly."

Isaak nodded and departed Frank's room relieved to have unburdened himself. He tried not to think what would happen now he'd told Frank, but Isaak was all the better for having shared the load he was carrying. By the pool, Naldo appeared not to have moved a single muscle since Isaak left, but he must have shifted by an inch, surely.

True to his word, Frank sauntered poolside and then the three Lagotti members returned to the summerhouse. A light flicked on inside and drapes were pulled shut, leaving Isaak and Naldo to stand and stare into the half-dark of the evening.

"How long do you think they'll be?"

"No idea but even if they don't want to eat, I sure as hell do. Mind if you cover me for a short while and I grab a sandwich?"

"Not if you make me one and bring it back out with you."

"Deal. Pastrami on rye for two coming right up."

FRANK'S FOCUS WAS only half on the planning taking place. The rest of his mind pondered over what Isaak had said. While he almost admired Mama's desire for violent and bloody resolution to the Markov problem, even he understood that whacking the guy was not practical—at least not now.

This meant Mama's ability to make rational decisions was flawed and so she needed to step down as head of the family. It was too dangerous to let her carry on as she was: the others were right. He dipped back into the conversation, unwilling to consider the implications of his own plan.

"Even if this pact only lasts a few months, we need a piece of their narcotics operation, especially if they have a New York side-deal already in place…"

But Mama wouldn't go voluntarily: she had no idea she had become unhinged. So there was no appealing to reason. And just pretend that somehow she was gone, who would take over?

Frank could imagine Alice wanting the job—her self-belief and arrogance would propel her into trying to run things, but that was not acceptable to him. He could see Bobby leading the outfit well, although Frank reckoned Alice would always have Bobby's ear over him.

Deep down Frank knew the only person who should be boss of the Lagotti family was him. So how to achieve that outcome? Alice wouldn't step aside—she'd need to be pushed. Same with Mama…

"We can't allow them free rein over prostitution either."

"To sweeten matters, we could offer a percentage point or two from our lottery scam."

Frank experienced a cold shiver down his spine just as he noticed a solitary drop of sweat trickle off his forehead. Pushing Mama aside only meant one thing: he was going to kill his mom. And maybe his sister too.

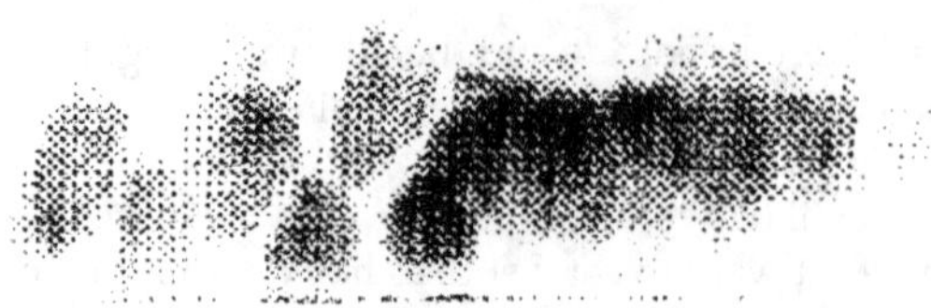

167

FRANK MENTALLY WITHDREW from the room, unable to believe what he'd just thought. That even the idea had flashed across his mind. And, despite his own horror, he was still prepared to countenance her murder. He recoiled and focused on the conversation.

"They already have points on the Lucky Lady and they're not getting another red cent—not after the effort we've put in building it up."

"Could the Queen of Sheba be offered, if only as leverage?"

"Points on it, you mean?"

"I'm not suggesting we give away the family silver. The aim is to offer him enough treats, so he doesn't notice when he's getting screwed. Within twelve months he'll be buried in the desert anyway, but in case we find a use for keeping him alive, we must negotiate in good faith and carve out a solid deal."

"Is there anything we could easily give up?"

"Our east coast interests."

"You're only saying that to goad Frank. Ignore her, will you?"

Frank nodded but did not respond as he was still consumed by the idea of killing his Mama. "Alice would do it if she had the chance," he thought.

MIDNIGHT AND THE planning was over. Bobby and Alice had figured out most of the major details although Frank had chipped in now and again. Alice walked straight up to her room and Bobby stayed in the summerhouse. Frank sat by the pool in the dark while Isaak remained nearby.

Frank lit a second cigarette off his first and stared at the stars. They looked pretty, twinkling away. Those miniature balls of light represented a tranquility he hadn't experienced on this planet, but he knew soon he would get the reward for his years of hard work and persistence.

"Isaak, come over here."

"Sure thing."

"On the day of the peace conference, I have a job for you to do. This is a special mission and is a secret that nobody else must ever know about."

"Okay…"

"You won't be in the meeting but will be located in a nearby building with a sniper rifle. Your target is Mary Lou Lagotti."

Frank wanted Isaak to soak in the news before uttering another word. When he saw Isaak blink, he knew the guy was processing his mission.

"If my sister gets hit too, that's a bonus, but the primary objective is the most important. Any questions?"

"And I'm doing this under your protection?"

"Yes. Once the deed is done, then I'll show my gratitude. Until then, you speak of this to no one. Understand?"

"I do. What about Bobby?"

"There is no need to take him out, but I will not be upset if he died in the crossfire."

"Who will protect you in the room?"

"Don't worry about me. I can look after myself."

Frank chuckled and then checked himself because Isaak was staring at him stone-faced. He was seeing the enormity of the task he'd been given and had nothing to laugh about. They had conspired to murder the boss of the entire family and this was set to happen in a handful of days, not in some theoretical future but before the weekend. Frank dismissed Isaak, lay back and stared at the stars once more. He was on the cusp of victory.

AT ONE IN the morning, Frank realized he hadn't moved and was cold, especially his fingers and toes. He hauled himself upright and slinked indoors, hands in his pockets. Through the conservatory and into the main body of the house. The living room sure was warmer but something was missing. There was a fire in his belly and he wanted companionship: either to share his hopes for the next few days or someone to fuck and he wasn't certain which he needed more. The answer was simple: Sammy.

Frank found Isaak and got him to drive to the west side of town and an unremarkable condo which was one of the many real-estate assets owned by the Lagottis for use as safe houses and crash pads. As she wasn't part of the family, neither Bobby nor Mama were happy for Sammy to spend all her time at home, but Frank had insisted they protect her and that she was nearby for him.

He'd had the presence of mind to call before he drove over—it was the middle of the night—so when he popped the key in the lock, Sammy stood waiting for him in the hallway. She had a bottle of French champagne in one hand and two glasses in the other, wearing only a dirty smile and a red G-string.

"Hi, baby. Figured you might fancy something with a bit of fizz."

"Sure do. Put those things down and we can get started."

SAMMY WOKE UP at four and wondered what the hell had happened. Her nose was next to someone's hairy shins and her crotch hurt and was bruised. She looked around, saw Frank and the recent past came rushing back into view. She'd sashayed into the kitchen to put the champagne in the fridge and when she turned round, Frank stood there as naked as the day he was born.

They licked, sucked and squeezed their way around each other's bodies until she sat on the counter and he forced himself inside her. Even though something didn't feel right to her, he only stopped when he'd come.

Sammy pushed him off and limped to the bathroom to be apart from him for a short while. When she returned, he was sat in bed with two glasses of champagne poured, waiting.

"You hurt me."

"Fuck-a-doodle-do. Sorry babe, I got carried away. Get under the sheets and I'll make it up to you."

IN THE MORNING, Sammy woke first and felt much better about herself. Frank lay sprawled out like a starfish and Sammy reflected how cute he appeared when he was sleeping. He built up a gruff exterior for most people, but she enjoyed being alone with him because he didn't bother pretending with her.

The sheets were on the floor. With goosebumps on her arms, she realized that was why she'd woken up—and she cast an eye over his arms, torso and legs.

"Good morning."

"Sure is."

"I've missed you."

"That's why I came a-visiting. I wanted you."

"Glad you did. You able to stay long?"

"Not really. Things still aren't safe but in a few days' time it will be different."

Frank let the idea hang in the air. He yearned to show off in front of his woman, but knew this was a mighty dangerous plan.

"How so?"

"We'll sort out all the family business. And when that's done, I'll be on top of the world."

Sammy giggled and snuggled into Frank, the thought of wallowing in the shadow of his glory a major aphrodisiac. She ran a hand over his chest and dug her nails into his skin enough to feel him but not to cause him discomfort. She wriggled until her lips were touching an ear and whispered.

"And I'll be on top of you as long as you want."

"It will be a great ride."

"You sure are."

They fooled around more until Frank got hungry and wanted to stop. Sammy hopped out of bed and prepared breakfast for both. Once he'd emptied his plate and glugged back his coffee, Frank made an announcement.

"Gotta go. Keep yourself hot and I'll be back as soon as I can."

He whipped out from under the sheets, threw on his clothes and hustled out the door and into Isaak's waiting car. Sammy lay there for fifteen minutes, then she showered, cleaned up the chaotic mess they'd created and carried on with her day.

168

ALICE WOKE UP and had breakfast in the kitchen, pleased Frank was nowhere to be seen. They were getting on better these last few days than ever before in their lives, but Alice thought they were just on their best behavior due to the Markov trouble rushing toward them at high speed. Once that moment passed—if it did—chances are they'd revert to past patterns. It's what people did.

She crunched her wheat toast and sipped her orange juice in silence, the sounds of her munching echoing around her skull. Irma breezed through and offered to make her a coffee, but Alice declined: she'd wait a little today.

Breakfast downed and OJ slurped, Alice noticed a dragging sound from outside: a terrible screeching of plastic or metal. She popped out to investigate although she knew it was nothing serious: the sentries would have taken care of any external threat.

Mama was hauling a sun lounger from one side of the pool to the other—for no real reason Alice could surmise.

"Let me help you with that."

"Thank you."

"Where do you want it?"

Mary Lou pointed to a shady spot that already had a recliner only ten feet away. Alice smiled but felt ill at ease with the illogical decision Mama had made. She picked up the lounger—none of them were heavy—and brought it past the diving board and over to the other side of the pool.

"There you go."

"Thank you."

Mary Lou shuffled over and placed her towel on the new seating, then she sat down and Alice watched as her body relaxed in the shade created by the summerhouse. Alice took advantage of the calm and rested next to her Mama using the lounger she'd recently spotted. The two women remained silent for a spell until Alice broke the moment.

"I'm worried."

"What about?"

"The Markov situation, of course."

"You don't need to be concerned, Cindy. Everything will be fine."

Alice froze and gripped the armrests of the sun lounger as she heard the name of the long-dead housekeeper: Mama had no idea who she was.

ALICE UNCLAMPED HER hands after three deep breaths and turned her head to face her Mama. Mary Lou was scratching at her elbow, idling the morning away. Her skin was red with the attention it was receiving.

"Don't scratch: it'll only make things worse."

Mary Lou acknowledged with a nod, but carried on gouging her nails into her flesh. Alice did her best to ignore it.

"Do you think we'll be able to get a deal with Markov?"

"Who?"

"Nikolay Markov."

"Oh, you don't need to worry about him. He will be dead soon. You can be sure of that."

"We're not killing him, we are negotiating a peace with him."

"If you say so, dear. But he'll be in the morgue within a week."

Alice ignored this outburst because it made no sense. Even Frank had come round to the idea that they diffuse the Markov clan now and only attack when all the heat from New York was off. Wasn't ideal by a wide margin, but it was the most pragmatic solution and was the surest way to save Mama's life.

Bobby walked past to get to the summerhouse and Alice looked up at him as he journeyed by. When she glanced back at Mama, a red river was trickling down her arm and she kept on scratching, regardless. Alice sprung up and rushed over, pushing Mama's hand out of the wound and holding the elbow up.

"Oh, Mama. I told you not to keep doing that."

There was anger in her voice, partly aimed at her mom and some at herself for not taking care of her better. Of allowing Mary Lou to harm herself right in front of Alice's eyes. She ran to the kitchen to get a towel and instructed Irma to bring a plaster. Five minutes later and everything was calm again— on the surface at least.

ALICE LEFT MAMA with Irma and returned to the house to find the number for the twenty-four-hour nurse. The time for talk was over. Her Mama needed to be cared for and watched over at all times. Since her reappearance at the Palace, all had seemed to settle down and they had become complacent. But no more.

Even though they needed someone over immediately, Alice accepted they'd have to wait three days before anyone reliable could be sent. This was not what she wanted to hear, but she knew she had to accept their fate. In the meantime, Naldo would stand guard around the clock. When he slept, one of the other fellas would take over. Alice would ensure Mama had the best care available and would stay safe.

A quick walk along the outskirts of the grounds and Alice found Naldo to issue him his instructions as a trusted compatriot. Then she went back to the pool to check on Mama: all was good, so she spoke with Bobby in the summerhouse.

BOBBY SAT AT the desk scribbling on a piece of paper and didn't appear to notice Alice was with him. Quarter of a page later, he looked up and nodded, then carried on writing.

"Sorry, I'll be with you in a minute. If I don't write this down now, I will forget it all."

"De nada."

Alice sprawled onto one of the armchairs, trying to remain as cool as ice, knowing she had terrible news to impart and had no idea what to say. Her lips were dry and her tongue stuck to the roof of her mouth. Bobby stopped, put his pen down and sauntered over to the couch, opposite Alice with a low table in between them. He picked up half a cigar from the ashtray in front of him and lit it for the millionth time that day. It had been a busy morning.

"You look like you want to talk."

"Yep… How d'you say Mama's been since we got back from the Palace?"

Bobby sunk into the couch a few inches more, his positive disposition floated out under the crack in the door. He sighed and sat forward in his seat.

"Between the Markovs and New York, I haven't given it too much of my attention."

"Me neither—until just now."

"And?"

"She didn't recognize me and gouged a hole in her arm."

Words floated around, but each one stuck in Alice's throat for an eternity.

"Mama has dementia and we're not helping her by pretending it's not happening. I'm talking about both of us: I am not blaming you for any of this."

Silence.

"I called the nursing agency we found but they can't send anyone over for a couple of days, so Naldo will mind her until then."

Bobby cast his eyes downward and squeezed himself into the smallest space he could fit in. Alice moved over and sat next to him, placing a hand on a shoulder. Tears rolled down his cheeks and he rocked forward and back. A man in pain.

ALICE WASN'T TOO sure what to do. She wanted to offer Bobby solace, but she was experiencing the same agony as him. Where was his comforting hand on her shoulder? He was meant to be the adult and she was the child in their relationship. That had broken down with Mama, but it didn't have to be that way with Bobby. She let him cry his heart out from the mental loss of his wife of over twenty-five years.

"It wasn't supposed to be like this."

"No, but she's alive and physically healthy. Our job is to make sure she survives past the weekend and lives a comfortable life. Some days she'll be with us and others… she will have left the room."

Now Alice couldn't contain herself any longer—all the anguish flooded out in salty tears and Bobby held her in his arms until her crying subsided. Then she kissed him on the cheek and they sat back to collect themselves together.

"You're a good man, Bobby Trevisan."

"That's what your mother used to say to me."

"Still true today."

"Kind of you, but I'm not sure you're right."

"Take the compliments when they land."

"Thank you, then."

"WHEN YOU AND Frank were little, we used to go on picnics and you guys would be content to play with a ball. Your mom and I would lie around watching you two and simply enjoy being in each other's company."

"Happy days. I don't remember that. Earliest memory I have is of a trip Frank and I took to a factory. Some bad guys locked us in a cupboard and Mama rescued us. I didn't know if it was real or a nightmare."

"Real. I'd been out of the business two years and met your mom three or four months before your cupboard ordeal, I think. Feels like it was a lifetime ago."

"For me it was."

Bobby laughed because Alice was right. She and Frank had only just learned to walk when they were kidnapped. All over a pound of heroin and a drug deal gone south. After that the Lagotti family made its mark once Mary Lou whacked Charlie Pentangelo. She had been one hell of a woman.

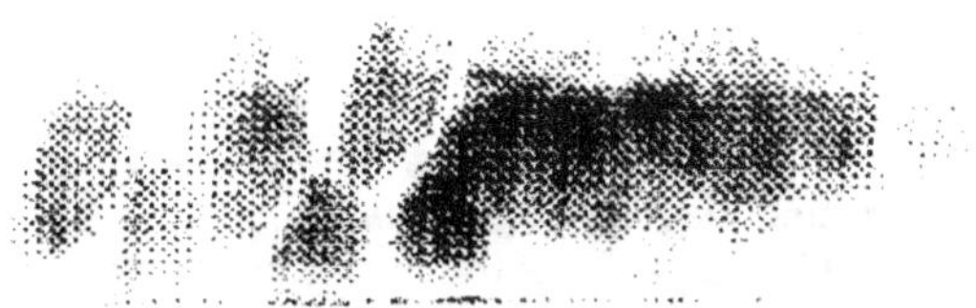

169

"ONCE WE'VE MADE peace with Markov, we will need someone to lead this family."

"Do you have anyone in mind?"

Bobby laughed.

"You, me or Frank. Or a combination."

"Makes sense. If we work together, we make better decisions."

"Yeah. Can the three of us operate as a team?"

Now it was Alice's turn to laugh. Bobby was asking leading questions, just so he wasn't the first one to nix Frank's name on the letterhead.

"I really can't answer. What d'you reckon?"

"It's not my place to stand between you two. Never has, but you guys have unresolved issues, so to speak."

"Been a long time since we agreed on anything. And he's too quick to temper: always looking for a fight. I mean, one minute we agree to negotiate a truce and before the words have left our lips, he runs off to San Francisco maiming, killing and setting up brothels. Those are not the actions of a team player."

"I hear you, but he gets shit done. He flew over to Boston then Atlantic City and created a quality revenue stream from nothing. Neither of us have achieved that."

"And what are the lottery cards? Chopped fucking liver?"

"Sorry, that's something I haven't achieved—not for decades, anyway."

"Better. Sometimes I wonder if anything I accomplish gets noticed. The effort to get the Queen of Sheba up-and-running nearly killed me. Mama was more interested in bailing out her precious Frank. Again."

"We knew how hard you were working and how difficult it was. As you're so reliable, we got into the habit of leaving you alone because you don't generally need hand-holding. Frank has been tied to his mom's apron strings for far too long. It's only since Boston that he's stood on his own two feet."

"So you're saying Frank should run the show?"

"DON'T PUT WORDS in my mouth. I'm just pointing out he's a lot more capable now than he used to be."

"So do you want him or not?"

Bobby sat back and inhaled on his cigar. He enjoyed having the prop in his hand because it was perfect excuse to give himself time to ponder. The end of the stogie glowed orange-red as he took the smoke into his mouth, rolled it around his palate and exhaled.

"He shouldn't run the family. Can't talk about the future, but he's not ready now."

"And what about me?"

"Do you want to? I mean, without me by your side?"

"Dunno. I like the idea of it, but I'm not sure if I am strong enough. Losing Sam hurt me more than I realized and I don't know if I'm weak at heart."

"Mary Lou and I have been an effective double-act for years. You and I could try the same thing—if you were up for it."

"At least until I regained my confidence. I used to say I was going to rule the world. Now I'm not certain I am cut out for global domination."

"You'll get there. The way you've handled yourself over Sam has been amazing. You have shown dignity and class when most people would have either hidden in their rooms or bitch-slapped her into the seventh circle of hell. You did neither and that takes guts. More than you give yourself credit for."

"HOW WILL FRANK react if we carve him out?"

"Not positively. He'd have to go."

For emphasis, Bobby stubbed out the remaining inch of his cigar in the ashtray, grinding it into oblivion. He flicked a piece of tobacco off his hand and it fluttered to the floor. They both watched the brown speck until it was motionless and looked at each other square in the eye.

"Let him keep his east coast businesses and cut commercial ties with him, right?"

"Don't know that'd work, Alice. We might need a more robust response."

That euphemism hung in the air, but Alice didn't want to deal with its implications: that they'd have to kill Frank to stop him from murdering them.

"I couldn't be a part of that. He's my flesh and blood. We are twins…"

Bobby stared at her with a bemused expression. The pair of them had been sparring all their adult lives and now Alice wanted to convince herself she could not deliver the final blow. So be it. If she wouldn't—or couldn't—take care of business then he'd step in and sort matters out to give the family the best chance of a sustainable future.

"Don't worry about it. We send Frank back to AC to empire build and everyone can leave each other in peace."

"Good. And Mama is our consiglieri on her better days."

"Yeah. We need to be careful not to show any weakness tomorrow in front of Markov so, if Mary Lou is able, she should appear to head up the negotiations."

"Cut a deal with Markov and then a smooth transition of power."

"Sounds like a plan."

FRANK HAD GOT himself a taste for Sammy and was spending time with her. While Alice and Bobby were discussing his future, Frank was penetrating Sammy from behind in the shower. Once he was done, they washed themselves and returned to bed to continue their gallivanting.

She didn't enjoy being held prisoner and had been feeling lonely and ignored. There was no point hooking up with a gangster if she was never given the opportunity to show off his fabulous wealth or to live in extremely comfortable circumstances. At least Alice had an amazing place in Malibu—Frank had dumped her in a crummy apartment and not been back for days.

So when Frank came over, her eyes lit up and she wrapped her limbs around his torso until she absorbed all his energy: he was a monster in the sack. For all Alice's intimate understanding of her body, she was a mild lay compared to Frank. Both had their plus points, but being with Frank was exciting and dangerous. Alice wanted to settle down and Frank just wanted fun.

That was the biggest difference between the twins. Sammy was aware of the irony because to the outside world, the greatest contrast was that one was male and the other female. Those details were uppermost in her mind as she went down on Frank again. His sheer physicality literally filled her head and the judders up and down her spine echoed how much he turned her on after she was finished with him and he had returned the oral favor.

MARY LOU SAT by the pool and stared into nowhere. She enjoyed the time by herself: she used it to reminisce about happier or clearer times. And to contemplate her conversations with Father Carmoody. That man sure had changed how she thought about the world. How fleeting was her life on the planet and how you risked an eternity of damnation if you made the wrong choices.

If it would save her soul, Mary Lou would hand the organization over to her children but she felt their own time in hell's fire would be affected. Perhaps they should wind down all their operations. That idea crossed her mind more than once, although she hadn't acted on it yet. A bad deal with Nikolay Markov could be precisely the excuse necessary to pass over the business to him and save her family from the Devil's clutches.

Then the memory of walking past all the cars in the lot, blood dripping off her skirt and her fingers, after her Frank was gunned down at Burbank Airport. Mary Lou recalled each vehicle: color, mark, which direction it was facing in its parking space.

Every little detail like it was yesterday. How she drove five miles below the speed limit all the way back to the hotel. What was its name again? The aroma of his dried blood on her hands. That acrid flavor of rust on her tongue.

Her entire world condensed into a journey across a lot to escape from the FBI and hang on to the takings from the Lansdowne branch of the First Bank of Baltimore. A personal fortune to start the family business which she'd turned into a small empire. Mary Lou and… what's-his-name. They'd done it together.

IN THE EVENING, Frank lay on the bed, head resting on Sammy's thighs. She made a good pillow and he inhaled the scent of sex which was smeared over both their bodies like a high-class perfume. He considered his plan for the peace conference, running through each element in his mind: rehearsing every moment. For him to succeed, he needed to execute a subtle play in the room and Isaak had to deliver the best marksmanship.

Sammy wriggled out from under him and propped him up with pillows. Then she nipped to the bathroom. When she came back into the bedroom, she sashayed off to mix them two cocktails, offering him one, which he gladly took—his mouth seemed parched.

He sank the curious green liquid in a single swig, smacked his lips together and announced his desire for a refill. Sammy shrugged and handed over her own glass as she couldn't be bothered to go off and mess about with the cocktail shaker and all that ice. Too cold and too much hassle.

She stopped right by the bed to reach Frank's hand with the drink. He knocked back the second cocktail, throwing the receptacle onto the carpeted floor causing it to bounce once and roll to a halt on the other side of the room. Sammy giggled as Frank turned around to face her. His head was inches from her groin and he placed a palm round her ass to draw her in nearer until she collapsed on top of him. As soon as he was done, Frank pushed her off and stood up to put his clothes on. Then his shoes.

"Been a blast. I'll be back tomorrow evening. Wear your red G-string for when I come over."
He closed the front door before Sammy had time to say a word. She dialed for a pizza and rummaged around to find a dressing gown before the boy with her food appeared wanting his tip.

170

THE PALLADIUM HOTEL used to be a go-to venue in San Francisco, but its heyday had long since receded. Nowadays, families occupied it in high season as a cheap alternative to one of the plush hotels in town. The rest of the year, sales reps and conference delegates took advantage of its competitive rates.

Half the rooms boasted a balcony view of the bay and a well-stocked minibar, comprising an array of liquor, bandages and prophylactics. Nobody assumed all three would be used at the same time, but this was San Francisco so no one judged.

The reason the Palladium survived despite its tawdry exterior was its location—and its competitive rates. This combination was the precise set of reasons Naldo selected the hotel for the peace conference. It was cheap, in the middle of town and there were loads of civilians milling all around in case anyone planned any funny business.

Both sides had scoped the meeting room on the second floor together. Each item of furniture subjected to a rigorous check: there was nothing hidden underneath, inside or elsewhere. Either Naldo or Lara Mikhailov slid a hand behind the mirror and the various paintings on the walls to ensure no blades were available for use if tensions arose. Once they were both satisfied, Naldo and Mikhailov stayed guard outside the only door into the place.

Bobby, Alice, Frank and Mary Lou arrived around ten and Nikolay appeared two minutes later. Everyone acknowledged each other, but no one shook hands. Coffee and water was served and everybody sat down, apart from Naldo and Mikhailov who continued to stand behind their respective leaders.

"If I had known so many of you were coming, I'd have brought my entire family this morning too."

Nikolay smirked and sipped his coffee. Alice ground her molars and held back the disgust she felt for this man. Mary Lou smiled benignly, because she didn't care about Nikolay's childish comment or because she had no idea who he was or what she was doing there.

"Shall we get on? We are here to broker a truce, not engage in idle chat."

"YOURS IS A large outfit with resources stretching from coast to coast. We are a small family with control over the Tenderloin and not much more."

"Nikolay, you do yourself an injustice. Your friends stretch all the way to Russia, so let's not pretend you have no reach. If you were just a cockroach, we'd have crushed you like a bug by now."

"Thank you for recognizing I am someone to be reckoned with. We all work hard in this pitiful country."

"The land of opportunity is big enough for all of us to carve out successful lives. We must agree how to slice up San Francisco."

"The way I see things, you came to my city, stole from me and killed my own. We agreed an accommodation and then you returned, took some more and attacked me again. You owe me and all we need to decide is how you shall pay for the harm you caused me."

Before Alice responded, Frank slammed his fist on the table, causing everyone to jump perceptibly and to rattle every cup of coffee in the room.

"Listen to me, little man: there has been damage done to both sides. What you need to consider more is how to make restitution for the killings with your name on it. If you think I'll bend over and take it up the ass from you, you're smoking more opium than you can sell."

Frank glared at Nikolay, who responded with a casual stare and gritted teeth. People didn't talk to him with such scant respect usually and survive. Mary Lou smiled benignly at the argument unfolding before her and Alice maintained her composure. Her primary aim was to prevent Mama from saying too much, so Frank's outburst aligned with her interests. As agreed, Bobby intended to remain silent for as long as possible, so there was one calm voice if tempers frayed.

"THE WAY I see things: we've got you by the balls because we have cut off your heroin supply and that musta hurt business. Without the brown sugar, how could you keep your skanks sedated enough to fuck the degenerates you get in your whorehouses? And your operations rely on the cash you generate from selling those bags too. So talk less about reparations and more about what you will do to convince us to open your franchises again."

"I am sure we are here to discuss, negotiate and agree, boy. If you want me to not make demands of you then you must stop laying down the law to me."

Frank stared through Nikolay and Mikhailov adjusted position to his right to get a better take on Frank's state of mind. Alice looked to Frank, then to Nikolay and finally on Mikhailov—in case she tried a move against Frank. No one needed to resort to violence given they were sat around a table talking.

"LET US BE clear. You admit you are blocking our supply lines, so the first thing you must do is to open our access to our own narcotics."

"Of course, we can do that but you get nothing for nothing in this life. What will you offer in return?"

Nikolay smiled again and glanced out the window as a boat motored across the view. Then his attention floated back inside the room and he focused on Frank and his challenge.

"What could I possibly give you that you don't already possess?"

"Someone in your position should have the imagination to make an offer and, even if you can't, you should be aware enough of your gang's actions to name something within your largesse. If you are the man, you think you are."

"Do not goad me, boy."

"Stop acting like the cheerleader who got fucked by the jock at the end of the prom and didn't expect anything to happen. You are here to negotiate and all you've done so far is to piss and moan."

Nikolay remained silent and drummed his fingers on the table. The annoyance seeped out of his fingertips until he regained his composure. Hard to tell if it was because Frank had called him on his behavior or because Markov would be forced to give something up. Frank remembered never to put out any number first in a negotiation, so was desperate to force Nikolay's hand, but the Russian didn't want to play ball. Maybe he'd received the same advice.

"PROSTITUTION. I CAN offer you a percentage of that San Francisco racket, if it was of interest."

"Always into making money out of fucking. We could open the supply lines for fifty per cent of your prostitution revenues and leave you to run San Francisco. Or we could accept only twenty cents on the dollar, but you would cease interfering with any of our whorehouses in town."

"A fifth for doing nothing. That's quite an offer."

"The revenue keeps your skanks alive and the smack flowing. Don't make yourself seem foolish: you understand the value of what I'm offering—and it's insulting for you to pretend otherwise."

"You forget why you are here, boy. Our biting at your heels so much has impacted your operations. Not just in this city, but your lottery racket is within our reach. So don't talk to me like a pimp to one of your whores. I am at least your equal and achieved more than you as I started with nothing while you were gifted your success by your mother."

Now it was Frank's turn to fall into silence and suck in the air until his pulse stopped racing. So far, all the two men had succeeded in doing was to goad each other, and they were no closer to any agreement than when they arrived. Alice was not impressed. If Frank wanted to preen his feathers, so be it, but they needed to bring Nikolay's plane safely in to land: no bumps, no bruises and no crashes.

"WHAT MY BROTHER is trying to say is that we respect all your achievements in the Tenderloin—and beyond. And what we agree here will have significant consequences for all concerned. I expect you would like to devote your energies into making more money and we want to do the same. So we need to draw a line under what has happened and figure out the best way to live side by side either by not elbowing each other or by working together, sharing risks and the rewards."

"My biggest concern is to get access to my heroin. The rest is just cheap words."

"If tens of millions of dollars are of no matter to you, then I underestimate the respect you deserve. For the Lagotti family that is a considerable amount of money at stake if we can't agree a reasonable resolution to our difficulties."

Nikolay raised his eyebrows and widened his eyes a fraction. Clearly he wanted to get his hands on that kind of green.

"Our lottery operation in California is the beginning of the adventure, not the endgame. As more states create legalized gambling, we shall take advantage with our fake tickets: the numbers racket reborn for modern times. There will be enough profit in the venture to allow others to dip their beaks in the trough. If you work with us—supplying drivers, protection and boots on the ground—we could give you five per cent of the gross. But if you harm our people or our assets, then you will have nothing and can peck on the floor with the rest of the hens. The choice is yours. The time to decide your future is now. Before we leave the Palladium either you are working for or against our interests."

Nikolay's cheeks reddened and he sipped his long gone cold coffee. Mikhailov tried to refill his mug, but he told her not to fuss around him.

"Let us take a break for a short while and stretch our legs."

171

NIKOLAY STOOD UP, put his hands in his pants pockets and took two steps to stand to look out of the window. The sky was blue and Alcatraz was easy to spot. Alice poured fresh coffees, walked over and handed one to him. The others hovered near the drinks table, murmuring and chewing on cookies.

"You need to cut a deal with us and I understand that you may not think much of my brother—or me."

"He thinks he is somebody because he can get girls to fuck for money. That just means he's a pimp. He has ideas far above his ability and doesn't realize how small a man he is."

"Not everyone in my family shares Frank's view of you and you should remember that."

"That may be the case but when we last met, you showed me tremendous disrespect."

Alice's pupils dilated as she recalled that moment in her hotel room.

"There is a world of difference between wishing to do business with you and wanting to fuck. You failed to distinguish those two things. That's not about respect; it's a question of your judgment."

"You chastise me like your brother did."

"No, he believes the best method to get his way is to strong-arm a person. I operate by letting people understand their options and leaving them to decide which consequences they prefer. You are free to do whatever you want—within reason—but accept what happens next."

"Are you really willing to let me share in your numbers racket? How do I know you aren't dangling a juicy worm in front of me now just to squeeze a truce out of me?"

"Bottom line is that you don't, but my word counts for something and the offer is genuine. We want to work with people and you have shown your mettle. All these matters boil down to trust. You have met me and seen me operate. And now you must decide if what I say matches what I do."

"YOU TALK OF consequences and you threaten me with extinction. Those are not the words of a business partner. You make it hard for me to trust you when your family reneged on our last detail."

"Did I return to the Tenderloin?"

"I don't believe so."

"I did not. And if you are serious about joining us with the numbers racket, then you need to get past being offended by Frank. There are many people who take issue with his manners and you're at the back of the line. Instead focus on what it would mean to run the operation in California or beyond.

That's the offer on the table—and to free up your narcotics pipeline in the short term. Keep your eyes on the prize, Nikolay."

Markov sipped and stared out the window some more while Alice continued to stand next to him. He was mesmerized by the sheer scale of the honey pot and that was central to their plan. If Frank had been in the summerhouse with the rest of the family and spent less time in Sam's condo, he would have known this too.

"Chuck the boy a bone and he'll stop yapping at your ankles. He wants to show what a great fella he is and I want a deal."

"AND WHAT MAKES your words more important than his in your family?"

"I'm older by four minutes…"

Nikolay smiled.

"…and I have the backing of the rest of my outfit. Don't underestimate me because I am a woman. Underestimate me because you only see a fraction of what I can do."

More silence and staring. If Nikolay had been more observant of his surroundings and less wrapped up in himself, he would have noticed that Alice had undone an extra blouse button before she went over to the window to talk to him. She understood how easy it was to play this chump and his eyes betrayed where his real focus lay. Sometimes all you needed was an attractive decolletage. Other times you had to threaten a man with death or poverty. Alice chose both options to hedge her bets.

"Your mother was more vocal at the last peace talks."

"She is doing her best to let others take the reins. Mama has worked hard all her life and deserves to enjoy the time she has."

"And who will take over from her?"

Alice smiled and shook her head.

"That's the kind of information we share with friends. When we agree a deal today, then I'll be happy to fill you in on our plans."

"Frank is a boy and Bobby is too old. Enough said already."

A grin ripped across Alice's face.

"If you know that, you appear to be a friend even now."

"Congratulations are in order and if this is true, then I apologize for my earlier behavior."

"Accepted, but not forgotten: not yet, anyway. Show me the man you can be at this table and then we shall discuss other matters further some other time."

She watched his eyes flit to her breasts and look at her face. Alice walked back to fill up her mug once more with gritted teeth and everyone shuffled to their seats.

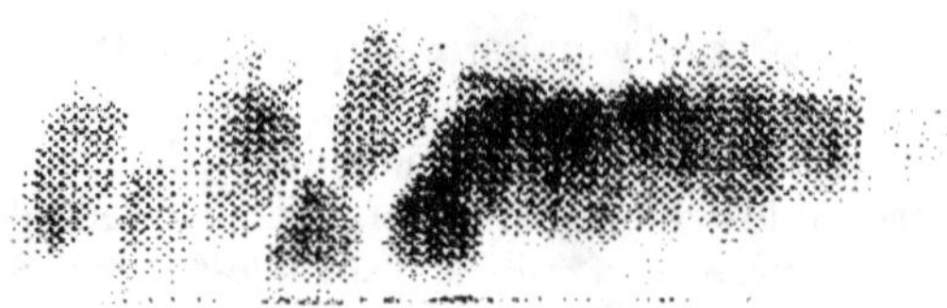

172

"SO HAVE YOU decided whether you will play ball?"

"Fuck you. I'll speak to the girl but not to a mook like you."

"What the hell did you say to him, Alice?"

"Nothing, Frank. Cool it."

"Don't you talk to me like that. You two are cooking something up between the pair of you."

Alice looked askance at Bobby, who stared back as confused as she was. Mary Lou continued to stare into space while Frank fumed. He stood up so quickly that his chair fell backwards onto the floor with a thud. Everyone watched as he muttered under his breath and stormed out of the room. Naldo picked up the seat and placed it without any fuss out of the way by a wall.

"My apologies, Nikolay."

"Sometimes children are best allowed out to play while the adults speak."

Markov cast a glance to Mikhailov who returned his look with a slight nod. All was good with everybody who remained, although Alice shifted her chair into the center with Mama to her left near the window and Bobby to her right nearer the coffee and cookie table. Once they had all settled down Nikolay waited a few seconds and then carried on.

"We were trying to agree how we can work together once you've opened up my narcotics supply."

"Indeed. We'll do that, but you have yet to say what you offer us in exchange."

"I shall open up the Tenderloin to prostitution for you if you enable me to join in your numbers racket."

"When we start in San Francisco, then you shall have fifty per cent of all the revenues you generate. For simplicity, we will keep our reps out of the city for the first twelve months. This gives your people ample chance to corner the market and means we can mop up any independent retailers who might have slipped through the net later on. The aim is to get every store on board: we are less concerned about who makes the sale as much as the product is sold."

"This is agreeable. And what about opportunities beyond the confines of the city?"

"Let's take one step at a time. Do well here and we will be happy to offer you other territories. If you need help with any other ventures, we ask—but don't demand—that you speak to us first. The more we work together, the greater our bond and that can only strengthen all here today."

Nikolay nodded and offered his open hand across the table. Alice stood up and reached over to seal the deal. And that was the point when the glass of the window was punctured by a bullet from who knows where.

THE SLUG WHIZZED through the air and into Mary Lou's orbit. She'd turned her head to stare out the window and the force of the bullet twisted her body round, whipping the blood departing the wound into an arc that caught Alice's cheek, shoulder and arm.

What was left of the shell spat out the other side Of her skull and into the wall. Mama's body tilted off the chair and headed down to the carpeted floor. The crack of the glass and the red-burst in the room caused Alice to hit the deck on pure instinct. Out of the corner of her eye, Alice caught the color scarlet near her Mama and saw a leg twitch.

Two more slugs entered the place. One landed in the mirror, next to the coffees and cookies, which shattered, shards of glass spraying out over Mikhailov and Bobby. The other bullet ricocheted off the coffee pot and pinged up into the ceiling. Alice kept her hands over her head as though that might protect her from a high caliber round.

Bobby wriggled over from his position past Alice and tried to cover Mary Lou's body to shield her corpse from the sniper. While trying to sink into the carpet, Alice swiveled around to survey the scene in the room and see who remained alive. In between table and chair legs, only Mama was lying still.

"Anyone else hurt?"

Naldo's voice of calm reason floated over the survivors. Without noticing herself do it, Alice grabbed the gun from her handbag, now nestling under a seat. Bobby's arms surrounded his wife, and he rocked her left-to-right with the first agony of her loss. His pain transformed him into a gripping, crying blob.

Alice glanced out of the window frame as though that would help her see the marksman. Then she stole another look around to see each of them holding weapons trained on the world outside the meeting room. Mikhailov had somehow got to the window and was bobbing and weaving, hoping to catch sight of the attacker. Alice saw Nikolay's lips move but she couldn't hear a word he said. She could tell by his expression he was getting increasingly frustrated. She swallowed and a wall of sound burst into her eardrums.

"What just happened?"

"We know nothing of this. My mother's been killed. You think I'd do that? To my Mama?"

NIKOLAY SHOOK HIS head and stared out the window while barking instructions to Mikhailov in Russian. They glared at each other then both turned in Alice's direction. A grim menace took over their demeanors—no mean feat given what had just happened to her Mama.

Alice looked to Bobby who had grown silent and now had a piece in his hand, finger on the trigger. For one brief second, Alice tasted hate in her mouth and she blinked at Bobby, his expression exactly the same as when he'd torture someone. They both understood what to do next.

Bobby planted a pair of slugs into Nikolay: first the heart and then the head. As he squeezed the trigger to take out Markov, Alice sent a bullet in the back of Lara Mikhailov's knee who screamed with agony and rolled over to face Alice. That gave her the opportunity to slam two cartridges into Mikhailov's torso.

Sirens wailed in the distance and Naldo was the first to react.

"We gotta get outta here."

Insistence in his tone, he crawled to the window and stared outside.

"I'll cover you but we have to leave right now."

He shot aimlessly out the window to give Alice and Bobby a chance to crawl to the door and make their escape. No one returned fire and he figured it would be safe to exit himself. With Bobby and Alice no longer in the room, Naldo first went over to Mary Lou's body to check she wasn't carrying any incriminating documents. Then he emptied the contents of her bag and did the same. He stuffed papers and a gun into his jacket and fled the scene.

THIRTY MINUTES LATER, the three survivors sat in Naldo's car near the edge of town, traveling at five miles an hour below the speed limit, heading back to Palm Springs.

"Who d'you think ordered the hit?"

"It's down to who wanted Mary Lou dead. Nikolay?"

"He looked as surprised as we were. Perhaps New York got impatient."

"No. If the mob called for the hit, they'd have whacked the lot of us to give Markov a free run of the city."

"Then who? Some rival gang we don't even know?"

"Unlikely. It will be somebody known. Someone close. Usually, very close."

Alice stared at Naldo who appeared to think more than he was saying.

"Do you have a name?"

"Can't say for certain, but who is among us yet not here?"

"Frank?"

The word left Alice's mouth as the quietest whisper ever uttered by a human being.

"Anyone seen Isaak today?"

Silence.

"Doesn't mean he was gunning for your mother. He could have had Markov in his sights and plain missed. Worse shit has happened in my lifetime."

Despite wanting to cling to the wafer-thin possibility that Nikolay was the target, Alice realized deep in her heart that it looked like Frank had murdered her darling Mama.

173

THE REMAINING PART of the day of the attack comprised bribing hotel staff and cops, constructing alibis and early thoughts about the morgue and a funeral. At home, Bobby and Alice sat in the living room trying to come to terms with the day's events but neither of them found that the least bit simple. Bobby was better at hiding his feelings, but even he would break down and cry regularly.

Naldo remained behind the wheel all the way to Oakcrest Drive and had done his best to leave the two alone since they got back indoors three hours earlier. But now the doorbell rang, which Naldo answered—Irma was in her room finding solace in prayer. He popped his head round the door to announce that Isaak was here.

"Where were you today? You were expected to be part of the security detail this morning."

"I've been in bed ill. When I was told about Mrs. Lagotti, I came straight over."

"And have you heard from Frank too? We haven't seen him since he walked out of the meeting shortly before some fuck blasted us with bullets."

Alice still couldn't bring herself to say out loud that Mama was dead. She detected an increased redness in Isaak's cheeks as she spoke. His eyes darted left and right and he could not maintain eye contact. That was when she knew he was the trigger man.

"Well, if you find him, remind him we're looking for him too."

"Sure thing."

"Can we get you a drink or some food? Maybe meds if you're still ill," interjected Bobby.

"A coffee would be good. It'd settle my stomach and ease my throat."

"Naldo, do you mind making him a pot?"

When the two bodyguards had moved to the kitchen, Bobby sat down next to Alice on the couch and whispered into her ear.

"We won't see that cocksucker again. I'll ensure Naldo deals with him after the funeral. There's no rush: we need to get the job done once he's less nervous."

Alice was pleased Bobby reached the same conclusion as her with greater presence of mind: she wanted to kill Isaak here and now.

FATHER CARMOODY SURFACED the following day, Saturday. He expressed his deepest sorrow for their loss and explained how Mary Lou had sought his counsel these past months.

"You are a Catholic priest? Am I right?"

"Yes, my dear."

"Are you aware of her early experience of the church and her views of the clergy in particular?"

"My child, your mother had a change of mind recently and wanted to let Jesus into her heart."

"You understand my wife suffered from dementia."

"Yes, my son. She spoke of how hard she found remembering the simplest of things and cried in my presence at not being able to recall the names of her own children."

Alice stormed out of the room: this man annoyed her, but she discovered over the coming days he inserted himself into their affairs. The only advantage of his existence to them was that he volunteered to liaise with the funeral parlor: arranging the release of the body from the pathologist, its transportation to Palm Springs and other more gruesome details neither Bobby nor Alice wanted to deal with.

The task they couldn't palm off to the priest was to contact everyone who knew Mary Lou to tell them what had happened. Given her dramatic end, news had traveled far across the country, but they took no chances: everybody needed a call. The only family Mary Lou had were Bobby, Frank and Alice, although somewhere her brothers and sisters might be still alive. No one had the desire to find them as Mary Lou turned her back on her kin when she left home.

FRANK APPEARED ON Sunday and refused to account for his whereabouts. Alice could barely stand to be in the same room as him and Bobby was taciturn even by his own quiet standards. Sensing the anger from his family, Frank left and visited Sammy instead where the welcome was warm and inviting, a red G-string the only thing standing between him and a willing bush.

By the end of the week, everyone stopped focusing on the cause of the funeral and fixated on the detailed organization of the church service and wake. Out of common decency, Bobby and Alice tried to include Frank in the decision making, but inevitably his was a minority voice on the rare occasions he left Sammy's bed. He wanted only the three of them there—and the priest if necessary—but Bobby understood Mary Lou was so widely known a small family affair was out of the question.

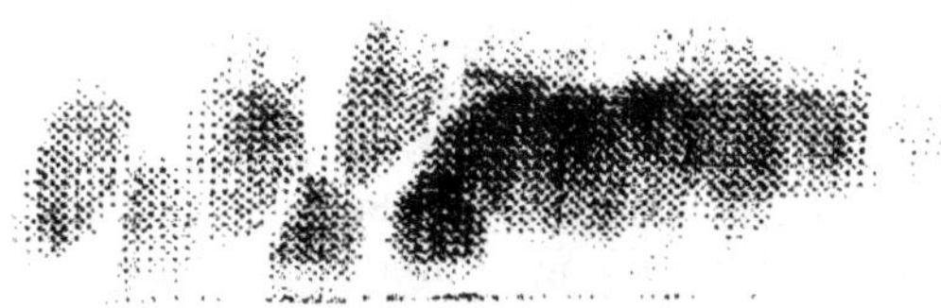

174

TIME TRICKLED BY until the day of the funeral. Alice awoke and felt guilty because for three seconds, she forgot Mama was dead. She cried yet again, got out of bed, showered and put on a black pants suit before heading downstairs for breakfast.

In the kitchen, Bobby was already sitting down nursing a mug of coffee, staring at a slice of granary toast supplied by Irma. Frank arrived and joined them to wait for the limousines, which were due at ten. The only noises were the clinking of crockery and the sound of Irma busying herself in the background.

The clock in the living room struck the hour and, in almost perfect synchrony, the doorbell rang as the limos were out front and waiting. There was one black stretch for Bobby, Alice and Frank with another for Irma, Naldo and a host of fellas. Bobby had nixed Naldo's suggestion to be in the same limo as the family for security reasons. The way Bobby figured it, if someone was going to whack him, they might as well do it today. While he didn't want to die, he didn't care if he lived. And he knew Alice was similarly inclined.

Outside the church were at least fifty mourners if not more—all come to send off Mary Lou. Frank wished they'd all just go away. He did not like his private grief being on public display. In contrast, Alice appeared heartened by the show of affection and respect afforded her mom by those attending. It showed how much Mama had touched so many lives during her brief visit to this crummy world.

THE SERVICE STARTED with a hymn and then the congregation stood and sat at the behest of Carmoody. After another song extolling the virtues of Jesus Christ, everyone sat and the priest began the eulogy.

"Mary Lou Lagotti, may she rest in peace, was a mother, a wife, a business woman. But above all she was a human being who died in tragic circumstances. She leaves behind two beautiful children— Frank Jr and Alice—as well as Bobby, her dutiful husband. She joined our community thirty years ago and she quickly developed into a fabulous contributor to our local charities. As her kids grew older, and her activities thrived, Mary Lou became a force for good in Palm Springs."

Frank disliked the hypocrisy of the man who met Mama only a few months before and knew nothing of her. He'd inveigled himself into Mama's life when she was at her most vulnerable. The guy's whole attitude sickened him to the core.

Alice remained too consumed with the pain of her loss and the reality of seeing her Mama's coffin in front of her. In that wooden box and its oak veneer was the body of her mother. Mama's corpse was almost within her grasp, but to acknowledge that meant Alice had to tell herself her mom was dead—and mean it—and that was too much for her to bear. So she cried again and waited for the juddering silent ache inside to subside enough to breathe again. And still the priest droned on while she curled up in her own thoughts.

AT THE GRAVESIDE, Carmoody issued a series of prayers and the coffin was lowered into the gaping hole awaiting it and the men used two shovels to heap the soil on top of the box. Bobby had the honor of throwing the first earth onto the wooden casket. The echoing thud as the earth slammed on the veneer sent a shiver down Bobby's spine. He focussed on the physical act of pushing the shovel into the mound of clay and dropping the contents into the abyss. He knew if he allowed himself half a second's thought about Mary Lou's corpse down in that pit he would break down completely.

When the coffin was no longer visible under the soil, Bobby, Alice and Frank walked away and back towards the church. Alice looked round for one last chance of seeing her mother and that was her undoing. The sensation of losing her Mama hit her knees and she collapsed to the ground. Lagotti men grabbed an arm each and hauled her to her feet, half dragging her through the cemetery.

The wake took place at the house which gave those who couldn't make the funeral a chance to show their respect. Irma had asked permission to get three waitresses in to help her serve canapes and drinks. An hour in and the food was eaten although there was still enough hard liquor to last four more hours.

BY THE TIME the final guests departed, Bobby was left slumped in the living room with a tumbler of Scotch in his hand. Frank and Alice were seated on sun loungers.

"We're orphans, Frank."

"Because both our parents are dead?"

"Yep."

Alice knocked back the remains of her whiskey and soda.

"Let's sneak into the summerhouse like when we were kids."

Frank followed Alice inside as she switched on the lights.

"Give me a hug. We're all alone, kid."

Frank stepped toward her and Alice opened her arms and engulfed him in a sisterly embrace. She squeezed that huge torso and leaned her chin on one shoulder. Despite the momentary comfort of her brother's biceps, Alice snapped awake to remember why her Mama was dead and who was the cause.

"I know what you did, Frank."

"Huh?"

"At the peace conference. No idea why but you killed my Mama."

"What're you…"

Alice pulled out a knife from her pants pocket and slammed it into Frank's stomach, twisting the blade as she plugged him. He gurgled, clutched his belly with one hand and swiped at his twin with the other. His palm caught the side of Alice's head and she almost lost her balance, but then she removed the metal and stuck it in his chest…

The sound of glass breaking and the memory of her Mama's blood splashing onto her cheek…

Frank fell to his knees, grabbing Alice's arms, torso, anything to stop himself hitting the ground. She reached out and scrunched his hair with a hand, yanking back his head. Then she took the blade and pressed its serrated edge over his throat to cut him open from one ear to the other.

Alice slumped on the floor, bouncing off Frank's body as she collapsed and sat in the pool of his blood until the red liquid seeped into her undies and felt sticky and uncomfortable. She rolled onto her side, huddled into the smallest ball of humanity she could make and she cried.

Alice sobbed and sobbed until she could cry no more—for her Mama, for Frank and for herself. She picked up the knife and wiped it clean on Frank's jacket. Then she stood up, one foot either side of his corpse, just as Bobby entered the room in search of the children. He looked down at Frank then sighed. Alice Lagotti, head of the family, stepped away from her brother's body and held out a hand.

Bobby went towards her, bowed and kissed her cygnet ring. The stench of Frank's gizzards heavy in the air.

"Get this mess tidied up: we've got territory in San Francisco to reclaim and a deal to close with New York."

THE END

THANK YOU FOR READING!

Get a free novella

Building a relationship with my readers is the very best thing about writing. I send weekly newsletters with details of new releases, special offers and other bits of news relating to the Lagotti Family and Alex Cohen series, as well as my stand-alone novels.

And if you sign up to the mailing list I'll send you a copy of the Lagotti Family prequel, The Stickup. Just go to www.leob.ws/signup and we'll take it from there.

Enjoy this book? You can make a difference

Reviews are the most powerful tools in my arsenal when it comes to getting attention for my books. Much as I'd like to, I don't have the financial muscle of a New York publisher. I can't take out full page ads or put posters on the subway. (Not yet, anyway).

But I do have something much more powerful and effective than that, and it's something that those publishers would kill to get their hands on.

A committed and loyal bunch of readers.

Honest reviews of my books help bring them to the attention of other readers.

If you've enjoyed this book I shall be very grateful if you would spend just five minutes leaving a review (it can be as short as you like) on the book's page. You can jump right to the page by clicking www.books2read.com/lagotti1-4.

Thank you very much.

Leo

OTHER BOOKS BY THE AUTHOR

The Case
The Death and Life of Penny Pitstop

The Lagotti Family Series

The Stickup (Prequel Novella)
The Heist (Book 1)
The Getaway (Book 2)
Powder (Book 3)
Mama's Gone (Book 4)
The Girl in the Striped Bikini (Short Story Sequel)
The Lagotti Collection: Complete Books 1-4

Alex Cohen Series

The Bowery Slugger (Book 1)
Eastside Hustler (Book 2 - Due 2020)
Midtown Huckster (Book 3 - Due 2020)

ABOUT LEOPOLD BORSTINSKI

Leopold Borstinski is an independent author whose past careers have included financial journalism, business management of financial software companies, consulting and product sales and marketing, as well as teaching.

There is nothing he likes better so he does as much nothing as he possibly can. He has travelled extensively in Europe and the US and has visited Asia on several occasions. Leopold holds a Philosophy degree and tries not to drop it too often.

He lives near London and is married with one wife, one child and no pets.

Find out more at LeopoldBorstinski.com.

www.ingramcontent.com/pod-product-compliance
Lightning Source LLC
Chambersburg PA
CBHW082125180726
48291CB00010B/2743